PENGUIN BOOKS

A NEST OF MAGPIES

Sybil Marshall was born in 1913 and grew up in East Anglia. As a villager all her life, she witnessed from the inside the breakdown of traditional village life in the post-war period, from new methods of farming to a different social structure of rural communities, and new values, particularly the attitude to sexual morality. It is the reluctant but inevitable submission of the old to the new that is lovingly and sympathetically explored in this novel.

Having been a village-school teacher, at the age of forty-seven she went up to Cambridge University to read English. She became Lecturer in Education at Sheffield University and subsequently Reader in Primary Education at the University of Sussex. In 1965, at the invitation of Granada Television, she conceived the 'creative' programme *Picture Box*, for which she continued to act as adviser and to write the teachers' handbooks until 1989.

As well as books on education, Sybil Marshall has written non-fiction books recording life in her native fens in their pre-war isolation, including *Fenland Chronicle*, *The Silver New Nothing* and *A Pride of Tigers*. She also won the Angel Prize for Literature for *Everyman's Book of English Folk Tales*.

Now retired, Sybil Marshall lives in Ely, Cambridgeshire, with Ewart Oakeshott, FSA, artist, author and recognized world authority on medieval weaponry and its usage.

D0419948

SYBIL MARSHALL

A NEST OF MAGPIES

PENGUIN BOOKS

PENGUIN BOOKS

Published by the Penguin Group
Penguin Books Ltd, 27 Wrights Lane, London W8 5TZ, England
Penguin Books USA Inc., 375 Hudson Street, New York, New York 10014, USA
Penguin Books Australia Ltd, Ringwood, Victoria, Australia
Penguin Books Canada Ltd, 10 Alcorn Avenue, Toronto, Ontario, Canada M4V 3B2
Penguin Books (NZ) Ltd, 182–190 Wairau Road, Auckland 10, New Zealand

Penguin Books Ltd, Registered Offices: Harmondsworth, Middlesex, England

First published by Michael Joseph 1993
Published in Penguin Books 1994
1 3 5 7 9 10 8 6 4 2

The lines from 'Just Making Conversation' by Harry Carlton on pages 342 and 431 are
reproduced by permission of Trudie Thompson, and those from 'Your Coffee in the
Morning' by Harry Warren and Al Dubin on page 349 are reproduced by permission of
EMI Music Publishing

Printed in England by Clays Ltd, St Ives plc

For Prue,
my daughter and my friend,
as loving as beloved

PART ONE

DOMINOES

1

Posted in Palermo. So that's where she was! I had recognized the handwriting, even before I had noticed the foreign stamp. Well, whatever you might think about her, you had to hand it to her in one respect. If ever there was a determined survivor, Johanna was it.

I had had my nose pressed flat against the glass of the landing window when I had heard the clink of the old brass letter-box, followed by the splat of yet another batch of Christmas cards falling on to the hall floor. The post came at any old time in the last days before Christmas. It must be at least half-past three, judging by the fiery gleams of the December sunset. I knew I ought to go downstairs and pick up the post and retire with it to my chair in the sitting-room. Sophie would not go home until she had brought me my tea.

We had been working side by side all day, preparing for my visitors, until Sophie had decided that I had done enough, and decreed that I should leave her to finish the preparations for tonight's meal by herself. She told me to go and have a bath and change my clothes, and then have a nice sit-down before anybody came. As if I were at least twice her age, or still only a child liable to become too excited.

I had obeyed her, as I usually did. She was nearly always right, anyway. But the landing window had trapped me on my way down, just as it used to when I was a child on one of my prolonged visits to Grandfather. More than forty years ago.

It was still the same beautiful, spacious half-landing at the turn of the same elegantly curved eighteenth-century staircase, and the huge window still presented the same glorious view.

There was the garden, planted when formal gardens were the fashion, and labour so cheap that any fairly well-to-do gentleman could indulge his taste to the full. Benedict's House itself was unpretentious, but its garden had been its pride. Lawns and yew hedges, walled gardens and terraced walks had been framed by trees and shrubs placed with judicious care to keep up a display of colour

3

whatever the season, enhancing each other's foliage by subtle blend-ing and startling contrasts of tone. The shrubs had mostly died of old age long ago, or had shot up into huge trees that now crowded against stands of pine, larch, silver birch and copper beech. The full-grown oaks still sturdily held their own against usurping bays and laurels, while blue cedars and deodars struggled against ever-encroaching cypresses; but the beauty remained undiminished. Who-ever had planned it had been careful not to put tall trees where they would obstruct the view from the landing window, so that even in high summer the squat tower of the old church was still visible two or three hundred yards away.

Elms enfolded the churchyard, and today they stood out in frosty silhouette against a duck-egg blue sky streaked with the sunset. I could see just a few yards of the narrow road that ran past the churchyard gate, and the lopsided gables of the ancient inn that faced the church. The cottages clustered round these two essential buildings were sending up columns of blue smoke, but otherwise they were invisible, being hidden by the trees.

Beyond the church, all one could see were fields — just fields and fields and fields that stretched gently away into the distance, rising very slightly to meet the sky on the horizon. It was surely just as it had been two hundred years ago. Even Ned, standing by his bonfire in 'the spinney', furthered that illusion. He was foreshortened by my view of him, and looked smaller and thinner than he really was, though his wiry strength was plain enough as he heaved up the fire with a long-handled pitch-fork to encourage it to burn out faster. His flat cap was pulled down over his ears to counter the keen air, but otherwise he made no concession to the fact that it was mid-winter. 'You can't work in a jacket,' he had said when I remonstrated with him about his bare arms. 'When I can't work hard enough to keep meself warm, it'll be time for me to give up.'

I looked down at him affectionately, as he shooed away his persistent pet robin with much arm-waving and, I guessed, a spate of good-natured imprecations. Oscar, our gander, was still planting his great red feet up and down the spinney close by, but the third member of Ned's normal afternoon entourage, my Siamese cat, had deserted. I guessed she had found the sitting-room fire.

The thought of the fire and the sound of tea-cups finally persuaded me to take my nose from the window. I fished for my handkerchief to rub off the little round greasy mark it had made, stabbed by a twinge of bitter-sweet nostalgia. Sophie still grumbled at me about it, just like her mother had done when she had been 'doing domestic' for my grandfather.

I heard the stump of Sophie's heavy lace-up shoes as she crossed the hall to the sitting-room, and she called up to me in a voice that was very nearly the command her mother would have used. 'I'm taking your tea in, now,' she said, with emphasis on the last word. I left the window, and went.

I never entered the sitting-room without a thrill of pleasure, even now. It was the most gracious room in a gracious old house. It was lit by two long windows facing south, and though it was large, and the corniced ceiling very high by modern standards, it was always warm and welcoming. A huge log fire crackled in the Adams-style marble fireplace, and holly and other evergreens from the garden were draped above pictures, mirrors, curtain-poles and overmantel.

Not even from the front windows did one catch a glimpse of the modern world. The house was two hundred yards from the road, reached by an avenue which ran across a field that Sophie and Ned still referred to as 'the front cluss'. The road went one way into the village, and the other way down to a little hump-backed bridge over a river, after which it continued for another three-quarters of a mile before it crossed another, much bigger river by a newer and more pretentious bridge; and only there did it join a major road, at the confluence of two waterways.

Beyond the second bridge, on the main road, lay the new town of Swithinford. This upstart had grown around the railway station in the middle of the last century, gradually overpowering the tiny community around St Swithin's church. When it had continued to grow, after the end of the second war, it had appropriated to itself the name of Swithinford, and the tiny hamlet in which I lived had, by current usage and post-office decree, become Old Swithinford: an ancient, poor relation, partronized by the brash newcomers because its age made it 'quaint', and tolerated, like a senile dependant, because it was there and couldn't be completely ignored.

Well, that is how it had been until this year, now at its end.

Old Swithinford resented Swithinford's existence, and the newcomers who lived there despised us. They were of the present and of the future, full of mechanized bustle and packaged entertainment. Until very recently, we had belonged to yesterday, and thousands of yesterdays before that. They pushed things forward; we just let things happen. Their outlook was urban, and they relegated all truly rural folk to the 'country-bumpkin' category. We who lived within

5

sight of the church clock never seemed to feel the lack of excitement, though. There had been more than enough excitement here in this last year. That was because we still retained a deep human interest in each other.

For all the understanding there was between the two Swithinfords, they might as well have been in different hemispheres. Though little more than a mile, as the crow flies, lay between our old church and their new one, contact between the communities was minimal. This may have been in some degree due to the extraordinary fact that they were separated by a third community lying a little to one side, which acted as a buffer between them rather than a link, and belonged in tone and lifestyle to neither.

After the Great War, a lot of people in towns had been deluded into thinking that a life of wealth and ease could be had for the price of a strip of land in the country and a few 'chickens'. So it had happened that between the two bridges over the converging rivers there had sprung up in the twenties and early thirties a dreadful scatter of four-square, pebble-dashed bungalows interspersed with mock-Tudor semi-detached houses.

As chicken farms, they had all failed here as they had done elsewhere up and down the country. But the dwellings had remained, creating a sort of new, half-baked village that had no real roots and belonged nowhere. Technically, this was now designated by the autocratic post-office authorities as Swithinford Bridges; to everybody in the locality, it was simply Hen Street.

I sat down in my armchair by the fire, and poured myself a cup of tea. It was still only four o'clock, and I could not expect anybody yet for two hours, even William. William was — well, in the first place, my step-cousin, his mother having been step-sister to my father. We were therefore, in fact, no relation at all, but we had grown up in a kind of emotional twinship. When we were little, and indeed even into our early teens, we had made secret vows to marry each other, because neither of us was ever so happy anywhere else as in each other's company. But the vows had not been kept. Grandfather had died, Benedict's had been sold, and our lives had taken off in different directions. In the ensuing confusion of the war, both of us had married and after that we had completely lost touch.

I had been reasonably happy, I suppose, until a German bomb had scored a direct hit upon the building in which my high-ranking Civil Service husband had worked in his secret, reserved occupation. He left me a widow with two small children and a good pension, in

6

an alien northern town which I could not leave because his shattered parents needed me and my children so much after the loss of their only child.

William had not been as fortunate as I. He had married while serving as a fighter-pilot, and his wife had not been at all prepared for the change in their lifestyle when on being demobbed William had returned to his academic post. She had been bored beyond endurance by her life as the wife of a scholarly university don. East Anglia was still one huge airfield, with a USAAF base more or less sandwiched between every two RAF stations. That is where her interests lay, and she had amused herself more and more until she had one day simply vamoosed with a Yank. William had been stunned, grieved, and full of remorse because he had felt too late that he had failed to observe how unhappy and ill-at-ease she had been. She had not asked to be set free, and he had been grateful for that, divorce being still a very dirty word, much frowned upon in academic circles, especially at the older universities. She had disappeared in person from his life, and he had retreated hurt and bewildered into the sort of bachelor existence that so many dons had been expected to live even as late as the early twentieth century. All of which had happened during the many years that I had been living and working, as Shakespeare would have said, 'in another part of the forest'.

I had adequate means, and I had always worked myself during the war, even when the babies were young. The publishing house I had just joined when I married was glad I was willing to do part-time work at home. By the time my parents-in-law died, I had far more financial security than I had ever deemed possible.

I wanted to go 'home', by which I meant somewhere in East Anglia. I had grown to love the industrial north, but every now and then I thought of the huge skies and longed for a whiff or two of my native air to invigorate me. But I seemed to lack the necessary energy and will-power to uproot myself until one morning a short, rather formal note came in the post from William, forwarded through my publisher, congratulating me on my latest TV script.

I was overjoyed, and started buzzing with activity like a clockwork toy when the spring is released. I tore off a letter to William, setting my problems before him, and asking, since he was still apparently in 'home' territory, if he could offer any advice about where I should start to look for a new place to live. His reply came by return – a very different kind of missive from the stilted one before. He plunged into it as if we had seen each other only last week, and began to describe a car journey he had taken recently to see a sick colleague. He had passed a signpost to Old Swithinford on the way back, and overcome by curiosity and a bit of nostalgia, had turned to go through the village.

Would you believe it? Benedict's is for sale. Again! It is *terribly* run down and neglected, and the garden is so overgrown that you can no longer see what you know must be there. I poked around, just for old time's sake, and for what my opinion is worth, I'd say that structurally the old house is as sound as a bell.

I have no idea what it is you are looking for, or how much you want to spend. You may be after a modern service flat in town, for all I know. But I can't believe you can have changed so much since we last met, and I've got a hunch that the thought of Benedict's will make your mouth water. Why not come down and have a look at it, even if you can't consider buying it? I'll meet you at the station, give you lunch, and then drive you out. We can wallow in nostalgia together.

Make my mouth water? I was very nearly choked with saliva! I went.

I wondered if I should recognize William after so many years, but he had raised his hat, held out his hand, pecked my cheek and taken my overnight bag from me before I had time to get both feet on the platform, or so it seemed to me. I was pleasurably disorientated, as if my life were a film from which a pair of giant cutters had just snipped out more than twenty years.

From the time the smooth young man from the house-agent turned the key in the huge lock on the old front door, I knew I had to have Benedict's. It was the only home I could ever be happy in again. I wanted to live the rest of my life there, and die in the same room in which three generations before Grandfather had died. I couldn't believe how we had all come to desert the house. We hadn't even bothered to bear it in remembrance. And there it still sat surely waiting for one of us to come and take possession of it again.

William asked the smooth young man if we could go round it alone. I blessed his intuition, and gave myself time to swallow any nostalgia that was threatening to subdue common sense. Again, William understood, and began to seek out the snags that I did not want him to find. His opinion was that the property as it stood could be bought very reasonably, but that renovation would cost the earth.

'Besides,' he said, 'how would you cope with a house this size? You can't get domestic help these days for love nor money. And what about the garden? It would need at least one man, full time. Where would you find such a man, even supposing cost were no object? And would you mind living in a big house like this all alone?'

He paused, looked startled and then embarrassed, and shot me a searching glance from under his full dark eyebrows. There was a hint of hesitation in his next question, as if it were something that had only just crossed his mind. 'I take it that you will be – er – alone?'

I answered a bit waspishly, though I couldn't have said why. 'Of course I shall be alone. I'm a widow, and my children both have homes of their own. And I'm certainly not contemplating marriage again, if that is what you're hinting at. As for domestic and gardening help, I shall cross each bridge as I get to it. I want this old house, and I'm going to have it!'

I think I must have been glaring at him, because I realized he was grinning at me with one eyebrow raised and the other lowered – a trick he had learned when very young – just as he used to when we were about fourteen, and I had begun to throw my feminine weight about. In spite of that bush of wavy white hair that now contrasted so vividly with his still-dark eyebrows, and the slight academic stoop of his shoulders, it was 'my' William standing there in front of me.

'Still the same old Fran,' William said. 'Still knowing just what she wants, and as determined as ever to get it. All I can say is, don't blame me. I know you of old, when you look like that! So go ahead and ruin yourself. I shan't try to stop you. In fact, I'm beginning to think it's a good idea. I suppose you'd let me visit now and again, to see how it's all going?'

'Don't be daft,' I said, holding out my hand to him. 'If I get it and come back here, of course it will be the family home again. So welcome back to Benedict's! Jess, too, whenever she wants to come. I haven't seen her, either, for more than twenty years.'

Jess was William's half-sister, and my own first cousin; but in spite of the blood tie, she had never been so dear to me as William. We had always tended to leave her out of things in our childhood partnership, and as we grew older the slight rift had widened a bit. To think about it now made me feel guilty. I would do my best to put it right as soon as I was settled, wherever I was, but especially if I were here at Benedict's. I asked William about her, and he told me briefly of her marriage to a man of great charm who was a genius *manqué*, an adept at everything except providing them with a good living. They were at present living in a crofter's house on the island of Barra, because Greg had a commission for a book of poems and paintings inspired by the scenery and the birds.

Looking back, I think now that William did not believe I could possibly achieve the ambition he had watched me conceive, and which was to a large extent his doing. But things worked out better than I could ever have dared to hope. Indeed, I have often found myself thinking recently that never before have I been so happy and contented as I am now. I am almost fearful of giving the thought expression, lest I tempt a well-disposed Providence to alter its mind. On the other hand, I think that if by Providence I mean the same as Sophie does when she invokes ''Im Above', I wonder why whoever he is doesn't get thoroughly fed up with those who can never accept gifts without wondering when and how they will have to pay for them.

Being happy has always had the effect on me of setting off a surge of creative energy that releases itself by attempting some outsized project. There are so many such schemes lined up in front of me at present that I couldn't get them all into three lifetimes, let alone the second half of one. William has teased me about it, declaring that I must have found Zeus's herb of immortality in the garden at Benedict's. Perhaps I have, because the thought of the future, near or distant, no longer bothers me at all. I am far too contentedly occupied all the time, as now, this Christmas Eve.

Sophie stumped in and drew the curtains, switching on the light. 'I'll be a-gooing 'ome, then,' she said, 'if you're sure you don't want me to do nothing towards 'is tea, or their supper when they get 'ere.'

She almost always called William 'he', though with no disrespect or sarcasm intended. We had all played together as children, when we had been 'Fran' and 'Bill' to her, and she 'Soph' to us. It would not be right, in her eyes, for her now to be so familiar; but neither could she bring herself to address me as Mrs Catherwood, or William as Professor Burbage. So she compromised by calling me 'you' to my face, and 'she' to anybody else. Jess had been as much of an old playmate as William or I, but Sophie had real difficulty with her. The trouble was that Greg, Jess's husband, had a surname that was unusual. Though pronounced Tolliver, it was actually spelled Taliaferro — and Sophie had chanced to see it written down before she had heard it spoken. She had decided that he was to be given his full title, and that his name should be pronounced, 'like other folks', as it was spelt, which resulted in her calling him 'Mr Tallyhofearo'. She got round her difficulty with Jess by calling her 'Mis' Tolly'. Collectively, they were 'they' or 'them'.

Sophie fussed about, poking the fire unnecessarily, moving cushions, straightening the hearth rug. I knew all the signs, bless her. She didn't really want to leave before my guests came. The trouble was that she had no previous experience of a Christmas spent mostly by herself. She had bought herself a radio, but it would not compensate her for the family gathering that had been the ritual since she had been a child. If she had stayed, though, it would only have been to wait on us, because nothing would have induced her to sit down with us. It was best to let her go. I knew she wanted me to open the Christmas cards one by one, and show each to her, and tell her about the sender; but some instinct warned me against it.

'Do go home, Sophie. It will soon be pitch dark.'

She gave in reluctantly. 'Well, you know where I am if you want me,' she said. 'Not that I shall come tomorrow, bein' as it's a 'oly day. I met Thirz' this morning and she said as she'd be expecting me to dinner tomorrow, same as usual. I'm glad as she's asked me, though I don't really want to go, after the row at 'er 'ouse. But I shall. Mam would ha' wanted me to.'

She was gone at last, and as soon as the door closed behind her, I turned over the batch of cards and began to open them. The envelope from Palermo was of the expensive quality I should have expected from Johanna if I had thought she might send one, but that had never entered my head. I had taken it for granted that she had gone out of our lives for good. Of her devotion to me, personally, I had no doubt; but to almost everybody else, she had brought trouble, like the child who knocks against the table on which another child is building a house of cards.

She wasn't my sort of woman, nor I hers, as Sophie had told me in the first place; and but for the machinations of a mischievous fate, the threads of our lives would never have crossed at all, let alone tangled the village into a knot that could not be unravelled, and had

11

had to be cut to pieces. Honesty bade me reflect that she had not foreseen, and certainly had never intended any harm – but then, neither does the fly that carries cholera. She had never done me any harm at all, and I had become very fond of her – that I had to admit. It was just that she managed to leave a lot of misery behind her. The wheel of her fortune had revolved round me at the hub, while its rim had run over a great many others, bruising and crushing them as it turned.

I was reluctant to open the envelope. I did not want even the thought of her to intrude into this Christmas that I had been looking forward to so much. So I tucked it down beside me in my chair, and enjoyed the rest of the cards.

But she had already intruded, and my thoughts returned to her again and again.

'Cat,' I said aloud, at which Cat raised her head from my knee and inquired in her throaty Siamese voice what it was I required of her.

'No, not you, puss,' I said, pulling her ears. 'Me. Sour grapes. We can't all be as elegant and beautiful as you and Johanna are, and some of us just aren't. That's all!'

2

William's predictions had been right; the asking price for Benedict's was within my means, but estimates for restoration of the house and the garden rather took my breath away. It also threatened to be a considerable time before I could start living there.

Well, hadn't I told William that I would cross my bridges when I came to them? I signed the contract for the purchase, put my present home on the market, made arrangements to store my furniture and hoped for the best. The moment a buyer turned up for my house, I headed south, authorized the renovations, and continued south-east to Kent where my daughter and her husband lived. I rang William to tell him work was starting immediately, and asked him to keep a watching brief on the job because I had no firm plans for the immediate future.

I had only been with Kate for about a week when William rang to say that the first difficulty had arisen that he was not prepared to make a decision on without consulting me; in fact, he really thought I ought to see for myself what the problem was. So of course I went, booking myself in at the best 'hotel' Swithinford could offer. After two days, I knew I had to make better and more permanent arrangements. It was quite clear that the snags were going to be many and various, and equally so that my presence on the spot would be a major factor in determining both the cost and the length of time before I could move in; but it was also obvious to me that I could not, and would not, endure life in what was only a rather nasty, tarted-up modern pub for a day longer than I could help. I clung to a stubborn optimism that because I was truly 'going home', the Lord would provide.

I spent a morning battling with an obtuse plumber who wanted to take pipes in full view across the landing, and went outside to cool off. It had been in my mind for days to go and poke round the churchyard, to look up some of my family, as it were. I knew where Grandfather lay, so I visited him first, noting with surprise the neatness of his grave, and the fresh flowers by the headstone. There must be a lot of earlier Wagstaffes down in the oldest bit, I thought, so I began to make my way towards that overgrown corner reading headstone inscriptions as I went. A particularly obnoxious black marble headstone caught my eye. It overtopped its neighbours by about ten inches, the extra height being in the shape and form of an open book – a Bible, no doubt – resting on the top of the curved top. I stopped to read its inscription. The bold gold lettering read:

Sacred to the Memory of
our Beloved Parents
Zedikiah Wainwright, born 1880, died 1918
and Kezia Mildred, his Beloved Wife,
who departed this life on 1 May 1956
aged seventy-four years
GOD'S WILL BE DONE.

Kezia! Our Kezia. So it must have been Thirzah, and Sophie, and Hetty, the three little girls for whom Kezia had slaved and saved all the long years of her widowhood, who had thus made certain that their progenitors should be less insignificant in death than they had been in life. What must that gravestone have cost? It was high time I made myself known again down in the village. I looked up at the sound of approaching footsteps, and saw Kezia herself bearing down on me.

The likeness was so striking that my first impulse was to run from a ghost who had come to upbraid me for my arrogant criticism; but the ghost was remarkably solid, from the black felt hat to the thick-soled, high-laced shoes, and was carrying a bright green watering-can in one hand and a sheaf of early outdoor chrysanthemums in the other. Its grey eyes met mine in gentle recognition, as she set the watering-can down on the black marble chippings.

'Sophie!' I gasped.

'Ah! Tha's right,' she said. 'We 'eard as 'ow it was you as 'ad come back and took the old 'ouse again. I knowed you the minute I set eyes on you, standing a-looking at Mam's headstone. We give 'em quite as good as anybody else 'as got, didn't we?'

'Better,' I lied. Sophie was gazing at the horrid memorial with tears in her beautiful eyes, and a pride that covered me with shame.

'I all'us come with fresh flowers every Friday,' she said. 'And I all'us bring enough for your grandfather as well. She'd ha' wanted me to. She brought 'em 'erself, and kept 'is grave tidy, as long as ever she could. It seemed only right, like, after she'd gone to go on doing it for 'er.'

So that's who had been caring for Grandfather, Kezia till ten years ago, then Sophie. I was struggling to find the words to thank Sophie without giving offence by overdoing it, when she said, 'Here's the Rector a-coming. Seen you from the Rectory winder, I dare say.'

So it proved. The charming old gentleman, nearing eighty, I guessed, had come out to welcome me, and greeted Sophie by name as if she had still been a child. A sudden thought struck me. The sooner I took up residence in the village, the better. Was there any chance that somebody might have rooms to let? I asked.

Sophie shook her head immediately as if to repudiate at once the suggestion than anybody in Old Swithinford could possibly have sunk so low; but the Rector's face lit up with pleasure at being able to offer a bit of help, however vague.

'It is a strange coincidence that you should ask,' he said. 'Only yesterday, my lay reader at Swithinford Bridges was telling me about a lady there who is in financial difficulty because of her husband's desertion, and who had asked his advice about the possibility of taking in paying guests. A Mrs Brookes – or perhaps it was Rivers.' He turned his placid, benevolent gaze on me, smiling in self-deprecating fashion. 'I am ashamed to say that I leave all my pastoral duties in Swithinford Bridges to Mr Birch, these days. I am sadly out of touch with my parishioners there. But I dare say Sophie would know.'

(I found out in the course of time that it would have been more truthful if the Reverend Howard had said he left all his duties there to Hector Birch, and neglected the rest of them everywhere except for the very minimum of services; but at that moment this did not concern me at all.)

I looked towards Sophie, hopefully.

'Oh, 'er,' she said. 'No, I don't know 'er, but I know of 'er, as you might say, on account of our Hetty living cluss to 'er. I doubt it would be suitable.'

She was, I felt, trying to convey some sort of message to me with her eyes. I reflected quickly that in Sophie's book, which was probably taken direct from Kezia's, any sort of matrimonial dissension must inevitably be read as scandal, and be the fault of the woman. In matters of this nature, village women were strangely unsupportive of their own sex, and unrelenting in their lack of sympathy.

Well, it really would not matter to me what the true facts were, if the deserted wife would take me as a paying guest for a few weeks. I tried to ignore Sophie's blatant hints, and thanked the Rector for his suggestion. He beamed on me with benign pleasure.

'From what Hector Birch has told me,' he said, 'this Mrs – er – Waters is a charming, rather superior sort of person. You go to see her.' He lifted his rather battered old hat, and bowed himself backwards out of the conversation.

I said, sensing opposition in Sophie and wishing to nip it in the bud, 'I have to go to London this afternoon, so I can't go and see the lady today. But if you can tell me her name and address I will write to her at once.'

She did, but added, 'But I doubt if she'll suit you. She ain't your sort o' woman at all. And I shouldn't ha' thought as you'd ha' wanted to goo and live in Hen Street!' Disapproval was written all over her.

'Dear Sophie,' I said. 'I am not proposing to live there. All I want is a bed and a roof over my head till I can move into my own house. There is so much to do, and I must be near to keep my eye on things. I must get to know people again, and I have to find somebody to do the garden, and to help me in the house.'

She looked, for a moment, so deeply offended that I quailed, and began to wonder if Mrs Brooke's establishment were truly a den of iniquity after all; but the dignity with which she replied informed me that my offence was of a very different nature.

'You've only got to tell me when you want me to start,' she said. 'Wainwrights 'as done domestic for Wagstaffes at Benedict's since the first Wagstaffe come there, and I worked for them as bought it when your grandfather died, though not when it was that wartime hostel place. Since then I've made up with bits and pieces, like, washing-up in the caff at Swithinford, and doing a bit at the Rectory. I ain't starved, but it'll be nice to be 'ome again in the big house. I've all'us 'eld meself ready, like, to go back to Benedict's if anybody ever did buy it. And when I 'eard as it was *you* . . .' Her voice broke, and the grey eyes filled with tears.

'Oh, Sophie,' I said, 'I just can't tell you how happy I am!'

'Ah! So am I!' she said. 'Thanks be to 'Im Above. Mam all'us used to say that when He shets a door, He all'us opens a winder. Just let me know when you want me to start.'

She turned and plodded away, quite abruptly, to fill her green watering-can at the standpipe by the hedge, and I beat a hasty retreat to hide my own exultation. Wait till I could tell William! I was over my first domestic bridge before I had even thought how to begin to tackle it.

I did not much like the prospect of becoming a paying guest. But it would not be for long, and the re-discovery of Sophie had boosted my confidence a lot. I wrote to Mrs Brooke, and was soon in receipt of a reply. The handwriting was firm and decorative, rather large for a woman, with a lot of flourishes; it merely stated that she would be pleased to welcome me as her paying guest if the accommodation and her terms suited me. She would be at home on the Thursday following, in the afternoon, if I would care to call and see what she could offer.

I spent a good deal of time till Thursday conjecturing about what I should find at Bryony Cottage. It turned out to be a most uncompromising four-square bungalow with some odd bits stuck on, built in the thirties, and standing in a large and well-kept garden that included several beautiful, full-grown old trees. I had little time to take anything else in, because as I approached the front door, it opened, and Mrs Brooke was standing on the step to greet me.

She was about as unlike my idea of a landlady as it was possible to be, for she was dressed with an elegance that made me feel old, dowdy, fat and rural. The simple afternoon dress she wore was of excellent quality and cut, and fitted her small, neat figure to perfection. Her expensive shoes drew instant attention to a pair of most beautiful legs, trim ankles and exceedingly pretty feet.

The long fingers of the small hand she extended were tipped with tawny-orange nail varnish, and her dark-auburn hair was so carelessly natural that she must surely have come almost straight from a professional hairdresser. The overall impression I received was one of neat, compact beauty, though as I glanced into her face as we shook hands, I could see she was not as young as I had first thought, or indeed as I had expected her to be from Sophie's hints. There were lines about the mouth and eyes that no make-up could disguise. Her eyes were brown, but not the dark, melting brown seen so often in East Anglia. They were instead of a transparent, golden brown, almost startling in their effect under that hair and her darker brows and lashes. At that particular moment they conveyed nothing but a slight apprehension at the coming interview, a feeling I shared and with which I wholly sympathized.

She asked me in, and we passed through a short passage which in that sort of bungalow is up-graded to 'the hall', and into the sitting-room. It was much like the lady in so far as it was small, compact and attractive, though neither so fashionably nor expensively dressed as its owner. The walls were of the same shade as her writing-paper, eau-de-nil, although what had been delicately feminine in one seemed rather coldly and icily blue in its larger expanse. However, a three-piece suite loose-covered in a large Jacobean pattern of browns and oranges somewhat counteracted it.

The room was certainly comfortable, and my only momentary – and trivial – qualm was caused by the prospect of having to spend evening after evening in contemplation of an overplus of carved soapstone ornaments.

In all other respects it suited me very well. I hoped I might manage to be able to camp out in part of Benedict's by Christmas, but I was consoled to realize that if that were impossible, I could be comfortable enough here till spring. And in the meantime, with Sophie's help I could be integrated with the rest of the village again, and find out how much or how little I wanted to have to do with the brash new town next door.

Mrs Brooke rose with a studied dignity that left me floundering in my deep chair like an old hen in a dust-bath, and offered to conduct me round the rest of the house. She showed me my bedroom, which was less pretentious than 'the lounge', but quite acceptable. Then we had a brief tour of the dining-room, bathroom, kitchen and her own bedroom, plus a tiny boxroom. We went into the garden, and she explained that as she had no car, I could have the use of the garage.

17

'Your garden is beautiful,' I said, remembering the tangled confusion at Benedict's. 'However do you manage to keep it so spick and span and well-kept everywhere?'

'Oh, I have a man to do it,' she replied. 'I couldn't do it all myself, even if I knew anything about gardening, or even liked doing it.'

We returned to the lounge, and she made tea accompanied by delicious home-made scones. There was no doubt about her ability to cook. I considered myself very lucky to have found such a comfortable *pied-à-terre*, and said so.

That she was much relieved at my decision I could tell, and she delicately introduced the subject of 'terms'. She would provide breakfast and an evening meal during the week, but not lunch; she would prefer not to cook on Saturday evenings, and lunch would be at midday on Sundays, with a cold snack in the evening. For this she was asking ten guineas a week, payable in advance.

I was conscious of being surprised. Ten guineas was considerably more than I was paying at the pub, but I was quite willing to pay whatever she had asked, because of the convenience she offered.

I reached for my handbag and took out my wallet, extracting from it two five-pound notes. I looked up to ask her if she would prefer a cheque, and surprised her gaze riveted on the cash in my hands. The tawny eyes were lit from within by such a feverish intensity that she reminded me of a starving animal at the sight of food. I made no mention of substituting a cheque, but added the ten shillings in silver and passed the money across to her. Her hands closed round it like the talons of a hawk.

I left soon after that, having arranged to move in at the weekend. She stood at the gate to wave me away, still clutching my first week's board-money.

As I drove away, I tried to think objectively about her, and the interview, and the whole situation, but I was baffled. I suddenly realized what it was that had repelled me when we were discussing the terms; it was not what she had said, but the steel that had crept into her voice. She was either a miser or quite desperate for money, though the extravagance of her wardrobe didn't bear out either theory. There would be a lot to find out in the coming weeks.

3

I moved into my new accommodation on the following Saturday, a warm, still, golden early September day. Mrs Brooke came from the garden to welcome me, wearing a lime-green sundress of such silken simplicity that it almost shouted Paris. She had been sitting in the sun, and was warmly flushed and very slightly tanned.

As soon as I had dumped my suitcases in the bedroom, she suggested tea in the garden, and quite delightful it all proved to be. The only fly in the ointment as far as I was concerned was the presence at close quarters of 'the man' doing the garden. He was a chap of about fifty-five, of middle height and as lean as a greyhound, browned all over by the elements and as full of wiry energy as a coiled spring. He had the most startlingly blue eyes I ever remembered seeing, in a lined but merry face, and whistled tunefully and sweetly as he worked with a will and a rhythm that was a joy to watch. He could not have been more than six feet from the card-table on which our tea had been set out, but Mrs Brooke absolutely ignored his presence, and made not the least attempt to make him known to me, or vice versa. My village upbringing was warning me that she might be getting me off to a bad start, so I smiled at him and got what I can only describe as a furtive salutation in return.

We talked of trivialities, as women sparring to get to know each other do, of the weather, my journey, of her preparations for my arrival, of the progress (or lack of it) at Benedict's. She got up to go into the house to refill the teapot, and the gardener straightened up, following her with his eyes. As he started to work again, true and sweet as a blackbird came the sound again from his pursed lips, though the tune had changed. It was quite unmistakable, though I felt certain the choice was absolutely unconscious on his part.

> Did you not see my lady
> Go down the garden singing . . .

I looked at him with new interest, but my hostess came back and coolly dismissed him again from our female scene.

When the clock of Old Swithinford church chimed the hour of six very faintly in the distance, the man straightened up, and took from his waistcoat pocket a large silver watch. 'Dear oh dear,' he said, 'Time I wasn't here. I shall catch it proper from the missus if I ain't on time for my Sat'day supper.' Mrs Brooke did not appear to have heard him. His broad East Anglian accent warmed my heart.

Her attitude towards him had made one thing abundantly clear to me — that she was not country-born, or 'of' the village, though of course that must apply to the majority of Hen Street's inhabitants. No genuine countrywoman would have dreamed of treating a local workman as she had treated her gardener.

'What a delightful man,' I said, when he had gone. 'Who is he?'

'Who? Oh, the gardener? His name is Ned Merriman, but apart from that I know nothing about him. He heard I needed help in the garden, and came to offer himself.'

'Oh *dear*,' I said. 'I do wish you had introduced us. He will think I did not want to recognize him, but of course I remember him as a youth about the village. It didn't occur to me that he might be from Old Swithinford. I must put it right when he comes tomorrow.'

She looked hard at me, as if she suspected me of something, though I couldn't think what. Unless it was that she disapproved of the idea of me hobnobbing with a menial, however much I might remember him or his family. That was the only interpretation I could put on her expression, which was of apprehension rather than anything else, I thought. Perhaps she really was a distressed gentle-woman, having difficulty in finding her new level, and clinging desperately to the last few strands of former status. She was certainly not out of the top drawer — so what was she? I found such social snobbishness difficult to cope with, to tell the truth, and liked her less for it than I had been prepared to.

After I had unpacked, I was on my way back to the lounge when I glanced through the kitchen door and saw her standing at the sink doing the washing-up. Her hands were encased in clumsy, shocking-pink rubber gloves, and she had a lighted cigarette stuck between her scarlet lipstick. Her eyes were screwed up to avoid the smoke, and she looked real, warm, human — utterly different from the hard, polished woman quoting her terms on Thursday, or the *grande dame* who could look straight through Ned Merriman without seeing him. After that domesticated glimpse of her at the sink, I decided that I quite liked her, if for no other reason than that she interested me so much, though I had to admit to myself that Sophie had probably been right in her estimate that she was not the sort of woman to suit me. I wanted to know more about her, and intuition told me I should not have to wait long. In this I was right. Once the remains of our cold evening meal had been cleared away, the social hoarfrost began to melt.

'Do call me Johanna,' she said. 'Even if your house goes ahead as fast as you want it to, you will still be here with me for the next three months at least. We might just as well make the most of it, and get to know each other properly.'

I did not reciprocate by inviting her to call me Frances, let alone Fran, because I have never been one to rush into first-name terms on five minutes' acquaintance. Nevertheless, there was something very attractive about her that prevented me from attempting to hold her at arms' length. (She was calling me 'Fran' within a few days without any feeling about it on my part.)

She knew all about my circumstances; the grapevine via Sophie's sister Hetty and Ned Merriman had supplied what details I had not made known when I wrote to her. All I knew about her was that there were matrimonial difficulties.

I had hoped that I should not be required to make polite conversation among the soapstone ornaments every evening of my stay under her roof, and had decided to make it clear from the start that I liked to read, and to use my hands. In this, however, she forestalled me on that first evening, by reaching behind the arm of the settee and producing a bag of very domesticated knitting.

'What are you making?' I asked, seeing at a glance that it could not be a garment for her own elegant wardrobe.

She laughed — a genuine laugh full of gentle humour. 'I'm finishing a pullover for one of my neighbours,' she said. 'She keeps on starting bits of dreadful knitting and getting stuck by the time she gets to shaping the armholes. This must be at least the sixth pullover I've had to rescue, but she never learns.' After a pause, her tone changed and she heaved a deep sigh. 'I suppose I do it because I miss having a man to knit for.'

This was so blatant a lead that I felt it would be churlish not to follow it with a bit of interest.

'I am sorry,' I said, clumsily. 'The Rector told me that you were living alone.'

She paused to light a cigarette, then took up her knitting again, staring down at it without moving the needles, as if to gain control of herself before speaking again.

21

'My husband is in Australia,' she said, 'or he was when I last heard from him, six months or so ago. He emigrated nearly three years ago, when the firm he was working for got a big contract. But it had bitten off more than it could chew, and went bust. He had gone over first to find his feet, and was going to send for me when he had found us somewhere to live. That is how I come to be in a dump like this! We sold our lovely home in Essex so that he could buy this and still have some to put down on a flat overlooking Sydney Harbour. When the firm packed up, he tried to get another job, but he couldn't, and wrote to say he would have to come back. He hadn't been able to send me anything to live on — and that's where things began to go seriously wrong. You see, he had gone out on an assisted passage, and before they would release his passport to let him come back, he had got to pay for his passage out as well as his passage home. So he asked me for £500 of what we had in the bank. Well, I got a bit windy, then, and only sent him half of what he had asked for. You see, some of what we had was mine — a legacy I had had left to me. And I had had to have quite a bit out to live on when he wasn't sending me any. He turned nasty, then, and wrote saying it was plain that I didn't want him back. Since then, I've only heard from him three times, each from a different place. But one of his mates did come back, and came to see me, and told me Dave had taken up with another woman as soon as he'd got over there, and had never had any intention of coming back. He just wanted to get money out of me!'

Her voice broke, and she produced a tiny lace-edged handkerchief, and cried.

I did not know what to say. It was, unfortunately, the sort of sorry, sordid story one heard far too often, now.

'I never thought I should be reduced to taking paying guests,' she said. 'But the house is all I've got left. I have to make it work for me somehow. Of course I have been to see a solicitor, and he says I might be able to get a court order for maintenance. But it's one thing to obtain a court order, and quite another to make a man pay up. While he chooses to stop in Australia, I should still never be sure of anything.'

'Not even if you got a divorce?'

The handkerchief came into play again. 'Oh no!' she almost wailed. 'I won't! I don't want to! He's *my* husband!' She sobbed, and again I felt helpless, though not so sympathetic as I had been. A husband irrevocably lost of his own volition on the other side of the world didn't seem to me to be a very valuable asset. All the same, I recognized the essential feminine quality of her argument. I had heard it many times before.

'Dave insisted that we put this bungalow into joint names,' she said, 'because I had put all the money I had into our first home. And my solicitor says that if he continues to default on maintenance, I could in time possibly get it made over to me completely. But you came along just in the nick of time. I really don't know what I should have done if you hadn't.'

I could see that she was in a mess, and was facing a very nasty set of circumstances with both common sense and courage. But I felt that she was subjecting me to a kind of moral blackmail. I had not yet spent one night in her house, but she had already made it clear that if for any reason I left her, I should be a deep-dyed villain condemning her more or less to starvation. I was irritated.

She had a good deal more to say about 'her Dave', who was apparently all that a man should be physically, and a loving companion into the bargain. She was certain that he still loved her, but that 'some Australian floosie' had got hold of him, and wouldn't let go.

I murmured words of condolence and sympathy, and then she got up and excused herself, making apologies.

When she returned, she had made up her face again, and brought in some bedtime drinks. If she had looked after Dave as well as she had started looking after me, I thought, he was probably a fool rather than a knave.

Next morning was Sunday, with no reason for rising early. Johanna knocked on my door about seven thirty, and came in with a cup of tea and the Sunday paper. I slipped on my dressing-gown and went along the passage to the bathroom, pausing with my hand on the door. The kitchen door was slightly ajar, and through it came the sound of two unmistakable East Anglian voices engaged in good-humoured banter of a characteristically beefy village nature. One was undoubtedly that of Ned, the gardener; the other I did not recognize. The timbre of it was that of the wide-open spaces, and the dialect the one that I had heard and loved from my childhood. When I came out of the bathroom the door had drifted a few inches wider open, far enough for me to satisfy my curiosity about the other occupant of the kitchen.

The morning sun was brilliant, and was streaming into the tiny kitchen through the half-glass door that led into the conservatory. At the corner of the kitchen table sat Ned, with a cup of coffee in front of him and a cigarette in his hand. His blue eyes were fixed on the doorway, where his companion must be standing, and the admiration in them was not to be mistaken. Nosey I might be, but I had to know who it was that was causing that expression in the eyes of such a man as I had judged Ned Merriman to be yesterday, at seven thirty on a Sunday morning. I moved silently to get a wider view.

Framed in the sunlit doorway stood Johanna. She wore a ravishing pale pink negligée over a matching nightdress, and both were, to say the very least, revealing. Like Rodin's girdle, the translucent clinging material drew attention to more than it concealed. Unintelligent auburn women, I had noticed, tend to go for blues and greens; the truly seductive ones know that pale pink is their colour. Johanna's pink concoction was enhanced by a froth of exquisitely fine écru lace all down the front opening. The garments were so essentially feminine that one felt Eve might have found them more useful than none when tempting poor Adam at the dawn of love.

I stood stock-still with surprise and disbelief, and a mixture of other emotions in which distaste, dismay, and shame at my own Peeping Tom role were mingled. I was just about to risk slipping quietly by the door when Johanna spoke. She had turned to face Ned, and said, 'Naow what a-yer gawpin' at, Ned Merriman? You've seen many a woman in 'er bedgown afore, I'll be bound!' Her imitation of the dialect was perfect, and I could only recall with disbelief the distant Lady Bracknell Johanna addressing the very same man in the garden yesterday afternoon. I was past the door and on my way back to the bedroom when I heard Ned's answer. 'Ah! That I have. But none to touch you in that thing with the pig's fry all down the front.'

And even as I blushed at the only inference I could put upon the badinage, I heard the laughter of both ring out — Ned's a deep, hearty chuckle and Johanna's as bell-like as an innocent child's. Just enjoying a bit of fun together, no more. Nothing made sense. There must be a good deal more to Johanna Brooke than met the eye, and I saw that I was going to have difficulty in knowing where to pitch my scale of values with regard to her behaviour while I was a guest under her roof.

An hour later, when we had breakfasted, Ned came to the door with some newly dug vegetables for our lunch, and Johanna's manner towards him was what I can only think of as 'ordinary'. There was neither the stand-offishness of yesterday nor the too easy familiarity of this early morning. I decided that I was turning into a nosey old frump who no longer understood the changing social patterns. It was the only explanation I could think of.

My days were very fully occupied, and once I had settled down with Johanna, comfortable and even enjoyable. Much to my architect's disgust, I had insisted in having my finger in all his plans for my house. I had no intention of allowing him to try any modern tricks with it that would rob it of any of its period charm, or of its nostalgic memories for me. When we had planned the restoration of the main part of the house, there were still some rooms left over. They were mainly at the back, and had once been the servants' quarters, with a separate staircase and a door leading out to the kitchen garden. For some obscure reason, they were in less need of repair than any of the main rooms, though one and all needed touching up and redecorating. Wandering through them during the first week of my life with Johanna, I was struck by an idea. If I could get a couple of them cleaned and aired, I could get bits of my furniture out of store and camp there so as to be always on the spot when needed. I sought out Sophie, and asked her to come down with me and give me her opinion about the feasibility of my plan. She saw at once what I was after, and said she would start on the rooms as soon as ever she could give up her job in Swithinford. The next week she was back in her own element at Benedict's, setting about her Herculean task with a will.

Not everything was going so smoothly, though. The architect had sub-contracted the building work to a large firm who in turn had sub-contracted a firm of plumbers. This chain of service broke down whenever the plumbers failed to turn up, which was far too often, wasting precious days. The garden was also starting to worry me a lot, because it needed to be tackled at once, this autumn, so as to give it any hope of being licked into shape before spring. The architect had promised to give me a list of the best landscape gardeners near enough to take it on, but I had not so far received it. When I rang to ask about the plumbers' continued absence, the smoothy who answered – my architect was on holiday – said that that was 'really the builder's baby'; the builder said yes, it was, but he could do nothing without the architect's instructions.

This is the sort of situation that in your helplessness makes you feel alone; I wanted someone intelligent and interested to discuss it with. The answer, of course, was William, but I was a little afraid to lean on our 'cousinhood' too heavily. However, I took my courage in both hands, and rang him. His reply was that he would come out on Wednesday as soon as he could get away, just after lunch, meeting me at Benedict's to inspect the progress that had been made. He would then like to take me out to dinner and deliver me again to Bryony Cottage on his way home, hinting that he would rather like to see my new quarters.

I told Johanna, and asked permission to bring my cousin in, even though it might be a bit late in the evening. She appeared to know all about him — again via Ned, no doubt. She expressed her pleasure at the thought of meeting any of my friends, indicating that they would be welcome at Bryony Cottage any time.

As I drove out of the gates on Wednesday to go down to Benedict's, I saw a woman leave the 'semi' two doors away and turn, on foot, towards Old Swithinford. She was solid, middle-aged and shaped oddly like a pear, with most of her weight at the bottom end. There was something about her that amused me. She had a habit of putting each foot forward a long way, and then drawing it back again before transferring her weight to it. It gave her feet a sort of scratching motion, and caused her large posterior to wiggle from side to side.

I stopped the car, and offered her a lift. I introduced myself as Mrs Brooke's new lodger, and as we chatted she seemed bent on eliciting my opinion of Johanna. I was on my guard about her innocent-sounding gambits; but to my surprise, my passenger was warm in her praise of Johanna as a good and friendly neighbour.

'Nice woman,' she declared. 'Neat with her fingers she is, too, always willing to do what she can to help you. Many's the time she's put my bits of knitting right, when I have got into a muddle, and she looked after my husband so kind, when I had to go into hospital. She hasn't been here all that long, of course, and there's some who don't care much for her, but I must speak as I find. She's a real good neighbour, and I think it's a real shame about that husband of hers going off like he has and leaving her to fend for herself in a place where nobody knows her.'

Luckily, we had reached the end of the drive down to Benedict's, so I pulled up, and was not obliged to answer or make any comment. My new acquaintance scrambled out of the car, reiterating her thanks. I waved goodbye and was beginning to move when she suddenly started padding along beside the car, rapping on the passenger-side window. I thought she must have forgotten her handbag, and hastily applied my brakes. She opened the door and

26

said in a hoarse whisper, 'But don't lend her any money!' Then the door closed again, and she had gone.

I was startled and a bit shocked by this strange turn of events, but at that moment I heard the toot of William's car as he drew up behind me and I put the incident from my mind, as I drove on up to the house with him following.

4

Sophie was making the dust fly in what had once been the kitchen when we got to the house. I took William in and re-introduced them. She greeted him with the same pleased, unruffled calm with which she had first encountered me in the churchyard, dispelling any doubts I might have had about a new relationship between three adults who had once played together as children. She behaved as if she and William might have parted only yesterday, while at the same time managing to convey that they were now on a different footing.

'Them plumbers ain't 'ere again today,' she said. 'If you was to ask me, I should say as you'd do a sight better to sack 'em and get somebody as lives clusser to.'

'I've thought the same thing,' I said. 'But are there many reliable local plumbers?'

'Well, there's Arf and Hully,' she replied. 'They've been doing plumbing work since the day they was breeched. I know as some folks think as they're a bit slow up top, like, but most folk in the village have 'em if they want any plumbing work done.'

'And where can I find them?'

'Down in the village. Where the old blacksmith's forge used to be. Folks round 'ere know 'em as Arf and Hully, 'cos them's all'us been their nicknames, but their real names are Arthur and George.'

William looked in his breast-pocket for something to write on, and asked, 'What is their surname?'

Sophie had turned her back on him to get on with her work, and answered him from amid a shower of loose plaster and dust that she had just brought down from the ceiling.

'Gawn,' she replied. 'G—A—W—N.'

We scuttled out of the old kitchen to avoid another plastery shower, and proceeded to inspect the rest of the house at our leisure, before retiring to Swithinford to find a café for a cup of tea.

'I believe Sophie may have a good point in suggesting you use local workmen,' William said seriously. 'They may be the old type of skilled rural craftsmen, and it would get you off to a good start in the eyes of the village. Why don't we go and pay Arthur and George a visit, now? We've got plenty of time.'

'Arf and Hully,' I said, idly, and then choked on my tea. 'Oh, William.' I caught his eye, and the slight distance there had been between us closed up with a snap. We had always laughed together at the same things. 'Sophie said some people thought they were a bit simple! Their surname is Gawn – Arf Gawn and Hully Gawn! Can I possible employ people who answer to names like that?'

All the same, after visiting the brothers, I felt that I simply could not do better. And emboldened by their grasp of the situation and their skilful suggestions, I asked Arf, who seemed to be the senior partner, if he could recommend anybody local who might undertake the first blitz on the garden. He directed us to a firm of odd-jobbers called Bean, and before we left for an early dinner at the Coach House, I felt that at last that I was beginning to make real progress.

We ate our meal in a warm glow of nostalgia and shared childhood reminiscences, but got away early so as to give William time to stay long enough at Bryony Cottage to be reasonably polite to Johanna before having to leave.

She opened the door to us, and I almost felt the shock that ran through William's frame at the sight of her. This time she was wearing the kind of elegant 'little black dress' that costs a small fortune and makes women of her colouring glow like highly polished old copper.

William continued to look dazed as he followed us into the lounge, and watched Johanna's deft little hands dispensing coffee and liqueurs. She followed his gaze when in an effort not to appear rude he dragged it from her person and fastened it in a desperate attempt at politeness on a bit of soapstone. Then, watching the momentary pained look on his sensitive face, she let out a peal of laughter as melodious as a chime of tubular bells.

'You don't like my monstrosities, Professor? Neither do I!'

'Then why do you keep them?' I asked, because I had truly always wanted to know. She stood looking at them, and her face softened: her tawny eyes had a moist, melting quality that I could see was calling out all the essential maleness in William. I felt on edge, as if I were suddenly the odd one out among the three of us.

'My father collected them bit by bit when I was very small,' she said. 'He loved them. Some do, and some don't. I happen not to. But I can't bear to throw them out, so I have no choice but to stick them all in this little room and overwhelm everybody with my dubious taste. Have some more coffee.'

She was a splendid hostess, and set herself to charm William, and she succeeded. I took myself to task for feeling 'narked' by his so obvious admiration of her. But while she flirted openly with William, who seemed to me to look much younger for the treatment, I experienced a sensation I had expected never to feel again. I wasn't jealous of her figure or her looks, and goodness knows I had no reason to envy her in any material way – but William was my acquaintance, and I had only just found him again, 'my' William, over lunch that very day.

I had to snap out of it. William was only 'my' William because he had offered to help a so-called cousin who had been a childhood friend. I had no claim on him, and I must never, never, even in my most private thoughts, delude myself that I had. He was a man of the world, perfectly capable of taking care of himself. No doubt a modern university was full of sirens of the Johanna variety, and for all I knew William had had plenty of experience in either yielding to or fending off their blandishments. I saw him for the first time as a man, rather than the boy I had grown up with, now a bit older. It gave me a considerable jolt somewhere inside me to become so suddenly aware what a sexually attractive male he was.

Johanna had fixed a cigarette in a long ivory holder, and William was leaning forward to light it for her, caught and held in that ultra-feminine web.

'She's a man's woman,' I told myself. 'She makes no bones about it. At least in that she is absolutely sincere.'

That was it – one could never find the core of complete sincerity in her. You could never grasp the essential Johanna, because there were as many Johannas as there were different situations to act as settings for her. She appeared to be ninety-nine per cent sincere in any setting, but always there was something held back, kept secret, covered up – a real self so deep down that perhaps she herself didn't really know it well enough to recognize it.

'Penny for them,' said William, putting his hand over mine. It was like an electric shock.

I collected myself together guiltily, seeking a scapegoat in the bushes. 'I'm sorry,' I said. 'I'm afraid I had gone off chasing my own preoccupations again. Do you,' I asked, addressing Johanna directly, 'know anything of the Bean family?'

'I only know them by sight. One of the brothers is long and thin, and the other shorter but more thickset. I don't know their names — no, wait a minute, I do. Ned told me that their names are Kenneth and James, but nobody ever calls them that. They have always been known as Kidney and Jelly.'

'Oh, really!' I expostulated. 'Are you expecting me to believe that in one day I have engaged the services not only of Arf Gawn and Hully Gawn, but of Kidney Bean and Jelly Bean as well?'

The atmosphere had changed, and become less charged.

'I must go,' said William. 'I had no idea it was as late as it is.'

'Have another cup of coffee before you set out,' said Johanna, jumping up. 'I'll go and make it.'

She disappeared through the door William had sprung to his feet to open for her, and we heard her clattering about the kitchen. William deliberately closed the door, latching it.

'Why didn't you warn me?' he said. 'I would have polished my armour and put it on.'

There was a strained silence.

'I'm sorry, Fran,' he said. 'She caught me off guard. I hope I haven't been making too much of a fool of myself, but I can't say I haven't enjoyed the evening. I think you never met Janice. They are as alike as two peas from the same pod — and not only to look at. It was like meeting Janice for the first time all over again.' He made a wry face. 'Once bitten, twice shy.'

'But the attraction still holds?'

'A man wouldn't be a man at all who didn't rise like a fish to that sort of fly,' he said. 'But I hope I have learned something from experience. How do you react to her?'

With the inconsistency for which women are notorious, I now felt bound to defend her, and that female dominance she could bring into play over the opposite sex.

'I like her,' I said stoutly. 'If I had a face and a figure like that, I doubt if I should be half as nice to other women as she is. She's a duck.'

William was looking more serious than the occasion demanded, I thought. He played with his car keys for a minute or two before looking up at me and replying.

'She's as deep as a well and as fragile as cat-ice,' he said. 'Don't get too involved. You'll get hurt.'

I went to see William off, and when I returned to the house the domestic, easy, capable Johanna had replaced the polished hostess and the siren. Even her voice was different.

'I saw you pick Margaret Ellis up this afternoon,' she said. 'She's the one whose knitting I am always having to put right.'

'Yes, she told me so.' I smiled at the remembrance of the strange little woman. Johanna caught the smile, and chuckled.

'She and Stan are about the only ones left in Hen Street who actually keep chickens,' she said. 'They've been at it so long that they both look and sound like chickens themselves.'

She set down the tray she was holding and stuck on her head the old kitchen tea-cosy that she had hastily secreted earlier in her knitting bag when William and I had arrived. Then she began to walk up and down the room, her feet 'scratching' in the way I had noted Mrs Ellis's doing, her slim behind waggling and her head making pecking movements. While I was still gasping in astonishment at this startling bit of visual clowning, she spoke, greeting and thanking me in a voice that was at once that of Margaret Ellis, and the cackling of an agitated hen.

Of course – that was exactly how Mrs Ellis looked and spoke. I hadn't seen it this afternoon, but I could see it now. I laughed aloud while my landlady calmly took off the tea-cosy and straightened her body till it was its own slim self again.

'Johanna,' I gasped. 'That was priceless! You should have been an actress.'

'Of course I should. I've always wanted to be. It just wasn't in my cards.'

'Don't you make any use of a gift like that at all?'

'Not now. How can I? I used to do a lot of amateur theatricals, once. I believe there is an amateur theatrical society in Swithinford, but I couldn't get there, even supposing they would welcome me, or be good enough anyway to interest me. Though I would try them, if I had a car.'

She sat down again, gazing sadly and regretfully into the dying fire. I felt so dreadfully pampered and selfish that I thought I must do something about that. If she could drive, she could at least borrow my car for the coming autumn season. I was opening my mouth to make the offer when revelation suddenly burst round me like the light on the road to Damascus.

Johanna never stopped acting! Everything, but everything, she did was a part being played. That's why I had felt I could never find the real Johanna. Perhaps I had never yet met her. Those changes of voice I had heard – Lady Bracknell, the village wench, her silky purr for William – were all put on as much as Margaret Ellis's persona had been a minute or two ago. The act of tear-restraining self-control I was watching now was being brilliantly performed, worthy of a great tragedienne, and it had nearly fooled me; but disbelief had come from somewhere, and for the next few minutes could not be suspended.

I heard again in my distant consciousness Madge Ellis saying, 'Don't lend her any money', and William's voice in my other ear, 'She's as deep as a well. Don't get involved.'

Johanna had stubbed out one cigarette and lit another. She stood up and began to pile things on the tray.

'But you can't let a talent like that go unused,' I said. 'There must be some way of getting into Swithinford, surely? Any local amateur society would give its eyebrows for a member with your sort of gift.'

She didn't answer, but picked up the tray and screwed her eyes to avoid the smoke from her cigarette again. That, at any rate, was not an act. I softened towards her, thinking, 'Now she is real. A born home maker without a man to make a home for.' I was glad to have discovered the real Johanna for myself. It would make the rest of our time together less edgy, and more enjoyable.

It was only after I had gone to bed and lay thinking in the dark that it occurred to me that perhaps the 'real' Johanna, to use my own banal phraseology, had other aspects too. Had I not once surprised a money-hungry predator's gold-flecked eyes gleaming at the sight of its prey? Sleepily, I concluded that it was none of my business. I didn't like her any the less for being such a consummate natural actress – why should I, now that I knew? On the other hand, it deepened my interest in her very much. My last thoughts before sleep overcame me were that Johanna was certainly 'one too many' for her rural or pseudo-rural neighbours to comprehend. The likes of Sophie, or Arf and Hully, could only put their own construction on her behaviour. Was it a cuckoo or a kestrel they had in their nest?

5

My days were remarkably full. During the following week, the Bean family began their assault on the garden, and I spent a lot of my time standing at the landing window looking down on them, as yard by yard they revealed more and more memories of my childhood. There were bits I had forgotten, like the set of three semicircular steps that led from the old, raised, walled rose garden to the rectangle of lawn that ran alongside the huge herbaceous border. Jelly Bean had, in fact, fallen down them in my sight because he had had no idea they were there, so overgrown with cushions of saxifrage, clumps of camomile, tangles of wild strawberry and bushes of purple mallow had they become. He had turned in anger and slashed them down, pulling up the dark green clumps of saxifrage and hurling them aside to assuage his own discomfiture, like a child kicking the leg of the table he has just bumped his head on. And there, as he did so, he revealed the glowing old steps of red brick which my grandfather had told me had been imported from Sussex specially for the purpose. There were three other sets on the three sides of the rose garden that Jelly had not yet tackled. It was on this particular lot that Jess and I had sat when we learned one of the world's great secrets.

A woman from the village had come up to help Kezia to turn out the cellar. At around midday, her daughter had appeared, carrying the baby, a boy about eighteen months old. It was a sunny spring morning, and Kezia had told the girl, who was about twelve, to take the baby out into the garden and let him run about there till his mother had finished what she was doing, and could see to him.

So the girl, whose name was Grace, had come into our view, and put the little boy down. She saw us and we saw her, but although we knew her by sight, she was some five years our senior and not one that we ever played with.

The baby toddled up and down, unsteady yet on his feet, so that every time he tumbled he sat down suddenly on his little swathed behind. He had not yet been breeched, and every time it happened, the great clout of diaper under the dress he was wearing slipped a little lower, until suddenly there he lay on the grass with the whole wet bundle round his ankles, the dress up round his shoulders, and himself bare from the waist down.

Jess and I nudged each other, caught in the grip of absorbing interest accompanied by acute embarrassment. We had never before been privileged to view a member of the male sex in his entirety.

Grace made a lunge at the baby, to pull up the offending bundle; but Tommy's little bottom had sensed freedom, and he got up and stepped neatly out of his sartorial encumbrance and began to run towards the lily pond. Grace went after, caught him, and carried him back to us, setting him down close to us while she picked up the wet bundle and looked around for somewhere to sit while she put it back on again. We made room for her on the steps, and looked our fill at his extraordinary appendage as the boy lay struggling across her knees.

I could not restrain my curiosity any longer, whatever the retribution might be. (Instinct warned me I was on forbidden ground.)

'Grace,' I said, going hot all over and blushing, 'what is that funny little thing at the bottom of his tummy?' (I wasn't allowed to say stomach, let alone belly.)

Grace let out a guffaw that made Jess and me cringe.

'Cor!' she said. 'Don't you know nothink? Fancy gels o' your age not knowing that!'

'Tell us, Grace, please,' I said, determined not to let this golden opportunity vanish, however much derision Grace showered upon us.

'Lay still, bor, else I'll slap you,' she said to Tommy. Then she hid the fascinating object from our view, and said casually, 'Tha's what all little ol' bors have. Gals don't. Tha's 'ow you know the difference.'

Well! How many times had I asked to have that very thing explained to me, and how many times had I been put off by a simpering mother or giggling maid telling me that their heads were a different shape, or their eyes a different colour! I was angry at this deliberate adult deceit, and even more anxious to learn as much as I could while I had the chance.

'What is it called?' I asked.

Grace stood Tommy upright, fully clothed again.

'Tha's got a lot o' names,' she said. 'Some ol' bors call it their willie, an' some call it their dickie, an' some say their charlie.'

How interesting! So far Jess had not said a word, though she had been all eyes and ears. Now she cogitated over Grace's information like a judge weighing up evidence.

'I shall call it Sid,' she said. That had become the accepted euphemism to us, now.

How had our parents ever expected any of us to grow up into normal men and women?

As I watched Jelly clear the steps Sophie came and stood by my side, looking down too.

'Jelly's found the steps,' I said.

'Ah! So I see,' she answered, in a tone that I can only describe as tender. Was she also enjoying glimpses of herself as a child in the garden? I turned towards her to look into her face as she stood close to me, and found the grey eyes unmistakably moist and sad as they rested on the sweating Jelly.

I collected my thoughts quickly. Sophie and Jelly were much of an age. They must have grown up together, been at school together, been young together before the war. What village romance had I unwittingly stumbled upon?

'I don't remember the Beans being in the village when I was a child,' I said, seeking some way of easing the silence while still satisfying my curiosity.

'Well, you wouldn't, would you? You knowed us 'cos we used to come down 'ere with Mam, but you didn't goo down to the village to play. Me and Jelly went to school together.'

I nodded, to show her I understood more than she had told me, and I took her hand. 'And then he married somebody else in the war.'

The tears spilled over as she shook her head. 'No,' she said. ''E ain't married. 'E still lives at 'ome.'

I thought I dare not pursue the topic any further, but, to my great surprise, she did. 'I am still got two bottles o' wine put away, left over from the lot Mam made for my twenty-first,' she said. 'Jelly come up to see me the day arter it, to our 'ouse, while Mam were up 'ere at work an' I were all by myself. So we set in the garden, and I give 'im a glass o' wine what were left in one o' the bottles we had opened at my party. And when he'd drunk it, 'e says to me, "Tha's a jolly good drop o' stuff, that is, Soph! Is there any more on it left?" And I says well no, not opened, but there were two whull bottles as hadn't been uncorked.

'"Keep 'em safe," 'e says, "They'll be real good come our weddin'." And then we 'eard Mam comin' in the front gate, so 'e went off over the back 'edge so as not to meet 'er. An' that night, I stole them two bottles o' wine and 'id 'em among the rest o' the things in my bottom drawer, as true as ever I stand 'ere.

'Well, come next day, Mam, she looked high and low for 'em, and counted the empty bottles again and again till I thought as I should have to give in and put 'em back somewhere when she weren't looking. But I never. She kept on about it, and blamed everybody from Thirzah's 'usband to old Sam Blatch as lived next door for stealin' em, but at last she forgot 'em — and there they still are.'

I was at a loss to know what to say in reply to this confidence, for such I knew it to be, and that I ought to feel humbly proud that Sophie should honour me with it.

'And that was all?' I asked at last.

She shook her head again. 'No. You see, we had a real good do here for the peace celebrations in 1945. There were sports and things in the daytime, an' a social in the school at night. Mam weren't well enough to goo at night, so Thirz' come and set with her, so as me and Hetty could goo to the social. Hetty and Joe 'ad been courting for a tidy while, then, so Mam let Hetty go with Joe as long as I were there to keep a eye on 'em, as you might say. So Hetty went off and danced with Joe, and left me settin' by myself under the window. Then Jelly come and set aside of me, and put 'is arm round my waist, and kep' it there all the whull evening. And once 'e whispered to me, "Ay yer still got that wine, gal?" and I nodded, 'cos I had.

' "We'll drink it, yet, you see if we don't," 'e said . . . I shall never forget it.'

It was almost more than I could bear.

'What happened?' I asked.

'Mother got to 'ear about it,' was all she said.

'But Sophie!' I expostulated. 'You must have been quite thirty by then! And what about Thirzah and Hetty? One was married and the other courting.'

She was still gazing out of the window, though no longer at Jelly. 'P'raps that's why,' she said. 'P'raps it was because they'd both gone as she didn't want me to go an' all. She wanted one of us left to look after 'er, at 'ome.'

'But that—' I swallowed. I knew that I must not so much as hint at any criticism of her mother, which would have made her suffering seem to have been in vain, but I had to make some sort of protest. 'She must have known she would have to leave you alone before long,' I said.

Sophie's tears were now slipping unchecked down her face. She nodded. 'Ah, I knowed that. I couldn't a-bear the thought o' leaving 'er, even if I 'ad 'ad the chance — but I didn't. Jelly never spoke to me no more — well, only to pass the time o' day, like, if we met each other by chance. Not even after Mam were dead. Not that it would ha' made no difference, then. We couldn't ha' gone against 'er wishes once she'd gone, could we? Not after all she'd done for us.'

The last sentence identified the 'we'. She would not have been allowed her freedom by Thirzah, who had stepped into her mother's shoes.

She shook her duster and dried her face on it, and then left me to get on with her work. I continued to stare down at Jelly, filled with the pity and terror of human tragedy. Like the Greeks, Sophie and Jelly had both accepted the machinations of the gods without point-less struggle, if not without question. The Romantic in me wanted to write another act, here and now; the Realist told me to let well alone, and count my own blessings.

Arf and Hully had been to inspect, and were so full of common sense and practical suggestions that I rang the builder at once to instruct him to sack his chosen plumbers.

So I engaged the Gawns, and found that their experience with Aga boilers and septic tanks was worth all the architectural advice in the book, and their work much better value. I was kept so busy that I rarely got back to Bryony Cottage before supper-time, and slept when I went to bed as I had not slept for years.

After the Gawns had been there for about a week, they had everything so much under control that for the first time I had an afternoon in my diary with no appointment in it. It was time I went to explore Swithinford, and do some bits of personal shopping. When I said so at breakfast-time, I saw at once the hope in Johanna's face. I had no option but to ask her if she would like to go with me. She accepted like a child offered an unexpected treat. I was going to be at Benedict's in the morning, and so we arranged for me to pick her up *en route*. Not that I minded; it was just that I was aware of an uncomfortable feeling that the gods were idly and mischievously tangling the threads of our lives together as relentlessly as they had kept Sophie's and Jelly's apart.

When I drove down to pick Johanna up at around two thirty, I was quite surprised to find her dressed up in a Lovat tweed suit and a pale pink jumper, with immaculate gloves and a pair of slim-cut brogues polished till they could have served Perseus as a shield. I had not changed to go out. I felt very much like a poor relation as we left the car and went up the side street together to where it met the main shopping area and centre of the town.

She looked a bit uncomfortable, and stopped as we reached the turning. 'Which way are you going?' she said, in a way that made it plain that she would not be coming with me. In fact, I was being politely dismissed to go about my business alone.

'Tell me where and at what time you want to meet me to go home,' I said.

'I'm going looking for shoes,' she replied, 'and I am very hard to please. Shall we say back at the car park at five o'clock?'

I was dumbfounded, because it was only a little after three, and I had had no intention of making a whole afternoon of it. But I agreed, weakly, and she set off at a brisk walk.

By four o'clock I wanted a cup of tea, and noticed a café, so I made towards it passing as I did so a large, stark, red-brick building plastered with notices. I stopped to glance at them, and saw that one was to the effect that the Swithinford Amateur Dramatic Society was meeting for the new season on Friday, and would welcome new members. I resolved to tell Johanna, and to offer to lend her my car. Then I went into the café.

Right up in the farthest corner, tucked into an alcove, was a table at which sat Johanna and a man.

I had no reason to be embarrassed, but I was; afterwards I realized that my embarrassment was a reflection of theirs. It was instantly covered up by expressions of welcome from Johanna.

'Hello,' she called gaily. 'Do come and join us.'

Rather reluctantly, I did so. The man stood up – a rounded, pink, well-cared-for man somewhere around the fifty mark, with a smooth baby face and a shiny patch of balditude showing through his carefully arranged hair as he bowed over my hand. His attire was just a little too flamboyant to have the stamp of good taste. Johanna had become in an instant a completely poised middle-class lady.

'I don't think you know each other,' she said. 'May I present Hector Birch? Mrs Catherwood, who is going to live at Benedict's.'

We sat down. 'Of course we know all about you, Mrs Catherwood,' he said effusively. 'We are so pleased to have someone back there who has a genuine interest in village life.'

I decided at once that I absolutely detested the man, though I had every reason to be grateful to him for finding me my pleasant temporary foothold. His voice was as pink and plummy as the rest of him – pleasantly modulated, educated, even cultured, but tinged with enough condescension to make my hackles rise. Playing at being a parson, and overdoing his act. Which reminded me.

'Johanna,' I said. 'I've just seen a notice that says the Amateur Dramatic Society actually wants new members. You really should join. Did you know, Mr Birch, what an absolutely marvellous actress Mrs Brooke is? She should have been an actress – a professional one. And she was telling me how much she has missed amateur dramatics since coming to live in Swithinford Bridges.'

Mr Birch's face registered a whole range of expressions. Interest, speculation, pleasure – plus a hint of doubt or vexation.

'Now that is a fascinating coincidence,' he said. 'My business in Swithinford this afternoon is connected with that very thing.'

He went on, holding the conversational floor, as it were, as if he might have been in the pulpit. 'The Dramatic Society meets in a hall that was built in the first place by a group of public-spirited people on a semi-business footing. It doesn't pay its way now, but it can't be sold without the unanimous agreement of the original "smallholders". One of them, still alive, vetoes the sale. So we are stuck with it.'

'Us?' asked Johanna. 'Does that mean you are involved personally?'

'Only by proxy, as it were. The Rector is one of the original shareholders, but he is too old to attend meetings now, so it has become part of my duty to stand in for him. As it happens, I am the Treasurer of the company that runs it. The Dramatic Society really does put on some good productions. It is a very long time since I trod the boards myself, but I have said I will join again this year. My wife is not one for social affairs, but in any case her time is fully occupied with the women's and the children's side of my church.'

Oh dear! Now all my first dislike had returned. 'Trod the boards?' Pompous idiot! And 'my church'! It was only a hut with a red painted corrugated iron roof, always referred to by Sophie as 'that there place as Het calls a church'.

He had turned towards Johanna, beaming. 'But my dear lady, can I persuade you to join? I could so easily take you to and from rehearsals, as I shall be going myself. There is another of my young people who wishes to join as well, if the society will accept her – a girl called Wendy Noble. She is not yet seventeen, but stage-struck, as so many at her age are.'

While Johanna was thanking him very prettily, my thoughts were elsewhere. Why should the name of Wendy Noble mean anything to me? Oh – of course! Sophie's sister Hetty's daughter. How much things must have altered, that one of Kezia's brood should even know enough about the stage to be 'struck' by it. To Kezia, all actresses were 'bad women', and the amateur ones were of the worst kind because they were more likely to be let loose among respectable folk, such as other women's husbands.

There was much cool, affable courtesy between Johanna and Birch as we said goodbye, and they made a firm arrangement for him to pick her up to take her to the first meeting of the SADS on Friday.

She was carrying a bag containing her purchases, and later I asked her if she had bought the shoes she had gone for.

'Oh, *yes*,' she said. 'I found exactly what I was looking for.' She leapt up to fetch the shoe-box, and took from it a pair of delicate, high-heeled, sandal-like emerald-green shoes.

'Aren't they absolutely *ducky*?' she said, bending down and slipping one on to show how it looked on the end of her lovely leg. 'Pricey, but once I had seen them, I simply had to have them.'

She slipped off the shoes and replaced them in the box. 'Supper in five minutes,' she said, and went happily into the kitchen.

I sat and sipped my pre-supper sherry in none too affable a mood. I thought she must consider me a stolid middle-aged dowd of questionable taste, especially with regard to clothes. I couldn't help feeling decidedly 'narked', mainly on account of the amount of undeserved sympathy I had been lavishing on her. Where did the easy-go money come from to uphold her *amour propre* to such a ridiculous degree? I supposed that just at present she was making it out of me — but that wouldn't last a day longer than I could help.

We chatted through our meal about the good luck that Hector Birch should be able to provide transport to the SADS. She was truly excited at the prospect, in such high spirits that she charmed my churlishness away.

Before I slept that night, though, I remembered that she had at no time offered any word of explanation as to why she had been having tea with Hector Birch. The more I thought about it, the more the unlikelihood of it having been just a chance meeting struck me. The café was almost empty when I went in and surprised them — they had not shared a table by anything but choice, and they had shown how disconcerted they had been to see me.

Suspicious, nasty-minded female that I must be turning into, I could only put two and two together. From whichever point of view I looked at it, I could only see that their meeting had all the outward signs of a hastily arranged assignation.

6

On Friday evening, when Birch sounded his car hooter outside, Johanna came in to tell me she was off, and I noticed with approval how carefully she was dressed for such an occasion. Though she looked, as always, trim and well-groomed, she had, if anything, taken trouble to tone down her normal striking appearance. She probably knew from past experience how such small-town societies worked, and had no wish to set up the backs of those who had kept the show running for so long by stunning them with her looks or showing off her acting ability. I hoped Hector Birch would also have the nous to let her stay in the background until the old-stagers had had time to get used to the bird of paradise that had strayed into their poultry yard, and to understand without envy just what an asset she could be to them in future if they let her.

I had been looking forward to a quiet evening with a book, but once she had gone I found it difficult to concentrate on the printed page, and my thoughts wandered.

Up at Benedict's things had been very busy. Though whenever you caught sight of them, singly or together, Art and Hully appeared to be moving like full-fed ponderous bullocks — 'mortaring in and out like a couple o' stray-dogs at a school-treat', as Sophie said — they had worked wonders already. Outside, too, Kid and Jelly had been clipping and scything and raking and burning till the layout of the garden as it used to be was once more visible. It was emerging day by day like an oriental dancer from beneath her seven veils. It was naked and unkempt, but full of lovely promise.

All the workmen used me as an errand boy, but I still found time to stand by the landing window and gloat. Sometimes, when the blue trails of smoke were drifting up from Jelly's bonfires to meet gold-braided and feather-trimmed clouds, and the brisk October wind was tossing the rooks into a game of 'breakneck' as they flew homeward, I was overcome with a sense of awe, thinking that nobody had the right to be quite as lucky as I was. It was a feeling that I often had to wrestle with, because I knew quite well that the English, and East Anglians in particular, still retained a curious streak of Puritanism. I had, anyway — and I repudiated it vigorously whenever I thought seriously about it. It seemed to me to be on the same level as a child refusing to accept a longed-for present on the grounds that he might one day lose it or break it.

Sophie had made terrific inroads into the task she had undertaken. She had reacted with indignation to my innocently expressed intention of getting the decorators already engaged in the main part of the house to finish off the rooms she had cleaned and scraped bare of damp wallpaper and flaking paint.

'Pay them fancy prices for doin' a bit of paper-'anging as I'm been doing since I was fourteen?' she asked, scandalized. 'I all'us look forward to *paperin'* a room! It's no 'ardship to me, if that's what you're a-thinking. On the other 'and, if you're afraid as I shan't do it well enough . . .' Her silence and her look made me quail.

'What about the painting?' I asked weakly, trying to remember from my one brief visit to her door what her own papered walls had looked like. I couldn't remember, though I found out later. Sophie's tiny living-room was so crammed with pictures and mirrors and wall-clocks and fading photographs and framed texts and pinned-up funeral cards and Palm-Sunday crosses that there was no room left for any wallpaper to show through. I thought perhaps I ought to point out to her that the decorators might not be willing to take on only half a job, the painting without the papering.

'Waste your money if you want to,' she sniffed. 'Easy come, easy go, I dare say. But I know as I shouldn't be paying no fancy town prices for slapping a bit o' paint on while I'd got Kid and Jelly 'ere on the premises a'ready.'

She had her own way, naturally. She papered and the Beans painted, on days when it was too windy or wet to get on in the garden. Sophie was put on her mettle by the proximity of Jelly, and although they had very little to say to each other, he was never above giving her a hand with awkward bits of wall where the old house showed its character. If the result was not absolutely as professional as it might have been, it was a great deal cheaper; and sentimentally, I was glad.

My day-dream of getting into and occupying these rooms by Christmas began to look quite possible. If Arf and Hully could contrive to get some sort of kitchen and one bathroom in working order in the back part of the house, I could make a sitting-room and a bedroom in what I referred to now as 'Sophie's wing'.

William would be surprised at the progress we had made. He hadn't been out for three weeks, but proposed to come next Wednesday. Not that I must allow myself to become dependent upon him for anything, even for an overdose of shared nostalgia. He had been very kind, and very helpful, and had seemed as pleased to renew old cousinly acquaintance as I had, but that was all it was. He had his work, and his own circle of friends — for all I knew, lady friends as well. It was hardly to be expected that so attractive a man had remained either lonely or celibate in this permissive age, with no wife in evidence. He had told me nothing about himself, and I had not asked, being, as I now realized, completely wrapped up in myself and my own affairs.

But I also realized, with a sort of shock, that I had been taking it for granted that he would always be there if and when I wanted him, and that that was not the case at all. What were my feelings towards him, then? No more than old-friend-and-cousinly. Some of my conviction on that score rose from the fact that I had accepted my age, and that, with my particular brand of physical make-up in these days when females were supposed to look like flat boards, no man would ever again look at me with the gleam I caught in every male's eyes when they rested on Johanna. But part of it rose also from my long-held views on the subject of marriage. I was ardently for it, as an institution upon which so much of the solid foundation of society rested; and bitterly and irrevocably against it as it seemed to affect the lives of so many otherwise wonderful people. I had had to conclude that it all depended on the people involved, and what you meant by 'marriage'. The legal and religious commitment of it seemed to be irrelevant; it tied people together like the torturers of the middle-ages did, to kill each other because they couldn't escape. The sexual side was inordinately over-rated, unless 'a marriage of true minds' existed between the couple already. In the few cases where that feeling of emotional oneness already existed, everything else came right. The sad thing was that most people never found the other halves of themselves till they were tied hand and foot by 'marriage' and offspring to the wrong one. I had been married. I had had a good, kind husband who had been a friend and a protector, and I had had two children. I had played my part in creating them, and they had given me so much love in my life that they had soon filled the gap their father had left. No, I was not contemplating matrimony again.

All the same, here I was once more relying emotionally on a man, 'cousin' though he might be. In William I had found again the male complement to my own particular brand of femininity which when we were young had been like a spiritual compound, so very different from the uneasy mixtures that so many marriages are. Argue as I might with myself about my female independence and more than comfortable circumstances, I had to admit how nice it was to have a man of one's own around again.

And there was the rub. William was not 'my' man, in any sense whatsoever.

I was glad to have thought it all through sensibly before I saw him again, and certainly before I moved into Benedict's, because the chances were high that once he had seen me safely installed there, he would gently drift out of my life again and back to his own. I should regret it; but one learns to bow before the inevitable. You can't have everything; and if I was feeling regretful at not having a man about after so short a time of knowing again what it was like, what must Johanna be feeling?

Perhaps I had never given her enough sympathy. She needed male attention and company as a plant needs light. She turned towards it whatever its source, from Ned or William — or Hector Birch? My mind went back to the picture of them seated together at the café table. In retrospect, I could analyse the situation. Johanna, cool but provocative; Birch, warily and faintly embarrassed, but definitely pursuing. Her eyes held invitation, though the rest of her kept a distance between them. He, too, was observing a metaphorical no man's land, but his eyes gave him away. They were not those of a man of the church who had by chance encountered one of his parishioners whom he knew to be in some distress.

There I went again — the worst of having a creative turn of mind is that you see round corners that are not yet in view. I picked up my book with resolution, but before I had read half a page I was startled to hear the kitchen door open, and a tuneful signal-like whistle. I found Ned inside the kitchen, hovering as if waiting. He had laid on the table five packets of Johanna's brand of cigarettes. My appearance, instead of Johanna's, obviously disconcerted him.

He seemed very much put out at hearing that Johanna had accepted a lift from Hector Birch. I was quite surprised by the vehemence of his reaction. Why on earth should Birch's name have had such an effect on Ned? I sat down cogitating once again. It was — it must be — that Johanna's sex appeal affected every man she encountered, even poor old Ned. I thought of her effect on William, sophisticated man of the world that he was, as much her superior in intellect and culture as she above Ned. I had underestimated the strength of it, because it was something I did not have. I didn't know then whether I was sorry or glad that it should be so.

Johanna came in a bit later, bright, breezy and happy. She went straight to get us a hot drink, as she did so giving me brilliant and amusing thumb-nail sketches of the society's stalwarts. They had decided to produce a play in which she had taken the lead before, but she had declined to put herself forward, asking to be allowed to act as prompter and general understudy for all the female parts since she already knew them all backwards. How sensible of her. She was such a nice woman in so many different ways.

I told her of Ned's visit, and his promise to come again on Sunday morning. But on Sunday morning, she had one of her occasional severe migraines, and could not get up. 'Tell Ned I'll see him again next Friday night,' she said.

'Won't you be in Swithinford again next Friday evening?' I asked, drawing her curtains against the light.

'Yes, of course. Tell him to come up any other evening,' she said, turning her head into the pillow.

So when he came, I delivered her message for her. 'Ah, I see,' he said, calmly. 'As long as I'm here, though, I might as well go and get the rest o' them 'taters up.' And away he went, whistling 'Sheep may safely graze' – just like the Ned I had known before Friday. I came to the conclusion that I was putting a black and white film of everyday mundane life into glorious Technicolor and making it into a great epic.

Next Friday, Johanna brought Hector Birch in for a drink when they returned, and with them came Sophie's niece, Wendy Noble. I had forgotten about her – I had not met Wendy before, and studied her with interest. She was tall, like Sophie, but inclined to juvenile plumpness, and unlike Sophie, fair and rosy. She spoke well, and appeared to be quite intelligent. Johanna had already worked her personal magic on the girl, who was, it was plain to see, in the first throes of hero-worship. Her charm had put the girl at ease, and though she was shy, she was certainly not gauche. In spite of her ash-blonde hair, she had Sophie's deep grey eyes, a most unusual combination of colouring.

Johanna had produced a bottle of sherry (mine, incidentally), and was pouring it out. She hesitated before including one for Wendy.

'Wendy?' she asked.

Birch looked as if he intended to answer for her, but Wendy shook her head. 'They'd smell it on my breath,' she said. 'I shall be in trouble enough as it is, for being late.'

'Shall I take you home now?' asked Birch, jumping up.

Wendy hesitated, and then shook her head defiantly. 'No, thank you,' she said. 'If I'm old enough to go out to work and get my own living, I'm old enough to be out till ten, I reckon.'

I drew her into conversation, and learned that she served in a stationer's shop in Swithinford. A nice girl, I thought, though there was a smoulder in the depths of her eyes that betrayed more fire than one might have expected from her Wainwright blood and the kind of upbringing she must have had from one of Kezia's children. It was perhaps a good thing that Birch and Johanna were channelling some of that pent-up energy into a sensible creative outlet.

Before they left, a whole new project had been conceived. The church was in need of funds, and Hector Birch was toying with ideas for fund-raising.

'Why don't we put on a concert?' Johanna said. 'I'm sure we could get enough talent together. I would do some monologues, and we could probably get enough young players for a sketch. What could you do, Wendy?' It was, I knew, only a way of letting the girl know she was not being left out of this adult conversation. We were all surprised by the blaze of interest that lit up her face.

'I could sing,' she said, simply stating a fact.

Birch nodded, in condescending acquiescence. 'Wendy has a sweet voice,' he said. 'She sings in my church choir.'

Wendy shot him a look of such intensity that the contempt and dislike in it were barely concealed. Johanna caught the look, and interpreted it correctly.

'What sort of things would you like to sing?' she asked.

'Pop songs. Songs from the shows. That sort of thing.'

Without a word, Johanna got up and crossed to the upright piano standing in the corner. She sat down and began to play, expertly, by ear, beckoning Wendy to come to her side. Wendy went, without the least trace of that reluctant embarrassment that usually greets such an invitation. Johanna began to play 'I Could Have Danced All Night' and Wendy began to sing. No wonder that she had made no fuss. Singing was the one thing that Wendy knew she could do well: her voice was rich and full and exciting, grating on the ear though the Americanized pop-singer diction in which she rendered the lyric might be.

'Bravo!' I cried.

Hector Birch clapped feebly, not quite sure he liked the turn events had taken.

46

Johanna jumped from the piano stool and put her arms round the girl, giving her a warm understanding kiss. Wendy blushed a deep, glowing rosy red that turned her into a beauty, like a rustic Venus caught bathing in a dew-pond. The light of elation blazed from her and around her, only to be extinguished the next moment by the sound of a clock somewhere striking the half after eleven.

'Lawks! I shan't half catch it!' she exclaimed, her East Anglian accent released in full by her dismay.

Birch jumped up and he and Wendy beat a very hasty retreat.

'Well,' I said. 'Life in Hen Street is full of surprises. Whoever would have thought it?'

Johanna, lighting her last cigarette of the night, nodded vigorously and happily. 'That girl is going places, if I know anything about it,' she said. 'She's got what it takes.'

7

Friday evenings usually ended with Birch and Wendy coming in with Johanna after rehearsals. Johanna was coaching Wendy with everything she knew about diction and stage presence, and the girl was a quick learner. Wendy was also taking part in a farce that Johanna was producing for the proposed concert. Johanna preferred to have the rehearsals in her own home rather than the cold, unheated church hall. This somewhat disturbed my comfort, but she did her best to arrange them on Wednesday evenings, when I was often not there.

William had rung up full of apologies for his long silence, and invited me out to dinner again with him on the following Wednesday. In spite of all my resolutions, I was happy to see him again; and when after the first Wednesday he suggested tentatively that we should make it a weekly fixture, I found myself only too happy to agree. After all, I told myself, I had so few friends and no real home in the area yet, and he no doubt realized it. It was kind of him, and we both enjoyed it. So why not?

Usually we got back to Bryony Cottage after Johanna's theatrical young hopefuls had left, and William would drop me at the gate and drive straight on. But early in November we had chosen our dinner venue badly, and were not prepared to sit over a mediocre meal in uncongenial surroundings for long, so we left early and when we reached Bryony Cottage I suggested he came in for a drink. Just as we stepped inside the lounge, Johanna began to play a medley of dance tunes from the thirties, and Wendy to sing. They both stopped abruptly at our entrance, but William cried, 'Go on! Oh, do go on!' and they did. I peeled off my coat and perched on the arm of the settee just inside the door, while William dropped his coat outside in the hall and came to stand close by my side. Having been a dedicated ballroom dancer before the war, I adored dance music. It was physically impossible for me to sit still while Johanna slipped from a waltz to a tango and back again to another waltz. The beat was throbbing in my thigh muscles and my feet, and running down my shoulders to my hands. I looked up at William, whose eyes were on the group at the piano, but I could actually see the rhythm pulsing through him. He looked down and caught my eye, then reached out a hand to pull me up. Johanna was playing a waltz, and away we went, making the most of the small space the lounge floor provided.

Wendy had stopped singing, wide-eyed at this unbelievable spectacle, but Johanna, delighted, slipped from the waltz to a slow fox-trot — that very difficult dance for those not able to hold the exact beat and the perfect balance it requires. We took it in our stride, as if we had been practising for weeks, though it was at least twenty years since I had last performed it. Then our pianist wickedly swung into a quickstep, and I was amazed at the way my feet could still anticipate my expert partner's every intricate move. I couldn't bear for Johanna to stop, but when the quickstep came to an end with a rapid twirl, and I stood, a bit breathless and a bit giddy, still being held up by William's arm around me, she started to play again: that slow, dreamy waltz that had so often been used as 'the last dance' in those long-ago days — 'Sweetheart, sweetheart, sweetheart' ... Memory was almost unbearable, yet I forgot everything but the joy of the present when William gathered me up again, holding me closer than before as we glided into that most evocative of all romantic rhythms.

When the dance ended, we stood looking at each other, finding it difficult to come back over twenty years to that little bungalow's tiny lounge again.

'Where did you learn to dance like that, Fran?' he asked. 'Do you know that I have *never* danced with you before?'

I shook my head. 'Where did *you*?' I asked in turn. 'I have never thought of you on a dance floor!'

'We all danced before the war,' he said. 'And don't forget I was in the RAF.'

I wished he hadn't reminded me. Of course, there was that whole long period of his life that belonged to Janice, and in which I had had no part; but tonight nothing could cloud the delight I had felt in yielding to the spell of moving to rhythm again, and of the still greater delight of finding yet one more aspect of William's personality so marvellously dovetailing with my own. Johanna was still sitting at the piano, surveying us with a tiny wry smile on her lips. 'Off you go, Wendy,' she said, getting up, 'or you'll be in trouble again.'

When William went, I did not accompany him to the door, nor did he wait for Johanna to see him out. I was still in a haze of pleasure that any goodbye must have shattered.

I found that William was not very favourable to my plan to move into the only partly finished house before Christmas. Not having been occupied for so long, it would be damp and cold he said; neither would it be safe — the unfinished part would give far too easy access to any intruders. Was I really contemplating spending the Christmas holiday there, all alone? He was going to Italy with a group of post-grad students and he couldn't possibly get out of it — but in any case he could not have stayed there with me, nor be close enough at hand in the middle of the night if I had been attacked or taken ill. I laughed at all his silly apprehensions, wishing he would not make it so plain that I was becoming a nuisance to him, an obligation, a load he had to carry because there was no one else to do it.

But I found everybody else against me, too. Sophie was plain horrified, and asked me if I had taken leave of my senses. Kate and Jeremy were hurt that I apparently preferred my own company in a cold, damp, lonely house to theirs and that of my grandchildren; and every time I mentioned it to Johanna, she looked so miserable and woebegone that I began to feel guilty at the thought of leaving her alone wherever I went. Time and time again I found it on the tip of my tongue to tell her I would stay with her at Bryony Cottage, but I truly didn't know how much of her desire for me to stay with her was emotional, and how much financial. I must make my own decision.

I asked her, when the time drew near, what she would do over the holiday, telling her that I had more or less made up my mind to go to Kate for three or four days, and then straight to my own temporary quarters at Benedict's when I returned. She was distressed, and cried — in a way that wrecked her looks. Her acted tears only enhanced her sex-appeal; her genuine ones made me uncomfortable.

'Same as last year, I suppose. I went to Madge and Stan Ellis for Christmas Day, and helped them to eat one of their scraggy old cockerels. Ned came up on Boxing Day in the morning, and I had Madge and Stan in for drinks in the evening. Some Christmas!'

'At least you'll have Wendy in and out, this year,' I said, determined not to yield my own freedom of movement to anyone.

'It's not being able to look forward to you coming back after Christmas that I can't bear,' she said. 'And William coming in occasionally as well.'

My sympathy took a buffet, and reeled. I had never heard her call him 'William' before; I was aware how much he attracted her, partly just because he was male, but partly, I guessed, because his old-fashioned brand of respectful courtesy was something she did not often encounter. I could not help but remember that he, too, seemed to be attracted. It was in his eye, in the way he lit her cigarette, in the overall change in him when she was present — quite different from his easy style when there were just the two of us. It was as if he were always on the alert.

Sophie was adamant in her opposition to me moving into my rooms at Benedict's. 'It's tempting Providence, that's what it is, to come in afore it's ready,' she said. 'I don't say as you wouldn't be safe enough and comfortable enough b'day, but who knows what might 'appen b'night?'

I could see the argument, though not very clearly. As the days continued to shorten, I had to go back to Bryony Cottage earlier and earlier, and I was getting restless with longing to have some of my own things round me again. In the end, I compromised. I would get my rooms furnished and comfortable as soon as I possibly could, so as to be able to spend my days there; but I would keep my status as Johanna's paying guest and go back there for supper and to sleep. Johanna was delighted, William relieved, and even Sophie less agitated.

As Sophie and I were waiting for the furniture van to deliver the pieces I had asked for out of store, I explained that I would be back before the New Year. 'I mustn't miss the concert, and Wendy's singing.'

I knew that Wendy was the apple of Sophie's eye, though she professed to find fault with her, and the way 'our Het' had brought the child up. Wendy was the only sprig of Kezia's tree to carry on the Wainwright line, Thirzah never having produced any children. So Wendy, poor child, had had three mothers – or perhaps it would be truer to say that she had had one silly mother, one severe grandmother, and one strait-laced great-aunt, because both Sophie and Thirzah were in many ways very much behind the times. Wendy's father, Joe Noble, was by all accounts a gentle, easy-going chap who took the course of least resistance with regard to the interference of his wife's sisters in the bringing-up of his only child, who could do no wrong in his eyes.

I was really taken back by Sophie's reaction to my mention of Wendy's part in the coming concert. She snorted, pursed her lips, opened them as if to speak, coloured up, and shut her mouth again with a snap. She opened the window and shook her duster out with a vigour that suggested she was ridding the house of a tarantula, or something equally poisonous and objectionable. When she had shut the window again with a decided bang, the words she had bitten back before burst from her.

'Concert!' she said bitterly. 'It's a pity as our Wend' ever got mixed up in such a thing. Bad'll become of it, mark my words! Thirz' thinks so, and so do I, but you can't tell our Hetty.'

'Why, Sophie,' I exclaimed, really shocked by the virulence of her outburst, 'whatever is wrong with it? It's a village do, for the church – and it can only be a good thing for Wendy and her friends to have something to do these dark winter evenings.'

'Not for the *church*, it ain't,' she snapped. 'I don't call that old hut a church no more than I call that 'Ector Birch a parson. But it ain't that, it's what's come over Wendy. No 'olding 'er, there ain't, since she started this 'ere singin' and play-acting. Throws 'erself about for nothing, and don't know which way 'er be'ind 'angs, if you'll excuse the saying. Won't do nothing only as she likes, an' not even that if it ain't what Mis' Brooke 'appens to like an' all. She's the real trouble. We don't care for any gel of our'n to be mixed up with a woman like that.'

Sophie was on the verge of tears, having said a good deal more than she intended, and afraid she had upset me. The last thing I wanted was to get on the wrong side of Sophie but I felt that I simply must stand up for Johanna against this unjustified, bitter, ignorant and prejudiced attack.

'I think you are being most unkind,' I said at last. 'Mrs Brooke is taking a great deal of trouble with all the young people in the social, but especially with Wendy. She believes that Wendy has real musical talent, and so do I. Whatever can possibly be bad about them visiting Mrs Brooke's house to practise? As for Wendy's tantrums, they are just part of growing up. You can't keep her a little girl for ever, you know. At seventeen, it's natural for her to want her own way a bit.'

'Ah, well. Tha's as maybe. As long as it ain't the same way as that ginger-'eaded dink-me-doll at Bryony Cottage. She ain't our sort, and we don't want none of 'er!'

'What are you suggesting?' I said sharply. 'You really mustn't say such things about Mrs Brooke just because she is beautiful, and dresses well!'

'Where's she get the money from for all them posh clo'es? Where's 'er 'usband? What's that there Birch doing a-creepin' round 'er, all day an' every day? She's a flashy, dolled-up sort o' woman, and I'm sorry to say it, but it's a bad job as you ever got mixed up with 'er yourself. I'm said so from the first, and I'll say it again. She's no good, and the sooner you're away from 'er, the better for us all.'

'Mrs Brooke is my friend, Sophie,' I said firmly, sitting down. 'I cannot and will not listen to any more wicked talk about her.'

Then Sophie sat down, too, and began to cry, blubbering into her duster. I got up and went to her, putting my arm around her shoulders.

'And you are my dear, dear Sophie,' I said, 'and I should stick up for you if Mrs Brooke or anybody else dared to say a word against you. I am sure she is no bad influence on Wendy — though if Wendy is being a bit cheeky at home I can understand how you feel. But don't spoil the social for Wendy — she is looking forward to it so much.'

The arrival of the furniture vans brought the unhappy incident to a sudden end, and for the rest of the day Sophie worked as if she had the will and strength of two women. By tea-time, we had got the rooms straight. While Sophie went off to make a cup of tea, I sat down to enjoy my new temporary sitting-room and the extraordinary scene of this morning returned to my thoughts. What had Sophie meant about Hector Birch? He was a fairly frequent visitor to Bryony Cottage just at present, what with the rehearsals at Swithinford and the arrangements for the concert. He usually came in with Johanna on Friday evenings, but always accompanied by Wendy, and I was there too. Was the whole village agog with the same rumour,

I wondered? Or was it only Wendy's immediate family looking for a good reason to withdraw their chick from Sodom and Gomorrah before the wrath of 'Im Above fell on Johanna and all her theatrical brood?

As far as I had gathered, Birch was generally regarded as a kind, conscientious, hard-working man with far too many duties thrust upon him by reason of the Rector's age and infirmity. The only bit of gossip I had ever picked up about him was that he tended to overwork his wife, who was a poor, meek little woman, hardly ever seen except on Sundays. I remembered being sorry for her, and thinking that it was probably she who bore all the brunt of his overload of work. I couldn't say I liked the man, though he had always been the soul of discretion and politeness in my company.

I was later than usual leaving, that day, and after dropping Sophie at her own gate, I drove on to Bryony Cottage. I fished for my key in the dim light, but could not find it. So I went round to the back and in at the kitchen door instead, as I had often done before. There Johanna and Hector Birch stood, between the cooker and the table, very close together. The light was failing, and if I had been on trial for my life I could not have said with conviction that they had been even closer before my entrance, or that they sprang apart at my intrusion; but the feeling came, and remained with me, that I had interrupted something of a much more personal nature than yet another detail of the concert. Though in the name of heaven – what?

I apologized, Johanna snapped on the light, and Birch greeted me with his usual effusion, and I went straight through to my bedroom. But for Sophie's outburst this morning, I should not have thought twice about it. I longed for the time to pass quickly so that I could shut my own door on the village and its concerns, and keep my own counsel on the other side of it. I ought to have known then that it was only an impossible dream.

8

I returned to Old Swithinford when the new year was only two days old. William had been wrong. Sophie had kept the central heating going, and my rooms were cosy, warm and delightful, in spite of the dark days and the wintry weather. The skies were overcast, and there was a strong east wind sweeping across from the sea, its biting progress from the Ural Mountains unimpeded as it crossed the icy continent and the flat lands of the fens right into the heart of England.

'Too cold for snow,' was Sophie's first comment when she came out to meet me. I knew these freezing, penetrating winds of old, though I had forgotten them. Very often they yielded only to heavy snow, when at last the temperature rose; but while they lasted, it was as if they had a shrivelling effect on life, all nature, including man, needing to shrink inside itself to escape them. The thick, solid eighteenth-century walls of the old house kept the heat in and the cold out in a way that no jerry-built bungalow in Hen Street ever could, as I discovered when reluctantly I left my own delicious solitude and took myself down to Bryony Cottage for supper. It was, to use our East Anglian expression, 'perishing'.

The lack of warmth was not entirely due to the thin walls and ill-fitting doors. Heating was at a minimum that I had not noticed during the mild autumn. My bedroom was an ice-house, having had no heating at all for more than a week. The small electric heater, put on, I guessed, no more than an hour before my arrival, served only to bring out the clammy, clinging cold. I was tired and hungry, and inclined to feel a bit aggrieved. After all, I had paid Johanna my full board and lodging for every week since I had become her paying guest, whether I had been there or not.

I soon found that the drop in temperature at Bryony Cottage was psychological as well as physical. Johanna had been undisguisedly glad to see me, and had soon produced a good hot meal, for which I was very grateful. She chatted brightly as we ate, but I could see she was having to make an effort; I didn't dare ask her about Christmas, at least until the meal was over. When, however, we sat down before the apology for a fire in the lounge, and she lay back against the settee and wearily closed her eyes, I accepted it as a direct invitation to my sympathy that I could no longer refuse.

'What's the matter, Johanna?' I asked. 'You are not your usual self. Not sickening for 'flu, I hope, especially with the concert so close, now.' It had been arranged for the second Monday in January, Plough Monday, when from medieval times there had been some sort of ritual celebrating the return to work after a long enforced holiday during which labourers who couldn't work were not paid.

'Damn the bloody concert,' she said, suddenly sitting upright with a burst of hard laughter. 'I haven't yet reached the point of such bumpkin mentality that I could get myself upset about a village concert.'

The contempt in her tone made me want to bite back, to tell her in no uncertain terms not to include me in her attitude toward 'bumpkin mentality', unless she cared to regard me as one of the bumpkins. I refrained: I knew I should now get the tale whether I wanted it or not.

'Oh, it's just the same old things. Being alone again at Christmas, dependent upon the squawking and cackling of Madge Ellis for company, counting the hours till you got back and knowing that you won't be here much longer, even at nights. I don't know whatever I shall do, then.'

I felt guiltily uncomfortable, though part of my guilt was for being a hard-hearted bitch who suspected that her tears were not genuine. I was sure, though, that if they were, the reason she had given me for them was not the only one. I said nothing, and after a few minutes she mopped herself up and went on.

'I was sure I should hear from Dave at Christmas. Last year, he timed a cheque to arrive with a Christmas card, and he had put in £10 as a present, as well. I expected a cheque for all the back pay he owes me on Christmas Day if nothing extra. But not a word, damn him! I'll bet he's sitting on some sunny beach with his Kangaroo Mathilda, not caring a brass bugger about me in this bloody dump without enough money to buy a hundred-weight of coal . . .'

She stopped and coloured as I had never seen her do before. Perhaps my face had registered the distaste I felt at the stridency and vehemence of her outburst. She knew that she had let herself down with that coarse and vulgar tirade. It didn't matter to me, except for the embarrassment it was now causing both of us. I had to say something.

'It really is too bad,' I said. 'I am sorry, especially if you were relying on it coming.'

'Don't lend her any money,' said Madge Ellis's voice in my ear; perhaps just in time, for I was on the point of offering to do exactly that. However, for my own peace of mind and my own comfort, I offered as delicately as I could to pay the next two weeks' board in advance, and the effect on her was little short of miraculous. The tears vanished the moment that she had the notes in her hands again. It was my turn to feel unhappy; I had not thought that she was sailing so very near the wind financially. I reflected that if I had been stony broke, I should not have had a telephone, dressed like a duchess, or smoked at least twenty cigarettes every day. It must surely be only some temporary circumstance that had put her into such sore straits.

Wanting to change the subject, I asked how the preparations for the concert had gone during my absence.

Johanna frowned. 'I don't know,' she said. 'Something's gone wrong. I can't put my finger on it, but it's lost its "go". The other kids are just as keen as ever, but young Wendy is acting very queer. She still comes round now and again, but she keeps on saying she "doesn't want to be in it". If it had been any of the others, I should have put it down to stage-fright – but not her. She could face a West End audience or a television camera without a quiver, just like I could. And she has suddenly taken such a scunner at Hector Birch that if he comes anywhere near, she bolts like a scared rabbit. But why, don't ask me! I hope she'll soon come to her senses, because she is going to spoil it for everybody if she keeps this up. She's the star, after all.'

'Perhaps that's all that is the matter,' I said. 'It's gone to her head. She's playing at being the prima donna.'

Johanna nodded. She was quite herself again now, and, somewhat to my rather cynical surprise, was genuinely concerned both for the concert in its entirety and for the success of her protégée in particular. I recalled Sophie's tirade to me, and concluded that Wendy was being got at all the time at home, and pressure was being put upon her to fall out of the show. I thought I should do no harm by dropping a hint or two of what I guessed might be the case.

'Perhaps she's staying out later than her mother thinks she ought,' I said. 'They are very old-fashioned. Perhaps they regard any performance in public as such a snare of the devil that even Hector Birch's presence can't prevent Wendy from being caught in it.'

'I'm sure you are on the right track,' Johanna said. 'In fact, I know you are, because I had a visit from Wendy's mother while you were away. What is worrying me is that she let out more than she thought, and I don't know what to do about it.'

'Tell me,' I said. I could see we were both going to enjoy a dramatized version of Mrs Noble's visit. I had not yet encountered Sophie's youngest sister Hetty, whom I remembered only as a runny-nosed, whining nine-year-old. After the performance Johanna gave me, I felt that I should recognize her anywhere. I laughed myself almost warm, but once it was over, Johanna became serious again.

'What she was getting at was that she objected to Wendy being up here so much — both the frequency of her visits and the late hours. She had come, she said, to ask me not to encourage her so much, and to send her home to bed earlier, because Wendy had been so tired and "lawless" — I'm sure that was the word she used — just lately that it had been "'oss's work" to get her out of bed in the mornings. So of course I promised, and apologized, and said it would soon all be over and she would then only be coming here on Fridays, after Swithinford rehearsals. So Mum was a bit mollified, and went. But what I didn't tell her was that Wendy had not been here when her mother thought she was. She didn't come to a single rehearsal all last week. And I had been very careful, after Hector dropped me a hint, not to keep her later than nine o'clock. In fact, he came once or twice himself to make sure she left on time, But her mother said it had been after midnight when she got in several times.'

'She's probably got a boyfriend for the first time, and is using you for cover. If I were you, I think I would have a word with Wendy and tell her you won't give her away so long as she stops it now and doesn't involve you again.'

Johanna agreed. She wanted the concert to be a success and so did I, for her sake. If it went well, it would give her the entrée she needed to whatever heart Hen Street had. She might have to live there a long time, yet — indeed, I feared so.

I went to bed cold, and could not get warm enough to sleep. The discomfort strengthened my resolution to move out by next weekend.

When I told Johanna of my intentions of moving out on Saturday, she played the scene exactly as I had foreseen, weeping real tears, attempting to change my mind for me, and finally accepting it and assuring me of her undying friendship and her help if ever I should need it. I responded in kind. I did like her, very much, and found her extraordinary moods and changing personae fascinating. If I couldn't say I always *approved* of her, it was because I had been brought up so differently, and in my way retained many of the same sort of values that Sophie and her sisters did, I was honest enough with myself to admit as well that though I could not say I envied her in any way, the grapes were a bit sour when I looked at that slim, exquisite figure, those gorgeous legs, that wonderful hair, those fetching eyes, and the vitality that seemed to burst through into some new talent at any minute for want of other outlets. I had nothing to grumble about with regard to my own energy or talent, if it came to that, and I had many other blessings to count that she had not. But the fact remained, that though there was little between us in age, Johanna was still essentially a desirable woman, and in that particular respect, I felt a had-been. I counted on my common-sense, my usual philosophic outlook, my family, and — not to put too fine a point upon it — my extra education, to help me accept that fact, and to deal with it. There was hardly likely to be any competition between us on that score. If she liked to practise feminine wiles on Birch, or Ned, or any other male, let her. It wasn't in my nature to enter the lists against her, anyway, even if I had been equipped to do so. Did I really mean 'any other male' though?

The break was made easier for me by Birch reporting to Johanna that the church hall had now been heated, and the last few rehearsals could be held there. Johanna asked if I would mind having my hot meal at midday. That suited me fine, because I could stay as late as I liked at Benedict's, just going back to Johanna's to sleep till Saturday came and I could stay in 'the flat' for good.

Johanna gave me a message from William to say he would be out as usual on Wednesday, providing it was possible weatherwise.

'Did you tell him I should be at the old house?' I asked.

'No. I'm sorry, but Hector was banging on the door, and I rang off before I gave it a thought. But I can send him straight back there when he comes.'

'Don't bother,' I said. 'I might as well come here to change'.

So it was back to the old pattern on Wednesday, for the last time. I left my cosy hide-out at about 5.45 p.m., and drove back to Bryony. William's car already stood in front of the bungalow. I ran my car down into the garage. The sky was clear, and the stars brilliant, though a long way away. The freezing wind had, if anything, strengthened; no snow just yet, I judged, hoping that it might now hold off till I was safely ensconced in my own house and with no need to go out at all if I didn't want to.

The orange curtains of Johanna's lounge were drawn against the cold, and the window glowed in the surrounding darkness. The curtains were cheap and ill-fitting, and as usual they did not quite meet at one corner of the ugly little square-bay window. I had found this chink useful on many previous occasions, because I never thought to look for my door-key until I got to the door; it also provided a peephole into the lounge, through which I could see if Johanna had visitors.

I stepped towards the chink tonight, found my key at once, and looked through the gap in the curtains.

Johanna was sitting on the end of the settee nearest to the door, and William sat on the arm of it. While I stood frozen on the spot with a numbing coldness that was both internal and external, he put back into his breast packet the cheque book he had been using and, leaning down, put a cheque into Johanna's hand and folded her fingers over it. She looked up at him with the Mary Magdalene glance of her kind throughout the ages, adoring and provocatively humble, rubbing her face gratefully against his sleeve like a well-fed cat. I couldn't see his face, because his head was bent, but I did see his arm go round her shoulders for a moment before his hand ruffled her glowing red head.

I have always noticed that when anything happens to tilt one's world on its axis and throw it suddenly off course, there is a sort of automatic pilot ready to take over. I went on moving towards the door, and fitted my key into the lock, as if what I had just witnessed made no difference whatsoever to me or to my outlook on life. Yet in those few seconds, it seemed as if time had taken on new dimensions. I have heard that drowning folk see their whole lives unrolled before them in the three minutes or so it takes them to die. In ten seconds I had had to readjust my outlook – on the past, on the present, and on the future.

There had been one moment of utter disbelief. Oh no, not William! It just wasn't possible – that white-haired academic, nearing fifty? But of course, I had reasoned that all out before, and decided it was not only possible, but likely – only not in the context of Johanna.

Then there came another throb of utter revulsion, against him, against her, against God or whoever it was that had set up a sex urge so powerful that it very often overrode every other considera-tion. I wanted to be sick. If William had 'fallen for' Johanna, openly, as he had done for Janice in the past, I felt I could have endured it. But the money changing hands? Had he known from the first, then, that his innocent cousin had landed herself in the web of a high-class prostitute? If so, why on earth hadn't he told me so? For the very obvious reason, I supposed; how could I have been so blind, thinking back to all those other Wednesdays when he had been there before me? Was this what Sophie and Hetty knew, but couldn't bring themselves to say?

And now? Was I to pretend not to know, or renounce both of them? What was it to do with me?

Well, I ought to have known that things were too good to last. Everything had gone along so swimmingly that I had lowered my guard against the inevitable setback that must come sooner or later. Not that in my wildest imagination would I have conjured up the revelations of this awful moment.

The automatic pilot was still in control as I opened the door into the lounge. They had obviously heard the front door. Johanna sat in her accustomed place at the other end of the settee, and William stood in the middle of the room with both hands outstretched in greeting. The offending cheque had been whisked away out of sight.

'You're trembling, Fran,' said William, concern in every line of him. 'Are you OK?'

'Shivering, you mean,' I answered lightly, marvelling at my own self-control. 'It is absolutely freezing out there. As Kezia would have said, "It's enough to freeze the hairs off a gooseberry".'

Oh God! Why had I said that? What had an innocent gooseberry got to do with freezing or being *de trop*, as I was now? Except that it was green, like me. In another minute I should start to cry.

'I'll go and get into something warmer,' I said, and made my escape before I did.

It was not a happy evening. As the numbing effect of the shock wore off, I found it harder and harder to be natural with William, and to make conversation. The lovely, comradely, satisfying relationship between us had gone as if it had never been renewed.

We finished our meal almost in silence, and William ordered coffee and liqueurs. He knew that in the ordinary way I didn't take spirits, but tonight he did not ask.

'Now, tell me what's the matter, Fran,' William said, gently.

'You tell me,' was all that I could find to say.

'What have I done wrong?' he said, looking at me searchingly.

I longed to be able to blurt the whole of my dilemma out to him, to beg him to deny it, to put the clock back, two hours, a week or even a year to the time before he had come back into my life again. Of course I couldn't do that, partly because a peeping Tom must always have difficulty in making use of any information so clandestinely come by, and partly because the last person I could let know what a dreadful effect his fall from grace was having on me was William himself.

Besides, I knew now that I did not want to face a future at Benedict's in which he had no part. If I were ever to show by word or deed, that I regarded him in any way as 'mine', or as a necessary part of my new life, he would withdraw altogether, if not in fright, then in circumspection. 'Half a loaf is better than no bread at all,' I told myself miserably. He was no longer my shining, perfect new friend – but he was still the beloved companion of my childhood, whatever flaws I had discovered in him.

'I am worried, and a bit overtired, that's all,' I said. 'I have been so cold at nights since I came back after Christmas that I haven't been able to sleep. Did Johanna tell you that I'm moving out on Saturday? I must say I'm glad – for all sorts of reasons.'

He nodded. 'She's quite upset,' he said. 'I really believe she thought you wouldn't go until you could take over Benedict's all complete.'

'She may well be upset,' I countered, with some bitterness in my voice. 'She's been getting ten guineas a week out of me for very little. She'll have to rely on selling her services elsewhere from now on. I don't think she'll have much difficulty.'

William shot me a penetrating glance, concealed under a heavy frown, and his voice was cold. 'Just what do you mean by that?'

'Oh really, William,' I said. 'You are a man. I'm only a fuddy-duddy middle-aged woman, but I am neither blind nor stupid. How does she manage to be so well dressed, and smoke and drink like she does on a non-existent allowance from an invisible husband? Sophie's been trying to warn me. That's why Hetty is so distressed at Wendy's friendship with her. If I stay with her a day longer than I have to, I shall be tarred with the same brush. I wouldn't be surprised if I am already, if the truth be told. It isn't exactly the start I had hoped for, back in the village, but I dare say I shall live it down in the course of time.'

I was jamming things into my handbag with trembling hands. When I looked up, I saw that William's face was suffused with a deep red flush that ran right up into his white hair and made him look quite ferocious, his eyes cold and hard. I hadn't seen him look like that since we were sixteen. He had always been angry when he felt guilty – and the worse the guilt, the greater the anger.

'I think it's time you went home and took yourself in hand,' he said icily. 'I must say I never expected such a narrow-minded, sus-picious, one-track village-yokel attitude from you, Fran, even if your facts were substantiated, which I doubt. From what I can gather, you are basing your nasty accusations on nothing more than gossip, surmise and a bad bout of winter-time blues. I think you are being very unfair.'

'Oh, am I?' I retorted. 'How do you know? Of course you will stick up for her. You haven't seen her in Hector Birch's arms, or in her see-through nightie deliberately titillating Ned Merriman, or . . .'

'Or what? Now stop it, Fran.' He rose. 'I don't want to listen, anyway.'

We drove back to the bungalow in terrible silence. When we got there, William got out and opened the car door as courteously as ever, but he was stiff and white-faced in the starlight.

'Goodnight, Fran,' he said, with the slight inclination of his body that he used in lieu of raising his hat when he didn't happen to be wearing one.

'Goodbye, William,' I said, and slammed the front door on him.

Johanna, by the grace of God, was not yet home from her rehearsal. I left her a note, and went to bed, to cry over the ruins.

9

Next morning I got away as soon as I could, and went via the village shop to order a stock of supplies for my own larder. The wind had died, and a hard frost had set in; the skies were clear, and the sunshine bright and brittle. It was exhilarating, and as I worked beside Sophie I cheered up – till every now and then I remembered what a great gap in my future there would be left by William's absence from it. There would be the concert on Monday, but I was not looking forward to my first Wednesday in my new home. Nothing was ever perfect, as I had told myself over and over again before the rift.

Saturday morning was as traumatic as I had feared, when I took my last suitcases over her doorstep, and Johanna stood there in tears, saying that once Monday was over we must 'make arrangements to keep in touch'. Then I was away, and on my own feet again, at last.

I kept myself very busy all day, determined not to think of what lay ahead except as I had done when I had first decided to come back to live in East Anglia. William had not been part of the picture

I had had in my imagination last summer. I knew how foolish I had been to let him become so dominant a feature in it — but even without him in the foreground, the scene was still a very pleasant one. I had got what I had wanted then — and far more. I had wanted to get settled before I began to write a play which had been more or less contracted. I forced myself to think about it again, set out some clean paper and my pens and typewriter on the desk in my new study, and determined that after breakfast on Sunday I would sit down and start on it. I slept well, and woke happier. As Sophie did not come on Sundays, my first whole day there would have to include domestic chores — washing up and cooking my own lunch. Actually, I had always found them conducive to creative thought, so in a way it was no hardship at all.

I did actually write a page or two before wandering into my little sitting-room to enjoy it in the morning sunshine. I had put the kettle on for some coffee, and was standing in the kitchen when I heard William's voice outside the window.

'Fran! Fran? Where are you? How do I get into this rabbit warren?'

I flew out of the room, down the back corridor and unbolted the back door, which was at present the only way into my retreat. I didn't know whether to laugh or cry, but what I did do was to hold out both hands and say, 'William! I am so glad to see you!'

He squeezed my hands, and said, 'Me, too. I was worried, and couldn't sleep because of thinking of you coming in yesterday all by yourself, and wondering if you would be all right when it got dark, and how you would feel about sleeping here alone after all. So as soon as I could this morning, I came to find out.'

'How nice of you,' I said lamely, leading the way into my 'day-room'. I gave him some coffee, then blurted out, 'Oh, William! I am sorry!'

'So am I,' he said. 'I don't know what got into us. Let's put it down to the cold. What had Johanna done to get you so worked up about her?'

The air was charged with danger. One wrong word might cause an even worse explosion than last Wednesday's. I had seen what I had seen, but I simply had to forget it.

'She had been miserable, and bitchy, and different, somehow. I saw another side of her — almost crude and common,' I said. 'But I think the real trouble was that she was making me feel guilty about leaving her. You warned me not to get personally involved with her — but it's almost impossible not to. She made me feel that by sticking to my own plans, I was taking the bread out of her mouth.'

'Mm. She certainly was in the dumps when I arrived on Wednesday. I found her in tears, sitting on the settee surrounded by unpaid bills. To tell you the truth, I was pretty sure she had set the scene up deliberately for you to walk in on. My early arrival nearly threw her.'

'Bills?' I queried. 'She never mentioned any bills to me – but of course I ought to have guessed. They always come in shoals just after Christmas. No wonder she was so glad to get my two weeks' board in advance.'

'Twenty pounds wouldn't get her far in the face of that lot,' he commented a bit wryly. 'She had no idea at all what she was going to do except to ask you to lend it to her.'

'Well, she didn't, and she hasn't since,' I replied. I was about to tell him about Madge Ellis's warning, when the revelation came. 'William,' I said, 'how was it that she was so cheerful and lively on Thursday morning?' I looked fixedly at him, and refused to shift my gaze till I had the enormous satisfaction of watching that brilliant flood of colour creeping up to the roots of his white hair again, though this time it filled me with gloating relief and joy.

'She was going to ask you,' he said guiltily. 'I just forestalled her, that's all.'

'You silly man,' I said. 'You aren't nearly so clever as you look. Don't you see that I might just possibly have got some of my money back – but you'll never get a penny? She won't "offend" you by offering to repay it, even if she ever could. And what's more, she has now got you just where she wants you. You can't drop her acquaintance, or even be cool towards her, because she knows perfectly well that "a gentleman like you" would never let a sordid thing like money change a relationship. She has read you like a book. It's a back-to-front kind of blackmail, aimed now at both of us.'

I was so relieved to have had my unworthy suspicions blown sky-high that I could have forgiven Johanna anything.

'You didn't admire her much on Wednesday evening,' he said. 'In fact, you threw out some very nasty insinuations.'

I nodded. 'I know. I admit it. I thought they must be true, then. Now I don't know again. I just don't understand her. Why try to keep up the style she does when she knows there is nothing coming in to pay for it? She's not stupid. She knows as well as I would that the day of reckoning must come.'

He stretched out his long legs before the fire, perfectly relaxed, and put up both hands behind his head. I watched him with a warmth inside me that made up for all the cold on Wednesday. He looked so comfortably at home there, sitting deep in thought.

'Maybe I do understand her, better than you ever could,' he said. 'You and she don't really have much in common. But she and Janice might be twins. It's a state of mind they grow up with, and not really their fault. Because they are as they are, they think they confer a blessing on mankind just by being alive. Perhaps they do. But in time they come to believe than mankind owes them a living in return. Without the props, they can't keep the show on the road. So they have no alternative. Like Queen Victoria, they do not admit the possibility of defeat. In their case, defeat would mean the day when they couldn't find any way of meeting their commitments. Somebody always comes along in the nick of time to save them. As you so ungenerously suggested, they do have other goods to sell if the worst ever comes to the worst. But from my observation, they don't resort to that line till they are really forced to. They put the goods on show, so to speak, and are interested in advance bids. But any actual sale has the effect of devaluing the remaining stock.'

'I'm glad you said "a blessing on *man*kind",' I said.

He laughed. 'I don't believe you are really such a puritan as you make out,' he said. 'You know as well as I do that there are two sorts of women that every man wants and needs. No man with an ounce of red blood in his veins can wholly resist the Johannas and the Janices. That's why lucky men have both wives and mistresses. Every man needs a Johanna in his life at some time or other — but if he's got any sense at all, he doesn't marry her.' There was a bitterness there that Johanna could not account for.

'Yet Johanna herself seems to want a firm, secure relationship within marriage,' I argued.

'Yes. Security is the keynote. That is what her present husband isn't providing. There has to be a safe, placid, unexciting husband in the background to pay bills now and then when all other help fails, and to keep the nest warm for the gay little moth to flutter back to when the present candle flickers out — what are you laughing at?'

'Your terribly mixed metaphors, Professor,' I said. 'Say no more. Johanna is the jam, and I'm the dough!'

He began to protest indignantly that he had said no such thing, but he was laughing too. 'I'm glad to see you laugh, Fran, after the other night. But I'm serious, for the moment. I want to tell you about Janice. Do you mind if I go on?'

'I'd like to know,' I said.

'Well, you see, I'm the fool in the background, the one with the cheque book to make sure the security is in place. I didn't understand her. I was too dull to keep up with her. I had work I loved, and I never suspected her of anything worse than blatant flirtations – just like Johanna. It was only when my cheque book failed her that she sold her stock – if we can stick to that metaphor. I failed her first – that's why she failed me. So she is still my wife. Why? Because she can't bring herself to cut the link that still gives her a base of security. And I can't because for one thing divorce is still frowned on, and gentlemen don't sue for divorce. They take the blame. And if ladies divorce their husbands, it doesn't go down too well in the academic world. But in any case I still feel responsible for her.'

'Because you still love her?'

He stared into the fire for what seemed an eternity, before slowly shaking his head. 'Since you put it so bluntly, no. But I was crazy about her, once. An old flame! That's the cliché, but it's a very apt one. The fire dies down, and goes on smouldering. Meeting a woman like Johanna fans a few sparks from the embers, and then they burn out. Janice belongs to the exciting part of my youth, along with flying and the war. Bygone excitement. She's still my legal wife. I still help to support her. But if I ever had the chance again I'd choose a real wife.'

'You would have to be sure you didn't still love Janice – or the memory of her – at all,' I said. 'You can't love two women at once.'

'That's what you women always say,' he answered. 'If they dare tell the truth, most men will say it is perfectly possible. As I said, the lucky ones, like the French and royalty, have the best of both worlds. It just hasn't been my luck.'

I didn't really know how seriously to answer him. It seemed that he was dealing lightly with what was to him a very serious matter. I was afraid of hurting him, or of destroying the confidence he was putting in me as a friend to whom he could talk freely and openly about his deepest feelings.

'I think you are talking about two different things,' I said. 'I still say you can't *love* two women at the same time. I take it that what you really mean when you say that men want the best of both worlds is that they want comfort from a wife and sexual excitement from a mistress.'

'That's putting it crudely,' he said, 'but essentially that's it.' He brought his faraway look back to me, and sat up. 'Perhaps I was wrong. Perhaps the lucky men are those who can get both sorts of satisfaction in one special woman. He gives her his heart, and all the rest follows. His sweetheart and his wife in one.'

I nodded. 'That's Love with a capital L,' I said. 'Very few of us are so lucky.'

'I wasn't,' he said. His voice hurt me somewhere deep inside.

'Thanks for telling me about Janice,' I said. 'It does make me understand Johanna a bit better.'

'I wouldn't worry too much about her, if I were you,' he said. 'There are a great many fools about, still. She'll find one, sooner or later.' He smiled, as if dismissing the subject. 'Show me round,' he said, getting up and holding out his hand to help me up; but at that moment there came a furious clatter of blows on the solid front door of the main part of the house. They sounded impatient, almost frantic, and in spite of myself I was alarmed. I didn't let go of William's hand. 'Who on earth can that be?' I asked. 'Nobody knows I'm here.'

'Nobody knows *I'm* here,' he said grimly, 'but it's a good thing that I am.' He let go of my hand. 'I'll go. You stay here.' He went — but nothing could have kept me from following him into the front hall, stepping over bags of cement and lengths of tubing and negotiating my way round a wheelbarrow and a shovel. William pulled back the huge brass bolts and heaved open the door, to reveal Hector Birch with one hand raised to seize the old iron lion-headed knocker again. The plump lay-reader looked startled and foolish at confronting William. He and Birch had never met, so I had to come forward and take charge.

'Mr Birch!' I said, in great surprise. 'Do come in if you can get in.'

'No! No!' he said, in great agitation. 'Thank you all the same, but there isn't time!'

He was white, and shaking. In spite of the cold, his baby face was wet with perspiration, and he mopped it and his head with his handkerchief before replacing the hat he had lifted when I appeared.

'Is something wrong?' I asked, thinking immediately of Johanna. 'Are you sure you won't come in?'

He stepped inside the door, leaning up against the wall, as if to give himself support. 'I am sorry to intrude,' he babbled. 'I have had some very bad news, and I need help. My mother has had a severe heart attack, and is dying. She is asking for me all the time. I must go to her at once.'

'But of course,' I said, arching my eyebrows at William. What on earth had it to do with me?

'Where do you have to get to?'

He appeared quite dazed; but after a moment's hesitation, he replied, 'Oh, Liverpool. Well, not Liverpool exactly — Birkenhead, to be precise. And on a Sunday.'

'Mr Birch,' I said firmly, 'it has been a dreadful shock to you, but you must think carefully. Now do come in, and tell us what we can do to help you.'

He looked as if he might bolt at any moment. 'No! No!' he almost shouted. 'It would waste time! But I did come to you for help. You see,' (he started gabbling now, words tripping each other up as they tried to get out) 'my car is being repaired at the garage, so I must get a train — but I can't get to the station without my car. Then I thought that I must see Johanna, because I shall not be back for the concert, so she may want to cancel it. On my way to her I had the idea of asking you to take me to the station. But I had forgotten you were no longer there. When she told me, I just kept coming straight on to find you.'

His words were rattling out in spate, now, building up in excitement like a train nearing the end of a tunnel. He was trembling so much I was afraid he might collapse. How strange, I thought, that a man who spent his life finding banal words of philosophical comfort to others in this same state of threatened bereavement should so lack any inner resources when he was the one in trouble. The shock seemed to have robbed him of reason, including the most simple common sense. There must be many of his parishioners in Hen Street at home with idle cars on a Sunday morning; why on earth had he been daft enough to waste twenty minutes at least walking a mile in the wrong direction towards a comparative stranger? But he was obviously in such great distress that it was pointless to argue with him now.

William, untroubled by such extraneous thought, had become extremely practical. 'Liverpool — that means crossing London. I doubt if any branch-line trains will be of much use to you on a Sunday. I think you must get to a main-line station. Unfortunately, there is no telephone here yet — but you will need to go back home to pick up some things for your journey. I will take you home, and you can phone from there to see which of the two main lines will serve you best.'

Birch turned a shade of pale green, and his hands shook as he clasped them together. 'No, no!' he said. 'Every moment is precious! I shall go just as I am — my wife knows I have left. My poor mother!

I am afraid I have not been a very good son to her, lately. It must be nearly a year since I last went to see her. I must get there in time, so please Mr —?'

'Professor Burbage, my cousin,' I murmured.

'If the Professor will really be so kind . . .' Birch appeared suddenly and enormously relieved, looking at William as the proverbially drowning man must regard the straw he hopes may save him. He turned back towards me, surprisingly coherent, now. 'You must be wondering why I came to you for help, Mrs Catherwood,' he said, 'because of course I had no idea that Professor Burbage would be here. But as this is a Sunday, I have absolutely no way of raising the cash for my fare. In the ordinary way, Mrs Birch would have had quite a bit in the house, the Young Wives' petty cash, and so on; but everything was banked before Christmas. We couldn't raise more than five pounds between us. And to be quite honest, you were the only person I could think of who was likely to have enough cash to lend me till I get back, which of course may not be until after the funeral.' He was now mopping his eyes, but I had left him to run to my desk for my wallet.

I pushed the four £5 notes I had unearthed into his hands at the door, noting that William had already turned his car round in the drive. He came back into the hall to put his top-coat on. We stood together behind the door for a moment. 'It's already past eleven o'clock,' I said. 'What will you do when you have got him to the station – go straight home, or come back here? It's going to snow before long, I think.'

'Oh, I'll come back, if I may. What about lunch? Shall we go out, to make up for Wednesday?'

'I've got steak,' I said. 'There's plenty for two.'

'Fine,' said William, grinning. 'I haven't tasted your cooking since we used to cook bacon on sticks over a fire in the spinney.'

There was an agitated banging on the door, and Birch opened it a fraction. 'Please, Professor, may we get off?'

'I won't be a second longer than I can help,' William said to me. 'Coming,' he yelled to his now almost frantic passenger; and I heard the car draw away.

I returned to the sitting-room and poured myself a drink. It would take William at least an hour and a half to get back, so I needn't bother about lunch yet. I sat back and thought what an extraordinary morning it had been for my first day in my new home. Clearing up that silly misunderstanding with William – and then that confidential talk which I knew he intended to let me know exactly where I now stood in his life. Back, in fact, in the same loving, trusting, cousinly friendship that we had had when we were sixteen. It was lovely to think he would share the first real meal I cooked in Benedict's. The house now might be mine, legally, but he had a share in its heart, as much as I did.

How queer, too, that in the end I had not been requested to lend Johanna money, but had just handed all I had in the house over to the village lay-reader without any of the qualms or irritation that I should have felt in handing it to Johanna. I supposed because he had genuine need of it. And what would Johanna now do about the concert? I hoped she would have the sense to postpone it, especially in view of the worsening weather. She ought not to take on the chance of it being a total flop without somebody like Birch behind her to back her up. It struck me how lucky I had been to get out of her orbit just in time not to have to help her make decisions. I was free. I gloated, and spread my toes to a fire big enough to warm a baronial hall.

William was back just after one o'clock, and gave me an account of his trip while I cooked the steak.

'I've never seen a man of his age in such a state,' he said. 'I was jolly glad when we got to the station, I can tell you.'

'Did you stop to find out how long he had to wait for a London train?' I inquired, thinking that that broken apology for a man would be lucky to get himself as far as Liverpool Street in that state, let alone Liverpool.

'There was a train due in ten minutes,' William said. 'So I sat in the car, and watched him as far as the ticket office. Then he went through the barrier, holding up his hand to thank me. But I felt I had to make sure he was still all right. So I went to the barrier, and there he was, standing like a dummy on the down platform instead of the up-line one. I yelled at him to go across the bridge, and he heard me, because he held his hand up again and shuffled off. That's the last I saw of him. If I hadn't waited, he'd be well on his way to Harwich or somewhere by now.'

I couldn't help smiling. It had taken only the tiniest pinprick of ordinary human experience to deflate that terribly pompous pseudo-cleric and turn him into that soggy, shapeless, miserable and helpless creature.

'I hope you'll get your money back,' said William suddenly. 'Want to bet which of us ever gets any back first?'

'It wouldn't be a fair bet,' I said. 'He's a public figure. He couldn't risk a scandal. Nobody else will ever know about Johanna's debt to you. I've been thinking how often that sort of emergency happens on a Sunday. I must remember, and be prepared. It was such luck that you happened to be here today, but I can't rely on that happening very often.'

'Oh, I don't know, Fran,' he said. 'This is nice – eating in the dear old house again. It's the first time I've really felt at home for about ten years.'

He gave his whole attention to the steak then, and I watched him, to the neglect of my own. It was like watching the transformation scene in a pantomime, only in reverse. The academic robes had fallen off and the William who was facing me across the table with crooked eyebrows and twinkling eyes was a handsome, virile, satisfied and utterly contented man.

'Let's leave the washing-up for Sophie to do tomorrow,' I said. 'She'll be pleased to be part of the homecoming. Let's go back to toast our toes.'

10

'Here's Sophie!' I said, staring in disbelief. Sophie's solid figure had passed by the window, and was going round to the back door. She opened it without knocking, and came in. One glance was enough to tell me that something was wrong.

'Is Wendy here?' she asked, without waiting for me to speak, or greeting William.

'Wendy?' I repeated foolishly. 'Why on earth should Wendy be here?'

Sophie sat down very suddenly, as if her legs had been taken off by a *samurai's* katana.

'Well, it was only a chance. Hetty's Joe has just been up to mine. Seems as 'ow Het and Wend' had a bit of a row, this morning, 'cos Wend' didn't want to get up to go to Sunday school. She's been a teacher there since she were fourteen, y'see. She 'ad been out late last night an' she crep' in without waking 'em. Then this morning, when Het went to wake 'er, she tell Het as she were tired, an' she wasn't going to git up to go to no dratted Sunday school — only she didn't say "dratted". She *swore*, Joe said! Then Joe, 'e pulled 'er out o' bed, and she squealed and cried and shrieked an' swore till Hetty upped and slapped 'er good and proper. Arter that, she say all right, she will goo to Sunday school, an' she'll tell that there Birch as it'd be for the very last time, and why. So off she went all sulky and not speakin' to 'er Mam and Dad. Then when she'd gone, Joe 'ad to square Het up, 'cos she 'ad a fit o' 'sterricks. So they made up their mind, when she come back, as they'd have a straight talk to 'er, like. Joe said just the same as you said, that 'e reckoned as we'd all been a-keepin' 'er too much of a child. But she ain't come back yet!'

Sophie paused for breath. She didn't often make such long speeches, and I gauged the level of her distress by the way she had dropped deeper and deeper into dialect.

She got her second wind, and went on. 'So Joe got on 'is bike, an' went to look for 'er. 'E went fust to Mis' Brooke's but she say she ain't seen Wend' since Friday night, 'cos Wend' were at work yest'day afternoon when the rest of 'em went to get the church room ready for the do on Monday. So then Joe went to see Mr Birch, to ask 'im if Wend' 'ad been to Sunday school this mornin'; but Joe only see Mis' Birch, and she told 'im as she 'ad seen Wend' talking to 'er 'usband atween mornin' service an' Sunday school, in the churchyard. Mis' Birch say she expect it were only still one more thing about that dratted ol' concert so she never waited for him, but went 'ome along of 'er neighbour. And she went into 'er neighbour's 'ouse, like, for a few minutes, and when she did go 'ome she'd found a note to say as 'er husband's mother 'ad been took bad in Manchester, and 'e'd gone straight off to see 'er, without waitin' for 'is wife to get 'ome. Well, then Joe got on 'is bike an' went round everywhere again, but he couldn't see 'ide nor 'air o' Wendy. He didn't worry, like, 'cos 'e had felt sure that when 'e went 'ome, 'e'd find 'er there. But 'e didn't, and she ain't come 'ome yet. When Joe went in without 'er, Het 'ad another fit o' 'sterricks, an' he couldn't do nothing with 'er. He says she's got it into 'er 'ead that something terrible's 'appened to the gal, though she 'as only been gone for about four hours yet. But Joe couldn't deal with Het's 'sterricks an' be out lookin' for Wend' both at once, so by that, like, 'e come up to fetch me and Thirz. I said as I'd come 'ere first just in case Birch or Mis' Brooke 'ad sent 'er up 'ere with a message, or to borrow something, or anything else o' the sort.'

She stopped again, in tragic bewilderment, as if now that her tale was told, she felt like Columbus's sailors faced by a wide and empty sea leading only to the end of the world. I knew that she had never had the least hope of finding Wendy with me, or of gathering any clue to the girl's whereabouts. She had come with the instinct of a homing pigeon to the one place where she knew she could put her feelings into words, and at the same time be given a bit of sound advice without having to ask for it. I suspected that Hetty's ''sterricks' were turning a tremor into an earthquake. Wendy had rebelled, and was now taking advantage of her own daring to make a good job of it, on the principle that she might as well be hanged for a sheep as a lamb. But I had a most uncomfortable feeling that on the same icy winter day that had already seen one hurried departure, we might expect more trouble.

William stood jingling coins in his trouser pocket, and Sophie turned towards him, with a look of relief that told me she had only just taken in that he was there in the flesh. It was written all over her that in this kind of emergency, what you needed was a man. If I hadn't been so concerned for her, I should have laughed. Sophie, who had been brought up in a manless household, and kept away from the opposite sex as if they were all lepers, still bowed without question to St Paul's doctrine about their superiority over women.

When he spoke, William was more serious than I had expected him to be. 'Mr Birch has left for Liverpool,' he said. 'I put him on the train a couple of hours ago. If Wendy was the last person he saw before leaving in such a hurry, he may have asked her to go all round those who were helping with the concert, to tell them that it was to be postponed.'

Sophie looked so relieved that it really hurt me to have to knock the prop of hope away. 'I don't think so. He saw Wendy at the church, but he told us the telephone was ringing when he went into his house and that he had left at once.'

Sophie looked up. '*She* said Manchester.'

'Manchester? Who? Oh, Mrs Birch! No, he's gone to Liverpool.'

'She *said* Manchester.'

'Well, people round here do get them muddled up.'

Sophie's face set like plaster-of-Paris, all at once, into a grim contradiction which must have cost her a lot.

'I know she said Manchester, and she ought to know.'

William became very practical all at once.

'I don't suppose where he has gone matters,' he said. 'What

matters is that we find Wendy. There is only about an hour of daylight left, and we may have to organize a proper search. So where do you want to go? Down to Hen Street? We'll go in my car, and then if necessary we can help by going straight on to the police in Swithinford.'

At the word 'police' Sophie bit back a cry of protest, then stood up to go. We set out.

I had now been back in the district more than three months, but until today I had not encountered either of Sophie's sisters. I was sad that our first meeting had to be at such an inauspicious time. Hetty lived close to Johanna in a mock-Tudor semi that Sophie had told me was 'too posh for the likes of 'er.'

We were ushered into the living-room at the back, which was overcrowded with furniture as well as people, and reeking with the smell of overcooked greens from the still uneaten dinner.

Hetty was short, fair and well covered, with a rosy prettiness that Wendy had inherited. She bore no resemblance to either of her sisters; Sophie was tall and dark, and Thirzah uncompromisingly square, dark-skinned and very broad in the beam. Hetty prepared to go into hysterics at our entrance, and Joe hovered round her saying helplessly, 'Now Het! Now Het!' over and over again.

Thirzah sat like some Biblical matriarch, disapproval writ large in every line of her: she acknowledged us with a regal inclination of her head, saying sharply, 'Pull yourself together, Het, do! Don't make such an hexibition o' yourself! It's no use crying over spilt milk. You should ha' put your foot down weeks ago. It's all come about on account o' this play-acting, you may depend. If she comes 'ome, you want to turn 'er clothes up and tan 'er backside till she can't sit down. Now then! Mrs Catherwood and Professor Burbage will tell us what to do for the best.' Our unexpected arrival on the scene was being made to look as if she had planned it all.

'If she comes 'ome! If she comes 'ome,' wailed Hetty.

'I think we must inform the police at once,' I said.

'That we shall not!' said Thirzah, with godlike finality. 'No kin o' mine is going to be put in the paper on account o' the police having to be called out to look for 'er. She's just a-showin' off.'

Sophie's grey eyes sought mine in mute appeal, and Hetty's wails increased in volume. Calling in the police would be the last straw for them. I tried hard to think clearly. Wendy could not have got any great distance from the village unless she had an accomplice, since public transport on a Sunday was non-existent. Had her friends been questioned?

Again, I met Thirzah's veto. Nobody was to know Wendy was missing until all else failed.

William was getting impatient. Outside the little steamed-up window, the afternoon light was already fading as the thickening snowclouds curled upwards from the horizon to cover the last frail patches of egg-shell-blue sky. He spoke to Joe, but his voice was intended for the three women too.

'Listen to me,' he said – and surprisingly, they did. 'Either she is deliberately declaring her independence by going off with some friends without telling anybody, in which case she will be back safe and sound by bed-time. Or not so probably, but quite possible, is that she went off in a temper because of what happened this morning and dare not come back. If that is the case, she's probably hiding somewhere till it is dark and she can creep in without you knowing. She can't have gone very far, on foot. There are only two roads out of Hen Street, and I think you said Mr Noble has searched both those on his bike. She was not on the road to Swithinford when I took Mr Birch that way, which would be at about the crucial time. Is there any other way she could have gone?'

'There's the way down to the river, sir,' said Daniel, from his chair in the darkest corner, a tall, spare, handsome man, with soft, intelligent eyes. 'Quite likely some o' the young'uns might go down that way after Sunday school to see if the ice'll bear yet. They all know well enough as the river wouldn't be safe, but they can't come to much harm on the washes if the ice does bear there. There ain't enough water for it to be deep. If they went a-sliding there, and she went with 'em, it's p'raps like you say, sir, and she daresn't come back.'

From the look Thirzah gave him, I gathered that if we had not been there, she would have told him to hold his tongue. There was no doubt that Thirzah lorded it as of right over the Wainwright clan.

'Yes. Well, I think we had better try the river path. We'll take the car as far as we can, and then walk. Fran, you go along to see Johanna and get a list of all the youngsters in the group she's been coaching – and any sort of clues she may be able to supply. Then come down the river road and if we haven't got back to it by then, use my car to visit all the friends Wendy has seen lately. If we haven't found her, or got some idea where she is, by four o'clock, go straight to the police. You ladies' – William charged on, defeating Thirzah's attempt to forbid it – 'must stay here, in case she comes in.'

I ran all the way to Bryony Cottage, and told Johanna as briefly as I could what I was there for. She was surprised that Wendy could be quite so stupid, but thought it was just another of the strange fits the girl had been throwing lately.

'I expect she's just feeling her feet, and showing off,' she said, putting on her warm outdoor clothes to come with me. If we had to turn detectives and make house-to-house inquiries, two would do it quicker than one. 'Besides,' she said, 'all the concert lot know me well by now, but you are still a stranger.'

We hurried along the road, and took off to the left. At the bottom of a short, loose-gravelled lane the path turned into a rutty track across the low-lying ground to a point where, a quarter of a mile or so distant from the road, it petered out when it came to the river, and there joined what had once been a towpath. The path was now overgrown with coarse grass and encroaching reed, and willows that had strayed there from the washes now obstructed it, leaning out over the river in what appeared to be a vain attempt to link arms with those the other side.

William's car stood at the end of the gravelled track. We stopped for a moment before getting into it, partly to make sure my orders had not been changed or countermanded, and partly because, just at that moment, the clouds parted and a brilliant orange gleam lit up the prospect before us like a heavenly searchlight in action.

There had been a fair amount of rain before Christmas, and the washes had been flooded, though to only a very shallow depth. Clumps of coarse grass and tufts of sedge broke the surface of the ice that had formed in the last few days, and everywhere willows and sallows stood poised above it with their arms, like those of a *corps de ballet*, held in graceful if impossible positions. The wind had dropped now, and the keen afternoon was frozen into stillness. It was an incredibly beautiful picture the sudden fiery gleam had lit up, for among the trees and reeds and sedges the ice was dotted with brilliantly white waterfowl standing or sitting in ceramic attitudes of disconsolate patience; most of them were swans – and for that magic matter of seconds every one, along with every tree and every rush and every bent of grass had been repeated upside down in myriad reflections in the dark, glossy ice. Then the brilliant gap in the clouds closed again, and the first few flakes of snow drifted aimlessly down.

From a clump of willows by the river I caught the sound of William's voice, and, peering into the half-light, saw him running towards us, gesticulating and shouting.

'They've found something,' I said, my heart in my mouth.

'Stay there,' yelled William, and we stood where we were till he came up, the breath freezing in clouds before him as he ran.

'We've found her!' he said. 'No, she's OK so far, but we may need the police, yet. So hang on for a few minutes.'

I wanted to shake him for not blurting out all the details.

'Let me get my breath back,' he gasped. 'She was hiding down amongst the willows, as we thought, probably waiting for it to get dark. Her father saw her first, and called out to her – so I told him to go on alone to get her. Daniel and I stood and waited, but when Joe got about a dozen yards from her, she began to scream at him not to go nearer, or she'd jump in the river.'

I glanced involuntarily towards the river where ice had already formed a crust for the flakes of snow to rest upon. It was not yet strong enough for skating, but plenty thick enough to make Wendy's threat overcharged with awful possibility. East Anglian rivers are notorious for tragedy if anyone falls through the ice. Even when help is at hand, rescue may be impossible, because no one can get near enough to be of any use. The ice gives way round the edges of the hole, under the would-be rescuers. Shocked by the sudden immersion, paralysed with the cold, caught in the grip of cramp and lacerated by the razor-sharp edges of the broken ice, the victim gives up the struggle to survive easily and sinks under the ice. I shuddered.

'Come on,' said William, turning back. 'Perhaps you can persuade her to come down.'

'Come down?' I panted, trying to keep up with his much longer legs.

'Joe thought she was only trying it on, but he decided to get between her and the river. When she saw that he was still going towards her, she turned the other way, and climbed a tree. Then she crawled along a branch that hangs out right over the water, and there she is. She says if anybody goes close enough to try to get her down, she'll let go and drop into the river.'

'The police,' said Johanna, who had easily kept pace with my stumbling trot, 'or the fire brigade.'

'Yes, of course,' said William. 'Fran, take the car and go for both! Oh, no! God, no! Don't let them come any nearer! Stop them, somehow, whatever you have to do.' He was gone.

He pointed behind me as he ran, and turning on my heel I saw three figures battling through the gloom, like the three fates, separated from each other only by the nature of their particular grisly duties. First came Hetty, hatless and coatless, slipping and sliding and shrieking distracted, unintelligible cries. A few yards behind her, also unprotected from the weather except for a flowered overall, padded Sophie; and fifty yards or so behind came Thirzah, still wearing her best Sunday hat and coat, rolling and waddling from side to side of the uneven path like a Dutch barge wallowing in a gale.

I sprang back into Hetty's path, trying to intercept her, and shouting to Johanna to come and help me, but Johanna was nowhere to be seen. I grabbed Hetty as she tried to pass me, and threw my arms round her. She beat me with clenched fists until I began to fear that she must break my hold. When Sophie caught up and joined me, Hetty saw that she was outnumbered, and went limp, a sobbing rag doll. Thirzah drew breathlessly close.

'She's drownded, ain't she?' Hetty kept saying every now and then, struggling to break away. 'I know she is! Let me go! I want to see her!'

'No! No!' I said, shaking her fiercely in my vehemence every time I spoke. 'She's alive, but she's in danger. I'm going for help, but you mustn't go any further. Go back home—' I stopped. I could see what an impossible command that was to Wendy's three mothers, when they had no inkling at all of the situation. If I told them, they would simply push past me, and go forward. I appealed to Sophie.

'Sophie,' I said. 'You trust me, don't you? You mustn't let Hetty go on! If you can get Hetty back home, the chances are that Wendy will be there with you, safe and sound, soon. *Please* Sophie, *please!*'

Sophie raised her wide grey eyes to mine, and searched my face for truth. I shall never have to endure a more penetrating look, even on Judgement Day. I held her gaze, and I realized with terrible guilt that all three of the distracted women had until that moment believed that my efforts to restrain Hetty had been to prevent her from seeing Wendy's drowned or mutilated corpse.

'Come, Het,' Sophie coaxed. 'Come home, Het, there's a good gel. She is telling you the truth. Wend'll soon be 'ome now. Come on 'ome!'

Hetty came to life again suddenly. She was going to her child, dead or alive. She began her powerful straining against our hold again. To make matters worse, it now began to snow in good earnest, huge white flakes feathering down to make a speckled white curtain which the dim light was still trying vainly to penetrate.

When neither my failing physical strength nor Sophie's cajoling showed any effect of deflecting Hetty from her purpose, Thirzah joined the fray. She placed herself squarely in front of the three of us, holding up her hand for silence, and said, 'We shall ask the help of the Lord, the same as if we was at 'ome, so you 'old yer row, Hetty, else the Lord won't be able to 'ear me!'

Her two sisters seemed mesmerized into instant obedience. They stood, side by side, hands clasped and eyes turned down to the ground, though I was paralysed by embarrassment, and overcome by the unreality of it all. I ought to have been on my way to Swithinford to get real, practical help. I was about to say so, when I looked at Thirzah again. She was still waiting, the upturned brim of her black felt hat gradually filling with snow. How did I know that her faith was not worth more than the presence of a police-sergeant or a fire-officer?

The tread of feet behind me brought me to my senses. All three of the men were there, but no Wendy, no Johanna.

I pulled William aside, and asked what had happened.

'Wendy wouldn't budge,' he whispered. 'Then Johanna arrived from somewhere, and simply took charge. She said she thought that if we would let her handle Wendy alone, she could talk her down. So I persuaded the others to let her try, especially as it seems to be Wendy's family that sent her to the verge of insanity. We said we would come away as far as this, to be within calling distance if she needed us.'

'Hark!' said Joe, who had been telling the others the same tale. We listened. It was Johanna's voice, and we all reacted as one to the lack of any urgency in it.

'Professor! Professor!'

William turned and began to run, commanding us all to stay where we were. He was back again very soon.

'It's all right!' he called through the puthering snow. 'She's safe!' Hetty showed signs of keeling over. 'Take her home, Joe,' he said.

'I'm a-waiting till I see Wendy!' said Hetty obstinately, but William was prepared for that.

'She is coming now, with Mrs Brooke, as soon as ever you have gone,' he said. 'I will bring her home in my car. I can't get the rest of you in.'

All of them, even Thirzah, seemed a bit dazed by such a prompt answer to their prayers. They had done their bit, and like a bunch of sheep who suddenly give in to a sheep-dog, they decided to obey William's orders. Led by Daniel and Thirzah, with Joe and Hetty following, and Sophie bringing up the rear by herself, they stumbled away, heads bent forward against the snow.

William caught me by the hand and pulled me back. 'Go with them, and keep them occupied somehow,' he said in a low voice. 'Johanna only got Wendy to come down from the tree by giving her a firm promise that she need not go home. When they have gone, I'll take them both to Bryony Cottage. Then I'll come up and tell them, and try to persuade them all to go easy with her. She's still in a terrible state.'

I ran after the others, and helped Sophie prepare some hot tea while the rest in varying degrees gave their attention to Hetty, and took off their own wet clothes. Then, always with one ear cocked for the sound of the car that would announce the arrival of the prodigal daughter, they proceeded to 'talk it out' among themselves.

After heartfelt relief came the natural desire to punish the culprit for all the anguish she had put them through. Then came barely concealed resentment that Johanna had been involved, and that it was to her pleas, rather than those of 'her own flesh and blood' that Wendy had yielded. That boded ill for Johanna's reputation, I thought. They would never forgive her for being the person of all others to whom they were 'beholden'.

As the long minutes dragged by, the sense both of outrage and anxiety returned, and in the end it was Daniel, looking timidly over the rim of his teacup at Thirzah, who suggested that whatever was going to be done or said to Wendy had perhaps better be left till morning. The immediate and unanimous acquiescence of all the rest made it plain that this was what each of them had been feeling secretly, but had not dared voice for fear of losing face, especially in front of me.

It was Sophie who broke the ensuing silence. 'I wish they'd come,' she said. 'We don't know yet what it's all about, do we? It can't be just because of what 'appened this morning, surely? Wend' may be a bit headstrong, like, but she ain't daft.'

Exactly. That is what I had been telling myself for the last ten minutes. The storm had risen so unexpectedly, and had been so violent while it lasted, that there had been little time to consider what had caused it. Listening with half an ear to her family's speculation about it, I was astounded to hear Thirzah say that as long as the neighbours were none the wiser, no harm was likely to arise from it. Wendy had, no doubt about it, won the battle for her independence, simply by indulging in a bit of melodrama.

There came a tap on the door at last, and a charge of tension ran through the little room as all eyes turned to greet the return of the black sheep to the fold. But it was only William, alone.

He reported that no amount of cajoling would budge Wendy from Bryony Cottage. She was shaking with cold, fear and fatigue, he said, and he had advised Mrs Brooke to put her to bed at once with hot water bottles and aspirins, which she had done. Wendy was now lying there crying. Mrs Brooke had suggested that perhaps her mother and father might care to go along alone to see her and sit with her a little while. If having them with her would help her to fall asleep, no doubt she would be perfectly well again by morning.

The suggestion was received with silent resentment. Hetty stood up, as if to go at once, but catching Thirzah's eye, sat down again, awaiting permission from the chief of the clan, as it were. Thirzah said, reluctantly, 'You'd better go, then. We shall stop 'ere till you get back.' It was a dismissal for us and I grabbed at it. I, too, stood up and began to reach for my coat, but I caught William's eye, and he shook his head very slightly with a warning look. I subsided, I thought, exactly as Hetty or Sophie would have done had Thirzah issued such a sign. I was becoming light-headed, and suppressed a desire to laugh hysterically. Would this extraordinary day never end?

Joe and Hetty set off into the snow-filled dark. William spoke to Daniel. 'I think we ought to stay long enough to let them get there and see Wendy,' he said, 'in case my car is needed. We might still have need to fetch a doctor.' I wondered if the patient he had in mind was Wendy or Hetty. After about another twenty minutes of difficult, stilted conversation, he stood up.

'I think I might take you back to Benedict's now, Fran,' he said. 'Then I must get away, in case the roads get very bad.'

So we made our farewells, received from Thirzah grudging thanks, and left. William's car stood by the roadside, and as we went towards it, we heard Johanna's voice calling us to wait. She was running along the grass verge with an electric torch wavering in front of her, punching a snow-mottled circular hole of light in the featherbed of darkness.

'I am glad I caught you,' she panted. 'I must talk to you for a minute or two. Shall we get into the car?' We did.

'Don't stop just here, William,' I said. 'Drive on a bit. They will be peeping through the front curtains to make sure we have really gone.'

William drove about a hundred yards till we could pull into a gateway.

'Is Wendy OK?' I asked. 'I hope they won't get at her tonight, silly child. How did you manage to talk the mad Ophelia out of her watery death?'

'Don't laugh too soon, Fran,' Johanna said, and even in the dark I could tell there was no acting now. 'To answer your question, I swore at her. I acted on a hunch when I left you and followed William. I guessed that she had begun by staging a bit of an act, and had got carried away by her own performance. It's so easy to do, and I know you get worked into the part till you can't stop when you want to. I know how she hero-worships me, and I thought I should be the last person she would want to see her making a fool of herself. So I asked the men to clear out of her sight, and leave the job to me. I told her flatly that I had rumbled her, and she might just as well call her silly threats off, and if she'd come off it straight away, without any more fuss, I'd promise that somehow I would put things right for her at home.

'She was gazing down at me in a dazed sort of way, crouched on a branch far too near the thin end for comfort. And then she seemed all at once to come to, and realize who I was and where she was. Instead of coming backwards, she began to scream that I couldn't put things right for her, that nobody could, ever again. And she began to crawl *forward* towards the end of the branch right over the river. God, was I scared! I had let the men go and played my card, and lost. So I began to yell, too. At her. I was so terrified that I didn't know what I was saying, but when I heard myself, I was letting rip at her in a language I didn't think I knew — or at least that I had thought I had forgotten. But it worked. The shock of hearing me swearing like a Billingsgate fishwife was what saved her. She looked around her, and I think only at that moment became aware that she was in danger. So then I talked her backwards along the branch till she could get down the trunk, and after that it was child's play.'

'Well,' I said. 'It seems like a case of good coming out of evil. It does sound as if she really was mad enough to have jumped if her father had tried scolding.'

'Yes,' she said. 'They're with her now, though she won't speak. But I left them with her to try to watch for you coming out, to get a word with you. You see, when I got her down the tree she was frozen to the marrow and frightened to death, but what she was babbling so frantically to me was not to send her home, because she could never go home again. She's pregnant, Fran. By Hector Birch.'

The sound of the car's engine and the light of the torch went out together. The spent arrows of the snow fell hurtlessly outside the enclosed, thick, blacked-out silence. Neither William nor Johanna moved or spoke. They were awaiting the first reaction from me.

But my mind was blank, as numbed as a hand is by a sudden hard blow on the elbow, unable to feel or function. Then as sensation returns, and the first prickling of pins-and-needles makes itself felt in the fingertips, the sufferer is aware what intense pain must follow. It took a long time before the meaning of Johanna's words registered.

Since Wednesday evening, I had run the whole gamut of emotion; — of shock, disgust, jealousy, disappointment, disillusionment, despair, loneliness, shame at my own suspicious stupidity, relief, and the joy both of being under my own roof again and sharing my first meal there with William. Then Birch going and the search for Wendy . . .

The pain came flooding in. Now this. Now this. Now this.

As we found afterwards, when we were able to discuss that moment rationally, the reasons for all three of us being disturbed were very different.

William had helped Birch to abscond. There was no dying mother. A frightened man had run away, abandoning all responsibility, with my money in his pocket. (Not only mine, either, as we found out later, but also petty cash belonging to the church, the Dramatic Society, the Smallholders' Hall and even the Young Wives' Meeting.) Johanna was cursing chance (and me) for ever causing her to be dragged into a village scandal when she was not of the village in spirit or in truth; she was fearing for her own reputation, not that of her protégée. And I was suffering acutely, because I was the only one of the three who understood even a fraction of the devastation it would cause within Kezia's family circle.

Johanna found her voice first, urgent and practical. 'We can't discuss it now. They'll smell a rat if I am away too long. She says she can't tell them and won't tell them. She seems to think that in some miraculous way, I can save her. Ought one of us to break it here and now to her parents?'

'No!' I cried, as all feeling returned to me with a rush. 'We simply must not let on to them that such a thing ever crossed our minds. It's a question of their pride, you see. We mustn't damage it more than Wendy already has.'

'Don't be silly, Fran. You're talking like a mid-Victorian. Such a thing isn't the end of the world nowadays.'

'I know I'm right, Johanna,' I argued. 'We have got to let it be, and keep quiet till they find out.'

'And what happens if Wendy does put herself in the river after all? Where do I stand then? "Oh yes, sir," I say to the coroner, "the girl confided in me, but I thought it was none of my business"?'

'I know that sounds like sense,' I said, 'but I'm backing my instinct, and I *know* I'm right.'

'I must get back to them,' Johanna said. 'I'll talk to Wendy again tomorrow, and come down to see you, Fran. Maybe something will happen to sort it out. Thank God it means that that damned concert is off, anyway.' She got out, and ran through the snow back to the bungalow.

William, very quiet, delivered me back to Benedict's, and came in for a quick drink; but once he was warmed through, he put on his car-coat again, and prepared to leave. He stood for a moment in front of me, as if he were not sure of himself.

'I don't want to leave you,' he said, 'but of course I must. Are you sure you will be all right?'

'Of course I shall,' I said. 'I shall worry, but I'm not afraid. It is nice of you to think about me, though.'

He took both my hands in his, and held them. 'I think about you all the time,' he said, lightly, with his charming smile. 'It's more or less my fault that you are here, on a night like this, by yourself.'

He let go suddenly, and was gone out into the night.

Well! So much for my first day of 'peace' at Benedict's! But little did I know then what was in store for us all.

A log rolled forward in the fireplace, and I moved to stand up to deal with it. The cat on my knee protested loudly, and laid her slender weight against my effort to rise. I was always surprised at the strength in that feline sinuosity, and the wiry determination she could bring to bear against anything that disturbed her immediate comfort or threatened to deprive her of her own way. She was not above using her talons, either, if reduced to it. I sometimes wondered why I bothered about her, so much a slave to her imperious wishes had I become. I adored her. She gave me infinite pleasure to look at, and to try to understand. She was not 'my cat', because she was nobody's cat but her own. Just like Johanna, I thought as I heaved her up to dislodge her and she yowled her disapproval.

I replaced the fallen log, and added others to it, kneeling on the hearthrug but not really seeing what I was doing. I was still far away, back in the past, still trapped in the memory of that eventful first Sunday at Benedict's, and its consequences as time had passed. I poured myself a drink, and returned to my chair and my musing.

PART TWO

THE GAME

11

My memories had got out of sequence. I had rushed forward from the extraordinary first day in my new house, but I had to go back to that time to collect together all the threads that wove themselves into my life during the months that followed.

After William left, it began to snow in earnest, and before midnight it had turned to a real blizzard. Having had Sophie so constantly at my side during the last three months had bundled me headlong into a comprehension of the life of the village that even William, who knew it as well as I did, could not begin to recapture. Johanna would not have a clue. I should have to see her as soon as possible, and try to make her believe that I knew far better than she did how people living in such a closed community were likely to react to Wendy's predicament.

When I got up it was still snowing – not now driving as it had been in the night, but drifting down in a shaken blanket of huge flakes. I went to the landing window in the main house on purpose to watch it fall, hearing Kezia's voice in my ears like a muffled echo from far away.

> There's the old woman a-picking her geese
> And selling the feathers a penny apiece.

The snowflakes did look like feathers – as if 'Im Above had torn a great rent in His feather-bed and was emptying the tick of its entire contents down upon our heads. I wondered for the umpteenth time why it was that snowflakes looked black as they drifted towards you and so ruthlessly, puritanically white once they landed. Of course I knew the answer. It had been explained to me in a physics lesson on light when I was at school; but a scientific explanation couldn't and didn't wholly satisfy my questioning. The larger inquiry had to do with the whole concept of truth, with the difference between perception and knowledge, between illusion and reality.

Who could, or should, tell me whether snow was black or white? It depended entirely on my own viewpoint.

Thinking of yesterday's goings-on, and the terrible blow about to be dealt to Wendy's family, I felt the pain that I knew it must cause them quite physically. Why them? What was 'Im Above up to, to allow such suffering to those who so implicitly put their faith in Him?

Perhaps that faith would help them to understand and accept better than I ever could. Perhaps like Job, they would hear His voice, and in their simple faith understand both His words and His purpose. 'Where wast *thou* when I laid the foundations of the earth? Hast *thou* entered into the treasures of the snow? Wilt *thou* disannul *my* judgement? Wilt *thou* condemn me, that *thou* mayest be righteous?'

I knew that whatever final decisions they arrived at, they would still be guided by faith rather than reason. I envied them their trust, for though I feared that it might be badly shaken, it would survive. As I turned away from the window reluctantly, after taking one more long look at the black feathers swirling towards me, again there came the faint memory of Kezia's voice: 'He shall cover thee with his feathers, and under His wings shalt thou trust.'

The text in fact proved more to the point than I could have expected or hoped for in the next few days. It was as though the eiderdown of snow insulated us all from any immediate effects of the micro-crisis Sunday's events foreshadowed. The snow continued to fall until the countryside merged and softened to a world of dazzling crystal beauty, melting here and there into blue shadow as evening fell and the orange stars of light began to flicker from cottage windows. We existed, as it were, inside a padded cell of forced inertia. Roads were blocked and telephone lines brought down. Rail services everywhere were disrupted, and only essential supplies got through on cleared and gritted main roads. Work at Benedict's had to be suspended, and I was entirely cut off from the outside world. We were even cut off from Hen Street, except for verbal messages delivered by the postman on foot.

Sophie battled her way to me each morning from her cottage half a mile away in Old Swithinford, but even she flinched at the thought of trudging to Hen Street and back. Daniel had been sent on foot by Thirzah to inquire about any developments in the Noble household, and had reported that things were calm if none too comfortable there. Wendy had caught a severe chill on Sunday, and Johanna had flatly refused to allow Hetty and Joe to take her out of her bed to walk home through the blizzard. So she was still at Bryony Cottage, much to the chagrin of both her parents. I wondered as Sophie chatted on, how much of the chill was Johanna's invention. It solved nothing, but it did allow time for feelings to simmer down a bit all round.

I watched Sophie for any signs that the bomb which sooner or later must wreck their placid existence had fallen. As it happened, nothing of Wendy's escapade on Sunday seemed to have reached the old village, no doubt because Mr Birch's absence to his dying mother's bedside was already stealing the headlines. Nobody, not even Sophie, had any reason to suspect that it was in any way connected with Wendy and her antics; which made the load of knowledge on me all the heavier.

Sophie reported that Birch's wife had also left — it was taken for granted that she, too, had been sent for to the deathbed and the funeral. The continuing bad weather seemed to keep both gossip and official inquiries muted. When at last it did become a matter for the police, William's part in taking Birch to the station was disclosed, and my loan of money. Police questioning at the mainline station elicited a vague memory from the ticket collector that a man answering to the description of Birch had come tumbling down the steps from the bridge just as the train to the east was drawing out, and had flung himself upon it. So he had been making for the coast all along. If he or his wife were ever traced, the news did not reach us.

I found it more difficult every day to greet Sophie without giving a hint that I was expecting anything to disturb our new and happy routine at Benedict's. But the day came when she arrived late, sat down without removing her coat, and burst into tears. The bombshell had exploded.

I had to put on an act worthy of Johanna, as Sophie poured out her tale how Hetty had caught sight of Wendy undressing the night before, and had needed no further telling what the matter was; of Hetty's anguished cry, 'Oh my God!' repeated over and over and over again; of recriminations and accusations, of browbeating and what seemed like third-degree questioning, until the punch-drunk girl had at last sobbed out who the father was; of Hetty's instant bout of hysterics, during which she had lost all reason and had flown at Wendy like a wild cat, scratching and clawing at her until Joe had had to pull her away and slap her face hard; and then of him turning to Wendy in terrible, stern, cold fury, repudiating his erst-while darling's proffered love and pleading.

''E pushed 'er away,' sobbed Sophie, 'and 'e dragged 'er to the corner of the room, and stood 'er up against the wall, and made 'er stand there and read out o' the Bible about the whores of Babylon. Then 'e shut 'er in 'er room while 'e come up to fetch us, and when we got there 'e fetched Wend' out and made 'er read it out loud over and over again, like somebody gone off 'is 'ead. Even Thirz' couldn't stop 'im. I never see Joe do anything like that afore — 'e's usually so quiet and kind. It were awful to watch, Fran!'

May the gods pour blessings down upon Dan'el's tender heart I prayed silently, because I gathered that he had been the only one to stand up for Wendy at all. 'She ain't the first, and she won't be the last,' he had said, echoing the gnomic sentiment that seldom fails to soothe. I tried to appear sufficiently surprised and shocked while doing my best to comfort my poor distracted Sophie.

'A married man!' she kept saying. 'To think as our gal should go along of a man old enough to be 'er father, and a married man an' all! Whatever could ha' come over 'er? I'm sorry to say it, especially to you, but it's all that red-'eaded bitch's fault, with 'er singing and 'er play-acting. I told you bad would become of it. But not this 'ere! We shall never be able to 'old our 'eads up in Swithinford again. I can't abear it, that I can't!'

The agony passed eventually, as it always does, leaving behind it a dull, heavy, relentless pain. William and Johanna were frankly astounded at the depth of grief and shame Wendy's condition was causing her whole family. Perhaps they were more typical products of our time than I. They both failed to understand that whatever permissiveness modern society allowed at present with regard to sex, it could not change overnight the essential mores of a closed rural community, chain-linked as those mores were with the immedi-ate pre-war past and all the past long before. It might be that the first reaction in the village did have something of Victorian prudery in it, but it went much deeper than that.

I was personally involved because of my close daily contact with Sophie, and my growing affection and admiration for her. On the other hand, as day by day Sophie added more details of the drama I found myself puzzled by the way each of the main characters was behaving. As Daniel had said, Wendy's story was not all that unusual, in spite of the church's denunciation and the mothers' warnings, the social ignominy and the moral disgrace. Even Kezia's family would have accepted that such a thing was 'nat'ral', though wrong. They would all have stuck up for the daughter of any of their friends or neighbours as Daniel had defended Wendy; but their own they could not forgive. The new twist in the old story was that it had happened to them.

Sophie wanted to unburden herself to me, in every little detail; but we were up against a difficulty that I had not foreseen. Sophie was 'a maiden lady'; I was not. If there was one subject we could not meet easily upon, it was anything that related, however loosely, to sex. It was not for several days that I realized how she dropped her voice and almost whispered any confidence about Wendy's condition. When I asked her a question one day, she replied that she didn't know and added, 'Well, they wouldn't tell me, would they, me not being married, like.' She was not expected to know anything of the mysteries of sex – and if she did, or showed any interest at all, she was in danger of being called dirty-minded. So she was the odd woman out in her own close circle. Even Wendy had had an experience apparently to be withheld from Sophie. I did my best to squash this attitude once and for all. 'Sophie, you are not stupid,' I said, and went on to speak my mind. Wasn't it, I asked her, her God who had created men and women different just so that by this very act life on the earth might go on? Did Noah not tell the beasts about to leave the ark to go out and multiply? And here we were, two middle-aged women without a man between us, and if we could not discuss what God had decreed, then it was we who were at fault, not God. I will say for Sophie that if I ever got on my high horse with her, she usually showed her ability to think.

'I don't want to talk sex-talk. But you know very well from what has happened to Wendy that you can't keep it hidden. I don't propose to sweep it under the carpet here in my house just because you don't happen to have been married.' She took the point.

'I don't know what to think,' she said. 'Mam would never tell me nothing, and warned Thirz' and Het as they mustn't tell me when they were married. I don't know what 'arm she thought it could ha' done me, then.'

'I didn't mean to shout at you,' I said. 'Only to make you see that I am the one person you can talk to without either of us being embarrassed. So now, please tell me how Wendy is.'

Sophie said that the poor girl was being got at morning, noon and night. She looked awful, and wouldn't eat what they took her into her bedroom. 'She just lays there and cries, except when Joe makes 'er come out and read bits from the Bible.' It seemed as if he was taking it worse than her mother − possibly because he had loved her most. He refused to open his mouth to Wendy at all except to hurl Biblical imprecations at her. And what about Hetty, I asked?

Sophie's face, took on such an expression of scorn for her younger sister that she forgot herself, and Kezia's training of family loyalty.

''Er!' she said bitterly. 'It's my opinion as she can't be quite right in the 'ead! She spends all 'er time in that place she calls a church, down on 'er knees a-praying. Well may she pray, for we were all'us brought up to cast our burdens upon the Lord − but fancy 'er gooin' to that place, where that man as got our Wend' into trouble used to preach!'

Hetty would not, so Sophie said, speak or communicate with Wendy at all, and Thirzah had failed in her attempt to find out how advanced the pregnancy was, or when the baby was due. But she in her childlessness and Sophie in her virginal state were doing their bumbling best to start to provide for what Sophie in her hushed voice still referred to as 'come Wendy's time'.

Sophie begged me not to disclose who the father was. That had been Hetty's wish, repeated again and again with such fervour that in the end Thirzah had agreed.

When I told William of my conversation with Sophie, I remarked how strange it was that none of them seemed to spend any time or energy railing against Birch. Kezia used to say, 'I always blame the woman' and that pattern had held, although in this case the woman was the white hen's chicken of their own brood. But then, even in the garden of Eden, poor Eve had got all the blame! Personally, I couldn't find things bad enough to think or to say about Birch. Surely, I said to William, if blame had to be allocated, Birch must bear the biggest load?

William, to my surprise, did not wholly agree with me. 'It is the use of the word "blame", I think, that I stick at,' he said. 'To me, that implies some sort of deliberation, or intent to cause trouble. If you want to go right to the roots of the matter of blame, you have to establish the cause. In which case, I'd say that Johanna carries the can.'

'Johanna? How on earth can you saddle her with the blame?'

'Did you ever actually talk to Johanna about her own relationship with Birch? Did she like him? Were you ever given any explanation of finding them together, in the café, for instance, or close together in the kitchen?'

'Yes. Of course we talked about him. Johanna gave me the impression that she rather disliked him, but found him useful.'

'She's devastatingly honest, sometimes,' he said. 'Go on.'

'Well, she did say he was always pestering her to meet him somewhere "by chance", or on some pretext or other. And once they had started the amateur dramatics together, he had got a lot bolder in his physical advances. "Always looking for a chance to maul me," was how she put it.'

'Exactly,' said William. 'But she didn't send him off with a flea in his ear, did she? She just isn't capable of that. She led him on because she couldn't help it. *She* doesn't mean harm. But in this particular case, she did harm all the same. She amused herself with a chap who has probably suppressed his sex drive for donkey's years. Johanna once gave me an impersonation of his wife – cruel, but I guess pretty accurate: the sort of woman who thinks the Almighty slipped up pretty badly in arranging the method of human reproduction. Birch probably might as well have tried making love to a lamp-post! So what happens? Johanna protects herself by using Wendy as a chaperone. She makes sure that as often as possible Wendy is present when he has occasion to visit her. That doesn't prevent her from using every trick in the book to get him excited, but it does prevent him from doing anything about it. And when she's got him into a state where he's ready to rape her on the kitchen table, she sends him out into the night with Wendy – a kid so bursting with sex herself that she doesn't know what to do with it either. She'd go off like a firework as soon as he touched her.'

I was silent, because I couldn't refute him. Now that he had laid the situation before me so explicitly, I was staggered at my own past stupidity. I had witnessed it happening more than once and had never bothered to think of any implications. So I, too, was to blame! Though I could not have been expected to foresee what had now happened, I ought to have known that in a village – even a hotch-potch of a village like Hen Street – Wendy should not have been out with a married man in a car late at night, lay-reader though he might be. *That* was the real reason for Thirzah and Sophie's concern about 'this 'ere play-acting'. They had been helpless in their attempts to draw anybody's attention to the danger to Wendy's reputation, because of Birch's profession and the fact that he had known Wendy from her childhood.

'Johanna should have known better,' I said.

William shook his head. 'She isn't really to *blame*, either,' he said, 'as far as I can see. You see, it never occurred to her for a single moment that Wendy might also be a desirable woman with anything to offer a man compared to her own charms. She sees everything only in relation to herself. That's how she is. As I said, she can't help it.'

'But what you are saying is that none of us is really responsible for the misery we cause! I can't go along with that. What about Hitler – or a murderer like Christie or whatever?'

William did his eyebrow trick.

> 'As flies to wanton boys are we to the gods.
> They kill us for their sport.'

'Oh! No, no, no!' I cried. 'I can't and won't believe that! Do you mean that the gods – including the God that Sophie and Thirzah believe in so completely – just sit up there in their heaven working out for the fun of it the permutations of misery they can cause simply by throwing different sorts of folks in each others' way? What about the whole question of free will?'

'That's what I've been trying to say. If there is a definite will towards harm, you can apportion blame. In the absence of it, you have to blame the gods. I'm pretty sure that if I were a god with a character like Johanna on my hands, I should be tempted to toss her down like a cat among the pigeons, just to see the feathers fly.'

I handed him the drink I had been getting, and sat down again opposite to him, seeing him across the roaring fire.

'Well, thank heaven,' I said, 'as far as we are concerned, they have probably finished their little bit of fun. It's hardly likely that they will involve us in their next experiment.'

'Oh, I don't know,' he said, raising his glass to me. 'I should hate to have to go back to the dull sort of life I was enduring before you turned up again, Fran. And I am afraid that where you are, there will Johanna be also. And me, too. There's a nice explosive mixture!'

12

Snow or no snow, I had to see Johanna. So when on the second Saturday, the sun came and frost set in again, the scintillating panorama tempted me out of my dormouse nest, and I set off to walk to Hen Street.

96

The path to the back door of the bungalow had been cleared of snow and swept, so I took it, and having tapped on the door I stepped through the narrow conservatory and into the kitchen. My abrupt entrance nearly knocked Ned over, because he was standing on the doormat with a cup of steaming coffee in his hands. His face was black with coal dust, and a coalman's leather pad lay across his high shoulders. Though normally he worked as an agricultural labourer, I knew that his employer was also a coal merchant, and that Ned sometimes doubled as delivery man. It was the first time I had actually seen him in his coalman's gear.

Johanna was sitting at the kitchen table, looking as ravishing as ever in a pair of tight soft blue woollen ski pants that fitted her taut little bottom without wrinkle or crease. She looked even more feminine in trousers than she did in a dress. She wore a sloppy-joe pullover of misty grey over a blue blouse, and a deep-blue silk scarf was knotted so that the two ends coincided with the points at which her nipples just lifted the loose jumper enough to be seductively conspicuous. Even while I replied to her greeting, I took it all in, and thought that if I had been a man, that carefully arranged scarf would probably have been my undoing. There was a glow about her, too, a suppressed excitement that obviously had nothing to do with the conversation she was having with Ned.

She pulled up a kitchen chair for me. 'It's warmer here than anywhere else in the house,' she said. 'If I'd known you were coming, I'd have lit a fire, especially now Ned has brought me some coal.' She smiled a dazzling beam of warmth towards him. 'He's having trouble with his coal deliveries.'

'I'm not surprised, with this weather,' I said. 'I wonder anything has got through at all.'

'Well, that's how you'd think anybody might look at it,' said Ned, 'Anybody except Jack Bartrum, that is.'

'Who's Jack Bartrum, and what's he done?' I asked, seeing that this was expected of me.

Johanna replied. 'He's a small farmer whose land lies at the back, behind Hen Street, between us and Swithinford. His house is a little way off the Swithinford Road, and he doesn't have much to do with us. But he has got a right of way down between my bungalow and the next – that's where the gate leads to, that one the other side of my boundary hedge.'

'And yer see, ma'am,' Ned went on, 'there's three or four cottages out in the fields back there, that's easier to come at that way, than round through the farm they're on. So I brought chains for the old lorry, and I had intended getting them folks up there some coal if I could, like I'm done many a winter before. But when I got 'ere this morning, I found the gate padlocked.'

'But surely, if it is a right of way, this Jack Bartrum can't close it?' I said.

Ned shook his head. 'It's one o' them things nobody really knows the rights and wrongs on,' he said. 'Some say it's a bridle path, but Jack says it's his land and nobody else has got a right to set foot on it. He's all'us been nasty about it. That's his way. Wouldn't give anybody the droppings of his nose to save their lives, if he could 'elp it. Ah, a rum'un, Jack is. I've knowed him all my life. I doubt he'll change now. I shall hev' to be goin', though, an' see about it. Them folks still want their coal.'

He set his cup on the table, put on his dirty old cap and went off whistling the Hallelujah chorus.

'I don't know what I should have done without Ned,' Johanna said. 'He's been here every day, sweeping the path, chopping kindling, making the fire up, getting the coal in, fetching me cigarettes. All for nothing, of course. He knows as well as I do that I can't afford to pay him. He just keeps coming out of the goodness of his heart.'

I could well believe it. I could see that she fascinated Ned in the same way a bright picture may capture the fancy of a child, so that he will pore over it for hours in utter absorption while not comprehending its meaning in the very least. But then most men succumbed when she turned on the charm. They sat up like poodles and begged to be made use of. Even William.

She seemed to be following my thoughts. 'William phoned,' she said, lighting another cigarette. 'He said if I saw you to tell you that if the roads were passable at all, he'd be out as usual on Wednesday.'

'Good,' I replied. 'That's nice. I wondered if he had been trying to get in touch. But it was Wendy I really came up to see you about. What's the latest news?'

Johanna removed the cigarette, half-smoked, from between her lips, and stubbed it out, slowly and deliberately, in the ugly soapstone ashtray at her elbow. It was a theatrical gesture, performed to perfection, and conveyed most adequately all it was intended to: that she was not interested in Wendy. The whole act was indicative of indifference, boredom, even distaste, and implied withdrawal from a situation not to her liking.

'She went home on Wednesday morning. I haven't seen her since. They'll sort it out now. It's none of our business, after all, is it?'

I was shocked and nettled — shocked at the casual dismissal of Wendy, and nettled at Johanna's assumption that she expected me to follow her lead in the matter. She was so cool, so detached, so much in control of the situation, that I felt awkward and gauche, a country bumpkin outclassed in this sort of encounter by a suave woman-of-the-world. At the same time, it was this very feeling that served at that moment to cement my alliance with Wendy, instead of with the urbanized lady before me.

'Not exactly our business,' I said, 'but I can't help it being my concern. I'm involved, whether I like it or not. Did you get any details out of her? How far gone is the pregnancy? Can't be very far, obviously. I wish there was something we could *do*!'

Johanna looked at me with a very direct but wary gaze. 'About three months — missed a couple of times, and is being queasy in the mornings. She knows when it happened, all right, though from what I can make out, after the first time, it was a case of anywhere, any time though especially a Friday night treat. But look here, Fran — she's no concern of *mine*, and as for anything being done about it, as you put it, you can leave me out. Nothing doing! Don't tell me she didn't know what game she was playing, silly kid! I didn't mind looking after her while she was here, but I made it fairly plain when she went home that that was that. I got my fingers burnt over that bloody village concert, anyway. Everything's collapsed again, and I'm back where I started, thanks to Wendy and Mr Bloody Birch.'

I was appalled. When I had said I wished we could do something, I was merely expressing a wish that there was no need for secrecy, and that at least we could offer the girl and her family moral support. Johanna had taken me literally to mean I was seeking her connivance in arranging a back-street abortion.

I thought of Sophie in the churchyard, doubting openly whether Mrs Brooke 'would do'. Maybe I ought to have listened to her, but I hadn't, and here I was. I could no more cut Johanna off than I could Wendy, and for much the same reasons.

'It isn't as easy as all that for me,' I said at last. 'But I can see your point of view. Maybe when it's all out in the open, I shall feel better about it.'

She got up to put the kettle on for more coffee, and gave me a smile that might have melted the soapstone.

'Don't be cross with me, Fran, please. I can see how you feel, too.

Your feet are on the grass. Mine are on the pavement. You fall naturally into sympathy with people like Sophie and Thirzah. I can't get on with them, and don't, any more than they do with me. I just can't get myself worked up because some silly Hen Street child gets herself in a mess. It'll turn out OK in the end, without you making yourself miserable. You'll see. So stop worrying and let me tell you my news!'

I liked her again and I relaxed, quite willing to change the subject. But she hadn't quite done with it.

'I think that's really where Birch made his mistake, you know. Hen Street is not Old Swithinford, and I'm not a villager. Birch was trying to make this hotch-potch into a proper village, but only time will do that, time and a settled population. And that's really my bit of news. It's just possible that my time here is limited. I've had a letter from Dave!'

She looked so vivid, so intensely alive that I quite forgot that I been in contention with her five minutes ago. I found myself genuinely agog to hear the latest about her errant husband. She took my interest for granted, and went on.

'It was intended to get here for Christmas. He sent a cheque for the arrears, and £10 extra for me to get myself a present. He's got a job at last, earning good money, and is saving to come home. If his luck holds, he'll be here by the autumn or at least by next Christmas. He suggests we make a fresh start together somewhere else, and wants to know what I think about it.'

'And what do you?' I said.

'Well, anything to get away from here,' she answered. 'Even a fresh start with Dave.' She paused, and if it were not a gross exaggeration, I would have to say that her jaw dropped as she realized that she had said, or at least implied, more than she had intended.

I was surprised and blurted out, 'Don't you want him back? I thought you did.'

Having forgotten for the moment to keep up the act, she relinquished it, and spoke hesitantly, with real feeling.

'Fran – I wish I knew. When I married Dave, I thought he was all right. He turned up at the right time, I suppose. I was right down when he appeared, and I thought we'd rub along all right. But —'

'Well, go on,' I said. 'What?'

'It seems so awful to put it into words,' she said. 'He did his best, I know, but he couldn't make himself into anything but what he

100

was, any more than Ned could. No breeding, no education, no polish. Just enough to get by in a run-of-the-mill job. He earned a good wage, but whatever he'd earned we couldn't have made the social grade. The idea of going to Australia was mine. I thought we might make it, there.'

'I see,' I said. 'And it all went wrong. What about the other woman, now?'

'What other woman? Oh, did I tell you all that? I never believed it, really. It just wasn't like Dave, for one thing. That was part of the trouble — he was never out of my sight, nor I out of his. It wasn't that he was jealous. I don't think he has enough imagination for that. He was just so bloody *satisfied* — with me, with his job, with everything. I wasn't. I was bored and edgy all the time. It was like being forced to drink tap water when you're longing for a nip of gin.' She grinned the gamin smile that contrived to give her a wide-eyed childlike innocence even when she was caught redhanded in mischief.

'You can't have it both ways,' I said, soberly. I had no desire to take on the role of an agony column auntie for her, but I did know from personal experience how much it helps to take your feelings out of mothballs occasionally, and give them a good shake in the fresh air. And in one respect I could feel a good deal of sympathy with Johanna. Middle age has its disadvantages. The young don't expect anybody over forty-five to have any interest in the opposite sex; but when you reach that advanced age, you find that that certainly isn't the opinion of most folks, especially if you happen to be one of the unlucky ones left partnerless, whatever the reason. I sympathized, with her need to cling to her essential femininity, and to make use of the sex appeal she had been so over-blessed with. All the same, I couldn't help a twinge of prudish regret at her seemingly callous rejection of the sort of devotion her plain, unexciting husband had lavished on her till she had forced separation upon him as well as on herself. That had probably been an unconscious bid for freedom, though she had disguised it even from herself.

William had been terribly hurt when his tolerance had been abused, but even then he had tried to understand. I didn't know Dave, but I guessed his reaction would be that of a discarded pet dog, quite unable to reason for himself in what way he had failed or offended. He had slunk away at her command, hurt and humiliated. Now he wanted to creep back, just to be with her again. She'd learned something by his absence, but obviously not enough to cure her. So would it work? What was I expected to say?

'Perhaps being apart may have made a difference to your relationship,' I said. 'But I do think you'll have to be sure what it is you want, because I don't really suppose you'll find he's changed much. I think he sounds rather nice, though. Couldn't you sort of count your blessings?'

She swung round to face me, charged with such pent-up fury that she looked like an animal about to spring. Beneath her pelt of blue clothing I could see her quivering, and her eyes glinted with fiery-orange flames. To gain control of herself she disembowelled a new packet of cigarettes with taloned ferocity, but words broke from her before she could get one alight.

'Don't you dare sit there, like a bloody parson's wife, telling me to count my blessings!' she said. 'When did you ever have to count yours? You've got everything — enough money, position, talent, a lovely old house, a new car, even—' She struck the match, and lit the cigarette with hands still trembling, and was very near to tears.

I was flabbergasted and almost unnerved by her bitter vehemence. I hadn't intended to sound smug. I certainly didn't want to quarrel with her, and though I was angry, too, at her unprovoked attack on me, I recognized the depth of genuine emotion in it. My answer, when it came, had more asperity in it than I intended.

'No, not everything, Johanna,' I heard myself saying. 'I haven't got your looks, or your sex appeal. Nor have I got an adoring man waiting to come back to me. That's all I meant.'

'What sort of a man, though? That's what *I* meant! Adoring, perhaps, like a lop-eared old spaniel with its tongue out, and about as exciting as a suet dumpling. How would you like to spend the rest of your life with a man like that? You've always had interesting men round you, the sort I've always wanted. Like William — men with breeding, social standing, manners, education. Oh, they fall for women like me occasionally, just to amuse themselves with — don't I know it? But it's your sort they marry.'

'Don't be so utterly ridiculous!' I exclaimed. She was going to cry, I could see, and I was afraid I might too. It was all getting out of hand. I put my hand on her arm, and said, 'Don't let's quarrel, Johanna. I'm sorry you're upset, but it really isn't my fault.'

'Sorry, Fran,' she said, sniffing into her handkerchief. 'You are such a — such an *innocent*, somehow, that I have a job to make myself believe it isn't all a great act.'

'Well!' I said. 'For you to accuse me of acting really does take the cake! And as for being innocent — what do you mean?'

'Well, you don't know much about men, anyway.' She got up and to my surprise, leaned over and kissed me. 'I'm miserable without you in the house, Fran! I think that's really what's getting me down. Then I deliver the message that William's waiting to get here the moment he can to see you, and you say "Oh, that's nice," and forget it. I've been nasty to you because I envy you.'

'Well, surely not about William,' I replied. 'He's just my old long-lost cousin.'

'How "nice" for you,' she said. But there was no sting in her voice now. 'That's what's the difference between us. Things will work themselves out for you, but I have to push them the way I want them to go. That's what I have to do now. I'm worried in case I push the wrong way. But the thought of getting away from Hen Street ought to cheer me up, though it's a long time ahead to look forward to.'

'Don't wish time away,' I said. 'It goes all too fast for me, now. Look how it's gone this morning. I must go, or I shan't be home before Sophie goes.'

I stood up to go. I hadn't really got any further in the matter I'd set out about, but there was nothing more I could do, now, except wait and worry. The contretemps with Johanna had really shaken me.

Johanna slipped on her coat and threw a scarf round her neck. 'I'll come as far as the bridge with you,' she said. 'A breath of air would do me good.'

When we reached the gate, loud male voices, raised in altercation and well loaded with invective, were staining the sparkling, snow-covered stillness. Ned's coal lorry stood on the road at the end of Johanna's garden, and a well-worn Morris stood facing it. In the gateway of the right-of-way stood Ned and another man, obviously having what Ned would have called 'an up-and-a-downer'. They took no notice of us as we passed. Johanna whispered out of the corner of her mouth that this was Jack Bartrum, and I took in a lithe figure of a man about fifty, of average height and wiry, slim build, with a handsome ruddy complexion.

'I wonder what's wrong now,' said Johanna. 'It's two hours since Ned left us. He must have gone home to the farm and come back.'

'Mr Bartrum's keeping guard on his gate no doubt,' I said. 'I expect we shall hear more from Ned.'

Johanna laughed aloud. She had completely recovered. 'You really *are* interested in the parish pump, aren't you, Fran? You *honestly* want to know what they're yelling at each other for! Well, I'll listen when Ned tells me, and keep you informed, though I can't say I shall lose any sleep over it.'

We parted, and I walked on alone. I concluded that Johanna was right in her estimate of me. I did have a village mentality. I was reminded of Rabbit, in the Pooh books, 'whose life was made up of Important Things'. All sorts of oddments that Johanna tossed aside like burnt matchsticks were Important to me.

13

I didn't interfere with the way Sophie worked in my house. Not that it would have made much difference if I had. She worked not by the hour, but by the job, so to speak, setting herself a task and finishing it before going home, working at her own pace. She made it her business to begin wherever I happened to be, and unburden her budget of news and chat before either of us got down to serious work. I could see that I was setting up a pattern that in future would never be broken, and the truth was that I didn't care in the least. To be quite honest, I liked it. Without Sophie, in these early days, I should have probably been lonely, in spite of all my protestations, and she usually kept me up to date with any goings-on.

She had been very upset and quiet, but gradually became more like her old self again. She told me of the ongoing row between Ned Merriman and Jack Bartrum, regarding the use of the right of way. The old village and Hen Street were both solidly behind Ned.

'There's no two ways about it,' Sophie had declared. 'That old road's been a right o' way to them cottages since time out o' mind. When we was children, we all'us used to goo that way to the wood a-Good Friday, and nobody never stopped us. And that were in Jack's father's day, and 'e were such a nasty old man that I'm sure 'e would ha' stopped us if 'e could ha' done.'

'But if it is a footpath, Ned certainly would not be within his rights to take a lorry down it,' I said.

'No — that's what Bill Edgeley, 'im as is Ned's boss, told him. He forbid Ned to take the lorry that way — though Jack Bartrum brings tractors up and down it just as he likes. But Bill told Ned as 'e didn't want no argy-bargy wi' Jack Bartrum about it, so Ned 'ad better take the coal the long way round. But Ned said them folks 'ad got to have coal, and if Bill wanted it to go the long way round, 'e could take it hisself. So then Ned and Bill 'ad words – but that's nothing fresh. Ned's a peaceable enough man till 'e's roused, as you might say, but when 'e is, 'e don't give in easy. I've knowed 'im all my life, and 'is wife, Ethel Turner-as-was. A poor thing she is now, never well, like. You see, she's never been the same since their old boy got drownded, when 'e were fifteen, seven or eight year ago now. Been to the 'sylum three or four times since that 'appened, an' every time she's took they think it'll be for good. Ah! That were a bad job for both of 'em. You can't wonder if Ned lets 'isself goo now and then against other folks, can you? Bill Edgeley understands 'im, though, so they never fall out for long. It'll soon blow over.'

I had had no idea at all of that tragedy lying behind Ned's ordinary cheerful presence. Besides, an ailing, listless wife of his own could very well account for his dog-like devotion to Johanna. I wondered if she knew his story. I hoped she wouldn't misinterpret his devotion to her, because I was sure he asked for no reward other than that she should be his 'ideal'. A man who had lost so much surely had a right to his dreams, and I was afraid Johanna might tread on them and hurt him even more.

'So she ain't to be relied on, if you know what I mean,' Sophie went on. 'She's as right as rain one minute, an' the next minute she's took. There is them as don't think Ned ought to leave 'er by 'erself as much as 'e does. 'E has to goo to work, of course. But there's many a time 'e could be at 'ome with her when he's doing somebody else's garden, or white-washin' a ceiling, an' such like. If he goos 'ome one day an' finds she's made away with herself, it wou'n't surprise me.' Sophie dumped my breakfast dishes into the sink with a sort of moral finality that would have made me laugh if I hadn't been so concerned. So the village was already talking about Ned's dancing attendance on Johanna?

Sophie was now tidying up my living-room-cum-study. She had her back to me, and did not notice that I had allowed my attention to wander. Now she was off on another tack entirely.

'– so he said per'aps I'd ask you. I don't like asking folks for such things, an' I said so, but after all, it is for a good cause.'

'I'm sorry, Sophie, but I'm afraid I missed the beginning of that, and I haven't quite understood what it is you have to ask me.'

Sophie turned round to face me, continuing nevertheless to dust the paperweight she had picked up from my desk.

'We had the meeting to arrange the church whist drive last night,' she explained. 'We all'us hev a whistdrive a-Shrove Tuesday night for the church restoration fund, 'cos we don't 'old with heving any such do's in Lent. We reckon to hev good prizes, so as folk'll come from Hen Street, an' even from Swithinford, but we don't allow no raffles. Mr Howard told us the Bishop was very down on games o' chance, and said as 'ow raffles was as bad as any other sort o' gambling. O' course, the prizes is all'us give, but it comes down to the same few to give 'em time an' again. So the rector says he'd had a idea that perhaps you'd give the ladies' first prize, seeing as you've just come to live here, and asked me to ask you for him.'

'Well, of course I will,' I said. 'I should like to.' But Sophie took no notice. She just carried on, having obviously taken my consent utterly for granted anyway.

'Then the rector said as he 'ad a'ready got the gents' first prize. He'd asked Jack Bartrum last week when 'e met 'im in the village, an' he said as he'd give one o' these new premium bond things. Then it 'ould be filled in to whoever it was who won it, d'you see.'

'What a good idea!' I put in.

'Ah. Well, we di'n't think so, me and Thirz'. An' we said so, Thirz' ups an' says that wou'n't be right, an' she wou'n't have nothing to do with it. She says them premium bonds is every bit as much gambling as a raffle is, an' if the Bishop's against one, he'd be against the other.'

'What happened?' I asked, as she paused.

'The rector said this was different, 'cos it were lending money to the gover'ment, but in any case he'd accepted it now, an' we cou'n't goo agin it. So me and Thirz' said we should hev to think about it. You see, we all'us do the refreshments, an' the washing up afterwards. But Thirz' said she didn't know if we should be there. She'll hev to make up her mind for both of us, nearer the time, 'cos I shan't go if she don't. I think she's right, at any road. I don't 'old wi' saying one thing an' doing another. I said so to Thirz'. You mark my words, I said. If he lets 'em use one o' them gambling bonds in a church do, bad'll become of it.'

'Oh Sophie,' I said. 'How could it? Whoever wins it need not keep it, if he doesn't want to. He can cash it after three months, and get £1 back for it.'

'Can 'e?' said Sophie, surprised. 'But that don't alter the gambling nature on it, does it?' She moved off to clear up the bedroom, and I went to my desk.

When the weather at last grew warmer, the workmen returned and Benedict's became such a hive of activity again that my interest in the minutiae of my neighbours' lives diminished. It was from Johanna that I learned of the next incident in the Bartrum–Merriman feud. She came up one afternoon. Sophie let her in, and opened the door into my den ungraciously, saying as she did so, 'I'll be going, then, now' – although it was a good hour before her normal time for departure. I understood that she would not stay under the same roof as the bad woman she blamed for Wendy's downfall, so I made no protest, and began to get Johanna a cup of tea myself.

'I've been having an exciting time,' she said, 'keeping the peace between Ned and Jack Bartrum. Or at least, preventing them from actually causing each other grievous bodily harm.'

I laughed. 'I thought you weren't interested,' I said.

'No, well, I'm not. But Jack Bartrum introduced himself to me that day in the snow, and he's been in and out of the gate next to mine several times since, and I've held my hand up to him. He came by one day when Ned was there, and raised his hat, so I called out something or other. Didn't Ned put himself out about it! I wasn't going to stand for that. His quarrel with Jack had got nothing to do with me, and I said so. Then Ned said he'd fix the bugger about that right of way, and show him who was boss. I hardly knew Ned could be like that, Fran. He nearly frightened me.'

So does any fire when it gets out of control. Johanna should know that; she played with it often enough.

'Go on,' I said. 'What happened in the next instalment?'

'Saturday afternoon,' she said. 'I was having a fag on the settee, with my feet up, about two o'clock, when I heard a lot of loud banging and clanking. It went on so long that I decided to go out and complain. And there was Ned, with one of those whopping great coal-hammers, smashing the padlock off the gate. He'd just got it to give way when he saw me. He picked up the bits and threw them into the ditch, and set the gate wide open. He didn't speak to me till he'd finished, and then all he said was, "I told you I'd get topside o' the bugger somehow", and away he went back towards Old Swithinford.'

'That doesn't seem to have achieved much,' I said. 'I would have thought Ned had more sense. Bartrum will only make him pay for the damage.'

'I haven't finished, yet,' she said. 'Ned was back again in about ten minutes, riding an old cart horse. He was sitting sideways on it, with four tiny little sacks of coal hung round him.

'"I'm off delivering coal to the cottages," he called. "He can't stop me usin' a hoss on a bridle path, I reckon. And he's got no right to bar the way against me using one, neither. Let him put his bloody padlock on as many times as he likes, I shall smash it off again." Then away he went on the horse, and I went back to my afternoon nap. But about an hour later, I heard voices raised and went to look out of the window. Jack had seen him up on the track, and had got his car out and come round by the road so as to be waiting for Ned when he got back to the gate. They'd started a slanging match, I could see, and before long both of them had started to peel their jackets off. So then I went out to stop them. It's a long time now since I saw a fist fight, but I knew well enough that it wouldn't be long before one of them kicked the other in the — where it hurts. So I got in between them, because I was afraid it would be Ned that would come off worst. Jack grabbed his coat and ran for his car, when he saw me, telling Ned he hadn't heard the last of it, and Ned put his jacket on again, and said I should have let him kill the so-and-so.'

'Have you seen him since?' I asked.

'Ned called next morning,' she said. 'His usual self. But I think he was ashamed of himself, all the same. He didn't stop long, because his wife is having one of her queer turns again. I think he's aware that his antics with the gate have upset her. I haven't seen Jack again yet. He's probably ashamed of himself, too.'

'Perhaps his wife is having something to say as well,' I ventured.

She laughed her merry, ringing laugh. 'He hasn't got one. A bachelor gay is Jack, according to Ned. And a handsome one, according to me. Too mean to get married is what Ned says, but I'd guess he likes to take his fun where he finds it.'

I hoped he wouldn't find it at Bryony Cottage, especially as David was now in the background again. I changed the subject, asking her if she'd made up her mind about his suggestion of a new start together. She was still undecided, and said, reasonably enough, that she'd like to see him again before she made up her mind. That didn't appear to be a very likely solution, I thought. It was good to see her so bright and cheerful again, though, and when she left I felt as if one responsibility had been lifted from my shoulders.

When Ash Wednesday arrived, Sophie came late to work. 'Me an'

Thirz' has been to church, to the service,' she said. 'We 'ad to start gooin' again some time, an' we knowed there wou'n't be many folk there this morning.'

'Poor Sophie,' I said. 'Do you really think what's happened to Wendy will make anybody think less of you and Thirzah? In another week they'll all have got so accustomed to the news that they won't even think about it.' She didn't answer.

'So you didn't go to the whist drive last night?' I hazarded.

She shook her head. 'Connie Potts and Lottie Corney done the refreshments. They're been wantin' the job for years. But do you know who won that there dratted premium bond as Jack Bartrum give?'

'Who?' I said, regarding a pantomime of facial, head and arm gestures from Sophie with surprise.

''*Im*,' she whispered – or perhaps hissed would be a better description of her powerful *sotto voce*; and following her head jerkings and pointing fingers, I looked towards the spot where Jelly Bean was busily pruning a tangled mass of climbing roses on the kitchen-garden wall.

'Jelly?' I said. 'How nice!'

'That's as maybe,' said Sophie, stolidly and primly. 'There's no call for 'im to be mixed up in gambling, is there?'

'Oh dear!' I said. 'I'd forgotten.'

'Ah, well I h'ain't! Seems that 'im and a chap from Swithinford 'ad to cut for first prize, an' Jelly won. 'E could have had a gent's hair brush wi' silver on the back, or one of the butcher's best big pork pies. But he choosed that there dratted bond.'

Scorn and disapproval could not have been expressed louder. That she still felt a proprietory interest in Jelly was evident, but that he had failed to live up to her ideal was just as plain. 'Bad'll become of it,' she repeated darkly, as she shook out her duster and prepared to 'do' my bedroom.

The Beans had been causing me a bit of anxiety, too. Their contract for bringing the garden under control had been faithfully carried out, and Kenneth, the older brother, had been to tell me that this week would see the work completed. He had then asked me who was going to keep it in order for me, once the growing season had begun. 'Them weeds'll grow heavens high atween night an' morning, again,' he said. 'And them lawns'll want cutting once a week reg'lar, and twice some weeks.'

'Yes, I know,' I said. 'I had hoped we might come to an agreement so that you would continue to do it for me.'

'Ah, I were afraid as you might say that,' he said, scratching his head with the hand that held his cap. 'It ain't so easy as all that, like. You see, Jelly an' me's been years a-buildin' up our business, an' we're got our reg'lar customers, come spring and summer – as many as we can take proper an' look after our own small-holdin' an' all. But if I may say so, ma'am, I reckon you're goin' to need a gard'ner full time, to keep this 'ow it should be.'

So now I really had come to the second of the bridges I'd been so scathing to William about. There were no spare full-time gardeners around. I should have to put an advert in the local paper, though I doubted if I should get anything better than a retired farm labourer or a failed chicken farmer who knew very little about gardening as such. I wasn't going to ask William's advice till I had to, though.

Work in the house was almost finished. In two more weeks, I could take possession. I made arrangements to get the rest of my furniture out of store, and lay in bed at night in a state of delightful anticipation, planning where I should put each piece, once the carpets were down.

My only regret was at leaving my dear little temporary home; I hated abandoning it, demoting it to being 'spare rooms' again. I had been so comfortable there, in spite of being a bit cramped. I had inherited so much furniture from my in-laws that there was still too much even for a house the size of Benedict's. I had been going to get rid of some. But why not leave the flat furnished, and take from there into the main house only those things that I had to have, such as my desk? No sooner thought of than decided.

How wonderful it was not to have to consult anybody else's wishes! For the first time in many, many years, I could be myself, solely and entirely. I was nobody's daughter, nobody's wife, nobody's mother (well, that is, nobody for whom I was any longer responsible); nobody's colleague, nobody's employee, nobody's paying guest! Just *me*! If Sophie knew how I felt, she would undoubtedly warn me not to tempt Providence – but I wasn't tempting him: I was praising him. Johanna might make me feel cheap and smug – but then, I shouldn't tell her.

I did tell William, though, how wonderful it felt just to be me again.

'But you are always you, Fran,' he said. 'That's what is so good about you.'

'That isn't what I meant,' I said. 'It's just so nice not to feel obligations and duties to everybody but myself! I didn't feel the restrictions until suddenly they weren't there any more. It's wonderful.'

'And how long is this euphoria going to last?'

'I can't answer that because I have no idea. I only thought of it last night.'

He sat regarding me with a crooked smile that was wicked and wistful at the same time.

'What's amusing you?' I asked.

'I was thinking there were a few other things you could add to your list. You need be nobody's neighbour, nobody's friend, nobody's slave, nobody's mistress, nobody's sweetheart —'

'Oh, don't laugh at me,' I said. 'I thought you would understand.'

'I'm not laughing at you, Fran, dear! I'm just comforting myself. I can see that the best thing for me to be as far as you are concerned is what I already am – nobody.'

'Idiot,' I said.

'Come on, let's go,' he said, getting up. Then he turned a much more serious face towards me, and said, 'I think I'm jealous of you Fran. Obligations to other people are the very devil.'

14

When the great day came, and I moved my personal belongings to my bedroom in the main house, and Sophie lit a fire for the first time in the elegant sitting-room, we managed to leave the flat a perfectly self-contained set of furnished rooms. I felt enormously satisfied. I had the same feeling that I used to have when I was a child and we 'broke-up school' at lunchtime on Friday to begin the long summer holiday. The rest of that Friday and the Saturday and Sunday following were special because they were bonuses, not part of the real summer holiday which didn't officially begin till Monday morning. A little bit extra at the front. Now I had a house with an appendage like Eeyore's tail, 'a little bit extra at the back'.

From that moment, the flat became 'Eeyore's Tail' in my mind, and I found myself referring to it all the time by that name. It made me laugh when after a while Sophie picked it up from me, and began to use it as freely as I did. She had no idea to what it referred, and I guessed that she probably thought it was some foreign appellation such as *'Mon Repos'* or *'Dulce Domum'*. She always pronounced it 'He-horse Tail', and I gathered that she considered it vaguely indecent.

It was on a Tuesday that I eventually made the move, and I spent a most delightful evening literally counting up the cost of my venture. It added up to far more than I had intended to spend, but I really could not bring myself to care. I had made a splendid financial investment; but much more important to me was the spiritual investment I had made. I knew I could be happy here, and that meant I could work, and I should. Ideas for new ventures with my pen chased each other through my mind so fast that evening that I had forgotten half of them by the time I went to bed.

When William came next day, I showed him round with enormous pride, and watched his face glow with pleasure as I opened one door after another. I told him about Eeyore's Tail, and had the enormous satisfaction of hearing him chuckle and catch his breath on it, just as he had always done as a boy when something had really tickled his fancy. We made short work of our dinner that evening in the hotel we had chosen, so as to get back to Benedict's for coffee and liqueurs to christen my sitting-room.

'I'll keep Sophie to cook us a house-warming dinner one day soon,' I said, 'and we'll christen the dining-room as well.'

'I shall be looking forward to that,' he said, as he rose to go at about ten thirty. 'Are you sure you are not going to be lonely in this vast house, Fran?'

I looked around the big, beautiful room, at the space behind my chair, at the distant corner where the Bechstein grand piano was half lost in the warm shadows, at the closed curtains that kept out the dark that I knew to be there outside the windows among the trees and fields.

'No-o,' I said. 'I'm not lonely – though I did feel a bit alone here, last night . . . if you see what I mean. I was conscious that I was the only live thing in the house. There, now I've confessed. I'm no more alone here than I was in Eeyore's Tail, but I don't feel able to cope yet with all the space around me in which there's no other movement but my own. It's because it's all so new, I expect. But thank you for asking. It's so nice that somebody understands.'

It was only after he had gone, and I was on my way to bed, that I realized I had taken it for granted that he would be continuing to come on Wednesdays now. I must give him every chance to withdraw if he wanted to.

I went shopping in the village on Saturday, and felt guiltily that in all fairness I ought to go and call on Johanna. Would she care to see my house, now that it was all furnished? Her outburst on the occasion of my last visit to her had betrayed a hidden streak of envy that I had not previously suspected. But in view of the way our relationship had developed while I was there, she would be justified in supposing that I was now simply dropping her if I did not make some sort of move towards her.

And when could I ask her to come to visit? It was all a bit difficult just at present. For one thing, Sophie was almost living at Benedict's, partly because of her delight in its restored glory, and her devotion both to me personally and my forefathers. But it was also partly because her only other refuge in these unhappy times was either her own lonesome fireside or that of the other members of the distressed family on whom such bitter disgrace and unhappiness had fallen. She resented my continued acquaintance with Johanna, and I knew she would be hard put to it to tolerate Johanna's actual presence in my house.

There were limits to how far I could allow her feelings to dominate my own, but if I chose to ignore Sophie and do as I liked, though she would probably respect me more in the long run, she would distance herself from me with the dignity which was one of her strongest characteristics, and make me feel a second-rate *nouveau riche* in my own and my ancestral house. Sophie was particularly vulnerable to any sign of uncaring just now, and to add to her pain and distress in any way was more than I could bring myself to do. If Johanna should arrive one day, uninvited, that would be one thing; but for Sophie to realize that I had invited her and gone to collect her in the car would be quite another. Sophie did not come to work on Sundays, though only because she would not deliberately break the fourth commandment – nothing else would have kept her away. I decided that I would invite Johanna up to lunch one Sunday very soon.

So I took the bull by the horns, and turned my car towards Hen Street. I banged on the front door of the bungalow, which was opened after a minute or two by a red-faced and slightly dishevelled Johanna, obviously under some sort of stress. She swept me into the hall with a gesture of urgency, and hissed, rather than whispered, 'Fran! God, am I pleased to see you! Saved by the front-door bell!'

'What on earth's the matter?' I asked, bewildered but, as always, intrigued.

'Listen!' she said. The back door closed with a bang. 'He's gone.'

'Who? What?' I asked again, as we went into the kitchen. It was empty. Johanna waved me to a stool, picked up two dirty cups and saucers and dumped them on to the draining board, filled the kettle and switched it on, then sat down and lit a cigarette with hands that trembled. This was no act.

'Bloody Jack Bartrum!' she said, 'Trying to rape me!'

'Oh, go on, Johanna!' I said. 'Not really? You can't mean it.'

'Can't I? I don't know what else you'd call it.'

'I didn't know you even knew him.'

'I don't — or at least, I didn't. He came round to apologize soon after that day I stopped him and Ned fighting. I asked him in and gave him some coffee, and I must say I got a really good impression of him: well mannered, and quite kind. Then he started bringing me things — vegetables, mainly, and once a brace of pheasants. But Ned must have heard about it, because he's been here as well, morning, noon and night — well almost. Like a guard dog. I've been scared to death that one of them would find the other here — but their silly quarrel about a gate has nothing to do with me. I just didn't want them fighting in my garden. But short of telling them both to stop away, what could I do?'

'What happened just now, before I came?'

'Well, I was upset when Jack arrived, because it's Saturday and, as you know, Ned always comes on Saturday afternoons, wet or fine. I was coolly polite to Jack, though he came in without being invited. I did wish he would go before Ned turned up. I began to feel really nervous. In the end I hinted to Jack that I could spare him no more time because I was busy, and got up. He was sitting where you are now, so I had to pass him to get to the sink. He just reached out and grabbed me, and began to maul me!'

She stopped, and looked at me, as if wondering how to choose her words to tell me the rest, as if I were a child who wouldn't understand.

'I don't mean just trying to stroke me or pat me or peck me like Birch was always doing,' she said. 'I mean *maul*. He shoved me up against that wall and started to claw my skirt up. I pushed him away, but that only made him more determined. He was shoving himself up against me and trying to pull my pants down. Oh, he meant business all right. He was saying things like, "Come on, now! Don't pretend you don't like a good bunk-up! It's a long while since you felt a hard'un like that, I know. I'll bet you're a hot little piece, and no mistake. You're like me – we've both got a bit of ginger under our tails, haven't we? Where's your bedroom?" And he was half pushing me and half carrying me towards the door – honestly, Fran – when you rang.'

I was silent, with surprise and disgust, but also because I had no idea what to say. There was no mistaking her genuine distress, and yet there was in me such distaste that I was unable to give her my full sympathy. Why did such things happen to her? Was it because she unconsciously half-invited them? By some coquettish trick or other put the idea into their heads that that was what she wanted of them? I could see for myself that everything about Johanna, every curvaceous movement, every sidelong glance, every witty remark had a vague 'come-hither' undercurrent. Surely most men didn't take liberties like that with every lonely woman – it had never happened to me, for instance, even when I was younger and attractive, not even when all sorts of emotions had got out of control in the excitement and stress of wartime. I had been wooed and courted like every other young woman, and by some who went as far as 'trying it on' to see how far they could get – but I'd never been assaulted in that crude fashion.

'How awful for you,' I said at last. 'What an absolute beast of a man he must be.'

'They're all alike, if you ask me,' she said angrily, and with real bitterness. 'Even Ned, if I gave him half a chance. Sometimes I feel nervous of him now, the way he looks at me. He never used to – it's only since Jack started to come here as well. I'm sure they think that any woman living by herself is fair game, especially if you once let them over the doorstep. But I can't go on, day after day, week after week, with never anybody to speak to but Madge Ellis. I can't! And I won't!'

'No, neither can I,' I said. 'That's just why I came – to ask you to come up and have lunch with me tomorrow.'

She looked like a small child offered a sweet, and my conscience smote me. I said I would come up and fetch her around coffee-time. I wanted to get the taste of Jack Bartrum out of my mouth, and changed the subject.

'Actually, I wanted to ask you about Ned.' I went on to tell her about the Beans giving me notice that they couldn't continue to do my garden, and that I had wondered if Ned would be willing to try to keep it in hand till I could find a full-time man to do it. 'The only thing is that I don't want to pinch his services from you,' I said.

'He doesn't come here for pay,' she said. 'I used to pay him when you were here, but he knows I can't, now. But I don't think he will neglect me altogether. He's bound to be here tomorrow when you fetch me.'

The next day proved to be one of those late February days that pretends it is already spring. Johanna was ready and waiting when I got there, but before she got into the car she said, 'Ned hasn't come again today. I think he must be ill. If you want to see him, why don't we drive round to his house on our way back to yours?'

'That's a good idea,' I said. 'Though I would guess that it is this fine weather that's changing his habits. He is probably at work in his own garden so as to be free to come and do yours later.'

It was a gorgeous morning, with a clear blue sky fluffed out with swansdown clouds like a pantomime backcloth. The sun had far more warmth in it than one could expect, and the air was as soft on the skin as a primrose-scented bubble-bath.

We set off to visit Ned, with Johanna telling me the way. We came to the end of a very narrow gravelled road, and at the point where the gravel stopped and it turned into a cart-track there stood a cottage that had once been twins, with two identical front doors and two identical little squares of window set into whitewashed lath-and-plaster under a red corrugated zinc roof that must surely cover beautiful but crumbling old thatch. The cottage stood well back from the road, and a brick path led from the wooden gate to within ten feet of the cottage, where it divided to sweep in two symmetrical curves up to each of the doors. Between the two doors was a slab of ancient stone that must, I thought, have once been part of the medieval monastery. Now it had come to rest where it provided a cool garden seat in high summer.

Ned's garden was as neat and trim as the man himself. The flower garden on each side of the paths was almost regimented, as if clumps of saxifrage and bulbs just pushing through were waiting at ease to bloom when Ned gave the order. I was surprised by this more than usual neatness — it lacked the rather careless profusion of charm that one usually connects with the English cottage garden. It was, in fact, too well cared for to be beautiful.

Yet I had seen Ned at work, and knew that he had the skill of gardening well. Maybe, I thought, what was wrong with this garden was that it got too much careful attention. Maybe what Ned needed was a much bigger garden that threatened all the time to get on top of him. This was, as I recognized at once, a form of wishful thinking.

I could hardly pinch Ned from a farmer for whom he had worked since he was thirteen, even if everything else could be arranged.

Ned was in his garden, in his shirt sleeves, with a fork in his hand. He did not turn, or acknowledge our presence in any way. I thought he looked sullen, hurt or angry – or maybe it was just embarrassment. Whatever it was, I began to feel a distinct unease before we were near enough to speak, so different was this Ned from the one I thought I knew. Johanna called a cheery greeting, which he barely acknowledged, bending down to pick up a drifting straw that nobody else would have noticed, so as not to have to look at her.

'Where have you been?' she said, gaily. 'I've been worried about you. Are you all right?'

'Ah, I'm all right. Nothink wrong wi' me,' he said. 'But I'm got things o' my own to see to. You ain't been without company, from what I hear, either. I war'n't coming face to face with Jack Bartrum, so I tell you straight. I'd rather keep away altogether.'

It was a long speech for Ned, and he delivered it without looking at her at all. I was dreadfully embarrassed, fearing, I suppose, a vulgar row. I need not have worried. Johanna put on a smile that would have changed the expression of a gargoyle, and her voice dropped a tone or two lower and softened as if it had been massaged with oatmeal.

'Oh, *Ned*!' she said. 'I needed you to stop him from coming, not the other way round. I can't be absolutely rude to him, can I? Your quarrel with him really doesn't concern me, you know. Anyway, it was really Mrs Catherwood who wanted to see you.'

Ned straightened up at last, and looked at me inquiringly. I was opening my mouth to speak, when one of the doors of the cottage burst open, and Ned's wife stood in the doorway, a white enamel bowl full of dirty water and potato peelings in her hands, one of which also held a short, well-worn kitchen knife. We all turned towards her, and my glance took in a small, fair, faded little woman with a round face and a pair of china-blue, doll-like eyes that fastened themselves directly on Johanna. Then with a sweep of her arms that seemed to be part of the same movement that had opened the door, so swiftly did it all happen, she flung the contents of the bowl towards Johanna, who leapt back with a cry, so that only a few drops of water reached her. Ned dropped his garden fork and sprang forward to clasp his wife with both arms round her waist.

'She's been took again!' he cried. 'Get off as quick as you can. I can deal with her.' He managed to pinion one of her arms, but the other was free, and she struck at him repeatedly with it, while the bowl fell to the ground and rolled clanging on its edge towards us down the bumpy path. Mrs Merriman began to scream and yell as she fought for freedom, trying to get out while Ned struggled to push her back inside the door. I caught words here and there among the incoherent shrieks, and distinguished 'red-headed whore' and 'Jack Bartrum's molly', along with 'my husband' over and over again.

Johanna, white-faced, ran down the path and scrambled into the car. I had started to follow her when the sight of blood on Ned's arms and shirt made me turn again. The free arm of the frenzied woman was the one that held the paring knife, and she was beating him with it, point downwards. His arms were already a mass of jabs and scratches and I could see that if she happened by chance to catch the artery at wrist or elbow, the result might be very serious indeed. I ran back towards the struggling couple, though with no idea at all what I could do to help. Ned had also just seen his danger, and taking advantage of the woman's frenzied attention being turned momentarily towards me, he let go of her waist and struck the knife out of her hand, deftly pinioning both arms again as he held her in front of him while he looked over her head at me.

'Send the doctor,' he said. 'I can manage now. Get *her* away as soon as you can' — and he nodded his head towards the car.

Of course, I must remove the source of the trouble from the premises, for there was no doubt at all that simmering jealousy had been brought to the boil by the sight of Johanna actually on Merriman home territory, tipping the uneasy balance between sanity and mental derangement. I stumbled down the path and flung myself into the driver's seat, pressing the starter as I did so.

'Doctor,' I gasped. 'Which way?'

Johanna had recovered herself a bit, and she directed me swiftly into the main street and down another turning to an old white house standing alone. By good luck the doctor was at home. I gave my message as coherently as I could, and had the satisfaction of seeing him backing his car out of the gate as I drove off towards Benedict's.

I got us both a good stiff brandy before anything else. We sat down in my sitting-room to recover, so far neither of us seeming to be willing or able to break the silence. Johanna's colour had come back, but she sat forward on her chair, tense and taut, while her eyes glittered with a feverish brightness that I decided was compounded of fear and anger mixed with a dash of contempt.

'Poor woman,' I said at last, unable to bear the strain of the silence any longer.

'Who? Her, or me?' she asked.

I wished she wouldn't nettle me so. The fear and anger were real enough, but so was the contempt.

'Oh, Johanna, how can you?' I said, involuntarily sharp. To my dismay, she began to cry.

'I suppose it doesn't matter about me?' she said. 'I'm not one of these simple god-fearing village folk. They can take my character away, call me anything they can lay their tongues to, and even attack me physically – but I get no sympathy. Do you suppose *she* thought all that up, for herself? I'll bet it's been on every old woman's tongue in both villages for the last three weeks. It isn't me that's sent her crazy again, it's them. I'll bet they've been "drawing it across her" as your Sophie would say, every time she's set foot in the village, that her Ned's had his nose put out of joint by Jack Bartrum. It isn't fair, Fran. You know perfectly well that none of the gossip's true. As if I'd let myself down by having an affair with a man like Ned Merriman! Or Jack Bartrum, either. There's no sense in it, and no reason. Just pure bloody nastiness. And jealousy, I daresay. I can't help it if they're all fat or look as if they're made of chewed indiarubber, can I? I don't want their bloody men. God, if only they knew!'

As usual, she had managed to swing my opinion round. There was a great deal of truth in her outburst. I was quite certain in my own mind that she had never egged Ned on sexually, for instance – at least, not deliberately. She hadn't really given a thought to any physical culmination to her attractiveness in that direction. Or in Jack Bartrum's, or Hector Birch's. To tempt them by her feminine provocativeness was second nature to her. There was no getting round the fact that she enjoyed her power, especially when there were any material benefits, however small or mundane, to be gained. I was sure that she really was quite fond of Ned, and liked to please him. His devotion hung at her waist like a scalp, and she acknowledged it; but his work in her garden and his errands for her were by no means negligible in terms of actual worth. Neither were Jack Bartrum's 'neighbourly' gifts. I was a bit puzzled about what Hector Birch had had to offer, but reflected that he had happened in her life at a time when she was very low indeed. My conscience couldn't really clear her altogether on that score, and once again my opinion veered a trifle.

119

'Drink your brandy,' I said. 'I'm going to put the vegetables on. Of course it wasn't your fault at all this morning. I expect it had been brewing up a long time and we just coincided with the breaking point. I'll be back in a minute.'

I went to the kitchen and busied myself about the lunch, trying to determine what line to take when I returned to her. I made up my mind that a bit of candid speaking coupled with some practical suggestions would be better than too much sympathy, especially as with the best will in the world I couldn't make the sympathy utterly wholehearted. I wished I could. But there was always that indefinable difference of outlook between us that prevented my crossing the gap between warm acquaintanceship and true friendship with her. In a great many ways, the thing that I wished most for my own sake, as well as hers, was for Dave to turn up soon and take her away.

When I went back to the sitting-room, I could tell that she had relaxed a great deal.

'You didn't tell me you owned a beautiful Bechstein grand,' she said. 'I can't wait to try it. But I want to be in the mood, and at the moment I'm too worried. I've got to stop in Hen Street for a while yet, and it seems to be getting too hot for me. What shall I do, Fran? What would you do if you were me?'

I laughed. 'If I were you, I should obviously do exactly what you would do. Because I'm not you, though, I may be able to see things in a way that you can't. Now forgive me, Johanna — you know I'm an old fuddy-duddy and a puritan into the bargain. You've said you don't understand the village folk, and don't want to. Neither do they understand you — but you are complaining because they apparently don't want to, either. You've got a fair idea of what their standards of morality are—'

'On the surface,' she put in.

'On the surface, if you like. They haven't really any idea where yours are. You have the undeniable advantage, there. To them, there are no shades of grey in sexual morality. It's all or nothing. I don't suppose it ever occurred to you that simply having Ned about your place while Dave is not in evidence was asking for trouble, but it was. You were asking for trouble with Hector Birch, and you got more than you asked for with Jack Bartrum. If I guess correctly, he, at least, thought honestly that you were asking — making advances, in fact. You do turn the charm on, you know, when there's a man about. Do you have to make it quite so obvious?'

As usual, I'd said more than I'd intended to, and I could see that I had gone too far. We went through the now familiar pantomime of grinding out the cigarette in the saucer I had provided her with, and the lighting of another.

'Sometimes you make me sick!' she said, with genuine anger and scorn in her voice. '*You* say the village folk don't understand me! Do you? Now look here, Fran. Do you suppose that if I had all this' — her hand indicated the house, the room, the fire, the piano, all in one comprehensive gesture — 'that people would be so ready to talk about me? Or if my grandfather had been "the squire" years ago? Do they talk about your association with William, and if they do, do you care? Not you. You're safe, but I'm fair game for every nasty tongue. I don't put on the charm, as you call it, as far as I know. I like men's company, and I miss it, I miss it terribly. That doesn't mean that I fall into bed with anything that wears trousers, or that I'm out to filch somebody else's husband just for the fun of it. And to accuse me of affairs with labourers like Ned, or morons like Jack Bartrum—' Her voice broke, but I felt it was with anger more than with indignation.

'Then why do you lay yourself open to such charges? Why do you invite it by encouraging men like Ned and Bartrum to your house? It just makes people talk.'

She blazed. That is really the only word for it. Her hair looked redder, and her eyes shot hard sparks. She clenched the arms of her chair and half pulled herself out of it, glaring at me across the room as if she really might be going to pounce.

'I *don't* encourage them! I'm there when they come, and short of locking myself in, I don't know what I can do about that. *I* don't have a car at my disposal, remember? I'm stuck in that miserable bungalow, day in, day out! I'm glad to see *anybody*, even Madge Ellis, even elephant-arsed Stan. If I had the choice, do you think I'd go for Ned or Jack Bartrum as friends or companions? Do you think I'd spend my life with a stick-in-the-mud like Dave, if I ever had the chance to meet the sort of man I've always dreamed of? What do you know about it? You've only got to hold out your apron and a man like William drops in your lap. I'd give anything to have that sort of chance.' She sank back in her chair and began to cry again.

'What are you saying, Johanna?' I exclaimed, startled by the insinuation in her bitter tone. 'William, as I've told you before, is a relative who has been very helpful while I've been doing the house up. I've been very glad of him, but I don't suppose I shall see much of him in future. He has his own work, and his own home. As for "falling into my lap" as you put it, you know because I've told you that he already has a wife.'

She snorted. 'A wife who left him donkey's years ago. He could get rid of her at the drop of a hat!'

'If he wanted to,' I retorted. 'Surely it's obvious that he doesn't want to. And if he did, it wouldn't be because of me.'

She had already lost some of her anger, and she now mopped up her tears and regarded me with a long, quizzical gaze. I felt as if I were under a microscope, and knew I was colouring up and almost physically wriggling under her scrutiny.

'I believe you honestly think that,' she said, at last. 'Though how any woman can be so innocent, or so blind, or know so little about men beats me. Especially somebody like you who has been about the world, been through a war, been married, had a job working among men——! Do you really mean to tell me you don't know that William is crazy about you?'

My heart stopped, dropping somewhere below my diaphragm, and then rose again with a thump that sent the blood to my ears. I stood foolishly with a bottle of sherry in my hand, searching dazedly with the other for a glass. The broccoli had boiled over on to the top of Sophie's spotless new cooker in the kitchen, and the strong smell drifted into the sitting-room. My back was towards Johanna, and I kept it that way, fumbling with the glasses, till I should decide how to answer. That sickening dereliction of my heart told me what I had not known previously and that I wanted what she had just said to be the truth; but my mind was racing forward, and I also knew that even if I half admitted the possibility, there would be no peace or contentment for me in future. I had to stamp on the idea hard, and at once.

'What nonsense!' I said, adding inconsequentially, 'The greens have boiled over.' I went to raise the lid of the saucepan, and to give myself time to recover. When I returned, she pursued the subject with wicked determination.

'See what I mean? William is the sort of man I'm talking of – a gentleman by old-fashioned standards. They include being faithful to his wife, whatever she's done to him. So of course he'll never tell you how he feels about you, unless you drag it out of him.'

'Which I shan't.' I exploded. 'Now stop it, Johanna. Stop being so silly. You haven't a vestige of proof, and whether you know it or not, you are upsetting me. I'm happy with my relationship with William as it is. I don't want it different, and I don't want it spoilt.' I was on the verge of tears, now.

She was right in one thing. I was certainly in no position to criticize her. She had caught me out, fair and square, at least to myself. I could hardly face the future without his Wednesday visits to look forward to, without the security of advice on tap, and that marvellous knowledge that somebody you trusted absolutely was there at hand. Johanna had showed me at a stroke all the things she was without. I had never missed them before, not even when my husband had been killed. I'd never *had* them, not even now, but I knew I'd been taking them for granted for the future, trusting that my relationship with William would go on from week to week as it was at present. I had been perfectly content. Now she'd wrecked it all. If she was right, the situation was impossible from a practical point of view. If she was wrong, then I had my own conscience to cope with.

'You think I'm making it up just to upset you, don't you? I told you you didn't know anything about men. I knew from the first time I saw you in each other's company, but it stuck out a mile the night you danced in my sitting-room. As far as I was concerned, William might as well have stepped to a microphone and announced it. And I thought then that you didn't understand. So if I'm jealous, you know why. Not of William himself, though if it weren't for you I'd get him, believe me – but of your luck.'

I sat down on a convenient chair, and poured two glasses of sherry. I took a swig at my own, and regained control.

'I am sure you are mistaken,' I said, 'but in any case it can make no difference. I would rather not talk about it any more, if you don't mind. Drink your sherry while I go and dish up lunch.'

She laughed, and I went out into the kitchen, seething with practically every emotion in the book, directed at the gods, at Johanna, at William, but most of all at myself. I did what I could to rescue our overcooked lunch, and called to Johanna to come. She appeared in a moment through the dining-room door, speaking in a voice not her own at all, and when I turned in surprise to look, I saw not Johanna but Fran Catherwood. I heard my own voice, that after all the years had retained its high East Anglian pitch and the trick of hitting some words a lot harder than others. I saw my own stance, my own head and hand movements, and heard my own suspect verbal reasoning coming back at me. The impersonation was marvellous, and in spite of myself, I collapsed in relief and laughter. She broke off, and gave me an enchanting smile. How clever she was to break the tension between us like that.

'Forgive me again, Fran,' she said. 'This morning's episode in Ned's garden really has upset me but I didn't mean to upset you.'

'Forgive me, too,' I said, 'for old-maidish interfering. I do understand what your difficulties are between now and the time Dave comes back – if you want him to come back. You still have time to decide that. But it seems to me you'll have to do something in the meantime. Why not sell up, and get a job somewhere?'

'Can't,' she said, eating appreciatively. 'I need Dave's permission to sell his half, and I'm sure he wouldn't give it. He's relying on the proceeds of the bungalow to buy us a place when he comes back. He wouldn't trust me with them.'

Of course he wouldn't. Ready money would disappear on dresses and shoes and handbags, not because she wanted or needed them, but because she couldn't resist them any more than she could resist giving men what would be vulgarly called 'the glad eye'.

Her ways were not my ways, but I was learning to sympathize with if not to condone all of them. My ways were not hers, either, and I didn't really want to conjecture what she thought of me. But I did realize, as we finished our lunch, that fate had tossed us together and that it would take a lot to disentangle our paths again.

As I served our sweet course, an idea occurred to me. 'Of course, as you said yourself, part of your difficulty is because you are always by yourself in your bungalow. Isn't the answer another paying guest?'

She nodded. 'Of course,' she answered. 'You sort of dropped from heaven. But who on earth would want to come and live in Hen Street unless they had a very good reason, such as you had?'

'I don't know,' I said. 'All sorts of people need homes, or at least accommodation. Would you mind a retired person, for instance? An old man or woman?'

'No – strange as you may think it, I like old people. And I don't mind doing things for people, either. I resent *having* to do it for a living, but I don't mind the work.'

'Well, why not advertise rooms with service? You don't know what might come of it, and in any case it couldn't do any harm. You needn't have anybody you didn't like the look of.'

'I'd rather have an old man than an old woman,' she said, thoughtfully. 'If I do that, and anybody answers it, will you promise to come and be with me when they come to see the place? At the interview, I mean, because that's really what it would be. I'm so afraid of landing myself into something I can't cope with. But I could do with the money as well as the company.'

124

I agreed to her suggestion and we drafted an advertisement for the regional newspaper over our coffee. By the time we had washed up and I had at last shown her round the house, the events and tensions of the morning seemed as if they were part of a distant dream. We were once again two women enjoying each other's female society. While I was getting a cup of tea before taking Johanna home again, I heard the sound of the piano, and stopped to listen. She was playing from memory, and at first I could sense the hesitancy, but after a moment she slid into a Haydn sonata, and I simply could not bring myself to break the magical spell. I made fresh tea when she came to the end, standing her cup and plate on the piano, in mute invitation for her to continue. The look that she gave me over the piano was one of gratitude and affection. Friendship with Johanna was like a brantub at a village fête, I thought. You simply never knew what might come out next.

15

I spent a restless night, disturbed by Johanna's mischievous interference with my peace of mind. Whether or not she was right, and whatever my response, there was no possibility that anything between William and me could be changed. He had explained his situation; I had accepted it. If we tried to change it, we could only lose a very precious friendship. Listening to the rain, I resolved again and again that it should make no difference whatever to my attitude to William in future, though at the same time doubting my ability to carry my resolution through. I was not so clever as Johanna when it came to putting on an act.

When I woke my window showed me a clear sky from which the colours of dawn were only just fading. Somehow, by the light of day I felt much more able to cope with everything, including my garden. If only my visit to Ned yesterday had been happier, and had had a more successful outcome. I wondered what had happened after we left.

I did not have to wait long to find out. Sophie began on the subject as soon as she came through the kitchen door.

'Bad job about Ethel Merriman, ain't it?' she said. 'Poor soul! They say it'll be for good, this time.'

'What do you mean?' I asked. 'I know she was taken ill yesterday, because I was at Ned's house at the time, and it was I who sent the doctor. But that is all I know.'

Sophie looked grim. 'Ah, I did 'ear as you and that red-headed dink-me— that there Mrs Brooke 'ad something to do with it.'

'We had nothing whatever to do with it,' I snapped. 'We just happened to call at the same time. It was probably fortunate that I was there with the car.'

Sophie sniffed, and for once I was really angry with her. It was to be expected that Johanna's presence would give the whole female population of both villages as toothsome a morsel of gossip to chew on as it had had lately. It was all very well to say that they didn't mean any harm by it. In the ordinary way, Sophie did not indulge in this sort of scandal, but when Johanna was concerned, she had a blank spot where her moral conscience usually resided. She could see I was vexed, and drew in her horns at once.

'Seems as Ethel had stabbed Ned's arm with 'er 'tater-peeling knife afore 'e could get 'er back inside the 'ouse,' she went on. 'But 'e got the knife away from 'er, and swacked it aside somewhere. Then 'e pulled 'er into the 'ouse, and made 'er sit down against the table. She were crying and moaning, so 'e started to make 'er a cup o' tea. He turned 'is back on 'er to fill the kettle, when she ups and squeals out loud, and grabs their old carving-fork as was laying there 'andy, and was a-stabbing 'erself in the chest with it afore Ned could get round the table to 'er. He were still struggling to get it away from 'er when the doctor got there, and 'e actually see 'er trying to make away with 'erself, like. Then Dr Henderson wouldn't listen to Ned no more; he said she wasn't safe, and would have to be took to the 'sylum straight off. So 'e sent for the ambulance there and then, an' they took 'er. And 'e told Ned as 'e doubts if she'll ever come 'ome again, now. They just daresn't risk it.'

'Poor Ned,' I said. 'I wonder what he'll do. He seemed very kind to her.'

'That's as maybe,' said Sophie. 'There is them as thinks he could ha' stopped at 'ome with 'er a bit more, and not left 'er so much by 'erself. But there's no telling what's right in a case like that, is there?'

She had talked herself into her normal, amiable, good-natured Monday-morning self again, and gathered up her cleaning tools to start work, while I went to my study. I sat at my desk, but all inspiration had deserted me. My mind strayed again to the problems the weekend had brought, and try as I might to tell myself that all of them were not my problems, I could not dissociate myself wholly from any of them. I was just a hexagon in a patchwork quilt made of other hexagons, touched on all sides by the lives of others, and part of the pattern whether I liked it or not. That I had one very personal problem and another practical one, to do something about the garden, only made me more aware of the others.

The morning was long. I went to the library in Swithinford in a half-hearted fashion, but was soon on my way home again, via Hen Street, having concluded that anybody's company was better than my own till the churning in my diaphragm had slowed down a bit. Johanna was, as always, pleased to see me. I found her sitting in the kitchen, struggling to 'unmuddle' yet another piece of Madge Ellis's handiwork, this time a shapeless mess of thick cream wool.

'Why the silly woman ever starts on them I can't imagine,' she said. 'I can only suppose it is a sort of unfulfilled ambition with her to finish just one knitted garment without help. Like it is mine to play the lead in some drama.'

I laughed. 'Do you mean on the stage, or in real life?' I asked.

'Well, I meant in the West End,' she answered, 'but just at present I'd settle for a bit of real-life drama, provided the rest of the cast was suitable and there was a happy ending.'

'And what would that consist of?' I asked, idly. She shot me one of those penetrating looks of hers that always jolted me, as if she suspected that my question had some deep probing significance.

'A man,' she said. 'A man of the kind I want. And money. Oodles and oodles of lovely lolly.'

As William said, she was most devastatingly honest sometimes. I reflected that if most women were to answer the question as honestly as she had done, the ingredients of their replies would be roughly the same. We chatted of trivialities. She was, in fact, in a much better mood this morning, cheerful and competent.

'I sent off the advert this morning,' she said. 'To get it into this week's issue. I wonder if there will be any response at all? Now I have committed myself, I feel as if I can't wait. Let's go into the lounge,' she said. 'I lit the fire there after lunch, but I needed a table to unravel this bowlful of ruined spaghetti.' She pushed the knitting aside, and cleared up our cups.

As we entered the lounge, we became aware of some sort of fracas going on outside. The noise of a blaring motor horn and loud male voices raised in altercation drew Johanna to the window. 'They're at it again,' she said, and as I joined her I had no need to ask who she meant.

Standing in the entrance to the right-of-way was Ned's old coal lorry, with Ned half in and half out of the driving-side door, waving his arms about in imprecation. Bartrum's Morris stood at the roadside, pointing towards Swithinford. Bartrum himself, thickset and powerful, leaned on the closed five-barred gate. It was my first real view of him, and I looked with interest. His hands were shoved deep into the pockets of his check-tweed jacket, and his pork-pie hat was shoved back on his head, so that the fiery ginger of his hair could not be missed. His assumed pose was that of a man prepared to stand there and block the way all day if he had to, but there was something so tense about him that he reminded me of a feral beast. I could have sworn that the hands in his pockets were clenched into fists, in spite of his seeming nonchalance. Ned made as if to climb down from his cab, and as his grim face and wiry body moved one could almost feel the compression of the air between the two men.

'Oh, *no! Not* again!' cried Johanna, apparently about to make a dash for the door and run out.

I grabbed her arm, and held on. 'Stay where you are,' I ordered. 'Don't be an idiot. You can't stop them — you'll only get hurt yourself.'

'I did before,' she cried, trying to pull away from me. She also seemed charged with the tension, her eyes glowing with repressed energy and excitement. The female of the species! She was like a wild creature, responding wholly and primitively to the sight of two males showing mutual aggression. Were all females in nature affected in the same way during the annual battles between the males for dominance, I wondered?

'Let me go!' she cried. 'They won't fight when they see me.'

'Things have changed since then,' I said. 'The sight of you now will only make matters worse. Besides, even if you don't get hurt physically, it wouldn't do you much good just at present to get mixed up in something else that involves Ned.'

Johanna didn't love me much at that moment; but my words told, all the same, and she yielded reluctantly to her own common sense.

Ned was shouting, though we could not hear what he was saying. He was waving his arms about excitedly, but not closing with the farmer. I hoped his anger might burn itself out in vituperation, because although he was tough and wiry, the fact remained that the thickset, sturdier farmer would make almost two of him. I was prepared to ring the police, Johanna or no Johanna, if blows were going to be exchanged.

Johanna gasped as Bartrum leapt, with the agility of a crouching leopard. But Ned's reaction was as quick, and even more surprising. He sprang, too, not towards Bartrum but into the lorry, slamming the door with the same movement. I understood now why he had maintained his strategic distance — the engine of the lorry had been left running in readiness. The vehicle, with its heavy load of sacks, lurched forward as Ned trod on the accelerator, and it took no more than a split second for it to reach the gate. There was a rending, splintering crash as the radiator hit the gate at the very place where a moment before Bartrum had been lounging. Gateposts and bars fell aside as the lorry charged through them and roared its way up the track. Bartrum, realizing too late that he had been tricked, had seized the door handle, but the lorry's sudden lurch forward had upset his balance, and he had fallen heavily into the mud of the churned-up gateway.

'Duck!' I yelled at Johanna, and to my surprise, she obeyed me. Only just in time, because as he picked himself up, his first glance was towards the window, to see if his defeat at Ned's hands had been witnessed. Bartrum was a man of violent passion and uncertain disposition — that much had already been made plain, and, I suspected, he would be a very nasty enemy. Johanna had already spurned his sexual advances, but he would try again, if Ned was right. If he thought she had witnessed the indignity of his fall, he would pursue her out of sheer vindictiveness. I peeped furtively after a minute or two, being the taller, and reported to Johanna that he had got into his car and made off towards Swithinford. To the police? or his solicitor?

'I'm afraid we haven't heard the last of that little dust-up,' I said.

'Fancy all that to-do about a gate,' she said. 'Good old Ned. I didn't know he had it in him. I shall enjoy the thought of that bastard going base-over-apex for many a day to come.'

'I hope it doesn't cause a lot more trouble for Ned,' I said. 'He probably wouldn't have done what he did if he hadn't been full to the brim with grief already. He had to get rid of some of it somehow. Somebody will have to pay for a new gate, most likely Ned, for one thing. But that's only a side-issue. It's the awful bad blood that disturbs me. It is what village feuds are made of — family against family — just as it has been right back to Anglo-Saxon and

Viking days, I guess. Luckily, though, in this particular case, neither of them has a son to carry it on. But somebody will be made to suffer for it. I don't want it to be you.'

She was aflame with scorn again. 'Such kid's stuff!' she said angrily. 'Every molehill in this damned hole is a mountain, according to you. It's a pity if they haven't got anything better to do than set up lifelong feuds because somebody locks a gate he thinks is his anyway. Whatever does it matter?' The contempt in her voice silenced me. So we both sat and drank our luke-warm tea each thinking her own thoughts.

My difficulty was that I knew, and guessed that she knew perfectly well, too, that the business of the right of way and the smashed gate was no longer the issue between the two men. She was. What was more, it pleased and excited her that it should be so, even gratified and in some strange way consoled her, that she still had such power. It all added up to making me distinctly uneasy: for her, for Ned, and for my own peace and tranquillity, which had been one reason for my choosing to live in such a rural community. I acknowledged to myself how silly I had been to harbour any such snobbish expectation, as though I thought country people were immune from strong emotions. That Johanna apparently thought them all too stupid to feel anything irritated me almost beyond bearing. Looked at rationally, there had to be less chance of a tranquil life in a small rural community than in a larger urban or suburban one, because the fewer the people, the more their lives impinged on each other's.

Well, I was used to it, and really rather glad to be part of it. Johanna was at the very opposite extreme. She despised what she considered to be the pettiness of issues such as Wendy's pregnancy or the scene we had just witnessed. I knew that they were anything but petty to those concerned. And in a small village, sooner or later everybody got drawn in. The same sort of events that made no stir in a town were earthquakes in a village. Things made more noise in a closed community, like a blowfly in a bottle.

We chatted about other inconsequential matters, and I left. Wednesday was now fast approaching, and I had problems of my own to solve.

The sun was setting, flooding my sitting-room with golden, rosy light, when I heard a knock on the back door. It was Ned Merriman. As I opened the door, he stood there with his back towards me, looking at the garden, and that expressive 'couldn't-care-less' attitude told me at once that in fact there was something very much amiss with him. He turned, and took off his cap.

'Why, hello Ned.' I said. 'Is something the matter? Can I help?'
My first thought was that he was in need of a chauffeur to go and
see his wife, though his workaday clothes seemed to rule that out at
once. He waved in a generally vague sort of fashion, with a very
pointedly sharp elbow still bent, towards my garden.

'Mis' Brooke's just told me you're a-looking for a man, full-time,
for your garden,' he said.

'Yes, so I am,' I said. 'Why, do you know of somebody?'

'Ah,' he replied. 'It so 'appens as I do. Me.'

'Full time?' I repeated, surprised. He nodded, and the braggadocio
seemed to ooze out of him like blood from a freshly opened wound.
I invited him into the kitchen, and suggested he should sit down.

'Tell me,' I said.

'I'm worked for Bill Edgeley since I left school,' he said. 'Been at
his beck an' call, I have, come wind, come weather, for more'n forty
year. When I got back to the farm the 'sarternoon, there 'e stood a-
waitin' for me, wi' Jack Bartrum with 'im. Bill an' me's 'ad many a
up-an'-a-downer afore now, an' all'us ended up better friends arter it.
But today were different. Jack were demandin' compensation for his
bl— for 'is gate as I smashed. Bill said 'e wou'n't pay a penny, an' I
said I never expected 'im to. I smashed the bloody thing, an' I
should pay for it. That seemed to aggravate both on 'em. Then Bill
asked if I were goin' to pay for a new radiator for the ol' lorry, an'
all. I said no, not nohow, 'cos it ain't fit to be on the road, anyway.
Besides, it's on'y a bit bent, like. Then Bill lost 'is temper an' begun
to call me everything 'e could lay 'is tongue to, an' I give 'im as
good as I got. I warn't standin' for that in front of Mr Bloody
Bartrum! So there an' then, Bill gi' me the sack. Told me to go up to
the 'ouse for me cards come Friday night. You bet I will, I says. O'
course, I know very well that come Friday, 'e'll expect me to ha'
forgot about it, like 'e will. But I shan't, this time. Let 'im keep 'is
bloody job. 'E wou'n't find nobody else to do what I'm done for 'im.
'E says to me, "An' you'll be a long while afore you'll find another
job, I'll be bound, but it wou'n't be no use comin' creepin' back
round 'ere." But I went round to do Mis' Brooke's garden to take it
out with a bit o' diggin' like, and she told me what you'd come up
to say yest'ay, afore poor Ethel were took. So I come straight round
to see you. I shan't hurt you for wages, that's one thing. Bill
Edgeley has never paid me more than the very least 'e could by law,
an' I can turn my 'and to most things you're likely to want round
'ere, I reckon.' He waited.

'I can't believe it, Ned,' I said. 'It seems too good to be true. When can you start?'

'There's no time like the present,' he said. 'I'll just have a goo a-making sure the mower's in good trim, then I'll be 'ere fust thing a-Monday morning.'

He stood up, and I went to the back door to point out to him where various things were kept. Five minutes later, going to the sitting-room window to close it, I picked up the whistled strains of a march by Handel, and found myself laughing aloud at the subconscious choice. If Ned thought of himself as the conquering hero, he must have come out of the whole affair unscathed. And I had got across the second of my two major bridges as easily as I had the first. Wait till I could tell William that!

I was dressed and ready to go when William's car drew up outside the front door next day. Normally, he just tooted and then turned the car while I locked the door and went out. Today, he got out of the car and had opened my door before I got there, so we met in the comparative gloom of the hall.

'Hello, Fran. Can I come in for a moment?'

'Of course,' I said, pushing open the door of the sitting-room, and wondering with sinking heart what could be the matter. Was William bracing himself to break it to me that this must be the last of our Wednesday outings? Well, if so it was no more or less than I had expected, after all. So much for Johanna's romantic notions! As I led the way into the sitting-room, I was conscious that alongside my disappointment and dismay, there was also something very akin to relief. If he was now withdrawing himself, there was no need for the resolution of any problem on my part of how to deal with him in the future. I squared my shoulders and turned to face whatever the next few minutes might disclose.

William was standing just inside the sitting-room door with his hands behind his back and an idiotic look on his face, like a child waiting for the presents to come off a Christmas tree. The blood surged back into my heart and nearly toppled my composure.

'Shut your eyes and open your hands,' he said, in the age-old formula of childhood. 'I've brought you a present.'

'William!' I said, sitting down suddenly in my armchair. 'Whatever for? It isn't my birthday, is it?'

'Let's call it a house-warming present,' he said, and put into my hands a square parcel like a glamorous hat box, all tied around with ribbons and bows. It quivered as I touched it, and from inside it came tiny scrabbling noises. I began to tear off the wrappings, but I knew before I lifted the lid what I should find there, because at the first movement of it there had come from the box a tiny, plaintive, muffled but unmistakable Siamese miaow. I eased off the top of the box gently, and looked in, though for a moment I couldn't see for tears. The white kitten fluff was only just giving way to sleek cream, and the points were well developed but not yet darkened, so that they looked like smoky shadows. The big blue eyes in the tiny pointed face looked straight up at me as I lifted the baby out and put it to my cheek. I was rewarded almost instantly with a purr so incredibly loud that William and I both laughed, though by now the tears were falling unchecked down my face.

'I'm glad to see you like each other,' said William, with genuine relief in his voice. 'Her name is Emmersbridge Viola and she has a pedigree as long as your arm. But I daresay you'll find a better name for her than that.'

'You bet I will,' I said. 'Oh, William, however did you come to think of such a marvellous thing?'

'Well, I remembered how crazy you always were about cats, and how you always longed for a Siamese kitten of your very own when you were a little girl. The thought of actually paying good money for a cat put it out of question, then. But when you said last week that you sometimes felt you were the only living creature in the place, the idea came to me like a flash. I'd been wondering what sort of a house-warming gift I could get for you.'

I simply could not answer. I held the soft little bundle up against my face, and then examined my present again as I put her down on my lap. She immediately began to play with the end of my scarf, and I ran my fingers up her thin little tail.

'She's slightly cross-eyed, as she should be,' said William, 'and I daresay you've found the kink in her tail.' I had. She was perfect. I looked up, struggling to express my thanks.

'Don't, Fran,' he said. 'Please don't. I don't know what I'd have done if you hadn't wanted her, because I've had her for three days, now, and it would have been more than I could do to take her back. Well, shall we go?'

'Go? Go?' I exclaimed. 'You don't think for a moment I'm going to go out and leave this tiny scrap alone here in a strange place all the evening?'

'Gosh, I hadn't thought of that,' he said. 'But what about dinner?'

'There's cold chicken in the fridge, or we can have a tin of soup and Welsh rabbit.'

'You sit and cuddle Viola,' said William, 'and leave the dinner to me – if you'll allow me the freedom of your kitchen and larder.' He was stripping off his coat, and I nodded weakly, sitting where I was in a daze of delight compounded of so many things that it was much like a pot-pourri, so blended together that it was no longer possible to disentangle the separate scents.

When William called me to the kitchen, I took little Viola with me on my shoulder, where she seemed happy to ride. We ate at the kitchen table, a meal of tinned asparagus soup, cold chicken and salad, and pancakes, which William tossed so expertly that I felt ashamed. It was a culinary achievement I had never mastered.

'Nectar and ambrosia isn't in it,' I said, finishing my second pancake with gusto. 'I fear I shall never have a figure like Johanna.'

William grinned his lopsided smile, and answered fervently. 'My dear Fran, the last thing I want is that you should ever resemble Johanna in any particular.'

The words were barely out before both of us tensed in unusual embarrassment. Was I showing what I felt at his words – that tingling upsurge of joy, fear and – oh, no, surely it wasn't *hope*? The past hour had been so pleasant that I simply could not bear this relationship to be spoiled now. Of anything more there was no hope, as I knew perfectly well. If it changed at all, it had to be for the worse. I was afraid I was going to precipitate a crisis by bursting into tears, but at that very moment Viola began to yowl in a tiny, frantic manner and looked beseechingly at me.

William leapt to his feet. 'I forgot to bring in the rest of the paraphernalia,' he said. He came back in a couple of minutes with a flat plastic tray and a bag of cat-litter. No sooner was it put on to the floor than Viola scrambled into it, made dainty little dabs at the litter with her smoke-tipped paws, wriggled her little bottom over the depression like a honey-laden bee at the door of the hive, and closed her eyes in a sort of ecstasy of relief. We were spellbound until we burst into simultaneous laughter.

'She won't need that once she discovers the garden,' he said.

'Garden,' I repeated. 'I'd forgotten what a lot of news I have for you. Let's make some coffee quickly and go back into the sitting-room, and I'll make my report on the week's doings.'

We discussed Johanna's problems, and my suggested solution, at some length.

'I'm sure that is wise,' William said at last. 'I was a bit afraid you were going to be soft-hearted enough to propose a different solution, and I should have been very much against that – if you'll forgive me for interfering.'

'What do you mean?' I asked, genuinely puzzled.

'Eeyore's Tail,' he replied. 'I've been afraid you might find yourself with a companion–housekeeper of the wrong kind who had tenancy rights of a self-contained flat into the bargain.'

'William,' I stuttered, horrified at the thought. 'Such a thing never crossed my mind.'

'I'll bet it's crossed hers a good many times,' he said grimly.

'But I couldn't – what about Sophie?'

'What about all sorts of things?' he retorted. 'It's a dangerous situation, Fran. She's got you summed up well enough to know you're as soft as wax where other people's troubles are concerned. Don't you see she only has to manoeuvre herself into a situation where she has no roof over her own head for you to rush to the rescue? Your conscience wouldn't allow you to live alone in a house this size – to say nothing of Eeyore's Tail – without offering at least temporary shelter and hospitality. And that would be fatal for you, but just what she would like. She'd pay you for the first month, but after that she'd be a permanent unpaying guest. It would be her entrée to the world she longs for, and you'd have her on your hands until such time as a man with more money than sense relieved you of her.'

'But her husband's coming,' I countered.

'So is Doomsday,' said William, flatly.

'What can I do?' I asked, giving in. I knew he was right, and that I was in grave danger of having my lovely new conditions terribly wrecked.

'Well, I've already worked out one solution,' he said, slowly. 'But I'm not at all sure if you'll like it. May I speak frankly – and personally – without upsetting you?'

I nodded, afraid to speak.

'I have only a few more years to go to honourable retirement. I like my work where I am, and don't really want to move. But before you came back, I'd got very restless. There was – there still is – always a chance that Janice will turn up again. When she first went, I tried hard to persuade her to come back, and I gave her my word that if she ever did, the door would be open, and the past forgotten. It was a very stupid thing to do, but it seemed then to me to be right. It was the way we were brought up. Marriage – even to the wrong person, was for ever. It's just part of what I'm about to suggest or I wouldn't have mentioned her.

'It isn't much to offer you, Fran — please believe I know that. But I love to be here. I feel at home here as I don't anywhere else. I can't go on sponging on you, and for obvious reasons I can't stay overnight unless there is somebody else in the house. But what if I were to rent Eeyore's Tail from you, on a legal basis — furnished as it is? I could pay Sophie extra to "do for me" and look after it while I am away. I should be able to come and go as I pleased, and have visitors of my own if I really wanted to. It would have some advantages to you — besides keeping Johanna out — because I could keep an eye on the rest of the place while you are away. I should have to keep on my flat as well — partly because it would be useful during term-time, but in case of the other eventuality as well. But I should think of Eeyore's Tail as my home.'

After what I had been preparing myself for, I was having some difficulty in readjusting both my emotions and my practical reactions.

'What would the village say?'

'I guessed that would be your first thought. I've considered it, too. No more than they are saying now, probably. They'll talk. You will have to make up your mind whether you want to take the risk. But I don't think it would be a very bad one. Sophie being about so much will help. They know her well enough to know that she wouldn't be in on it if she didn't see it as just a business arrangement. Then they all know quite well that it used to be my old home as well as yours. So what more natural? And then there's the fact that Benedict's in its own right offers you privileges that wouldn't be afforded to just any woman — well, Johanna, for example. Doesn't all that add up to enough to protect you from a bit of nasty gossip?'

'Not on your nelly!' I replied, with more truth and vehemence than elegance. 'But don't let that worry you. I shan't. It is an absolutely brilliant idea.'

'There are two snags that I can see, that I think we should discuss before being too sure,' he said. 'One is Janice. What happens if she should turn up one day out of the blue? If I am going to be here a lot — as I should be — we are going to get very used to each other being about. If she came into it, I should give up my tenancy at once. But I know how unfair that would be to you, Fran. I'm not flattering myself — but I can understand that it would put you back into the situation that may have prompted the move to Benedict's in the first place. A sort of personal isolation. But if, by happy chance, she stays out of my day-to-day life, I can go on being your tenant, your cousin, your friend and companion, and an escort if you need one, till the cows come home.'

I picked the kitten up from my lap and held her against my face, where she purred like a little steam-engine, to soothe myself enough to be able to answer steadily.

'I didn't expect any of those things when I came here,' I said. 'Of course I should miss you dreadfully – but it's a risk I'm prepared to take. I have never believed in mortgaging the present for an uncertain future. What's the other snag?'

A cloud passed over his sensitive face, but he held his gaze steady as he answered, 'That I must be equally prepared for the boot to be on the other foot. I can't, and won't, stand in your way if ever another man appears in your life. The moment there is any likelihood of that, I shall go back to my monkish cell somewhere. I want to say "God forbid", but that wouldn't be fair. You're free, and I will not be a dog in the manger. Think that over as well before you decide. Let's leave a firm decision till next week.'

Yes, that might be wise, though I knew already what my answer would be. What he was offering me was far more than I had thought possible, and although nothing had changed at all, we were starting again on a different footing. Johanna had alerted me to my own feelings towards him, and although he had been most circum-spect, I could no longer swear with truth that her suggestion was beyond the bounds of possibility. Our relationship had a new el-ement in it which neither of us dared acknowledge. But I was honest enough with myself to know I could not stamp on it and kill it, whatever future harm it might do.

It was not late, but he decided to leave very soon after we had washed up. I went with him to the front door, and he paused on the threshold, standing close and turning to look at me with the purring kitten on my shoulder. He put out a hand to rub her head, and then transferred his caressing finger from her chin to mine, struggling, I could see, for some form of words.

'I wish I could perform miracles, Fran. It's the Lovelace syndrome, I suppose.' He pecked my cheek as he always did, and was gone.

I closed the door behind him with the sort of yearning inside me that I had never expected to feel again; but I no longer felt alone. Apart from the little ball of purring ecstasy in my arms, there was the knowledge that I had not said goodbye to William for long. He would be back.

I could not pretend not to understand what he had meant by 'the Lovelace syndrome'.

I could not love thee, Dear, so much
Loved I not Honour more.

'Honour' didn't mean much to a lot of people in this post-war period, but William was not of it any more than I was, and he was steeped in medieval chivalry into the bargain. It was only after I got to bed, with a blissfully happy kitten on my chest, that I realized how wide the water was that he could not get across. It was not only his honour that forbade him ever to come closer to me than he already was: it was also his chivalric concern for mine.

I hoped I might always be strong enough to do what I had so nonchalantly advised Johanna to do, and count the blessings I already had.

16

I was no longer mistress in my own house. Within twenty-four hours my kitten had made it quite clear that her imperious wishes were paramount. If she wanted to ride on my shoulder, or be draped round my neck, only a door between us could prevent it, and then I had to listen to feline complaints in such a variety of tones and of such incredible decibel power, considering the size of her, that concentration on anything else was impossible, so she usually got her own way. I had said I would find a better name for her than Viola, but she never acquired another — for one thing, I liked the Shakespearian connection, but really because after the first few days, she simply became 'Cat'. There was only one like her.

Sophie had been brought up in the strict belief that animals, being without souls, should not be accorded any privileges kept for the race God had made in his own image; moreover, in Kezia's code of conduct, anything that gave you pleasure must necessarily contain an element of wickedness. That Sophie adored Cat nearly as much as I did was pretty plain, but she continually reprimanded me and chided herself for 'giving way to such feeling' about 'that cat'.

When, early in the week, my telephone was at last installed, Cat came at once on to my desk to investigate it, and installed herself there and then as its rightful guardian. She often sat with her forepaws stretched over it, and her smutty little pointed muzzle resting on them. I had been putting it off on one excuse or another, because I feared to make myself accessible and therefore vulnerable to her loneliness, but I knew I must let Johanna know I was now connected.

I moved Cat aside, and dialled. At the first sound of her voice, I knew she was excited. Her advertisement had produced a reply.

'A man rang up, and wants to come and view,' she said. 'He doesn't want it for himself, but for an old friend. He's coming at three tomorrow afternoon. Can you manage that?'

'Well, of course I will if it is really necessary,' I said. 'But I thought the idea was that I should help you to vet your possible PG. Is there any point in me coming just to meet the scout?'

'Oh, do please come,' she pleaded.

So of course I went. On my way it occurred to me that she probably needed some sort of ballast to counteract the first impression of her looks and personality, especially on an elderly newcomer; or even, perhaps, to add an extra touch of middle-class respectability.

She was got up to kill, with a vengeance. Her hair had been discreetly set that morning, and I had never before seen the frock she was wearing — one of baby-pink soft angora wool that clung to her figure at exactly the right places, and at others remained so seductively subtle that it set imagination aflame. I could see she was nervous.

'If the man is under ninety and at all impressionable, I guess you've got another paying guest,' I said. 'You look simply marvellous.'

'Who do you mean? The chap who is coming or the person he wants accommodation for? I'm a bit wary, Fran. Why didn't the one who wants it come himself? Where's the catch? Ought I to have looked housewifely, even a bit dowdy? I did think about it, but it seemed silly. I mean, you don't have to look like your Sophie to be able to boil an egg, do you?'

In her slight apprehension, she was being herself; that is, she was not acting, either consciously or unconsciously. When she was truly being herself, I had a genuine warm affection for her. Or, I thought, qualifying the admission, when she was being this particular self, all flowers; it was difficult to believe in the bird of prey when she appeared to be made of soft pink petals.

Her eyes widened as she looked out of the window that I had my back to.

'Just look at that car!' she exclaimed. 'A brand new Jag!'

She watched it, and I watched her. It was almost incredible, even to me who now thought I knew her, to see her assuming the character she had summoned up from nowhere at the first sight of the visitor. Gone was the hint of dignity and patient endurance she had shown to me; courage and gay defiance in the face of unmerited hardship had taken its place. The difference was in her stance, her walk, the tilt of her head; the Johanna who had been chatting to me five minutes before was as dead as her neanderthal ancestors. Like all great actors, Johanna never simply played a part — she became a different person.

The visitor was a big man, whose expensive, well-cut suit did a lot to minimize the tendency to heaviness in middle-aged men who like the fleshpots. He was tall enough, though, to give an overall impression of healthy manliness, with large hands and feet, and a slightly coarse but undeniably handsome face. His thick crop of very dark hair was inclined to wave, and only very lightly touched at the temples with grey; but it was something of a shock to encounter beneath those black, heavy eyebrows a pair of very hard eyes of pale blue. He towered above Johanna as she led the way in, and I felt, rather than saw, that already the magnetism was not all pulling one way. She was responding as much to his masculine physique as he to her ultra-feminine petiteness. When he caught sight of me, as Johanna made the polite introduction, it was easy to read in his face a slight irritation, or even disappointment that I was present.

He was sitting now, and opening an opulent gold cigarette case to me, while Johanna brought up side-tables and ashtrays. How she managed to maintain her act with such perfection amazed me. I could swear that not a hair had been changed or a thread of clothing disarranged, but she had gone out of the room to let him in looking chic, poised and coolly businesslike, and had come back in again seeming appealingly small and fluffily helpless. The first Johanna would have set the table down with precision, reached for the ashtray that was never more than a yard away from her, and placed both within reach with no more ado than it took her to breathe. The take-over version had managed to get the legs of the table entangled in the fringe of the hearth-rug, which necessitated him leaping to his feet to help her and receiving in return a dazzling smile of thanks mingled with pretty apologies. Then she had to search for the ashtray, giving her the opportunity of much display of beautiful leg and seductive figure, while at the same time somehow managing to convey that she couldn't remember where she had left the ashtray because she only smoked a very occasional cigarette. Cigarettes alight, he began to explain.

He had an elderly friend, a man who in the past had been very good to him. At present this friend was living in a private hotel in Scarborough; but it had recently changed hands, and Mr Ambrose was no longer happy or comfortable there.

'I went to see him recently,' said Mr Ellington, 'and it was clear to me at once that he had to move. It was his own idea that he would like to try being a paying guest in a private house, rather than a larger and more impersonal hotel, where they cannot provide the little extra individual attention an elderly invalid may require.'

I saw Johanna stiffen, and registered a wicked thought that the unwise choice of words like 'elderly' and 'invalid' would each cost him – or his principal – an extra guinea a week.

'Is he a relative?' she asked, managing to load the question with sweet moral approbation of a man who would take such trouble for an appendage like a sick elderly relative.

'No–o,' he replied, hesitantly. Then he took a manly plunge into the truth. 'I am a self-made man, my dear lady,' he said. 'I own a string of large garages all over the East Midlands and East Anglia – Monte Carlows, Ltd. I hope to make them nationwide in the next ten years, but I started as an apprentice when I left school at fourteen, in a tiny garage-workshop run by the owner, one mechanic and me. The proprietor was the man I am trying to fix up with accommodation – Mr Ambrose. When my apprenticeship ran out and I was twenty-one, I wanted to set up in business for myself, but I hadn't any money at all. He lent me the thousand pounds that gave me a start. When I offered to pay him back, he opted for some shares in my growing business; I bought him out of his garage, because his wife had just died and he had no children. He was free to travel; so I offered him a job as a sort of roving consultant, and it was good for us both. His knowledge was valuable to me, and I had provided him with a nice lump of capital and a comfortable if not large income. But he has had to give up the job, and now that he no longer travels, he needs a homely sort of place to be in. I feel responsible for his welfare, and he looks upon me as he might have done a son. He would like to be closer to me – though my wife for obvious reasons does not wish him to be too close. He is not a relative, after all, and in financial terms I have repaid him many times over.'

I couldn't help wondering if he had read Johanna shrewdly enough to take this confidential line, especially about money, quite deliberately, or whether it was natural to him. I decided on the latter. He didn't look like 'a self-made man', but he certainly sounded like one. He had taken pains to educate himself, but his Midland accent was strong, and one could sense that to some extent he was proud of it; certainly too proud to deny his humble beginnings. He had the direct hard-headedness of a man who had had to fight hard and take risks to get what he wanted. If his pride in his own achievement was plain, it was justifiably so. I began to like him better than I had thought I should.

'How old is he?' asked Johanna.

'Sixty-five.'

'Oh, not all that old.' Johanna had spoken so spontaneously that I was at a loss to know whether the fact of his age was to be entered on the credit or the debit side. One could not always follow her motives.

I put in my oar for the first time. 'If he isn't very old, how much of an invalid is he?'

Now Mr Ellington made play with his gold cigarette case again, and I suspected that I had dug in the right spot.

'He is reasonably mobile, and in no danger of becoming bedridden,' he answered. 'It is a case of several different complaints together making life difficult for him. He does need good medical care occasionally, but he needs daily comfort more. He doesn't walk at all well. That's one reason for him needing to be really comfortable at home. He has wounds from the war – the first one. He is subject to some sort of recurrent liver trouble brought on by a very bad attack of hepatitis – it lays him out for a few days now and then, and while it lasts he has to be careful what he eats.' He looked at Johanna with a question in those hard eyes, and I thought he was trying to guess what sort of a cook this beautiful but rather helpless little woman was.

At least I could speak truthfully on that subject. 'I can assure you that Mrs Brooke is a splendid cook,' I said. 'I was her first paying guest, and I speak from experience.'

The look of gratitude Johanna shot me told me that she had made up her mind to take the old man already. I thought I had now served my purpose, and said I must be going to catch Sophie before she went home. Johanna was quick to plead that I really couldn't go without having a cup of tea. I was becoming quite astute at reading Johanna, and I thought that though she had made up her mind, she was of the opinion that Mr Ellington could do with a bit more softening up before they reached the question of her 'terms'. Like me, she had sensed his ability to drive a hard bargain.

'Let me go and bring the tea in,' I said, 'while you show Mr Ellington the rooms.' She accepted, and after tea myself, I left.

I was not altogether easy in my mind as I drove away. I was anxious for Johanna to get another paying guest as fast as possible, more for my own sake than hers; but I was not sure I had done the right thing in helping to land a poor, sick old man at Bryony Cottage. I wanted her off my hands and my conscience, but I had hardly envisaged her burdening herself by taking in an invalid, whatever his means; there was also the question of his welfare. I suspected that Mr Ellington had played down his infirmities, and though she would feed him well, I had doubts about his comfort in the winter. But it was now spring, and if all went well the old man would have to move again before another winter, because of Dave's expected return. But I was quite sure Mr Ellington could look after his own.

When my phone rang later in the evening, I knew before I lifted the receiver that it would be Johanna.

'He stayed until nearly six o'clock,' she crowed, excitement in her tone. 'Wasn't he a *nice* fellow! We got on like a house on fire after you left, and I agreed to take the old man for a trial period of three months, at £50 a month. I do hope I've done the right thing.'

'So do I,' I said. 'When is he coming?'

'Next week, if all goes as planned. Monty's going to fetch him down by car.'

'Who?' I asked.

'Monty. Mr Ellington. He asked me to start as we were likely to go on, because Mr Ambrose always calls him Monty, and he is likely to be here quite a bit until the old man gets settled in.'

'No doubt,' I said. 'I'm sure he will.' She had the grace to laugh. I ought to have guessed the cause of that sort of excitement in her voice. At any rate, she never pretended that she didn't know how attractive she was to the opposite sex.

After she rang off, and I lifted Cat back on to my knee and picked up my book again, I sighed with satisfaction. I knew Johanna well enough to see that as Mr Ellington already had a wife he was not exactly in Johanna's sights; besides, I judged him well able to take care of himself. At least I could now enjoy my own roof over my own head without uncomfortable feelings that it ought to shelter her head, too; and an elderly old gentleman, however disabled, would be enough to keep Jack Bartrum away.

'If I could purr, Cat,' I said, 'I should.'

17

Spring had crept up on us, taking us unaware. My garden, that had looked so forlorn in September, had come to life again. I kept finding patches of gallant little flowers that had clung doggedly to life under all the tangled grass and matted weeds, and had even survived Jelly's onslaughts. There were clumps of green hellebore, spindly crocuses, windflowers and yellow aconites, the sudden blue of a patch of scyllas — all, it seemed, surprised to find themselves still alive and determined to flower even though their season had passed. Spikes of daffodils and narcissi from bulbs long hidden were appearing under every hedge and border, and the spinney was delighting me by pushing up primroses and the hope of bluebells soon to come.

Birds were busy everywhere in their self-imposed slavery of nest-building and young-rearing; and the pyrocanthus on the wall was so noisy in the early morning with the chirping of sparrows and the twittering of starlings that I sometimes sleepily wished them anywhere but outside my bedroom window.

Getting up on Saturday morning, I looked down on the garden, and to my surprise and delight saw Ned already busily at work there. My first surge of relief at the sight of his bare, sinewy arms, still speckled with scabbed-over cuts and scratches, wielding a fork in the rose-beds was checked at once by the remembrance that it was Saturday. Did that mean that his interview with Bill Edgeley last night had ended amicably after all, and that the only time he was going to be able to spare for me was outside his normal working hours? He looked up and saw me at the window, held up a hand in salutation, and immediately began to clean the earth from his boots in preparation for coming to the house to speak to me. I went down and met him at the door.

Ned stood on the doorway outside the back door, cap in hand, and told me in his own way what had happened while the spring morning sun showered us with gold. He politely but firmly refused my invitation to come in and tell me over a cup of coffee, thereby making his own distinction between working for me and odd-jobbing for Johanna perfectly clear.

He had gone to the farm last night, as arranged, in a conciliatory mood but with very mixed feelings. His partnership with Bill had been good, appreciated on both sides, but he was now up against a completely new set of conditions in his own personal life. There was very little hope that his wife would ever return from the asylum again, so he was now on his own altogether – and it made a lot of difference. He had paused, and was looking across the garden somewhere into the far distance, turning over the cap in his hands; I followed his gaze through the trees towards the churchyard.

'O' course, if I'd still got th' ole boy—'

The silence was painful, but he ended it by setting his cap back firmly on his head.

What it meant, he went on, was that he could now afford to take risks that he would never have dreamed of taking before, and he was restless, and 'gnawed at in his belly' all the time with memories and what-might-have-beens as soon as he was alone and without work to keep his thoughts as well as his hands busy. So he had made up his mind as he walked up to the farm that he didn't really care very much one way or the other what happened. He would play it whichever way Bill wanted to, because if it didn't work out he was now responsible to nobody but himself for what happened afterwards.

From what Ned recounted to me, it seemed that Bill was in much the same sort of quandary. He had an obligation to Ned that all the Bartrums in the world would not make him go back on, so in fact he had no intention whatsoever of actually giving Ned the sack. But he was worried: if Ned continued to work for him, coal would still have to be delivered to the cottages, and he knew Ned well enough not to hope that it would in future ever be taken the long way round. I was also made to understand that while friendship and loyalty put Bill on Ned's side, a sort of *esprit de corps* put him into Bartrum's camp at the same time. Bill and Bartrum were both smallholders on the edge of being in the farming hierarchy; Ned was, and always would be, a labourer. Bill could no more afford to make an enemy of Bartrum than he could of Ned, as far as his good name in the village went.

'Anyways, Bill asked me in for a glass o' beer,' Ned was saying. 'And then he says, "This 'ere's a rum do, I reckon, Ned. What'll you do if I don't keep you on?" That nettled me, and I said, "What'll you do if I don't choose to stop on, you mean! You won't get nobody else to be the fool for you as I'm been all these year. But you needn't worry about me," I says, "'cos it so 'appens as I'm got another job to go to come Monday morning — same money, less 'ard work." Well, he were took aback, but I could see how relieved 'e was at the same time. So I told him, peaceable like, about you and this 'ere big garden, and 'ow it would be just the sort o' change for me as I wanted. An' I could see as he understood 'ow I felt about Eth being took again and all that, more than he would ever say. Ah, I like old Bill. We've never yet had no do as we couldn't both get over in a few days. So he set still for a minute or two, and then he says, "Look 'ere Ned, I'll tell you what. You go and take your new job, and see how you like it, and give this row wi' Jack Bartrum time to die down. An' you and me'll make a bargain," he says, "that if you can't get on up at Benedict's for any reason, you can have your old job back again." Well, that couldn't be no fairer, could it? So I says, "Done, Bill! But," I says, "I reckon as I know Mis' Catherwood well enough to judge as it'll be a tidy while afore I come knocking on your door asking you to take me back. All the same, if ever you get into any sort o' difficulty where an old 'and as knows the ropes can 'elp you out, I shall be 'ere as soon as you send for me. And I feel sure as I can answer for Mis' Catherwood that she wouldn't stand in my way if you was to want me for a week or two over 'arvest, or if you should be laid up yourself like, and had to have somebody to do your own work".' He paused, at last.

'What a wonderful way of settling it all,' I said, blessing the practical common sense that had led both of them to such a conclusion.

'So I come up first thing this morning to tell you as I'll start for you, proper-like, come Monday. But I'm going up to Mis' Brooke's now. I can't let her down, neither, just 'cos I'm coming to work here full time. See?'

I did see. I saw plainly what Johanna would never notice, or give credit for if she did, that *noblesse oblige* had nothing to do with modern social standing. The *'noblesse'* was largely a matter of spirit that seemed bred into a lot of country people, like Sophie and Ned.

I had to give a lot of thought to William's proposal for Eeyore's Tail. It had seemed so perfect a solution last week that I had pooh-poohed any suggestion that what the village might think or say about it would make any difference to me. Now I was not so sure. His Wednesday visits and our weekly excursions while I was under Johanna's chaperonage had been noted, of course; that they had continued after I came to Benedict's, and that his car had been seen leaving fairly late at night would have caused a good deal of speculation about our relationship, I had no doubt. There must have been a lot of talk, some of it salaciously ribald, at our expense. That was the way of things, where everybody was interested in everybody else's private affairs. No real harm was meant by it. But we ought not to take it for granted that it could not have harmful effects.

Sophie and the rest of her family would have been at pains to explain our distant kinship, which to their own uncomplicated minds, their mother having had a powerful hand in bringing both of us up, would make any association between us as pure as the driven snow – that same snow that could appear very black indeed from a different viewpoint. There were also a lot of other folks in the place old enough to remember us both as children, and who would not have forgotten that in fact William was no more 'kin' to me than Ned was.

What William had really been saying, and with the help of Lovelace making quite sure that I understood, was that anything other than the relationship we now had with each other was absolutely out of question; the 'anything more' being a euphemism, legally sanctioned or otherwise, that contained a sexual element. It was nice of him to put it so tactfully, or even to put it at all, but he hadn't really needed to.

I knew now, since last Wednesday, that what he meant to me made what feelings I had ever had for any other man, even the one I had married, seem like something from Woolworth's in comparison. He was the other half of me, as he had been when we had been growing up together; I should never again feel completely whole without him. I had been caught off guard, and thrilled, that his quotation from Lovelace appeared to indicate that he, too, was not beyond dreaming of what might have been.

But under the circumstances that existed, as solidly and immovably 'there' as Mount Everest, not even William could have broken the puritan morality that still held me on a leading-rein in spite of all my 'educated' emancipation and reason. William was affected by it, too; that is why he would never attempt to free himself till his wife made the first move. There never was a couple less likely to be caught *in flagrante delicto* than William and me. But who was to know that? We could hardly go around explaining it to people. After all, even the law of the land was on the opposite side. In a divorce court, all that was necessary to prove adultery between a spouse and a co-respondent was that there had been opportunity for it.

It was, I must say, very difficult for me to look upon myself as an adultress just because William's car had been seen standing outside the house in which I lived alone, after dark; but I had to admit that, as usual, William was probably right: any damage to my reputation had been done already. His occupation as a tenant of Eeyore's Tail might, in fact actually make us more, not less, respectable. I guessed that Sophie's loyalty to the past would outweigh any possible moral doubts about us; but I considered it wise, before Wednesday, to float William's idea to her, and watch for any adverse reactions. If they did happen to be those of shock or doubt, maybe William and I should have to think again, or at least postpone any implementation of it. I smiled, a little ruefully, at the thought of elevating Sophie to the position of guardian of my reputation, as I watched her that morning stumping round the side of the house to the back door. And I remembered with some cynicism, too, that it was I who had seriously warned Johanna to be careful not to 'give people the chance to talk'.

Sophie was beginning to show strain with regard to the coming event in Hen Street. Wendy was now in the seventh month of her pregnancy, as far as anybody could judge; the period of 'disgrace' had been lived through, somehow, but the practical issues still had to be faced, and nobody seemed to be doing much to prepare themselves or the poor young mother for the birth. Joe had remained utterly implacable, and Hetty was more and more inclined to ''sterricks' and to long periods on her knees in church. She, too, had to some degree changed her attitude towards the girl, and, as reported by Sophie, 'seemed to have took agin her'. From all that Sophie told me, the poor child was getting neither sympathy nor practical help from the parents who had once been in such agonizing fear that she might have been drowned. One could almost hear somebody saying 'Better drownded, than this'. Thirzah the childless was 'doing her duty' by making such preparations as she had heard of from her mother, but her ministrations were accompanied by constant reproof and exhortation to the sinner to repent. Only Sophie, to whom all sexual matters were veiled in mist and mystery, and Daniel the soft-hearted, ever seemed to remember that Wendy was the same girl they had all once loved so much. It was certainly not the best time for me to ask Sophie to arbitrate on a delicate moral dilemma; but it might give her something other to think about than the ordeal ahead.

So I told her about Ned. I was pleased to see how genuinely she approved.

I then launched into the telling of William's suggestion and waited for her reaction. She finished her oat biscuit and daintily wiped her fingers on her duster, then with a moistened forefinger gathered up the one or two crumbs she had let fall upon the table and transferred them to her mouth. Her eyes never met mine, but concentrated on her hands and her cup. I understood that this was not evasion, but a sign of deep concentration and consideration. She was, I could tell, immediately on the wavelength, and was listening somehow to some private oracle before pronouncing her verdict. I stirred uneasily, suspecting and rather resenting the interference of Kezia's ghost into my private plans. When, at last, Sophie raised her eyes to mine and spoke, the banality of her reply almost reduced me to ''sterricks' of laughter, so down to earth with a bump did my high-faluting notions of difficulty come.

'That there door into the kitchen would have to be made to open again,' (she pronounced it 'uppen') she decreed, 'so as 'e could have 'is own door, like. And you'd 'ev to 'ev a key to the door into the 'all, and a bolt put on your side of it. Do, I can't see nothing against it.'

So a bolt would preserve my virtue, seemingly, just as 'visitors out by nine o'clock' had outwardly preserved the respectability of female undergraduates when I had been one. This time, I felt, convention was definitely on my side.

'If I was you, when the time comes,' Sophie continued, 'I should get Jelly and Kid to come up again with their van and tools and things to do the door and put the bolt on. Somebody down in the village is bound to ask them what they are a-doing up 'ere again, like, so it'll get round and stop folks talking afore they start, as you might say.'

'I'll talk to William when he comes again on Wednesday,' I said, 'and see if he wants to go on with the plan. He may have changed his mind. It will mean we shall have a lot to talk about though, so I was hoping you might be able to leave us a meal in the Aga so that we don't have to go out to dinner.'

She beamed with pleasure, and I knew she would do her splendid best for us. She got up to get on with her work, but paused to say in a very positive tone, 'I 'ope as 'e 'asn't changed 'is mind. You need a man about a place as big as this is, I reckon, and it would be nice for you to 'ev one o' your own kin.'

She had made up her mind, I could tell, that I was in no sort of moral danger whatsoever as far as William was concerned. I was perversely irritated with her. I hoped it wasn't because she considered that either William or I, or both, looked past it. It was much more likely to be her intimate knowledge of us both since childhood; and I did trust her knowledge of the village's reaction.

She came back into the kitchen with a question I didn't really know the answer to. 'What's the arrangements for Easter?' she asked. ''Cos I shan't come up a-Good Friday. We all'us treat it just like a Sunday, though a lot o' folks don't take no notice of it at all, now.'

'I'll let you know after Wednesday,' I said. 'I think William is going abroad somewhere during the holiday, and I have had so much on my mind this week that I forgot it was so near. But I won't rely on you. Thank you for telling me.'

I was apprehensive all day on Wednesday. William's declaration as he went last week, the tiny caress as he left, had put us on a different footing, whatever his overall message of 'no hope' had been. I was afraid we might not be able to maintain the easy comradeship of the past knowing that one false move or word could pierce its fragile layer and show what depths lay underneath. As it was, Sophie saved the day by refusing to go till we had actually finished eating the meal she had provided for us. By that time, we had both relaxed before we went into the sitting-room with our coffee.

'This is nice,' William said, stretching his long legs in the chair opposite to mine and looking with real appreciation at his surroundings. 'You mustn't do this too often, or you will never get rid of me.'

I told him how Sophie proposed to make sure we kept our respectability by a bolt on my side of the door.

He laughed, and looked ruefully at me over the rim of his cup. 'My dear Fran, if the village gossips only knew you better, there would be no need even for a bolt,' he said. 'Your own virtue surrounds you like the hedge of thorns in the fairy tale. It would take a braver prince than I am to try to break it down.'

Well, I couldn't have it both ways.

'What are you doing at Easter?' I asked. 'It's only next week.'

'I don't know. I have to leave for about a week on the Tuesday after Easter Monday. We set it up a long time ago – that's the worst of not being able to see into the future. But I suppose I am looking forward to it, really. We propose to make a sort of study of the English connection with the Duchy d'Aquitaine in the Hundred Years' War – based on Bordeaux and up the Dordogne to places like Bergerac, La Réole and Châtillon.'

'Sounds lovely,' I said lightly. 'I wish I could come.'

How difficult life was going to be! I hadn't meant anything more than a flippant reply, but I was surprised to hear him whisper as if to himself, 'No more than I do!'

I strove to take us away from the rapids I could see ahead, pretending I hadn't heard. 'So what about the Easter holiday itself? I have an idea.'

'Fire away,' he said.

'Well, before you actually decide on Eeyore's Tail, don't you think you ought to make a trial of it? What about over the Easter weekend?'

He put on a shocked expression. 'What, before the bolt is in place? And Sophie not here?'

'I shall take care not to compromise you, Professor,' I said. 'It has occurred to me that it is time Kate and Jeremy saw the house – and met their Uncle William. There would have to be their two children as well, of course, but that is really what I meant about trying out the flat. We could find out just how much, or how little, you could be private there. There has been a kind of unspoken agreement that they would come here for Easter instead of me going there. I was going to invite you over to dinner to meet them – but if you were in residence you could see as much or as little of them as you liked. And with my family here, not even the wickedest tongue could find a crumb of scandal.'

I was surprised to find him silent, where I had expected either an enthusiastic acceptance of my idea, or a polite but courteous backing-off. But I waited, and heard the break in his voice as he answered, very low, 'You offer me hope of water even in the desert, Fran.'

18

Easter was an unqualified success. The weather turned as warm as April at its best can be, and it seemed to lift everybody's spirits one notch above normal. I went to work with a will, to get as far forward as I could before the holiday, giving myself a chance to take time off from my desk with a good conscience. Ned was so busy in the garden, getting the lawns cut and trimmed, till they reached a stage of perfection I never remembered before, that he seemed to be healing himself with work almost as visibly as the scars on his bare arms were disappearing day by day. Even Sophie hummed as she went about her work. I caught the strains of 'All things bright and beautiful' more than once. She set herself to make Eeyore's Tail as spick and span in every way as was possible, to show her approval of the ultra-respectability of the try-out of William's more permanent tenancy.

We had agreed that William should arrive in time for dinner on Thursday evening, while Sophie was still there to cook and serve up a meal for all of us, after the children had been put to bed.

I had looked forward so much to Kate and Jeremy seeing my new home, having quite deliberately kept them away during the time it had been, as Sophie would have said, 'by the halves'. I had bored them with details over the telephone, talked of little else while I had been staying with them, and entertained them with reminiscences of our childish doings when Grandfather had been there. So they knew the old place by hearsay – but I was still unprepared for the gasps of admiration and delight that the reality brought spontaneously from them. When Kate had poked about a bit by herself, she came back to find me. 'Mum,' she said, 'it isn't just beautiful and grand. It's you. And it's home. It is so lovely I want to cry.'

'You look years younger yourself, Mum,' she had said. 'I think this old house has some sort of magic in it.'

'I think it's just glad to have us back,' I answered. 'It has been missing its family. It has even got Sophie back in Kezia's place, and you'll meet William tonight. I suppose you had better call him "Uncle William" in front of the children, though of course they'll be in bed before he comes.'

'I think I'm a bit scared,' she said. 'I mean, he's a Professor, isn't he? I hope Jeremy will be able to keep his end up. We're not exactly an academic family.'

'I don't think you need worry,' I said, and left it at that. Could it be that I had never said enough about William to them to give them any idea what to expect? There must have been some unconscious guard on my tongue with regard to him, but I was not going to change her preconceived idea of him now.

Sophie had been into the dining-room to see that the table was all in order just as Kate and Jeremy came down from putting the babies to bed; and I, having peeped in at them to say goodnight, had nipped into my bedroom and changed my casual garments for a more becoming frock. So we were all standing outside the sitting-room door together when Sophie cocked her head on one side and said, 'Ah! there's 'is car. William's, I mean.'

Kate and Jeremy froze into a sort of baffled incredulity, and it was Jeremy who said, in a strangled sort of voice, looking after Sophie's retreating back, 'She calls him *William*?'

'Not to his face,' I answered, still unwilling to spoil the surprise. 'But she remembers him from long ago, as well, you know. Come in and sit down.' I ushered them in, but we had not had time to sit down before we heard his step in the hall and I stood back to watch the meeting. He was looking particularly young, and extraordinarily handsome, I thought. His eyes sought mine to send me a message, but it was to Kate he turned.

'Kate,' he said, holding out his hand and imprisoning hers so that she could not withdraw it. 'I need no introduction. I would have known you in a crowd of ten thousand: you are so exactly like your mother.' And without asking, he pulled her towards him and kissed her – not the sort of peck he sometimes gave me, but a long, warm, welcoming one that, after the first shock of surprise, I saw her return. He shook hands with Jeremy, then crossed the room to take the drinks tray out of my hands and set it down. 'Hello, Fran. Let me do that – may I? You look too splendid in that dress to risk spilling sherry down it.'

I sat down weakly, and watched him dispensing drinks as if I, too, were seeing him for the first time. He was, I knew, going out of his way for my sake to take any edge of formality off this first family gathering, but I had got used to him so gradually that the shock of his powerful personality was almost as great on me as it was on them. I saw him afresh through their eyes, and liked what I saw as much as I could sense they did.

From that moment the whole weekend went like a dream. The children, able to be outside when they were not being fed or rested, had behaved like a couple of cherubim, giving their parents a real chance to rest and relax. William kept out of the way so discreetly that by lunchtime on Good Friday Kate was demanding to know where he was because if he thought he was going to become a recluse while she was there he had another think coming. She went to look for him, and took so long about it that Jeremy and I had fed the children and put them up to rest before the two of them came in sight again. 'What a splendid idea it is that Uncle William should have the tenancy of the flat,' she said. 'It sort of makes the family whole, somehow.'

'My dear girl,' said William, getting up and going round the table to kiss her, 'if you had tried to find something to make me especially happy, you couldn't have bettered that.'

It was as if they had known each other always; I could understand this from William's point of view, because, as he had remarked, she was so very like me, especially when I had been young; but it was with something of a shock that it came to me that he was fitting exactly into the space left empty all these years by her father's death. I hoped Jeremy would understand, too. It was only when William was helping me to wash up that I caught the look between Kate and Jeremy that told me how much they had already gathered about the strength of the bond between William and me. They did not know the facts; I should have to disillusion them before they took too much for granted. But I could not spoil this happy Easter.

On Thursday, William made his farewells all round. Me last, of course.

'Have a good time in Aquitaine,' I said, as lightly as I could.

'What? After this weekend? I can only do my best. 'Bye, Fran. And thank you. I'll ring as soon as I'm back.' He leaned out of the car window, and blew a kiss towards us all. I knew it was meant for me.

I felt very flat when they had all gone, and knew the only thing to do was to work hard. So I did. I went to my desk on the first morning, but had only been there a few minutes when Sophie appeared with the morning's post in her hand. Among the batch of no particular importance was a card of invitation for me to attend a coffee morning on behalf of the Red Cross, from the wife of our local GP, Mrs Henderson. To be held on May Day, indoors if wet, outdoors if weather permitted. There was to be a 'bring and buy' stall, raffle and all the rest of the usual ways of raising money.

I showed it to Sophie, guessing she would know more about such things than I did. She read it, and sniffed.

'So they 'ave got round to noticing as you 'ave come to live 'ere at last,' she said. 'I wondered 'ow much longer it would take 'em.'

I supposed she was right in some respects. Apart from having been asked to give a whist-drive prize, my presence in the village, let alone at 'the big house' had been entirely ignored. Nobody had called on me, and I had been asked nowhere. I asked Sophie what sort of people were likely to be there.

'I couldn't say, I'm sure,' she said primly. 'It ain't the sort of do the likes of me and Thirz' would get asked to. There'll be other doctors' wives from round about, I dare say, and parsons and their wives from far and near, and such as think they are somebody in Swithinford. And ol' Mis' de ffranksbridge from the 'All, I make no doubt, an' a few jumped-up farmers' wives from here and there. Them as run the Women's Institute'll very likely be there 'elping, and the schoolteachers from Swithinford if they still 'ave a 'oliday that day.'

'I think perhaps I shall go,' I said.

'You'd better,' she answered. 'It would be took amiss if you didn't, seein' as they 'ave got round to asking you. O' course, none o' them would want to look too eager, as you might say, because you are a newcomer after all, in spite o' your grandfather livin' 'ere all them years. It usually takes about five year for anybody to be treated as one o' the proper village folk, like, but I dessay it will be a bit different wi' you. They'll all be friendly enough, seein' as you are who you are, as long as you don't push yourself forr'ard, like!'

She got up to go, having, I felt, figuratively speaking wiped my nose, made sure I had a hankie, and instructed me how to behave at my first party.

So far, I had heard nothing from Johanna about the arrival of her new guest. It had been my impression that he was to arrive over the Easter weekend, and by the next Saturday I began to feel that I ought at least to ask. In spite of myself, I was interested; but I was not going to call till invited. However, she rang on Sunday evening, and asked me to go along any time I liked.

So I set out to walk the next day. I always think that the last week in April is one of the two most beautiful weeks of the year, the other being the first in November. Both, for me, always have a tinge of nostalgia about them, though I don't really know why. Perhaps it is something to do with the marking of time: another summer coming in in April; another summer gone again when the first wind after a frost strips the last leaves from the trees in November.

I arrived at Bryony Cottage just as Johanna and Mr Ambrose were having coffee in the lounge. She had seen me coming, and was at the door to open it for me, so as to be able to give me a lightning summary of what to expect while we were still in the tiny hall. In the five paces or so it took us to get from the front door to the door of the lounge, she put on a wordless mime of a rather dull, almost senile but very self-satisfied wreck of a man. Next moment, he was being introduced to me, struggling to rise but being very sweetly though firmly pushed back again by Johanna's hand laid on his shoulder while with the other she neatly rescued his half-filled coffee cup, which was chattering in its saucer as his trembling twisted fingers endeavoured to set it down.

Mr Ambrose was tall, with a big bony frame thinned down by pain and discomfort. He had probably when young been 'a fine figure of a man', which only served to make his present distortion more pitiable. He was pulled out of shape by some arthritic condition, I thought, because the knuckles of his huge hands were twisted and swollen, and it was a considerable effort for him to close his fingers enough to lift or hold a cup in one hand. He wore old shoes of good quality leather, polished till they glowed, but they were patched on both bunions and reinforced with a double row of saddle-stitching round the tops, which stood away from very swollen ankles. (Later, when he stood up, I saw how terribly misshapen his lower extremities were. He placed them almost sideways as he walked, in the position caused by 'trench feet'.) The least exertion caused him to pant for breath in a most distressing fashion, so that his speech came in short rushes, with hoarse in-drawn breaths between, and the words were punctuated with little bubbling puffs as he pursed his lips together and blew through them, even while gasping to take air in. I looked towards Johanna, but she would not meet my eye; I did not remember Ellington saying anything about a bad heart, but to my unmedically trained eye, it looked like that. To top the awful sight up, there was the old wound on the side of his head, above his right temple. His iron-grey hair was still abundant, but it was clear that the wound had been such a severe one that the hair had never grown back over it. There was an area about the size of the top of a teacup that was bald, scarred, and blue; and beneath the skin stretched tightly across this gruesome patch, a pulse beat visibly, like the fontanelle of a newborn baby.

I took all this in while being introduced, and I was horrified. Every feminine instinct in me rushed out in sympathy to this poor old man who was, in spite of all his disabilities, attempting to put on an act of gentlemanly courtesy. How would Johanna react to his obviously many and various needs? This was surely more than she had bargained for. She had asked £50 per calendar month, but £50 per week would not have been too much, I thought. He needed a trained nurse, not a landlady. What had smooth-tongued Mr 'Monty' been about, to deposit an old fellow in this appalling physical condition in the lap of an untrained, inexperienced woman of Johanna's calibre just because he had sensed how desperately she needed money? I reflected that she had agreed to the conditions only for a trial period; and there was always a possibility that Dave might turn up to rescue her – and the old man – from each other.

She brought coffee in for me, placing herself cleverly with her back towards him so that she could look at me without his seeing her face. She raised her beautiful eyebrows in a gesture expressive of everything I was feeling except, perhaps, my dismay. The dominant expression she registered was one of profound sympathy, and for the umpteenth time I was forced to acknowledge how little I really knew her. She had, I thought, to my own relief, accepted the challenge. She was going to show somebody – old Ambrose himself, or Ellington or me or even Jack Bartrum, or all of us – what qualities she possessed besides those of a natural seductress.

'Ernie knows all about you, Fran,' she said, turning to face him again. 'So he knows that it was your idea that brought him here.'

My hackles rose, unbidden. So whatever happened, the blame was already apportioned, but I guessed that if things went well, praise would not be so easily bestowed. It might turn out better than seemed possible.

Old Ernie was speaking, in his breathless puffing and blowing manner. 'I don't know how to thank you enough, then, Mrs Catherwood. I have only been here a week, but I can tell you it has been the nearest thing to home that has come my way for more than twenty years. She's a wonder, that's what she is.'

Johanna had just gone out of the room to refill the coffee-pot, and his last remark had been made more to himself than to me. He turned his battered face to follow her, so that I saw only his unmarked side with its normal, rather watery blue eye, but there was no mistaking the look in it. With what seemed almost like a physical jolt, I thought, 'Good God, he's succumbed already. The old fool's in love with her, in spite of his age and decrepitude.' I wondered, grimly, what the outcome would be. Maybe I had mistaken sincere gratitude for what I was so used to seeing in the faces of other men when their eyes rested on Johanna. I hoped so. Surely there must be an upper age-limit to sexual reactions somewhere? A time when the spirit is no longer willing to respond to the dying urges of such aged, mauled and mutilated flesh as Ernie Ambrose's? I didn't know.

William rang to say he was back in England, and would be over on Wednesday as usual. Sooner than I had expected him. Instead of being pleasantly filled with anticipation, to my dismay I found that I was apprehensive. The period of time coming up to Easter, and then the family weekend itself, had once more changed our relationship. I looked the situation in the face, and summed it up. Though he had never actually said so, he loved me, and wanted to be with me as much as he could. He wanted everything he could not have — with 'honour'. He was suffering, and there was nothing I could do about it except, for his sake, to pretend I did not know — and that I did not care. That was what was going to be so difficult, especially if he was going to be always within my sight, my hearing, my reach. He had said my 'virtue' surrounded me like a hedge of thorns and I found some comfort in that. It meant that he was not sure of my feelings towards him, and I knew that somehow, *I must keep it that way*. We could have everything except the crown on our love. There was no way out except for me to stick to my moral guns, and allow him to stick to his.

We both carried it off well on Wednesday. We talked about his trip, which had truly been worthwhile in every way, and I told him about old Ernie and the coming coffee morning — and so on. There was only one really difficult moment, when he thanked me again for letting him be part of my lovely family, and produced from his pocket a gift-box which turned out to contain French perfume such as I had never indulged in before. I didn't know how to thank him, and without thinking held out both my hands — which he took, held, laid his face on and kissed. But he let them go, and we returned to making plans for his tenancy of Eeyore's Tail. He would come for weekends when he could till the end of the summer term, though he did not expect to be free enough to do that often until the term was well and truly over, and the long vacation gave him a chance really to live and relax there. It seemed to me just the right sort of compromise to help me find the resolution I needed to hold the *status quo*.

19

May Day had arrived, and I was to make my début in the village. The weather was perfect, so I judged it would be an outdoor occasion. I dressed appropriately with some care, and set out on foot.

Dr Henderson lived in the oldest part of the village, in a lane close by the church. The house itself was long and low and thatched and whitewashed, and from its configuration it was easy to see that it had once been three small cottages joined together in a row. It stood rather close to the lane, but behind it was a beautiful garden that was large because that also had once been three, and it had retained that wonderful fragrance and feeling of peace and permanence that it takes any garden a very long time to acquire. Some of the trees looked as if they must have been there as long as the house had, though I could see that they had recently blossomed and that on some the fruit was already setting. As a backdrop to any village function of this kind, it was almost too good to be true.

The coffee morning itself turned out to be so exactly what Sophie had predicted that it was like experiencing *déjà vu*. There were a few men, mostly elderly, in panama hats and clerical collars, but they stood about like exhibits, leaning on sticks and raising their hats so often that I pitied them – they were doing their duty painfully when they would all so much rather have been at home. The different groups of women were easily identifiable, and all, in their different ways, were pleasant and politely welcoming towards me. After doing all that was expected of me in the way of spending money to help the cause, I bought a cup of coffee and retired with it to a garden seat under an old apple tree, a bit removed from the stall that was the centre of operations, and prepared to enjoy myself watching my new neighbours. I had barely sat down when a voice from behind me caused me to turn and look round.

'I'm in such a fantigue that I hardly know whether I'm coming or going,' it said, 'but I think you must be Mrs Catherwood. Well, of course, I know perfectly well that you are. For one thing because I remember you quite well from when you were a child, and for another because we have all naturally been agog with curiosity about you ever since we heard you had turned up here again. I'm Mary Budd, ex-schoolmistress of Old Swithinford School. You won't remember me, but your grandfather was one of the managers who helped to appoint me when I was young and just seeking my first post as a head teacher. He was a grand old gentleman. Most people who knew him loved him. That is something those of you who belong to his family should remember and be proud of. There aren't any like him to be found anywhere now. But I expect you know all that.'

Vague memories stirred in me, associated mainly with Kezia's children, and of Kezia and Sophie talking about 'Miss'. She was holding out her hand, and when I took it, it was warm and firm and somehow managed to convey in its touch a welcome and a friendliness of the kind I had been unconsciously hoping for. She sat down on the seat beside me, and I said with absolute truth how delighted I was to meet her.

I guessed that she would never see seventy again, but she certainly did not look, or act, as old as that. She was a rather short but small, compact woman, with a mass of long hair piled neatly and elegantly into an elongated oval bun. It was silvery-white over her forehead and temples, iron-grey over her ears, and still as jet black as it had always been in the coil of the bun. Her skin, wrinkled though it was, had the texture of youth still insofar as it was without spot or blemish and innocent of make-up except for the bloom and patina a vigorous outdoor life had given it. But it was her eyes that attracted one, dancing as they seemed to be with just the joy of being alive and active on such a perfect morning. Black as sloes, not the melting velvet brown of so many East Anglians, but the sort you can still meet unexpectedly in Wales, in a few people whose Iberian genes never quite succumbed to Celtic dominance. It was difficult to say whether they were, in fact, very dark brown or, like sloes, black tinged with blue, but as she talked they seemed continually to change colour, shape and expression. With her mouth, they enacted her thoughts so that one had the feeling that her speech itself was three dimensional, and that you could see all round it at once. She was asking me questions, answering them herself, giving me thumb-nail portraits of the different sections of society milling about the fast-emptying stall – in effect, filling in the background all round for me and at last making me feel I had a place in the picture.

'May I fill your cup again, Miss Budd?' A young woman, with 'farmer's wife' written all over her, stood before us with a coffee pot in one hand and a milk jug in the other.

Miss Budd stopped talking, and smiled. 'Thank you, Cynthia, dear,' she said, and as she held out her cup, I had a momentary impression of the years actually being rolled up and put away like the scenery in Chinese theatre, to reveal Miss Budd at her battered old teacher's desk, surrounded by red ink, rulers and attendance registers. As for Cynthia, she shrank to a plump, fair, hazel-eyed child of ten, as she carefully poured coffee and milk into the outstretched cup. Then she looked up at Miss Budd, and the look was charged with such reverent adoration as ascetics are wont to bestow upon symbols of their god. When she turned her attention to me, Cynthia smiled, and became again at once the adult she was.

'Nice girl,' Miss Budd said, watching her back as she retreated. 'Not a great deal up top, but none the worse for that. Married well, to young Tom Fairey. They were in the same class for years, of course, always sweethearts. But I was afraid his folks would want something better for him than a local blacksmith's daughter, especially as nobody wanted blacksmithing now and there was neither money nor land to come with her. But Tom knew what he wanted, and he's a lucky man. So is she, well, a lucky girl, I mean of course. I wish all my pupils showed as much common sense as those two. There wouldn't be so many divorces, then. Still, I suppose they were lucky, rather than clever. It just happened that way for them, in an old-fashioned sort of romance. Maybe the others are just as happy in their way. I'm the old-fashioned one, I dare say.'

'We're all old-fashioned, when it comes to a bit of romance like you've just recounted,' I said.

She nodded. 'Yes, I think so, too. Fashion in human behaviour is never much more than skin deep, is it? As that marvellous character of W. W. Jacobs says, "Human nature's a very funny thing." And like him – the Nightwatchman I mean – I can add, "An' I know, 'cos I've seen a lot of it in my time."' She chuckled.

I had no doubt that whatever claims the other ladies might make, the real doyenne of Swithinford society was the one sitting beside me. She had, tucked away in her mind, a complete knowledge of them, body, mind and spirit, and of course they were aware of it. She had known, and shared, their triumphs and disasters, their woes and their good fortune. She knew their family histories, their own struggles, and their peccadilloes. She could, I guessed, be a severe judge, but such deep knowledge and understanding breed tolerance, and her censure would, I felt sure, always have been tempered by mercy and love.

161

'Preserve me, O Lord,' she said, suddenly and irreverently in my ear. 'Whither shall I flee? Here comes Mrs de ffranksbridge.'

I had no time to ask questions. There was nowhere to hide from the newcomer, who was bearing down on us like the weather-beaten sail of a vessel making for harbour. She fetched up about a yard or so in front of my knees, ignoring Miss Budd's polite salutation. She peered towards me, looked purposefully down at the inadequate space on the seat between me and my companion, then transferred her gaze deliberately to the ex-schoolmistress, with a dismissive gesture that said 'Off' as plainly as if she had just found a stray dog sitting in her armchair. Miss Budd rose at once, glad to be excused, I thought; but I didn't want to lose her, yet, and in any case I shrank from being left unprotected beneath the newcomer's Gorgon-like gaze. So I put out my hand instinctively and caught Miss Budd's sleeve.

'Don't go, please,' I said. 'I have a lot I want to ask you.' She had already risen to make way for Mrs de ffranksbridge, so she patted my hand reassuringly as it lay on her arm, dropped a suspicion of a wink from a wicked black eye, and replied, 'I'll just get another cup of coffee, I think', and left me. I understood that she intended to keep me in view, and would come back to my rescue if necessary. All this happened in the time it took for Mrs de ffranksbridge to stabilize her equilibrium, approach the seat, and speak. Her voice was of the deep, full-throated 'county' type, her accent decidedly upper-crust.

'I am Mrs de ffranksbridge, Mrs Catherwood,' she announced. 'I told Mrs Henderson I would prefer to introduce myself. I knew your grandfather.'

If she had said she had also known Methuselah, I shouldn't have been much surprised, so incredibly old did she appear.

'Do sit down, Mrs de ffranksbridge,' I said, fearing she would fall. She sat, and I looked again, at closer quarters. It wasn't age – it was neglect that made her look as she did. She was dressed in garments that had seen their best days before anybody had ever heard of Adolf Hitler, and judging by the amount of caked grease round the collar, spots down the jabot front and mud round the hem, she had worn little else since that time. Her ensemble was completed by a shapeless brown toque, on which was pinned a magnificent tiger-claw brooch exquisitely mounted in gold. Below the hat coarse grey hair that had once been wavy escaped; but at her right temple, where the toque left her head exposed, the hair was so thin that her

162

scalp showed through the greasy strands, and it was speckled and crusted with age-old dirt. Round her scraggy neck hung a string of pearls of a warmth and colour that no cultured ones have ever attained, but to look at them cost an effort of will, because of the black lines etched by the wrinkles. (I could hear Kezia's voice, as she inspected William before bed. 'Go back and wash your neck again! You could sow onion seeds round it.') As she fumbled to open an old handbag, I noticed that her grimy fingers were laden with gorgeous rings. I followed the movements of those hands with a horrible sort of fascination as they scrabbled inside the old handbag, and at last produced what she was seeking, a grimy visiting card with bent corners and battered edges. She put it into my hands, and I read, 'Mrs Hugh de ffranksbridge, At Home, Thursday 3.30 to 5.00 p.m.' Down in one corner, the address was given as de ffranksbridge Hall, Swithinford.

I thanked her, realizing as I did so that she was almost blind, though she wore no spectacles. Her eyes were glazed in the pale way that denotes severe glaucoma, and though they were fixed on me, I doubted if she could see me at all clearly.

'I hope you will come and take tea with me,' she said in her exquisitely modulated voice. 'Any Thursday.'

'How kind of you,' I said, while my gorge rose at the very thought. There was no doubt about it: she stank.

'I shall expect you,' she said, 'on Thursday afternoon in two weeks' time,' and rose suddenly. She moved in a wide-legged, nonchalant sort of way towards the tree behind me, as if admiring its many clean and green-cheeked apples, till she was behind the gnarled old trunk. Then there came to my ears the unmistakable sound of liquid falling upon hard earth, such as in my childhood I had heard many times when at last Grandfather's old mare, long put out to grass, had got herself comfortably straddled into the right position. The flood over, Mrs de ffranksbridge moved off to mingle again with the folks still round the stall.

'Golly, I nearly got splashed,' said Miss Budd at my ear again. 'I was waiting behind the tree myself, to come back when she'd gone. I ought to have remembered. That's very nearly her party-piece, nowadays.'

'Poor, poor old soul,' I said. 'Tell me about her. She's invited me to tea. What shall I do? Shall I have to go? I can't be rude to the poor old thing. I couldn't be cruel enough. She's so obviously trying to do the proper thing.'

Mary Budd snorted. 'Poor old thing? Don't waste a moment's sympathy on her. When has she asked you for?'

'Two weeks today,' I said, showing her the miserable had-been of a visiting card.

'Hm. Time for you to think up a good excuse. Honestly, you're a better man than I am if you could face it. Apart from the danger of getting contaminated in any other way, she'd probably poison you with the mouldy remains of the cake she's buying at this moment.'

'Is she really so very poor? Who looks after her?'

'Poor? She's the village Rockefeller. That string of pearls round her scraggy old neck would save half the war orphans in Europe. That Hall is stuffed from end to end with antiques that would have been worth a mint of money if she hadn't let them all crumble with woodworm. Same with the Hall itself — fourteenth-century guildhall, beautiful — but gone quite beyond renovation now. Holes in the thatch that have been letting rain in for thirty years. She lives in one room.'

'Alone?' I said. 'Why?'

'Because she's too mean to pay anybody to do anything at all for her, and always has been. Can't bring herself to part with a penny of her income, let alone her capital. Expects other folks to do things for her for the pleasure of a word of thanks from Mrs Hugh de ffranksbridge. Not that they'd get even that. She simply expects service from "the lower orders" for nothing as her feudal right. There's one of my old pupils, married with a big family of her own, who is her nearest neighbour. Jean's got a kind heart, and every now and then it gets the better of her reason, and she goes up to the Hall to see if she can help the great lady. Once or twice she's been let in and allowed to clean up a bit, but the most she's ever been offered for her work is a bag of fallen apples.'

'But how terrible,' I said. 'I had no idea such people still existed.'

'It's a dying breed, and the sooner they're extinct, the better,' declared Miss Budd roundly. 'Don't get me wrong — I'm no egalitarian. But worth should be measured at least partly in human terms, I think. The de ffranksbridges had plenty to be proud of, once. The Old Hall was the real hub of the community in days gone by. Everybody was interested in their doings, and felt part of the family.'

'What happened, then? Sons all killed in two wars? Nothing left to live for?'

She shook her head. 'No, nothing so romantic or heart-rending.

Silly choice of a bride by Hugh de ffranksbridge, that's all. A pretty face and a proud nature, blue blood and only poverty to keep it company. Once she'd married the de ffranksbridge money, her husband as a man might as well have been a dog, for all the notice she took of him. Refused to have children — well, so "they" say — and that broke his heart, because he was the last of his line, and it went back to the conquest or some such. So he drank himself to death by the time he was forty, and she's reigned supreme with her money bags and her great name ever since. Once the war came, of course, she simply had either to pay up or do without service. She chose to do without. As I said, don't waste your sympathy. And don't go to see her. Honestly, I think it's dangerous to do so. She doesn't acknowledge my existence, of course, and most other people avoid her. But you would naturally be fair game as a newcomer, and because your grandfather probably held her stirrup once or twice at a Boxing Day meet.'

'I suppose I ought to consider myself honoured, then? Thank you for being so frank with the warning.'

'Look out,' she said. 'Swithinford's parvenu great lady also has her eye on you. The tall dark one with the Spanish-looking hat.'

The woman in question was buying at the stall, but looking our way every now and again, as if awaiting her opportunity to approach.

'She's waiting for me to leave you,' said Miss Budd grimly. 'I'm the last person she'd want to hand when she makes herself known to you.'

'Why?' I asked, really wanting to know.

'I've spanked her behind too many times in the past,' said Miss Budd. 'And not because she didn't deserve it, either.'

'Oh, she's indigenous, is she?' I was surprised. The lady was tall, slender, with a good, well-held figure that was most elegantly attired — much too much so, perhaps for an occasion of this nature, but the effect was good, all the same. She was beautiful, not seductive in the way that Johanna was at all, but eye-catching, and she knew it. She was ostentatiously spending a good deal, while the ladies behind the stall offered her this and that and she chatted rather condescendingly to them about her purchases.

'They were all at school together,' said Miss Budd. 'Well, at least until most of the others there went to the grammar school, and she didn't. She went off to London to work, at fourteen, then married a Yank in the war, so they say. Be that as it may, she came back to her parents at Swithinford with a child, a little boy. Her mother used to be the barmaid at the pub here, and married a shopkeeper in Swithinford. Then suddenly, out of the blue the village is ablaze with the news that she's marrying Loddy Thackeray. The Thackerays are the biggest farmers, in terms of acreage and success, for miles around — two brothers, both forty-odd, now. The younger one has everything it takes, including a charming wife. But nobody ever expected poor old Loddy to marry. He had a terrible accident when he was a baby — he pulled a pot of boiling potatoes all over himself. His head and face were so badly scalded that his hair came off and never grew again — he's as bald as a coot, and has to wear a wig. His face is puckered and scarred, and his mouth drawn all to one side. But the worst of it was that the shock, and the pain no doubt, caused a lot of psychological disturbance, too. He stammers so badly that in company he can hardly get a word out, and he is given to terrible moods of deep depression and isolation. All of which is perfectly understandable. His parents did their very best to educate him, and gave him every chance that love, and money, could provide. He resisted it all, except for work on the farm. But of course Michael, the younger son, was, and is, all that poor Laurence could never be after the accident. Michael adores his older brother, and they worked the farm together for years in perfect harmony, even after Michael married. Made a great deal of money, during the war, and bought up every scrap of land they could lay their hands on. Then Pamela Balls turns up again, and now she is Mrs Laurence Thackeray. Well, well. She's coming this way, in spite of my unwanted presence. Good afternoon, Pamela. Do you know Mrs Catherwood? Heavens! It's nearly one o'clock. I must go. Goodbye, Mrs Catherwood. Goodbye, Pamela.'

'Miss Budd,' I called after her — but she was gone, and I gave my attention to Mrs Thackeray. Mercifully, it was now evident that the gathering was at an end, so we dispersed, and I resolved to look Miss Budd up in the telephone directory as soon as I got back, because the thing I had wanted to ask her was if she would come to dinner with me at Benedict's before our newfound acquaintance had had time to grow cold. I knew I'd found a friend.

When, later that night, I heard myself singing 'Hark, hark, the lark', which I'd learned at school when I was about seven, I knew that in some way it had been subconsciously recalled by one of the many events of the day. I stood at the landing window, and tried to remember the song all through, bursting into audible laughter when I reached the line,

And winking marybuds begin
To ope their sleepy eyes . . .

How absolutely apt that she should have such a name!

20

During May, William barely had time to make his usual Wednesday visits, and though he came over once or twice at weekends to make up for it, he did not sleep in the flat. He was, I felt, keeping a very wary eye on Sophie, afraid to risk losing her approval by jumping the gun till the all-important bolt had been put in place. I was glad that he had plenty to occupy him, because I certainly had. I was behind with my own writing schedule, and in any case couldn't keep my mind on it. I was finding real live flesh and blood better than my own fictional characters.

I was anxious about Sophie. She was not her usual pragmatic, cheerful self, and though she didn't say, I knew she was getting tense as the birth of Wendy's baby drew nearer day by day. She didn't stop to chat with me between jobs, went home early, and every time the phone rang, she appeared with a face the colour of one of her own old washed-out yellow dusters – though who she thought might telephone her I couldn't discover. As there were about six more weeks to go before anything was likely to happen, I did what I could to calm her down, but it was a hopeless task. She had never been involved in anything of the kind before, and was very apprehensive. Joe was still aloof and Hetty more and more given only to prayer, and from what I could make out it was Daniel's experience as a cowman they were relying on for advice. Thirzah was to be present to assist the village midwife, and Sophie 'to be about, like' for every other chore. I had more sense than to try to interfere, even to offer advice not to worry, but every now and then I found myself being profoundly irritated: people had babies all the time.

I kept thinking about Johanna and her decrepit lodger, as well. Having for so long desired nothing better than to be able to rid myself of any moral obligation to Johanna, I now discovered that I was piqued not to be kept informed. The truth was that since I had entered the village milieu at the coffee morning, I had become a proper villager with what I considered a proper village outlook. I was interested in my neighbours, and wanted to know.

There was no way I could find out how she was coping, because Johanna wouldn't leave him to visit me, and if I called there, or rang up, he would be within hearing.

However, I was driving through Hen Street early the next week when I saw Johanna with a shopping basket on her arm. I pulled up the car and opened the passenger-side door, and she got in.

'Shall I run you home?'

'No – he's having a nap in bed, so he's quite safe. It is a marvellous chance for a word with you.' She lit a cigarette, and turned an amused face to me. 'It was a bit of a facer, when he appeared,' she said, 'but I can't help liking him. I think I would rather have him, completely dependent on me, than someone I was always having to mind my p's and q's with. And he certainly keeps me busy.'

'Are you going to be able to manage? What if he's really ill?'

'It's all being taken care of. We had a visitation from Monty. I suggested that the sooner Ernie got registered with a doctor, the better. You should have just seen the disgust at my suggesting that any friend of his should be left to the mercies of the welfare state! Poor old Ernie wasn't allowed any say in it. Monty had got it all in hand. A friend of his who is a Harley Street consultant and has a private nursing home somewhere around here will make it his business to call on Ernie once a fortnight. I said I wasn't happy with a doctor who was in London most of the time and twenty miles away at his nursing home, but I might as well have saved my breath.'

'Who's doing the paying for such expensive care?' I asked.

'Search me – I don't know. I don't really know what sort of means Ernie has. Overwhelming compared to mine is all I can say. But when Ernie asked what it was all likely to cost, Monty was quite sharp with him. "That's what was the trouble before," he said. "You know perfectly well you can afford to be properly cared for medically. I've arranged it" – and poor old Ernie gave in as if he were a half-witted child. Then on Sunday we had our first visit from the doctor. Archer, his name is. Very posh – about Monty's age but out of a different drawer. He gave Ernie a good going over, and reported to me over our drinks.' She caught my reaction, and grinned. 'Oh, we've got quite a cellar, now. Ernie gave me a blank cheque to go and set it up with. Makes a nice change from instant coffee, I must say.'

'And what did he make of the poor old man?'

She looked more serious than she had done so far. 'The breath trouble is emphysema,' she said. 'It will never be any better, but as long as he doesn't exert himself too much, it isn't likely to get much worse. As the doctor pointed out, he's used to it, and it's probably worse for us than for him. There's a steel plate in his head, but it has been there a long time and there's no reason to think that as far as that's concerned he couldn't still die of old age and nothing else. He needs painkillers for his arthritis, but not too many because they could upset his stomach.'

'And the liver complaint?'

'Made very light of it. It's a sort of jaundice, apparently. But Bob says he'll come once a fortnight to keep his eye on him. And Monty will come every Sunday morning.'

'Bob?'

She laughed like an excited child. 'Don't look so disapproving, Fran. Monty calls him Bob, and though he's Dr Archer to his face, I think of him as Bob.' She was in one of her honest moods. 'You just can't think of the difference it means to me to be able to look forward to having drinks with two men like that. Till now, my Sunday treat has had to be a cup of coffee with Ned.'

'Watch it!' I said, soberly.

'Spoilsport! I'm in no danger. Maybe you think they are?'

I shook my head. 'I don't want you to get hurt,' I said. 'I apologize, Johanna — honestly. I'm glad to see you so happy.'

'All very satisfactory so far,' she said. 'Like steak and mushrooms for lunch today.' She got out of the car, and I drove on. I didn't really understand why I should be disquieted. Drat the woman! She caused me almost as much effort to unmuddle her affairs in my mind as it took her to unmuddle Madge Ellis's everlasting pullovers.

I wanted to meet Miss Budd again, so I rang up and asked her to come to tea. She did, and we got on famously. I paid a return visit to her school-house down by the church. Through her I could be in touch with the entire village, and not just those elements of it that Sophie deemed suitable for me to hear about. We discussed everything, from the latest titbit of scandal to the newest trends in primary education, from the Rector's last fit of absence-of-mind to the poetry of John Donne.

'I've got to decide what to do about Mrs de ffranksbridge on Thursday,' I said miserably. 'I do dread it, but I suppose I shall have to go. You don't suppose she will have forgotten, do you?'

Miss Budd clicked her tongue in self-disapproval. 'Fancy me forgetting to tell you,' she said. 'She's ill. Some people report a true, physical illness, because of her being half-starved, and some say she is wandering in her mind. Either way, it lets you out.'

I breathed a sigh of enormous relief. 'I'll get some flowers, or fruit or something, and send Ned up with a note to say how sorry I am to hear she is ill,' I said. 'That would deal with it, wouldn't it?'

'Yes – though I should make your gift edible rather than beautiful. I dare say the starvation theory is the correct one.'

I took her word for it, and on Wednesday packed a basket of fruit, wrote a note and asked Ned to go up in my car to deliver it. When he returned, he came straight to the study to find me, looking anxious.

'I reckon somebody ought to send a doctor up there to her,' he said. 'She were wandering about that great wilderness of a garden when I got there, tottering on a stick, and trying to pick some apples. They're as green as grass and as hard as marbles yet, but she were cramming 'em into her mouth and trying to chew 'em, skins and all. When I handed her your fruit she started on it as if she hadn't seen victuals for a month. I give her the letter, but she just tore it up, and dropped the bits into the basket. Then I asked her if I could help her to get back inside the house afore I left her, but she said no, she was on her way to the bank to see her bank manager. I told her the bank would be closed, but she said they'd let her in because the manager was expecting her.

'Well, I looked at my watch, and I couldn't see how she was going to get into Swithinford, 'cos the afternoon bus had gone. I thought you wouldn't mind if I took her in your car, and I was just going to tell her so when she picked up her stick and clouted me with it, and asked me how I dare contradict her. She said the manager would be in his bank a-weighing up the sugar, "like he always is when the doors are closed," she said. Then I knowed as she must really be queer in the head, ma'am, though as different as can be from my poor Eth when she is took. So I left her in the garden, and come as quick as I could to tell you.'

'Oh dear,' I said. 'I'm sure you are right, Ned – somebody must send a doctor. But I don't think a comparative newcomer like me is the right person to interfere. I think I'll ring Miss Budd. She'll know what to do.'

It was an enormous relief to hear Mary Budd's vibrant voice at the other end of the phone. I explained, and she listened as I poured out the tale Ned had just told me.

'Hm,' she said. 'I agree that it wouldn't be wise for you to go – or me, either. She doesn't "know" me when she's well, and I think she will by now have forgotten you altogether. I know! I'll go up straight away and see Jean Howe, the girl I told you about, who has sometimes kept an eye on her before. She'll find out what the situation is, and then let me know, and if necessary I will then take the responsibility of sending Dr Henderson.'

She was as good as her word, and reported back several hours later. Jean had got the old lady into bed, and Dr Henderson had been to see her. There was nothing wrong that good food and a bit of care wouldn't soon put right. He had suggested a nursing home, but she had been quite clear-headed enough to tell him forcefully that she couldn't and wouldn't pay for such a thing. She wasn't ill enough for him to get her into a hospital, but she couldn't be left without somebody to look after her. As he said, if she could pay but wouldn't, which is obviously the case, they would have to take her to a geriatric hospital. Jean said she couldn't let that happen, and Dr Henderson said he would do everything he could to help, so she had agreed to look after the invalid till she was about again.

'Your Jean Howe sounds a brick,' I said. 'Fancy taking that lot on, knowing you'll never get paid for it, except perhaps by abuse.'

Mary sounded pleased. 'Yes,' she said. 'Jean's OK. I've got a very soft spot for her. She'll cope with life.'

Two or three days later, I had an unexpected visit from Johanna. Monty Ellington had arrived to take Ernie out for a ride with him, and had dropped her off at my gate. I stopped work, and we went into the sitting-room, where Sophie usually brought me some tea at about three thirty. I popped my head into the kitchen to tell Sophie I had a visitor, but I could tell from her set face that she was already well aware of the fact, and who my visitor was. When a little later she put the tray of tea down before us, her cold dignity made me irritated and uncomfortable. It really was silly for Sophie to behave like this towards Johanna. That she was being used by Wendy's family as the only scapegoat available, I could understand to some extent; but I resented Sophie making it so obvious in my house. I glanced at Johanna to see if she was hurt by Sophie's rudeness, but she hadn't even noticed. As always, she looked ravishing, in a

creamy-yellow dress piped with brown, her slim little waist accentu-
ated by a golden patent-leather belt to match. As I poured out the
tea, I thought, 'Feathers today, with a vengeance. I wonder why?'
She seemed to be on guard, but why, here in my house? It was long
after we had finished tea that I noticed her fingering her wrist-
watch, though she was not looking at the time.

'Johanna,' I said, unthinking, 'what a beautiful watch! I've never
seen it before.'

'No,' she said shortly, 'you are hardly likely to have done. It's
new.' There was an air of defiance about her as she added, 'Present,
from Ernie.'

I suppose I must have shown some sort of disapproval. I thought
it unwise of her to be accepting such expensive gifts so soon,
because they smacked too much of bribery to induce her to keep the
decrepit old invalid. And I remembered thinking when I had seen
them together that however old and disabled he was, she had still
stirred the hot blood in his veins. She was playing with fire again,
like a child who cannot be made to understand how dangerous it is
until he has been really badly burned. She read my look, and I
watched the defiance grow in her eyes and show in the tensing of
her fingers. I had reacted exactly as she had expected. All I said,
though, was 'How very nice!'

But she was not going to be put off what she had intended to
say. 'It's no use you putting on your vicar's wife act with me, Fran,'
she said, though taking the sting out of her words with her impish
smile. 'Look at it from my point of view. I really am doing my best
for him, and he's happy for the first time for years. He's got more
money than he knows how to get rid of, living in Hen Street – wads
of fivers in his wallet, piling up there because they are left over from
what Monty brings him every week. And God knows what a
change for me it is not to dread the postman coming. If he chooses
to spend some of his surplus dough on presents for me, why
shouldn't he? What, honestly, is there against it?'

Put like that, what was there? Yet I had a sense of foreboding. I
was struggling to find words to get us both back on to our casual
terms again, when Sophie opened the door and announced, with
slivers of ice in her voice, that I had another visitor at the door.
'That Mis' Thack'ray,' she said, in a hoarse whisper that carried
much farther than her ordinary speaking voice.

I jumped to my feet, astounded. 'Ask her in, please Sophie,' I said,
doing my best to convey to Sophie that I was as surprised as she

was, and not a great deal better pleased. Somewhat mollified, she went, and ushered in Pamela Thackeray.

As I introduced her to Johanna, I felt as if I had a couple of magnets in my hands. That there was instant force generated between them, I could feel, though for a second or two I did not know whether the poles would be towards or opposed to each other.

They were inspecting and appraising each other coolly as I asked the newcomer to sit down, pulling another chair up into the circle for her, and as she lowered her tall frame into it, I could see both ladies metaphorically drawing their skirts away from each other. They were more likely to be opposed.

I refilled the teapot, and offered Mrs Thackeray tea, which she took, more at her ease, if anything, than Johanna was. They could hardly have been more different — one tall, dark and Junoesque, the other petite and glowing with inward flame. My thoughts flashed to Mount Ida, and for the first time ever I understood properly the task that Zeus had laid upon poor Paris. How could one say that one was more beautiful, or more attractive, than the other? Mrs Thackeray's clothes, if anything, were more expensive than Johanna's, but Johanna certainly had the edge with regard to taste. Both seemed to exude the self-assurance that beautiful women well turned out seem able to command; but instinct told me that while Johanna's was worn, like a delicate veil that could be put on or taken off at will, Pamela Thackeray's was a skin, growing thicker as one after another the social barriers of Old Swithinford went down before her new status of Mrs Laurence Thackeray of Southside House.

She had called, she was saying, at the pressing request of Mrs de ffranksbridge, to thank me for my gift and to say that Mrs ffranksbridge hoped my visit was only postponed. As soon as she was about again, she would send another invitation.

'I'm glad to hear she is well enough to be bothered,' I said. 'I suppose you must have been to see her?'

'Oh, yes. As soon as my husband heard of her indisposition, he insisted that I should call to see if there was anything we could do. I have been in the habit of calling on her occasionally, in a social way, and as my husband says, such folks as us have to stick together. That's why I felt I had to come and give you her message, though it were out of my way.'

Johanna was looking like a ginger kitten watching a black one lapping up the cream. I was thinking that her grammar didn't match the put-on voice.

Mrs Thackeray rose to go, making much play of drawing on a pair of expensive gloves. There was no doubt about it. If the contest had been with tooth and claw instead of female sparring with arch glances, elegant wrist movements and studied crossing of ankles, Johanna would have been lying on the carpet with her tawny feathers ruffled, because so far the points had all gone to Pamela. I veered round in desire to support Johanna, who was my friend. Though her back was towards the window, I could tell that her thoughts were centred with almost cankerous envy on Pamela's smart little car standing at the door, and with which, in the next five minutes, she would contrive to deliver the knock-out blow.

Then all was reversed.

'Johanna,' I said wickedly. 'I think I see your car coming to collect you.'

She shot me a look of such fiery gratitude that I nearly forgot my courtesy as hostess to both of them, so great was the urge to laugh. Johanna rose with the grace of a Fonteyn, and turned on Pamela a smile that would have petrified a more sensitive woman. Then she tiptoed to kiss me goodbye. I hope I didn't show my surprise, because it was something she had rarely done before. Johanna was not the kissing type – but in the circumstances it was a bit of one-up-man-ship that I could but admire, establishing as it did her priority in the matter of friendship. Then she turned towards the window, and said languidly, in her most Dietrichlike voice, 'Yes, here is Monty,' as Ellington's opulent white Jaguar cruised into close-up.

It was, I felt, a slightly subdued Pamela that watched Johanna being driven off, and she left almost at once. I found that Sophie had waited to clear away the tea things, and was irritated with her for doing so, but I guessed she was afraid she might have upset me, and had stayed deliberately to make amends. She need not have worried. I had already seen enough of Mrs Laurence Thackeray to know that if I were in Sophie's shoes, and had sat with Pamela as a child in the same classroom, I should not relish having to wait upon the lady she had now become. Sophie and I exchanged a few comments about the visit, and I noticed that her attitude towards Johanna had softened noticeably. There were no flies on Sophie, and comparisons are always useful yardsticks.

I kept my nose to the grindstone in my study for the next week or so, and when Mary Budd rang to ask me to tea again, I was really glad of the break. Ned had been picking early plums in the old orchard, far more than Sophie and I could deal with, so I filled a bag for Mary and another for Johanna, which meant that I had to go round to Hen Street to deliver them.

'I can't stop,' I said, popping my head into the kitchen and putting the plums on the table. Johanna was fresh and rosy from the afternoon nap she always took if at all possible, and was sitting in her accustomed place at the kitchen table with the inevitable coffee and soapstone ashtray in front of her.

'You must, just for a sec,' she said, jumping up. 'I've got something to show you.'

She led the way to the sitting-room, pushing open the door for me to go in. The walls and the soapstone were as I had known them, but the rest had undergone a kind of pantomime transformation. A new carpet of thick dull gold stretched from wall to wall, and lush velvet curtains, professionally lined and hung under a shaped and braided pelmet, made the cheap little window into a thing of beauty. A new suite in muted brown had replaced the old one, and a baby grand piano stood in the corner where the old upright had been.

I didn't know what to say, or indeed what I was expected to say, but Johanna was so excited she didn't wait for me to say anything.

'Ernie,' she gurgled, and I could see that she was not at all apprehensive this time, as she had been about the watch, but amused and bursting to tell.

'After my visit to your house the other day,' she said, 'I told Ernie about Mrs Thackeray.' ('Told' was an understatement, I thought. I could imagine Johanna's impersonation in every detail.) 'Then, would you believe it, Ernie and I were in the village shopping and she swept down on us and insisted on taking us both home with her for a drink. Of course it was only to show off her house. But she was all over Ernie, and put on the dog so much she really got under his skin, I think. He was very quiet all next day, and rang up Monty to say he wanted to see him. The next I knew, Monty whisked me off with instructions and a blank cheque, to buy whatever I wanted to make the sitting-room "more comfortable for him". I had a whale of a time.'

'It's lovely,' I said, and I meant it. For the first time, the room looked warm and comfortable. If Ernie had needed an excuse to suggest some improvements for his own benefit, his determination that Johanna should not be completely outclassed by Pamela had provided it.

'It's working well,' Johanna said, as she came out to the car with me. 'Apart from all that,' (she waved a vague hand towards the sitting-room window) 'I'm really getting very fond of the poor old s— chap. Honestly, he is really very sweet, and so grateful for everything. It does make a nice change, not to be short of money all the time.'

I nodded. I could appreciate the relief she must feel, even if I still had vague apprehensions that somehow it was all unwise.

'Any snags at all, yet?' I asked.

She shrugged and grinned. 'Of course – plenty, but not serious. So far, Ned's the only real fly in the ointment.'

'Ned?' I repeated. 'What on earth—?'

'Well, he's still been coming regularly to help me since he came to work for you, just like he always used to, and as I told you, I never could pay him for what he did. Last Sunday, he was busy in the garden as usual, and Ernie went out to him. I didn't know anything at all about it, but Ernie suggested Ned should get the outside of the bungalow colourwashed and painted before the winter set in, and he, Ernie I mean, would pay for it. I don't know what Ned said to him, but the poor old chap came in quite upset, and then when Ned came in to bring my usual fags, he let rip at me.'

'Why?'

'As far as I can make out, because I hadn't asked him myself, and he wasn't going to work for Ernie Ambrose, money or no money. He was really nasty, the silly idiot. I put him in his place, of course. But the truth is that I just don't understand these yokels of yours, Fran. It just makes me mad when they get tetchy like that about nothing. You'd think we were insulting Ned, trying to pay him!'

'They're not "my" yokels,' I retorted, 'even if that's what you choose to call them in any case. But Ned's in a special category, I think.'

As I drove the short distance from Hen Street back to Old Swithinford, I tried to consider the matter all round as objectively as I could. How much Johanna accepted from Ernie Ambrose was her own concern, but I didn't want Ned upset, for my own comfort as well as his. Johanna had absolutely no understanding of the nature of Ned's devotion to her, or of his simple pride. Ernie's offer had offended against the laws of his chivalry, reduced him from Johanna's knight to her servitor. He had expected Johanna to understand how he felt, and she had failed him. In doing so, she had negated all his past loving services, too. I could but wonder what the outcome would be.

176

I enjoyed my time with Miss Budd as I always did. Apart from the fact that I liked her and found her intellectually stimulating, she fed my insatiable thirst for insight into the ways of people. She didn't 'gossip', because most of what she knew of happenings in the district were first-hand, established facts. She had no use for hearsay, and in any case was blessed with almost unlimited tolerance of human foibles. Through her eyes, one saw the community entire, though she could at any moment bring a pair of personal binoculars on to any detail within it. I was reminded of Thomas Hardy's analogy of the weave of a story being like the pattern on a carpet. Mary Budd saw the carpet whole, but she could at any moment put her finger on one colour or design, and trace it accurately through.

We were deep in a discussion of a play on the radio to which we had both listened when my hostess looked up in surprise and said, 'Here's Jean Howe — looking terribly distressed. I wonder what's the matter.' She was at the door almost before Mrs Howe knocked. Voices in the tiny front hall rose and fell, and though I tried not to listen, it was clear that the younger woman was crying in a quite distracted fashion. After a few minutes, Miss Budd came back into the sitting-room and said, 'I'm awfully sorry, but Jean really needs me for a little while. Will you excuse me?'

I jumped up, protesting that I would go home. For her to have a visit from an old pupil in distress was probably by no means unusual. The old-fashioned type of village schoolteacher often appeared to be much more accessible than the parson — though of course it depended upon the personalities of both. In our particular case, the Reverend Howard was a dear and charming old man, but years of self-indulgent bachelordom had removed him from the sphere of post-war youth and its difficulties. Miss Budd had never taken her fingers out of the community's pie as the mixture changed its nature, and took pastoral work as a sort of obligation attached to her past services.

Mary had pushed open the door, and Mrs Howe heard my reply. 'No, don't go, Mrs Catherwood, on account of me,' she said. 'I'll come back.' She was mopping her eyes with a man's large handkerchief.

Miss Budd caught her hand, gently. 'Come in, Jean, and sit down, and tell Mrs Catherwood all about it, too. You can take my word for it that she will tell no one else, any more than I would.'

Mrs Howe still hesitated. When Miss Budd spoke again, it was in quite a different tone of voice. 'Now come along, Jean. Do as you're told,' she said, teacher all over. Jean Howe gave her a wan smile through her tears, and came. Her mentor almost pushed her down into an armchair, and removed her headscarf, untying it beneath her chin for all the world as if Jean were still five years old and having trouble with the knot. Then she put a cup of tea into the woman's shaking hands, and sat down again by the tea table to finish her own scone.

I looked at Mrs Howe with warm interest, and saw a young woman of middle height, inclined to be plump, with a fair, apple-blossom skin underpainted with freckles. The headscarf had concealed a mass of wavy, ash-blonde hair caught up in a loose knot at the back, from which curly tendrils escaped to frame her face with its blotchy, red-rimmed eyes.

The tea was soothing her, and Miss Budd judged to a nicety the exact moment to ask her to begin her tale.

'You will remember, Mrs Catherwood, that it was I who suggested Jean should go and do what she could for Mrs de ffranksbridge. I'm afraid this is the result of all our good intentions. Begin at the beginning, Jean, and tell us exactly what happened.'

'Well, I went, and all the time the poor old lady was in bed I took her meals and done what I could for her.'

'Did,' said Miss Budd, absently.

'Sorry, Miss Budd. I did what I could, like cleaning up downstairs and turning out all the mouldy bread and milk bottles from the pantry and things like that. Then the doctor said she could get up an hour or two every day, so I used to make it my business to go down and get her up, give her a hot meal and a drink, and wash up before I left. Well, Wednesday of last week, I'd just got her meal on the tray ready to take to her, when in comes that — in comes Pamela Balls-as-was, all done up to the nines, with that child of hers. And if Mrs de ffranksbridge didn't order me to get them a cup of coffee! Just as if I was a maid, or something, instead of a neighbour doing what I could for nothing! You know, Miss — I didn't like to make trouble, but it put my hackles up good and proper to be ordered to wait on Pam Balls, whoever she's married now. But I done it — sorry, did it, for the sake o' peace and quiet. Pam, she barely said thank you — looked at me as if she'd never seen me before, instead o' me remembering when my mam had to ask you to move me away from her in school 'cos she were lousy, and mam didn't want me to have to have my hair cut off.'

'Sh!' said Miss Budd, soothingly but with a hint of reproof. 'That's all water under the bridge now, Jean.'

'Yes, of course, Miss. I'm sorry – but you really should have seen her putting on airs with me. I was that put out, that when I took the dirty cups and things out into the kitchen, I dumped 'em on the side o' the mucky old sink and left 'em. Let them as used 'em wash 'em up, I thought and off I went home.

'Next day, Mrs de ffranksbridge asked me why I hadn't finished my job, and I felt obliged to tell her, straight, that I wasn't being paid to wait on her visitors, and in fact I wasn't being paid at all. An' she made a very curious remark. She said, "I think you are seeing to it that you're not out of pocket." I couldn't think what she meant at all, but I forgot it because after all she is a bit queer in the head. But I gave her to understand that in future she could leave the pots on the sink, and I'd do 'em next day.

'Then, night before last, Pam Balls and her son were there again, so I left what I'd took for the old lady, and went home. Yesterday morning I made a batch o' cakes, and thought perhaps it would be a treat for her to have a couple fresh from the oven, so I nipped up to take her some. And there stood the poor old thing at the sink, trying to wash them greasy pots in cold water. I felt real bad at leaving 'em for her, that I did, so I put the kettle on and finished 'em, but I daren't stop to put them away or anything else, 'cos I'd left another batch o' things cooking at home.

'Well, come last night, when I got there, if Pam Balls weren't there again. So I told Mrs de ffranksbridge I'd go back and do the washing up later. Then Pam says, very snooty like, "No need for that, Jean. I'll help my hostess to wash up when she's finished." "Hostess," she says, for all the world as if she were really a lady, instead of a—' She caught Miss Budd's eye, and stopped short. 'So I went this morning, as promised, and that damned old woman was waiting for me. She shut the door behind me, quick as lightning, and then asked me what I'd done with her rings! "What rings?" I says, and she holds her skinny old hands out, bare as mine are except for her wedding ring. "My rings," she says. "My emerald hoop and my ruby cluster and my diamond solitaire, as I always wear." "I haven't seen them," I said. "Oh yes you have, my good woman," she answers, "because I know where I left them. They were on the sink top when you washed up yesterday morning. I was quite able to do the washing up myself, but you interfered as you are always doing, and made me sit down while you finished it. Of course I had taken my rings off to do the washing up. That was what you had been planning, and waiting for, I dare say. But you won't get away with it this time," she says, "because when Mrs Thackeray comes tonight I shall send her straight off to the police." And she told me to go home, and never go up there no more. How I got home, I don't know! I just set there crying when Tom come in for his dinner and we didn't know what to do. Then he says that as soon as ever the children were home from school, I'd better come up and see you and ask you what I ought to do.'

Her tale finished, she collapsed into a new agony of fear and indignation. Miss Budd's face was sterner than I had ever seen it before, and I judged from it that she was indeed very worried. She soothed Jean in every way she could, till the poor woman could once more speak coherently, and then began to ask very practical questions.

'I suppose you didn't notice the rings on the sink?'

'No, I never. But you see I was in such a rush, on account of them cakes I'd left in the oven. I wish I'd never gone near the place.'

I felt I had to say something. 'Don't forget, Mrs Howe,' I said 'that she is a very old woman who does do strange things. The police will want much more evidence than her accusation before they take any notice at all. She's probably put them in an ornament on the mantelpiece, or in the sugar bowl, and will find them when she isn't looking for them.'

'Now look here, my girl,' said Miss Budd. 'Nobody that knows you will take any notice whatever of such a tale, of that I am sure. But if Mrs de ffranksbridge does report her loss to the police — or to her insurance company — they will be bound to question you.' (Wails of terror from poor Jean made my heart almost turn over with distress for her.) 'On the other hand, as Mrs Catherwood says, she may find them, or simply forget the whole incident. Just you try to remember every detail that you can, and then when you are asked, tell the truth and stick to it. But no one else need know of it, so do try not to worry.'

'She'll tell that nasty Pam Balls, she will,' sobbed Jean, 'and then it'll be all over the village. She never could keep nothing to herself.'

'No one will take her word against yours,' said Miss Budd, but her tone lacked conviction, and Jean was quick to note it.

'They wouldn't have done when she was plain Pam Balls, the barmaid's daughter,' she said. 'But it's different now she's Mis' Thackeray.'

The despair in her voice made it sound like ice being scraped from a block.

'Her being Mrs Thackeray doesn't change the fact that everybody knows that Jean Howe is Honesty and Goodness walking on two legs.'

'Mud sticks, though, don't it, Miss? You may be as honest as the day, in a little place like this, but if somebody chucks mud at you, some of it sticks, and folks don't forget it.'

Assured of every bit of help, support and backing, practical as well as moral, that Miss Budd could offer, Jean at last took her leave.

'We need something stronger than tea, after that,' said my hostess, as she got out sherry and glasses. 'I'm sorry you have been subjected to it, but I think you being here helped. It probably curbed Jean's tongue with regard to Pamela, for one thing, and least said is always soonest mended.'

'And yours,' I said.

She shot me a penetrating glance from her blue-black eyes. 'Oh dear, did I show what I was thinking? I won't hide the fact I'm much more worried than I would have Jean believe. I don't like it at all.'

'Why?' I asked, bluntly.

She fingered her sherry glass, turning it round and round before replying. 'You met Pam Thackeray at the coffee morning, I think?'

'I did – and she has since called on me.'

Miss Budd's genuine surprise was almost ludicrous. 'No! Has she really?'

'Why are you so surprised?'

'Caught off guard. Like Jean Howe, my picture of Pamela is not that of a well-to-do lady who makes social calls. She's obviously got what it takes. Pity she didn't go and do it somewhere else, where nobody knows her.'

'It isn't like you to be so class or money conscious. It simply never occurred to me to look at her visit like that.'

Miss Budd looked hurt. 'I'm not class or money conscious at all,' she replied. 'A poor schoolmarm I'd have made if I had been. But I am character conscious. I did my best with that girl, because certain – shall we say "acquisitive" – characteristics were there from the start. But maybe I didn't smack her behind hard enough or often enough when I had the chance.'

'Poor Jean Howe,' I said. 'What a mess for her.'

She snorted. 'Don't waste too much sympathy on Jean,' she said. 'That girl is pure gold, and it will take more than a dotty old woman's accusation to stain her. If you have any feelings to squander, think of poor Pamela's husband.'

She became silent and a bit preoccupied, and I took it as a signal that she wanted to think things out in peace and quiet, so I began to make my excuses to leave.

'I'm sorry all this has happened,' she said. 'I wanted to tell you about the horkey, and beg you to come.'

'Tell me tomorrow,' I said. 'Come to lunch and enjoy some of Sophie's cooking. She'd adore that.'

'So should I,' she said as she waved me goodbye.

21

The speed with which news can travel from mouth to mouth in a sparsely populated countryside never fails to surprise me. The last fault that I could ever find with Sophie or Ned was that they wasted my time by gossiping to each other, so that when I went next morning to find Sophie to tell her of Miss Budd's impending visit for lunch, and found Ned inside the kitchen with her, I knew instinctively what they were talking about. They stopped the moment I opened the door, like two cats caught at the cream bowl. Sophie had enough sense to know that I should find the situation unusual, so she told me what they had been discussing.

'I knew already,' I said. 'Jean Howe came to see Miss Budd while I was there yesterday.'

'It's a real bad job,' said Sophie indignantly. 'Ned 'ere's got proof enough that that old gel's gone right off 'er 'ead this time. Nobody'll believe 'er, be she who she may — well, not about Jean, anyway. But no doubt, being as she is who she is, the police'll be brought in. And then them few as don't know Jean as well as we do'll have plenty to say.'

Ned went off and by tacit consent Sophie and I left the matter there. Any mention of the police was too much for Sophie's suscepti-bilities, especially in her present overwrought state.

Over lunch, it was Miss Budd who brought the subject up again — to my surprise, in front of Sophie. 'I'm in the mood for a bit of prophecy about it,' she said. 'I don't think it is going to be even a nine-days'-wonder. I prophesy that those rings will be found before this day is out. Where would you guess that they may be discovered, Mrs Catherwood? Come on, guess! And you too, Sophie. We'll see which of the three of us is the best fortune-teller.'

'Not me, miss,' said Sophie decidedly. 'I never did 'old wi' fortune-telling and such, not no'ow.' She went back to her kitchen.

'That girl's English is no better now than it ever was,' sighed Miss Budd. 'Come now, do make a guess at where the rings will turn up.' She seemed so strangely insistent on playing her childish game that she had me uncomfortably puzzled. '"In the sugar bowl or an ornament on the mantelpiece" is what you said yesterday. Which are you going to plump for?'

'I'll change my mind,' I said, to please her. 'My crystal ball tells me they are in the sink-basket under the dishcloth.'

She seemed satisfied at having made me reply, and soon after lunch excused herself, saying that she had to make a preliminary round of the farmers who usually helped her with a fund-raising effort for the Save the Children Fund.

It was almost bedtime when I answered the telephone to her, her voice, charged, or so I thought, with a mixture of triumphant satisfaction and relief.

'I thought you might like to know that I have just had a visit from Jean Howe, to report that the rings have been found.'

'Oh, I am so glad!' I exclaimed. 'Who found them, and where were they?'

Amusement crept into her voice. 'I'll give you the usual three guesses,' she said. 'Pamela Thackeray found them. Now you tell me where.'

'It couldn't be!' I said. 'Not under the dishcloth in the sink-basket?'

'Well, I did tell you to prophesy, didn't I?'

I was incredulous. 'Are you telling me that if I had said in the cat's dish or the toe of a slipper, that's where Mrs Thackeray would have found them?'

'Really, Frances! I said no such thing at all. But all's well that ends well.'

(For some reason I couldn't explain, I felt a glow of warmth all over at her use of my first name, in full. It was right. I was 'Fran' only to my nearest and dearest, which in fact now really only meant William.) I was not prepared to let her go without a bit more explanation. 'I trust your round of the farmers went off successfully this afternoon.'

She chuckled, quite wickedly. 'Oh, yes. Pamela Thackeray and I had quite a long chat about old times, remembering several occasions on which other articles had been mislaid by their owners. It was all very pleasant — for me, at any rate. It has been a lovely day. Thank you for my delicious lunch. Goodnight, Frances.'

May had slipped into June, and I still hadn't got the door to the flat reopened, or the bolt fixed. I had asked the Beans to do it, but it was, as they said, 'the growing time o' year', meaning that they had their hands very full with the one or two gardens they looked after and work on their own small-holding.

I hadn't seen much of William, but when I had, we were just about managing to maintain our old warm comradeship, which had been threatened for a little while after his qualified, 'honourable' declaration and my resolution not to show him how much I reciprocated his feelings.

Towards the middle of a spell of very warm weather in mid-June, he arrived unexpectedly one evening, so we went out to dinner and then back to sit in the garden.

'Only another couple of weeks, Fran,' he said, stretching luxuriously in the garden chair at my side, 'and I can come and relax here. Did I tell you that I have to go to the States for about two weeks towards the end of the vacation? A sort of pre-conference conference, I can't get out of it, worse luck. I am so looking forward to being here, messing about in Eeyore's Tail, catching up on reading and writing, and above all, being at home, where you are. You do know that, don't you?'

We sat in comfortable silence till it suddenly turned chilly and we had to go inside. I went to make him a drink before leaving, and when I took it to him, he said, 'I have been thinking that I really ought to go and see Jess. I've been neglecting her quite badly since Christmas. But I don't want to go. Much as I like the islands, I also like comfort. It hasn't mattered before, but now I want to be at home for as much as I can of my free time.'

'You don't say much about Jess,' I said. 'I should love to see her, too. Why don't we ask them to come here?'

'I don't think it would work,' he said. 'Don't ask me why now, because it's late and I must go. I'll talk to my own conscience about going up there — but my conscience has other things to occupy it. It isn't all that bothered about Jess nowadays.'

I was just getting up next morning when I caught a glimpse of

Sophie hurrying down the drive, and guessed the cause at once. I went down to meet her at the door. She was strained and nervous and started calling out her news even while still closing the gap between us.

'I shan't be a-coming to work this morning,' she said. 'You see, Dan'el's made it 'is business to go down to Hen Street every morning for this last week or two, what with Joe not having anythink to do with Wend' at all, and Het being as she is. And 'e's just come tearing back for me and Thirz', so Thirz' 'as gone straight off, and I come to tell you as I'm gooin' now. I'll come back to work as soon as ever I can, and I'll let you know when I know myself what's 'appening.'

'Come in a minute and get your breath back,' I said. 'Then I'll get the car out and take you to Hen Street.'

'No, thanks all the same. I'm in a hurry,' she said. And I could tell that she meant it. She was so agitated that to begin at once to walk would be infinitely more endurable for her than to wait even five minutes for me. So I let her go, murmuring what soothing encouragement I could.

She did not return, so it was clear that Daniel had been right in his judgement. I spent the day alone, and got a gratifying amount of work done. Then, at about six, Jelly Bean arrived in his old van, full of apologies for his sudden appearance and the lateness of the hour, but he had been meaning for days to come and get 'that there ol' door fixed' and put the bolt where I wanted it. Would it be convenient for him to do it now?

He soon fixed the door, which gave the flat a completely separate entrance, and began to put a bolt on the door between the old kitchen and the new one where I was preparing my supper. He worked away in his usual stolid fashion, whistling silently between his teeth, and we had very little to say to each other. I put my food on a tray, so as not to embarrass him by eating it, as I so often did, at the kitchen table in full view of him. I was about to leave the kitchen with it, when Sophie came in.

She was white and drawn, and looked drained and wrung out with emotion; but in her eyes was a light of triumph, of victory, of atavistic joy. I had no need to ask if the birth had taken place.

She had never before, in the whole of her nearly fifty years, been within sight or sound of this so-common miracle of birth, and it had, I guessed, been as much of an ordeal for her as it had for the mother herself. If she had endured with Wendy every pain and pang, she was now sharing also the moment of incredible elation and wonder. A closer look at her showed me that she was trembling with fatigue, and that the strong reaction of relief and joy after such a long day of tension was having a sudden and severe effect on her.

When she came into the kitchen, Jelly was out of sight, working on the other side of the door, which he was holding three-quarters closed. Then he opened it and came through to look at it from the inside, appearing as if by magic only a few feet from where Sophie stood. His sudden unexpected entrance was the last straw that broke the back of Sophie's hard-held composure. She sat down suddenly on a kitchen chair by the table, and began to cry.

I had never seen Sophie shed a tear since the day she had looked down from the landing window at Jelly working in the garden. Tears, in Kezia's book, were an admission of weakness, a yielding of spirit which could only invite further defeat. Maybe such rigid denial of Nature's safety valve was what had induced in Hetty her predisposition to hysterics: if she was not allowed to 'cop out' one way, she took another. I was glad to see Sophie cry.

I set down my tray, and turned back to put the kettle on again. A sympathetic ear, a willing listener and a strong, hot cup of tea would probably be the best medicine in the world. I plugged the kettle in without speaking, and while half-turning was stopped as if I had been 'touched' while playing the children's game of 'Statues'. Sophie had her head down on the table; her old felt hat was pushed to one side and her thick dark hair showed dishevelled beneath the brim of it. Her hands were clasped as in prayer, and her forehead rested on them, while her shoulders silently shook with deep, shuddering sobs.

Two feet away from her stood Jelly, with a huge iron bolt in one hand, a screwdriver in the other, and on his weather-beaten face a look of such ineffable tenderness that it sent a thrill of anguished awe through me, such as Moses must have felt as he stood before the burning bush that could not be consumed. 'Take off thy shoes from off thy feet, for the place whereon thou standest is holy ground.'

He moved, and I turned back to the sink, afraid almost to breathe lest I should remind either of them of my presence. I heard him lay the tools down on the table, and I heard his voice. I hope to this day that it was accompanied by some appropriate gesture, but I didn't see.

He spoke low. 'Don't take on, Soph'! Don't! I can't abear it.'

There was such a profound silence in the kitchen after his one anguished outburst that the bell of the grandfather clock in the hall broke it like the fall of the executioner's axe. I stared down at the kettle and cups and saucers in front of me, but saw nothing. Then I heard the door scrape, and knew that Jelly had gone back to his work. So I turned, too, and found Sophie sitting up with her head high, drying her eyes on a spotless handkerchief. She did not look towards Jelly, but gave me a wobbly smile.

'It's a boy,' she said. 'As beautiful a child as you ever did see, born just after four o'clock. I come up, as soon as ever I could, to tell you. But I shall have to be getting off back, 'cos Thirz' is about done up, and Hetty's gone all to pieces, now that it's all over. I shall have to tell you all about it another time.' She looked straight at me, and indicated by a slight inclination of her head that the details she was bursting to relate must in all modesty wait till there were no male ears to hear, Jelly's above all others.

'Drink your tea,' I said, putting it down in front of her. 'They'll manage without you for five minutes more. Then I'll take you back.'

She shook her head. 'Thanks,' she said, 'but it'd be better for you not to go anywhere near, not tonight, like. It would ha' been different if the little ol' boy 'ad 'ad a proper father. They'd have all been so proud then for you to be the first to see 'im.'

'But Sophie, I wouldn't dream of intruding,' I said. 'I would save you a mile walk when you are so tired already, and set you down without any of them even catching sight if me at all.'

She shook her head again, and I was beginning to lose my patience with her when I looked up and caught Jelly's eye. He shook his head, sending me some sort of message, and I deemed it best to give way. I did not understand in the least the niceties that forbade Sophie to accept my offer, but it was clear that Jelly did, and did not want me to distress her by insisting. So she finished her tea, stood up, told me she would be at work at the usual time in the morning, and then left without so much as another glance at Jelly.

He came to my side of the door, and made a good deal of play of making sure that the bolt slid easily and fitted without difficulty. I had a hunch that he wanted to say something but didn't know if he ought.

'I'm going to make myself a cup of tea,' I said. 'I need one, after that. Come in and have one with me.'

I didn't expect him to accept, but to my great surprise he came and sat down in the chair Sophie had vacated, hanging his old working cap over one of his knees. I made the tea, and we sat facing each other across the kitchen table.

He stirred his tea round and round with a vertical spoon, and I waited. He took a sip from his cup, carefully tapping the spoon on its side and laying it in the saucer as if he were performing some sort of task requiring perfect precision, like cutting a diamond, for instance. Then he took the plunge.

'I'd a-took 'er meself, in the van, only I knowed as that would be the last thing she'd ha' wanted,' he said. 'Worse than you taking 'er, if you see what I mean. It's been a real bad job for 'em all, that it 'as. What they can't abear is that it's caused talk about 'em, you see. Since it's been known on that Wendy were like to have this child, they ha'n't 'ardly been able to 'old their 'eads up, no'ow, specially as nobody knows who it belongs to. The talk 'ad all died down a bit, o' course, just lately. But now every ol' woman'll be peepin' through 'er curtains and seein' a sight more than there is to see. If you'd ha' took 'er 'ome, somebody 'ould ha' seen you, an' wanted to know what your part in it were. Sophie knowed that. What folks don't know, yer see, they'll make up,' he said. 'I'm got my own idea whose child it is — but then, so 'as everybody else. It 'ould ha' been a sight better for Soph' an' them if the silly gal 'ad let on from the beginning, but tha's 'ow it is. She wouldn't, it seems. The thing as they want to stop now is any more talk, so as it'll soon die down. If poor Soph' 'ad been seen gettin' out o' my van, it 'ould ha' set tongues gooin' again for weeks.'

He took a noisy gulp of his tea, picked up his spoon and began to stir it again.

'Ah,' he said heavily. 'It's Soph' 'erself as I'm concerned for, not the rest on 'em. If it ha'n't been for the rest o' 'er family, things 'ould ha' been different. That little ol' boy as 'as just bin born might ha' been our'n — well our grandson, by now, I reckon, but you know what I mean.'

I nodded, to show him I understood. I didn't want to break the flow of his unexpected confidences.

'Yer see, me an' Soph' was all'us sweethearts,' he said. 'But Soph' were the easy going one of the family, the one as 'er ol' mother could keep under 'er thumb. She di'n't like me 'anging round Soph', an' told me so. "Goo you 'um," she said to me one day, "and don't let me find you round 'ere no more." I told Soph' that night, as she'd 'ave to choose then, atween me an' 'er mother. But Soph' cou'n't make up 'er mind to leave 'er. So that were that.'

'But Kezia's been dead years and years, now,' I said. 'Why didn't you marry Sophie when she died?'

He shifted uneasily. 'I dunno. I reckon it were a sort of pride. I kep' earing that ol' bitch — beg pardon, missus — that ol' woman say "Goo you 'um" every time I thought about speaking to Soph' again. But I don't reckon it 'ould ha' been no use, anyway. She wou'n't ha' gone against her mother's wishes. An' anyway, it don't matter now.'

'It does matter,' I said, severely. 'It's a wicked shame for both of you to spend the rest of your lives apart, and face lonely old age, when you still care for each other.'

'Ah, but then I don't know as Soph' does still feel for me like she used to,' he said. 'Sometimes I think she does, but then again I'm frit to find out. We're p'raps better off as we are, for the time bein' at any rate.'

'Don't leave it too long,' I said. 'Why not risk it, an' try your luck?' I couldn't give Sophie's confidences away to him, of course. Nor, I realized, could I give her even an inkling of what he was saying to me. I could only encourage both of them in an oblique sort of fashion in future.

'You wou'n't tell 'er what I'm said, will you, Mis' Catherwood?' he said, suddenly blushing deep purple through his tan. 'I never meant to goo on like that, that I di'n't. I dunno whatever come over me.'

'Of course I shan't,' I said. 'But I do hope you'll think about how happy you and Sophie could still be together.'

'Ah, I shall that, 'cos I do, often and often, specially when I see her again close to again, like just now. But I can't do nothing about it — well, not now — not till all this is blowed over again. She'd think as I was sorry for her, and that would be the end of everything. I'm waited a goodish while a'ready, so I reckon I can afford to wait a bit longer.'

He got up to go, and I let him, bringing us down to mundane matters by asking him about the bill for the work. But as I ate my belated supper, after he had gone, I reflected that it had been a momentous day, and that the best of it had been Jelly's so unexpected declaration. If only there was some way I could let Sophie know. But perhaps she did know; perhaps she had always known. And, what would be would be, without my intervention.

It was, in fact, two or three days before Sophie could return to work, and only when she did was I able to hear about the drama there had been up at Hen Street the day Wendy's baby had been born.

When Daniel had warned Hetty's household that the time had come, Joe had not changed one jot of his sullen resolution not to have anything whatsoever to do with his daughter. Hetty's only reaction had been to say she would 'pray for guidance'. Only Sophie and Thirzah had shown the girl any consideration, and Thirzah's did not extend as far as sympathy.

Wendy, having been kept in ignorance of any sort of facts except what the school playground had provided, and still benumbed by what had befallen her, had not understood more than one word in ten of what the district nurse-cum-midwife had said to her on her pre-natal visits. So on that morning when the terrified seventeen-year-old had found herself with the first signs of impending labour, and had turned in fearful apprehension to her mother, Hetty had chosen to escape any maternal duty by staging a real berserk fit of ''sterricks' during the course of which she had pushed Wendy out of the door, thrown her clothes after her, and screamed at her to go and give birth to her bastard in a ditch like the whoring little bitch she was. It had taken all Thirzah's and Sophie's combined strength to overpower Hetty and lock her into the front room, where she continued to scream while Thirzah put Wendy to bed and Sophie went back on foot to Old Swithinford to fetch the district nurse.

It had been Thirzah, so Sophie recounted, who had in the end received the baby, cleansed and dressed, from the nurse's arms eight hours or so later. She had taken the bundle downstairs, till she came to where Joe still stood as stony-faced and unyielding as a gargoyle. And she had been filled, for once, with godlike inspiration. She had simply reached out and thrust the pliant little bundle into Joe's unsuspecting arms, giving the unwilling grandfather the choice of holding it or letting it fall. Joe, who in normal circumstances would not have hurt a fly, made a clutch at the baby, and held on. The battle was won.

22

Once recovered from the trauma of the birth of the baby, Sophie became herself again, with a glow of such contentment about her that she set the tone for us all. I sometimes wondered how much the scene in my kitchen had to do with it – but of course I should never know.

William was now installed in Eeyore's Tail; and it rather surprised us both, I believe, to find how well the arrangements were working. Both William and I had all sorts of commitments that did not concern the other, and till supper-time each day we barely knew the other was in the same house. William had made it clear from the beginning that he wanted to be in the flat in his own right as a tenant, so he made his own breakfast, and if at home, his lunch as well. But Sophie had made the decision that unless either of us had visitors, William and I should eat together in the evening, 'same as is only sensible,' as she said. She pointed out that it was no more trouble for her to cook for two than for one, and (with a reproving sniff) it was a good deal cheaper; and if we hadn't been brought up to think of such things, she had. I won't say we let her have her own way to please her, because it pleased both of us, too. Sophie left our meal in or on the Aga, and we ate it whenever and wherever we felt like it. From 7.00 p.m. onwards till bedtime, we behaved in the sort of relaxed fashion that any couple with their silver wedding behind them might have done.

I said to William one night that I couldn't ever remember being any happier than I was – so happy that I was almost afraid to admit it.

'You don't really expect me to say the same, do you?' he asked, quizzically. 'I am happy too, but I could be happier. And I wish you wouldn't say things like that. Why on earth should you be afraid? You really do have streaks of puritanism left in you. I think one of your great-great-great-great-grandmothers must have been chased round Ely Cathedral by Oliver Cromwell.'

'What you are suggesting, is that he must have caught her under the Porta – or I should not be exhibiting his puritanical genes, which I suppose is what you meant. I'll bet he wasn't half as much of a spoilsport as he is made out to be, anyway. Neither am I.'

He raised his eyebrows in mock surprise, and said, 'Well, I can't tell you how glad I am to hear it. Let me know when Jelly Bean has been booked to come to take down the hedge of thorns.'

'Idiot!' I said, and hastily changed the subject.

There came one Sunday morning so beautiful that I wanted to be out and about in it before the combine harvesters destroyed the golden panorama of the standing corn. I popped my head round William's door to tell him I was going for a walk, and he elected to come with me. The vacation was flying fast and he would soon have to be off to the States, so it was an unexpected treat for us both to soak up England together while it was at its most magical best. As we walked, I said that I hadn't had a visit from Johanna lately, and wondered how things were developing. He suggested that we call for a few minutes, if for no other reason than to scotch any plan she might have of coming up to Benedict's with a tale of woe as soon as he had left me, so to speak, at her mercy.

She was pleased to see us, and made us welcome in her newly furbished sitting-room, which William had not seen before. But I could see that she was a bit on edge, and remembering that it was Sunday, asked her if she was expecting Mr Ellington, because if so we would nip out again before he arrived. She nodded. 'And Bob – Dr Archer,' she said.

I drank my coffee quickly, and William took the hint, though Ernie had buttonholed him and begun on a long tale, wheezing and coughing with bulging eyes as a sort of punctuating chorus to his narrative. Before he had finished, the white Jaguar glided to the front door, and excusing ourselves abruptly, we rose to go. Johanna sprang to her feet and ran to open the door, and we followed, anxious to get out before they got in. So we were already in the passage-hall in time to see Monty Ellington greet Johanna with a hearty kiss, and to hear Dr Archer's well-bred voice saying in greeting, 'Well, fair lady? How's our patient this week?' as he put into her arms a huge bunch of expensive hothouse flowers.

'Oh, Bob,' she replied. 'How wonderful of you!' And as William said afterwards, her voice was so charged with warmth and familiarity that it was a wonder the flowers didn't melt.

'Oh, don't go,' she said, as I sidled past them in the narrow hall. 'I haven't introduced William to . . .'

'Sorry,' I lied. 'I promised to be home at noon to take an important phone call.'

'What on earth's the matter?' William asked, as I slowed down my pace once we were out of sight of the bungalow's windows.

'I don't know,' I said. 'Except that every now and then I have the most awful feelings about Johanna. It's as if I am playing with a kitten that may suddenly turn into a lynx. I don't know whether I'm afraid of it, or afraid for it. It's a kind of premonition that if you invite trouble, one day it will come.'

He was silent for a long time. 'You may be right, Fran, but if you are, there isn't a thing you can do about it. As far as Johanna is concerned, the moving finger has already writ in bringing you together. If you drop her now, it won't make a scrap of difference.'

'That's what frightens me,' I said. 'I don't want to drop her, anyway. I'm quite fond of her. If I weren't, it wouldn't matter so much — to me, at least. But don't worry about my bad manners and sudden exit just now. She wanted us out of the way, so that she could use her charm to the full to further whatever plan she has afoot at the present moment.'

I told him more than I had ever done before about the Johanna–Ernie axis, and felt a lot better for having voiced my misgivings. William brought to my story a much more pragmatic, male and worldly view than I was capable of. I was ashamed of my ability to blow things up out of proportion and said so.

'Let's forget her,' William said. 'I shan't be here next Sunday. By this time next week I shall be among the fleshpots of Boston's Hilton Hotel.'

'Which will be full of Johannas,' I said, miserably. 'Or worse.'

He stopped in the road, and looked at me half jokingly, but with an intent and searching gaze all the same. 'Am I hearing aright?' he asked. 'For a moment, you could have fooled me into believing that you could be jealous.'

His face creased into his enchanting smile, and he seemed so happy that it quite lifted my mood of apprehension. 'I don't know about feeling jealous,' I said, 'but the thought of fleshpots makes me feel ravenously hungry. Come on.'

'Something is giving you a most becoming colour,' he said wickedly. Drat the man. He was beginning to suspect the feelings I was trying so hard not to show.

After he had left for his conference, I was lonelier than I had been for a long time, and quite glad to see Johanna when she turned up one day. Monty was taking Ernie off her hands for the afternoon, and as usual had dropped her off to spend the time with me. We sat in the garden, at her choice — well out of reach of Sophie's ears, as I concluded afterwards.

'Still all well?' I asked.

She hesitated. 'I suppose so. I haven't been so free of money worries for years. I've only got to hint that I want anything, and I can have it. But it begins to worry me a bit. I thought — I honestly did, Fran — that he was lashing out on me like this because he was grateful for comfort and care and a bit of companionship. I couldn't believe an old man in his state of health could possibly have other ideas.'

'But he has?' I needn't have asked. I'd seen it for myself.

She squirmed with distaste. 'Oh, yes. Keeps catching hold of me and trying to rub himself up against me, or pulling me down on his knee when I take him a drink, and things like that. I have to go into his bedroom of course, when he's in bed, and I'm never sure what I'm going to see.' She grimaced with disgust, and I sympathized entirely.

'Then he caused a real scene the other day, when Monty came unexpectedly. Ernie was in his bedroom, and came out just in time to see Monty kiss me, as he usually does. They glanced at each other like a couple of stray dogs, and could hardly be polite to each other. I can understand poor old Ernie — he likes to think of me as his property. But Monty surprised me. He's always flirted with me, but he's never made any sort of approach — always the perfect gentleman. So is Bob, though he has got a roving eye.'

I was, as always, put off by her outright acceptance of her own sexual appeal to anything in trousers, while at the same time ruefully admitting that she was, after all, only acknowledging the truth. I knew she thought me as old-fashioned and strait-laced on the subject of sex as Sophie was, and liked to shock me, but in this her estimate of me was at fault. My reservations were that sex was something very special and precious, a crown — not a paper hat to be worn at any odd angle in any vulgar company.

'Why do you get yourself into situations — well, like Monty Ellington taking it for granted that he can always kiss you when he arrives? He wouldn't attempt to kiss me.'

She let out a peal of such childlike laughter at the incredible thought that I warmed to her again at once.

'I play the only cards I've got,' she said. 'Ernie staying on with me depends on me keeping Monty sweet. If that's the way to do it, so be it — as long as he doesn't get any other ideas. He knows I have a husband and I am well aware he has a wife. I'm sure that wouldn't matter a damn to him, and under some circumstances it wouldn't to me, either. But I am not throwing away my chance of getting out of Hen Street and back again into civilization for the sake of a roll in the hay with Monty Ellington or Bob Archer. I've got longer term plans than that.'

'Such as?'

She regarded me seriously for what seemed a long time, as if wondering how much she dare confide in me.

'I know what I'm going to say will shock you, Fran, but you asked, and with you I try to be honest. Ernie is crazy about me. There's no doubt about that — and if I play the very respectable married woman whose husband has let her into a difficult financial situation, I can keep him. In spite of his attempts to maul me, he doesn't really expect anything, for one thing because he considers me a cut above him, and for another because he believes me to be wholly virtuous, in the same way as you are, for example. In a way, he's old-fashioned enough to approve of me because of it. So I make him my care, and go out of my way to gain his respect. He's as proud of me when I show any sort of practical skill as if I were his daughter. I want to keep it that way. After all, he can't last for ever — and if I were his daughter . . .' Her cigarette had burnt itself out; she took her time getting another to replace it, while she let what she had just said sink in. 'Don't lecture me, Fran. I know what I want.'

'I wasn't going to,' I said. 'But I was thinking to myself of the old adage about the foolishness of waiting for dead men's shoes.'

'His wouldn't fit me,' she said, stretching out her gorgeous legs and waggling her pretty feet, today encased in expensive crocodile brogues. In spite of myself I laughed, remembering his huge, patched, shapeless footwear, and she looked relieved. She rose to go, saying that she had arranged to be home with the tea ready when Monty and Ernie got back.

'See you,' she said, and went off, swinging up the drive with the grace of a deer, her hair and colouring blending with the golden sunshine and the yellow fields like a corn goddess, a primeval woman in spite of her smart summer suit and her neatly shod, purposeful little feet.

A few days later, I asked Mary Budd to come up and have lunch with me. I knew I was assured of interesting conversation, and on this particular occasion, she needed no prompting. As soon as we had finished eating, she began to tell me about what she referred to as 'the horkey'. I had heard the word a good many times before the war, though even then it had been an anachronism; as far as I knew, it had meant the traditional harvest supper. I said so, and Mary took up her explanation with enthusiasm.

It seemed that though it had long gone out of fashion in most other places, with her encouragement the farmers in Old Swithinford had managed to keep it going right up to the outbreak of war. It had, of course, lapsed during the hostilities, but once the conflict was over, she had had the idea that the old custom could be revived with good intent and effect, and had found a lot of willing support. For the last five years, she had organized a get-together with enough resemblance to the horkeys of old for her to feel able to continue using that word. The evening consisted of a community supper with some sort of jollification to follow. The farmers supplied most of the food and drink, the women did the work, and Miss Budd herself was in charge of the entertainment. Tickets were priced reasonably enough so that no one should be excluded on the ground of expense; donations welcome, and all profit to the Save the Children Fund.

'The last Saturday of next month,' she said.

'So soon?' I said. 'How much do you want?'

She looked both hurt and dismayed. 'I wasn't asking you for money,' she said. 'I want you to come. You see, it began very well, but the last couple of years haven't been so successful, socially, that is. The farmers' wives have worked hard, the farmers have been just as generous, and the rest of us ordinary mortals have had a good meal and some homely fun. But the spirit has gone out of it. Last year I had increased donations, some of them quite large, but the people who gave them didn't turn up: some of the farmers, and some of the professional people. Of course I want the money for the Fund; but I also want to keep the community together, while I can. At least just once a year. I should be grateful if you would buy a ticket, but that isn't really what I want. I hope you will show up at the do in person – and enjoy it.'

I had my doubts. I didn't somehow trust that sort of forced *bonhomie*, with the Rector dancing with his housekeeper, and the doctor singing 'Why am I always the bridesmaid?' I had a lot of faith in Miss Budd's common sense though. If there was anybody who really understood the village, it was she.

'This year we've got something rather special: a real honest-to-God barn dance, except that I'm calling it a country dance for a particular reason. But it is going to be in a barn, as a horkey should be. Have you met George Bridgefoot? Lives in Swithinford, but farms the family farm here, and owns other land including the Old Glebe Farm, which has the most beautiful old tithe barn. George has been restoring it, and there it is, standing ready, empty, swept and garnished. It really was too good an opportunity to miss. It even has lighting, and the Rector has agreed to lend his piano, so all is going fine. Do say you'll come.'

I still hesitated to give her my promise. The thought of enduring a whole evening, sitting like a middle-aged and fading wallflower watching other people dance was anything but a pleasant one to me. I marvelled at Mary's energy and enthusiasm, considering her age. I saw that she was regarding me with amused understanding.

'I know exactly what you are thinking, Frances,' she said. 'You are wondering why I am still trying to flog a dead horse. But you see, village life — real village life — is not dead yet. Not quite. Before easy transport and modern means of communication changed everything, the people in villages had to rely on each other. And there were all sorts and conditions of men then, just as there are now. There were farmers and there were labourers, rich and poor, those with education and those with none at all; some voted Conservative and some Liberal, some went to church and others to chapel. They all rubbed along together, and the different groupings criss-crossed each other all the time — like in a country dance. Old Swithinford is like that still. But now we are all educated and all mobile, there's danger that there will soon be only two groups — a polarization between rich, Conservative, Church of England farmers and the few professionals on one hand, and the rest who vote Labour and go to chapel on the other. As soon as that becomes the pattern everywhere, there won't be any villages any longer — not proper villages. While I can I want to do everything possible to make people see what they're losing before it's all too late. I don't belong to any of the groups; I'm a sort of link, or a buffer, between them all. I belong to both of the potential sides, or to neither. Nobody can classify me. That's why I am still an asset to the community, even at my advanced age.' She twinkled at me, but I knew she was being serious on a theme she cared deeply about. 'Oh dear, am I boring you?'

'Far, far from it,' I said.

'Well, I don't often get a chance to ride my hobby horse with anyone who will listen intelligently. These are things we just can't afford to lose — and while there's life, there's hope. I believe that any community can really only function well through the interdependence of all strands of society within it. I do not believe in all this false modern so-called equality. Nobody who has taught three generations of children in a village school could ever truly *believe* such clap-trap, whatever lip-service they may pay to it. About all children being "created equal" I mean.

'I grant that "equality of opportunity" is a very different thing, and sounds good in principle – but what does it mean in practice? Can a child of a dim-witted couple who really only think in terms of beer and fags and bed ever get an equal opportunity with a child of parents, however poor, who give him love and attention? Or take somebody like poor Loddy Thackeray: he can never have equal opportunity with his brother, can he? That's really why I say that in some ways we have regressed, not progressed at all. In the sort of community Old Swithinford once was, there was a sort of in-built equal opportunity – the chance for everybody to do what he could do best as well as he could do it. To use his head or his hands or both to some general good and get some personal satisfaction out of doing it into the bargain. People have to be dependent on each other. We all are, whether we want to be or not, though we no longer acknowledge it. Look at you and Sophie – could you honestly tell me which of you depends most on which? But it's all politics now – so one mustn't point to living examples. Only old dotards like me think in terms of real people. I hate politics – which is why I want to keep Old Swithinford human as long as I can. Of course I know that it must change – but over my dead body! Closing village schools was what finally killed off all hope of retaining the best of rural values. Done with all the best intentions, but by people with no real understanding. Gosh! What a speech I'm making! Do forgive me, Frances. I can't think what came over me.

'I must go,' she said. 'I hope you won't think I'm running away because I have been foolish and unmannerly but I must use this fine afternoon to go and see the Rector, to make sure he has remembered that he has promised to let his piano be taken down to the barn before the man comes to tune it.'

'Who plays?' I said. 'Do you hire a band?' I had been forming a vague hope that perhaps I could be allowed to pay for the band rather than buy tickets and have to attend.

She snorted a laugh. 'Now who do you suppose plays?' she asked. 'Me, of course! Hire a band? Whatever next! One of these raucous modern "groups" wouldn't supply the right sort of music.'

'But won't the youngsters want to do the twist, or whatever the latest craze is?'

'Doubting Thomas,' she said. 'What makes you suppose that I couldn't oblige with a bit of rock or twist or whatever if it should be called for? But I really doubt that it will be. Many of those who will be present have at some time or other been my own pupils, and I shall rely on them all knowing how to Strip the Willow or lead off the Gay Gordons. Arthur and George Gawn will support me nobly, as usual.'

'Arthur and George Gawn?' I was astonished. 'What, lead the dancing?'

'Oh, no,' she said. 'I mean with the music. They are both simply natural musicians. 'Arf plays a fiddle that would almost rival Amphion's and make the churchyard yews dance; and Hully is no fool with a mouth-organ, but for the public dos he brings out his piano accordion or his father's old concertina. Wasted talent in a couple of country plumbers? Well, perhaps it is — but not if the rest of the community can make use of it. That's what I meant, see?'

And while my mind boggled at the thought of the two men that even Sophie had referred to as 'a couple o' bullocks' in the new role Mary had created for them, she was gone. There were so many things I still had to learn; but I thought gratefully that I could have no better teacher than Miss Budd.

23

I saw no more of Mary after that, because she was getting busier and busier as the horkey drew nearer and nearer. I hated to disappoint her, but I could not face the thought of going. In fact, I was dreading it so much that if it had not been for my knowledge that any day now I could expect William's return, I should have asked Kate to invent an emergency at which my presence was urgently and crucially needed. It was a measure of my feeling of cowardice, I think, that though I usually consulted Sophie when in doubt about any village matter, on this I hadn't, and I didn't.

When, though, it was drawing dangerously close, I sat in my lovely sitting-room one evening and told myself firmly that if going to a village 'do' to please a new but valued friend was part of what I had to pay for being so lucky, then I had to pay my dues willingly, and not try to escape them. I went to the telephone to ring Mary and ask her to send me a ticket, but before I had had time to pick up the receiver, I heard the crunch of a car on the gravel, and the letter 'F' sounded in the morse code on a motor horn. That had always been William's way of announcing his arrival at my door, since his very first visit to Benedict's after I took up my quarters there.

I could hardly believe my ears, because William was at least two days earlier than he — or I — had expected him to be. We hadn't corresponded since he had been away, except that he had sent me a postcard with the Hilton Hotel in the background, but with only one female in sight, and she looked like a fat grotesque dressed incongruously in long, tight Bermuda shorts, floppy open sandals, and a peaked baseball cap. Its message was plain. A shared sense of humour must be the best glue possible in any relationship, I thought. I had not known when exactly to expect him back.

I bustled about and got him a cup of hot chocolate — the drink he liked best of all when nobody else was there to see. He was as glad to be back, I think, as I was to see him, and soon went off to unload his things back into the flat. It was always kept ready for him to arrive at a moment's notice, Sophie regarding this as some sort of holy obligation because he paid her whether or not he was about to require her services. He was very tired, having flown home from America and driven from London airport. So all talk to catch up on the interval had to be left till the next day.

Over a late breakfast, which he had to take with me because his own cupboards were bare, I asked him about his travels. He was very non-committal — almost to the point of reticence. I was beginning to feel quite apprehensive, when he suddenly looked at me across his toast and marmalade.

'I think I don't want to talk about it because I'm so glad it's over that I want to forget it. It has been quite an experience for me to find out how much the events of this last year have changed my outlook. To tell you the truth, Fran, I've been bored and fed up most of the time. Till now, I've looked forward to the long vacations for most of the rest of the year — new places, new faces, new courses to run, new ideas. Now I know that all that was really only sugar on the pill — something I invented to make three months of non-routine time palatable. Anywhere was better than being by myself in the flat which was never really home. This year, I grudged every minute away from Eeyore's Tail, and Benedict's, and you. There were a few good patches, and one or two bloody awful ones. I don't want to talk about them. But the good patches were nothing compared with this' – he waved the toast about to indicate the kitchen in the house, the house in the garden, the garden in the village, the village in East Anglia, till a splodge of marmalade fell off and landed on Cat's head where she was gazing up at him in the hope of a titbit. She looked so indignant that we both laughed, and I grabbed her up and took her to the sink to clean the sticky mess off, very glad of the excuse to be able to turn my back on William and deal with the lump in my throat at the same time. It was all very well to feel so happy, but just how long were both of us going to be able to maintain the status quo without cracking somewhere?

'And what have you been up to?' William was saying. 'That is much more important.'

Forcing my thoughts down again, I launched into a tale of all the trivialities that had happened since he went, from the last visit of Johanna to the horkey and my own reluctance to be present at it.

'I'm afraid I shall hate it,' I said. 'I don't feel part of the village enough to go and join in properly, and I certainly don't want to go in a patronizing sort of fashion.'

'I'm looking forward to meeting your Mary Budd,' he said. 'I just remember her when she was young – I can't imagine her any different from what she was. Cheer up, Fran – let's go determined to enjoy ourselves, and see what happens. It may be fun of a kind I haven't had for years.'

'William!' I said unbelievingly. 'Do you really mean that you will come too?'

'You try leaving me at home,' he said.

At that moment Sophie appeared purposefully with a look that told us the kitchen was her province, so I went back to my study wondering what one wore for such occasions, and whether anything I had was at all suitable.

William had a good deal of work to do in preparation for the new term, and I had a deadline for a script getting dangerously close. We didn't spend a great deal of time together, though he came to tea the next time I invited Mary Budd, and they got on famously.

She took my question with regard to dress for the horkey quite seriously. 'We've deliberately called it a "country dance", not a "barn dance",' she said. 'Country dances have been held in barns, I dare say, since the Middle Ages. But "barn dance" is now associated with the films, and the American west. I hope people will understand the difference.'

'I see,' said William. 'You'd rather I came in a collar and tie than a loud checked open-necked shirt.'

She looked at William as a child looks at a sweet, all delighted anticipation and approval. 'Do you mean to say you are *coming* to my "do", Professor?' she squeaked.

'Dear Miss Budd, of course I am! In a good old-fashioned English collar and tie! But I don't know why it should cause such surprise. Am I not a resident of Old Swithinford? With as many ties to it as Fran has? In fact, I was here before she was, being the elder of the two. May I book a dance with you, Miss Budd?'

'I wish all the men in Swithinford were so gallant,' she said. 'I shall be at the piano all the evening, I fear. But if a chance to dance should arise, Professor Burbage, I shall certainly keep you to your offer.'

She turned to me. 'Dr Burbage has hit the nail on the head,' she said. 'What I don't want is for it to turn into an American-style square dance occasion. So please choose a pretty dress, in keeping with a barn dance, English style.'

'Will Johanna be present?' William asked later, when Mary had left.

'Can you imagine it?' I asked. 'It is just the sort of affair that she would do her very utmost to avoid if she knew about it. It makes me really mad when she puts on that superior townee attitude and looks down her pretty nose at all such village bumpkins as me.'

'What's she done to upset you?' he said. 'You keep hinting at dark doings somewhere behind the scenes.'

I told him the gist of her schemes. 'You can't judge her actions by your own standards,' he said. 'You can't see through her eyes. But let's talk of more exciting things. Have you decided what you are going to wear to the horkey next Saturday? Let's have a mannequin parade so I can help you choose.'

It was fun. I dragged out dresses that hadn't seen the light of day for years, and spread them out while we made a short list. Then I tried them on, one after the other, while William sat by the first open fire of the autumn in the sitting-room, and I made entrance after entrance in one frock after another, complete with accessories dug out of boxes, drawers and cupboards here, there and everywhere. On one occasion the interval between my appearances was so long that my catwalk turn was wasted, because the only greeting my entrance got was a muffled snore. But when he did come to, he said at once, 'That's it! You can't better that. It makes you look like a better-class of gipsy. All mysterious inner fire. You need some huge drop earrings, and a flower in your hair.'

'Some hopes,' I said. 'Don't forget I'm nearer fifty than fifteen.'

'I don't,' he said. 'I should hate it if you were fifteen. Promise me you'll wear that one.'

'If you say so,' I answered, glad that nobody else was by to hear me so meekly acquiescing to male domination. But I had begun to look forward to Saturday.

He went off next morning for a week of the interminable meetings that always precede the opening of a university term, and left me to the small concerns that seemed now to be taking over a large part of my thoughts. Such as Sophie's request to be allowed to borrow half a dozen sets of cutlery for Saturday's horkey.

'I had no idea you were involved!' I said.

'Well, I ain't, not really, not on my own, as you might say. But Thirz' is, and I all'us help her, specially this year. You see, Dan'el works for George Bridgefoot so Mis' Bridgefoot asked Thirz', like, to be in charge o' one o' the tables. She'll lend all the knives and forks and things she can, but I said as I was sure you'd let us have some. An' Thirz' sent a message as 'ow she 'oped you'd sit at our table. Miss Budd'll sit wi' the Rector at Bridgefoot's other table, seeing as George Bridgefoot's lending them the barn.'

It gave me enormous pleasure to be counted on in this way — treated as of the indigenous, rather than one of the professional fringe.

'Of course you can borrow what you need,' I said.

William rang on Saturday to say he would be later back than he had expected to be, only just in time to change and get us down to the barn in good time, so would I please be dressed and ready when he got here. I felt reasonably satisfied with my appearance. I heard William's car arrive and went down to wait in the hall while he changed. I felt somehow that I was a different me — just a woman again without the burden of years or too much weight or respectability or experience of life. I felt young — that's what it was.

'Stand still,' said William as soon as he appeared. 'I've brought you some earrings.'

He pinned them on me, and I turned to look in the hall mirror. They were only cheap, costume jewellery, but they were exactly right with the dress, and for the occasion. We locked up, and set off for the horkey.

24

From the moment the looking-glass showed me the gipsy William's earrings had made of me, the evening of the horkey seemed enchanted, as if some spell had given it an extra dimension. It became an iridescent bubble of time in which I was enclosed, suspended somewhere between reality and fantasy. I couldn't say now that it was like a dream, even if I wanted to rely on the cliché, because it wasn't. However bizarre the events of a dream may be, at least you are able to believe in them while still dreaming. The horkey was happening around me in solid, three dimensional fact, and yet it didn't seem real, and I was unable to believe it. All the same, it did have some of the qualities of a dream – that enhanced receptivity of all the senses, for instance, and the ability to register impressions and think about them on a detached plane while still functioning normally on the ordinary one. I suppose it is because I was bombarded with such a barrage of acute sensations that I am able to recall it all now with such detailed clarity.

It was a lovely, warm, mellow evening, and the doors of the beautiful old barn stood wide open as we approached them on foot, having parked the car in the adjacent field. I was embarrassed, partly I suppose because I was appearing in full view for the first time with William as an escort, and partly because I was afraid I might have paid too much attention to Mary with regard to dress, and overdone it a bit. I was a little apprehensive, too, of what sort of an evening lay ahead of us. In spite of my fondness and admiration for Miss Budd, I couldn't help a sneaking feeling that she was unwisely attempting to keep alive a bit of the past that was too near to extinction to be worth trying to revive.

I wished we needn't have come – but we had already reached the doors and William had given up our tickets. We were led to our appointed places at the Bridgefoots' second table. My nose was assailed at once by a smell that jolted me almost physically into the real past. There is no other scent on earth quite like that of an old barn where year after year for centuries corn has been stored. It is in the walls, the floor, the beams and rafters, and no amount of scrubbing and sweeping can eradicate the haunting association with harvests long since past. The smell that wafted to me that night as I stepped over the threshold — quite literally the thresh-hold — was the same that must have greeted Potiphar's wife when she slid into the Egyptian granary to beguile Joseph.

Then the sight before me almost brought me to an amazed standstill. The length and breadth of the barn floor was set out with tables all covered with white damask. Every one had a centrepiece of wheatears, barley and oatbells arranged in a cornucopia of twisted straw. At the end of each table stood a tea-urn. Until that moment I would not have been made to believe that so many tea-urns still existed in the whole of the British Isles, let alone in one small village. They were of every size and shape, in brass and copper and even of silver. Behind each tea-urn a farmer's wife stood ready to welcome her guests, supported by two helpers to serve.

Our temporary hostess was George Bridgefoot's daughter-in-law. He and his wife were at the next table, at which Miss Budd, the Rector, Dr and Mrs Henderson and another couple I didn't know were already seated. Behind our hostess Thirzah and Sophie hovered like a couple of animated Dutch dolls. They were scrubbed and polished till their faces shone as if they had been varnished. I was struck by the family resemblance between Sophie and Thirzah to-night — the black sleek hair drawn back without an errant wisp from a centre parting, the high cheekbones and the hollows under the polished, shining cheeks. Both seemed a trifle rosier than usual, probably as the result of recent exertion, though no doubt the many kindly-intended inquiries about Wendy and her child were also a little responsible. In deference to the occasion, they wore grey lisle stockings and low laced-up shoes, and their dark dresses were covered with identical bibbed aprons in blue and white checked gingham.

In the few seconds it took to walk the half-dozen yards from the door to the table I had collected and collated all these, and other, vivid impressions, while still acting as normally as was expected of me. There were the sounds, too — the clattering of crockery and cutlery, of chairs and benches being scraped back, of a general hubbub of voices from which some rang out clear as greetings directed especially towards us, and others we were not supposed to hear filtered through to lodge in my ears.

'They say he's her second cousin or something' I heard clearly from somewhere behind me, and from the next table, Mary Budd's stage whisper as she sought to refresh the Rector's failing memory for names.

'No, not Burdock, Rector. Burbage — Bur-bage,' just as she might have corrected a child stumbling over his reading primer.

The organization of the cold meal was superb. The food had been prepared before in the various farmhouses, and transported in wicker clothes-baskets or tin baths, covered with freshly laundered cloths. Whoever used either wicker clothes-baskets or tin baths nowadays? Were they still kept just for occasions like this? Plates piled high with homemade bread were being placed on the tables, and as we sat down, Sophie leaned over from behind and put right in front of me a dish of butter that was to the eye a bowl of butter roses, so perfectly formed as to be indistinguishable at a glance from the one real rose set amongst them on their bed of real rose leaves. I caught Sophie's eye and thanked her wordlessly for memories long neglected of the cool feel of thin petals of butter being lifted from a bowl of iced water. Butter sculpture was an accomplishment Kezia had learned in her youth as a dairymaid, and had used to grace Grandfather's table on the rare occasions when he entertained. While she was making her sculpture, she would give Jess and me a bit of butter to play with, while we tried to emulate her beautiful creations. I had no idea that Kezia had taught Sophie her craft, but of course I might have known it. Could any of the scene spread out before me still exist in ten years' time?

There appeared in front of each of us as if by magic a plate piled high with the traditional cold meats of rural suppers — home-cured ham, pink roast beef, cold steamed chicken, pork-pie. The aroma reached my nose, and saliva gushed into my mouth, though I had not known I was hungry. Now I felt ravenous, and in no ladylike fashion, either.

There was a scraping of chairs, and a sudden hush. Sophie and Thirzah, caught with a plate of meat in each hand, lowered them on to the table without a sound like the old campaigners in this field that they were, and clasped their folded hands together. At the top table, George Bridgefoot rose. Not the Rector? The next moment I knew why.

'Welcome, all,' said George, briefly and to the point. 'We shall now sing grace.'

Miss Budd went to the piano. I felt that we were all her pupils, standing as generations had stood before her, 'hands together, eyes closed' every lunchtime in school, to sing the same words to the same tune.

'Be present at our table, Lord.
Be here, as everywhere, adored.
Thy creatures bless, and grant that we
May feast in paradise with Thee.'

Certainly feasting in Paradise could have little edge over the meal that followed. I enjoyed every mouthful, making conversation with the other people at the table, and still being able to gain vivid impressions of all sorts of other things happening around me. I was like one of those huge dish-like astro-telescopes, receiving willy-nilly all kinds of bits and pieces from the stars, incomprehensible at the time but full of meaning if and when they could be deciphered.

There was beer and shandy available for the men, and tea for anybody who wanted it — just right to end such a meal, I thought. But how had they conjured up those urns of scalding tea?

Looking towards the end of the barn, I saw a shirt-sleeved Jelly taking the emptied urn from Sophie, and disappearing. Minutes later he was back with the urn replenished from some outer source. I never did know from whence. Ned, also in his shirt sleeves, Dan'el, and others were likewise engaged. The team-work was miraculous, but of course they had been doing it, on and off, since they were teenagers. And before that, they had helped their fathers and mothers, their grandfathers and great-aunts — I kept coming back to it. This was continuity!

When the Rector had said grace at the end of the meal, we stood up and retired (with our chairs and benches) to the sides of the barn, and watched another minor miracle of organization as tables disappeared, cloths were folded up, dirty crockery stacked in the baskets emptied of food, and the dining hall turned into a dance hall. Miss Budd was fussing round the piano in one corner, and Arf and Hully, perspiring a bit in unwonted collars but otherwise quite businesslike and calm, were unpacking their instruments and conversing with Miss Budd like seasoned troupers in the world of entertainment.

While we remained in this limbo between the two halves of the occasion, Sophie and Thirzah appeared before me, no longer Dutch dolls but their solid Sunday selves again, with coats on and hats pinned to their buns of hair.

'We're just come to bid you goodnight, like,' Sophie said.

I was, in some curious way, utterly disappointed. 'Why Sophie,' I said, 'surely you are not going so early?'

She nodded. 'We're a-gooin' to do some o' the washing up, first,

like, in the Rectory kitchen,' she said. 'Then we shall get off 'ome.'
(She nearly said 'um', and I sensed in her slip into the brogue of her
childhood some measure of hidden distress.)

'Why don't you come back and enjoy the music, if not the
dancing?' I said.

'No thank you. Not tonight,' said Thirzah, taking it upon herself
to reply for Sophie. 'Come on, Soph'! We shall 'ev Dan'el a-waiting
for us.'

Sophie signalled from her wide grey eyes that she was going
against her will, but Thirzah stumped out in such an 'Onward
Christian Soldiers' fashion that it brooked no disobedience. At the
door, Sophie stopped to speak to Jelly, who, I thought, had been
waiting there on purpose. 'Come you on, Soph',' I heard Thirzah
say. 'Whatever next!' The mantle of Kezia had certainly fallen upon
Thirzah, as far as poor Sophie was concerned. Jelly looked crestfallen,
too. I guessed he had been looking forward to tonight for a chance
to sit with Sophie a while and have a bit of a chat with her, if no
more. I couldn't really imagine either of them on the dance floor, in
spite of what Miss Budd had said. Then I found her compact little
body beside me, asking me if I had enjoyed my meal. While we
chatted, and William was being introduced to some of the other
farmers, I noticed how the barn was clearing of people, with good-
nights being said at the door. I was quite concerned on Miss Budd's
behalf, but she was quick with an explanation.

'It's mostly the older ones leaving,' she said. 'They'll go home to
supervise the washing up in their kitchens, and the sorting of china
and so on. Most of them will be back by about ten o'clock. And in
the next half hour or so, there'll be others to take their places –
those who couldn't come to the meal or wouldn't, and those who
feel they must show up for an hour or two, like Pamela Thackeray.'
Her lip curled.

She was right though, of course. Small parties began to drift in,
and before she went back to the piano, there was a full complement
again. The duties of Master of Ceremonies were being shared by
George Bridgefoot's son Brian, and Michael Thackeray, whom I had
met that night for the first time.

'We shall begin, as we ought to, I suppose, with a barn-dance,'
announced Brian, adding, 'And if anybody doesn't know how to do
it, just follow Rosemary and me, or Michael and Peggy. We've been
well schooled so as to show you how.' (Miss Budd took few
chances!)

The musicians struck up, and away went the two lead couples. In a minute, the floor was full.

'Will you dance with me, Fran?' said William, his eyes on the couples as if almost afraid of my reply. Did he really think I should refuse? From that moment on, the evening became utterly enchanted.

I was waltzing with George Bridgefoot – a huge man who in spite of his sixty-five years was surprisingly light of foot – when Johanna appeared in the doorway, with Ernie Ambrose shuffling behind her on his sticks. She was wearing a white frock with a vivid blue and green scarf knotted skilfully at her throat, and my first vivid impression was that she looked like a candle, her red head and tawny eyes aflame at the top of a slim translucent column. I was surprised, to say the least, to see her, knowing how she despised village functions in general, and to speak truth, I was not at all pleased. I did not want to be bothered with her, nor to have to share William with her, tonight. I was afraid Johanna's presence would spoil it.

She came to us, while willing hands found Ernie a comfortable chair close to the piano.

We made a few introductions, though most of the indigenous villagers knew who Johanna was, and therefore, of course, all about her paying guest. If they felt any surprise at her presence among them, they didn't show it.

'He would come,' she whispered to me as soon as opportunity came. 'Somebody sold him some tickets one day when he was out with Monty, and he insisted on us coming. Hired a taxi from Swithinford to get us here! I refused point blank to come to the bean feast, but he seemed so set on being at the dance for an hour or two that I had to give in. But it really isn't my scene, is it?'

I introduced her to Miss Budd, who had heard all about her, of course, but had never actually met her socially before. There were only a few minutes between dances, and it was during one of these brief, chatter-filled gaps that Pamela Thackeray made her entrance. She was in full evening dress with the usual touch of sultry Spanish about it, and was flanked by two men, both in dinner jackets. A single glance identified her husband, with his scarred and puckered face and rather obvious wig. He appeared ill at ease, and looked sullenly resentful. The other man was Jack Bartrum.

The impact of their arrival was almost physical, like a sudden blow to the head. The silence it produced lasted only a split second, but as the talk flowed again my acutely tuned senses gathered impressions from all round me — sniggers and earthy remarks, for instance, in voices only just subdued reached me clearly from my side; Michael Thackeray, too, and he turned away in dull red embarrassment, not having had time yet to regain his carefully nurtured self-control. Miss Budd looked purposefully blank. I heard Johanna suck in her breath, and say in broad Cockney, 'Gorblimey!' with a wicked little laugh. I shivered. As the folk all around me would have said, a goose walked over my grave. If Johanna was the naked flame, here was the gunpowder. I could only hope that tonight, at any rate, they wouldn't come into contact.

Pamela was explaining to somebody in her slightly loud voice that they had been to a dinner somewhere else, but had felt they ought to leave early 'to support the village hop'. The condescension was not well received, especially by Miss Budd, but Mrs Thackeray appeared quite impervious to any change of atmosphere.

Loddy sat down by the wall, looking grim and patient, while his wife swept into a valeta with Jack Bartrum. He was a good dancer, and it was obvious that she was trained at 'Old Tyme', which was having quite a revival. The exaggerated movements and arch posing were competition, not enjoyment based, except that she was thoroughly enjoying giving an exhibition. Johanna danced with William, and as Brian Bridgefoot came to claim me, we passed in front of Ernie Ambrose. His gaze never left Johanna's lithe little form, any more than Ned's did, where he stood watching the dancing. Both men appeared rapt in admiration, starkly different from Loddy's gaze riveted on his wife's antics. When the dance ended, Johanna went up to Miss Budd, sure of herself and at ease. It was as though Pamela's showing off had brought out all the best in her, the fun-loving, capable, warmhearted side for the moment obscuring its obverse. This was the Johanna I loved — and it came almost as a shock to me that my thought was a true one. I was very fond of her — and tonight everything was Technicolored.

'Would you like a rest, Miss Budd, or a chance to dance?' she said. 'I'll play for a spell, if you would.'

I was afraid she would be rebuffed. Did Mary know how talented Johanna was?

It was William who robbed the situation of any potential disaster. 'Miss Budd, I claim my dance!' he said. 'You promised, you know, if there was a chance.' Mary was obviously caught in a quandary. She rose reluctantly, with one eye on Arf and Hully, to see how they would take the change. She needn't have bothered, I think. They were both dazed with the delight of making music again, and wouldn't have cared if Old Nick himself had suddenly appeared on the piano stool. Johanna ran her hands over the keys. 'What do you want, Miss Budd? A waltz?'

'No,' said William without hesitation. 'A polka.'

Miss Budd was hesitating – a most unusual thing for her. Michael Thackeray, who was taking his turn as MC, attempted to force the issue by announcing, 'Ladies and gentlemen, by special request, the next dance will be a polka.'

Johanna whispered to Arf and Hully, and they plunged into 'O, dem Golden Slippers' with a will. A look of pure delight spread like a beam of sunlight across Mary's face as she reacted to the expertise in Johanna's fingers. A few other couples had taken the floor before William finally persuaded Miss Budd to let him lead her out. The atmosphere changed, charged with a new excitement, as realization trickled through that their old mentor was indeed going to let her back hair down and dance with 'the professor'. The moment they were well committed, Johanna and her allies changed to 'You Should See Me Dance the Polka', and the joke was not lost on the rest of the gathering. They began to clap in time to the beat, and one by one the other dancing couples retired to leave the floor clear for William and his sprightly partner. Only one other pair remained – Pamela and Jack Bartrum, made conspicuous, and a bit ridiculous in any case, by their formal dress. Everybody expected them to retire as well, and at first believed that they had not noticed what was happening. To me, it was obvious that Pamela was simply not capable of understanding. I was again aware of that shiver of apprehension. This evening was proving too perfect, like those glorious long summer days that farmers distrust as 'weather breeders'. Seeds were being sown that might, like parsley, go to the devil three times before they germinated, but germinate they would, somehow or other. Michael Thackeray, a moment before all smiles, was scowling, and I heard him murmur to his wife, 'God Almighty! Has the bloody woman no sense?' Loddy sat with his head against the wall, a ventriloquist's dummy figure in his dress suit with a stretched, artificial grin set on his face, and his bow tie slightly awry as he plucked nervously at it. I knew from Mary Budd what an intelligent, sensitive man lay beneath the scarred mask, and of the psychological results of his disfigurement.

Johanna brought the dance to a crisp finish, and Mary gasping for breath, tottered on William's arm back to the piano stool. Roars of applause rang round the barn, and Pamela, two fingers on Jack's sleeve, turned this way and that, acknowledging it with deep curtsies.

A little later, fear gripped me again. The MC announced a ladies' choice, which would be a waltz. I grabbed William's hand to claim him at once, because I knew Johanna well enough to realize that she was without scruples of the kind I would have had about pinching somebody else's partner. She was certainly not the type to be a wallflower, and I wondered who she would choose. I could hardly believe my eyes when I saw her making her way purposefully round to the spot where Jack Bartrum stood talking to the Faireys. Surely she couldn't be going to risk a public snub?

His back was towards her as she approached him, and with a thrill of apprehension I observed Pamela making her way towards him from the opposite direction. Much as I disliked all I knew of him, at this moment I felt sorry for him. I was watching Johanna, and it occurred to me that she was not risking anything. She was completely sure of herself. She knew quite well that compared to Pamela's overdressed and self-advertised glamour, she was Cartier compared with Woolworth. Perhaps I deprecated the streak of vulgarity that enabled her to make use of her superiority — I honestly don't know, but I rejoiced in it all the same. Bartrum was caught off balance by surprise. Johanna had stopped in front of him, but did not speak. Pamela took hold of the sides of her full skirt, dropped another elaborate 'Olde Tyme' curtsey, and said, 'May I have the pleasure?'

William was waiting for me to join the dance, but I could not move. The man was looking in an agony of embarrassment from one to the other, when Johanna said in a low voice, 'I apologize. I made a mistake. I understood it was to be a *ladies'* choice.' I hoped there was not going to be a scene; but it appeared that no one else had taken in the innuendo — certainly not Pamela, though probably Jack had. Mrs Loddy Thackeray had a hide like that of a rhinoceros, which made any poisoned verbal arrows as innocuous as paper darts.

I wondered afterwards if Johanna had planned it all, to avenge Pamela's behaviour about the polka. Or had she really intended to hold out the olive branch to Bartrum?

I was relieved to flow into the waltz, and put the unpleasant little incident out of my mind, but all the same I watched with interest to see what Johanna would do. With complete aplomb she simply walked forward, past the fuming Bartrum and his waiting 'lady', to where Jelly still propped up the wall, and asked him for the dance.

I almost had to cling to William for support when I saw that he accepted — it had simply never entered my mind that Jelly would or could do anything that I did not already associate with Sophie. He was not an accomplished dancer, but he was no blunderer, either. Then, I reflected that in all probability he would not have succumbed to any other woman in the barn. Johanna set the pattern, and men followed.

Ernie, leaning on the piano, was waving a five-pound note at an astonished Miss Budd. 'This is for your fund, if you will play a special request for me,' he said.

'What a marvellous idea for making extra money!' she answered. 'Why have I never thought of it before? Special requests at five shillings a time. I can't possibly take five pounds.'

'I'm offering it to you,' he said. 'Play "I'm For Ever Blowing Bubbles" just for me.'

'I'm afraid I don't play very well by ear,' she said, still looking dubious.

Johanna was quick off the mark. 'You take the money, Miss Budd,' she said, 'and I'll play it for him.' She sat down and began to play, and Ernie, standing beside her, leaned on the piano and attempted to sing the banal lyric, gasping and bubbling and very painful to watch. I thought that few people would hear what words he managed to get out, but I remembered it too well not to know what they were — about bubbles, like dreams, floating high and beautiful until suddenly they were gone. Oh dear! Poor old man. His dreams at the moment were all about Johanna, who was as beautiful as a soap bubble and just as likely suddenly to disappear.

Poor Johanna, too? It wasn't all honey to be like she was, though I thought she had been happy tonight. I had been, and I still was, utterly, deliriously happy. I hadn't realized how much I had missed the sheer animal delight of dancing — which I had given up when I married a non-dancer after the war began. I couldn't help but wonder, now, how on earth that had happened. Especially when everybody else was still dancing madly to forget why all potential partners were suddenly wearing airforce blue — at least, that's how it had been in East Anglia, which was just becoming one huge airfield. It had been a sad time for lovers even before the war began — you met somebody on a dance floor who for one evening was everything you thought you had been looking for — and after the dance you arranged to meet him outside the cinema on Saturday, only to find that he did not show up. Then you learned from one of his friends that he had been posted nobody knew where, or, worse still, had crashed and been killed on a practice flight. Perhaps that was why I had left home, and gone north . . .

And I had never had William as a dancing partner before. It was as though we only had one mind and one pair of feet between the two of us.

But even such evenings of enchantment as the horkey must end.

We offered to give Johanna and Ernie a lift home. Johanna stood in the barn doorway, throwing a wrap round her shoulders against the night air. Ernie, struggling to keep his balance with two sticks, was solicitously trying to help her, his adoring old eyes never for a single second leaving her glowing face.

Jack Bartrum passed, on his way out with the Thackerays. The look he gave her was one of speculation: he had probably taken the incident earlier in the evening as an invitation. I had seen the same look in his eye before when it had rested upon her.

We dropped Johanna and Ernie off, and drove on home. The half-moon was just setting, and the night was soft and luminous, with Benedict's like a ship at anchor in an ocean of trees. William stopped the car in the drive for us to enjoy the sight of it.

'What a lovely evening,' I said. 'Bless Mary for making me feel young again.'

William turned towards me, and put an arm round my shoulders, pulling my head towards his own. 'I wish it didn't have to end here,' he said, kissing my ear. 'I can think of other ways of saying goodnight.'

So could I. The whole evening had been one of pure physical delight, and with William's face so close to my own, and the touch of his lips still tingling on my ear, I just wanted to give in. The thought of finishing this wonderful evening lying in William's arms was almost more than I could bear. He took his other hand from the wheel, and turned my face towards him. I started to speak, but he closed my lips with his own, and we clung and held each other for a long moment, star-high. Then he let me go, and we sat, in silent communion with love and each other.

'Sweetheart,' he said, with his lips still close to my ear, 'why do we have to go on pretending? Are we fooling anybody but ourselves? I can't pretend I don't love you. You can't fool me, after that, by pretending that you don't feel the same about me. Need you keep up the pretence? Who would know?'

I caught the hand that was stroking my face, and kissed it. But I had regained control of myself. 'We should,' I said. That was the hedge of thorns. The sexual mores of our youth. My virtue and his honour.

I felt him wince at the finality of my answer. I knew that he understood, as probably nobody else could, or would, why I couldn't take the modern way out and throw convention to the winds.

'It could be years, Fran,' he said. 'Tell me why it matters.'

'Do I have to? It's because we have so much, I'm afraid of grabbing more in case we lose what we already have. Like the boy with the apples in the fable: in trying to reach the biggest one from the top of the tree he dropped all the rest. If he had waited, he could have had that one, too, perfect and not bruised or spoilt. That's what I want.'

'I wish I had your strength of character,' he said. 'I want you now.'

'Darling, no more than I do. But I want it perfect. It couldn't be, yet – I might still have to be prepared to give you up to Janice. I couldn't – afterwards. We've got to go on as we are. Haven't we?'

'I shall have to, if you say so. I daren't even kiss you again.'

He didn't try. If I was disappointed, I was also relieved. I wasn't sure my resolution could have held out.

'Come in and let's make some coffee,' I said. 'You'll be glad tomorrow morning that I am still only your old frump of a cousin who pretended she hadn't any interest in the proposition.' He kissed my ear again, and drove up to the front door.

We had come a long way tonight. That kiss had given me away, and he knew we stood on equal terms, now. If it made some things worse, it would make other things better.

I had to admit that my refusal was really because I was me – the me I had been so glad to discover again. And it was 'me' he loved. I had been right to hold back. How had I been able to hold out, when everything in me had craved for him as much as he for me?

Being me, I still wanted to be able to look Sophie in the eye without any feeling of shame.

25

I woke next morning worrying that I had been too optimistic last night, in thinking that after what had happened, it would be possible at all for William and me to maintain the situation as it had been. But there were only two alternatives; for William to move out, or for us to try. We should go on trying. I hoped he had come to the same decision.

When we met again at supper-time, it was a rather silent meal, and neither of us wanted to discuss the horkey, but the first slight strain of over-stretched emotion gradually wore off a bit, and after supper we listened to some music and didn't talk. We had been up late the night before, so we went early to bed after the ritual shooting of the bolt on my side of the door. It seemed almost an insult to William, but I thought privately that if there was any danger, it was of me creeping into his bed, not the other way round. I doubted if he would ever broach the subject again, unless something occurred to change either the situation or my resolve.

I had worried that someone was bound to tell Sophie about Jelly dancing with Johanna; but to my great relief, when she came on Monday morning, she was her usual self, full of how well the horkey had gone off, and asking if I had heard how much 'Miss' had made for her fund. Nothing there to worry about. I told William at supper-time, that if this lovely weather lasted, I had every intention of taking a day or two off from my work.

'Splendid,' he said. 'I'm up to date as well. Let's make a holiday of it tomorrow. Let's go to the seaside for the day.'

I was so taken by the idea I could have cried with excitement. 'Hunstanton,' I said. 'Like we used to go once a year when we were children.'

'Huns'ton it shall be,' he said. 'I'll ring up the Lion and book lunch. Can you be ready by nine o'clock?'

I was childishly excited at the thought of seeing those strange red-and-white cliffs again. Besides, I felt that William's suggestion was a sort of earnest that we could go along as we had been doing before Saturday evening's lapse, in good companionship and friendship that was really a sort of marriage without sex. Quite the opposite of the modern trend.

In the middle of our lunch at the Lion, I remembered Sophie's birthday — only two days ahead. I had done nothing about it, which was a matter of much moment, as I knew that she would be considerably hurt if I did nothing to show her that I remembered, though she might pretend to despise modern birthday customs. Finding an acceptable present might be difficult but I had to find some sort of token.

I put my dilemma to William, who was tucking into a huge slab of kirsch torte with the gusto of a man quite content with the world as it was and most things in it. He looked at me over a forkful of cream-laden chocolate cake.

'A pot plant,' he suggested. 'The biggest aspidistra in the world.'

I laughed. 'She's already got that,' I said. 'It really is huge because it was already old when Sophie inherited it from Kezia. But I think you've hit it. A pot plant it shall be. I shall have to get it today, though. Bother! That means going into the town.'

'So what? The day's our own.'

A good one, too, so far. We had driven direct to Old Hunstanton, and from there we had walked along the beach, under the cliffs, towards the pier. It was surprisingly warm and sunny for the east coast, but it was already late September, and though it was a beautiful day, the beach was well-nigh as empty as it used to be on the very rare occasions in the past when William, Jess and I had been allowed to join the village Sunday-school day trips to the sea. We found on these annual outings what 'going to the sea-side' was all about — fat and elderly grandmothers and aunts paddling with their skirts tucked up round their waists; beef-dripping sandwiches (gritty with sand) eaten with gourmet delight while Sophie and her sisters munched with equal pleasure through the ham and tongue ones we had willingly exchanged. Ginger beer out of a bottle with a marble in its neck which we eyed as longingly as Tantalus might have done the unobtainable food, remembering instructions that glass bottles must never be broken on the beach because of the danger. (Other children broke them 'by accident' for us, sometimes.)

William and I almost cried with laughter at the memory when we passed the exact spot on the beach where Kezia had once lost her dignity altogether. She had been paddling with some other women, all swishing their bare feet in the sea and enjoying the unaccustomed feeling of cold water between the toes. A very fat lady from the village trod on a sharp pebble, and stumbled. Her behind took Kezia amidships, and tumbled her over just as an extra large wave rolled in. Next moment, a mazed-looking Kezia was on her feet again with her skirts lifted high and her dripping blue bloomers clinging tight to her wide buttocks, above which her faded pink corsets with their criss-crossing of lacing back and front were displayed to our goggling eyes. In the train going home that day she had padded herself under her skirts with clean newspaper, assured on all sides by the other women that sea-water never caused chills. We nudged each other with our elbows and giggled like the brainless little idiots we were, reminding each other with each elbow-dig that we had actually seen Kezia's knickers. How were the mighty fallen, that wonderful day!

Such delightful occurrences were very far removed from our annual 'official' holidays by the sea on the south coast. Those times were so carefully planned and mapped out for us, so rigidly controlled, so formal, so dignifiedly middle-class, so restricted by the wishes of parents, that for us children who provided the excuse for such large expenditure they were merely boring gaps to be endured till we could return to the general pleasurable excitement of summers spent with Grandfather.

We left the Lion and strolled into the town in search of a florist's shop. We passed a jeweller's shop, and I stopped to look in the window. (Is there a woman who can walk straight past a jeweller's window?) I looked for the tray of second-hand trinkets that almost always lies somewhere among the display of more expensive modern offerings. Apart from the chance of a bargain, I was always moved by the pathos of that second-hand tray. Who had those rings, bracelets and brooches belonged to? What joy and delight had they been the symbols of, when new? For what reason had they been disposed of? I always felt that each and every one of them could probably tell a tale better than any novelist could make up, if it could only be extracted from the heap of precious metal and stones lying so forlornly ticketed there.

My eye was caught by the glow of a pair of coral-drop earrings. Victorian, without doubt, mounted in gold and very beautiful; too delicate for my robust looks, but they absolutely pleaded to be hung against Johanna's creamy neck. I had a tremendous urge to go straight in and buy them for her, an urge so strong that reason went only a very little way to demolish it. Why on earth should I feel that I had to lavish an un-Christmas, un-birthday gift on somebody like Johanna who was being showered with much more expensive presents all the time by a doting old would-be sugar-daddy anyway? Yet I still wanted to go in and get them, seized by some superstitious belief that they had some important significance in the general scheme of things. I gave myself a metaphorical shake, and turned to go. William was standing patiently by my side. I had forgotten altogether how much men usually hate women's propensity for window-gazing, and looked up at him guiltily, surprising a look of such warmth and affection – no, of such unequivocal love – that I understood why it was I wanted to rush round buying presents for Sophie and Johanna: I had to share my happiness today with somebody before it overflowed into sentimentality and spoilt everything.

'What's the matter?' asked William, startled into awareness of my overcharged emotion. 'Have you seen something you want?' He looked so eager that I was quite sorry to have to disappoint him.

'Not for myself,' I said, and pointed to the earrings, in my embarrassment pouring out all I had been thinking about Johanna, though reserving to myself my reason for wanting to buy everybody else presents.

'Don't spoil a good intention,' he said, quite soberly. 'It's usually a mistake to kill instinct with reason. Look, we've got more exploring down on the beach to do yet, and time is flying by. You go on and find a florist and get Sophie's plant. Wait there with it till I come to pick you up – there can't be many florists close. We'll take it to our car by taxi. I'll go in here and find out how expensive the earrings are, and if they are not too bad I'll buy them while there's the chance. You can please yourself afterwards whether or not you still want to give them to Johanna. If you don't, I think they would make a lovely Christmas or birthday present for Katie. So off you go!'

I obeyed, and spent ten minutes trying to find a plant that would not die for want of light, or be suffocated by the plethora of other things surrounding it on the top of Sophie's chest of drawers. William arrived in a taxi almost at once, and we had soon deposited the plant in the boot of our own car. Then we went back to the place, remembered of old, from where we could climb down to the bottom of the cliffs. We sat down with our backs to them, and stared out to sea. The warmth, the peace, the solitude, the ease were beyond all expectation. Words were intrusive, and we sat in silence while the sea rolled away from us to its appointed limit and began its relentless return. A speck of sand alighting in my eye caused me to reach for a handkerchief from my handbag, but William caught my hand and held it in his own. I blinked the sand away, fearful of appearing to withdraw.

He spread out my fingers one by one, stroking each in turn until he reached the third. My wedding-ring had worn a deep groove in that finger and was almost obscured by the bloodstone Wagstaffe ring which I had worn constantly since my father had died. I rarely took either of them off, or gave them a thought; now I looked down at them on the hand lying in William's, almost surprised to see them there. William pulled at the signet ring, and it slid easily up my finger, leaving the wedding-ring exposed.

William raised his gaze from my hand to my face, compelling me to look back at him. 'Did you love him very much, Fran?' he said.

What answer could I make? Truthful it had to be, and I wasn't sure what the truth was. I groped for it in my mind, and for words to put it into.

'I thought I did,' I said at last — 'or I shouldn't have married him. And we were happy, I think. But I don't *know*. How can you measure love, or happiness? As far as I know, there's no standard for either.'

I didn't want to be disloyal to Brian, or to his memory. He had given me two beautiful children, and it had not been his fault that he had had to leave me so much alone, even while he had lived. My only criterion for measurement was comparison — with what it might have been if Brian had been William, and that I could not say. He understood, and said it for me.

'But not so happy that it couldn't have been better if circumstances had been different.'

I nodded.

'I'm sorry, Fran. Sorry for making such a mess of things for both of us.'

'It isn't your fault, any more than mine.'

'It is now. You're free. Most women in your place would give me an ultimatum. I know what I ought to do — what most men would do — but I can't bring myself to go back on a solemn promise, even if there were not other difficulties about divorce. If she would only ask, it might be different. How you must despise me!'

'I don't!' I said hotly. 'I love you as you are, and I don't want you to be anything but yourself.'

William lifted my hand and kissed the palm, carefully avoiding the finger that bore my husband's ring. He bent each of my fingers separately back over the palm as if to keep the kiss safe there for ever.

'When you expect to be killed before another morning,' he said, 'you don't stop to ask yourself what you are doing. My heart was never involved with Janice. How could it be? I gave her everything else, but what I didn't have, I couldn't give. You had my heart all the time.'

I nodded again, staring out to sea. He had said everything for me, too. I knew now why I had always felt my marriage to Brian somehow incomplete. A bit of me had never gone into it, because, though I hadn't known it then, it had been left with William.

'I have absolutely no right to say any more, Fran, but I must. I am a dog in the manger. I'm afraid that while I dither about doing what both of us seem still to regard as "the honourable thing", some other man will appear — and take you from me. I want a pledge from you that you won't let that happen. Will you marry me, Fran — if and when the time comes? And until it does, will you pledge me with your heart, that I think belongs to me already, just as mine belongs to you? I need an answer, sweetheart. Please.'

He was smiling, but I knew how serious the moment was. I couldn't speak, but I held his eyes and nodded again, so that the tears that I had been trying to hold back spilled down over my face. He opened my hand again and planted another lingering kiss there, before sliding the heavy old signet ring back into place. Then he mopped up my face with his handkerchief, as if I were a child, and sprang to his feet.

'Come on, let's go along to the end of the pier,' he said, and I came crashing down from the high peak of romance to find myself a rather too plump female covered in sand and trying to get to her feet without emulating Kezia's display of underwear. William reached down a hand to help me up. He didn't seem at all aware of our bathetic plunge from romance to reality, and set off down the beach with gigantic strides that had me running to keep up with him. He looked like an elongated cork released from under water, bobbing about in the air in an ecstasy of freedom.

We got to the pier in silence, and started to walk along it, straight into the sunset.

I had forgotten that curious phenomenon that somehow the two of us now seemed an integral part of — that standing on the east coast just there and looking out to sea, you can watch the sun sink into it, against all probability and all reason. We reached the end of the pier, and leaned on the rail. The sky ahead was aglow with a Turneresque riot of colour, framed in East Anglian space. Surrounded by frilly clouds of delicate pinks and mauves, the disc of the sun slipped down through washes of duck-egg blue and lemon yellow towards a reef of orange-red crimson that floated on the horizon. We watched, standing close together, until the golden ball was poised to slip away behind the reef. Then William dropped his hand over mine as it lay on the rail. Gently he pulled at the old signet ring until it came right off. I made no protest, entranced and enchanted as I was by the sunset's magic, when he pulled at the wedding-ring next. To my surprise, that, too, yielded and slid up over my finger, helped, no doubt, by the fact that the evening had begun to turn chilly, and my hands were cold.

I looked up at William, who stood quite still, looking at the little gold circle that now lay in the middle of his palm. Then he drew back his arm, and sent the ring spinning in a huge arc towards the sun. I saw it for a split second silhouetted against the sky, a speck of my past life in a vast ocean of light, before it dropped into the sea. I felt numbed, incapable of thought or understanding, accepting everything with the dazed commitment of a sacrificial victim in some ancient orgiastic rite. The sun, having turned from orange to crimson, was preparing to touch down into the sea. I didn't want to miss the moment of its going, but I could not take my eyes from William, who still held my left hand. His other hand was in his jacket pocket.

'Watch the sun,' he said, in a low, intense voice. It took an effort to wrench my eyes from his face to the glory before me; but at the moment when the rim of the sun's disc touched the horizon, I felt another ring being slipped firmly into place on my finger, and could not help but look down. It was simply another brand-new plain gold band. William lifted my hand and kissed the ring, and then putting his arm round me, turned both of us back to watch the sunset. We did not speak or move until the sun had gone. Then he spoke.

'I just couldn't bear to see you wearing another man's ring any longer,' he said. 'I am not asking anything else of you, Fran. It just makes me feel safer and happier to know we are both committed.' He pushed the old signet ring with its big bloodstone back into place. 'No one but the two of us will ever know the difference,' he said, adding anxiously, 'Fran, you don't mind?'

'Mind?' I repeated, looking down at my hand. 'Of course I mind! I mind *marvellously!*' And I flung myself at him, into his arms, so that our two figures merged tightly into one on the very edge of the day. He lowered his head and kissed me, the same long, clinging, passionate lover's kiss that on Saturday night had stirred every feminine instinct in me into vibrant longing.

We began to walk back along the pier, holding hands.

'Isn't it going to make it all more difficult?' I asked. 'To maintain the *status quo*, I mean?'

'Perhaps — I don't know yet. Look at it like this. We have been "engaged" to each other since we were children. My ring on your finger is a symbol of a love that has always been, and will always be, whatever happens now. We live under the same roof, and enjoy all the companionship that couples who have been married since they were twenty have. But often that is all they have left, because they have worn out their desire for each other with use. We haven't, my darling. We've still got all that to come. And it will, it must. If you can only wait for me.'

'For ever, if I have to,' I said. 'As I have told you once before.'

'Yes, I know. I won't try to tempt you again to come off your gold-standard. Only I am a man, and sometimes it's almost too much to bear. But I can't believe it will be long. I believe in Love.'

'So do I,' I said. 'That's the only sort of god I have any real faith in. Let's trust in him.'

'I said I wouldn't ask anything of you,' he said, 'but I do want just one small token from you, as a sort of constant reminder of our pledge to each other, just to keep me going. I have to guard my tongue all the time not to let out endearments, when Sophie or anybody else is around. Can I claim Sunday as a day of rest from the restriction on my tongue?'

'Darling Sir Galahad,' I said.

He stopped again and took me in his arms. 'My precious, darling, wonderful, sweetheart,' he said, planting a punctuating kiss on my lips between each word. A couple passing us turned and stared and tossed their heads in disbelief when they registered my figure and William's white hair. We burst into laughter, our hearts as light as the breeze that was just beginning to spring up.

'Come on,' said my white-haired swain. 'Race you to the pier entrance!'

We arrived home tired but happy. We sat one each side of the fire Sophie had lit before she went, like the old married couple William had envisaged.

'Can I have another look at the earrings?' I said.

The expression of utter blankness that crossed his face told me all, and I let out a sudden laugh that sent Cat scurrying from her place on my knee to take refuge under the piano.

'I forgot even to ask the price,' he confessed. 'When I got into the shop, the first thing I saw was a tray of wedding-rings. The idea came to me, and I acted on impulse.' His rueful gaze sought mine for reassurance.

'Well, at least we got Sophie's plant,' I said. 'We weren't meant to buy the earrings. They were just the means to an end that Fate had thought up for us.'

'No, not Fate,' said William. 'Call it Love.'

When at last I lay in bed, I took off the bloodstone, so as to be able to lay my face on William's ring, and I thought, gently but without regret or guilt, about Brian. That part of my past was dead. Whatever the future might bring, I was committed to it. I had made a bargain with Fate or with Love, and I must now stick to it.

Grandfather's old long-case clock in the hall struck the hour, bringing me back to the present with a jolt. It was only an hour since Sophie had left me, but my reverie had covered almost a year. What liars and deceivers clocks and watches are, pretending to measure out our lives for us in standard units of time! As if real Time had anything to do with the minutes or hours or days. For most of us, Time is measured by events. A split second was all it took for a gloved finger to press a button over Hiroshima, or to pull a trigger in Dallas, and the history of the world was changed. Then on the other hand, months drag on with nothing at all that future historians would regard as worth recording. And as with the world at large, so with our tiny corner of it, and with every single individual in it.

That night of the horkey, for example. Who would have suspected that during an evening of such innocent pleasure the spark of antagonism between two women could have caused an explosion big enough to wreck a lot of lives, and the foundations of a community at least a thousand years old?

Yet I could only look back on that enchanted evening through a glow of rosy nostalgia, as if it were a kitchen lit by an oil-lamp and filled with the scent of home-made blackberry jam. Like jam, my relationship with William had reached its setting point that night. It would keep, sweet and wholesome, till opened.

The fire crackled as flames rose from the red heart of it. Cat stretched her furry stomach luxuriously towards it, as if there was nothing more she could possibly desire. Yet I knew that if I were to stand up, she would spring to her feet and slink kitchenwards all eager anticipation pleading for an extra titbit as if on the point of starvation. Though not expecting anything, she never gave up hope. But the adage that in people hope never dies isn't true. Sometimes it is killed outright.

26

Summer was loath to die. It was the end of September and 'the nights were drawing in', but still the mellow sun warmed us all by day, and the moon that had been only half a moon on the night of the horkey had risen like a red balloon and sailed serenely up into a clear sky to take the sun's place as the harvest moon by night, so huge, so brilliant, so near that one could believe implicitly that only a century or so ago the corn had been garnered by its light.

I was deliberately avoiding Johanna, because I did not wish her to use her sharp nose to detect any change in me or in the atmosphere at Benedict's that would cause her to probe into the closer, more comfortable relationship between William and me that had settled over us since our day at Hunstanton. I rang Mary, wanting a chat with her, but she had gone away. So I worked on and off till Friday, when I had to go to Swithinford.

My bank was in charge of a manager nearing retirement who cared more for golf than finance, so the place was more or less run by his assistant, a man named Jevons. Against that dark, wavy-haired, bespectacled and pompous little individual, I had taken an instant scunner. I would always rather do business with the newest raw young clerk than have to sit in Mr Jevons' office.

There was, as usual, only one grille open when I went in, and several people waiting. I hated people breathing down my neck when I was conducting my affairs, and always tried not to do it to others. So I stood well back, waiting my turn. Then the door from the street opened again, and Jelly Bean came in. He was in his working clothes, with his old cap pulled well down, his collarless shirt open at the neck, and in spite of the warm weather, his feet encased in the huge rubber boots that he had worn when at work in my garden. Just at that moment, another clerk appeared behind the counter, and Jelly moved straight towards him, beating me to it. He had obviously not seen me, so I stood behind him, ready to speak when he should turn. He held a long brown envelope in his hands.

'It's the manager as I want to see, I reckon,' he said. There was a kind of nervous tension in his voice, and indeed in his whole person, that I had never seen before, and his face was flushed with a most uncharacteristic embarrassment. He looked so much like the proverbial fish out of water that I concluded Kid must be the businessman of the brothers' partnership, and Jelly completely unversed in looking after financial affairs.

The clerk looked him up and down, dubious. 'I don't know if that will be possible, sir,' he said. 'You have to make an appointment to see the manager, you know.'

Jelly looked dogged. 'It's 'im as I want,' he said.

Mr Jevons appeared on the scene. 'Can I have a word, Mr Jevons,' said the clerk. 'This — er — person is demanding to see the manager, without appointment.'

'Quite impossible!' said Mr Jevons, also looking poor Jelly over and deciding he didn't like what he saw.

'Are you one of our regular customers?' asked the clerk.

'No,' said Jelly. 'We bank at the Co-op. But I reckon I shall need another account, like, see. That's why I want to see the manager.'

Mr Jevons bustled up again. 'My good man,' he expostulated, 'if you really wish to open an account here, we should need a sponsor for you, and someone to identify you. You can't walk into a bank and open an account just like that, you know.'

His manner was more pompous and patronizing than ever, and my irritation with him, as well as my anxiety for Jelly, were rising every second. Could Jelly possibly be in some sort of financial difficulty that it was necessary to keep from his brother? I stepped forward.

'I shall be happy to identify, and to sponsor Mr Bean,' I said, as coldly and crisply as I could manage. Jelly turned and saw me, and the dull pink of his face turned to a deep brick red. I had, I feared, put my foot right into it, and didn't know how to get it out again.

'Good afternoon, Mrs Catherwood!' said Mr Jevons, brightly. 'Of course, if you know this gentleman and will be prepared to sponsor him, that alters the situation. I will see Mr Bean and Mrs Catherwood in my office in ten minutes, Mr Ashby. See that the necessary forms are prepared for signature.'

He swept off to the nether regions like a Grand Vizier about to witness wholesale executions, and left me and Jelly standing. Jelly had obviously made up his mind.

'Thank you,' he said, taking off his cap again. 'You see, it's about this 'ere, what come this morning.'

'There's no need for me to know your business,' I said. 'All I have to do is to swear that you are who you say you are, and that you are an ordinary respectable citizen who can be trusted with a cheque book, I think.'

He looked humbly pleading. 'Mis' Catherwood,' he said. 'I feel as if I'm got to tell somebody, like, what it's all about, an' if you don't mind, I'd as leave it be you as anybody I know. Only I shall have to ask you to promise as you'll never tell Soph' — well, not unless I ask you to, special like.' He was in a sort of excited distress, or distressed excitement, that I could see, but I couldn't decide which it was. I moved to the back of the room where the row of signing booths gave us a bit of privacy.

'I promise that I won't disclose your business to Sophie or anyone else,' I said. 'And if I can help you, of course I will.'

He opened the envelope with steady hands, and passed the contents to me. It was as well that I was leaning up against the booth. 'ON HER MAJESTY'S SERVICE' caught my eye and the word 'Congratulations'. Then I looked at the cheque attached to the letter. It was made out to Mr James Bean and the amount it was drawn for was ten thousand pounds.

'Jelly!' I gasped. 'How absolutely wonderful for you!' He took the cheque back.

'I dunno,' he said. 'I dunno as it is. Is it right, d'yer reckon, Mis' Catherwood? I mean, does it mean as I've really got all that? Or do I 'ave to do anythink else to get it, like? That's what I wanted to see 'im about.' He jerked his head backwards, to indicate the obnoxious Jevons.

'Of course it means what it says,' I assured him, still so dazed by the shock of such an unbelievable event that I was unable to think more than one step ahead. But Jelly was now talking freely, in a low, intense tone.

'It's that there dratted premium bond as I won at the whist drive,' he said. 'That's the trouble. You remember, p'raps, how down on me Soph' was for takin' it. She said bad would become of it, an' told me to my face as I hadn't got no business to be mixed up in gamblin'. If she ever got to know about this 'ere, I know she'd never speak to me no more. Just when I was beginning to think as you comin' back, an' her being so 'appy working for you again, and what's 'appened to Wendy an' everything might ha' made a difference to us again. But if Soph' ain't to know about this 'ere, I can't let nobody else know, either, not even Kid. That's why I left off work as soon as Kid had gone 'ome to his dinner, and sneaked off to put it in 'ere without nobody else knowing. Will they keep the secret, do you reckon?'

'If you tell them to, they must,' I said.

'Will you come in wi' me, an' see it done, proper like?' he said.

We were called in almost immediately, and Mr Jevons was such a mixture of polite deference to me and supercilious patronage to Jelly that I found myself wishing Johanna could have seen it, to add to her repertoire. The forms all duly signed and witnessed, he addressed himself to Jelly.

'And now, Mr Bean, if you will just tell me what it is you wish to open the account with, I think I can pass you back to Mr Ashby, and deal with Mrs Catherwood myself.'

'I want Mis' Catherwood to stop, and see it done proper,' said Jelly. And he handed the cheque to Jevons. Whatever disquiet or worse the knowledge of Jelly's secret might bring me in the future, I thought, it would be well compensated for by that moment when Mr Jevons looked down at the cheque in his hand.

'My dear sir,' he squeaked, holding his hand out to Jelly, who ignored it. 'Congratulations! We shall be honoured to look after your business for you. Well, what a thing to happen in sleepy little Swithinford! Why didn't you tell me what you wanted, Mr Bean? Wait till I tell the manager.' As Jelly was once again showing signs of stubborn distress, I stepped into the breach, and explained on Jelly's behalf his decision to keep the matter a close secret, that only the bank, myself as sponsor, and his new customer were to share. Then I left Jelly with him, occupying if not enjoying for the first time in his life the privileged position of the wealthy customer face to face with an ingratiating official, and went home.

The full burden of my knowledge really only made itself felt as Sophie hovered solicitously round me, getting my tea and chatting. It seemed to me that my relationship with Sophie had taken a new turn. On Saturday night I had apparently made her, without her knowledge, the arbiter of my sexual morals; now I was willy-nilly the custodian of her happiness – or at least of her hard-won contentment with the situation as it stood. I knew that I should be overwhelmingly tempted 'just' to tell William, and was equally aware that I mustn't. It was an all-or-nothing situation, and it must be all. If the news of his stupendous wealth, in comparison to his previous means, were ever to leak at all, Jelly would know it could only be from one of two sources. But I also dimly realized that the measure Jelly had taken could only be a temporary one. In spite of myself, I wanted to go back to yesterday, when this strange event had not happened, and my mind and peace had not been troubled with it.

I hadn't seen Johanna at all since the evening of the horkey, so one day in the next week I went round to Bryony Cottage on my way home from Swithinford. It was mid-afternoon, and Ernie was resting. I found Johanna sitting with Mrs Ellis at the kitchen table, once more engaged in 'unmuddling' a shapeless mass of knitting. Almost a year ago, I had first watched her performing this same neighbourly act. She was just the same Johanna, of course – yet very different. The urgency of distress had left her, and she was a much more consistent and secure character. The need to act all the time was now a spiritual rather than a material one. The presence of Ernie, his weekly payment and his extra-contractual generosity had seen to that. I liked this new Johanna a lot, and hoped the security might last long – at least till Dave came back.

Madge Ellis finished her cup of tea and left, and Johanna and I moved into the sitting-room with a freshly made pot.

'I'm glad Ernie's out of the way for a few minutes,' she said. 'It's so difficult to get a minute or two with you when he's not about.'

'How is he?'

'Fine – getting better in health all the time, I think. Monty seems quite delighted – at any rate he's given up looking for "something better" for Ernie. I must say it's nice to feel settled for a bit.'

'What if Dave comes home?'

She shot me a defensive look, much more like the old Johanna unsheathing her talons in case there was going to be a fight. 'I've told him to hold off a bit,' she said, carefully not catching my eye. 'There's too much at stake. I told you.'

I tried not to look either surprised or disapproving.

'More than you know, actually, Fran,' she said. 'It isn't just a question of waiting for dead men's shoes, as you put it once before. It's the present as well. I don't want Dave to upset it by coming back. After all, he stands to benefit in the long run.' She didn't wait for me to make any sort of reply, for which I was thankful. Instead, she said, 'Is Ned all right?'

'Ned?' I repeated a bit foolishly. 'As far as I know he is. He was busy in the garden when I came out. Why?'

'He hasn't been near here since the night of the horkey,' she said. 'Just simply stopped coming. Of course, he was already sulking, before, about what Ernie takes it on himself to do, and pay for – but he still used to come, Saturday afternoons and Sundays, same as always. Then suddenly, not at all.'

I knew instinctively that Ned could not, and would not, forgive her voluntary approach to Jack Bartrum on the dance floor.

'Not that it matters,' she said, 'except that I don't want the place to get overgrown again, in case I do need to sell in the spring. Ernie suggests we get the Beans to take on all the odd-job work. He'll pay, of course.'

I hope Johanna would never hear about Jelly's win! We could hear Ernie moving, so I made it my excuse to leave. Cat came to greet me, and I picked her up and put her on my shoulder.

'Midas has ass's ears,' I whispered to her.

'Talking to that there cat again as if it was a child,' Sophie said reprovingly. 'If the Lord 'ad wanted cats to be talked to, He'd a-give 'em a voice to answer back with. I can't say as I 'old with it, myself, putting dumb animals above their station, as you might say.'

'Oh, I don't know! But perhaps you're right, Sophie. What's for tea?' I said. I was learning how to mollify Sophie's worse strictures about Cat, because I knew quite well that part of her grouse against it was her own unwilling devotion to the demanding little creature. Half the time, it seemed that Sophie just parrotted Kezia's dicta without thinking at all. If it weren't for Thirzah, I might find a way even round the prejudice about the Premium Bond – but the time was not yet. I had to leave well alone for the time being.

27

It could never be said of Sophie that she indulged in scandal, but she had the average countrywoman's interest in the affairs of her neighbours, and was certainly not above a good gossip about them. The fine distinction between harmless gossip – if there is such a thing – and scandal lay in Sophie's own judgement of whatever it was she was talking about. If, according to her knowledge and view of the subject and the people involved, it was likely to be true, she regarded it as no sin to pass gossip on, even with allowable exaggeration. If she considered it unlikely, or blatantly untrue, she 'wouldn't let it pass her lips'. In this way, the ordinary goings on of the village and its inhabitants were pretty well sifted before they reached me. So I heard in detail of Dr Henderson's far from warm welcome when he decided to keep his eye on Mrs de ffranksbridge, of Ned's desertion of Johanna and of Jelly and Kid being called in to take over the garden at Bryony Cottage. It was at this point that a bit of malice crept in — but by Sophie's rule what she was about to say was fair comment, and therefore not scandalous.

'It's to be 'oped as she'll pay Jelly for what he does — well, better than she's ever paid Ned, by all accounts.'

'Now Sophie,' I said, as always needlessly rushing to defend Johanna when anybody else showed signs of attacking her. 'How do you know what she has paid Ned, or not paid him? Has Ned grumbled?'

'No, not Ned. But Eth used to, afore she was took. Said 'e never did get nothing for what he done up there. An' it's my belief as that's why 'e's stopped going, now.' She looked at me, as if to ascertain whether this statement was news to me or not.

'Ned has said nothing at all about it,' I said. 'And I can't see any reason why he should. It really is no business of mine what he does when he isn't here.'

Sophie has the most expressive sniff of anybody I know. She stood up, prepared to get on with her work. The sniff told me that she understood the rebuff, and doubted my truthfulness. I should be out of favour till coffee-time at least. I went to find her, and inquired if Mrs de ffranksbridge had given any cause for Dr Henderson to be worried enough to call unasked. Sophie toyed with her biscuit, crumbling it in her long fingers and staring at the bits, making up her mind how much to tell me.

'Well,' she said at last, dropping her voice a fraction to indicate that what she was about to say she would not have told me if I had not specifically asked.

'You know as after that do about them rings, Jean Howe said as she'd never go near the old you-know-what again. But all the same she's kept one eye and one ear open, like. Mind you, she's never been up there, because Pamela Balls-as-was still goes, and she often see'd Pam's car go by. Well, one day this week Jean was taking her youngest down to the surgery, an' while she were there, Loddy Thackeray come in with 'is hand wrapped up in a handkerchief, dripping blood all over the place. So the doctor had him in first. Jean 'eard 'im telling the doctor as 'e'd get Pam to drive 'im to the 'ospital as soon as she come back from seeing old Mis' de ffranksbridge. Seems Lod 'ad cut 'is 'and real bad when a carving knife slipped, or something. Anyway, when Jean got 'ome she felt bad about not telling Pam straight off as she were needed at 'ome wi'

231

the car, so she swallered 'er pride for Lod's sake an' went up to the Hall, but Pam weren't there. She see the old lady, an' accordin' to Jean she's gone real queer in the 'ead again, like she was afore. She said she hadn't seen Mis' Thackeray for more than a week, an' Jean said come to remember, like, she hadn't seen Pam's car go by, neither. Anyways, when Jean took her little ol' boy to the doctor again, she thought she ought to tell him what sort of a state she'd found old Mis' de ffranksbridge in, though she told 'im straight as she wasn't goin' to look after her no more. So by that, as you might say, 'e went 'isself.'

Sophie was, as I knew quite well, 'going round by Will's mother's' in order to tell me something else that she didn't want to approach directly.

'And what about Mr Thackeray? Is he all right?'

'As far as 'is hand goes, he is. Michael took 'im to the 'ospital, and they stitched it.'

'Now Sophie, what do you meant by "as far as his hand goes"? What else is wrong?'

Still she was reluctant. 'Well, I don't know the truth on it, so I don't like to repeat it. But Thirz' 'eard that when Pamela got 'ome, late, like, he'd got back from the 'ospital, and 'e asked 'er where she'd been. So she said as she'd been up at the Hall, visiting the old girl. "Ah, same as you 'ave been two or three times this last week or two," he says. "That's right," she says. "You know she relies on me." Then he ups an' tells 'er as 'e knows she hadn't been there at all. There were a terrible row, it appears.'

'Where was she then?'

Sophie shot me a glance such as an anxious mother might bestow on a child inquiring about the facts of life for the first time. 'Out a-meetin' Jack Bartrum somewheer, no doubt.'

'Jack Bartrum? Do you mean—' I paused. Surprise had got the better of my common sense. This really was scandal.

'Been goin' on now for a couple o' months or more, so they say. Everybody knowed about it except Loddy, it seems.'

I remembered Loddy's sullen, resentful look as he sat by the wall at the horkey, and wondered if he had suspected something even then. I had been in such a seventh heaven myself that I had failed to remember the vague apprehension I usually felt when things went too well. But the seeds of unhappiness had been there on that lovely evening, in Loddy's wife's antics, in Johanna's brush with Pamela and her unwise public approach to Jack Bartrum, in Sophie's disappointment and Jelly's dance with Johanna. Clouds no bigger than a man's hand, and certainly not threatening me personally. Yet every man's unhappiness diminished my own content. Such things hadn't impinged upon me when I had lived in town. This was part of the price I paid for realizing my dream and returning to Old Swithinford. Drat it, there I went again, always ready with my emotional cheque book before the demands came in.

I said to Sophie, 'What everybody knows often turns out to be a good deal more than there is to know, doesn't it? I expect it's all very exaggerated.'

'You asked me, else I shouldn't ha' mentioned it at all,' she said defensively. 'Jack Bartrum all'us 'as 'ad a bad name as far as women go, 'cos 'e's never married none of 'em.'

'And if you give a dog a bad name, you may as well hang it. I suppose the same applies to Mrs Thackeray. They would only have to be seen together once, and the fat would be in the fire.'

Sophie pursed her lips, but said no more. We let the matter drop.

I was restless. William was now staying away all the week. It certainly made Sundays special, and we both grudged the intrusion of anyone else on that day. It was a strange arrangement, for though he took the opportunity of letting an endearment slip now and then, by a mutual if unspoken agreement we kept things on a very cool, low level most of the time. But my unease was nothing to do with that; it had started the day I had met Jelly in the bank, and I could not throw it off.

The mornings were misty, now, and the nights decidedly cooler. I loved the autumn, and never minded the winter, though one can never help a twinge of regret at the end of another summer, and by November the metaphorical shadows can be as blue as the real ones under the hedges and trees are.

But before the end of this month, I should have another birthday, my first back at Benedict's, and I could perhaps have a family gathering over the nearest weekend. I should have to get on with making the arrangements at once. Cheered up by the thought, I decided to go to Johanna first, straight after lunch, on my way to Mary who had invited me to tea. In the afternoon, Ernie took a nap, so there was a chance of finding her alone. She was looking happy and relaxed.

'What's the news?' I said, really meaning, 'How is everything going?'; but she took me literally.

'Oh, things are fine, as they are now.'

'What happens if Ernie leaves you for any reason?'

She smiled. 'He won't. I'll see to that. Of course, he may die, but I have been assured that there would be a bit of income for me if that should happen. Don't look so disapproving, Fran. I shan't kill the poor old sod for the sake of a couple of pounds a week.'

'I wasn't looking disapproving at all,' I retorted indignantly. 'All I was doing was looking for a possible snag. If he's happy and you are happy, it's nobody else's concern.'

'Nobody but you would know anything about it,' she said. She looked at me hard, half smiling, half serious. 'We used to have a poker-work plaque on the wall when I was a little girl. It said, "A friend is one who knows all about you, and loves you just the same". That's why I tell you things, Fran. I tell you the truth because I know you well enough to think that you'll still love me as I am.' She didn't expect me to answer, and I was glad. She got up and went into her bedroom, returning almost immediately draped in a gorgeous new musquash coat that dwarfed her petite figure and gave her lovely legs a birdlike look, like those of a puffed-up robin on a snowy morning. The effect was breathtaking. While I took it in, she pirouetted and gurgled her urchin laugh.

'Now this, my dear old-fashioned friend, I cannot keep secret from you for ever, even if I would. Or from Pamela Thackeray. I have a lot to thank that nasty bit of work for.'

'Whatever can it possibly have to do with her?'

'Well, I've seen her going up the right of way towards Bartrum's a few times lately. Why she doesn't go the top way round I don't know, because this way she has to get out of her car to open the gate.

'Of course, since the dance there's been no love lost between her and me, as Ernie knows, and he saw her last week when she went up the lane. She was wearing a fur coat, warm as it was — one of those cheap-looking long-haired sorts, and Ernie called me to look. She took a long time about the gate, and I guessed she'd only put it on in the hope that I might see her. When she had gone, I said, "Well, she usually shows a lot better taste in clothes than that. I've always wanted a fur coat, but I've never had one because if I couldn't have a good one I'd rather not have one at all. I wouldn't be seen dead in a thing like that." So here it is.'

'You look a million dollars in it,' I said.

'It's a secret for the moment. You won't say anything about it, will you?' she said. 'I don't think he wants Monty Ellington to know about him buying it, yet.'

234

She went and took it off, while I sat wishing everybody wouldn't load me with their secrets. It could only be because I looked such an unimaginative lump of uninteresting womanhood, I thought, and felt far from flattered.

'Do you mind if we have a cup of tea in the kitchen?' Johanna was saying. 'Jelly Bean is at work in the garden, and I usually make him a cup, and ask him in to have one with me, before Ernie gets up. Jelly will talk to me, but he dries up if Ernie's there.'

Jelly came in and greeted me shyly, his cap in his hands. Johanna was 'joshing' him gently in her teasing fashion, and he was completely at his ease: more so, in fact, than he ever was in my kitchen with Sophie present. That Johanna attracted him was quite plain, just as she had done Ned, whose place he had apparently taken. With Ned, she had always acted the grand lady who could on occasion meet him on his own level for a bit of fun. Ned was nursing hurt pride and a sense of disillusionment, but there was no question of wrecked hopes of any kind, because I would have staked my life that he had never entertained hopes of repayment in terms of any personal favours from Johanna. Jelly had many of Ned's characteristics, but I wasn't so sure about him. There was a glint in Jelly's eye as he looked at Johanna that I had never seen in Ned's, though most other men were unable to hide it. Suddenly I was only too aware of the awful truth that if she did by any unwitting move knock aside his scruples, he was in a financial position to offer her as good a deal as Ernie Ambrose could, without requiring her services as housekeeper, cook and nurse. I prayed, if wishing till it hurts can be counted as prayer, that Johanna would be so intent in keeping what she'd already got that she wouldn't be tempted to use any dangerous wiles on Jelly.

Johanna said, suddenly and apparently without any ulterior purpose, that she hoped Jelly would tidy up the garage a bit. It hadn't been used since I had taken my car out nearly a year ago.

'Are you thinking of buying a car?' I asked, jokingly, because I knew of old that she was always thinking of buying a car, which was as far as she was ever likely to get, as she said.

She laughed. 'You know I'd give my eye-strings for a car of my own again,' she said. 'That's just a pipe dream, still. But once or twice Mr Ambrose has hinted that he would like to be a bit more independent, and when he found out I could drive, I believe it gave him ideas. Of course, it would be his car, so I suppose he'd only buy some big lumbering sort of model that would drive like a hearse.

Not that I'd grumble at anything on four wheels. But with Mr Ellington being in the car trade, I do think it's just possible. I'm keeping my fingers crossed.'

Jelly was interested. I'd heard Sophie say he had always liked cars, though all he ever drove was the old van he used for work. 'What sort would you have, then, if you could have just what you wanted?' he asked.

'Well, not the sort Mr Ambrose wants,' she said. 'Let me see now. I shouldn't look right in a Rolls or a Bentley, or even a Mercedes or a Buick. Jaguars are too masculine, I think, and Rovers are too sedate. I know! What would really feel like me would be a bright red sports car, a real rip-roaring hot-rod only not too big – like an MG or a TR2 or something. But can you see Ernie in one of those? So I shall be happy to settle for a little Austin 1300, or something of that kind, if I get the chance. But what a hope!'

Jelly finished his tea, and thanked her, and went back to work.

'I do think Ernie may have it in his mind,' she continued, 'but of course I keep quiet about it. You see, as it is, he's dependent on Monty to take him anywhere, on business, for instance, and that means Monty has to know more or less what he's doing, and I know that aggravates him, sometimes. Most of his money is tied up in Monty's car business, so you'd think Monty would be in favour of him having a car of his own, but so far he doesn't seem too keen on the idea. Maybe he's got a thing about women drivers.'

'I'd guess Mr Ellington's playing it a bit cool till he knows for certain that the old man's settled permanently with you,' I said. 'Old people can be very unpredictable, and change their minds at the drop of a hat.'

She nodded. 'Yes, I think that may be the reason, too. He really is very good to old Ernie, because after all the obligation is only a moral one.'

'Has Ernie no relations at all?'

'Yes – I think there's a nephew, somewhere, and a niece he hasn't heard of for years. They'll be in like vultures if he dies without a will, no doubt. Monty doesn't need anything – he's obviously got far more than he knows what to do with anyway. Which is why I see nothing immoral in me buttering the old fellow up, making him happy while I can, and getting what he likes to give me while he's alive. Then if he wants to make his will in my favour – but that's another pipe dream I won't indulge in. Oh! I can hear him getting up. I shall have to go and get him some tea.'

So I left, and as almost always when I drove out of the gate of Bryony Cottage, I had a confused mixture of feelings about and towards Johanna. She was shrewd enough to know that I did love her — but I feared her hawk beak and talons, not so much for what they could or would do to me, but for the effect on others less able to understand her than I.

Mary Budd was full of titbits of information, which were interleaved with more serious topics of discussion. It was all as good an antidote to my recent restlessness as anything could have been.

We discussed the horkey, and I said how much I had enjoyed it. So had she. 'Of course,' she said. 'Polka-ing with your William was the highlight of it for me.'

'He's not "my William",' I said, unnecessarily, angry at myself for feeling the colour rise to my face.

'No?' she said. 'Well, if you say so. But you're a foolish girl if he won't be one day. Anyway, as I say, it made my evening for me.'

'I think it was the high spot for almost everybody present,' I said, 'unless perhaps for Mr Thackeray.'

Her face clouded. 'Poor Loddy.' She seemed to be hesitating whether to go on. 'I'm afraid his marrying Pamela was a sad mistake — but she obviously seemed to offer him the chance of home and family, which I suppose every man wants. His father and mother weren't very happy at his choice, I know — but very happy that he would have a normal married life. After all, there's nothing wrong with him physically other than the awful scars on his face and head. The old couple offered to move out of their lovely old farmhouse to let Loddy and his wife have it, but she preferred a new, modern one. She would. There's no shortage of money, of course. That's what she was after, not poor Loddy.'

I nodded, to show I understood.

'So now,' said Miss Budd crisply and matter-of-factly, 'she has Loddy's money and the prestige of being Mrs Thackeray, and amuses herself elsewhere.'

'You mean Mr Bartrum,' I said.

'Do I? I don't know, and I don't care much who. I do care that Loddy is being made unhappy. And he is.'

'I thought he looked utterly miserable at the dance,' I said. 'But I don't suppose he cares for social functions much anyway.'

'No,' she replied. 'He never went anywhere till Pamela married him. But it's worse than that, I'm afraid. They've apparently taken to having violent quarrels.'

'Oh – that's probably idle village gossip, patchworked together because she danced with Jack Bartrum.'

She had been refilling the teapot, and she came back and sat down opposite to me looking very serious.

'Frances,' she said. 'I'm worried. I'm quite used to having my old pupils turn to me when they are in trouble. Usually I can take an objective look at what is bothering them, and often it is a storm in a teacup and of little consequence to anybody. But this is different. May I tell you, in confidence?'

She didn't wait for me to reply, and in any case I didn't know how to ask her not to.

'I was sitting here reading, last night, well after midnight,' she said. 'I know that must sound daft, but I really do need very little sleep, and I often don't go to bed till well after midnight. I usually lock the doors, though – but as it happened, last night I didn't. I heard a car stop outside, and loud voices, one of them unmistakably Pamela's. The next minute my front door opened, and Loddy fell in – literally – flat on the hall floor. I was scared to death because it might have been anybody, but I was so surprised that I didn't think very quickly, I fear. My first thought of course was that he was drunk. I heard the gears of the car grind as Pamela drove off, so I knew I was alone with him, anyway. My next thought was to get the police, but I was not really anxious to be mixed up in an affair of that kind, or to give Loddy away, if it comes to that. Then he began to pick himself up and I saw that his face was a mass of blood, running from a gash on his temple. So I took him to the bathroom, and cleaned him up. It wasn't really very bad, once I'd stopped the bleeding, but I should say he's got a good, ripe black eye and a severe headache today.'

'What had happened? Car accident? Was he drunk?'

She shook her head. 'They'd been out to some social function connected with her Old Tyme Dancing, it appears. She'd really made an exhibition of herself, flirting with some man who is her "official" partner for dancing medals, Loddy said. He'd been so embarrassed that on the way home he'd taken her to task about it, as well as about a few other recent happenings. He was driving, and they had had a terrible quarrel. Then she said she was going to throw herself out of the car, and leaned over her seat towards the back. Well, you know what farmers' cars are like – they've always got a variety of gear thrown in the back, and there was a big, heavy old tractor spanner lying on the seat. She grabbed it while he was stopping the car, just as they were going by here, and hit him with it as hard as she could. Luckily the car had stopped by then. He tried to scramble out of the car and saw my lights still on. She hit him again while he was trying to get out, and as soon as he began to stagger to my door, she got into the driving seat and made off.'

'How awful for you,' I said.

'Oh, you can't be in charge of a school full of youngsters for forty years without learning how to deal with emergencies. I got him cleaned up and gave him a cup of tea and then a good tot of whisky, and he was soon well enough to walk home. I offered to drive him, but all he wanted was to keep everything hushed up – from Michael and the rest of the family mostly – till he'd decided what to do. So he wanted to get back without anyone else noticing.'

'How lucky for him that it happened outside your door,' I said.

She nodded, 'Yes, I think so. He came to me as a child – to school I mean. Loddy was in and out of hospital till he was about eight, you see. He stopped with me till he went to a special school when he reached transfer age. A bright, lovely boy with a sweet nature, but of course with all sorts of other hang-ups mainly from shock in the first instance and embarrassment as he began to be old enough to realize his disfigurement. It had to come out somehow though, and it did, as time went by, in periods of dogged resentment, or occasional violent rages. Now he's a man, and a strong one. I didn't like the look in his eye last night at all. I tell you, Frances, I'm worried. I can't interfere, of course, but I can't just sit here and let two of my old pupils attempt to kill each other, can I?'

'My dear Mary,' I said. 'He probably went home and made it up with her in bed. Married folks do quarrel.'

'No,' she said. 'I'm afraid it's more serious than that. I know Pamela. I doubt if she shares his bed now – I guess that once she'd married him and got what she was after, she wouldn't give a damn about what he wanted. And I know Loddy, too. What she said to him in the car hurt him a lot more than the spanner did. She just turned the knife good and proper in the old wound about his looks and social inadequacy. I fear for them both. Oh dear!

'I shall feel better for having told you,' she said. 'Perhaps I may even be able to see some way to help. I ought not to have betrayed Loddy's confidences, even to you, I know. But really, keeping other people's secrets can be a burden, sometimes.'

As if I didn't know. I assured her, of course, that I would honour her trust in me, and left soon afterwards. As I drove through Old

Swithinford on my way back to Benedict's, the concept of village life had lost some of its charm for me. I saw it as I might have seen an anthill that had been kicked over by a horse, with all the normally busy workers scurrying about to save themselves and the future of their community from the awful, uncomprehended and to them incomprehensible disaster of being disturbed.

I forced my mind on to other things, mostly the celebration of my birthday. William agreed that evening that it was a lovely idea, so invitations went out by phone to Roland and his wife Sue, and Kate and Jeremy for the whole weekend. As almost always, Roland and Sue had a previous engagement, but Kate and Jeremy accepted with delight. Not the coming weekend, but the next. That gave Sophie and me plenty of time to plan and prepare.

The celebratory meal would be on the Saturday evening, late enough for the children to have been put to bed first.

'I shall ask Mary,' I said. 'But what about Johanna? I can't, and won't have old Ernie at the table – it is awful to watch him try to eat; and anyway, he isn't my friend – but she won't leave him behind, I'm sure. And I must have Sophie's willing help but it would spoil it all for her if Johanna were here.'

'What about asking her to bring old Ernie up for coffee and liqueurs after dinner?' William said. 'Then tell Sophie the arrangement and she needn't stay after she's washed up.'

'I think that's a good idea,' I said. 'You do have a way of solving my problems. I wish you could think of a magic way of getting Jess here, too. I feel sort of guilty about her.'

He got up from his chair opposite to me, and sat down on the floor at my feet, in silence, until the hall clock struck midnight. Then he looked up at me, and took my hand. 'Now, my sweetheart, it is Sunday and my tongue is unbridled. Please don't involve Jess in anything. The time isn't ripe. I haven't told her much about Benedict's, except that you have taken it over, and that I have the tenancy of a bachelor flat in it. She is stand-offish and distant about everything – even with me. She has tried so hard to made Greg into a success and it hasn't worked. She's gone bitter. I hoped you wouldn't ask too much about her. Time may help.'

'Poor old Jess,' I said.

'Darling – don't be too sorry for her. She has got a lot that we haven't.' He opened my hand, slid up the signet ring to the top of my finger, and planted a kiss on the plain gold band, closing my hand again when the bloodstone was back in place. 'I intend to go on doing that, my sweetheart, every Sunday till I can take the deed for the will. Forget Jess for now. Two's company. Jess was never happy as the third.'

28

It turned much colder by the weekend of my birthday party. To my great delight, Kate and her family arrived on Friday evening, and so did William, so we had the extra bonus of a whole evening just to ourselves. If I had asked for a special birthday present, it would have been that Kate and William would still get on with each other as they had before. They did and I thanked whatever gods there were that at least I did not have to face a choice between them.

When, on Saturday, Sophie announced that the birthday dinner was ready, we trooped into the dining-room for a meal into which Sophie had put all her devotion as well as all her considerable skill. In fact, she had excelled herself — and it was just the sort of happy, family occasion I had envisaged. We were back in the sitting-room before Johanna and Ernie arrived.

She came in wearing her new fur coat, sweeping through the door in a flurry of high spirits and fun, singing 'Happy Birthday to You' in her clear, musical voice, as excited as a child at a pantomime. Ernie shuffled in behind her like a clown attendant upon the fairy princess. Behind me in the sitting-room, William and Jeremy both rose to their feet. Kate, who had been sitting on the arm of her husband's chair, had to stand up to let him out. Only Mary remained seated, nonchalant and free, an observer on the sidelines. I glanced at Kate, seeing her for a moment as I hoped Johanna would: a tall, young woman well-covered by reason of contentment, goodlooking in a fresh and wholesome way, with a calm face lit from within by deep-seated happiness. 'Good enough to eat,' William had said when she had come down the stairs before dinner after putting the children to bed. But decidedly not beautiful in the way that Johanna was.

As she slipped off her coat in the hall, I saw at a glance that Johanna's whole outfit was a new one bought for the occasion — a cocktail dress in the most ravishing array of pinks, more suitable for dinner at the Ritz than a family party in a tiny rural village. But somehow Johanna never looked overdressed.

I felt a sudden premonition, an apprehension so sudden yet so strong that I wanted to stand in the doorway and block the meeting I had planned before it could take place. But of course, I did no such thing. I went on automatically making hostess sort of noises to my guests, and turned to precede them into the sitting-room. I was thus facing the men, and Kate, as Johanna made her stage entrance. I saw the expression on William's face as he moved forward to greet her, and that prompted me to glance at Jeremy. Kate was looking at him, too. Johanna saw him, and their eyes met. A change came over Johanna that it is impossible to describe. In the hall, she had been a most beautiful, cheerfully uninhibited, middle-ageing neighbour. From the moment her predatory eyes lighted on Jeremy's vigorous male-hood, she became a sinuous stream of allure. Kate watched as she saw her husband move forward to fall into and be swept away by the charm. The atmosphere curdled.

How I ever got through that evening of misery I don't know, except that I was conscious that William was aware of my distress, and always there, it seemed to me, to avert potential disaster by turning the conversation, offering fresh drinks, inveigling Mary into telling yet another tale, and so on.

In my innocence, I had envisaged that we might get Mary to play for some dancing — the room was quite big enough with the furniture pushed back — and that I might be able to persuade Johanna to do some of her lighting impersonations. But I had reckoned without the catalystic effect of Jeremy's young male beauty.

At about ten o'clock, Johanna sat down at the piano, and began to play. As if drawn by a pulley, Jeremy rose from Kate's side and went to lean over the piano. Kate got up, too, and said, in a low, brittle voice, 'If you will excuse me, Mother, I think I shall go to bed.'

Really! I felt more like slapping her than I had done since she was six and wouldn't swallow her ration of free cod-liver oil.

'Come into the kitchen,' I ordered her, urgently, and went that way myself. She followed, defiant, with a bright patch on either cheek.

'Don't be a stupid child, Kate,' I said. 'You know perfectly well that it doesn't mean anything.'

'I know perfectly well that I don't like your new friend, and that

242

nothing will induce me to stay in her company for another five minutes.'

'Kate, darling, don't spoil everything for me.'

'She looks more like spoiling everything for me!'

'You are being stupid! Don't be so childishly silly. She's old enough to be Jeremy's mother. But in any case she is just being herself. She can't help it. She's just a very beautiful and feminine woman who knows it.'

'She's just a bitch on heat. A sly, crafty, designing bitch! I congratulate you on your choice of friends.'

Her voice rose with bitter sarcasm, tears in her throat. This was dreadful. I *couldn't* quarrel with Katie. On the other hand, the rules that govern friendship and hospitality were ground into the very fibre of my being: Johanna had been accepted as my friend, and invited as a guest into my house. Besides, I knew that if Johanna sensed that she had aroused Kate's jealousy enough to cause her to lower her tail and run away to bed, the pink paddy-paws that had so far only patted Jeremy would turn into cruel talons designed to strike and hold fast.

'You stupid child!' I said. 'Get back in there and hold your own, before it's too late. In another minute I shall have to go and explain our absence, and then of course everybody will know there is something the matter.'

'I can't! I won't! They know now. Especially her.'

Her lip was quivering. I hoped she wouldn't cry, because if she did, I certainly should, and that would defeat all hope of us being able to cover the incident up.

'Am I intruding?' said Mary from the door. 'Kate, I hate to break into your conversation, but I've just been upstairs to the bathroom, and your baby is yelling his head off. I'm afraid I must have disturbed him.'

Kate was gone in a flash. I sat down and looked at Mary as a condemned man on the steps of the gallows must have regarded the messenger bringing a reprieve.

'What a mercy!' I said.

Mary nodded. 'I pinched him,' she said. 'It was lucky that Kate let me help her to put him to bed, so I knew exactly where to go.'

I began to laugh, hysterically, but Mary stopped me. 'Sh!' she said. 'Kate's coming.'

Kate reappeared with a screaming baby over her shoulder and a grizzling toddler clinging to her other hand, rosy from sleep, but

243

puzzled at being disturbed. Kate had gained complete control of herself again.

'I can't think whatever roused him,' she said, shushing the baby.

'It's just the strangeness, I expect,' I said. 'Then he cried, and woke Helen. Don't put them back for a little while. Let's take them into the sitting room.'

Kate understood. The moment that Jeremy caught sight of his family he jumped away from the piano, all concern and attention, as if some spell had been broken. He looked sheepish, like Bottom feeling for his erstwhile donkey's ears. Mary was doing a sort of schoolmistress act of organizing everything back to normality.

'I'm sorry to break up such a lovely party,' she said. 'But I am an old woman, and I'm afraid I must be going home.'

'And we must get the children back to bed,' said Jeremy.

I was afraid that Johanna would be too thick-skinned and selfish to take the hint; indeed, I believe she was, but old Ernie had also had enough of seeing her give all her attention to another man. He struggled to his feet, and said that they, too, must be going. Would William please call the taxi he had ordered?

William did, and brought in Johanna's coat. Though I was very disappointed for my party to end like this, I was quite sensible enough to let it.

Next morning, Kate was all contrition. We sat together in my study while William and Jeremy took the babies for a long walk.

'I am sorry I spoilt the party,' she said. 'But really, Mum, I am surprised at you getting yourself tangled up with a woman like that: I shall worry about you like anything, now that I've met her. She's got you just where she wants you. Look out that she doesn't pinch Uncle William from right under your very nose.'

'I don't think there's much danger for Uncle William,' I said. 'She's after bigger game, at the moment.'

'Hm,' said Kate dubiously. 'Jerry and I quarrelled, last night, for the first time ever about another woman. He was nasty because he knew he'd made a fool of himself. I was nasty for the same reason. When we made it up, I promised him I would come clean with you this morning. We love to come here, we love you and Uncle William – but we agreed that we won't accept any further invitations that would mean we had to meet Mrs Brooke again. As far as we are concerned, she is the wicked fairy at the feast. We can't risk what she might do to us, apart from the sort of phobia I've now built up about her.'

I sighed. 'Darling, you know that you come first,' I said. 'But I must say I don't care for being issued with an ultimatum like that. I've put my hand to the plough of friendship with her, to use a handy cliché. I don't see how I can possibly just withdraw it.'

'No need to. Just be careful. You needn't invite her in future when we are here, need you? Cheer up, Mum. All sorts of things can happen before we come again.' She came and put her arms round me, and we hugged and kissed each other, everything once more comfortable between us.

We heard the chatter of Helen's voice, and baby Andy's gurgling. The men were back. William opened the study door, and came in.

He came over to where we still stood, arms round each other, and put his arms round both.

'That was a lovely walk,' he said. 'Kate, my love, I have been lecturing Jeremy about experience being the best of all teachers. You should be thankful that he met a woman like Johanna Brooke in a situation where help was at hand. He knows now why and how such women are dangerous. They shine like brilliant lights, and rob you of reason. Just like the lights that wreckers used to hang on the rocks to lure ships to their doom. Fools like me make for them headlong, and get wrecked. A lighthouse is just as bright and more beautiful. You are Jeremy's lighthouse, Kate. He's a lucky man, darling, and he knows it.'

Before William had finished his monologue, Kate had turned her face into his chest and was crying quietly there. Then while Kate watched, he turned to me, and kissed me. 'Are you all right now, my sweetheart?' he said, and Kate knew he didn't mean her.

She looked from one to the other, and smiled, a deep warm, glad smile. He let us both go, and said lightly to Kate, 'I have an agreement with your mother, Kate, that on Sundays I can come a little closer to her, if only in word.'

'You are both idiots,' she said, 'but such darling idiots that I don't want either of you to change. Specially if it would make Mum feel like Johanna Brooke.' And away she went, to find Jeremy and her babies.

William became very practical all at once. 'We must get some lunch together, because they want to be off.'

As they were getting ready to leave, Kate said, 'Are you very busy at the moment, Mum?'

'No,' I answered. 'Not a bit, really. Why?'

'I want to be with you. Could you come down to us for a few days? Soon?'

'Why not?' said William quickly. 'I'll hold the fort here.'

'Tuesday?' suggested Kate.

I hesitated, but I wanted to go. So we fixed it, and I went.

On Friday, William rang. I could tell at once by his voice that something was wrong.

'Tell me,' I said, my mind galloping apprehensively from fire to burglary, from dire accident to Cat to the sudden and unexpected advent of Janice. But I was totally unprepared for what he did say.

'Nothing immediately to do with us,' he said, 'but I think Sophie needs you. Jelly Bean was killed in a car crash on the bridge on Wednesday night.'

29

William was waiting for me when I got home. Sophie had been to work as usual, exactly as if nothing had happened, so he said.

'Did you talk to her?' I asked.

'Oh, yes,' he said. 'Of course, I wasn't supposed to know that Jelly meant any more to her than any other neighbour, so it was a bit difficult. But I couldn't ignore the matter, obviously. So I told her how shocked I was to hear from Ned of the terrible accident. All she said was, "Ah, it's a bad job, and no mistake." And then after a pause she added, a bit grimly, I thought, "I just 'ope them as is responsible for it'll get what they deserve. God don't play 'is debts wi' money" – and then she stumped off.'

'What did she mean? Was the other fellow drunk, or something? Jelly's been driving that old van of his for years.'

William looked surprised. 'You haven't heard the details, of course. I forgot. Jelly was driving a brand new MG sports car that he'd only picked up from the garage half an hour before. Nobody else was involved at all. He was travelling very fast, it seems, and just drove into the bridge. It broke his neck and completely wrecked the car.'

I sat down. My knees didn't seem to want to support me.

'What colour was the car?' I asked – but I knew the answer before William told me. He was concerned about me; I could see my apparently stupid question had worried him. I tried to cover up my gaffe.

'What time is it now?' I said helplessly, vaguely aware that I must do something.

'Just after six. Why?'

'I'm going to see Sophie,' I said. 'Will you drive me down to the village?'

'Of course. But have a drink first — and something to eat.'

'No,' I said. 'Oh, William, don't you see? It's two days now since Sophie heard about Jelly, and she hasn't been able to say a word to anybody. As far as Thirzah is concerned, Jelly is taboo. Always has been. You weren't supposed to know how she felt. As far as Sophie knows, I am the only person who understands what this means to her. And I wasn't here when she needed me.' I was full of anger at the silly twist of fate that had taken me away unnecessarily just at the wrong moment. 'It's all that silly Pamela Thackeray's fault that I wasn't at home!' I burst out.

From the look of concerned bewilderment on William's face it was plain that he thought shock and fatigue had robbed me of my wits.

'Pamela Thackeray?' he said. 'Don't tell me you're involved in that, too!'

'Involved in what?' It was my turn to be bewildered.

'She's gone. Vamoosed about four days ago, so Ned tells me. And now I suppose you are going to say you know where she is, and why.' He set a cup of coffee in front of me, and I automatically picked it up and took a sip. It was scalding, and brought tears to my eyes.

I shook my head. 'It was a silly remark,' I said. 'I'll explain some other time. What do you mean, vamoosed?'

'Gone off with her dancing partner, and most of her husband's portable valuables,' William said.

'Not with Jack Bartrum?' I could have bitten my tongue, but it was out.

'So you do know more than you pretend to.'

'Look, William,' I said. 'I don't know anything except what my eyes and ears and Mary Budd told me. I'm sorry for poor Loddy, but it is no concern of mine. Sophie is. Let's go now, please. I'll walk back, so you needn't wait. I might be a long time.'

He brought my coat, and hung it round my shoulders. Then he closed his arms round me, and I was undone. I put my head on his chest, and cried. Jelly had been to Sophie all that William was to me. Perhaps we understood each other because for entirely different reasons, our situations were utterly similar. But William was still there — the feel and the smell of him, the sound of his voice, the knowledge that somewhere he existed all the time. Jelly didn't, any more. He was lying in his coffin, and Sophie would never again have the knowledge that he was out there waiting for her.

I pulled myself away and we went out into the dusk.

I knocked at the door of Sophie's cottage and she opened the door to me. She had been expecting me, I think, and showed no surprise.

'You'd better set there,' she said, indicating Kezia's vacant chair on one side of the old black-leaded range, in which a little fire glowed dully. Sophie poked it mechanically, then sat down in her own chair on the other side of the grate, and clasped her hands in her lap. An open Bible lay among the souvenirs and photographs on top of the cupboard at her side. She had no doubt been seeking solace from it when I knocked.

I knew better than to try to make any physical contact with her. I sat down, and tried to find words.

'Oh Sophie, what can I say?' I said at last.

'There's nothing to be said,' she answered. 'The Lord giveth, the Lord taketh away. It's His will. But I'm glad you're 'ome. I'm glad you've come.' The dull pain in her voice hurt me. She rocked gently, as if to ease some physical ache. I was filled with rage and hate — against Kezia, against her dead hand still held menacingly over Sophie, against their Lord whose moral restrictions, misapplied as they had been in this instance, had so much to answer for. If Sophie hadn't been so constrained all her life by that damned fifth commandment, she and Jelly might have had children to honour them.

I had to get Sophie to talk. Anything would be better than this dumb resignation. Besides, until I found out how much Sophie knew, or even suspected, about the mystery of Jelly's having been driving an expensive brand new sports car, I couldn't even guess the nature of her emotion.

'Tell me how it happened,' I said. 'I only got home about an hour ago. I came as soon as I could.'

She nodded. 'Well, I haven't been able to ask all the questions as I should like to, you understand,' she said. 'So I'm only been able to glean what I could from what folks is saying, like. Het came to see me today. She knowed plenty as she were pleased to tell me, but I wasn't goin' to let 'er see as I wanted to know nothing. Like as not Thirz' sent 'er to see 'ow the land lay with me. I ain't seen nothing o' Thirz', but she'll be at the funeral, I make no doubt. Apart from what Hetty said, all I know is what Ned told me this morning. It seems that Jelly went to Swithinford a day or two ago, an' see that new car in a garage show room. Then, night afore last, 'e left off work early and got dressed up an' went and bought it. Ned reckons it were 'cos 'e didn't know how to manage that sort o' car. Ned said 'e believes as Jelly just put 'is foot down 'ard on the exhilorator, like 'e would ha' done in 'is old van, and then 'e couldn't 'old it.'

As simple as that? So it wouldn't have happened if he had bought 'some lumbering model that drives like a hearse'. But it was only Ned's surmise, and the inquest might reveal some mechanical fault, or something. I hoped so. I found myself needing Sophie's Lord to pray to, to beg that that might be the case, and that Sophie might never know what I couldn't help suspecting.

She had fallen silent, waiting for me to reply. But I was concerned about a further question to which I needed some answer. Surely the whole village must be agog to know where Jelly got the money from to buy such a car on the spur of the moment. I had to take the bull by the horns.

'Sophie,' I said hesitantly. 'Are you wondering how he came to buy a car like that? And how he could afford it?'

'No,' she said, smiling wanly. 'No more than you are. I know, same as you do.'

I gasped with astonishment, utterly astounded.

'You *know*?' I said. 'How?'

''Cos Jelly told me, same as 'e told you,' she said.

She got up, and began to move about the crowded little room, picking things up and putting them down again. She picked up a photograph framed in seashells and stood looking down at it. I could see, even from a distance, that it was an old one of Kezia, and I was relieved to see Sophie's tears splashing down on it. It would do her good to cry.

'I know as she acted for the best according to her lights,' said Sophie. 'But 'ow did she know what was best for me an' Jelly?'

She laid the photograph back on the chest of drawers, face down. It was a pitiful gesture of defiance against the animosity of fate. Then she came back to her chair, and cried quietly into a large handkerchief. Her grief seemed all the more bitter for being kept in such a low key, even now. I would rather she had screamed, and sobbed, and railed. But after a few minutes she dried her eyes, and began again.

'A few days ago, just after you went, a knock came at my door after it was dark, and when I opened it, there stood Jelly. I were so surprised an' took aback, I couldn't believe my eyes. So I says, "You'd better come in, quick," I says. I didn't want nobody to see 'im standing on my doorstep so late at night. So by that 'e come in, an' set down where you're a-sitting now.

'Then 'e said, "Soph', are you still got them two bottles o' wine?"

'"Ah," I says, "I'm still got 'em, though 'eaven knows why. I don't."

'"Well I do," 'e says. "I reckon we're goin' to need 'em soon, after all. What do you say, Soph'?"

'Well! I could ha' fainted, very near. I set down 'ere, and Jelly told me about him winning a lot o' money with that premium bond 'e got at the whist drive. I couldn't believe it. "Well, you ask Mis' Catherwood," 'e says. "She knows. But I asked her myself not to say a word to you, 'cos I knowed 'ow you'd feel about it. An' I wanted to tell you myself."'

'Did he tell you how much it was?' I asked.

She shook her head. 'No — but 'e said as it was a nice little bit as would set us up proper with all that we wanted like. Might even ha' been as much as five hundred pound, the way 'e talked. "So what about it, Soph'?" 'e says.' She smiled at the recollection, savouring that moment of her delight over again. '"I know 'ow you feel about gambling, gel," he says, "and 'ow set you are about goin' against what your mother and Thirzah made up their minds for you. But Thirz' 'as got a 'usband of her own, and your mother's gone. It's up to you and me now, Soph' surely," 'e says.'

Sophie got up again, and wandered about. She came close to me, and looked down. 'I can't 'elp saying it, not to you, anyways. I knowed then as 'ow 'e was right, and they was wrong all the way along. I just couldn't say no to 'im no more. It come over me, like, 'ow 'e'd waited for me all these year, an' never looked at nobody else but me. An' I thought to myself as I'd been wrong to listen to Thirz' all this time, since Mother died. Then there was that money. It wasn't as if 'e'd stole it, or anything. You said you didn't think as it were really gamblin', either, to have these 'ere bonds or whatever they are. An' I thought to meself that when things go wrong, we say, "It's the Lord's will." But we don't ever say that when things go right. We don't give 'Im Above any credit for such things as Jelly winning all the money. An' if the Lord had arranged it so as Jelly could come an' ask me to marry 'im, who was I to go against what He'd done? Besides, I knowed very well as Thirz' 'ould think different when she knowed about the money.'

(I thought that if Thirzah knew the whole truth, the very magnitude of the sum would have made such wealth wicked again in her eyes. How wise Jelly had been not to tell Sophie all the truth, but to tempt her with an amount she was able to comprehend.)

'So you accepted him,' I prompted.

Sophie nodded. 'Only I asked him to wait a bit,' she said, 'till I got used to the idea.'

'"Lawks, Soph'," 'e said. "Ain't I waited long enough a'ready?"'

'"Long enough so's a bit longer won't hurt you," I says. "Till folks get used to us bein' seen together again, like, an' I can tell Thirz' and Hetty, and Mis' Catherwood an' all." So by that 'e agreed. And we was 'appy, till I made 'im go. I didn't see much of 'im after that, though he did come up for a few minutes twice more. But for one thing I didn't want to set folks a-talking, though I reckon they were, a'ready, from what Het were hinting at, today. And for another, he'd took some work on down in Hen Street – at Mis' Brooke's house, – as 'e 'ad to do evenings an' weekends when Kid didn't want 'im. But you know all that. Anyways, I was a bit put out when 'e couldn't come 'ere 'cos 'e 'ad to go *there*, but Jelly only laughed at me. "Lawks, gel," 'e said, "we've got all the time there is to be together now. And *I* shall go to work, even when we are married if you don't."

'"Ah, but I shall," I says. "I shan't let Mis' Catherwood down, married or not married." You see, Jelly reckoned as 'e could afford to buy us a new 'ouse – even hev one built, 'e said – but I said no, let's stop in my little 'ome and be cosy. I don't know 'ow we should ha' worked that out, I'm sure. But it don't matter now. Anyway, it were on account o' that Mis' Brooke an' 'er 'ouse paintin' that we never got it settled one way or the other.

'"There's time", 'e said. Little did 'e know!'

We fell silent. I had the feeling that she wanted to say more, but my unease at Johanna's name being brought in kept me quiet. As if she read my thoughts, she suddenly burst out again. 'Our Het' told me this morning that 'e was sweet on that red-'eaded dink-me-doll. Het' said as everybody knowed it, 'cept me. She said it was '*er* as wanted one o' them fancy cars. Het' gossips with that Mis' Ellis as keeps fowl, 'cos she goes to that same place a-Sundays as our Het', and Mis' Ellis, she told Het' that Mis' Brooke 'ad said many a time to 'er that what she wanted was one o' them just like Jelly killed 'issself in. An' Het' said everybody reckons 'e drawed all 'is winnings, an' went an' brought that car just to please 'er! An' 'er a married woman!'

Sophie turned her back on me, and clasped her hands in front of her, holding them to the pain inside her. Then she burst out again. 'Oh Fran, I do wish as Het' hadn't told me that. If only I didn't know that, now 'e's gone. To think 'as 'e went an' spent the money as was going to buy us a 'ouse on a car just to please 'er. I can't abear it. I can't! I can't!'

I couldn't either. Her use of my Christian name wrenched me as nothing previous had done, partly because it demonstrated the depths of her own distress, and partly because it emphasized the ties that bound her to me from our childhood. She sat down, and gave way to her feelings. I got up, and throwing caution aside, knelt beside her. If there was one person in the world she would believe, it was me. She must be made to believe what I said, lie as I might have to.

'Now listen to me, Sophie,' I said. 'You know that Mrs Brooke is my friend − but you are a much older, much dearer friend to me than she is. I would not stand up for her at your expense, and you know it. She is nothing to me compared with you. Do you believe that?' She nodded. At least that part of my tale was utterly true, and I hoped it lent conviction to the rest. 'You simply mustn't believe what Hetty said this morning. You wouldn't, you know, if you weren't already so upset. You would know it was just nasty, malicious gossip. Hetty has never forgiven Mrs Brooke for what happened to Wendy, though it was not her fault at all. But your Hetty is a silly woman in some ways, and she would not miss a chance of repeating scandal about Mrs Brooke. She'd also probably got an inkling of how things were moving between you and Jelly as you said, and about him having got a bit of money. She put two and two together, and was probably jealous enough to want to hurt you. You see, until now she could always rely on you to be there if she or her family needed you. Besides, she was a married woman with a man of her own, and you weren't. She could look down on you. The thought of you being a married woman better off than she is narked her a bit, I should think. She didn't stop to think how she was hurting you − she doesn't think at all. You know that.' (She nodded again. Between us it had always been tacitly agreed that

Hetty was a bit wanting in the cerebal region, besides having been petted and pampered by Kezia till what sense she'd been born with was atrophied.) I could see I was making some headway with my arguments.

'Well, I don't know, of course, where this silly idea of Jelly drawing all his money and buying that sort of car to please Johanna started. But, Sophie, I do know some other things that put quite a different light on the silly rumour. In the first place, what do you imagine Jelly hoped to get from Johanna Brooke? As you said, she's a married woman. Do you honestly believe that after waiting all these years for you, and having finally got you to agree to marry him, he would just throw it all away like that "just to please" Mrs Brooke? He'd know you would throw him over if you even suspected he had anything to do with her. Give him credit for having some sense, and for the loyalty he's shown to you all these years. You're not being very loyal to him, are you — allowing a bit of silly women's gossip to make you doubt him as soon as he's not able to stand up for himself? (That went home. I felt her stiffen as she took my point).

'And then consider it from Johanna's side. All right, she "has a way" with men; I don't deny it. She may have even flirted with Jelly, if talking and joking with him when he was at work has to be called flirting. But that's as far as she would go. She's a hard-headed woman, and *she* didn't know Jelly had got any money. Besides, as I happen to know, she's expecting her husband back from Australia any day now. There — that's something *you* didn't know.' (Lie number one, but I was able to offer it with enough conviction to make it register.)

Sophie was responding; I must keep my pleading going.

'And about the car. It could just be that Johanna has talked to Mrs Ellis about cars, because again, I happen to know that Mr Ambrose is considering buying one, so that she can drive him about a bit. I was actually there when they were talking about it, and Mrs Brooke said that what she thought he ought to get was a Morris 1300. Come to think of it, I believe Jelly was there at the time, too, having a cup of tea with us in the kitchen. So much for her wanting one like Jelly bought. That was a real *sports* car, Sophie — a man's car. People who drive sports cars are usually men who are car crazy, and love the mechanical power of them. That's not the sort of car elegant women like Johanna Brooke care for, believe me!

'But it is *just* what a man like Jelly would go for, if he could afford it. You've told me yourself, many a time, about Jelly's way with cars, and how he's always been mad about them. I don't suppose Jelly ever thought he would own a car like he bought last week, because they are very expensive. But that's where we come to the last bit of what I know, and you don't. In fact, I don't suppose anybody else does now, except me and the bank manager at Swithinford. You see, I promised Jelly that I would never tell anybody, but especially you, what he told me about his winnings. But I'm breaking my word to him for your sake, and his. You just can't go on believing he'd spend what he'd promised you for a house on a car. Sophie — listen to me. I *know* how much Jelly won on that premium bond. He could have bought three or four houses and still had enough to buy himself a car. He won *ten thousand pounds. That's* what he was trying to lay at your feet, Sophie. And you're doubting him, just because that silly sister of yours passes on a bit of nasty spiteful gossip! How can you?'

Sophie sat white-faced and rigid, her expression blank. She was incapable of comprehending a sum of ten thousand pounds. But after a minute or two, she turned her face towards me and turned on me the searching gaze I had been expecting. Her soft grey eyes, darkened with grief, caught and held mine till I felt like an insect under a microscope. I returned her gaze, and didn't wriggle. Then she dropped her head, and sat looking at her hands in her lap.

'I think I'd better go, now,' I said.

She nodded. I understood that she actually wanted me to go and leave her alone. I was on my way to the door, when she stopped me.

'Wait just another minute. There's something as I want to do, an' it'll be easier, like, if you're here.'

She got up and, moving with the firm deliberate step of a man determined not to show fear even at the steps of the scaffold, crossed the little room to the chest of drawers on which Kezia's photograph still lay face down. From the bottom drawer she took two bottles, each wrapped in tissue paper, and together enfolded in an old towel. She took off the coverings, and held them for a moment in the crook of her arms, as she might have held twins if her Lord had been kinder. Then she took them to the sink in her tiny kitchen and unhurriedly uncorked and emptied them. The silence was intense and stifling apart from the gurgling and plopping of the sticky golden liquid.

She put the empty bottles in the dustbin, and swilled the sink clear, washing her hands as she did so. I opened the door softly, and crept out.

30

After my visit to Sophie, she seemed to want to avoid further talk. She came to work as usual, calm-faced and stolid, determined not to show even an inkling of her feelings to the nosy world. But she was subdued and quiet, and it seemed kinder to her not to force myself on her, though I didn't want her to think I was avoiding her; so I sometimes went out in the middle of the morning. I couldn't bring myself to go to visit Johanna, and went to call on Mary instead.

She launched at once into the subject of Jelly's death, mourning her old pupil sincerely. But she was, I could see, in one of her waspishly wicked moods, when she was more inclined to slap her erstwhile charges verbally than to offer loving excuses for stupid or reprehensible behaviour. A handsome old queen wasp, I thought, seeking sweetness out of life wherever it might be found, but always with a sting at the ready when provoked or irritated. She didn't mince her words. In her opinion, Jelly's 'tragic' death was a pointless end to a pointless life.

'It would have been quite different, and truly tragic,' she said, 'if he had done what he should have done years ago, and married your Sophie and raised a brood of happy youngsters. But I suppose one can be glad for Sophie's sake, now. At least she's not left missing what she's never had.'

She caught my look of surprise. 'Oh, didn't you know of their attachment? No, I suppose not. Why should you? They've always been in love with each other. I used to catch them holding hands in school, when they were seven. I had to punish them for such wicked behaviour, then, of course. Sophie's mother would have had me sacked if I hadn't stamped on such sinful proclivities.'

The sting was definitely out this morning. Her chatter prevented me from having to answer, and lie about my ignorance, or reveal my knowledge of the anguish she felt Sophie had been spared.

'Those two really had the genuine article called love, you know,' she said. 'It never came to anything because of that old dragon. Now that's what I call sin: making innocent people suffer for no reason.'

I loved Mary in this mood. The conversation required nothing from me but an occasional prompting. I guessed there were further revelations to come, about doings in the community that Jelly's death had stirred up. I reminded her that I had been away when the accident had happened, and invited her to put me into the picture.

The shock of the accident had cut off at a stroke the buzz of excitement Pamela Thackeray's elopement had caused. Mary reported this with pursed lips, thereby informing me of her own feelings about Pamela, together with her censure of the talk it had set going. It was a long time, she said, since folks had had such a juicy sexy morsel to chew over, and they had made the most of it. Even the men, it seemed. They – that is, the men – respected the Thackeray family. Pamela, now voluntarily detached from their prestige and its protection, was fair game. The jokes at her expense, and that of her 'fancy man' were getting riper and riper, according to Mary, when the news of Jelly's fatal accident had stopped the gossip at a stroke.

'If it hadn't been so tragic, it would have been funny,' she said. 'They went looking guilty and ashamed, just like a roomful of children when the headmaster appears. But the latest news has set them all going again like a nest of magpies,' she said, on her way to the kitchen.

I called after her, idly, to ask what the latest news was.

She appeared for a moment at the connecting door, coffee-pot in hand. 'Do you mean you haven't heard?' she said, and then disappeared tantalizingly, without telling me, calling it out from amid the clatter of cups and running water, and leaving me to digest it as I might. Jelly, according to the latest rumour, had died 'worth' more than ten thousand pounds. She appeared for a second at the opening of the connecting door.

'And to crown it all, he's gone and left it to somebody nobody's ever heard of.'

This bit of information really did startle me, so that I had no need to feign astonishment at hearing of Jelly's tremendous wealth. I was surprised even to hear that he had made a will. Country folk usually shy away from making wills, out of superstitious fear. I had naturally supposed that under the circumstances, as I had believed I knew them, Jelly's aged parents and his living brothers and sisters would benefit.

Mary came back. 'I can't remember when there was such excitement before,' she said. 'Not since Tom Tatt's wife had four babies in eleven months! The place has been buzzing with talk like a beehive being robbed. You see, there's no guilt in it, this time, to stop anybody repeating what they've just heard. Just wonderful righteous indignation.'

'Tell me all,' I said, leaning back with my coffee. There was a twinkle in her eye now. She had, I realized, the true gift of laughing with the folk she loved and understood so well – laughing among them, rather than at them.

'I must tell you that I can only repeat what my informants told me,' she said. 'And the chief of those is my char, Mrs 'Opkins.'

Kid was the oldest brother, and Jelly's business partner, so it obviously fell to him to see about sorting out Jelly's affairs. But two sisters who hadn't been home for donkeys' years put in an appearance and made it quite plain that they were staking firm claims to their share of anything that might be left. The insurance on the car, for instance, and what few bits and pieces of personal possessions Jelly might have had. Kid was indignant, and Beryl, Kid's wife, was making no bones about what she thought of their grabbing attitude. She had already told several of her neighbours what she and Kid were going to do with the insurance money, to which she was certain they had absolute and exclusive right because of the business association. The neighbours weren't quite so confident. 'Kid ought to see a lawyer,' they opined. Which, of course, Kid was making arrangements to do as fast as he could.

So, it appeared, Kid had presented himself to a solicitor and stated his case. He just wanted to know how soon he could collect what Jelly had left, and whether he could share it out as he thought fit.

The solicitor had made inquiries from his partner then dropped the bombshell. Not only was Jelly's estate very considerable (he was indiscreet enough, apparently, to mention the figure). Of course nothing whatsoever could be done until probate had been granted to the executors of Jelly's will. All this was double-Dutch to poor Kid. He took in only vaguely what the solicitor was saying, still being in shock about the size of his legacy.

'Do you mean as I can't get the money, like, till you say so, then?' Kid had asked indignantly.

'I'm afraid it means that nobody will get anything for some weeks, even months. And then, of course they will be informed.'

'What do you mean,"they"?' Kid had asked.

'Those people whom your brother named in his will,' the solicitor had replied. 'The beneficiaries.'

'Well, that's what I guess happened from the garbled accounts I got,' said Mary. 'Kenneth could get no more out of the solicitor, and went home troubled. Slow he may be, but he is shrewd and, as they say round here "close" about his own affairs. To discover the size of the legacy that it seemed she wasn't going to get after all robbed Beryl of what self-control she had. She rushed out and told anybody who would listen what the lawyer had said, reviling poor Jelly for "passing his own over" till one of the neighbours felt obliged to rebuke her for speaking so ill of the dead. There was very nearly a female tooth-and-nail scrap, it seems. But they all wanted to know what Beryl could tell them, and she repeated what Ken had told her, with variations and additions.'

I was really only half listening. If Jelly had made a will, and it wasn't in favour of his immediate family, who had he left his money to? Could it be one or other of two women? And if it were, I wondered fearfully which would he have done the most harm to, whichever way the answer fell.

'It seems he had a very big win on Ernie,' Mary went on, 'and the bank manager persuaded him to make a will at the same time they had invested it for him.'

'Who has he left it to, then?' I said, not being able to await her time to tell me. She showed some surprise, even a bit of distaste, at my eagerness to know, and in retrospect I realized that I had not evinced the required element of surprise at his wealth. Surely Mary had said Jelly's will had named somebody the village had never heard of? Then it couldn't be either Johanna or Sophie. So who? I began to see Jelly as a very dark horse indeed.

'Who is the unknown legatee? Was Kid told?'

Mary's face broke into a broad grin.

'As the tale of poor Jelly's testatory misdemeanours reached me via Mrs 'Opkins, the person named on "Jelly's paper" was somebody called Ben Fisher.'

'Oh no,' I said, giggling in spite of a mouthful of hot coffee. You've made that up! I don't believe it.'

'Honest to God, that's what Beryl was making the fuss about.'

Send three and fourpence. We are going to a dance. 'Of course, somebody with a bit more nous soon put the mistake right, but that didn't clear up the mystery as to who is going to benefit. Whoever it is will be informed soon, of course, so they'll know, then — but

258

whether the rest of us will is another matter. I have to admit that even I am curious.'

So was I. And anxious, too. Jelly couldn't be so silly, surely! As I left Mary's house, I obeyed a sudden impulse and went on to see Johanna. I felt I simply had to know whether she had been implicated by word or deed, knowingly or unknowingly, in Jelly's choice of new car.

One glance at Johanna as she opened the door told me that she was in a state of suppressed agitation, though the smile of welcome was dazzlingly genuine, and the warmth of her hug dispelled some of my apprehension.

'I heard from Madge Ellis that you were back,' she said. 'I meant to ring, but I've been so busy. I've had my hands more than full, one way or another.' She indicated the sitting-room with a graceful tilt of her tawny head. 'He's been under the weather.'

'You mean he's been ill?' I asked, keeping my voice low to match hers.

She nodded. 'Depressed, too. I think Jelly Bean's accident upset him, and played on his mind. It was sad though, wasn't it? What on earth possessed him to buy a powerful sports car like that? Madge was full of talk about him leaving a lot of money — thousands and thousands, she said, according to Wendy's mother. Won a lot on a premium bond, Madge said. But come in.'

'I suppose Mr Ambrose doesn't like being reminded that we are all mortal,' I said.

'Mm. And aggravated that Jelly didn't get the garden done before he killed himself. But most of all, I think, because he had really made up his mind to buy a car. Now he's inclined to change his mind again, drat it. Says if an experienced driver like Jelly can kill himself in a car, it's too dangerous for a woman. I keep pointing out that the sort of car any sensible woman would want here is very different from Jelly's hotrod effort, but I'm afraid I've got to start the persuasion all over again. Oh dear, I was so looking forward to feeling free again. Let's go and sit down.'

'Wait a minute,' I said. 'Surely you are not letting that really upset you? Something's the matter, I can see. So tell me quick before we go into the sitting-room.'

She laughed. 'I can't hide anything from you, Fran, can I? I told you you knew all about me. Let's go into the kitchen. I'll tell him you're here and that I'm getting us all a drink.'

She went to talk to the old man, and I went on into the kitchen.

She was right about one thing. She couldn't act with me now, at any rate not well enough to deceive me, probably because she didn't try. So I was much relieved as I sat down against the kitchen table. She was in no way implicated in Jelly's affairs, even in my suspicious and apprehensive mind, and even if an idle remark of hers had set ideas going in his head and finally led to tragedy. That was Fate, not female machination.

'Things have been moving pretty fast,' she said. 'Poor old Ernie had a really bad attack of his liver complaint, whatever it is, and it made him feel low. Then Jelly killed himself, and I think the two combined to make him realize all over again how old and frail he is. Anyway the upshot of all this was that he began to worry about changing his will in my favour. He talked to me about it. He was prepared to leave practically everything he had to me, on one condition – that I kept him with me till he died, and that while he was alive I had no sort of relationship at all with any other men. He was sweet, really, poor old thing. He said he knew perfectly well I couldn't ever fancy him, but he just wanted to think of me as his, and if I wanted what he could leave me, he had to be able to think of me as his alone. So I have to make the decision. There's enough money to make me independent and comfortable for the rest of my life. But Fran' – her voice was urgent – 'I'm already fifty. He might last another twenty years. And there are times when I know I'm a woman.'

I was silent. I knew how she felt. There were times when I longed to be seventy myself, and not know I was a woman still full of life and sexual energy.

'Besides, I know you think I'm a Mercenary Mary all through, but even I have some scruples. I might as well sell myself in a public market place for sexual purposes as sell myself quietly at home for promising not to have anything at all to do with men. Oh dear!'

She ruffled her lovely hair up round her piquant, lively face, and looked helpless, all flowers and no feathers at all. It would certainly be a wicked waste of what a woman like her was intended for if she accepted the bargain – and what might it not do to her?

'That cheap Pamela Thackeray obviously thought a bit of you-know-what was worth more than all Loddy's money,' she said. 'That's enough in itself to make me want to take the opposite line. But suppose I turn him down, and then he goes and dies in six months' time?'

'You'll accept,' I said. 'I know you. You are a gambler by nature. I'm not.'

'You have never had any reason to be. You've got simple tastes and the means to supply expensive ones. It isn't my fault that I'm just the opposite. Yes, you're right, I suppose. When I think of all that lolly on one side, and the chance of being back to the sort of penury I was in when you came, on the other, there's no question in my mind. To hell with scruples! I'll take what I can get while I can get it, and if anybody tries to stop me, let them look out.'

She looked up at me suddenly, eyes blazing tawny red as if I were likely to try to dissuade her. Her hands, orange-tipped, untied and retied the silk scarf at her neck — the same talon-like hands that I had flinched from when I put my first week's board money into them. Feathers now — beak and claws at the ready. Whichever way she decided, it wasn't going to be easy for her or anybody else. I found myself wishing for the hundredth time that I had obeyed Sophie's instinct in the first instance, and stayed clear of her.

'They used to tell me at school that the love of money is the root of all evil,' she said. 'What rot! It's the lack of money, not the love of money, that makes me evil. So I shall avoid that possibility by accepting what is being offered to me on a plate. There's just one snag.'

I waited. She got up and stood like a sparrow-hawk on a fence, alert and watchful.

'Which is?' I prompted.

'What do I do if Dave turns up? There was a letter from him a couple of days ago, saying he was actually on his way home. I can't reach him to put him off. If he walks in, he'll ruin it all. Fancy him just deciding to come back *now*. You can always trust him to put his big feet into my plans. If he had come before I was reduced to having Ernie here, I should have been so pleased to have him home, with a chance to get out of this dump. Now he'll just wreck the best chance I've had for years. Oh Fran, what shall I *do*? Ernie thinks I'm a deserted wife bravely trying to keep my end up.'

I could not stem the tide of distaste, almost of revulsion, that was creeping over me, and I was furiously angry with myself, suddenly, for being the sort of woman everybody else wanted to take into their confidence.

'Don't look so distressed, Fran,' she said, 'I know you don't approve, and in any case you can't help, even with advice. I shall find a way of dealing with it if a situation with Dave does arise, I'm sure. I'm not going to let such a chance slip through my hands. After all, it would be to Dave's advantage in the long run, wouldn't it? He'll just have to do without me for a bit longer, even if it is another twenty years.'

Ernie called from the sitting-room, and she listened, her face full of kindly concern for him. 'I must get those drinks,' she said.

'Do you mind if I don't stay after all?' I said. 'I really only popped in for a minute, and I've been here half an hour already. Sophie expected me back ages ago.'

She let me go without protest.

William's term was in full swing, and Eeyore's Tail was unoccupied the next weekend. I was lonely and restless, and cross with myself for being so. Wasn't this isolation what I had longed for once? I tried to work, but was too depressed to lose myself in it. About eleven o'clock on the Sunday morning, I acted on impulse and unlocked the connecting door to Eeyore's Tail. I made coffee in William's kitchen, and sat down in his armchair to drink it, and gave myself up to thinking – about him, and about me, and our situation, which was both difficult and a bit silly. About Johanna and her problem, which wasn't so much silly as sordid – yet I wondered how I would act, if I were now in her place. And I thought about Sophie, no doubt at this moment on her knees in church, declaring the responses in the loud, firm voice she and Thirzah together led the rest of the congregation with – stolid, calm, showing no sign of the anguish the withering wreaths on Jelly's grave must be causing her. Just at that moment I heard footsteps and Sophie's voice inquiring for my whereabouts. I jumped up, guilty at being found alone in Eeyore's Tail, and answered.

'I'm in here,' I called, opening the door. Sophie came in, dressed in her Sunday best, with the tiny forget-me-nots bobbing on the brim of her black hat and her black-gloved hand clutching a well-worn Book of Common Prayer.

There must be some reason for this visit, but she didn't seem unduly distressed, so I concluded at once that I was not needed to take Wendy's baby to hospital, or anything of a similar urgent nature.

'Come in,' I said, adding truthfully, 'I felt lonely, and a bit miserable, and came in here to make coffee, just as if William was here. I often have coffee with him in here on Sunday mornings.' (Now why on earth should I feel it necessary to say that to Sophie? I didn't need to explain my actions to anybody, did I?)

But Sophie didn't react in any way. She peeled off her gloves, and laid them on the table.

'Get yourself some coffee,' I said. 'I'm sure something's the matter, or you wouldn't be here – but I'm glad to see you, all the same. Sit down and tell me what it is.'

She filled a cup and sat down primly, as befitted her best clothes, in 'my' chair, facing William's.

'It's this 'ere,' she said, opening her capacious black handbag. From it she took a long white envelope – and handed it to me.

'Come by post yist'day morning. Give me a real turn. But you read it. I don't know as I'm read it aright. That's why I thought I'd come round to see you on my way 'ome from church.'

I opened the typewritten letter, and as soon as my eyes fell on the printed heading, I knew what the letter contained. A part, at least, of the identity of Ben Fisher had been established. The letter stated briefly that under the will of the late Mr James Bean, she would inherit one-third of the residue of his estate, the estimated amount being around £3,000.

'Sophie!' I said, selfish misgivings arising in me as I wondered whatever I should do without her, and how I should replace her. 'How wonderful for you! And you see how right I was – Jelly was thinking of you all the time. He must have made this will even before he asked you to marry him.'

'So it does mean that, really, does it? It really means that I shall have £3,000 of my own – all on account o' that dratted bond what killed Jelly? It ain't right! I won't hev it, that I won't! Whatever would Thirz' an' all the other folks say? They'll say as I'm a bad woman, an' as Jelly's been a-visiting me on the sly all these years, like. Why should 'e go an' leave me 'is money, for nothing, as you might say? Nobody'll believe it. 'Ow can I stop it? Who am I got to tell as I don't want it? Will you take me to see this 'ere lawyer? Or else write a letter for me?'

'Oh *dear*!' I said, getting up and stamping round William's kitchen in irritation. 'Sometimes you are a very stupid woman, Sophie! Not want it? Don't be so *silly*!'

I spoke more sharply than I had intended in my exasperation with her, and to my utter dismay she broke down and began to sob distractedly. There was Johanna a mile or two away, fretting to get money out of a will that she had no valid claim to be on, and here was Sophie, fretting to fight and decline a legacy that would have set Johanna wild with excitement. Well, as George Eliot remarked, there's no denying women are queer creatures. I let her cry, and made a strong cup of tea, which I knew she would prefer.

'Come on now,' I said firmly. 'Drink that tea and let's talk it out.

We'll face all the facts as far as we can see them, and then make a decision what to do. You can't decide while you are in a state like this, but you'll see it differently soon, I'm sure.'

She dried her eyes obediently, still shuddering and sobbing but at less frequent intervals. 'I'm tired,' she said. 'I didn't sleep a wink last night. I should a' come up yist'day, only I thought he'd be 'ere, an ' I didn't want to bother you. I prayed and prayed, but for once it didn't seem as if I could get no answer. Tha's what made me feel so down, I reckon. I felt as if I hadn't got nobody at all to turn to.'

'Well, you have,' I said firmly. 'And I only wish William were here to help me convince you. If we try to sort it out for you first, I've no doubt your next lot of prayers will be answered.'

She nodded, setting the little forget-me-nots quivering as if a breeze was sweeping across them, and even found a wan smile. 'Yis. Tha's what mother all'us said. God 'elps them as 'elp theirselves.'

I began to try to make her see why she must accept her unexpected windfall, arguing among other things that she would cause much more talk by refusing the legacy than by letting it be a nine days' wonder. 'But of course it will be talked about,' I said, 'and as far as Thirzah is concerned, you can please yourself how much you tell her about Jelly.'

Her mouth set firm. 'I shan't tell her nothing,' she said. 'She and Mam spoilt things for me and him.'

I was pleased, out of all proportion, by this sudden belated stand against Thirzah's domination.

'There will be a lot of nastiness and envy in the village,' I said. 'But on the other hand, by their standards you'll be a wealthy woman. You'll find that will make a difference.'

I don't want there to be no difference,' she said. 'It won't stop me coming and doing for you and 'im for instance. Where is 'e?'

'Who?' I asked, not catching the connection in my relief at her last declaration.

''Im,' she said. 'William.'

She only ever used our Christian names when under great stress, as if a reversion to our childhood status of close and equal initmacy gave her extra security. 'He's too busy to get out at weekends just at present,' I said. 'That's why you found me in here. I was lonely.'

She looked at me over her cup of tea, her grey eyes, still wet and a bit red, full of utter sympathy and understanding.

'I know folk'll talk about me an' Jelly,' she said. 'I know as they'll hint as I'm a bad woman as 'e's bin a-visiting at night, an' such like, all these year. It won't 'urt me much, neither, come to that, though it ain't nice, is it? But what I keep thinking is that in all them years Jelly never so much as kissed me till that night as 'e asked me to marry 'im, an' then I was so took back I pushed 'im away. An' now 'e's gone, an' we shall be painted as black as if we'd both lived real bad lives, on account o' this money. So I keep saying to myself, why didn't we, then? Why didn't I let 'im come an' see me when 'e liked? What difference would it ha' made, now? I heven't even kep' my good name – or at least I shan't when this gets about.' She inclined her head towards the solicitor's letter still lying on the table.

'Now there's you an' William. I know as it's none o' my business, but I can't 'elp saying it. I know you both better'n most folks do, and I know you an' 'im feel about each other just the same as me an' Jelly did. An' folks is talking a'ready about you an' 'im being 'ere together at weekends, by yourselves when I ain't about. Het told me, a long while ago, what they were a-hinting. O' course, I shut 'er up good and proper, and I ain't 'eard no more, never. But such scandal as that don't lay down easy. So I thinks to myself as I come 'ere, why don't they be 'appy together while they can? They might just as well, seeing 'ow folks expect 'em to anyway. *I* know as you keep one each side o' that there locked door o' nights – but what's the use? If you ask me, you want to make the most o' what time you're got left together. I shan't split on you, that I can tell you.'

I was utterly astounded, and embarrassed – not at what she said, but that she understood it all so perfectly, and had the moral courage to say so.

I kissed her cheek, and took the cup out of her hands.

'Dear Sophie,' I said. 'Fancy you thinking about us in the midst of all your own trouble! I wish I could tell him what you've just said, though of course I can't. The trouble is that none of us can get away from the way we were brought up in a different age altogether. William and I wouldn't be happy, any more than you and Jelly would have done. We should feel guilty and that would spoil it all.'

She frowned. 'I know some – 'specially one – as were born well afore the war as wouldn't think twice about going to bed with any fellow she fancied, specially if 'e 'appened to 'ave a bit put by. And all I can say to you now is that I know as you'd feel different if William was to be took away from you for ever – same as I do, now. You'd think about it different, then, and wish you'd acted different while you 'ad the chance.' I never expected to see the day when Sophie of all people urged me into immorality – if that is the right word. I was quite out of my depth, and rather abruptly reverted to the real object of her visit.

'If you think it is right,' she said, 'I will do as you say. But I shall go 'ome and pray about it again afore I decide. After all, I needn't spend it, need I? I could hang on to it for Wend's little ol' boy, pr'aps.' The thought caused the first smile I had seen on her face for many days.

'Make up your mind tonight,' I said, 'and tell me in the morning. Then I'll take you to see the solicitor, or write a letter for you, whichever you would rather.'

After she'd gone I went back to my own part of the house; but I couldn't work. It seemed utterly stupid for me to be sitting there inventing characters and events when what was going on all round me in truth made any fiction I could create as uninteresting as photographic negatives.

Later I went to bed still pondering Sophie's startling bit of philosophy about William. The thought of him never being here again was absolutely unbearable. I wanted him so much that the empty space on the other side of my double bed seemed like the bottomless pit of misery.

31

It would have been nice to have gone to bed in my beautiful bedroom and enjoy a bit of private contemplation; but I spent a very restless night bothering myself about Sophie and the problems she was facing with regard to Jelly's legacy. I had to concede that she knew the village better than I did, so her fear of scandal was not imaginary; yet it would be out of question that she should refuse to take the legacy on such ridiculous grounds.

At five a.m. I went downstairs and made myself a cup of tea, taking it back to bed. Cat, always delighted to see me again after the separation of the night hours, sat on my chest and pushed her hard little head under my chin, purring like a tractor, and preventing me from tasting my tea while it was still hot.

'Cat,' I said, 'you are an unmitigated pest. An incubus. I detest you!' She increased the decibel power of her purr at the compliment, till she vibrated from head to tail with the effort. Then she shoved her muzzle against the rim of the saucer, and made me spill tea on the sheet.

'Get off!' I said, giving her a little push while I strove to mop up the mess. She rolled over on to her back with her little black paws in the air, squirming with pleasure, and exposing the exquisite cream fur on her underside while turning her head to one side with one browny-black ear flattened against me. Her gentian eyes were watching every moment, and her paws were at the ready to leap on any movement I made.

'You are the most beautiful and adorable creature on earth,' I said, resignedly setting down my cup and rubbing vigorously the bit between her back legs. This always had the effect of doubling her up into an ecstatic ball of fur, scrabbling at my hand with all four sets of claws.

'I don't know why on earth I put up with you,' I told her. 'You and Johanna are a good pair. I've got you and I love you and that makes me responsible for you, but you both twist me round your little paws. Every decision I make about either of you is against my better judgement. Why should I be bothered with either of you? Tell me that.'

She let go of my hand suddenly, and extended herself lengthwise in a voluptuous, lithe, feline stretch, opening her pink little mouth and letting out the most endearing of all her many voices, something halfway between a purr and a mew.

'OK,' I said. 'You win. Both of you. Now tell me how I can persuade Sophie not to be silly enough to refuse her windfall just because she is afraid what the neighbours will say.' But Cat was preparing herself for sleep, with her soft little head in the crook of my arm, and so as not to disturb her I lay still as well until I felt dozy again. Among the muddled thoughts that came to me before I slept was one that told me I was a fine one to reproach Sophie for not taking all that was available to her because of what others might think or say.

When Sophie arrived she came in with the firm tread and a set look on her face which I had come to know meant that she had made her decision.

'Well?' I said, indicating a chair on the other side of the table. She sat down and looked at me, bright-eyed and resolute.

'I shall take it,' she said. 'I prayed and prayed, and it seemed for all the world as if it was Jelly 'isself that answered me. I could 'ear 'is voice in my 'ead as plain as I 'eard it that night when 'e set in

Mam's chair and said as 'ow we might as well get married. "You take it, gel," 'e seemed to say, over and over again. "Another two or three months, and it would ha' been your'n anyways, when we were married. So whose is it b'rights now, if it ain't yourn? You take it, and let 'em talk if they must. Your conscience is clear enough — that I do know." And I thought to myself, "Ah," I thought, "so it is, and the Lord knows it as well as you and me do."' She paused, and her next remark was made direct to me.

'So what does it matter what folks say? *You* won't believe 'em.'

She spoke as if I were the final arbiter on all questions of morality, whereas I had come to think of her as just that.

'What about your sisters?' I asked.

'Thirz'll go on a bit, but Dan'el's got plenty o' common sense when it comes to it. Het's different. She'll have 'sterricks with jealousy. She never could abear me 'aving anything she 'adn't got. But she's got a lot as I'm never 'ad, and never shall 'ave, now. I shall tell 'er so, If I 'ave to.' She looked grim. 'As for the rest o' folks, let 'em say what they will. That's what Jelly said to me last night. while I were on my knees aside o' my bed. "Let 'em talk, and be damned to 'em," 'e said. Fran, I 'eard 'im!'

She brought out what she considered the swear word in such a prim and prudish fashion that I just could not suppress the smile the sight of her mouth brought to my own.

'I do wish I had known your Jelly better,' I said. 'I am so pleased that you have made up your mind so sensibly.'

'So you'll write that letter to the lawyer for me, then,' she said, and got up to go to work. The matter was settled, and we spoke of it no more. It took me some time to adjust to the knowledge that Sophie was now a 'monied' woman. The strength of her character was such that it made not a scrap of difference to her appearance, her manner, her routine, or her way of life. It must surely have been that very factor that killed stone dead any gossip in the village, because for once this extraordinary event seemed to pass over everybody's head.

A day or two after Sophie had made her momentous decision the unmistakable sound of car wheels on the front gravel caused us to wonder who it could be. We were not expecting visitors.

'I'll go,' I said to Sophie, warned by some instinct. In my hall stood Johanna, wrapped in her musquash coat, having let herself in, and there, behind her, was Ernie Ambrose, looking like a child who has just caught sight of Father Christmas.

'Come in quickly,' I said, 'out of the cold. Johanna, you look like a million-dollar film star.' Ernie's face broke into a great beam of appreciation as he wheezed and gurgled in a vain attempt to agree with me.

'No, you come out. We've got something to show you,' she said.

I guessed of course, what it was. I had heard the wheels on the gravel, so I grabbed a coat and went out to look. There it stood, a gleaming, brand-new Austin 1300. So she, like Sophie, had reached her decision. She had opted for the bird in the hand. That car was a dream come true, and she was glorying in it.

I took them into the sitting-room, where Ned had already lit a fire – I never asked Sophie to wait on Johanna – so I went to warn her. When I went back, Johanna and the old man stood together by the window, still looking out on the car. His arm lay round her fur-coated shoulders. She turned away impatiently, and drew off her gloves like a Noël Coward heroine. Ernie indicated the car with a sideways nod of his wobbly old head.

'Brand new this morning,' he said 'All for milady there.'

'Milady' was haughtily pretending she had not heard. I felt quite sorry for the silly old man.

'It's lovely,' I said. 'Come and sit down, and tell me all about it.'

'There's nothing to tell,' he wheezed. 'Milady wanted it, so she had to have it. And anything else she wants. It's hers.'

Johanna looked anxious. 'No it isn't,' she said. 'Don't go giving people wrong ideas. It's yours. I'm only the chauffeur.'

She was taking no chances. There would be tax and insurance to be paid.

'It's all one,' he said. 'I can't drive it, so you might as well call it yours.'

Johanna gave him a sweet and grateful smile, which contained a good deal of genuine warmth. I knew how she felt. A car at your disposal does confer a degree of freedom and independence.

She made good use of it, too. In the days that followed, she was always buzzing about at the wheel, usually with Ernie sitting huddled but proud beside her. But it was not long before she was off and out without him – so it was reported.

'Early Christmas shopping, probably,' I said.

'Quite likely,' said Sophie, 'She seems to have plenty to spend, nowadays. Don't know which way 'er be'ind 'angs since she 'ad that there car.'

'She likes to take old Mr Ambrose out when he's well enough to go,' I said.

'And when it suits 'er. There's times when it don't.'

I should have to slap her down. 'Now what are you hinting at?' I asked, coldly.

Sophie took the snub, and coloured, but she held her ground. 'Well, she's been a-going out, days and days, just lately, leaving 'im all by 'isself. Het told me as that Mis' Ellis is paid to goo in and git 'is dinner, and set with 'im.'

'Where does she go?' I asked.

Sophie shrugged. ''Ow should I know? But Het told me as one of her neighbours from Hen Street see her meeting somebody off a train at Cambridge station, and watched the chap as she'd met get into the car with 'er and drive off. Then another day somebody seen her saying goodbye to just such another man at Huntingdon station. Het said it sounded like the same man, from what she could make out of it. Tall, they said, a real good figure of a man.'

'It's a pity they haven't got something better to do than watch and tell tales about their neighbours,' I said.

'You asked, or I shouldn't ha' said nothing about it,' Sophie countered. 'It don't matter to me 'ow many fancy men she 'as. She ain't my friend. It's you as I'm thinking about.'

'Really, Sophie!' I expostulated. 'I suppose in a minute you'll be quoting the Bible at me about not coming near pitch without being defiled. I am sorry I asked. I know you don't like her, but I won't believe ill of her just on hearsay and imagination from such feather-headed gossip-mongers as your sister Hetty. The man was very likely a solicitor, 'and the business she was on not her own, but something Mr Ambrose had trusted her to do for him. People always want to think the worst. It makes me angry.'

She took my rebuke in silence, secure in the knowledge that I knew she very rarely parroted gossip that she could not substantiate.

She hooked out her dusters and polish, and extracted the vacuum-cleaner from its cupboard before replying. At the kitchen door, she paused, as if hesitating whether or not to have the last word.

'You may be right, o' course,' she said. 'Such as me and Het don't 'ave much call to goo about meeting lawyers, like such folks as you and her do. I didn't know as you 'ad to 'ang round their necks and kiss 'em goodbye in the way o' business, as you might say. But even fools learn!'

What was Johanna up to, now?

There were now only six weeks to Christmas. I had been vaguely looking forward to my first Christmas in Benedict's, but now the time had come, I was filled with apprehension. I had, as yet, made no friends hereabouts other than Mary and Johanna. Kate had made it quite clear that it could not be a family Christmas if Johanna was even to be invited up for a drink. Although Sophie was turning such a brave face to the world, she went about quiet and subdued, a little more bitter than was her wont, and I could hardly expect her this year to throw herself into my family festivities as she might have done if things had been happier for her.

William was worrying me, too. He seemed tired and preoccupied, as if there was something on his mind that he was not prepared to share with me. Yet he had become 'the man of the family', and I could not make any arrangements for Christmas that did not include him. Commonsense told me that he might be staying away more than he need because he found the present situation between us pretty nearly intolerable. Sometimes I did myself. I could not face the possibility of a long Christmas holiday with none but the two of us in the house, and the bolt still between us. Nor could I suggest going away myself, and leaving him alone. He had not fixed anything else for himself this year, no doubt because he expected to be here. But for Cat, we could both go to Kate. Put her into a cattery I would not.

After Sophie's revelations about Johanna, I thought I should find out how things were at Bryony Cottage.

When I rang, it was Madge Ellis who answered. Johanna had gone out and she was looking after Mr Ambrose.

'Cat,' I said to her severely as I laid the receiver back in its cradle. 'I'm worried. I don't like it. I just hope this isn't the calm before the storm.'

I heard Sophie come in, and hastily picked up my pen. Sophie disapproved of my elevating Cat to the rôle of confidante. I turned to greet her.

'Morning,' she said. 'Pamela Thackeray's back again.'

That was just like Sophie. When she chose of her own free-will to repeat a bit of gossip, she 'outed' with it at once. It meant she was absolutely sure of her facts. She had seen the lady, bold as brass in the post-office.

'Is she?' I said. 'Where is she staying, then?'

'At 'ome, of course. Just walked in and set down, as if she'd only been out for the day a-shopping. Seems Loddy were glad to see 'er, and just made 'er welcome. "and no questions asked", as the sayin' is. Ah, well, it's 'is affair when all is said and done. But I reckon 'e'll rue the day, that I do.' She went briskly away to work.

Poor Loddy. He had my sympathy, and so did the rest of his nice family. The return of the prodigal wife would cause them a lot of embarrassment and heart-burning. And wasn't there a child somewhere in the picture?

This bit of news was in no way connected to my own problems, yet it increased my disquiet. I needed a good long talk with somebody. Two days later, Sophie brought the next instalment. The errant Mrs Thackeray had gone again.

Sophie regarded her erstwhile schoolfellow as a non-person who had put herself beyond the bounds of decency and tolerance. Her tongue, therefore, was loosed, and she was prepared to tell all — and I let her run on.

Pamela, she said, had found that her 'man' was very short of funds. She had sold her car to keep their spree going, and when that money had run out, she had come back 'to get her bottle filled'. This time, when ready to depart, she had ordered a taxi and piled her suitcases into it — full of Loddy's family silver and any other *objets d'art* worth money — and driven off again.

'Left Lod a note, as said she was going to spend the rest of her days with a real man. And away she went.'

'Back to her dancing partner,' I said gullibly, not quick enough to see that Sophie's unaccustomed relish in telling her tale meant that she had not yet got to the end of it.

'Not she!' said Sophie, witheringly, pleased that I had fallen into her trap.

'As Mam used to say, "If one ain't enew, twenty's too few". Up to Jack Bartrum's! Bold as brass monkeys, the pair of 'em. So there you are. Better one 'ouse spoilt than two troubled. They'll make a good pair, I don't doubt. Where there's a Jack, there's a Jill. Sich wayses!'

The censure she managed to put into her voice was incredible. The interlarding of her tale with folk-sayings gave her strictures a sharper edge. She waved her regional speech about as a flag of defiance against modern trends of morality.

Pamela represented all those trends that she — and I, too, in my old-fashioned way — found so reprehensible about post-war society. It really boiled down to the change in attitude towards sexual relationships. What had begun, and been forgiven, in time of war had accelerated since the close of hostilities, but until now it had not actually washed out as far as places like Old Swithinford. Those of us who had been born and were through our teens by the outbreak of the war still had our feet entangled in the web of yesterday's moral values. In spite of myself, I found this latest turn of events not only unexpected, but disturbing. I gave in to my restlessness, and went to visit Mary. I found her, too, wanting to talk, and admitting it.

We talked of Pamela's latest move, and of poor Loddy. Mary was distressed by it all, partly because she felt in some way responsible for Pamela's character, having been her teacher. I asked her to tell me more about Pamela's child.

'I don't know the child at all,' she said. 'All I know is that when Loddy married her, he adopted the boy. They sent him to a tin-pot "prep" school in Swithinford till he was seven, and then to a second-rate boarding school. It got him out of the way. Jean Howe says he's a little horror – but I wouldn't count on even her word being unbiased about Pamela.'

'Complicateder and complicateder,' I said. 'So if Loddy adopted the boy legally, he is now either lumbered with a responsibility he may not want, or with the prospect of fighting his wife for the custody of a child he cares for but who is not his own.'

'Whichever way, it'll be poor Loddy who suffers. I can't see Pamela wanting the child, or giving him a moment's consideration, poor little brat. And I don't see Bartrum as a father-figure, either. No, the Thackerays are lumbered with him all right.'

'It really is awful for them all,' I said. 'Is she going to live openly as Bartrum's mistress? I mean, right here, in the middle of folks who know both of them, and where she is likely to meet Loddy or his family whenever she goes out?'

She snorted. 'You underrate Pamela if you think she'll worry about a little thing like that! They'll just brazen it out for a couple of months, and then she'll start calling herself Mrs Bartrum, and that'll be that. Before long the Rector will be calling on them to ask her to open the church fête.'

'Don't overdo it Mary,' I said, 'Surely they will both be cold-shouldered by people who know Loddy's family – and everybody here does. There are still some standards left!'

She stirred her tea, meditatively, before replying. When she looked up again, the slightly flippant tone had gone.

'Whose standards, though, Frances? We are behind the times, you and I. We live in the swinging sixties, but we are not of them. All our standards were set up before the second war – even yours.

Mine, before the Great War. *Autres temps, autres moeurs.'*

'But why?' I said. 'Either our values were all wrong, or the permissive society of today is wrong. They can't both be right.'

'Why not? Circumstances alter cases. What actual validation was there, ever, for Victorian morality? With regard to the matter of sex, for example?'

I had to think. 'I suppose it all boils down to the ten commandments, doesn't it?'

'And whose commandments were they — and what shaped them in the first place? Exactly the same motives that were behind the rubric of Victorian society. The material welfare of the tribe. The original commandments as laid down by Mao Tse Moses were designed to keep the masses worshipping the god of property. "Thou shalt not commit adultery" really meant "Keep what you've got in the family". Victorian middle-class families lived up to it to the letter. They married their cousins till some of them ought to have been prosecuted for incest, but most of the men had mistresses. I'll bet 'their wives considered that adultery. The men didn't. They could argue that it didn't threaten family property.'

'People still cling to their possessions,' I said. 'That wasn't a peculiarly Victorian trait.'

'Hm. You are confusing possessions with property. People who have property are becoming fewer and fewer — the politics of envy have seen to that. But this affluent society has smothered people in possessions. The difference is that you don't try to stick to mere possessions — indeed, to keep up with the Jones's you have to replace them all the time. And you can't leave expensive holidays on the Costa Brava to your heirs.

'But there are a lot of other reasons for the sudden let-up in sexual morality, aren't there? Women fighting for a bit of equality; easy travel and communication, making the possibilities of an *"affaire"* so much greater; and I suppose this new contraceptive pill. Perhaps, above all, the safety-net of the welfare state. Put together, the pill and social security have removed the fear of any material consequences. Without the fear, what chance has the church of applying any moral sanctions? The young of today just laugh. Every girl will soon be given a packet of contraceptive pills with her first wage-packet — like the men in the Navy hold out their hats upside down for a packet of condoms with their wages before going ashore.'

I must have shown my surprise. Mary was amused at my naiveté. I sighed.

'My grandchildren will be falling in and out of bed with anybody and everybody,' I said. 'There seemed some sort of excuse for it in the war – but I can't help thinking such promiscuity reduces the value of any sexual relationship. The young "have sex" now like they have coke or ice-cream – synthetic sex, as it were, ersatz emotion. Not the real thing. I think they are losing something precious.'

'You are speaking by the book, you know, Frances. You aren't really thinking. How many of your generation ever had the real thing? Not many, I think, because they didn't have any till they were married. And then what, if they found they had married the wrong person? At least the youngsters of today have something. Erzatz coffee and dried egg in the last war were better than no coffee or egg at all.'

She had jolted me a bit. You tended to forget, when talking to Mary, how old she was. She must be one of the thousands of women doomed to be old maids because the loss of a whole generation of young men had meant there weren't enough left to go round. She knew what she was talking about. I felt guilty.

'But what about *love*?' I said. 'Doesn't that enter into it somewhere? What you are talking about is just self-gratification.'

'When they find a loving relationship, they don't want to play around any more. What has gone before doesn't change it. I can't see any reason for asserting that more people found real love in the past than happens now. It's a pearl of great price, and not to be picked up on every doorstep.'

'Or under every hedge,' I countered. 'But if married couples didn't get the best of it, there was a fair chance that they would make the most of their bargain and try to keep it – not involve others in a chain of misery like Pamela Thackeray is doing. And is there no longer anything called self-respect?'

'Depends on what you mean by self-respect. Pamela respects herself all right: she's a megalomaniac. If she does it, then it must be OK. That is why she is a danger to society. It's what old Thomas Traherne said: "Souls be like apples, One being rotten rots another."'

'So you do agree that it's rotten?' I said, triumphantly 'You've been arguing for modern ways!'

'No, no, no!' she said, vehemently. 'I am surprised at you, Frances. You are not using anything but emotion in your arguments. I do not condone it, but I do try to understand it. All my reactions are against it – but you see, it doesn't affect me personally, so I can reason without difficulty. You obviously can't. Surely in the end it must be a question of every one having to consult his own conscience? People born before the war were given a touchy conscience that those born since the war don't have. As Mark Twain said, they only know what they do about conscience from hearsay. They grow up now without a conscience, like animals do. You don't censure cats for having sex on the tiles, do you? Why should you blame young human beings who have no more conscience about it than cats?'

'That's a horrible thought,' I said. 'Just copulation.'

'Mm. Not love. That's what you were trying to point out a minute or two ago. What you mean by love is a matter of the spirit. What today's youngsters mean by "lerve" is only of the body. Even the mind doesn't matter enter into it much. But you know, Frances, there's no way of holding back the sort of change that is happening now. You break yourself, trying to hold it back. You can only go with the tide in the sure knowledge that it will ebb again. Not in our time, perhaps, but ebb it will. Meanwhile we live in Rome, and must accept what the Romans do.'

I was silent.

'Not that I propose to go and live with the Rector,' she said. 'All I have really been saying is that forty years ago, Pamela and Bartrum could not have got away with it. Now they can. That's all. They've pushed the business on. Nobody can push it back. It's done.'

Then why were Fran and William holding back? I left Mary more depressed than I had been. She had rubbed it in that whether I liked it or not, I was living in Rome.

She knew. 'It doesn't affect me personally,' she had said, 'so I can reason. *You obviously can't.*' I felt I could trust her not to class me with Pamela Thackeray, and a hypocrite into the bargain. Some people did. Sophie had told me so. Well, like Sophie, I had so far a clear conscience; but all that brought me little comfort.

When later I heard William's tooted greeting I wanted to rush outside and throw myself into his arms; but the sight of him gave me other things to think about. I had never seen him look so old, or so tired. Was it my 'self-respect' that was causing him to look like that?

He sat down, and I waited on him, glad to do what I could to make him relax. He did.

'It is good to be home again,' he said, after supper. 'It's been a gruelling week. I can just keep going on the thought of coming back to this.'

That must mean that he was not too unhappy to go on being a Greek or a Gaul in Rome; but my discussion with Mary had unsettled me.

32

Johanna's car had given her a new lease of life, and I was glad; though it meant I was always threatened by visits from her and Ernie. It was to stave off just such a visit that I called to see her instead – though I also wanted to hear what she had to say about Pamela's latest move.

She didn't want to discuss it, though Ernie made one or two attempts to introduce the subject. He was a bit subdued, but she was all solicitousness: nurse, daughter, hostess, companion and mistress-like in turn. No man could have withstood that fivefold onslaught and not felt better for it. As I was leaving, she came to the door with me, and silently beckoned me round into her bedroom.

'It's done,' she said. 'He's made a new will, leaving everything to me. Signed and sealed last Thursday. Gordon Crane came here with it all ready drawn up, and Monty and Bob came specially to witness it. So it's all out in the open, too. They were so nice to me – kissed me all round and thanked me for making him so happy. I just can't believe it!'

'I'm very glad for you,' I said. It sounded flat and bald, but what else was there to say?

She grinned. 'I wonder which of us has got the better bargain, me or Pam Thackeray,' she said.

Next day, I had a telephone message that Ned's wife had died, very suddenly, without any prior warning, When I went out to break the news to him all he said was, 'Oh dear, Oh dear!' still poking about with a garden fork and barely looking up. He appeared unmoved, even indifferent, though I knew that could not be the case. Sophie had just arrived.

'Just leave him alone,' was her advice. 'That'll be for the best.'

I found it extremely hard advice to follow, so engrained was my training to show sympathy to the bereaved even if had to be fabricated. But a little later, Ned looked into the kitchen to tell Sophie he was leaving to 'go and see about things'.

Sophie watched him go with sadness. 'Ah,' she said, 'it's a bad job. But there, the Lord moves in a mysterious way His wonders to perform. Who are we to say as it ain't all for the best?'

The funeral took place the following Saturday, and William went with me to the service, but when the cortège moved to the grave, we slipped away. Ned's grief was plain for all to see, but he was more than well supported by his friends and neighbours. We felt outsiders.

We were surprised, at first to see him busily at work in the garden on Sunday morning, till we realized that Sundays were going to be 'loose-end' days for Ned from now on; he would be far happier at work than anywhere else. Cat stalked outside, apparently to inquire what he was doing there when he shouldn't be and rubbed round his legs till in the end he stopped work and picked her up to fondle her close to his lean face. She had often attempted to carry on conversations with him, but I had never before seen him caress her. He now had nothing else left to love.

Just after lunch that same day, the telephone rang, and I answered it. An agitated Madge Ellis at the other end was clucking like a broody hen disturbed by a fox. She apologized for ringing me several times, every time repeating that she didn't know what else to do.

'It's Mr Ambrose,' she said. 'He's asleep, and I can't wake him. I've tried and tried – I've shook him and shouted at him, but I just can't rouse him.'

'Where's Johanna?' I said, realizing the futility of the question almost before I'd spoken the words. 'Is he breathing properly? How long has he been like that?'

Johanna had gone out for the day, as she had done several times just lately, and Madge went in to get 'his' dinner. Johanna told nobody where she went.

'Perhaps you ought to get a doctor,' I said. 'Shall I ring Dr Henderson?'

'Well, I don't know. I came just after eleven o'clock, but that friend of his, Mr Ellington, and Dr Archer were both with him in the lounge, having drinks. I went straight to the kitchen to get on, and Dr Archer came and asked me where Mrs Brooke was. I told him I didn't know, but she'd said she wouldn't be home till tea-time. And he seemed put out, because he said he had got to change Mr

Ambrose's medicine, and he had wanted to give her strict instructions about it. "But not to worry," he said. "He's really very well, and I'm quite pleased with him."'

'But when I went to tell him his lunch was ready half an hour or more ago he was asleep with the newspaper over his face and his glasses on his forehead. So I tried to wake him, like I said. He's still the same, and his dinner's spoilt. I don't know what to do!'

'Gosh,' I said. 'It is difficult.' Her irritation with Johanna was plain. I sympathized wholly. We had to do something. 'Is he safe to be left for a few minutes?'

'I think so. He can't fall out of his chair.'

'Well, my guess is that he has probably had a drop too much drink,' I said. 'I don't think he should be left alone. Could you slip home and ask your husband to go back with you? Then if he doesn't rouse soon, give me another ring, and we will come round. We'll give it till three.'

Madge was calmed and soothed with help waiting in the wings, and rang off. We couldn't relax, though, so I rang at three o'clock. Madge informed me that he was just the same and hadn't moved a muscle.

'Damn!' I exploded, violently, as I put the receiver down. 'What does Johanna think she's up to, leaving him for us to look after?'

William looked grim. He wasn't at all pleased with Johanna for spoiling his Sunday.

The old man was as peacefully asleep as a baby. William felt his pulse, and pronounced it strong and regular. His breathing was deep, but rhythmic and not at all stertorous. His forehead was damp, but not clammy.

'He seems just to be asleep,' said William. 'But it's funny we can't wake him. I think we ought to stay a bit.'

So we sat down — Madge and Stan Ellis, William and I, like a party of Victorian corpse-watchers, only it was a living sort of corpse we had in front of us. At four-thirty I stood up, and announced that I was taking it upon myself to go down to the village to see Dr Henderson and explain the situation to him. William said we should have done it an hour and a half ago. I had only got as far as the door, when Johanna drove into the yard.

She looked anything but pleased to see the reception committee in her lounge, and swept into the house saying, 'What's the fuss? Can't I leave the place for five minutes without him kicking up a shindy?'

279

She was quickly (and coldly) apprised of the situation by William.

'Silly old fool!' she said contemptuously. 'I'll bet he's been at the whisky bottle. It always makes him sleepy.'

'Like *this*?' I said, indicating the still-comatose old man.

'Well, no. To be honest, I've never seen him like this before. I should think he's had a lot more than usual.'

She leaned over him, shook his head quite roughly from side to side several times, then slapped his face hard. He sighed, opened his eyes, gurgled, gasped, coughed and wheezed, and then caught her hand and held it, rubbing his gaunt blue cheek against it.

'Hello, my little lady! You're back sooner than I expected. I thought Mrs Ellis was going to give me my lunch. Oh, are we having a party?'

He was struggling to sit up. Johanna helped him, giving us all a comprehensive glance of such scorn that I felt a physical urge to wriggle away from it. Before she had got him on to his feet, I had dragged William away, leaving what explanations were necessary to the Ellises.

I was furious, and William's stifled sniggers of amusement, as he remembered us all sitting so solemnly round a chap who was only just innocently sleeping it off, did nothing to appease my intense irritation with Johanna.

A couple of days later, she arrived, alone, raging with anger.

'I have just been called over the coals about Sunday,' she exploded. 'By Monty, damn his impudence! Told me off for daring to leave Ernie alone — as if he had a right to give me orders! Why doesn't he take the old fool home with him, if he's so concerned? He was only asleep, after all.'

'How did he know about it?' I asked, noting that she had not evinced a word of thanks to me for our trouble.

'Turned up without ringing first, just like he did on Sunday. He usually rings to let me know when they are coming. Said he "just happened to be passing" and didn't like to go by without popping in to see Ernie. Of course Ernie was full of what had happened on Sunday, and told Monty all the details as if it was a great joke. But Monty took a very different view of it. Called me into the hall, and just let into me. Asked me what I thought I was being paid for, and threatened me — honestly Fran, he spoke to me as if I were a char caught sweeping the dust under the carpet! As good as told me that I'd better watch my step. Really! It isn't his bloody money I'm putting up with Ernie for. I shall tell Ernie word for word what he said. I'm not going to be blackmailed by that lecherous humbug, especially now that Ernie's committed himself.'

She was ablaze, and wonderfully handsome in her crackling anger.

'He tried to make out that Ernie had had some sort of a seizure, and must never be left alone again for a minute in case he has another. Well, I am not going to be tied hand and foot to him. Even a skivvy has one afternoon a week off. I had talked about it to Ernie, and we agreed that Sunday was the best day. Monty comes in the morning, and Madge is more willing to come on Sundays. What's the car for, if I can't use it? Besides, he wasn't exactly left alone, was he?'

She smiled, a mocking smile that made me want to hit her. 'You and William were in attendance, to say nothing of Hen-Len and Cock-Lock. If everybody had minded their own business, and just let him be, he would have slept till I got home. It's all so unnecessary. That's what is making me so mad.'

I really couldn't speak, and she got up to go. 'I had better get back on duty in case the Archangel Montagu calls again on his way home to make sure I am obeying instructions.'

She picked up her handbag and made for the door, anger still flaring out of every line of her.

I said goodbye to her with as good a grace as I could command, though I, too, was very angry. If that was what one got for being willing to help one's neighbour, I should certainly think twice in future. Whatever interpretation she chose to put on the incident, I still thought it exceedingly strange, and in some way sinister.

Next morning, a very contrite Johanna rang to apologize. 'The truth is, Fran, that I felt guilty, and that always makes me behave badly. Having the car has gone to my head a bit. I ought not to have left him for so long, and I won't again.'

I was mollified and to be fair, she had made adequate arrangements for him to be looked after. It occurred to me that some of my own anger with her, apart from her ingratitude, was that she had not offered a shred of information as to where she had been. I had secretly suspected that the 'solicitor' she had been seen meeting might have been Monty or Bob – but I had been proved wrong in that. And in any case, those sightings had taken place before Ernie had made his new will, and she had made her bargain with him. She surely had more sense than to risk being seen again with any man so soon? It was just not in Johanna's nature to jeopardize her welfare so blatantly. But where on earth did she go, if there were not a man in it somewhere?

*

I had my breakfast always at the kitchen table, so that I could see the view down the garden to where the church tower stood just above the treetops. I noticed that during the weekend, the last of the leaves had left the trees, and the view was almost better than it was in summer. I loved the tracery of bare branches against a sky as it was that Monday morning, their delicacy enhanced by the few solid patches of dark green yews and conifers.

Ned was out there already, making the most of the fine November weather. I had heard that he had once more returned to Bryony Cottage to finish what Jelly had had to leave undone. Well, why not? Ethel was no longer about to chide him for dancing attendance on 'that red-headed whore'; nor was Jack Bartrum likely to encounter him there, now that he had Pamela as full-time housekeeper or whatever other euphemism one cared to use.

It was funny how very quickly that scandal had died down. Even when she met Loddy or his family face to face, it passed without comment. People had simply written her off. She was not born a villager any more than Johanna was, so they could, and did, choose to ignore her 'goings-on'. Besides, they thought the Thackerays well rid of her, and hoped that Bartrum, though a native, 'would live to see his mistake'.

Sophie came in full of Monday-morning bustle.

'Did you 'ear the fire-engine, then?' she said, while still taking her coat off.

'No! Where? When? Why?' Fires were a legitimate cause for excitement.

'Last night, about half-past eight. Down at Loddy Thackeray's place. That silly child of Pam Balls's lit a fire in the summer 'ouse, when Lod thought 'e were safe in bed. Then 'e couldn't put it out. O'course they was all frit that it might spread to the farm buildings, but it never. They got off lucky, if you ask me.' She said no more, but went off to work in righteous indignation.

I saw Mary for a few minutes during the afternoon when I had to go down to the village post office. She was, surprisingly, full of the fire at the Thackeray house, and showed more concern than I thought it warranted.

'It was a naughty prank,' I said, 'that could have led to a disaster. But it didn't. I mean, aren't all children likely to get up to some mischief or other of that sort sooner or later? I know mine did.'

'Yours were normal children,' she said, 'if Kate is anything to go by. But I don't think young Melvyn is.'

'Really? Why not?'

'He hasn't had a proper chance. If ever a child has had reason to feel unwanted by his mother, that boy has. And I think the Thackerays, nice as they are, are having difficulty in making him feel one of them. I'm worried about him experimenting with fire, that's all. I should feel better if I dare warn somebody. But if I tried to, they would probably reply that all Melvyn needed was to have his backside tanned till he couldn't sit down. I am sure that corporal punishment is the one thing that must not be applied to that particular child. I can't interfere but it won't surprise me if there are more fires somewhere soon.'

I had other things to think about. William reported a long letter from Jess, in which she had admitted that she and Greg were at a very low ebb financially, and she feared they might have to come south again, but to where and to what she had no idea. In spite of what I had said previously to William, neither he nor I had done anything to bridge the gap, geographical or metaphorical, that seemed to be growing between her and us. I knew that William and I were being selfish. It was not that I grudged the possibility of material help, if she could be persuaded to accept it; but that, without expressing it to each other, what we feared was the intrusion of anybody — even Jess — into the peace and comfort we seemed to have achieved.

It left me feeling uneasy. I felt that in its tiny way it was an act of hubris that could only attract Nemesis in time. I was becoming smug, I thought. Everything was booming smugly everywhere. Great changes were taking place so rapidly that we had to accept them without question because before we had had time to digest them we had to be ready to swallow the next. Everybody felt so smugly secure these days that nobody was shocked by anything any longer; well — except for a few old fuddy-duddies like me and Sophie. No again; perhaps like me, because of my middle-class susceptibilities, but not like Sophie. She could be disapproving, but her life had been lived too close to hard reality for her to be shocked. She just thought it reprehensible for folk not to live up to the ten commandments when and wherever possible, like she did herself; but she accepted necessity as a reason for breaking the code. 'Have ye not heard what David did, when he had need, and an-hungered?'

She could make fine moral distinctions and did; she considered the evidence before giving her verdict. Her Bible-based values were overlaid with a much deeper, more rational covering that turned her from an uneducated bigot into a wise woman who saw through to the heart of things.

33

'Frances?'

'Yes.' A thrill of apprehension made me clutch the telephone tight. Only one person ever used my name in full, and whatever could Mary Budd want with me so early in the morning? I hadn't even finished breakfast.

'Hello, Mary. What's the matter? Is something wrong?'

She laughed. She had the most entrancing laugh, low in her throat and effortless, the crystallization of pure amusement. The sound of it immediately relaxed my tension.

'Why, am I so utterly transparent?' she asked. 'No, nothing is wrong, yet. But I do have a problem.'

'Not one of your own, I guess,' I said.

'Really, Frances, I do deplore your use of Americanisms. You may guess, and you may even guess correctly, as it happens. But you didn't mean that you were guessing. You meant to imply that you had already reached a conclusion. That is not guessing.'

'Quite right,' I said. 'And I apologize. I hate Americanisms quite as much as you do. It just came out. But you didn't ring me up at 8.15 a.m. to correct my use of English, I'll be bound – as Sophie would say. Or is that taboo, too, for being too colloquial?'

'No, I'll accept that. It is English made respectable by age and usage. Like good old clichés. It makes me so angry when people – jumped up critics, mostly – object to writers using clichés. They make such a song and dance about communication, these days, and then object to a phrase everybody understands just because it is commonly enough in use to be understood.' She dropped the school-marm's tone she had been using as we sparred, and said in her 'private' voice, 'I am worried, Frances. I need to talk to someone, so as to be able to hear my own arguments. Could you spare me an hour?'

'As many as you like,' I said. 'When, and where?'

'I hope this morning', she replied. 'And if you don't mind, I'd like you to come here. That's one reason I rang you early. Your Sophie has sharp ears. I'm afraid it may take all the morning, though. I could give you a cold collation at lunch-time, if that would do.'

'"Cold collation" it shall be,' I said. 'It always makes me think of Paul Dombey's christening party. I hope your problem isn't as serious as all that.'

Her voice changed again, a grave tone having now been added. 'Well not *yet*,' she said. 'But it does concern a child, and his future. May I expect you about coffee-time?'

I agreed, and went back to finish my cold toast. I could guess the identity of the child, I thought, though I couldn't see how Mary could be involved, but I remembered how much she had Loddy Thackeray's welfare at heart.

I decided it would do me good to walk down to Mary's, so I changed into some stronger shoes, and set out.

'Well?' I said, when we had settled to talk.

'It's about that boy of Pamela Balls',' she said.

I nodded. 'I thought so, probably.'

'It is, of course, properly speaking no concern of mine at all,' she began. 'But there comes a point when loving one's neighbour includes poking one's nose into his business uninvited. Suppose, for instance, I happened to be on top of Beachy Head and saw a blind man striding straight towards the edge of the cliff. I should obviously rush forward and warn him before he stepped over to his death. In that hypothetical case, nobody would accuse me of interfering; what's more, if I saw the tragedy about to happen, and didn't interfere, I should undoubtedly incur censure from the public at large. Wouldn't you agree?'

'Of course,' I said. 'So what?'

'If I look into the future by reason of a bit of specialized knowledge and a lot of human experience, and see a terrible domestic tragedy in the making, have I a moral right to do something about it?'

'Not just a right,' I said. 'I'd say almost a moral duty.'

'Mm. That's just what I think. But it isn't so easy to do as to talk about. Or as easy as stopping a man from stepping off a cliff. The folks concerned don't know they are in danger. How can I rush in waving a red flag and yelling "Stop"? Right into their private lives, treading on feelings here, there, and everywhere?'

'You are speaking of the Thackerays, I presume,' I said.

'Yes, and more. Have you heard what happened at the end of last week?'

'No. What? Has young Melvyn been playing around with the matches again?'

She nodded grimly. 'He had been with Loddy at the farm, as you know. But on Friday evening, Pamela rang to say she wanted the boy with her at Bartrum's place for all Saturday and Sunday. Incidentally, this is all in confidence.

'Loddy would like it not to be known at all, but I doubt if that's possible,' she said. 'I know because Loddy came round to see me on Friday after he had put Melvyn to bed – to ask me what I thought he ought to do. He trusts me just because I treated him just like any other normal child. He was very upset. He doesn't want to have any contact at all with Pamela if he can possibly help it. When Pamela phoned, he tried to talk sense to her. He told her how he felt, and asked her for everybody's sake to leave him and the boy alone. She was very high and mighty with him, he said, and said he needn't think he was going to get rid of her as easy as all that. As for the child, she would remind him that Melvyn was her child. Her maternal heart was wrung for the poor orphan, it seems. She wanted to clasp him to her ample bosom.'

'Careful now!' I said. 'You're making it up.'

She turned suddenly and came to sit down again, facing me. 'Tch!' she said. 'That woman does get under my skin. The cheek of it! Yes, of course I'm exaggerating, but that was the drift. She's decided to use the boy as a lever to get all she can out of Loddy. She knows perfectly well that he couldn't face, and his family wouldn't want, a long-drawn-out public squabble about custody. She's calculated that they'll pay up in cash without a fight if she offers to sell her son quietly to them. I'm sure Loddy hasn't got as far ahead as seeing the next move, but I have. If he made a fuss about letting the boy go to her for a couple of days, when asked, she'd threaten Loddy with an appeal to the local magistrates. You know what they are, these days. Loddy wouldn't stand a chance at all, as an adoptive father, against today's sentimental twaddle about the real mother having first rights, and the clap-trap of a child needing its mother above everything else, whatever she happens to be. Pamela would roast the child alive if she could sell him at threepence a slice! Anyway, she'd win, and she knows it. But the Thackerays would never let it get to court, nor would they part with the boy Loddy had made himself legally and morally responsible for. She'd ask for "compensation", and pretend she'd thought it over, and that after all it was in the boy's best interest to remain in the Thackeray camp.'

286

'Till next time,' I said.

'Exactly. You see why I need you, Frances. The Thackeray family are so — so genuine in all their dealings that they simply wouldn't understand the nature of the blackmail. Now on Friday, of course, Loddy wasn't concerned with any of this at all. What was bothering him was whether or not the boy would want to go, next morning, and whether or not he ought to let him go, or to make him go, or whatever.'

'So what did you advise?'

'It was difficult. You see, I saw through Pamela's motives in a flash. But all that I've sketched out would drag in the old Thackeray couple, and Michael and his wife and family. I thought that this was a case where prevention was better than cure. I didn't spell out all I've said to you to Loddy. Instead, I said how pleased I was to hear that Pamela still had some feeling for her child, and that it was only natural that she should want to see him occasionally. I put it to Loddy to ask himself whether some of his reluctance to letting the boy go wasn't a desire to punish Pamela a bit. Poor boy. He looked so guilty, and I felt such a cruel hypocrite for making him admit it. But I had decided that Loddy's only real chance of avoiding blackmail was to spike Pamela's guns at once. I told Loddy that of course he must let the boy go — indeed make him go, if he had to — just this once. Loddy was distressed, I could see, by my judgement, but bless him, he trusts me. So he agreed to do what I said.'

She wore a deep frown of concentration, and looked more depressed than I had ever noticed before. I thought that she'd probably had very little sleep since Friday.

'And what happened next day?' I asked gently.

She began again. 'I heard no more till Sunday night, quite late, when I had a long telephone call from Loddy, nearly frantic. The boy himself doesn't make the situation any easier,' she said. 'I don't claim to know him, but I've seen enough of him to make some sort of judgement. On the surface he is a reasonably likable child — speaks well, and has superficially good manners, though he's always quiet. But you can sense the wild creature underneath — wary, wily, inclined to be vicious when cornered, I'd say. And of course, he has reason to be. He's quite old enough now to understand the situation concerning his mother, and naturally he doesn't like it. Loddy says he's obedient but sullen. Bottling it all up, I should say. Anyhow, when told on Saturday morning to prepare himself for a visit to his precious mother, at first he sulked and said he wouldn't go. Then he

287

turned on Loddy and said he knew when he wasn't wanted, and he'd go anyway to get away from where he was. Loddy was trying to reason with him when Pamela drew up in Bartrum's car, bold as brass, and Melvyn just picked up his bag and ran out to her without saying another word to Loddy. Poor old Loddy — he was upset by the boy's attack on him. I had to explain that I understood the turmoil inside the child, and told him not to take it too personally. They get on well together as a rule.'

'And that's all?' I said, as she paused.

'All? That's hardly the beginning. I told you it would take hours.

'Loddy spent a miserable weekend, a bit worried over the boy, and very anxious about the future. I can understand why he doesn't want to lose the boy. He'll never have any of his own, now, and this one does give him a bit of a stake in the future. That's why I regret never having been married you know. People with no children really only operate on two cylinders, the past and present. Those like you, Frances, can work on all three. You don't know how lucky you are.'

I was silent, though I agreed absolutely. Nor did she know how lucky I was, though she may have had an inkling.

'Nothing had been said, it seems, about what time Loddy was to expect Melvyn back, but he had taken it for granted it would be fairly late on Sunday. So Loddy went across to have tea with his mother in the afternoon, and got back home again just after five. He found Melvyn sitting huddled in the front porch, with his jacket collar turned up all round his ears, and a scarf wound round his neck. He tried to get up to run away when he heard Loddy's footsteps, but he stumbled and Loddy caught him, and pulled the scarf off. He'd got a black eye, and a cut lip, and two of his front teeth were loose. Loddy said the child was quite dazed, and white and shaking. As soon as Loddy touched him he began to cry, and Loddy showed a great deal of common sense. He cosseted the child, got him some tea and food, made much of him and suggested a bath. The boy, he said, seemed incapable of doing anything for himself, and just went on crying quietly and despairingly while Loddy bathed him. He was a mass of weals and bruises from head to foot. But at last he began to calm down, and Loddy asked him what had happened.

'He'd hated it "up there", he said. He hated his mother, and he hated "him" worse than the devil. They'd tried to pump him about Loddy and his affairs, but he had refused to answer. Then they'd shouted at him for being sullen, and he'd said he wanted to go home.

'"This is your home," his mother said. The child seemed to sense that he was being used in a game the grown-ups were playing – he told Loddy he could see they didn't really want him. But when he said he wasn't going to stay with them, his mother said she'd see about that, and Jack Bartrum shouted at him to keep his mouth shut. Just then, the telephone rang, and Bartrum went to answer it. Pamela took the opportunity to slap her son's face and tell him to behave, and not to upset Jack, because he'd got a very nasty temper. Melvyn pulled away from her, and ran out. He went into the farmyard to hide till he could slip away and go home. They called him once or twice, but he kept quiet, and they soon gave up.

'Strange as it sounds, that seemed to upset the child more than anything so far. He must have concluded that nobody cared enough about him even to bother to look for him. As usual, he had a box of matches in his pocket. So he set fire to a little heap of straw next to a big barn, and felt better – or so he told Loddy. But the fire ran along the loose straw, and threatened the barn on one side, and a huge stack of straw on the other. He could see he had started a blaze that would burn the farm down, house and all. The poor child was desperately trying to beat out the flames when Pamela and Bartrum appeared. They soon got the fire out, and then Bartrum lost his temper and set into the boy. He thrashed him with the handle of an old yard broom that happened to be lying about, and punched him in the face again and again. It seems that Bartrum was quite beside himself. He hit Pamela and told her to go into the house and leave her brat to him to finish off. The child didn't remember much, after that. He said he thought Bartrum picked him up and put him in a car, and he half-remembered trying to get into Loddy's house. When he couldn't open the door, he'd been sick and then sat down in the porch, where Loddy had found him.'

I remembered with horror the look on Jack Bartrum's face when I had watched his altercation with Ned. I could not bear to contemplate that fury turned against a defenceless child half his size.

Mary had paused in her tale, and we sat in silence, she looking out of the window, but seeing only the problem, and I looking at her. It truly was the first time, ever, that I had considered her 'an old woman', so lively and vital was her intelligence, so humorously knowledgeable and critically tolerant of human nature was she. She looked drawn, and tired – ill. I began to show my anxiety, evidently, because she suddenly caught my glance, and smiled.

'I'm tired, Frances. I haven't slept well since Sunday, and I am in my eighth decade, you know.'

'It isn't fair,' I said. 'It isn't your problem, after all.'

She shook her head. 'I think you are wrong, there. It has to be somebody's, and Loddy can't take it alone.'

'He has a family,' I said.

'They are part of his problem — and certainly they are part of mine, as I'll explain in a minute. On Sunday evening, poor Loddy had a set of problems stacked up in front of him, and had to deal with the nearest first. That was that he now had a sick child in bed, and couldn't leave him alone in the house — which is why I heard all this by telephone. It was, I think, the mercy of Allah, because his natural instinct was to get in his car and seek Jack Bartrum out. I dread to think what sort of a *crime passionel* might have resulted. He told me that he had thought of going and telling his parents all that had happened, but something — pride, probably — shrank from making it a family affair. I dare say there is a lot of hidden feeling about this marriage, and his adoption of the boy. After all, Michael has children of his own — direct heirs to the Thackeray land, as it were. The old people, and Michael, must feel a bit bitter about Melvyn standing in line to inherit Loddy's share. One can see why he doesn't turn confidently to that quarter for unqualified understanding and support.'

'But they are bound to get to know,' I objected.

'Well, that was one thing Loddy desperately needed advice about. Should he go to the police and make out a case of assault and battery against Bartrum, or keep silent and try to hush the whole thing up? Should he send for Dr Henderson to see the boy, and his condition? Or could he hope that everybody had been taught a salutary lesson that would prevent trouble in future.'

'What did you advise?' I asked.

'As usual, reason and instinct were at odds,' she sighed. 'The desire to see Bartrum exposed for what he is, and for Pamela to be warned off from attempting any more little schemes, was very strong. But it would only have been a short-term solution, and I shrank from all the publicity on behalf of the Thackerays. I also happened to know that Dr Henderson was away, so it would have meant getting a doctor from Swithinford. So my advice to Loddy was to pretend the child had flu, and keep him in bed till he could take him back to school. If he still shows signs of his beating, then, I thought the boy would have enough sense to make up some tale about getting into a fight with a bigger boy, or something. To put it bluntly, I thought that to hush it all up with a few lies to cover the spot was the wisest course. Least said, soonest mended, as the old proverb has it. So far, all is quiet, and nothing has leaked.'

'So what is worrying you to the point of making yourself ill about it?'

She flashed me a smile of gratitude. 'We are back to the hypothetical blind man on top of Beachy Head. All I've done so far is to make him pause in his path towards destruction.'

'Have a glass of sherry – or whisky,' I said.

'Do you know, I believe I will.'

She fetched the drinks, pouring herself quite a stiff tot of whisky.

'If I'm right, what has happened so far is only a taster of what's to come,' she said. 'Can I start right at the beginning?'

'Please do.'

She proceeded to tell me how, after the war was over, she had taken a whole year's refresher course, which had included a lot of psychology that hadn't been discovered when she'd first done her teacher-training. 'I found myself studying the problems of those children termed now "socially maladjusted". What the psychologists said made a lot of sense.

'It was the war, you see. There were so many children whose childhoods had been wrecked. They were terribly difficult to deal with – naughty in ways you couldn't believe. But they weren't stupid. In fact, most of them were very intelligent. They had been so hurt that they wanted to hit back – though I'm sure many of them were not really conscious of their motives for disobeying society's rules of behaviour.

'I went to spend a week in a special school, just set up for such children. To look at them, you'd never know anything was wrong – but they were just writhing bags of hate inside. In fact, the place was crammed with Melvyns. Am I boring you?'

'Far from it. Do go on.'

'I learned a lot from the folks who ran that school. Their main aim was to supply the love that others for different reasons had failed to provide. "Love is kind, and suffers long", as the hymn says. They had been trained not to react angrily, *whatever* their charges did. And the things they did were legion. Among them was setting fire to things. This wasn't common, but once a child had started doing it, he had to be watched.'

'I can see how it all fits,' I said. 'If you are being burned up inside yourself with hate, fire seems to be the appropriate form of destruction.'

'Yes. Fire rages, and flames, and crackles – sort of gives out all the physical signs of hate. And it causes a lot of damage to other folks. So fire draws such children. They become addicted to it – indeed, some schools, I believe, actually have spots into which they put things of no value, inviting the pyromaniacs to get rid of their urges in relative safety. Now back to Melvyn. As soon as I saw the boy, I read the symptoms, but he was about to enter, for the first time, the very conditions most likely to bring about a cure. He now had two parents, and had acquired two more grandparents, as well as uncles and cousins. He was old enough to understand the adoption procedures, and intelligent enough to work out that somebody actually wanted him. Conditions seemed ideal, and until last spring I could have sworn that he would grow up to be quite normal. Then things began to go wrong.'

'When his mother took up with Jack Bartrum?'

'I think before that, actually. It probably didn't take him long to realize that there was a certain amount of resentment towards him from Michael and his family. And with the best will in the world, the old couple probably couldn't disguise the difference in their feelings towards him and their real grandchildren. When things began to go wrong between his mother and Loddy, I feared some sort of outburst. When those rings disappeared from old Mrs ffranksbridge's sink, I knew almost instinctively where they'd gone.'

I was quite thunderstruck. 'How wrong can you be!' I exclaimed. 'I could have staked my life that you thought Pamela herself had taken them.'

'No. I didn't think she could be such a fool, though in other respects I wouldn't put it past her. But theft is a way of making up for something that is being taken away from you. I was right in my surmise, of course. I told Loddy and Pamela what I suspected, and they questioned Melvyn at once. He owned up, so I extracted a promise from Loddy that he shouldn't be punished, and we arranged for Pamela to go up to see the old lady, and put them where they'd be found. So that all ended well, though I must say I've been a bit apprehensive of repercussions. And of further outbreaks from Melvyn.'

'And now?'

'Well – what I feared most was anyone offering physical violence, even quite mild, to the boy. I thought I could trust Loddy. He's such a good man, at heart, and I thought I'd given him some inkling of Melvyn's mood. Pamela has probably clouted the boy ever since he was born. From her, a bit of violence was accepted, I think. What I could not have foreseen was a thrashing from an outsider like Bartrum.'

She got up, and moved about the room again.

'I prophesy that as soon as that boy is on his feet again, something will go up in flames – with a vengeance. You see, the boy himself doesn't understand the origin of his need to set fire to things. He'll just act on impulse, somewhere, anywhere. So there is my chap on top of Beachy Head. I can see it happening, but I don't now where or when. And if I try to warn anybody, they'll think I'm mad. What am I to do, Frances? If any terrible tragedy should result, I shall feel like a murderer, for not preventing it! I've thought, and thought, and thought, but I can't see any way round it. I'll go and get our cold collation on the table. Please think about it.'

She went, and I did think. I had a great deal of admiration for her in every way, and I did not doubt her genuine anxiety, or her absolute sincerity. But try as I might, I could not take the issue as seriously as she was doing. Surely, Mary had got the whole thing about Melvyn out of proportion.

She called me to lunch.

'Well?' she asked, as we sat down and she piled up my plate. 'What does the oracle say?'

'Be fair, Mary. When you asked me to come, you said you just wanted to hear yourself speak. You didn't warn me that I was to sort of jury.'

'No. And I have no right to involve you, or to lengthen the chain of worry, as it were, to include you. But all the same I'd like to know what you think.'

'So be it.' I tried to find ways of softening what I had to say. I didn't want to upset Mary any more than she was already.

'I can see clearly that your theories about Melvyn's condition, and what may happen, are very plausible ones, and that they are soundly based. But they are only theories, all the same. Your analogy of the chap on top of Beachy Head isn't really very apt. That would be fact – his blindness would be fact, the drop from the top of the cliff is fact, and so on. Melvyn may be a socially maladjusted child – but that is only your theory. He hasn't been medically defined as such, has he? And at present you can't know what is going to happen. You can't make yourself ill worrying about something that may possibly happen at some unspecified future time to people you don't know. And as to trying to warn people – that's out of the question. Apart from convincing folk that you had taken leave of your senses, you'd have the entire village in a state of jitters. Look. You've already played your part in supporting Loddy. You'll no doubt have to go on doing that. But I'm sure you ought not to involve yourself in any further developments. Snap out of it! There, I've said my piece.'

'And if something awful does happen? What then? What about my state of mind then?'

'My dear Mary! You can't prevent it happening, can you? After all, you're not God.'

I spoke, perhaps, more vehemently than I had intended to, and to my utter dismay she pushed her plate aside, and began to cry.

I had never before seen the least suspicion of weakness in her, and I had no idea how to deal with it. I just sat quietly, and after a minute or two she blew her nose, wiped her eyes and managed a wry smile.

'I do apologize,' she said. 'I can't think what's the matter with me. And you did hit hard, but you are quite right, of course. I am not God. I suppose if I had any true religious belief, I could pray, and leave it all to him, instead of trying to do his work for him.'

'Sophie would,' I said.

'I haven't Sophie's strength of character,' she replied. 'So far, I've been able to get along reasonably well by trusting in Mary Budd. She's letting me down.'

'Is anything else worrying you?' I asked.

'Physically, I'm OK, I think. I'm just depressed, and a bit tired. And I do have another problem, strangely related to the first, as it happens. I just can't face starting on next year's fund-raising effort. I'm sure you realize that I always have to start organizing the next as soon as the last one is over. Some people are already saying we ought to have another dance like this year's. But that isn't possible.'

'Why?'

'Well, the barn will be in use, for one thing, so it would be difficult. I'd face the difficulties if I thought the spirit would be there — but it can't be. This year, the farming community was still whole. Now it is split, right down the middle. The Thackerays wouldn't want to run the risk of Pamela turning up with Jack Bartrum — and she would. So they just wouldn't take part. And if they don't, the others will find excuses not to. I know. Then look what else has happened since the horkey already — like James Bean's death, and Ned Merriman losing his wife. I doubt if Sophie would come with any heart, though she would do her duty. But I'm sure I have said enough to make you see what I meant about it having lost its spirit. No, last year's dance cannot be repeated.'

'It was an enchanted evening,' I said.

'Magic can be evil as well as good,' she said. 'It had in it the seeds of all those things I've mentioned.'

'So it had,' I replied. 'I remember thinking so at the time.' There was a short silence, after which Mary's voice sounded much more like her own.

'So that's it,' she said, suddenly firm and decisive. 'This year's horkey was my swan song. I am bowing out. That is quite final. Thank you, Frances. I knew when I asked you to come that somehow I should resolve that problem at least.'

'You will be got at from all sides to continue,' I said. 'They won't let you out as easily as all that.'

'Yes,' she said, 'but more out of courtesy than a wish for the gathering to continue. The end had to come. I must present them with a *fait accompli*.'

'How?'

'I haven't thought. By not being here to arrange it, perhaps.'

'Take a long holiday,' I suggested. 'I think you need one'.

'A hotel at Bournemouth in mid-winter, all by myself? Surrounded by other lonely senior citizens? I should go mad. I should be back home in less than a week.'

'Haven't I heard you speak of a brother overseas — somewhere in Canada? What about Christmas in the Rockies?'

'Why couldn't I think of that myself! It's my baby brother, Harry, and if I don't soon go one or the other of us will die. That's it! I am going to Canada as soon as I can possibly arrange it. For as long as I feel like stopping there.'

'Well, I seem to have done some good,' I said, amused at the way this elderly lady could make her mind up without a hint of the to-ing and fro-ing so many of us indulged in about every little thing. 'Now, you won't go back on that decision, will you? Get a letter off to your brother tonight, and I will take you into Swithinford tomorrow to see about booking your flight. The sooner the better. You can always cancel if it isn't convenient for Harry.'

I left her much cheered up and full of busy anticipation. But before I reached home, her depression had transferred itself to me. I hated the thought of the rest of the winter without her. Even turning William's ring on my finger for once didn't lift my vague apprehension and foreboding. Knowing she was within call was like

knowing Mother would be downstairs after the bedroom light had
been put out and you were left in the dark alone.

34

Mary left within a week. Her going seemed to me a watershed.

I had made no decision about Christmas. The practical problem
that faced me was what to do about Cat if we went to Kate. If we
could solve that, we would go.

When William came at the end of term and there was more time I
told him at once how restless and apprehensive I felt, though I
couldn't put my finger on the cause.

'I think you are probably bored,' he said. 'It has been an exciting
year, all in all. But the house is completed, and things are now going
along smoothly. A change is probably all you need to get you off
to another new start.'

Change. Yes, that was the key word, though not in the way he
had meant it. Change was in the air. Mary's conversation about the
horkey had pinpointed it. In early autumn, that wonderful occasion
had been possible; at Christmas, it was possible no longer. Events
between had brought us to the watershed between two eras. Before
the horkey we had belonged to the past; we had now crept into the
present, and were being pushed towards the future – a different
future, and one that I was not at all sure I was going to like.

It was funny, I thought, that I hadn't noticed any of this happening, until all of a sudden it had happened. I had been far too much
wrapped up in myself and my own affairs to notice the straws in the
wind, such as the crop of television aerials that had sprung up
everywhere. In Queen Anne farmhouses and medieval cottages, in
brash new dwellings like Loddy Thackeray's and in the row of council
houses – the inmates now shut themselves away from their neighbours to become citizens of a very different world. Sophie had said
how dramatically the attendance at church had dropped this winter.
She put it down to the Rector's failing health and the unpopularity
of the new lay-reader; I thought it was much more likely that some
popular TV programme coincided with the time of the service.

Even Sophie was different. Jelly's belated proposal, his death and his legacy had wrought small, subtle changes even in her constant soul, which were manifested mainly in her attitude towards her sisters. Whether they understood it or not, the difference was that she was no longer 'poor old Soph'' who had never been desired by a man. She knew now that she had been wanted, and her pride in the knowledge refused to allow her to kowtow any longer to Thirzah's inherited domination over her, or to give in to the weakness of Hetty's escape route of 'sterricks'. She now stood a little aloof from them, head held high, despite her suffering.

And I? I supposed I must have changed too, but it is difficult to know oneself. What was plain was that my role in the village had changed. I was no longer an object of interest — either as a newcomer, or as 'the old Squire's' granddaughter, or as a writer, or as the doubtful character who more likely than not slept with her cousin. Was I suffering chagrin because of it? If so, I ought to be ashamed of myself. I had got everything I had ever expected, and much, much more.

To know that William was under the same roof made me feel less like a boat dragging its anchor. We enjoyed a Saturday of busy companionship, catching up on all the week's tiny doings. Sunday, as always, was special; we had our lunch together in an atmosphere of gentle domesticity, and washed up together. William then said reluctantly that he really had to go to his study and write a Christmas letter or two if they were to reach his overseas acquaintances in time, so I opted to sit by the roaring fire in the sitting-room with a book.

'See you at tea-time, sweetheart,' William said, and when Cat settled on my knee and prevented me from reading, I sank back and felt at peace with myself and the world for the first time for many days. I slipped off into a contented snooze.

William had tried to prevent the telephone bell from disturbing me, but when he looked into the sitting-room, it had already roused me, and I was wide awake.

'Sorry, Fran, my darling. But it's Pertelote. From what I can make out, Reynard has got into Bryony Cottage and carried off Chanticleer.'

Still a bit dazed from sleep, I laughed at the reference until William's face told me that he did not regard it as any laughing matter.

'It's Madge Ellis,' he said, 'clucking and squawking worse than usual. I didn't want a wild-goose chase like the last one, so before I disturbed you I tried to find out what exactly was the matter. But she was quite incoherent, and all I could establish clearly was that Mr Ambrose "had gone". She wanted to talk to you.'

'She means that he has died,' I said, shocked. 'Perhaps Johanna has left her to look after him again, and she has found him dead.'

'She's hanging on,' he said. 'Go and find out what you can while I get coats ready and the car out.'

'Frances Catherwood, Mrs Ellis. What's wrong?' I said into the mouthpiece. But I got no answer. I could hear Madge's hen-like tones in the distance, confused with hysterical sobbing and gabbling in a voice that sounded a bit like Johanna's.

'Now, now!' I heard Madge say. 'What shall I tell her, then?'

There seemed to be an argument, of which I could only hear two rising voices. Then the receiver was picked up, and Madge said quite distinctly, 'I can't do anything with her. Please come!' The line went dead.

I conjectured, once we were on our way, that the shock of Ernie's death had robbed Johanna of all self-control. 'Madge Ellis wouldn't be the best of supports at such a time,' I said.

William was not looking particularly sympathetic. I couldn't help but feel guiltily how unfair it was to him to have to face another extraordinary situation because of my so-called friendship with Johanna — which I had to concede was beginning to look more and more like pig-headed obstinacy on my part. I didn't wonder that his patience with it and with me was exhausted.

He looked down at me sideways, as if debating how much he should say. 'I'm afraid your interpretation of the situation is too simple — almost naïve,' he said. 'I am prepared for something far more complicated than what you think. Have you forgotten the old man's will? Do you really think that if he had slipped his cable with no fuss or bother to her, Johanna would do anything but rejoice?' He looked at me quizzically. We were almost there.

'Perhaps she is afraid of death,' I said. 'Or perhaps she is having hysterics because of shock combined with relief.' I still felt an absolute need to defend Johanna against his cynicism.

'We shall soon know,' he said.

I went straight into the lounge, with William close behind me. She was sitting in her usual place on the corner of the rather too large new chesterfield. Madge Ellis was vainly endeavouring in her fussy way to thrust a cup of tea upon her.

'Oh, clear off, Madge! Leave me alone! What did you have to rouse the entire village for? I'm all right, I tell you. Just go away and leave me by myself for a few minutes.'

Mrs Ellis turned and saw us, and set the cup down. She looked as if she might have hysterics, too, at any second. I looked quickly round for some evidence of what had occurred. At least the old man had not died in his chair. So where was he?

William picked up the cup of tea, and put it into Madge's hands. 'You drink it,' he said and to my astonishment, she obeyed him. He took the cup back from her. 'We'll be in the kitchen when you want us,' he said to the back of Johanna's head, shepherding Madge and me to the door as he spoke. 'Now,' he said, pulling up the stools round the kitchen table, 'tell us what has happened while you have the chance.'

His calm, purposeful manner worked wonders on Madge. She fished a handkerchief from the sagging pocket of her old cardigan, and wiped her mouth.

'He's gone,' she said. 'While she was out.'

'How awful for you,' I said. 'I suppose you found him dead?'

Her mouth opened wide, like an old hen with the gapes. 'He's not *dead*,' she said. 'Just gone. Cleared off! Vamoosed! Clean as a whistle! Bag and baggage.'

William's glance at me said 'I told you so' so plainly that I longed to hit him.

'Begin right at the beginning,' he said to Madge, and she did, keeping her voice low so that Johanna shouldn't hear.

Ernie had had one or two more queer turns, but Dr Archer had not seemed unduly worried. Johanna had insisted on having one day a week free, on which days she, Mrs Ellis, was paid to look after him. However since 'Rip van Winkle Sunday' (as William had tagged it) she had not usually gone away on Sunday when Monty Ellington or the doctor was likely to call. But this week, they had turned up unexpectedly yesterday, Saturday, so Johanna had gone today because it really was the most convenient day for Madge. 'I got here early to give him his dinner, and he was OK – ate every bit of it. I took him to his chair and gave him his Sunday paper and his glasses, and told him I'd come back later, 'cos me and Stan hadn't had our own dinner then. I sat down with a cup of tea after I'd cleared up, and I dropped off. But he never liked me to disturb him in the afternoon.

'Then, about four o'clock, Johanna comes bustling up to ours asking what's the matter and where is he. I thought straight away that he must have been took bad or fallen down, so we both ran back here as fast as we could. But we couldn't find him anywhere. Then I saw her sort of start, and go white, and she told me to stop where I was while she went into his room again. When she came back, she flung herself down on the settee and started crying and calling him such names . . . So I went to look myself. It was all left very neat and tidy, which was why we hadn't seen it when we were looking for him. But everything has gone! All his clothes, and shoes, and his hair-brushes, and papers – just gone!'

We were silent. It had all the signs of having been a carefully planned operation. He had probably got fed up with being left alone, and had arranged to be evacuated in her absence. I said so.

Madge shook her head. 'No, I don't think so. He couldn't have known what time I was going to get his dinner, could he? Besides, he was daft about her – you know he was. And I know he hadn't packed anything, because he asked me to get him a clean handker-chief, and everything was just ordinary in his bedroom then.'

'But it doesn't make sense,' I said, loudly and vehemently.

'Oh, yes it does,' said Johanna from the doorway.

We all turned towards her, like three marionettes all on one control. She was a bit dishevelled, and very pale, but her eyes were ablaze with anger. Her voice, too, came out hard and stony, like chippings from a mason's chisel. 'I know what's happened. He's been kidnapped, by Mr Monty Bloody Ellington. I am sure of one thing – that he has not gone of his own free will.'

'Police?' I said.

William shook his head. 'Not till we know more,' he said. 'For all Johanna says, he may have gone willingly.'

Johanna looked at him as if he might have been a tarantula sitting on her kitchen table. 'I don't want the police snooping round, thank you. I can manage by myself.'

She looked round at all three of us, making sure we had got the message clearly. She didn't want anybody snooping around. And again, just as if the puppeteer had moved his control, we all stood up together.

'It would have been better all round if nobody had known any-thing,' Johanna said. 'But I could not stop Madge from calling you. Now the only thing any of you can do to help is to keep your head shut till I get him back again.'

No word of thanks. She was too angry for that. We slipped away like embarrassed children who had been discovered doing naughty things in the lavatories. I wondered if William would find it funny this time.

We didn't speak till we were nearly home, and I had sat thinking how anger had taken the polish off Johanna's voice and left the raw soapstone showing.

'I wonder what her origins really are,' I said aloud.

'You took that thought straight out of my head,' William replied. 'Irish washerwoman married — or not married, as the case may be — to a Billingsgate porter would be my guess. But what a looker! I was just thinking that I had never seen her looking so — so fetching. I don't think there is a man on earth who could resist her.'

'Not one?' I said, sounding as miserable as I felt.

'Well, maybe just one,' he said. We had reached home, and he had stopped the car and turned out the lights. He put his arms round me, ruffling my hair.

'Don't get upset about this business, Fran darling. You can't afford to, because this is only the beginning. When she finds out what she is up against, she'll be round here like a shot for the help and support she knows she'll get. I'm sorry to say so, sweetheart, but I am afraid your beautiful friend's other name is trouble.'

'I'm not sure she is my friend,' I said (very grateful for the fact that it was still Sunday).

'No? Well, I'm quite sure she thinks you are hers.'

'I'm sorry,' I said humbly. 'I know you don't like her.'

'I find her devastatingly fascinating,' he said brutally. 'But I warned you not to get involved, didn't I? Now you are, and you have got to see it through.'

He let go of me, and gave me his handkerchief. And then he added, 'And so have I, because what concerns you also concerns me. You may have forgotten, but I haven't. You are my wife. So don't worry about having to involve me. I think she is right in her surmise. Monty Ellington has "rescued" or "liberated" Ernie against his will, though what the motive is I have no idea. But I'll bet my last sixpence that she'll never see Sugar Daddy again!'

'Oh, William,' I cried, as the full implication of what he had said welled over me. 'What will she do?'

'She'll survive,' he said, opening the car door for me. 'The real question is, who will go under to make sure that she does?'

I knew he was right. Johanna was now an unexploded bomb under us all.

301

35

Two whole days passed with no word from Johanna; on the third morning, I was alone in my study when she rang, and proved William right.

'Can I come round?' she said. 'There's too much to tell you on the phone.'

'Of course,' I said, overcoming my resentment. 'I'll have coffee ready.'

'Coffee? It's the brandy bottle I shall need,' she said, and rang off.

Johanna looked tired and strained, and when I stood both the coffee-pot and the brandy bottle by her side, she seemed on the verge of tears.

'I don't know what to do next,' she said, plunging straight in. 'As soon as you had gone on Sunday, I rang Monty's house. His wife answered – the bitch! She said he was not there, and put the phone down on me. So I tried Bob Archer – same result. In its way, it was reassuring. It was so obvious that both women had been briefed what to say. So it had all been prearranged. It meant that they had got him – it was no use going to the police.'

I waited. I knew her well enough by now to know that she would tell me what she wanted to, and no more.

She exploded suddenly into furious tears of anger. 'Damn him! May he rot in hell for all eternity! To think of all he's got, and he still grudged me every little thing Ernie chose to give me. Didn't I earn it? Who else would have looked after that miserable and helpless old sod like I did? It isn't fair!' She was crying in earnest now, real tears of misery.

'Go on,' I said. 'What happened next?'

'On Monday, I kept ringing Bob Archer's number till his receptionist answered me. She had been briefed, too. Mr Ambrose had been admitted to Dr Archer's private nursing home. I asked why, but of course she didn't know. I demanded to know what the home was called and where it was. So I went there, straight away. I asked to see him, but they said Dr Archer had given specific instructions that he was to have absolutely no visitors, because he was under heavy sedation. I asked what was the matter with him, and do you know

302

what they said? "Nothing that good food and attention couldn't put right." Can you beat it? No further information.

'So then I went directly to Monty's place, and bearded him in his office. He swore that they had called again on Sunday "quite by chance", and had found him in a coma again. So Dr Archer had made the decision there and then to take him to the nursing home.'

'And they stayed long enough, with the poor old chap still in a coma, to clear his wardrobe and his desk and all the rest?' I said. 'That doesn't make much sense.'

She ground her teeth. 'Especially his desk,' she said. 'I'll bet Archer had to give him a shot to put him out, first. He had nearly four hundred pounds in his desk, in cash. He told me he had put it there especially, so that if anything did happen to him suddenly, I was to go and get it before letting anybody else know. It was put there specially for me. I was very careful never to touch it, or to let him spend it on me. It was going to be mine in the long run, anyway. But now it's gone! Oh, Fran, what *am* I going to do? I can't get along without his money. Of course, I shall be all right when he dies, but he may last for years and years.'

I doubted it, and said so. If he were conscious but in their power, he would be in such distress that it would soon kill him; if they kept him sedated when he didn't need it, that would soon finish him, too.

'It can't be long,' I comforted. 'And you must have got things a bit sorted out since he has been with you, haven't you? If the worst comes to the worst, you still have a room to let again. And it can't be long now till Dave arrives, can it?'

I know how irritating such platitudes can be, though what else was there for me to say? But she stood up suddenly, scorn and distaste reflected from every curve of her.

'I didn't expect you to be able to understand,' she said. 'Why should you? You've never had to cope with anything. But I didn't expect you to talk exactly like Madge Ellis.'

I was angry, but it was no time to quarrel with her, so I apologized. 'I am sorry. I do understand – but I'm as helpless as you are.'

'Don't worry about me. I shall find a way out by myself. That idiot Madge should never have rung you on Sunday – while your precious professor was with you. You've always got him around to turn to.'

Now I was very angry, and I suppose I showed it. It was she who apologized, coming close and smiling through her tears like the consummate actress she was. She probably expected me to hold her and comfort her, so that she could break her brave resolve not to burden me further with her troubles, and then do exactly that. But it didn't work. I was still too angry, and she was intelligent enough to see that it wasn't going to. When she spoke again, there was a very steely core to her tone.

'As I said on Sunday, all I ask of you is that you keep quiet. I don't know what I'm going to do yet, but do something I shall. So I warn you. And don't expect me to play my game by your ladylike rules, either. It's tooth and claw for me from now on. 'Bye, for now. I'll let you know when there is anything fresh to tell you.'

I let her go, still fuming myself. She had made her message to me quite clear: keep off the grass. She needn't have worried on that score. I intended to.

I reported to William when he came back. 'She'll win,' I said. To my surprise, he was not so sanguine.

'I'm not so sure. You see, Fran, he is in his own doctor's care. Nobody can get him out of that but himself. And they will take good care to see that he is in no condition to act on his own behalf.'

'But that would be criminal! And should two men, one a professional, do a thing like that?'

'There's money involved. Professional men suffer from greed as much as other folks do. They thought they had got that poor old man just where they wanted him – and then he goes and falls for Johanna, and all their little scheme goes awry. It's that will of his that has put the cat among the pigeons.'

'Well, he has made it, so that is all safe,' I said.

William snorted.

'Oh William! They couldn't!'

'We shall see. I don't suppose they will go as far as murder, though if they wanted to it would be easy enough. In the meantime, they've got him, and they'll keep him. It does seem to me to smack of personal animosity towards Johanna as well, though.'

'Yes, I think so. She was too clever for them: they didn't expect a country landlady to turn out like that. And since Ernie made his will, with its condition, she has held them both off physically. They both thought they only had to wait for time and opportunity. They don't like their advances being rebuffed.'

'They don't know Johanna, if they really hoped for that,' he answered. 'She is after the really big game. Ernie was just a hillside goat to keep her aim in trim till the tiger appeared in her sights. Maybe the mysterious man who enticed her to take her eye off Ernie is the tiger she's been tracking. We shall have to wait and see.'

As I was paying Ned in the kitchen on Friday afternoon, he suddenly asked me if I knew when Mr Ambrose would be back.

'I'm afraid I don't,' I said. 'All I know is that he has had to go into a nursing home.'

Ned turned his cap over in his hands two or three times, while deciding what line to take. Then he brought his startling blue gaze directly upon me, and said, 'Well, that's as maybe. But if he ain't coming back, who's a-going to pay me?'

I was horrified. All my foreboding returned in a flash.

'Oh, Ned!' I said. 'You don't mean they owe you for what you've been doing all this time?'

'I ain't had a penny, yet,' he said. 'She set me on, saying as the old man 'ould pay me all at once when I'd finished. That seemed to me to be a good idea, like. But once or twice I've had my doubts, 'cos he's sometimes made funny remarks like hoping I hadn't spent all I'd took last week buying fags for her, and such like. And once he asked me how much longer it was likely to take, because it was costing him more than he'd intended. What I mean is, he spoke as if I'd *had* the money, somehow. But he were a queer old fellow in some ways, so I didn't take much notice o' what he said.'

'So you haven't been paid all the summer?'

'Worse than that, ma'am. You see, she asked me in the first place to paint the house, outside and in. "You get what you need in the way o' paint," she says, "and Mr Ambrose'll settle it all when you've finished." So I did. Then she asks if I'll do the big lawn afresh. "It wants returfing," I says, "to make a good job on it." So the same thing happens. I get the turf, an' pay for it, an' give her the bills. About a hundred pound, altogether, with my work, an' cheap at that. An' that don't take no account of all the packets o' fags an' bottles o' sherry she's asked me to pick up for her from the pub.'

'Oh Ned, you *fool*,' I exclaimed.

'Ah. I know. Kill all the fools an' the wise 'ould soon starve, as the saying goes. But there, fools never learn – specially if they don't want to. Anyways, I should like to know when he's coming back, so as I can have it out with him, like.'

'Sit down a minute, Ned,' I said. I had to decide what I should tell him. It was quite obvious to me that Johanna had taken the money to pay Ned from Ernie in cash, and had simply spent it on something else, trusting to Ned's devotion to her to keep him at his job. Where was all the money going? I think I felt more disgust towards her than I ever had done before. But I was angry with him, too. He

305

really should have had more sense! I was a bit comforted by the knowledge that he wasn't exactly in want himself, so he could spare the actual money better than most. I told him what I knew, without any details. He took it all in very quietly. 'So you know where he is, if you want to send a bill,' I said.

He looked at me again, this time with the ghost of a twinkle.

'It's never no good floggin' a dead 'orse,' he said. 'The thing is, 'e's paid it once, an' she's spent it.'

'But it's terrible, Ned,' I said.

'Worse things 'appen at sea,' he replied. 'I shall know better next time.' He stood up. 'I reckon she's changed a lot since that old chap come to live there,' he said. 'She used to be that full o' fun, I'd a-done anything for 'er, whether she ever paid me or not. She were so different, like. I hadn't never met anybody like her afore.'

Poor old Ned, to have his beautiful dream so shattered by reality.

Next Monday morning, Ned sought me out in my study. He had decided to go up to see Johanna and ask her outright whether or not he was ever likely to get his money.

'The door was locked, so I knocked and banged, and at last she come to answer it,' he said. 'She opened it just a crack, 'cos she were only in her nightgown. She could hardly speak, and just croaked at me that she had got the flu, real bad. I asked if there was anything I could do for her, and she said no, only go away and let her go back to bed. I thought as somebody ought to know as she's there, bad in bed, all by herself.'

I thanked him, and told him not to worry. 'I expect Mrs Ellis will be going in and out,' I said.

He looked uncomfortable. 'I've heard as they have had a real barney with each other,' he said, 'the day after Old Ambrose went. Mis' Ellis won't be doing nothing to help her in future. That's why I thought as I ought to tell you.'

I was more or less speechless. Ned put on his cap, and prepared to go out. At the door he turned, and said, 'Sophie tells me as you want to go away at Christmas, but can't leave your cat,' he said. 'I shan't have nothing nor nobody else to bother about, this year, so if you like to leave her to me, I'll see as she's all right. If it's all the same to you, I'll come up here and sit with her, like, an hour or two morning and night.'

He was gone before I could take in his marvellous offer, which of course we should accept, sad though we were to consider the cause of it.

'Let him use my sitting-room in Eeyore's Tail,' William said that evening. 'I'll show him how to use the television. What a splendid idea.'

I told William what Ned had said about Johanna's flu. He looked sceptical, but had to admit that it was just possibly genuine.

'I suppose you want to rush to the rescue,' he said, with some asperity. 'It's no good me trying to stop you. I, personally, could strangle the damned woman with pleasure.'

'Don't be cross with me, William,' I said. 'It isn't my fault.'

'Go and ring her, my dear girl,' he said. 'You won't be happy till she's made you miserable again.'

But he was grinning at me, and I did exactly what he had told me to do. Her voice was a ghostly whisper, and it was evident that she was crying.

'Shall I come down?' I asked.

'Let yourself in,' she said.

I told William I thought it best to go alone.

36

She was lying in a darkened room, with the curtains drawn. There was no welcome from the lump beneath the bedclothes.

I called, 'Hello. Can you bear the light?'

She raised her head from the pillows, and said, in an urgent voice, 'Switch it on if you like, but don't draw the curtains.' Then she started to sob, great gasping sobs which told me she had been crying for so long that tears were exhausted.

'Johanna,' I cried. 'Whatever is the matter?' And I pressed the light-switch.

When one uses the word 'transformation', one thinks of it only working one way – the ragged Cinderella into the jewel-clad princess, or the ugly frog to the handsome prince. What had happened to Johanna in a few days had been in reverse gear. Always petite, she had shrunk. The face peeping above the crumpled sheet was that of a wizened little witch with red swollen eyes. Her hair hung loose and bedraggled round her ears, and even older than the tear-sodden face were the tiny, claw-like hands clasping and unclasping the top of the sheet. She didn't look at me, but pulled the sheet up over her face, and began to wail.

I rushed to the bed and sat down upon it, and she sat up and threw herself into my arms, gabbling incoherently. The only word I could distinguish was 'car'; and then what sounded like, 'They've taken the car.'

Whatever the matter was, its origin was no kind of virus. 'Let me get you a cup of tea, or some brandy or something,' I said.

'There isn't any,' she said. 'Brandy, I mean. I've already drunk every drop of alcohol there was in the house. There may be some tea. You can look.'

I found some tea and made a strong brew, then I fetched face cloth and towel, and supplied some astringent eau-de-cologne sachets from my own handbag. A hairbrush completed the first stage of restoration, and though she didn't look a great deal better for my efforts, she had at any rate stopped her incoherent babbling, while the shuddering dry sobs were becoming less frequent.

'Now tell me,' I commanded.

She had been in no doubt, she said, when she had left me at Benedict's, that sooner or later she would hear from Ernie, asking to be fetched 'home'. But she could not communicate with him at all, and growing increasingly worried – mainly about her own financial position, though there was also some concern for the old man – she had decided that her best bet was his solicitor, Gordon Crane. She visited him, and the blow fell.

'He told me that it had been decided that Ernie was no longer in a state fit to conduct his own affairs,' she said, starting to cry again. 'So he had been persuaded to sign some legal document passing the entire handling of all his affairs over to Monty. Then I kept ringing Monty till I forced him to speak to me. Fran, he was so *nasty* – apart from what he told me, which was that as far as Ernie and his money was concerned, I could forget it.' Her voice dropped to a wailing whisper, if there is such a thing, as she added, 'And he has changed his will. Oh, Fran, what shall I do?'

What indeed? My mind was blank. 'We'll think of something,' I said. 'After all, we did before.'

'What a bloody stupid thing to say!' she flared at me. 'And look where it's got me! I've never been in such a mess as I am now in all my life. You haven't heard the worst, yet.'

'Go on,' I said.

'Damn him! Damn him!' she said, over and over again. 'Damn them, all of them! They are all in it. At least I should still have somebody, if it hadn't been for that bloody will. I nearly went mad, after Monty put the phone down. I started to drink, until I had finished all the bottles they had left. Then I came to bed. I've been here virtually ever since.'

'Have you had any food?'

She shook her head. 'I'd eaten everything there was in the house before I rang Monty. I didn't want anything afterwards. Ned came, one night − I can't remember when it was − but I told him I'd got flu. This came on Saturday morning.' She fished under her pillow, and brought out a letter with Gordon Crane's letterhead. It was to inform her that Mr Ellington had sold Mr Ambrose's car to a Mr J. Bartrum for the use of his wife. Would she have the keys, log-book etc. ready for Mr Bartrum to pick up the car on Monday morning?

'They came, this morning,' Johanna said. 'I can't stand it. To have to see her of all people − that blowsy tart − driving my car! How could they do it to me?'

I was appalled by the situation I now had on my hands.

'Johanna,' I said. 'I must ring William. He will be worried about me. How much may I tell him? Sooner or later he will have to know what has happened.'

'Everybody will soon know,' she said. 'So what does it matter? Tell him what you like.'

'In that case,' I said briskly, 'I shall tell him to make a thermos flask of soup, and bring some milk and the brandy bottle.'

She made no protest, so I briefed a rather glum William as quickly as I could, and returned to my 'patient'. It was time for somebody to be positive about something. This crying of woe was getting us nowhere.

'To say I'm sorry doesn't mean much,' I said, 'though I am. But we must try to think what you are going to do. It really is awful for you to be set back again like this, more or less to where you were before I came.'

'Only worse,' she said.

'I suppose it must seem worse, because you have had things you wanted in the meantime. But you aren't in debt now, for one thing. At least you can start again with a clean slate.'

'That's what you think,' she said bitterly. 'I'm up to my eyes in debt, everywhere. Much worse than before, because all the tradespeople would let me have anything or everything, on the strength of Ernie being here, and obviously so well off.'

'But what have you done with all the money that he did give you?' I had asked the question out of sheer alarm and disbelief. I think it was the one and only time I ever saw Johanna look genuinely ashamed. She coloured, a dull red that ran down her neck and up to her forehead. For a long moment she was silent; we heard William's car arrive.

'Dave,' she said hurriedly, as if she wanted to confess before William came in. 'You know I told you he was coming back, just after Ernie had arrived and got settled. Well, he came. Only before he landed, old Ernie had made that damned will, with its one condition. I had to see Dave somehow, and try to explain it all to him.

'He wasn't very pleased, I can tell you. His morals are as old-fashioned as yours are. I couldn't persuade him that it was for his good as well as mine in the long run. So I don't know what would have happened if Ernie hadn't had that funny turn that Sunday. I had seen Dave before that day, and he had said he was not putting up with it, and was coming to blow the gaff on me. So I had to keep on meeting him. But when Ernie had that queer turn, I thought it was very likely the beginning of the end. I hadn't really any intention of ever going back to Dave once I had seen him again, but I thought that if I could keep him quiet and out of the way till Ernie snuffed it, I should get the money and could do as I liked. Dave hadn't got a penny or a job. So I gambled on Ernie not lasting long. I took Dave every penny I could lay my hands on, pretending it was for him to save to set us up together again.'

I could hear William rattling crockery in the kitchen. I felt I couldn't stand much more of this without his support, and tried to stand up; but she was intent on finishing her confession, and grabbed my hand and held on to me.

'Then it isn't as bad as it might be,' I said. 'Gosh, Johanna, I am glad. Where is Dave? I am sure William will go and collect him — now, today, if you want him to.'

She gave me a look composed of such contempt that I instinctively drew away from her. It said quite plainly that she was one step ahead of me, and knew that self-interest had prompted my relief quite as much as any thought for her future welfare.

'Sorry, Fran. Barking up the wrong tree, as usual. I'm not going to spend the rest of my life with Dave! And anyway, last Saturday Bob

Archer gave Ernie a real good going over, and told me that he was good for at least another five years. Well, that altered things, didn't it? I arranged to go to meet Dave and tell him how things stood. He said I had to choose. I said I should choose Ernie, and the money. Fran, you don't understand! Dave couldn't satisfy any of my cravings – for beautiful clothes, and beautiful things around me, and real conversation. All the things I envy you for. If I am ever going to get any of them, I can't have Dave round my neck. There was an awful scene, but in the end we made a bargain. I told him he could use all the money I'd taken him to go back to Australia again, on condition that he would keep quiet about ever having seen me in England. Then I could start divorce proceedings at once, on the grounds of desertion from the time he first went. And I made up my mind that once I was free, I should marry old Ernie and make everything absolutely safe. When I got home, Monty had kidnapped him.

'So as soon as I had got rid of you all, I tried to ring Dave to tell him I had changed my mind – just to keep him in view till I found out what was happening. But they said he had left his lodgings, and didn't know where he had gone. So I've burnt my boats as far as Dave is concerned, as well.'

'Can I come in?' asked William from the door. I could hardly have welcomed the Archangel Gabriel more fervently. He was wonderful with Johanna – especially as he had only this morning professed his desire to strangle her. He coaxed her to eat and we all made quite a good meal, picnic style on Johanna's bed – which, considering what the day still had in store for us, must have been providential.

The winter afternoon was now drawing in fast; as I went to find some glasses, I was surprised to find how late it was. Somebody had to make some sort of decision before long as to what we should do about Johanna.

She finished her brandy, and William poured her another. He caught my eye, and I saw that he had the situation summed up, and was dealing with it in his own way. With food and a noggin or two of brandy inside her, worn out as she was, she must soon sleep, and we could then go home. I would come again in the morning, having had a chance to consult William.

The plan, however, did not work out. Instead of making her drowsy, the brandy loosened her tongue. 'So here I am, back where I started, with nothing but debts and nobody to turn to for help. And my best asset not worth much now either. I mean me.' She

311

laughed, a bitter, cynical laugh, crushing her cigarette end into the fast-filling ashtray. 'You don't know anything about me, do you? I don't tell people who don't ask, and when anybody does ask, I tell 'em lies so well that they believe me.'

'I hadn't thought about it,' I said.

'Now you're lying, Fran,' she said. 'You have both thought about it, and talked about it, too. I can almost hear you saying, "I wonder what her background really is?" Well, I'll tell you! Then perhaps you'll understand.'

We made demurring noises, but there was no stopping her.

'These,' she said, picking up the soapstone ashtray, 'are all I've got left of the one person who really loved me and didn't expect anything in return. The man who brought me up, though he wasn't my father. He was a junk dealer from Bermondsey. For some reason he adored soapstone, and if he ever got a bit, he kept it. It was all he had to leave me when a bloody German bomb got him in the war. I'd already left home, by that time, of course. Into the army.'

'Don't, Johanna,' we pleaded. She took no notice, but just talked on. The man she called 'Pop' had had a yard, filled with the junk that went in and out. One night he found he had uninvited guests – a girl with a baby. 'Me and my damned bitch of a mother,' Johanna said, taking another swig at her brandy. A fifth-rate actress – talented and very beautiful, who'd been kept by a young upper-class blood apeing royalty. She was pregnant and demanding a settlement when he was killed in a bobsleigh accident on the Cresta run. It was too late to dump the baby unborn, so she decided to dump it anyway at the first real opportunity, somehow or other, so as to get back and start again.

'So you see my inheritance, don't you? Good looks, a talent for acting, and a goddam need always to be going back to start again.

'Anyway, luck hadn't been with her, and she'd gone down her few reserves till there was nothing left. What she was doing in Bermondsey was never revealed – but feeling ill she'd crawled into Pop's yard for a rest, and there he'd found her, and taken her in, and looked after her till the pneumonia cleared itself up and she'd regained her looks, by which time Pop was her slave and wanted nothing else but to keep her and the baby for ever. She used to taunt him by telling him about her other man – everything except his name. My father, I suppose. But I sometimes wonder. She was a good actress, and a good liar, like me. I've got no proof. For all I know, the young aristocrat never existed, and my real father might be a scene-shifter who never even bothered to take his cap off. She cleared off and left Pop and me when I was about six. Gone to start all over again, no doubt. Pop never got over it, or her, though he didn't try to find her. But he kept me. I adored him. We used to make plans about what we'd do when my name was up in lights in Leicester Square. Perhaps I might have made it — I don't know. But by the time I left school, the bloody slump had set in. Pop wouldn't let me go and try my luck at acting. I think he was afraid of losing me. So of course, I ran away. Poor old Pop.'

She was crying gently now, still cuddling the soapstone ashtray. She précised the rest: failure to find work on the stage, return home to loving, welcoming Pop. Marriage, at twenty-one, to a flashy commercial traveller; failure, back to Pop. Keeping an antique shop, stocked with the best of Pop's buys, and some real hopes of success, especially as male customers came again and again to look at the most beautiful article of all in the shop.

'That's what Pop used to say — and declare that I ought to have a tag on me saying "Not for Sale".' She looked suddenly up at me. 'Believe it or not, Fran, but I wasn't. And I really was happy, for a little while. We had some beautiful pieces, sometimes. Pop had got me a rackety old piano when I was seven, and found that I could just sit down and play it. So he got somebody to teach me "proper", and made me practise. While we had the shop, he came by a lovely little Broadwood boudoir grand one day, going cheap, so he brought it home. After that, I didn't really want to go out. I had Pop, who loved me, and my lovely things in the shop, and my piano.' She stopped, put the ashtray down, and lit another cigarette.

'What happened?' William prompted, gently.

'Oh, the bloody lease ran out. We moved, but couldn't find another place for a shop. I suppose I got bored. I started going about with a young RAF officer who was a bit posh — too posh to take home to meet Pop, anyway. So I went to work in a shop in Oxford Street where I could live in, and be about to meet Tony when he was on leave. I went home to Pop at weekends when Tony was on duty. I think Pop knew, but he never said a word, so I'd cook special things for him, and play the piano to him, and he'd show me what he'd picked up in the week. And we planned for the time we could start up the shop again, though I knew all the time it would never be. Tony had begun to talk about us getting married, just before the war broke out. But you must remember the sort of legacy of bad luck my mother left me. Her man was killed in a sporting accident. Mine went west in a plane crash. So I went back to Pop, to start again.'

William and I sat silent. It was by now late evening and Johanna showed no signs of sleepiness. We were prisoners, like Coleridge's wedding guest, hypnotized by both the tale and the teller.

'Then the war broke out. I joined the WRAC. It seemed better than going into a munitions factory. So of course I left dear old Pop alone again, in London, by himself. I fell on my feet, for once I suppose. As soon as my talent for acting and my ability to play the piano was discovered I joined ENSA. Pop felt he had to do his bit, too, so he gave up the business and went into the factory, which was where the bomb got him. I cleared everything out of the old home except the bits of soapstone and my piano. That I put in store – but it went up in flames in 1944. After the war, I tried to run a teashop in Kent, on the coast, but I hadn't enough money to do it well, so I failed again. Then I met Dave. Any port in a storm is better than none. The rest you know.'

We were still silent, worn out, bruised by the tale, of which neither of us doubted a single detail.

She sat up, suddenly, and reached for my hand. 'I'm glad you know, Fran,' she said. 'You are the nearest thing to a real friend I've ever had.'

I squeezed the hand, still not wanting to commit myself to banal words. A friend is one who knows all about you, and loves you just the same – as her poker-work plaque had said. Whatever the risk, I should have to help.

'You must go home,' she said. 'I'll be OK. In fact, I shall probably sleep the clock round, once I get off. I feel enormously better for talking it all out.'

'I shall bring you a meal round about six tomorrow night,' I said, 'and we'll decide then what's to be done next.'

I tucked her in, and leaned over to kiss her. To my surprise, she clung to me, pressing her lovely face against me as if I had been the mother who deserted her at six years old. I could feel her shoulders tense and shaking, and was afraid my gesture of affection had undone the control she had managed to achieve. However, after a minute or two she let go, and lay back.

William came back to say goodnight to her. She had already closed her eyes, and was breathing deep and calmly.

'I think I'm going to sleep,' she said drowsily.

'Good. We'll go quickly, and put the catch on the door. See you tomorrow.'

She raised a languid hand in farewell, and we left. In the car, I said to William, 'Well. At least we know the truth, now.'

'Mm. Nothing but the truth, I'd say, but probably not the whole truth.'

'Whatever makes you say that? I'm sure none of that was an act.'

'If it was, it was a brilliant one. But I think — I'm not absolutely convinced. The curtain tag was a bit much.' I was tired, and couldn't fathom his meaning.

'She wasn't asleep, or even sleepy,' he said. 'Now why did she put on that act?'

'She wanted to get rid of us, suddenly, I suppose. She'd just had enough — if you are right, which I have to admit you generally are. I don't know and I don't care. All I want is my own bed — and some sort of inspiration to put to her tomorrow.'

'Your heart's too soft,' he said. 'Do be careful, Fran. It would be much too dangerous.'

'I know,' I said. 'Like keeping a pet tiger.'

37

We were crossing the first bridge, on our way home, and in consequence raised a few feet above the surrounding low-lying ground, when I happened to glance over my left shoulder. Tired as I was, an alarm bell rang in my head.

'Isn't that *fire*?' I asked. 'Over to the left.'

William slowed the car, and looked. Then he stopped, and went back to the bridge to get a better view. There was no doubt. About a mile distant across the fields was an unmistakable orange glow lighting up the horizon, with an occasional burst of flame playing on the clouds of smoke rising above it.

'Not in the village,' William said. 'A straw-stack gone up, I should think, where some idiot has thrown a cigarette end.'

I was trying to get my bearings, not very successfully.

'I suppose we had better report it when we get home,' William said.

'William,' I said hesitantly, still struggling to place the locality of the blaze, 'am I wrong, or is it in the general direction of old Mrs de ffranksbridge's place?'

The car came to a screeching halt, and William got out again. 'I'm afraid you may be right. Good God! What now?'

'It's quite late. We may be the first to have seen it. Where's the nearest telephone? There's a kiosk back over the bridge. Report from there, and then we ought to go on to see if we can do anything. The nearest cottages are at least a quarter of a mile away, and that crazy old woman is there by herself. Everybody will be inside if they haven't yet gone to bed. Oh, do hurry!'

William executed a perfect three-point turn, and we sped back to the kiosk. I could hear his urgent voice, but he returned to the car without hurry.

'It had already been reported,' he said. 'And it is the de ffranksbridge place. There's nothing we can do, so let's go home.'

'No!' I cried. 'We must go on and see! We can't just go home and not even try to help, or to find out what's happening!'

'Haven't you had enough drama for one day?'

I didn't know how to answer, how to make him aware that for some reason I simply had to go back to that fire. My need to go was almost physical. After the long, draining day and evening, I could not think clearly, but I felt that it was my moral duty to be there. Somehow or other, I was already involved. Then understanding came to me in a flash.

'What day of the week is it?' I asked.

'Whatever difference does that make?'

'It does! Melvyn must have broken up school for Christmas on Friday. What can we do?'

William was quite dumbfounded. I had said no word to him of Mary's fears, in which, to be truthful, I had not put much credence myself. I thought she had got herself so worked up, especially about Loddy and Pamela, that Melvyn was being used as an Aunt Sally for all her misgivings about 'her' village. I could only assure William that I had not gone mad: that Mary had foreseen the pyromaniac child setting fire to something possibly quite unconnected with himself or his family, and that this might well be the explanation of the fire at the de ffranksbridge Hall tonight. I was possibly the only person who knew that Melvyn might be responsible.

'So what?' said William, shaking me. 'It won't do any good for you to go blurting that out in the middle of the conflagration, will it? Darling, my darling, you mustn't get involved! Mary isn't here, and if she were, it would not be her responsibility. It certainly isn't yours. That crazy old woman is lucky that she hasn't burnt the place down years ago. She is probably safe and sound by somebody else's hearth by now. And if she isn't— It's a sad end for her to come to, but you can't help it. Don't be silly!'

I was struggling to get free, beating my hands against his chest, desperate because he was being so obtuse and wasting time.

'But where's Melvyn?' I yelled. 'Don't you see? If he did set it alight, he may still be in there. He may be trapped in the house, and nobody aware that he is anywhere near! Fire fascinates him. Once he had started a good blaze, he wouldn't leave it, and he wouldn't have any real understanding of his danger.'

I could feel that I had got through to William at last, and that he was thinking swiftly and clearly what to do for the best.

'I really don't see what good you going to the fire would do,' he said. 'For all you know, the child is at home in bed. And I can't see us knocking the Thackerays up to ask them if they know where he is. After all, you are not supposed to know anything Mary told you, are you?'

'But I do!' I wailed. 'I can't un-know. How can I just not do anything? Suppose we do nothing at all, and the child is burnt to death?'

William held me close, though only to steady my trembling. 'Look, Fran, you are beside yourself. I'm not surprised, what with one thing and another. But whatever happens, *you-are-not-to-blame.*' He emphasized each word with a little shake. 'You have got to believe that now, this minute. I suggest we drive down to the Thackeray farm. If it is all quiet and peaceful there, we shall turn round and go home. If we see anybody about, I give you my word that I'll think again, though God only knows what we can do.'

It took us less than three minutes to reach the farm, where the old farmhouse sat in the middle of the complex, with Loddy's opulent new house on one side and Michael's Victorian one on the other, close to a huge old barn. One glance told us all we needed to know, and that long before we actually got there. Lights were ablaze in all three dwellings, and the double doors of Loddy's two-car garage open wide. His car had gone.

William, grim-faced, turned the car and took me back to Benedict's. 'They know already,' he said. 'I insist that you keep out of it.'

From our landing window, the blazing house was quite visible, lighting up the skyline in a most lurid fashion. William lovingly urged me away, but I was rooted there, like a member of an ancient Greek audience chained to his stone seat by the tragedy being played out before him, though he had known the story even before the action had begun. Wasn't that the very essence of tragedy: the knowledge that the gods had set up a situation from which there was no escape?

In no way did what was happening over there touch me nearly – yet if tragedy it was, then I was for ever part of it, because of the row of hooks that had linked Pamela's wartime offspring to Loddy, Loddy to Mary, Mary to me. It was all unforeseen and inexplicable, leaving me utterly blameless, yet full of formless guilt, like those snowflakes I had watched, neither black nor white, nor both – except for one's perception of them. I cried and cried and it was a long time before I allowed William to pull me gently away from the window, and turn my face into his chest. He made it plain that he was not prepared to be separated from me for the rest of that night. We should make up the fire again, and rest in our chairs. He sat on the arm of mine, holding me and stroking me, and at last I began to relax and went to sleep with my head on his shoulder. He left me to sit in his own chair only when I had at last succumbed to weariness and the comfort of his presence.

He was up and about in the morning before Sophie arrived, warning her of where I was, and why. I heard them talking to each other at about ten thirty, and went to join them in the kitchen.

William came close to me, and gave me a chair; but I had already seen his face, and knew that my fears of last night had been justified.

'It's bad, Fran – worse than we could have guessed.'

'Is she dead?' I asked, turning towards Sophie.

She nodded, setting a cup of tea down before me. 'They got her out, but she died nearly straight off.'

'She was old,' I said. 'And friendless. From that point of view, it could have been worse.'

William reached for my hand, and held it fast. I looked from one to the other.

'Who else?' I said, in a small voice.

'Poor Loddy Thackeray, and that boy of Pamela Balls',' said Sophie flatly. 'Burnt to death when the roof fell in.'

Oh Mary, how did you know?

When the shocked silence had passed, Sophie took up the tale. 'It was Loddy got the old woman out, and then went back for the boy – at least, that's what they reckon must have happened. Everybody wants to know what the child were doin' there so late at night. I dare say a lot'll come out at the hinkwest. But they'll all 'ush it up as much as ever they can, the Thack'rays, I mean.'

'Hush what up, Sophie?'

She looked uncomfortable, and I knew the signs too well for her to be able to deceive me. She had said more than she intended, and was now 'biting her tongue'. But she sensed that my question had to be answered, that it meant a great deal to me to know the whole truth.

'Well, if I tell you what I know, you'll have to keep it to yourselves for ever, as you might say, 'cos Dan'el would never forgive hisself if Loddy's good name got fly-blowed because of 'im. They went to school together, and Dan'el's all'us stuck up for Loddy. So 'e made me and Thirz' promise as we would never breathe a word to anybody about what 'e told us. But I shall tell Dan as 'ow you asked me, and that I told you. 'E wouldn't care about you knowing, 'cos 'e would know you wouldn't let it go no further.'

I felt that if Sophie did not soon tell me I should shake it out of her. There was this mysterious involvement of Daniel in it; Daniel did not work for the Thackerays, and never had done.

'Of course we won't tell a soul,' William said.

'William must speak for himself, Sophie,' I said. 'If you tell me, I must be allowed to tell Miss Budd. She was very, very fond of Mr Thackeray. If I can't tell her the true details when I write, I would rather not know myself.'

This was moral blackmail, because not to be able to open her bundle of knowledge to me now would have been a sore trial to Sophie, though her strength of will was quite able to deal with it if she had decided that way. It was not, however, my blackmail but offence that I should dare to consider Mary a person unfit for confidences that pricked Sophie's tongue into action again.

'I'm knowed "Miss" longer that you 'ave,' she said severely, 'and a sight better, as well. And I'm never knowed 'er to tittle-tattle to nobody about nothing yet.'

I was going to scream at her if she didn't tell me quick. I took a deep breath, and kept my voice under control as well as I could. 'Please, now tell us what Daniel told you. However did he come to know anything about it?'

Her expression said, very plainly, that it was no good me trying to force the pace. Tragedy or not, for once she held centre-stage, and she was going to make the most of her moment of importance.

'Well. As you know, Dan's been Bridgefoot's cowman, and there ain't much as 'e don't know about cows by now. He's never worked for Thack'rays, but Bridgefoots and Thack'rays 'ave all'us been the best o' friends, an' last year some time, Bridgefoots and Thack'rays decided to go into partnership to buy one o' them special French cows as is all the rage now. It were a thoroughbred heifer, in calf. The bargain was that Thack'rays should 'ouse it and feed it, but Dan should look after it special, keeping 'is eye on it all the while, and be there when it come to the time for the calf to be born. So by that, 'e's been back'ards and for'ards to Thackerays a goodish lot, just lately.

'So, come this last weekend, like, she's due to calve, and Dan thinks 'e'd better find Michael or Loddy, to warn 'em like. But just as 'e got to the cowshed door, who should drive into the yard but Pamela Balls-as-was, looking for that child of 'ers, who had come 'ome from school for Christmas the day afore. And Dan'el didn't want to meet '*er*, so 'e dropped back inside the cowshed. And nobody knowed 'e were there – but 'e see and 'eard everything. Everything as none o' them will ever want nobody else to know, now.' There was no stopping Sophie now. In and out the roundabout tale unfolded, and from among the bales of extraneous padding William and I picked out and pieced together the threads of that tragic evening.

When Pamela had driven in in her newly acquired car, Michael himself had come across the yard, just in time to meet her. She had got out, 'all la-di-da', and told Michael she had come to fetch Melvyn. She had phoned Loddy, who had told her Melvyn would not want to go with her, and in any case he was playing in the barn with his 'cousins' – Michael's children, of course. So she had come across to get him, wherever he was. Pamela went to the edge of the yard and called Melvyn several times, but got no answer. Then, looking down at her high-heeled shoes, she had suggested to Michael that he should go and get her son for her. Furious at her thick-skinned cheek, but maintaining cool civility, he had compromised by shouting for his own children, a boy of nine and a girl of seven. The boy reported that Melvyn had heard his mother calling, but wouldn't come out of the barn. The girl had piped up and repeated Melvyn's actual words – which hadn't helped.

Then Pamela had lost her ladylike temper, and said she would find the little so-and-so, and he'd go with her if she had to knock him out and carry him. She started off across the mucky yard, and

Michael tried to stop her, but she kept going until he told her she was trespassing, and ordered her off.

'She just laughed in 'is face,' Sophie said. '"And 'ow do you make that out?" she says. "I'm still a Thackeray, ain't I? And don't you forget it! I'm still your brother's lawful wife, I'll 'ave you know!"' This had been more than Michael's temper could stand, and there was a slanging match, after which she got in her car and drove off, telling Michael that he hadn't heard the last of it. Michael had then gone across the yard yelling at the top of his voice for Melvyn. He came back after a few minutes dragging the child after him.

(It became evident to me, from the next part of Sophie's report, that Michael had known about Melvyn's exploits up at Bartrum's farm, and of his passion for lighting fires. Of course neither Daniel nor Sophie had the least inkling of what had prompted the next, to them inexplicable, scene.)

Michael had ordered Melvyn to turn out his pockets. The boy refused, but the man, already tried to the limits of his patience, had grabbed him and held him, and emptied his pockets for him. Among the other contents were two or three little matchbooks.

'I don't know why,' said Sophie, 'but Dan'el said as the sight o' them matches was like wavin' a red rag at a bull. Michael just clouted 'im – 'it 'im so 'ard that 'e nearly knocked 'im over. Dan'el says as in all the years 'e's knowed Michael Thack'ray, 'e 'ad never before knowed 'im to lose 'is temper, let alone 'it a child.'

The blow had, it seemed, had the effect of turning Melvyn into a shrieking little demon who had let out all his pent-up misery, especially about his position as an outsider in the Thackeray camp, in such a string of invective that Sophie said she couldn't, and wouldn't repeat it. And when Michael, who was still holding him, took hold of his shoulder to give him a good shaking to make him stop, Melvyn had turned his head and bitten Michael's thumb till the blood ran.

It must have been the gods who sent Loddy out of his house to call Melvyn in for his supper at that very moment. When Loddy saw Michael striking his adopted son, he rushed to the child's defence, and a bitter quarrel between the two men had finally turned to blows. Daniel had no idea how to stop the fight, but shrank back inside the cowshed so that they should never suspect that anybody else knew about it. The noise had reached the main farmhouse, though, and both their old parents had come out into the cold to beg them to stop, and to reason with them; but by this time Loddy's blood was up, and Michael almost beside himself.

At this point the tears began to trickle down Sophie's face. 'Ah! It was grievous to 'ear 'em, so Dan'el said. You see, Michael let his tongue go and told Loddy 'ow all of 'em 'ad all'us felt about 'im marrying that b— woman, that Pam Balls. And 'e said that after what 'ad 'appened tonight, 'e'd go to law if it cost 'im every penny 'e 'ad afore 'e would ever let that there little 'ell-'ound of 'ers 'ave a foot o' Thackeray land. And their poor old mother went to 'im and tried to stop 'im from saying anythink more, but Michael turned on 'er and said as she 'ad all'us favoured Loddy, and 'e knowed very well as 'e had never meant nothing to 'er. Then the poor old man broke down and cried, and took 'is wife back into the 'ouse, and left 'em to it. Dan'el said it was *awful.*'

Michael had made Loddy's nose bleed, and the blood had brought the actual scrap to an end. Loddy went into his own house, taking Melvyn with him. Michael went home without even looking into the cowshed. So Daniel was left alone to cope with the heifer, and about an hour later, was very surprised to see Michael and his wife 'all dressed up to the nines' come out and set off in the car.

Then after about two more hours, Daniel had begun to be a bit worried about his so valuable charge, and he felt Loddy should tell the local vet that his services might be needed. Loddy had answered Daniel's knock at the door as if nothing out of the ordinary had happened. He told Daniel he would call the vet, and then come across to the cowshed himself — but he might be a minute or two because he would have to go upstairs to tell Melvyn where he would be. So Daniel went back to the cowshed, but Loddy didn't come. The vet soon turned up, though, and it was not long before he and Daniel had their hands too full to think about anything else than getting the precious calf born alive.

Then Loddy came running to the farm, shouting for Melvyn, because he had found he wasn't in his bed where he ought to have been. Michael and his wife came back, and saw the vet's car, so Michael went straight towards the cowshed. But he heard Loddy calling, and turned to go to help his brother instead. Daniel said neither of them said a word about the quarrel — they just acted like they had always done, helping each other as if it had never happened. When they had searched all over the farm, Loddy asked Michael to go and see about the cow, because he had just thought where young Melvyn might have gone. He had run off once or twice afore, so it appeared, and he was pretty sure he'd find Melvyn up at the Hall with old Mrs de ffranksbridge.

'Nobody knowed then, though it's all come out since last night, that there ol' boy had struck up a sort o' friendship with that crazy old woman as were in 'er second child'ood! It seems as she were all'us glad to see 'im, and would play marbles and dominoes and silly card games like "Draw-the-well-dry" and such with 'im for hours at a time. Just after 'is mother went off, he'd done it whenever 'e was 'ome from school, getting out of 'is bedroom window while Loddy were watching television.'

When Loddy had got there he was too late. The place was already well alight. Loddy had raced back and knocked up the Howes, and while Jean's husband phoned for the fire brigade, Loddy went back to rescue the old woman. He still hadn't seen Melvyn, and thought he was hiding in the garden. He carried the old woman outside, very badly burned, but still alive, and left her with Jean Howe, and it was then that they saw Melvyn at one of the upstairs windows. He didn't hesitate a minute, but went straight back into the blazing house to get the boy. They were fighting their way down the stairs in the great hall when the whole of the burning thatch fell in.

'And they say that there's nothing left standing this morning, only them two great brick chimneystacks, one at each end of the house.' Sophie got up and went on, 'The Lord giveth, the Lord taketh away,' she said. 'It ain't for us to question His ways. I never thought poor Loddy Thackeray would end doing a brave thing like that any more than I expected my Jelly to kill hisself in a new car. It is 'ard on the old couple, though. And worst of all for Michael. And you can see why Dan'el 'll never say a word about that quarrel. But we must all abide by the Lord's will.'

38

Silence is golden? Silence is a great black vacuum into which random thoughts rush to stem the pain of facing reality.

With the tears still drying on her face, Sophie started like an automaton to provide our mid-morning drinks.

'No, thank you, Sophie,' William said. 'Whisky in my study, Fran.'

He opened the door, and I obeyed him, grateful that for once I could follow, and not be expected to lead. William knew that I had to go on talking about it – it was the only way I could ever come to terms with it.

'Michael will never get over the awful guilt of having his wish for the Thackeray land to be kept in the Thackeray family granted so swiftly in such a terrible way. He'll be haunted by that quarrel with Loddy for as long as he lives.'

'He'll be lucky if he only has his own guilt to cope with,' William said, soberly. 'There's Loddy's wife. She actually taunted Michael that she was still legally a Thackeray – and of course, she is. She won't give up her rights in a hurry.'

'But surely Loddy would have altered his will when she left him?'

'Possibly. But who would he name as his heir? His adopted child, Melvyn. And he is dead too. In the moment of their deaths, his estate will have passed to Melvyn – who died intestate. And who is Melvyn's next of kin? His mother. Not a very pleasant prospect for the Thackeray family.'

'That poor old couple,' I said, appalled by William's foresight. 'Michael must have heard about Melvyn's passion for setting things alight,' I went on. 'But nobody can ever prove now that it was Melvyn who set the Hall on fire, can they?'

William swung round on me. 'My dear Fran, a lot of folks know Melvyn carried matches in his pocket. So did I, at his age. So does every boy till he gets found out. But *you* are the only one who knows that he was a real pyromaniac. Well, you – and I because you told me – and Mary who isn't here. You simply must not be heard suggesting to anybody that he was even possibly the culprit.'

'Another damned secret to keep?' I said, bitterly. 'This bloody village is full of secrets. And they will all tell them to me!'

'I'm afraid it is your lot in life,' he said. 'You somehow invite it – it isn't your fault, though I do think you sometimes lay yourself open to it more than you need to. With people like Johanna, for instance. I'll bet she is furious with herself this morning, for having spilled all the beans to us last night.'

'Johanna!' I exclaimed. 'I had completely forgotten her! I said I'd go to her at six. And I must write to Mary first. I must soften the blow to her as much as I can. She will think she ran away just as the blind man reached the edge of the cliff.'

'She couldn't have prevented it any more than you could. I'm glad she's out of it.'

I had thought of something else. 'I wish you hadn't reminded me of Johanna. It's partly her fault. If she hadn't set up a rivalry with Pamela to see who was the sexiest, if she had played honest with Dave, and fair with old Ernie, she would still have had that car, and Pamela couldn't have driven it down to show it off to Loddy and taunt Michael and upset Melvyn . . .'

'That's what history is made of. The storm that wrecked King John's fleet, the stroke that killed Edward the Fourth at forty-seven – all chance. But thousand upon thousand of ordinary people bore the suffering that followed. Sophie calls it "the Lord's will". We fight it, because we lack her faith.'

'And life has to go on, even for the poor Thackerays,' I said.

'And for us, too. You are in no fit state to do anything. You are going to bed till tea-time. You are not going to get up till I call you.'

I was so dumbfounded by this masterful man that I didn't attempt to argue.

Sophie woke me with a cup of tea about four o'clock and I felt a great deal better, and as she went out of my room I called her back.

'Sophie,' I said. 'What happened to the calf?'

'Twins!' she said, from the door. 'A bull calf and a heifer calf! Dan'el just can't get over it!'

William came in. 'Sorry I wasn't here when you woke up,' he said. 'I suddenly remembered that I ought to get the car filled with petrol, and I hoped I should be back before you came down.'

He was still full of forceful purpose. 'I have told Sophie that Johanna is ill and that you are going to see her; and asked her to stay to get us a meal ready for seven o'clock. That will mean you will have to get away from Johanna fairly quickly whether she wants it or not.'

I looked at him in amazement – I had never before seen the Professor at work as head of his department.

'And I have written your letter to Mary for you, incidentally,' he said. 'You can just add a postscript. Can you cope with Johanna by yourself?'

Well, really! There was no doubt who was in charge at this moment, but I bridled a bit at the insinuation that I had overnight become a spineless ditherer who couldn't find my way to Hen Street and back without my guardian. 'Of course I can!' I said. 'I might as well put the food and things together, and go at once.'

I noticed as I drove into the gates of Bryony College that the curtains at Johanna's bedroom window were still drawn, and took it as a sign that she was still in bed in the dark. The front door would be locked, but she would have left the back door unlocked for me to get in. So I ran round to the back door, surprised at the absence of any lighted windows. Luckily, I carried a torch in my handbag, and fished for it to guide my steps on the path. On the back doorstep was a large stone, under which she had always left her instructions for the milkman. Under it now was a thick eau-de-nil coloured envelope. It was, as I saw by the light of my torch, addressed to me, in Johanna's large flowery hand. Just like her, I thought with irritation, to waste expensive notepaper and an envelope on me, and still owe the milkman for her latest pint. I guessed it was to tell me that she would rather not be disturbed. I tore it open — and the length of it warned me that my surmise was wrong.

> My dearest Fran,
>   If you ever read this, it will mean you have proved yourself to be the only woman friend I ever had, one who now knows all about me, and is still willing to do what she can for me without a hope of ever getting anything in return, not even proper thanks. So forgive me, before you read any more, for doing what I must in my own way. If I could have done it without hurting you, I would have done, and my only regret now is that I am saying goodbye to you.

My heart had begun to pound in terrible panic, though it was so impossible to think of Johanna as a suicidal type. She was too tough, too resilient — and yet? I must read on.

> What I told you last night was the truth, but not all of it. The real truth is that I am in a worse fix than you could ever imagine, because about three months ago, Ernie had the bright idea of making himself absolutely secure with me by paying off my mortgage — which means that I no longer have even a roof over my head. The money I was taking Dave was really to keep him quiet about his half-share of the bungalow — I had to pay him in cash so that when I was ready to move, he had no tags on me of any kind.
>   What it means now is that I have no assets, either to meet my debts or to start again with. So I have got to disappear, and quick. You mustn't know where I have gone, even if I

could tell you, but as it happens, I can't, because even I don't know. If any of my debtors or the police do question you, you will be able to answer with absolute truth that I just cleared off, and left you flat. That's a good thing, because you really are such a very poor liar. But I know you well enough to think that you will worry about me, so I must tell you one last thing. I lied to you last night, because I could only see one way out, and had already decided that I should have to take it. Dave *had* left me a forwarding address, in case I changed my mind. And a telephone number; so first thing this morning I rang him, and he is on his way to pick me up in a hired car that nobody will know any minute now.

Think of me sometimes, and if ever a chance does arise, I'll let you know that I am still alive. I doubt if I shall ever set foot in Old Swithinford or Hen Street again – well, not if I can help it. Wherever I get to, I cannot possibly be more of a fish out of water than I have been here. It's your element, Fran, but it isn't mine. You can keep your rural beauty and your simple village way of life. I've got to start again.

Cheerio, then.

Love,

Johanna.

Stunned and unbelieving, I ran round to the front windows. The curtains there were not drawn across, and I shone my torch beam into the lounge. Every scrap of soapstone had gone.

When I arrived home, I was punch-drunk, and unable to feel or think any more. I told William briefly and flatly what I had found.

'May all the gods be praised!' he said, as he helped me off with my coat and placed a chair at the kitchen table for me. 'Now eat your supper like a good girl, and then go and pack. Sophie is waiting to help you. As soon as ever you can put together what you need, we are starting for Kate's – yes, this very night. She is expecting us, and it is a clear, fine night. We shall be there by midnight. I have briefed both Sophie and Ned about Cat, and I am not taking any argument from you about it. We are going to enjoy Christmas and leave all Swithinford's troubles behind us. When we come back, it will be another year – a new start for everybody.'

PART THREE

THE SCORE

39

Christmas proved to be as delightful as the run up to it had been distressful.

I had been very surprised, and a bit piqued, to tell the truth, at having my arrangements for the holiday taken so completely out of my hands by a William that I barely recognized, so – well – *bossy* is the only word I can think of that describes the change. He really was acting in a high-handed fashion! An extraordinary suspicion struck me, and I spoke it aloud.

'William,' I said, 'you are not *kidnapping* me, are you?'

A bellow of laughter greeted my remark. 'Of course I am. It is no good for you for help to scream, for nobody at hand is to hear. It is in my power you are! My wicked way with you at last I shall have!' He had dropped his voice to the deep guttural tones of Peterson the villain in the Bulldog Drummond books, which as adolescents we had adored. 'My dear Fran,' he said, in his ordinary voice, 'why didn't I think of it myself, and act on it? Nothing so romantic, I fear. We are simply on our way to Kate for Christmas a few days earlier than planned, that's all.'

'Why, William? Nothing else awful has happened that I don't know about, has it? I mean, you haven't heard that Mary has died, or anything like that?'

We were passing a lay-by, and he drew in and stopped the car. 'If you command me to, I will turn round here, and take you home. But I hope you won't. I spoke to Kate while you were gone to see Johanna, just in case I could persuade you to leave before the plague of misery hit Benedict's. You see, my love, you had soaked up so much sorrow already that I thought you might go under. I was simply not going to let it happen. Once you had gone down, the first thing you would have said was that it was all because the gods were displeased, with everybody in Old Swithinford, including yourself. You would have seen yourself as the greatest sinner, the Jonah whose presence was wrecking the village. Why? Because you have a man under your roof at nights to whom you are not married either by civil or church rites, and to whom you cannot be without him committing bigamy, that is. You would probably have accused yourself of committing adultery – I can't help hoping so anyway – because of what Sophie's "good book" says about the thought of adultery being as bad as the deed. And what would this conscience-stricken deep-dyed-sinner of a Jonah have done? Cried herself silly, and given the poor innocent man who has never had a hint of an invitation to sin in that way his marching orders there and then! Spoilt your own Christmas and mine and Kate's and everybody else's. Am I not right?'

I didn't answer, and he turned towards me in the dark and drew me to him. 'Fran, darling – I am exaggerating and being facetious about it now because I am so relieved to have got you away before it happened. I was so worried I rang Kate up to ask her advice. She told me to "be a man" and give the orders myself for once.' I sat in silence, thinking. I knew that both he and Kate were right. I heaved myself up from the seat, wrapped my arms round his neck, and I think for the first time ever, I kissed him instead of the other way round. I kissed his forehead, and then each eye, and finally his mouth, and then slid back into my seat. 'Drive on, Sir Galahad,' I said.

The car became a magic carpet that soared over and away from the troubled world we had left behind, and from that moment everything was all that Christmas should be. As the days passed, if sad thoughts did return, at least they were kept in perspective.

We returned to Benedict's refreshed and looking forward, in time to see the New Year in there together, and to start to pick up the loosened threads of our existence back in the subdued village.

There is always a low after Christmas, when bad weather usually sets in and the worst of the dark time of the year is still to come. Last year the weather had been nothing short of dramatic, but this January was only dark, dull, raw, and cold. Sophie had given graphic details of the funerals that William's determined action had spared me – of a church filled to overflowing for Loddy's, arranged with simple dignity by his sole executor, Michael. And of Melvyn's body having been claimed by his mother, who had followed the little coffin alone, dressed in the deepest black, into a church almost empty except for the ghouls who made it their business to attend every funeral just to see the sights. The saddest piece of news was that old Mrs Thackeray had collapsed before setting out for Loddy's burial, and had not been out of bed since. She was pining away; and in the first week of January Sophie arrived one morning with the news that she had died in her sleep. In itself it was nothing to be sad about, but it brought back all the rest of the grief that, to put it bluntly, William had made me run away from.

I tried to shake off the gloom that was threatening to settle on me again, telling myself that all that was amiss was that without Mary and Johanna, I was simply missing female company.

William was to leave soon for the USA. I could detect, however, that he was preoccupied with something other than work. We were both edgy.

We were alike in a great many ways, but in one respect we were absolute opposites. When anything was causing me anxiety, I wanted to talk it out, on the principle that a worry shared was a worry halved. William in the same state put a clamp on his lips, on the opposing principle that there was no point in doubling the trouble by loading anybody else with it. I sought a patient listener; he only wanted to be left alone.

In normal circumstances, each of us took the role best suited to the other; but when by some unlucky chance we were both worried at the same time, each thought the other selfish and unsympathetic, and tension rose till somebody's patience snapped and it ended in a row. It was almost always my fault, because I simply could not wait for the mood to pass. I either badgered him beyond endurance to tell me what was the matter, or shut myself away from him and let my fertile imagination create situations to account for what it was he couldn't or wouldn't tell me.

On Friday evening, William was so quiet and preoccupied that he didn't appear to hear what I said, and replied to my attempts at normal conversation with the same reflex courtesy that made him raise his hat in the street to any female acquaintance without ever registering the fact that they had passed each other. I tried hard to be patient, but my need of somebody to talk to was surely as much to be taken account of as his to be quiet. He showed no sign of being aware of my need, and that hurt me. By Sunday morning, I had a raging volcano of anger inside me, threatening to erupt, and suddenly, without prior warning, it did. Between a silent breakfast and what looked like being an unshared coffee-break, I just marched into his study and demanded to know what was the matter. The result was an iconoclastic row such as we had never had before, a violent clash of fire and ice that went on for hours and hours and shook the very foundations of our world. Then, exhausted with fury, grief and frustration, I subsided at last — and sat back to view the scene of desolation my outburst had wrought. The worst of that was that as far as I could see, I had achieved nothing at all. William, white and stiff with the effort of self-control, still bore the same blank mien of non-communication that had set me off in the first place. Though evidently hurt and shaken by the transformation of his normally happy and pleasant companion into a blubbering virago, he did not seem a fraction of an inch nearer to offering me any explanation. I sat silent.

I wanted to scream, and to beat my head against the wood of his desk. He still had no idea what had upset me, after a whole morning during which I thought I had laid bare my whole being and my most secret self. I controlled myself as well as I could, and began again, though this time without the anger that had so exhausted me. And at last he gathered some inkling of the cause of my distress.

'So what do you want to know?'

'What it is that you are so worried about.'

'My dear girl, is that all? Why didn't you just ask?'

'Please tell me now. Whatever it is. Everything. Is it *us*?'

'Good God, NO! Well, no more than it always is. To love you and be so near to you, yet not near enough to be your lover, doesn't exactly make me deliriously happy. But that is no worse now than it always is.' He smiled, for the first time for hours. My consequent relief was so complete that I was myself again in an instant, in spite of my tear-blubbered face and swollen eyes. I could think and behave as rationally within the next minute as if the quarrel had never been. That was me; but William was different. It would take him days to recover, but to go on telling me now would help him most.

'Our situation is just the background that makes all other worries seem worse. I'm so helpless to *do* anything!'

'You have heard from Janice again. Is that it?'

'Oh dear, Fran darling, must you be so suspicious? You know you have my heart absolutely. If you won't take the rest of me, there is nothing I can do about it. I just have to put up with it. But I wish I could do something.'

'So it is Janice.'

'No — except that Johanna has made me realize that there is even less hope than I thought. They both want to have their cake and eat it. Janice regards me just like Johanna regards that faithful old Dave of hers — a sheet anchor that she neither needs nor wants in fair weather; but if she thought the anchor-chain was likely to break, she'd act quick enough to prevent it. I daren't suggest divorce, because I can see all too plainly that she wouldn't do it willingly or sensibly. Her one aim would be to get as much money out of me as she possibly could. Just like Johanna would in the same situation.'

'Mm. Does she know about us?'

'She doesn't know you exist, as far as I am aware. What is there to know? That I rent a flat in the house of my widowed step-cousin. That's all there is to it, and it looks like staying that way. Even I can't make up my mind what it is you really want.'

'If she could once but catch sight of me, it would cure her of any fancy idea that she has a rival with the same sort of values as her own,' I said. 'If that is what is worrying you, forget it! I am never going to help her turn your voluntary maintenance of her into Yankee-style alimony.' The thought of money in the equation made me catch my breath.

'William,' I said in tones of horror, 'it isn't money you are worried about, is it? You are not thinking that because of what happened at Hunstanton, you ought to be helping to support *me*? Oh dear! I thought we had settled all that sort of thing, and understood each other.'

'Don't blaze at me again, Fran! I can't stand any more. But no, of course it isn't anything like that. If I can't give you what you want, at least I don't insult you by supposing you value my love for you in money. But there is a financial element of sorts in my present anxiety, as it happens.'

He held out his hand to me, and I went over and sat down on the floor at his feet, holding his hand. We were both far too drained for any other show of reconciliation.

'So what else?' I said.

'Well, work. I can't work up any enthusiasm for it, now. As my students would say, I'm fed up, browned off, cheesed. Before you came back, it was all I had, and it expanded to fill the empty places left in my life. Now there is only one thing that will do that. Even my precious research is just a load of useless lumber that I don't know how to get rid of — like Janice.'

'Give it all up, then. Retire, and write the books you want to.'

'I can't. I can't afford to.'

I was surprised. I had never thought of William as in any way short of money. How could he be?

'Truly? I mean, is that a fact, or are you what Sophie would call "maunch-gutting"? I know all academics complain about how badly paid they are, but you've been at the top for a long time.'

'I don't complain. I'm all right while I still have a salary – I'm not so sure how I would cope on a pension. My commitment to Janice, for example, wouldn't stop just because I retired.'

I was silent, while all sorts of thoughts drifted uncalled for through my head. Were there other commitments I didn't know about? I dare not speak in case I broke his resolution to confide in me, and at last he said, in a way that told me what an effort it cost him, 'As a matter of fact, I do have other calls on my purse. It has been rather bad just lately, and I am afraid we may have reached a crisis.'

'We?' It was out before I could stop it. Whom did he mean by 'we'?

He smiled, very wanly. 'Suspicious again? Why, Fran? "We" means us, you and me. I see no way of solving the problem that doesn't involve you.'

'Then for heaven's sake!' I exploded. 'You know you can count on me for whatever it is, now and for ever. And if you don't want me to start screaming, for God's sake tell me: who or what is draining your resources beyond the limit? Whatever it is, I can take it, so long as we are in it together. What I cannot stand another minute is not to know.'

His reply, after all that – nearly three hours of it – was so banal that the quarrel had been like using an atomic bomb to clear a wasp's nest.

'Jess. And that hopeless husband of hers.'

My relief was so great that it stunned me. I was on the verge of hysterics, started to laugh, felt the tears welling up, and in an effort to regain control of myself, stood up too suddenly. Then I turned dizzy and I put out a hand to prevent myself from falling, but immediately found two strong but very loving arms supporting me. When the world had stopped spinning, I looked up into a face that was 'my' William's again, only agonized with concern for me.

'Is that all?' I said.

'It's plenty. There, my darling, are you OK now? I expect you are hungry. Do you know it is already past two o'clock?'

'What a waste of our precious Sunday! We must get something to eat,' I said. We made our way towards the kitchen.

The January day had darkened even more as the sun lowered itself behind a bank of unbroken cloud towards the west; but the kitchen, with all the lights on, was warm and welcoming. There is something atavistically soothing about a hearth, and food cooking on it. There was no focus for family life without a hearth or some other fireplace emanating warmth. The best nowadays was often a radiator — until the television set became the focal point in the room. No wonder so many children were disoriented and unstable.

'Now you can tell me all about it,' I said, as I looked for something for lunch. 'Whatever it is, we are in it together. Even if it is the soup that we're in.'

'Soup sounds like a good idea,' he said.

40

I'd always been left in the dark a little about Jess and her husband. Now, briefly, I learned that William had been keeping them going financially for years. It had begun innocently enough, with him offering loans while Greg 'wrote a book' or 'finished his research' or 'got enough pictures for a one-man show together'. He admitted that in those days they had not asked, but he had detected then (and which he still affirmed now) a streak of real genius in Greg that he had wanted to gamble on. As he said, at that time his own life was concentrated on his work, and his means were more than adequate for his commitments, even including Janice. Jess was his only near relative, his only real care, and he liked Greg. It seemed only right and natural that they should share his academic success and the comfort it assured. Jess had a job as a secretary, and managed to keep normal household expenses going, but William had had to be responsible for securing a roof over their heads — the deposit on their house, the solicitors and removal expenses of their constant moves, repairs on their old car, and so on. The amounts advanced were always 'loans', and had always been accompanied by agreements, signed by Greg with good intentions, to pay interest on them at a low rate, and the capital by instalments when whatever project was in hand reached fruition. Of course, it never did, and once the agreements were signed and Greg had been helped over the immediate crisis, he had rarely mentioned money again till next time.

'Don't get Greg wrong,' William said. 'He's not a dishonest man. He's one who never really makes contact with hard reality. You'll love him, I know. He's witty, intelligent, educated, courteous, and a brilliant artist with pen or brush. As far as I know, no serious vices, either — but ineffectual. Neither publishers nor the art world takes him seriously because he just never delivers the goods. Somehow or other he has managed to survive on charm, without ever getting anywhere.'

I could see how much he hated to explain the gradual steps by which his willing help had deteriorated into a sort of extortion by emotional blackmail. First Greg, and then Jess, had appealed for little extra loans, begging William not to let the other know, each offering somehow to be responsible for paying him back. When Jess had been ill William had undertaken the mortgage payments till 'something should turn up'. When it didn't, Greg had come up with the idea of selling their house and going to Barra where they could live cheaply while he wrote a novel that would solve their problems, and at the same time do the book about birds, with pictures (of which I had heard), in which a publisher was interested enough to offer a contract and a reasonable advance. Greg had anticipated that it would last them until he could deliver the book, when a second instalment would be due. Jess had said they should pay William a bit out of it, as a token of their intentions, but he had refused.

'I did take the opportunity, though, of telling them that I felt I had reached the limit of what I could be expected to do for them, and that once they took the step of going off into the wilds like that, they were on their own. Greg was utterly charming about it, said he understood completely how I felt, and that of course he would cope from now on. Jess went silent, and never said a word. I could see how I had wounded her pride by alluding to their indebtedness, and wished I'd never mentioned the damned money. She's never asked for a halfpenny since, and I've never been able to get a word or a hint from her about how they've been managing.'

'I expect you read her all wrong,' I said. 'She probably knew quite well that they were setting off across the desert with no water-bottle.'

'Both, I think.'

In the event, the clearing-up of their mortgage in England, the move itself, the renting of a cottage, etc. had left them with very little in reserve, and although Jess had never appealed again for help, it had been only a matter of months before Greg had done so behind her back. The amounts had been small and William had optimistically believed that their heads had been kept just above water. Delivery of the book was due very soon now, deadline already extended once. William had gathered from Jess's bright letters that life had been hard, reduced to bare necessities; but had not been prepared for what he now knew.

'I feel so *guilty*,' he said. 'Once you came back, and I began to feel this was my home, I stopped regarding Jess as part of my life, I think. If you hadn't been here, I should have made a point of going to see them. As it was, I didn't want to be bothered. You've often asked why Jess didn't come to see me — us. I didn't ask her. I suppose I didn't want her, but I was also a bit scared. Once back here in civilization, they might not have returned so comfortably to their isolation.'

'So now?'

He took a letter from his pocket, and handed it to me. Then he got up, and went away, leaving me to read it. There were pages and pages of it in Jess's distinctive writting, and it laid bare the true facts in detail. Resolution broken, she was turning to her only source of succour, asking for nothing still, but letting him know, nevertheless, that they had reached the end of the road. There was no condemnation of Greg. She simply stated facts. The book was hardly begun, and she could see no prospect whatever of it ever being finished, however long they stayed on the island. But that was the rub. They could stay no longer. Their money had run out after the first six months, and since then their only source of income had been social security payments. 'Greg has managed to chase up old debts a few times,' she wrote, 'and produced a sizeable sum from this source that has always seemed to come just when we had reached rock bottom. Without that bit of luck, the end would have come before now.' (Old debts, indeed! I wonder how much Jess guessed.) Now the blow had fallen. The old woman who owned their little cottage had been living with her daughter. She had died, and the daughter had also been widowed. She wanted to move into the cottage herself, and as she was now the new owner, there was not much they could do about it. 'So we're destitute, to put it bluntly. There's no chance of work for me here, of course, which has been one of the troubles. But where to head for, and what to do next, I have no idea. The winter is upon us, and the cold is intense. It seems to have numbed Greg altogether. He just sits wrapped in an old coat and a blanket, and dreams dreams, curiously unperturbed by our predicament. This time, though, I doubt if the Lord will provide, and I'm at my wits' end. I am *not* asking for money, but it seemed silly not to ask your advice. And also to beg you to keep your eye open for any sort of job at the university that I might be able to do, even cleaning or serving behind a bar.' And much more in the same vein.

I looked at the date on the letter. It was already ten days old. No wonder William had been distraught.

I washed up, and took the opportunity to prepare a few things towards our evening meal. We both needed time to think before we met again.

We had finished our evening meal, and were back in my sitting-room before I broached the subject again. I handed him back Jess's letter, and said, 'There's only one answer, isn't there? They'll have to come here.'

'No.' His vehemence was unexpected. 'I knew you'd say that, but it isn't on.'

'Why not?'

'Because you haven't seen Jess, or had anything to do with her for twenty-five years. You don't even know if you like her as she is now. And you've never met Greg at all, have you? You're suggesting that you take what amounts to a couple of destitute strangers into your home. It just wouldn't work.'

'Jess is my first cousin,' I said. 'We always got on well as children.'

'Wrong again. She was always the odd one out. It would be a recipe for disaster. And have you considered where they'd sleep, put their personal belongings, and so on? Do you want them under your feet all day and every day! No, Fran, no!'

'That's all very well,' I countered. 'But I can't see how you can occupy two residences, and me one the size of this, and let your sister and my cousin be homeless! Jess isn't a stray cat! She's one of us, the nearest thing to a sister I've ever had.'

'Don't rub it in. I've thought of all that, too. But I obviously can't let them have my college rooms, and I won't give up Eeyore's Tail to them. I can't! Let them wreck everything? Go back to spending weekends and vacations in my rooms, giving up my home to them? Are you really suggesting that?'

'Don't be silly! Of course I'm not suggesting anything so drastic or so stupid! Let them have the flat, and you move in here with me. We could make you a study upstairs in one of the back bedrooms, and you could use the guest room.'

He looked at me with a sort of resigned patience. For a moment the cobweb threads of our rapport with each other were strained almost to their limit. Then he pushed Cat roughly from his lap, and got up, striding across the hearthrug till he stood over me, and I turned my head to look at him. I was amazed at the sudden change in him.

'And sleep – I said *sleep* – like some faithful old sheepdog, on the mat by your door, and never be let inside? Dear God, Fran! Have you no idea what makes a man tick? How I feel about you? What torture it is for me to live here with you, be near to you, be *married* to you in every respect except the one that makes a man feel like a man? I would change it if I could, but if I were to throw over all my principles about Janice, I'd be throwing yours over as well, and you wouldn't be any happier. I know you! You want my love and my companionship, but as far as I can see, you don't really want me unless we can go and stand in front of some old fool like Howard, with all the village out to gawp at us.

'So far, we've managed – or let me say I've managed, somehow. Sophie's bloody locked door, supposed to act like the sword they used to put between medieval lovers in bed. But I'm at the end of my tether. I've been hoping for a miracle, I suppose, but I'm too old and disillusioned now to believe they really happen. And there you sit, coolly suggesting that I voluntarily turn the rack several notches tighter! Oh – I know I'm the one with the encumbrance that prevents us from being "honourable", as you put it; I can't help it. But that's only one part of the problem, and you know it. Doesn't it affect you at all? Or are you trying to tell me that you want us to stay in this respectable platonic friendship for ever? Because I can't, and I won't. Perhaps the best thing would be for me to get another job abroad somewhere. All right! Let Jess and Greg have this flat, and I'll clear out! Is that what you want? Is companionship all you want from me? Is that why you are so bloody satisfied, and I'm not? I'm telling you, Fran, I can't stand it any longer. I'm a man, and I love you. I've always loved you, and I always shall. But I'm not a bloody plaster saint. Just how much longer am I expected to go on pretending I am? No – don't touch me! I won't answer for the consequences if you do.'

He sprang out of reach as I put out my hand towards him, and went and leaned on the piano, with his head down on his arms, white and shaking.

I was afraid to speak, or move. We were both already so drained by the quarrel of this morning that neither of us could endure another outburst. The gap between us hurt like a gaping wound.

I tried to remember if I had ever shown any willingness, let alone eagerness, to let him through the hedge of thorns that our Victorian ancestors had planted round my 'honour'. Perhaps I never had. His own 'honour' forbade him take anything for granted. But it was also part of that code that so coloured my more rational thought that no 'nice' woman ever made any sort of advance. I looked miserably at the back of his head, seeing there not the white head of the academic but the crisp black curls that had crept out under his RAF officer's cap the last time I had ever seen him before the war had separated us. Why, oh why, had we not thrown our arms round each other then? What a wicked, wicked waste of precious years! And it was I who was now making us go on wasting our love. Why? There had been a popular song in our young days that had said it all, except that I didn't know then how near a lyric could get to the serious heart of things. I did now.

We can't go on for ever, counting stars in the sky above,
Just making conversation when we ought to be making love.

'Well?' said William. 'It seems to be up to you. What is it to be?'

The destiny of Benedict's and all that it meant hung on my reply. It was where all my new plans had begun; I loved it as I could never love another place. But what would it be to me now without William to share it with me? A garland of ashes.

I stumbled to my feet, and went blindly towards him. He caught me in arms made hard by passion, and began to kiss me, long, hard, lover-like kisses that turned my blood to liquid fire. He buried his face in my neck, holding me so close that I could hardly breathe, and I could feel the urgency in his loins rising to meet me. My knees weakened as I responded. He freed a hand and began to fumble for the buttons on my blouse. I offered no protest as his lips travelled down my throat towards the opening his fingers were making. I wanted to fling myself down on the hearthrug with him, there and then. This was what I had always wanted. This was my erotic adolescent fantasy suddenly coming true. How many times had this happened before in my dreams? But this was for real. The buttons were all undone. I yearned for him to make the next move, though reluctant to let go of this moment of throbbing, thrilling anticipation. 'Fran?' said William hoarsely, trembling, and gently pulling me down. 'Oh, Fran!'

He had got his answer. My clinging body said it all. Besides, my knees were giving way. My head was swimming in complete consent, when at our very elbows the telephone rang, shrill, strident, unrelenting, shattering. Gasping, we came apart.

'Damn,' said William. 'Let it ring.'

You can say 'Let it rain' because you know you can't stop it. You can say 'Let it go' when you know there is no way of retrieving whatever it is. But as far as I know, there is no way you can say 'Let it ring' and mean it. The harsh bell had punctured the magic moment like a stone thrown at a mirror.

I lifted the receiver, listened, and replaced it.

'Wrong number,' I said flatly.

I sank weakly on to the nearest seat, which happened to be the duet-sized piano stool, and instinctively strove to do up the buttons that William had undone. After a moment or two, he came and sat beside me, holding me gently and stroking my head as he pulled it on to his shoulder.

He was still white and he looked spent, but the terrible tension had gone out of him. 'I can't be sorry for that, Fran, darling,' he said. 'It told me all I wanted to know. You do love me — and you do want me, as a man, I mean.'

'Fathead,' I said, kissing the only bit of him I could reach, which was his chin. He grinned, still fighting for self-control and reason. He got up, and went to sit down in his own armchair, looking dazed. I wanted to be close to him still, and I knew we had not yet finished with the episode. I sat down on the arm of the chair.

My heart was still 'hung out' between him and me. I was thrilling yet to his lover's touch, wanting the few seconds of ecstasy back, though quite aware that to recapture it now was impossible. I had to get my own sanity back, and somehow restore us both to some sort of normality. He leaned his head against me, and rubbed my hand against his cheek, finally opening my fingers and imprinting a kiss in the palm. The Love it stirred in me was infinitely wider in extent than his passionate kisses of the peak we had reached when the telephone bell had brought us crashing down. While that mighty range of Love still stood, the towering summit of it was always 'there' waiting to be climbed when we chose, or when conditions were right.

'So what happens now, Fran? Where do we go from here?'

I cradled his head against me, and stroked his forehead, while I began to talk — Fran-like, really only expressing my thoughts aloud as they occurred to me.

'We have loved each other for thirty years now, even if we have been apart for most of that time. I didn't really know what love was, till you came back. I never wanted any man as I want you – but I know that I have been wanting you always – more than just physically. Time's passing, and we can't have what we waste of it back. Why do we run such an awful risk of ending up like Sophie and Jelly, with one of us having to live out an existence regretting love that was never satisfied? Do you know that when Jelly was killed Sophie actually took me to task about you, and advised me to take what I could while I could? She knows and understands what we feel, and why we are risking everything that matters to us – because, like her, of the way we were brought up. And still I hesitate, even after what happened just now, because I'm confused and don't know any answers.

'We've put our lives back together again like a beautiful jigsaw, with every bit fitting perfectly, except for the one bit that would – will – make the picture perfect. When I come to you as your "wife" I want it to be perfect. I'm afraid of getting it wrong now and pulling all the rest apart again. I don't want the romance I've been dreaming of for thirty years spoiled now by anything, or anybody. I don't think I could bear a tinsel crown after waiting so long for a gold one. I know you'll think this silly, but . . . I'm superstitious about it, now. I feel as if that wrong number was our guardian angel calling. He's arranged everything for us, and we were about to spoil his plans by grabbing them out of his hands.' I shivered.

He didn't speak, but turned his head against me, snuggling up with a sort of childlike trust that hurt and almost defeated my resolution.

'So what could change? It will be even worse, now, that I know what I do know.'

'Darling, I believe Time is really on our side if we leave it to him. Don't let's try to force his hand.'

'As long as he doesn't forget us. I really meant what I said: I can't go on much longer like this.'

'I promise. As soon as ever we get things sorted out. Trust me?'

'With more than my life,' he said. 'With my reason for wanting to live. I just wish I could understand what's holding you back, if it truly isn't the existence of Janice.'

'It isn't, not any longer. She doesn't exist for me now, any more than Brian does. She's no longer a threat to me, so I don't fear her like I did. Not that I have ever hoped for any solution from that direction. I can't, and don't wish her any harm.'

He looked searchingly up into my face. 'Don't you? Don't you honestly, Fran?'

I shook my head. 'Then you are a better man than I am,' he said grimly. 'I do, often!'

'William! You mustn't! You know we should both be horrified if she were to step under a bus. There'd be no golden crowns for us then — just a couple of paper hats out of Old Nick's Christmas cracker.'

'Is there any hope, then?' He sounded weary and defeated.

'Yes. There must be. And look — about the money side — it isn't you by yourself any longer. It's us. Maybe we shall have to sell Benedict's and start again. It might have advantages, to go where nobody knows us.'

He was gazing at me with a look compounded of consternation, disbelief, admiration and adoration.

'Do you really mean that you would be willing to give up Benedict's? For me? You would be willing to do even that for my sake?'

'What on earth would it be to me now, without you?' I said.

He sat up, and closed his arms round me in a circle of love so close and endless that I knew it could never be broken. 'Where Love is, God is.' That was it. We had only to trust in our own particular god.

'Have it your way,' he said. 'What does a bit more time mean, now? You keep telling me you are nearly fifty. So what? You are as full of fire and glow as a lighthouse. My lighthouse. And if you were ninety you would still be the only woman I want to be with, all day as well as all night. But we'll find a way without sacrificing Benedict's. We belong here.'

'When the right time comes,' I said, 'we shall know.'

'Yes. But if I leave it to you to choose the time, I want the privilege of choosing the place.'

'Isn't that usually the male's privilege?' I asked, picking up the lighthearted reference to yet another of those songs of our dancing years. 'May I know in advance where it is likely to be?'

'Where do you think? Here, at Benedict's of course. Where else?'

I laughed aloud, the first real sound of *joie de vivre* that had been heard in the house that day.

William responded by dropping his voice to take on Peterson's guttural tones. 'After which breezy interlude, let us to business get,' he said. 'What are we going to do about Jess and Greg?'

*

It was taken for granted that it was up to us to mount some sort of rescue operation.

'I can't see anything for it but to have them here, at least for the first week or two,' I said. 'Let them come as my guests, so that you needn't move. I shall have to leave the decision to you. After all, as you reminded me, I don't know Jess as she is now, and Greg not at all.'

The fact that we were who we were, and living still under Grandfather's roof, was part of our difficulty. William was not of Grandfather's own blood, but even he had been part of 'the squire's family'. Benedict's was still at the very heart of the 'old' village, whether we knew it or not, and whether the village acknowledged it or not. The very fact of me being here had held the old social mortar in the cracks a little longer. The church had lost its influence, what with old Howard's feebleness and Birch's defection; the school had closed. The pub only remained — and that indefinable social hierarchy that 'outsiders' like Johanna could not understand even if they would. The general dislike of 'Pamela-Balls-as-was' was not altogether because she was vulgar by nature. In marrying above her rank in that old ordered hierarchy, she had threatened the community. Even the farmers, who were the very backbone of it, were in danger if such as Pamela could infiltrate their solidarity.

I had never before actually formulated all these thoughts, but I knew now that I had apprehended them all the same. William understood; that we were fighting a losing battle, neither of us could doubt, but we didn't want to feel like deserters.

Jess, like me, was of the old squire's own blood-line. It was no use us trying to guess how the pattern might be changed when she returned. Anybody who has ever played with a kaleidoscope knows that one extra piece introduced produces an infinite variety of new patterns. The only thing you can be sure of is that you will never see the old patterns again.

When William began to talk about Jess, I gathered somehow that he was warning me that she had a tendency to regard him as her own particular source of love and comfort, and might resent my reappearance. She had, as he reminded me once more, always been the odd-one-out when we were children.

He had certainly given her a lot of justification for claiming him now as hers first and foremost. Whatever sort of show of pride and independence she had put up, the fact remained that she had also relied on him a lot for material help. Was she going to regard me as a danger? How much had he told her about me?

I asked.

Very little; well, hardly anything at all. He had reported bare facts, deliberately contriving to present our relationship as no more than cousinly. He had found me 'just the same, only older'.

'But *why*?' I said, over and over again. 'I don't think you credit Jess with much intelligence,' I said. 'She won't have forgotten how close we were in the past.'

He could see that I was piqued, even hurt. Was he ashamed of our relationship, I demanded? That hurt him. He strove to make me see it in the same light as he did. Look, I had turned up again suddenly, out of the blue: a successful career woman with every material advantage that Jess hadn't got. Why should he elaborate on anything that would invite comparison with her own acute penury? While they stayed hundreds of miles away on a remote Scottish island, there was no way she could discover for herself what the true situation was. Besides, he had never intended it as deliberate deception as far as I was concerned. He had not then even dared to hope that there could be a place for him in my new life. 'I felt,' he said 'like people in the old fairy tales who somehow came by a purse of gold: if it turned out to be faery gold, all they found in the purse the next day was dust. I daren't let myself believe that it even might still be gold next morning. If I'm touchy, it's because I'm still afraid. That's why I'm apprehensive about Jess. I can't see any logical reason for her wanting to spoil things for us; but I wish this needn't have happened.'

I was glad our guardian angel had been on duty this afternoon. If Jess was not going to turn out to be a natural ally, it was just as well that she had not stepped into the middle of what she would most likely have regarded as 'a sordid *affaire*' between us.

'So tell me exactly what is about to happen, as far as you know,' I commanded. My firm tone seemed to hearten William. He answered without hesitation or equivocation for the first time.

'I have suggested that they should come south as soon as possible, and that I will do my best to find them somewhere, even if it has to be a hotel room, till we can make more permanent arrangements.'

'So they are almost on their way?'

He nodded. 'This coming Saturday.'

And I had wondered why he was *distrait*!

'When have you got to go away again?'

He sighed. 'I have been trying to get out of going to the USA this time, but I can't. The Vice-Chancellor himself put my name up as the British representative at this International Seminar, long before you turned up again, and I accepted. Short of pretending I'm bedridden with gout, or prematurely senile all of a sudden, I don't see any reasonable way of getting out of my obligation. Everything just goes on getting more tangled up, like the skeins of wool Kezia used to make us hold for her to wind.'

'But the tangles did all come out in the end,' I said. 'Go on explaining. You are unwinding yourself very nicely. Don't stop now.'

'Well, till this business with Jess and Greg, I had had a sort of dream that I could take you with me – on our honeymoon, as it were. I hadn't given up hope of the miracle happening. But it hasn't happened, and it won't happen, so that's the end of that dream. We can't go unmarried. We couldn't be together, and there wouldn't be much point otherwise. We should be "sussed out" as they say now, and branded as a couple of adulterers without a shred of moral principle between us. I can't, and won't subject you to that. So I go alone.'

'Truly?' I asked, unbelieving. I knew that Oxbridge still wore the facade of such moral strictures, but in America, in the 1960s?

'Truly. I may not tell you things that I ought, perhaps, but I'm not in the habit of telling you lies. Are you being suspicious again? Do you imagine it is an excuse for me to slip off and visit Janice on the sly? No, really, darling. I don't wonder you are surprised. We don't properly understand our American cousins any more than they do us. They hop into bed with each other as often as they eat hamburgers – getting divorced and remarried between bites. But married they must be if they are to be seen together after dark in the context of their older universities. A chap can get the push for indulging in a bit of open adultery. He can be divorced and remarried and divorced again till the cows come home, but "living in sin" can put him quite literally beyond the pale. They've never got beyond the Pilgrim Fathers in some ways.'

'Well,' I said, 'that's obviously what Don Marquis meant: how does it go?

> that stern and rock-bound coast felt
> like an amateur
> when it saw how grim
> the puritans that
> landed on it were.'

William laughed, standing up and slapping his thigh in pure enjoyment. 'Where Sophie can always produce an aphorism, you can

348

always come up with an apt quotation,' he said. 'That's one of the many things I adore about you! You couldn't bore me if you live till we're ninety, not for a single minute. It's also why I want you with me day and night, now and forever. I don't want to go anywhere without you. Must I?'

'Yes,' I answered. 'Just this once more. There are too many obstacles, apart from the Pilgrim Fathers.'

'So. When will you be my wife, Fran? Before I go? And then have to face an eternity of separation?'

'Can I quote again?'

'Could anybody stop you?'

'Well, it wouldn't be for eternity. We should both be looking forward. Remember what Shakespeare wrote

> . . . for hope to joy is little less in joy
> Than hope enjoyed.'

'I can cap that with a contradiction from the same source:

> O who can hold a fire in his hand
> By thinking on the frosty Caucasus?
> Or cloy the hungry edge of appetite
> By bare imagination of a feast?'

He stopped, and came close again. 'That puts it in a nutshell. I'm hungry. I've been hungry for thirty-five years. Now I'm like poor old Tantalus. What I want is within my sight, within my reach, but not within my grasp. I think what you are saying is that you would rather not be a "lovely weekend" sort of wartime bride. Forget what I said. It's settled. I go alone. But when I come back, my darling—' The kiss he gave me was too highly charged for safety. He drew away, and said lightly, 'I shall be looking forward, too, to bringing you

> Your coffee in the morning;
> And kisses in the night.

'There, I think I've won that quotation game. Now I shall go and get our bedtime drinks. We still have to do something fairly quickly about Jess and Greg.'

He returned bearing our hot drinks and we sipped them gratefully. The gamut of emotions we had run that day left us both exhausted.

349

'They will be leaving Barra in less than seventy-two hours from now,' he said. 'We'll play it by ear what they do on Saturday. Though I suppose I had better reserve a hotel room just in case. I can always cancel it. But we ought to make plans for them after that. They won't be in any condition to solve the problem for themselves.'

'There really isn't much of a problem,' I said.

'Now, Fran, wait a minute. I have no intention of starting again where we began twelve hours or more ago!'

'I think I've had an idea,' I said.

'Oh? I know! You'll move in with me to Eeyore's Tail, and let them have the rest of Benedict's to turn into a bed and breakfast place. Well, I won't play, so there.'

'If we hadn't been in such a state about our silly selves, we should have thought of it at once. Bryony Cottage is empty — already furnished, too. I should think Mr Monty Ellington would be over-joyed to let it on a short lease. He needn't know who they are. Fix it up through your solicitors.'

The simplicity and relief of it stunned us both.

'Till I come back at any rate. And when I come back, will you try to solve our problem as easily?' His tone was bantering, but his eyes belied it.

'I will,' I said.

He held me close as we stood at the bottom of the stairs before separating for the night. 'Was that a promise, Fran? Did you really mean it?'

What could I swear on? I said the first 'holy' thing that sprang to mind.

'I promise,' I said, 'on my grandchildren's heads.'

We looked at each other, but the result was hardly what either of us might have expected at such a moment. Each saw that the other was struggling not to laugh. Then we burst simultaneously into the mirth that could not be suppressed. Both of us on the fifty mark, in love with each other for the last thirty-five years, living under the same roof with that love still unconsummated — in the permissive days of the second half of the twentieth century! Stupidly clinging to old ideals that went out with Maurice Hewlett and Jeffrey Farnol! But then, their heroes and heroines were always 'sweet young things' with very little experience of life. Never before, surely, had the heroine promised her knight fulfilment by swearing on the heads of her grandchildren.

The peals of helpless, uncontrollable laughter coiled themselves lovingly round the carvings on the newel-post and up along the polished wood of the banisters to reach the empty rooms above. The very walls seemed to echo with the sound as William closed his door and I ritually shot the bolt on my side. The scrape of it had obviously set him off again, because a whole male-voice choir of deep chuckles followed me all the way upstairs. Axel Munthé was right. The Devil himself could do nothing to you as long as you can still laugh.

41

William's solicitor had no trouble in fixing up a lease on Bryony Cottage, though they would have to remain at Benedict's until they could take over there. When Jess phoned with details of their arrival, he was able to tell her that they would be his guests in the flat, while he had one of my spare rooms. I told Sophie as much as was absolutely necessary, that Jess and her husband would be our guests for a week or two.

She said suddenly, 'It'll be nice to see her again, after all these year.'

'It will, ' I agreed. 'I wonder how much she has changed.'

'It's her new name as I can't git over,' said Sophie. 'As houtlandish a name as I ever did 'ear. I don't see 'ow I shall ever git my tongue round it, try 'eavens 'ard as I may.'

'It's pronounced Tolliver,' I said. 'That's easy enough. You have known people called Oliver all your life. Just put a T in front of it.'

'Sich foreign wayses!' said Sophie shortly. 'I don't 'old with 'em. Why don't they spell it Tolliver if that's 'ow they say it?'

I felt it quite beyond my powers to explain the mysteries of esoteric pronunciation to Sophie, and was irritated by her making an issue of it.

As she got up to go back to work, she turned and said, 'What's 'e like?'

'Who?'

'That there foreign Eyetie as Jess 'as gone and married.'

'I don't know. I've never met him; but William says he's charming.'

Sophie swallowed a sound like a disapproving grunt. "Andsome is as 'andsome does, if you ask me,' she said darkly. 'I can't say I like the sound of 'im a lot.'

She had made me uneasy now. How, 'in the Lord's blessing' as she would have said, had she managed to pounce upon the fact that Jess and Greg were in some sort of trouble?

'Do you reckon as Mis' Whatever-'er-name-is'll remember me?' she asked.

'Of course she will! You don't forget old friends just because you change your name.'

That seemed to satisfy, and even please her. 'Ah! That's what Mam all'us used to say.

> Make new friends, but keep the old.
> One is silver. The other's gold.'

She was gone again, and I was relieved that at least half the impending couple would be welcomed without reserve.

Saturday seemed to be as long as a normal week. William had stayed in his rooms on Friday night so as to be on hand if plans were changed. Sophie came on Saturday, as she sometimes did, and we spent the morning making preparations.

When all was ready, she said, in her most matter-of-fact voice, 'If tha's all, I'll be a-gooin', then. I dessay they wou'n't be long, now.'

I was overwhelmed with relief. Her fine sensitivity had made her aware of my mixed feelings about meeting Jess again, after so very long. It had also warned her that her own presence would be *de trop*.

'I'll see 'em a-Monday morning, when they've 'ad time to take everything in, like.'

I went to dress, and on my way down stopped at the landing window. My thoughts turned back to Sophie's strange reaction to the subject of Jess. Perhaps she was glad of somebody or something to take a few of her suppressed feelings out on. She had continued to show such an unaltered face or mien in spite of all that had happened to her in the last twelve months that we, too, had let things pass without considering her enough. That blow to the family's pride I had shared with her, and the waiting for the birth of Wendy's baby. Jelly's fortune, and his consequent death, she had so firmly bottled within herself that I had been forced into a sort of conspiracy of silence, of going along with her in pretending to all and sundry that those events had had no more effect on her than they had had on any other of Jelly's contemporaries. It was only three months ago that Jelly had been killed; barely two months still since Johanna's disappearance and the Thackeray tragedy. It was as if a whirlwind of misery had spiralled round Benedict's without yet touching it. I hoped it had blown itself out, but I doubted it. Sophie seemed to be feeling in her bones that there was still more to come, as the old who have rheumatism already can detect a 'low' over the Atlantic even before the weathermen announce it.

There was, of course, still a bit of bad feeling between the three sisters, both with regard to what had happened to Wendy, and because of Jelly's legacy. I had gathered that Hetty had taken out her jealousy and umbrage at Sophie's sudden 'luck', by warning her off from making any too close claims on the child. It had been made plain to her that if she had money, Het now had something she could never hope for — a grandchild. And Hetty was going to see that Sophie's 'wealth' did not buy what was hers. Thirzah, too, had been made to understand that she had played her part, and that Het and Joe could 'now look after their own'. Not that the village in general was allowed to know that a breach had been made in the walls of solidarity in Kezia's family.

She had been unrepentantly glad that Johanna had taken herself out of my life. She didn't exactly say 'I told you so', but she meant it all the same. That had brought up the old grievance with regard to Wendy.

'Our Wend' ain't the same gal as she was before she got in with that Mis' Brooke,' Sophie had said. 'She won't look for another job — just sits about at 'ome doing nothing, as you might say. You'd think she'd be pleased to goo out an' earn something to 'elp keep the baby. But Joe's that soft about 'im that 'e'd spend their last penny a-keeping the boy afore 'e'd let anybody else 'elp. And Het told me to my face as she didn't want no charity from me on that account. The way she pushes that child about Hen Street in its pram, showing it to anybody she can stop and gossip to, would make you think she had something to be proud of. Wend' don't do nothing at all for that child. She wouldn't try to feed it herself, and it's got so Het's its mother, an' Joe's its father. All Wend' does is to sit about making her face up with that powder and lipstick and stuff, and curling 'er 'air, and polishing 'er nails, just like that—' she caught herself in time, and said no more. 'I can't abear to think what Mam would ha' said.' she finished. 'Look arter Hetty,' she said to me and Thirz' many a time. I do believe as she knowed our Het wasn't quite right in the 'ead. She's actin' now as if she never 'as been more than 'levenpence 'apenny in the shilling. But we shall all'us do our best to keep the fam'ly together, for Mam's own sake.'

I heard the car on the gravel and went down to face the present. I was feeling distinctly nervous. I reached the bottom of the stairs and Jess was there. I kissed her, and I felt how cold her face was, and realized that apart from the trauma she was enduring, she had now been travelling for more than forty-eight hours, and must be absolutely worn out. I took her by the hand and led her into the breakfast room, where central heating as well as an open coal fire provided both warmth and welcome. In the bright light, I looked at her, and she looked at me. I don't know what she saw, or what her first impressions were. What I took in of her appearance gave me the foolish feeling I might have had if I had found myself embracing a complete stranger in the middle of a London street.

Jess was as poised and self-possessed as a Victorian grand-dame leaving her calling-card on a new acquaintance. I don't know what I had subconsciously been expecting – a ravaged old woman showing signs of all the years of wear and tear, perhaps even a sort of middle-class version of Thirzah, since Jess when young had been the sturdy one who might later run to fat. The woman in my chair stretching brown, capable hands and long, slender feet towards the fire came nowhere near that image. Jess had fined down to a taut slenderness. Neither the petite slimness of Johanna, nor the tall curvaceousness of Pamela Thackeray. She always had been beautiful, but the rosy plumpness of girlhood had disguised the lovely bone structure I saw now. Her dark hair had greyed a bit at the temples, adding a touch of elegant distinction; it was swept up into a French pleat that left her jawline clear to view. A brown face, with only a suspicion of make-up, and not weathered, only naturally a bit tanned. There was the broad, high forehead that I remembered, and the Celtic eyes, grey-blue or blue-grey, with their dark ring round the iris. The high cheekbones were rosy now with warmth after cold, and beneath them lay the lovely hollows that an Italian peasant had once described as 'beauty-holes'. Under the firm, straight nose was a mercurial mouth ready to turn up or down according to her mood, and a strong jawline ended in a pointed chin that was still being held high. She was wearing a polo-necked jumper of fine Scottish wool that fitted her closely without making her femininity obvious in the way that Johanna's always did, tight-fitting ski-pants, and flat, sensible shoes. She was certainly no object for charity.

I went into the kitchen to check that all was ready, uneasily 'wasting' time. I then went back to Jess.

'What a marvellous surprise, to come back to dear old Benedict's,' she said. 'I can't take it all in yet. You haven't changed much, Fran. I hope the house hasn't changed any more than you have.'

I laughed, glad to find easy conversation. 'It hasn't *spread* like I have,' I said. 'It's still itself, but it has had to be made over. I'm beyond that.'

She didn't contradict me, I noticed. 'I'm glad,' she said, not making it clear whether she meant the house or me, or both.

I was a little afraid of going on much longer in this tête-à-tête way with Jess. 'Where are the men?' I said. 'What on earth can they be doing?'

'Coming now,' said William's voice. 'As we had to take in the luggage I thought I might just as well introduce Greg to their quarters at the same time. Come in, Greg, and meet Frances. It's about time you knew each other.'

I turned, and saw Greg. Nothing could have been more different from the image I had conjured up of him. I have no idea why I should have expected the genius manqué to be tall, thin and cadaverous, with pale grey eyes looking always away into the mist somewhere, but I did. The man who stood before me was of middle height, thick-set, well-fed and prosperous looking, with a pair of black eyes hidden behind heavy horn-rimmed spectacles. He was as wide-awake and sure of himself as the yard-bird cockerel at dawn. He came forward with his square-cut artist's hand extended, and eyes that even through the glasses showed no hint of poetic melancholy. He took my hand, raised it in a theatrical gesture, lowered his head over it, and kissed it with a courtly bow that would have done Olivier credit.

'Frances, Lady Bountiful,' he said.

My immediate instinct was to hit him, and behind me I felt, rather than saw, how William stiffened with disgust. But before I had had time to register either properly, Greg had shed his stage costume, swept off the concealing glasses to reveal the merriest pair of sparkling eyes I had ever seen, and pulled me into his arms to plant a hearty kiss fair and square on my mouth.

'Hello, Fran,' he said. 'I need no introduction to you or the house, really. Jess has talked of you so much that my only fear was that she was making both of you up for my entertainment. Now I know you are both real. Go on – why don't you clout me with that wet dishcloth you are clutching?' I looked down at my left hand, and found to my dismay that there was a wet dishcloth in it. He kissed me again, holding me close, to whisper a fervent 'thank you' into my ear under the cover of William and Jess's laughter.

He let me go, and I said, 'I shall clout somebody, soon, unless that somebody gets us all a drink. Then we can eat — because if nobody else is hungry, I am.'

The ice was broken, as Greg had intended it should be. I looked at him again, furtively, and met his twinkling eyes engaged in the same pursuit. We both chuckled, and I yielded to his enormous charm. He had claimed another victim, and I felt a momentary twinge of disloyalty to Jess and to William. But I needn't have worried. Jess was looking on, amused and pleased, while the set of William's shoulders as he set down the tray of drinks told me how pleased he was.

The meal went forward in the spirit of a lovely family gathering. William and I maintained our relationship at a friendly, cousinly level, which was a bit of a strain because I hadn't realized quite how much we had dropped into the habit of using endearments to each other. Now we were both biting them back, or catching them just before they slipped out. I hardly dared look directly at William in case we giggled like fourteen-year-olds. I declined Jess's offer of help with the washing-up.

'Sophie would never forgive me for not letting her have at least that privilege of helping to welcome you back home,' I said.

'Sophie? Not Kezia's Sophie? You can't mean it!' Jess exclaimed. My eyes thanked William for leaving this bit of information for Jess to find out. It was the bon-bon after the feast.

I nodded. 'Kezia come again!' I said. 'Except that Sophie has a heart twice as big and three times as tender as her mother's.' I turned to William. 'Jess is drooping with weariness,' I said. 'Take them away and settle them in for a good night's rest. They shall see everything else by daylight tomorrow.'

They made no demur to being thus dismissed, and went off to the flat like obedient children. I heard William shoot the bolt on what was now 'our' side of the door. I wanted him to myself for a moment so that he could put me wholly into the picture before we all met again next morning.

'Quite a day,' he said, sitting down at my feet and resting his white head against my knee. 'Much better than I had hoped or expected. No questions asked that I was not prepared to answer.'

'But we must go on being circumspect?'

'Aren't we always? Even when we are alone together, like this?'

'Bed,' I said, yawning.

'Don't do that to me, Fran,' he said, half bantering, half serious. 'I thought you were making what the *News of the World* would call "a certain suggestion" to me.'

'Rubbish!' I countered. 'You are as tired as I am,' I said.

'Good thing, too,' he said, pulling me to my feet.

'When they appear,' William said over breakfast, 'I think we'll embark at once on the proposed tour of the house, before coffee time; then, if you agree, I will take them in the car for a ride round the village, and on to Hen Street to have a quick look at Bryony Cottage from the outside, before committing them to it. I think it might be better if I took them alone, don't you?'

I was mightily relieved at the last bit. 'If I had my way, I would never set foot in Hen Street, let alone Bryony Cottage, again. It's the canker in Swithinford's rose, as far as I am concerned. It means Johanna. She seems to stand for everything that has happened. It all stemmed from there in the first place.'

William's fears of any sign of envy in Jess did not materialize in that first week; nor did Jess seem to show any interest in any relationship we might have set up with each other. In fact, if anything, everything had so far been too easy.

Greg wandered round in a daze of delight, just drinking in every bit of beauty or pleasure as it came. He stood, just as I did, for long periods at the landing window, soaking up the view. He held my various bits of pottery or other *objets d'art* in his hands and adored them. Cat sent him into a kind of physical ecstasy with her feline grace and her tactile sinuosity. He picked up bits of old wood in the wood-shed, and with an ordinary shut-knife turned them into tiny sculptures of her while listening enraptured to Beethoven on the record-player. It was exceedingly difficult to believe that this lively, cultured man was the same one who had, only two weeks ago, been sitting mute in a Scottish croft, wrapped in rugs to keep out the highland cold, and subsisting on porridge – or its equivalent.

They wouldn't be under my roof for much longer. The only real fly in my ointment was the knowledge that however pleasant this time was, it was passing, and hour by hour bringing the day of William's departure nearer.

I was in the garden with Jess towards the end of that first week, when we looked up and saw Greg standing dreamily at the landing window.

'He's thawing,' said Jess. 'He's coming back to life again.'

'William avers that he's a genius,' I said. 'And geniuses are few and far between, not like us lesser mortals. I don't think Barra can have been very good for him.'

'What is genius?' asked Jess, her mouth a bit grim. 'My teacher used to say that a craftsman worked with his hands, an artist worked with his head and hands, and a genius—' She looked up, with a somewhat cynical expression, to where Greg still stood by the window.

'And a genius,' I finished for her, 'works with hands, head, and heart. Does that make Greg a genius?'

'No, Fran, it doesn't,' she said, ruefully but bluntly. 'He doesn't work at all.'

We walked on; there seemed nothing I could say. But after a couple of minutes, she brightened up and stuck out her firm chin again.

'Every time he has a new idea, I think, "This time it will work". And it may be that this period of thawing is what he has always needed and has never before been able to have — thanks to dear old Bill, and you, of course. But it mustn't last too long, or he'll melt in his own warmth, and then congeal again when we move, like ice-cream that's got too runny to put back in the freezer.'

She changed the subject abruptly, so abruptly that I was unprepared to deal with it.

'Bill doesn't want to go away,' she said. 'I can see that. But why? He's never minded going before. In fact, he used to look forward to it from one time to the next. I think Janice still draws him, but he's giving up hope.'

Was this idle chatter, or was she fishing for my reaction? I felt, for the first time, the 'alien something' in Jess that William had mentioned. Something had alerted her to the fact that the subject of Janice's existence was not a very welcome one for discussion at Benedict's, and she had deliberately chosen to bring it up with me in order to find out more. I remembered that she actually knew Janice.

'I never saw her, you know. What is she like?'

'Beautiful. Lively, Clever. Unhappy. Born dissatisfied, I think. I mean — just think what she could have had, now: a husband like Bill, adoring her, lovely children, the pleasant life-style of a don's wife in an old university. Everything. But it wasn't enough. And she could still have it all — except perhaps the children, if she would.' She blazed suddenly with an emotion I wasn't quite sure I could interpret.

'She's ruined Bill's life! Anybody can see he isn't happy. Still wanting something he hasn't got. Still hoping she'll come back to him one of these days, and so she should. She married him. And marriage is for good and all, for better, for worse. For what you don't expect as much as for what you do. Don't I know! If only she would come home with him this time, they've still got time to start again. Sometimes, when I catch him with that yearning look, I feel like writing to her, and telling her what she's missing.'

I dare not tell her how wrong her diagnosis was. Either William and I had played our parts too well, or there was, after all, a streak of jealousy in her that made her want to disturb me. There was an edge of something more personal in her outburst than concern for William, and to me it had sounded anti-Fran. But perhaps that was because I had a guilty conscience, both about my real relationship with William, and our secrecy about it. It wasn't going to be easy, having her even as near as Hen Street, while he was away.

I was smarting, and glad, for the first time, that they would soon be moving out of my house. I had to revise my feelings about Jess. I came to the conclusion that though I still felt affection for her, I didn't particularly like the woman I had found living under her skin. Perhaps I never had known her very well. People do change with maturity. Neither of us could take the other for granted.

42

Next Monday morning, Sophie and Ned both arrived early, bursting with news, and trying to beat each other to the telling.

Sophie won, because she came direct to me in the kitchen, while Ned had to find an excuse to come to the house. But she had barely got her coat off before he knocked and she let him in. Ned stood waiting for Sophie to begin; but she was in no hurry to oblige him or to disclose her tit-bit too quickly, and put on her apron with slow deliberation that caused Ned (and me) intense frustration. If she didn't soon speak, he would explode like a firework with too short a fuse for safety. Yet in both faces I read anxiety and distress.

'What's the matter?' I said.

'Thack'rays,' said Sophie. 'They're a-gooing. We shall never be the same no more.'

'Sold out,' said Ned. 'Lock, stock, and barrel.'

'To a foreigner, from Birmingham way. Not even to anybody from these parts. And not even waiting till Lady Day. I'm never in all my life 'eard of a farm changin' 'ands only at Michaelmas or Lady Day.' Sophie's voice indicated how scandalized she was at this terrible rupture of the culture she understood.

'Well, you see, them as are bought 'em out made it worth their while to oblige,' said Ned. 'After all, there's spring crops to be sowed yet, and the new folks want to do it their way. Start as they mean to go on, like.' Even Ned was grimmer than one might have expected.

'Who have they sold to? Sit down and tell me all you know.'

'It's one o' them farming syndicates,' Ned said. 'A chap o' the name o' Choppen seems to be the one doing all the business, but there's a lot of 'em in it. Want to grub up all the 'edges they can afore they sow spring wheat, like, and turn a lot o' little fields into a few big 'uns so as the combines can 'arvest quicker, and such like. It's all goin' to be farmed by machinery from now on.'

Between them, they succeeded in putting me into the picture. Woman-like, Sophie was concerned about the emotional side; Ned kept returning to the agricultural nuts and bolts.

'Michael's never been the same since the fire,' she said. 'Never could get it out of his 'ead that it were 'is fault as Loddy and that poor child was killed. Then his poor old mother and father followed Loddy to the grave. And Michael's been like a man mazed, Thirz' says, ever since. The whull fam'ly's stopped gooin' to church, for one thing. That I do know. And all on account o' that Pamela Balls-as-was! There's been Thack'rays up at that farm for 'undreds o' years. But never no more, now.'

I looked towards Ned to give me the reason why the pattern had been broken now.

'It goes back to Loddy being like he was from a child,' he said. 'Old Thack'ray wanted to make sure as Loddy 'ould get a fair deal, like. I reckon he could ha' trusted Michael, but when a man's married he can't all'us do as he would, and there were no telling what sort of a woman Michael might marry. So when Loddy turned twenty-one, and Michael were eighteen, the old man made the farms into a company, and made Loddy and Michael partners in it while he should live. What it amounted to really were that he made over to Loddy and Michael some o' the land for their own, like, there and then. So's the two boys would have it all arranged to go on being equal partners when him and his wife were gone. No doubt he reckoned on it all coming back together again, one day. To Michael and his children, yer see, 'cos it could be expected as Michael would get married afore long. But nobody ever thought as Loddy would get married.'

'I can see old Mr Thackeray's point of view,' I said.

'Well, I can't,' snapped Sophie. 'We could ha' told 'im that no good could come of it. Gooin' against all the proper old ways. Father to son that farm 'as been 'anded down from generation unto generation, as the Bible says, but never till now hev' the sons expected to take over while their father was above ground. Flyin' in the face o' Providence, I call it.'

Ned let her get her indignation off her chest before taking up his tale again. 'Well, d'yer see, when Loddy went and got killed up at ffranksbridge 'All, and Lod's wife were carrying on the way she was, the old man went off to make sure that everything went back to Michael and his children. But it appears as it were too late, now that Lod were dead. There warn't nothing as he could do about it. That's really what finished the old man off so quick. The lawyer said that Lod's share would go direct to Lod's widder, whether or not Lod had made a will.'

'That Pamela Balls-as-was will have a lot to answer for, come God's good time,' said Sophie darkly, but with more than a hint of satisfaction at the thought in her voice.

Ned continued doggedly, not allowing Sophie's moral commentary to deflect him. 'So it appears as Michael went to Loddy's wife, and offered to buy all Lod's share o' the land back. He got his lawyers to offer her top price and a bit over. Lod's land were that parcel as lays between the main farm and what Bill Edgeley's got. The bit Bill Edgeley farms comes right up to 'em. It were done like that a-purpose, so that when Bill had to give the land up, him having no sons to follow him, it would just go back into Thack'ray 'ands, and make Loddy's farm up to the same size as Michael's.'

'So Bill Edgeley is only a tenant farmer?' This was news to me.

'We all knowed that, surely,' said Sophie witheringly. 'Bill's father had it, and his grandfather, in your grandfather's time. But there's only about sixty acre, and that ain't enough for folks, these days. That's why Bill started the coal business. But it's still Thack'ray land, all the same.'

'Tha's right,' Ned agreed. 'It were Bill as told me the news, last night about Michael and them clearing out straight away. But Lod's wife wouldn't sell. Not at no price,' Ned went on. 'So then Michael offered to hire it from her, at twice the rent he gets from Bill Edgeley. But she wouldn't budge. Said that as Loddy's widder, she had a right to be a partner in the firm herself if she wanted to, and have her say in how things should be run from now on. That were a facer for poor Michael, and no mistake.'

Sophie and Ned both fell silent, their faces full of grievous concern for a man they had known and respected from his birth. His dilemma was theirs, too. They were part of the same warp and woof as he.

Sophie took up the tale. 'So by that, Michael went to see if George Bridgefoot would buy his half o' the land, 'cos he wanted to give 'is old neighbour first chance. But George couldn't see 'is way clear to buying it. I know that's the truth, 'cos last night when the other news come out, George told Dan'el when he went up to do the milking. You see, most o' what we know now 'appened as soon as Old Thack'ray died. It seems Michael made up 'is mind to leave all 'is mem'ries behind 'im, an' start afresh. And 'e didn't 'ave no trouble, 'cos this 'ere man Choppen were on the look-out for just such a old place as 'e could make over from the beginning just as he wanted it to be, houses and buildings and all the lot.'

Ned intervened. 'Of course, Loddy's wife had to know, sooner or later. Michael got the papers all drawed up, but 'e just couldn't bring hisself to sign away that land what had been his father's and his grandfather's and a long way afore them. He kept waiting and hanging on, in the 'opes that Pamela Balls would see reason.'

'Or find out for 'erself as bein' a partner weren't all sunshine, bein' responsible for losses as well as gains, like,' said Sophie. 'That fly-by-night 'ad enj'yed being Loddy's wife, 'cos that way she got the best of everything. But that ain't the same as watchin' a beautiful crop of upstandin' wheat being laid flat in a storm, or a herd o' cows as you're reared from calves being put down 'cos o' foot-an'-mouth. I reckon Michael were banking on that, and hoping she'd take the money and clear out back to London where she come from if 'e waited long enough.'

She was coming, I could tell, to the dénouement of the story. 'Then by Sat'day's post, Michael got a little box o' wedding cake, "with Mr and Mrs Jack Bartrum's compliments".'

We sat in silence. The trump of doom can hardly produce a profounder one.

'You can understand what that meant to Michael,' Ned said at last. 'You see, it was a warning that he hadn't got a woman as knowed nothing about farming for a partner no longer. He'd got another farmer as he had all'us disliked and didn't trust, and the very one as had cost him the life of his brother and mother and father.'

'It just couldn't be beared,' said Sophie, her anger turning to grief. 'So, accordin' to Thirz, who had it from Dan'el, who had it from George Bridgefoot, who had it from Michael hisself, he rung up this 'ere Choppen there and then, and told 'im as 'e would meet 'im this very morning and sign the papers. And that's when Choppen offered him a lot more to go without waitin' till Lady Day, because apart from wanting to take the 'edges up and get the drillin' done while this spell o' spring weather lasts, it seems they want the old house done up immediate, and that there big old barn next to it, special. I don't know what for. But Thirz' said she'd 'eard that we can expect them bulldozers and things to knock the old place down any minute.'

She rose slowly, to pick up the coffee cups. 'Old Swithinford will never be the same no more.'

Ned put on his cap, and went out. I went upstairs, and paused to look out across the village from the landing window. Somehow, the village itself seemed to have shrunk like an old woman in a cold wind. It was all very well to resent change, but we couldn't hold it back. I thought of Mary, and how much till now she had symbolized the wish of most of us to hold change at bay as long as possible — till with her usual brand of extra experience and foresight, she had recognized the moment when resistance was of no further use. The decade we were halfway through had brought the inevitable to our doorsteps, and now its force could no longer be withstood.

It was a fine, bright day for late February, and in the distant fields I could see tractors at work. The new owners of the Thackeray land would pull up trees as well as hedges, no doubt. The whole landscape would be changed. Even the fields at the bottom of my garden might be in danger. Thank Heaven I had stretched my resources, in the face of all advice, to include 'the front cluss' in my purchase of Benedict's. The avenue of black poplars that ran from my island to the road was a causeway I could, and would, defend to the last. My island of peace was threatened from the outside — and a twinge of apprehension told me that I feared for my island's inner tranquillity, too. Jess had managed somehow to get under my skin, and I should be relieved when the end of the week took her and Greg off to Hen Street.

I saw little of Jess and Greg all day, they having kept to the flat and I not feeling particularly in need of company, so I had no chance to relate the news till we were all seated round the supper table.

'Isn't it awful?' I said. 'I can't take it in, so I know what a shock it will be to everybody.' I waited for some sort of response, but none came, except a murmur of understanding from William, who was busy carving.

'What I'm worried about is what these new owners will do to the village as a whole, with their new-fangled, up-to-date methods of farming, and their interference in all the old ways. It doesn't seem right to me that a farm like Thackerays should be run by people who don't know the men that work on it, or anything about them, for one thing. Then there's the fact that some of the people putting money into the syndicate aren't farmers at all. They are just business men looking for a good investment. They don't care about the land: all they'll care about is what it will do to their bank balances in the short term. When it was a family affair, they always had one eye on the future as well as all the past to look at. The land and the folk went together, didn't they? You didn't separate the land from the people who owned it, or the labourers that worked it, because they just went on from father to sons as well. Choppen appears to be going to live here, or he wouldn't be in such a hurry to do the old house at Monastery Farm up; but he won't belong like the Thackerays did, however much he lives here. And what he'll do once he gets here doesn't bear thinking about.'

'He won't upset you, will he?' said Jess. 'So I don't see why you are making such a fuss. You are safe enough. In fact, I should have thought it strengthened your chance of becoming the village headman again, to have the Thackerays removed altogether.' The tone of her voice surprised and chilled me, as if I had been doused with a fall of wet snow from a rooftop. I looked up at her in startled surprise and dismay. It was not what she had said, but the curl on her lip and the edge in her voice that stung me.

Greg rushed in to prevent trouble. 'Will it affect you, Fran? I mean, isn't Benedict's self-contained?'

'Yes, of course it is. But I'm not. I don't have any ambitions to be the President of the Women's Institute, or a churchwarden, or anything like that, if that's what Jess means. But I belong to the village, all the same. What affects people like Sophie and Ned affects me. My roots are here, and I've just got them re-established. I don't want them disturbed.'

'So are mine,' said Jess, cuttingly. 'But then, I don't happen to be the lady of the manor. I should have thought it was a good thing for everything to be brought up to date. It's one thing to be Fran, with all this and ample means to support it. But I'll bet there are a lot of people down in the village whose roofs are leaking and whose chimneys are smoking and who would get out to better conditions like a shot if they had the chance. Fran can afford to be a romantic, indulging in notions of dancing round the maypole on the village green on May Day. They can't.'

'I believe all that's worrying Fran is that the change will be too sudden and that it will affect things too much,' William said, still trying to prevent a difference of opinion from turning into a quarrel; but Jess's choice of words had already curdled the atmosphere. 'Gradual change is one thing. Upheaval of their entire lifestyle is another.'

'I can see Fran's point,' said Greg, perhaps unwisely. 'It is a bit of a blow to anybody to find his whole mode of life altered overnight: the people he works for, the place he works in, the routine of the work he does, the tools he has been used to . . .'

'I don't know how *you* can possibly know anything about it,' snapped Jess. 'When did you ever have a pattern of work that could possibly be changed?'

Greg had flushed to the roots of his hair, though whether from anger at her pointed personal attack on him, or embarrassment at her equally barbed attack on me, I couldn't tell. William, too, was distinctly uncomfortable, sorry for Greg, fearing a scene, and not daring to be seen taking sides. His eyes were sending me mute pleading to let the matter drop; but I was both hurt and angry, and for once in no mood to oblige him. I gathered up the dirty plates and cutlery, and went with them to the kitchen. William followed me with the remains of our first course. He found me at the sink, and put his arms round me.

'Don't!' I said pushing him away. 'I can't take it! Besides, I'm quite capable of defending myself, thank you. I think this is mostly because she suspects more than she's been told. Don't give her the satisfaction of finding out that she may be right.'

Now it was William's turn to flare. 'May be? What do you mean by that?'

'That she will obviously do her utmost to see to it that if she finds out that she is right, she'll do her best to stop it,' I said. 'While she is around, I can't feel safe any more.'

'I see. You are lashing yourself up now to think there are two women in my life who count more than you do. Well, you are wrong. So to put your mind at ease, I had better go straight back in there and explain just what the position is. If it is still as I thought it was.' He was preparing to march off, but I caught his arm.

'No, don't be silly. Look, I'm sorry,' I gave him a quick kiss and handed him a hot pudding, so he was at some disadvantage to reciprocate. I didn't want him to, lest my hurt pride crumble into tears. 'Leave it to me,' I said. 'I can deal with it. Sh! Listen!' I said.

We stood close together, straining our ears towards the breakfast room. The voices coming through the closed door were raised and angry, though no words were distinguishable.

William said, 'I guess they have been at loggerheads all day. She just took it out on you, sweetheart. Don't quarrel with me about it, please, Fran.'

'No, I won't. But please don't expect me to just sit mum and take it, simply because she's Jess, either. I can't.'

We returned bearing the second course, like butler and parlourmaid. I was seething with indignation at Jess's apparent rejection of all we had been trying to offer her. She had no right to embarrass William in front of me, or spurn my hospitality. She knew better than that, so I had to conclude that her attack on me was deliberate.

Jess and Greg sat in strained, sullen silence. I dished out the sticky syrup sponge and sat down again, now deliberately playing a lady-of-the-manor hostess role.

'As it happens, Jess,' I said, coolly reintroducing the subject all three of the others would have preferred me to drop. 'Old Swithinford doesn't happen to have a green to be danced on. I should have expected you to remember that, since, as you claim, your roots are here as much as mine are. And as to me being able to afford to have romantic notions, it so happens that everything I have here is the result of my own effort. It isn't a legacy from Grandfather, if that is what you suspect. My interest in the village is, though. So in fact, your surmise is right, Greg. I, as well as Benedict's, am quite self-sufficient, thank you.'

I smiled a 'hostess' kind of smile at Jess, and added, 'Of course, Jess, you have an absolute right to your opinion. I'm just sorry we can't agree, though — because I have just as much right to mine. I live here permanently. What a good thing it is that you won't have to be living in such a quaint old place much longer. Hen Street isn't bothered by the spirit of the past at all. So you ought to be comfortable there.'

I watched with grim pleasure as the colour rose in Jess's face, the appreciation in Greg's, and the surprised but admiring expression on William's. He didn't know this Fran, who could use her able tongue like a rapier, gracefully pinking her victim at will. Well, Jess had deserved any hits I had made. I felt it would be a long time before we were on easy terms again.

Jess and Greg went off back to the flat as soon as courtesy allowed, and time spent silently in William's company soon soothed me. By common consent, we did not hold a *post mortem* on the incident at supper time; but we held hands as his head rested against my knee – the carpet at my feet was always his favourite place to sit – and I poured out my forebodings about the fate of the village to his sympathetic ears.

'By the time you come back,' I said, 'you won't recognize it.'

'As long as Benedict's with you in it is still here,' he said, 'I think I could even bear that. Don't get me wrong, Fran. I do understand – though we mustn't flatter ourselves that we can do anything to stop the tide. Remember that.'

'I will,' I said. 'I'll remember Lot's wife, too. She looked back. I'm only going to look forward.'

'Good. I should be sad to have to spend the rest of my life with a pillar of salt,' he said, 'because, if it's the Bible we are going to quote, I shall quote the Book of Ruth: 'Whither thou goest, I will go . . . Thy people shall be my people, and thy God my God. Where thou diest will I die, and there will I be buried.'

He had begun in jest, but he couldn't keep it up. He turned his face into my hand, covering his eyes until he had himself under control again.

I felt a twinge of guilt that in view of all that I had got, I had allowed Jess to upset me.

'You know,' I said, 'I think that Jess hasn't got enough to do. What she needs is a full-time job she can be interested in, so that she takes her mind off what Greg is doing – or not doing, as the case may be.'

'Keep out of it, Fran my darling. Let events take their course.'

Jess and Greg could move into Bryony Cottage on Saturday. I

learned from Sophie that it was also the day appointed for Michael Thackeray to leave, and hand over to Choppen. Sophie reported sadly the arrival of furniture vans to the Thackeray house on Thursday. All Jess and Greg had to move were their personal belongings and Greg's portfolio and art materials, which William could move in his car. The first event was nobody's business but ours: the second disturbed the peace of everybody. Nobody knew what to expect.

As far as I was concerned, Saturday couldn't come fast enough. On Friday, Sophie arrived in the gloom of a particularly dark morning threatening tears as clearly as the heavy sky threatened rain. She was not to be put off from telling her story. The furniture had been packed on Thursday, and Dan'el had been lent to help put together the few pieces of farm equipment that Michael wanted to take with him. But when Daniel had got there early today, Michael's car was not in the garage. He and the family had slipped away overnight, unable to face the farewells of friends and neighbours.

'What can't be cured must be endured,' she said. 'The only Thackerays left 'ere now, after all them years, are a-laying side by side in the churchyard. It don't seem right, but as Thirz said this morning, "If it's the will of 'Im Above, we must abide by it." So I'd better be gettin' on. Is 'e going back to 'is own place when they're gone, come Sat'day?'

'I don't know,' I said. 'I'll find out.'

When William set off with Jess and Greg to Hen Street, he said he would stop till they had unpacked, and make their first cup of tea there. That gave me a whole afternoon to do as I liked in. I was 'high' on the pleasure of having our house to ourselves again; but until William returned from Hen Street, I couldn't take it as an ordinary day. There was no point in trying to work, so I decided to take advantage of the nice afternoon, and go for a brisk walk.

I turned instinctively away from the direction of Hen Street, towards the village. Past the church was the lane that led up to Monastery Farm. Empty, now – all of it. No longer 'the Thack'ray place', but 'a valuable freehold property'.

So it was from that door, or that window, that poor old Mrs Thackeray had watched her two sons fighting it out, and her poor helpless old husband trying to part them. I wished I could forget, but standing there, on the scene of Sophie's graphic narrative, had suddenly made it all more real than ever before. I went round the end of the house to go and look at the front. End on to the length of the main part of the house – in fact, a sort of continuation of it, though separated by a gap of fifty yards or so — stood a most beautiful old barn. It was, by any standards, a very large building, built of stud and mud, and thatched. The thatch was old and straggly, but had been covered with wire-netting to prevent the worst ravages of nesting sparrows. Though not as big as George Bridgefoot's tithe-barn, it was quite as old, I thought, and more beautiful.

I went between the house and the barn, and round to the front, which I had never seen at close quarters before. It was three rooms long, and two storeys high, with a thatched roof from which rose two sets of unmistakably seventeenth-century chimneys. The front was completely clad with ivy and Virginia creeper, amongst which other thick green foliage had fought to climb up as far as the roof. They gave the house a dark and foreboding appearance, only relieved by the windows. The ivy had been kept clipped away from them to let light in, and just now they were catching the afternoon sun and reflecting it, bringing everything to life as eyes do in a human face. Then I noticed that from the bedroom window nearest the end of the house, the creepers had been stripped enough to show what the walls were like under the growth. It was a black and white timbered house, and to my amazement I saw that the upper storey overhung the lower. Elizabethan! With chimneys added a century later, and windows changed a century later still. What a beauty it would be, properly restored! I prayed that Choppen and Co. had enough sense not to leave its restoration to their female partner.

I wondered, with a pain that was almost anguish, whether it had been a Thackeray who had had it built four hundred years or more ago.

There is no armour against fate.

Fate, in this case, using as her weapon a pot of boiling potatoes. I couldn't wait to get back to the safety of Benedict's and William. He was not back when I got home, so I made myself a cup of tea and allowed myself the luxury of a few tears, not for myself, but for all humanity faced as it was with inexorable time and circumstance. Monastery Farm was a crystallized symbol of the inevitable. But its eyes were still open, so there was still life to be revived there. As I myself had restored life to Benedict's.

43

Things began to happen immediately at Monastery Farm; not the
iconoclastic bulldozers predicted by Sophie, but a professional firm
of house restorers, and more furniture vans. Mr Choppen was certainly not one to allow the grass to grow under his feet.

The furniture vans were to install the gentleman hinself, plus a
'housekeeper', into the house that Michael had vacated, and then to
move Jack and Pamela Bartrum into the new one built when she had
married Loddy. Sophie and Ned resented that more than anything
else. As Sophie said, it didn't somehow seem decent. It offended
them that she had married again too soon after Loddy's demise
(albeit she had left him for Jack months before his death had set her
free). To them moving back into the house she had shared with him
and which was legally now her property, finalized her unaccept-
ability. Their contempt of her was plain every time they referred to
her as 'that Pamela-Balls-as-was'. I could detect no sign of envy, nor
of self-righteousness. She had simply offended against their holy
laws. The curious thing, as far as I was concerned, was that I found
myself in agreement with them. I was on their side, and I couldn't
help it. I came to the conclusion that my dislike of her was both
instinctive, and rational. I had heard too many details from Mary; I
had championed Johanna against her, and would do so again; and,
ruefully, I confessed to myself that if I had not been wholly on the
side of the village before my brush with Jess, I should be henceforth.
She had put my back up, and in this matter it would be a long time
before my hackles went down again.

That he did not propose to pull down the old farmhouse earned
Mr Choppen himself some grudging respect. The speed with which
the restoration progressed was startling. An army of skilled workmen
simply descended on it, and proceeded to *do it up*; not in the
hesitant, halting, frustrating, hit-or-miss way I had had to endure at
Benedict's, either. It was more like the way in which an expensive
beauty salon can admit a middle-aged, greying, wrinkled and nonde-
script female at 9.00 a.m and turn out the same woman as an
elegant model at midday. Mr Choppen's money wasn't just talking.
It was shouting through a megaphone.

Suspicion was rife that he intended to sell it, especially when the old barn was included in the face-lift. Sophie, however, had a hot-line via Thirzah, Daniel, and the former Thackeray cowman, who had agreed to continue to work for Choppen. Sophie, feeling she could believe anything transmitted by this route, did not mind passing it on.

'They say this 'ere Choppen's a widder-man wi' two growed up child'en. The oldest as is a gal as works in London, and the other a boy as works for 'isself. So by that them two are going to live in Thack'ray's old 'ouse.'

In midweek, it was to Ned she delivered the latest news.

'There's no gainsayin' it,' she was saying as I paused to listen. 'They're at it this very minute, grubbin' up that 'edge as lays atween Thurstan's Furlong and Priorspingle! And Dan'el's been told as they're going straight on to throw Great Windigow and Little Windigow in with them, all into one big field!'

'Oh dear, Oh dear!' Ned was expostulating. 'Them old 'edges that have been there for 'undreds and 'undreds o' year. And them fields. Fancy ploughing them all into one!'

'Don't seem right, does it? I mind the time we all'us used to goo pickin' cowslips in Little Windigow to make Mam's cowslip wine with. Clifted all over with 'em, it 'ould be, so thick as you cou'n't set your foot down without treadin' on five or six. Same as in September wi' blackberries from them 'edges as they're a-pullin' up.'

Ned nodded, remembering. Sophie went on. 'An' in spring, Monksacre 'ould be purple-over wi' cuckoos. They weren't no good for nothing, like cowslips or blackberries, but they looked and smelt so nice we used to pick 'em till our 'ands was full and we couldn't carry no more. Mam never wanted 'em in the 'ouse, 'cos she couldn't abide the smell of 'em, so we used to steal jam-jars out o' the cupboard where she kept 'em, and go and put great bunches o' them cuckoos on the old graves in the church-yard — graves o' folks as 'ad been dead 'undreds o' year — just to get rid o' the cuckoos we'd picked.'

Sentimentally, I liked the sound of that. The people in the graves had no doubt picked them from the same fields in their own childhood. That was the sort of continuity that all three of us treasured, and resented being broken.

'You don't see them cuckoos nowhere, now, do you?' Ned was saying.

Sophie was shaking her head sadly. 'Nor yet vi'lets, neither! Up

Church Lane and Little Lane they'd be so thick as you could pick all day, purple and white, and some as 'ad got mixed by the bees, and next day you couldn't see where you'd been, 'cos there'd be just as many again. Now, you don't see one! Them council men come round with great sprayers and spray all the roadsides as if it were a sin to see a wild flower a-growin' there! I've said to Thirz' more than once, that somebody ought to suffer for destr'ying what 'Im Above 'ad set there for child'en to pick. And there ain't no milkmaids, neither, down in the low places. Pretty things them milkmaids was, though they did wilt quick, like, when you pulled 'em.'

They parted, sad-faced, to get on with their work; but they left their regret with me. I had been included more than once in those cowslip or blackberry-picking expeditions, and had picked, as she said, more than my hands would hold of the strongly scented 'cuckoos'. It was true; they had all gone, from under our very noses, literally, without anybody making a protest as to what we were robbing future generations of. And those distinctive old fields, with their evocative names! A history book in themselves for any who chose to read it.

But there, we had been through a war. Human beings can't eat wild flowers. All the same, as the Bible says, 'Man cannot live by bread alone' . . . Somehow, it was Mary that came to mind, and her efforts to hold back the inevitable as long as possible. But she was wise. She knew when she was defeated, and it was time to give in. Sooner or later, we should all have to accept.

It was a difficult time for me. I didn't see much of William, who was very much occupied with preparations for his work in the USA. That weekend, he suggested tentatively that we ought to go and call on Jess and Greg, to see how it was working out. I rebelled. Surely the obligation was on them?

'I think,' I said, 'that if Jess wanted to see me, she would have walked down, or phoned. What you are forgetting is that she doesn't think of us as a couple. We took pains, if you remember, to give her no hint of our feelings for each other. So why should she expect us to visit her together? I suggest that you go and visit her. Then, if you think it advisable, I will ask them down for a meal just before you go. Wouldn't that be sensible?'

Reluctantly, he agreed. And the next Saturday afternoon, he set off to see them alone.

I felt restless and bad-tempered. I decided that the thing to do was to go for a long walk, to blow the cobwebs away. Looking out of the landing window, I was surprised to see that the cloud was lifting from the west, where a patch of blue sky quite big enough to make a Dutchman a pair of trousers was already on show. If I took the loop-road I could see what progress had been made at Monastery Farm, then turn towards Hen Street and take the road down to the washes. By that time, with any luck, the clouds might have lifted enough for there to be a lovely East Anglian sunset. Once I began to walk, I felt better – that is, until I reached the farm.

The old house, stripped of its appendages of ruined out-buildings, dog-kennels and creeper, stood revealed in all its sixteenth-century beauty, its beams standing old and proud against its new coat of white emulsion, and the roof glowing with gold where the new thatching had already been started. I could see very well that when they had completed their task with the traditional local decoration, Benedict's was indeed going to have a rival in the 'lovely old house' stakes. Pamela and Johanna all over again, I thought, so different were their styles, both so outstanding in their particular ways. Except that the older house had none of Pamela's vulgarity. It was exquisite, as I was forced to acknowledge.

Following the loop-road, I took in the front of the house, too, and it was at the new gate that I got the shock which counteracted all my previously soothed feelings about the changes that had been wrought. What stopped me in my tracks was a newly painted noticeboard. It was large, square, and glossily black, with its legend in startlingly white paint and fancy lettering. It read:

OLD MANOR FARM
MANOR FARMS LTD. (Registered Office,
Southside House, Old Swithinford)

with the details of the telephone number, etc. below.

I was unbelievably angry. How dare they? Why on earth did anyone want to change a name as meaningful as Monastery Farm to one as banal as Old Manor? It was not, and never had been a manor, let alone *the* manor. That was the appellation of the remnant of the farm Jack Bartrum had left, reduced though the house itself was to a couple of old walls and a mean Victorian dwelling. I could only suppose that Choppen had no knowledge of or feeling whatsoever for history.

My new and optimistic mood had vanished at the sight of that notice-board. It symbolized everything I dreaded. I walked on, striding along in an anger that quickened my step but robbed me of any pleasure in my surroundings. I had reached the road down to the washes where last year we had stood while Thirzah had prayed and Johanna had sworn at Wendy till she had come down from the tree. I stood still on the very spot, and thought about it. I remembered how I had felt for Sophie, bringing up the rear alone, when Jelly should have been by her side as Joe was by Hetty's and Daniel by Thirzah's. Now she would be like that for ever. Last year there had still been hope. Now there was none.

And today, this afternoon, I stood here alone, while William, who had been at my side on that Sunday afternoon, was visiting the one person who would try to use her influence on him to patch things up with Janice.

I had to trust William, and Love. I felt better as I turned to go home. And just as it had on that January day last year, the light streamed out suddenly across the washes; but this time the clouds did not close up again. The patch of blue sky had been stealthily growing while I had stood there doubting, till only one last bank of rose-edged purply-blue cloud had been left obscuring the setting sun. Most of the sky was now clear, though intensifying its colour against that brilliant ball of fire dipping towards the west. I thought of us on Hunstanton pier, and took off my glove to make sure the ring was still on my finger. As I knew, that last bit of cloud would soon break up into a myriad small, gold-flecked scraps, and stretch out sideways like a cat on a hearth-rug offering its furry length to the fire. Then there would be tiny puff-balls of pink floating amongst them, till the huge falling sun turned them all to deep crimson, and if I was lucky, put on that extraordinary corona of brilliant green it wore occasionally just before disappearing below the horizon. I stood like a supplicant awaiting a sign. Yes, there it was!

And now the afterglow, when the glory spread right across the heavens, reflected on the last wisps of cloud over to the east.

It would be dark before I reached Benedict's again, and William would be worried if he got there first and couldn't find me – but I was transfixed by that skyful of glory, and did not move until the brightness at last began to fade. Then I strode off again with a new lightness in my step, towards the bridge over the river and the mile-long road that bordered it which still lay between me and the loop-road home. The sky had darkened now to a luminous deep blue, cold and distant, and I knew I could soon watch for the first twinkle of the never-failing stars. But as I turned over the bridge and along the bank, another miracle happened. The breeze had dropped, and the keen air was still. Yet from somewhere there came a murmuring, rhythmic sound that I could not recognize. It seemed to be coming from above me, and I looked up. High over my head there flew a swan, its long neck stretched forward, its feet trailing, and its huge wings drumming on the air. Just as that unknown old Anglo-Saxon who penned the riddles in *The Exeter Book* must have seen one twelve centuries ago! There was continuity for you!

> I can be carried: high over house-tops
> By my own garments: and upsoaring air.
> Whiles I am wafted: strong as a storm-cloud
> above all mankind: wandering wind-waif
> whilst I rest neither: on flood nor furrow
> my feather finery: murmurs melodious
> making my music: singing in splendour.

I was bewitched into stillness, as I watched the swan descend towards the washes, straining my ears for the last beat of its wings; but behind me came the same sound, louder than before; and I looked up again at two more swans, then four – then more and more and yet more. The music of their wings on my ears was hypnotic, and still I stood rooted till the whole firmament was as filled with the repeated pattern of their shapes and the air was filled with the drumming beat of their wings. And always as they sailed over my head, they began to descend to their meeting-place on the washes. Then they thinned out, as the few tired stragglers made for water on which they could rest. It was only when all had passed and I brought my eyes down to earth again that the true wonder of it hit me. They must be sitting on the water, now pure porcelain-white – but I had been looking up at a skyful of swans that were jet-black against the blue. So what was truth? What was right? What was wrong? Love had sent me a sign, as surely as Thirzah's God had answered her prayer. It depended where you stood whether anything was black or white. As magpies were black and white, or white and black, according to how you saw them. The old rhyme, about which I was as superstitious as most East Anglians, rushed into my head.

> I saw seven magpies in a tree,
> Six for you and one for me.
> One for sorrow, two for mirth . . .

What, I wondered, for a hundred or more swans?

William reported his visit, briskly if a bit drily, while we ate supper.

'I had a feeling that Jess was afraid Greg would blurt something out to me that she didn't want him to say. She was on edge, and kept shutting him up almost before he spoke.'

'I'll ask them to supper next Saturday,' I said. (That would be the last weekend before William left.)

They came, and all went well; the four of us were quite comfortable together, until the meal was finished, when Jess turned to William and asked, in an all-too-casual way, if he had made any plans to see Janice while he was in the USA. I hoped she hadn't seen him stiffen, as I had, though he answered her lightly enough.

'I've been too busy to think farther than the work I have to do,' he said.

'But you know where she is?'

'Not all the time. Any change of address is always notified to my bank, though.'

'I'm sure you should go and see her. Get to know her as she is now. You have changed a bit, lately, and maybe she has, too. It's daft for you to go on living in this no-man's-land between work and a lonely bachelor existence, when all the time you actually have a wife that you still love. She is probably just waiting for you to make the first move.'

I dropped my napkin on purpose, so that I could bend to pick it up, and not catch his eye. He was not so good at dissembling as I was; but he had himself well under control, although his mouth hardened as he replied. 'I'll think about it,' was all he said.

I got up to remove the dirty plates and take them to the kitchen, quite expecting William to leap to his feet and follow me, as an escape. Instead, it was Greg I found at my elbow. He was looking the picture of contentment.

'Can I do anything, Fran? I thought I had better leave those two together to finish that conversation. Did you know old Bill's wife?'

'No,' I answered, baldly and flatly.

'Neither did I. All I know is what Jess tells me. An absolute corker for looks, it seems. But till just lately I'd always got the impression that Jess didn't care much for her. I wonder why she's so anxious all of a sudden for him to get her back?'

He prattled on. I didn't need to answer him, especially as by this time he had picked up Cat, and was enacting a feline love-duet with her. I liked him more and more – but my first warm feelings towards Jess were cooling distinctly. My consolation was that for once I did not blame myself. If there was going to be any falling-off in our relationship, it was her fault. We went back to our meal.

Then Jess said, in that careless way that warned us she was about to say something of importance, 'I think you might drink to me, and congratulate me. I'm going to have a full-time job.'

I thought Greg was going to drop his cup. He spun round towards her as if he had been hit by a bullet. Whatever she was about to disclose, we needed no telling that it was as much news to him as it was to William and me.

'I didn't know for certain until this morning's post,' she said, mainly for Greg's benefit. 'I am going to be Mr Choppen's farm-secretary.' Her eyes were bright, almost glittery, and her handsome clean-cut chin jutted out at what one could only call a belligerent angle, as if she was prepared for opposition. The moment of stunned silence that followed her announcement reminded me of the odd occasions in the long ago days when the projector in the local cinema broke down. So she had openly gone over to 'the enemy', had she? History was going to repeat itself. She was about to take over Johanna's role as well as her house.

William, first to recover, exclaimed, 'Jess! How splendid for you!' and leaned across to kiss her. I murmured something, though I don't know what. It had to be good news, surely, in spite of my first reaction. But did it mean that they would be staying on indefinitely so near to us? Always intruding on us? Spoiling our delicious isola-tion? That was something that neither of us had ever comtemplated, and I guessed it would be no more welcome to William than to me.

Greg was hurt. She had neither consulted him, nor told him till now. In their straitened circumstances, not to apply for a job that had so fortuitously presented itself would have been foolish, looking a gift-horse in the mouth. But why the secrecy?

Having had cause to reassess Greg, I now saw how much this might hurt his pride. She might just as well have declared outright that she had no faith in him to do anything towards recovering their independence. Well, she knew him better than I did, but there was no need to humiliate him in front of us. It was all part of her dangerous mood. It was I who recovered first, enough to ask her to tell us all about it. Of what, for example, would her work consist?

'The company has far-reaching plans, for buying up more land when and where they can. Some to farm, some to develop for other schemes. I shall do all the correspondence, look after the telephone, keep the accounts, and so on.'

'Where will you work?' William asked.

'Michael Thackeray used one of the rooms in his house as a kind of office. They have plans to extend it out into the garden, if they can get planning permission, and in any case they will redecorate and refurnish it with all the latest office equipment. I still can't believe my luck.'

'And how are you going to get to and fro?' asked Greg.

'I've got legs, haven't I?' she said, stretching out her shapely limbs in their slim-fitting ski-pants. 'But I hope it won't be long before we can afford a car. Actually, there's quite a good chance that I can buy that little green one Mrs Bartrum drives.'

I felt a goose walk over my grave, as the country people said. Johanna's car, back in Johanna's garage? And its owner lying in Johanna's bed? It was uncanny.

The rest of the evening passed pleasantly enough, however, till they were putting on their coats for William to drive them back to Hen Street. While we stood in the hall, three things happened all at once. Greg came to kiss me goodnight, hugging me in his usual ebullient fashion. He held me close to him, and whispered right into my ear, 'Don't worry, Fran. He'll be back.' I kissed him again, to let him know I understood what he meant, and though she wasn't watching, I felt that Jess saw the incident. Beware, Fran.

Then William said, almost thinking aloud, 'I think I've just had a very good idea. I'm going to be away for six weeks. My car will be standing idle, so why shouldn't you two use it?'

They were both overwhelmed at this last bit of good fortune. They drew close together, as if pinching each other to make sure they had heard correctly, and started on thanks, but William cut them short. A rosy glow had returned to our gathering, and was gently spreading over us all, till in relief at the happy outcome of his suggestion, William dropped his guard.

'That's settled, then. You can pick it up when you're ready. We shan't need my car before I leave on Wednesday, shall we, Fran, my darling?'

I watched the endearment strike Jess, distorting her face momentarily like a twinge of toothache. William was quite unaware of his gaffe, and she kissed me goodnight — at least, we kissed each other — as if neither of us had noticed the cold nip in the air between us. What good actresses all women can be when they choose to!

Neither of us wanted to spoil William's pleasure; in that, at any rate, we were still at one.

44

Three days later, William left. I took him early to the station and was back at home before Sophie came. I did not feel half as low as I had expected. The sooner he had to go, the sooner he would be back. I was lazily making up my own breakfast when Sophie arrived.

She was reassured, and went about her work. We were both relieved to be back to something like our normal routine. I missed William, of course, but days slipped by without too much loneliness – though Mary was away and Johanna gone. I neither saw nor heard from Jess. I thought it strange that Sophie did not remark on that, because I was pretty sure the whole village must be aware of Jess's new job with Manor Farms Ltd by now.

I was in my study one morning in mid-February when Sophie arrived looking far from her normal placid self. One glance at her grim face told me that all was not well. I guessed at once that she had heard at last of Jess's proposed employment. We had kept any mention of it from her till William should have gone, and then I had waited for her to broach the subject to me. That had been a mistake.

'I suppose you've knowed about it all the way along,' she said, managing to make it sound like a reproof while still asking a question.

I didn't pretend that I couldn't guess what she meant. 'If you mean about Jess and her new job, yes,' I said. There was a long silence. 'I don't like it any more than you do. But we must be fair to Jess. She had to get a job sooner or later, and this one cropped up as if made for her. I think she doesn't understand at all the way we feel about what's happening. She didn't know the Thackerays. She thinks Mr Choppen is just what Old Swithinford needed to give it a push towards progress.'

She sniffed. 'Them as still live in what used to be Thack'ray's cottages won't think so,' she said. 'That they won't!'

I couldn't believe my own ignorance. I had known the village from my early childhood, and had taken what I found around me for granted. People who worked on the land lived in those fairytale cottages, some traditional white with thatch, and others, mostly also thatched, a deep rosy red. It had never occurred to me to inquire who owned the cottages.

'Do the farmers still own the cottages, then?' I asked, innocently. The look Sophie turned on me would have floored a rogue elephant, so flabbergasted was she by my abysmal stupidity.

'*Course they do,*' she said. 'Some few folk 'as seen fit to buy their places, if they come into a bit of a legacy, like, or 'ad managed to save up enough. But the old sort o' farmers like Thackerays and Bridgefoots never turned nobody as were too old, or in trouble of any sort, out o' their 'omes if they could possibly 'elp it. Since they started building them new council 'ouses, there ain't really been no need. The young folks would rather 'ave 'em than them tumbledown little old cottages. Tha's one thing that 'as worked out well.'

'So which cottages belong to Monastery Farm, and which to the Glebe?' I asked.

'You can tell 'em easy enough apart if you use your eyes. Them as belong to Glebe are all pink'uns, like Thirz's, and them as belong to Monastery are all white like mine.'

'Sophie! Do you mean that your home still belongs to Monastery Farm?' I couldn't believe it.

'Yes. My father worked for old Thack'ray till 'e died o' lockjaw when a bull gored 'im and dragged 'im through the muck in the yard. Dad were only thirty-eight. But Thack'ray weren't a man to turn a widder-woman with three young child'en out of 'ouse and 'ome, be the cottage never so tied. So by that, we paid our rent reg'lar, and 'e let us be. Same with old Johnnie Cullup next door. 'E were born in that little 'ouse, and so were 'is father and grandfather afore 'im, and they'd all worked for Thack'rays as long as they could work. Johnnie's well past eighty, now. It wasn't very likely as they would turn 'im out when 'e got past work, was it?'

New and awful thoughts began to assail me. Picturesque cottages in the country were being much sought after nowadays, as second homes for the affluent urban middle class. I couldn't see Jack Bartrum or his wife letting sentiment stand in their way if there was any chance of turning crumbling stud-and-mud into hard cash.

'What about Ned?' I asked.

'Oh, 'e's all right,' said Sophie comfortably. 'Is 'ouse is his'n, 'is very own, like. It come to 'im through Eth, d'you see, 'cos her father owned both. So Ned 'as all'us been 'is own man, if you see what I mean.'

That was good news. Sophie was concerned for her old neighbour, Johnnie Cullup, as well as herself. My concern for her set me thinking and I wasn't listening to her. When I picked her tale up, we were, apparently, in the middle of some story of long ago, before the birth of next-door-neighbour Johnnie, who had been an only child.

'When she'd been married five year, and 'ad never fell for a child, she give up 'ope an' never expected to 'ave none. But she felt it very bad, and so did 'er man. Then one day, a gipsy-woman came to her door, selling things. She didn't want to buy nothing, but the woman woul'n't go away. She kept looking at 'er, close like, an' at last the woman says, "I can see you're got a great sorrer, on account o' never having 'ad a child. Cross my 'and wi' silver," says the gipsy, "an' I'll tell you what to do. Come next barley-harvest, you shall hev' as fine a child as any woman could wish."

'Well, from what Mother told us when we was growed, Mis' Cullup couldn't find a thruppeny-bit anywheer in the 'ouse an' 'ad to give the woman sixpence. "For that," says the Romany, "I can promise you a fine boy." An' sure enough, she had Johnnie just as they was beginning to cut the barley next July. Eighty-two, he'll be, come his birthday this year.'

'What a lovely story,' I said. 'But what did the gipsy tell her to do?'

I ought to have known better. Sophie blushed to the roots of her hair, and looked decidedly uncomfortable.

She struggled with her embarrassment, though she finally allowed her desire to tell to win. 'Mother never did tell me, but I 'eard Thirz' telling Het', after Het' were married,' she said. 'She woul'n't mention such things to me. What that gipsy woman said were this, "Go you to bed with your man," she says, "an' as soon as it's over, do you get up an' eat a apple, as big and rosy as you can find. But save the pips. Then next day, choose one o' them pips, an' set it in your garden, and make water on it there an' then. Do that pip grow, so will your babe," she says. Well, Mis' Cullup begged some big rosy apples from the vicar's garden, an' that very night arter her husband 'ad his way with 'er, she got up an' ate one o' them apples, and went out in her nightgown and planted a pip, and then made water on it, then and there, just like the gipsy woman told 'er to. And there's old Johnnie to prove it, and that old apple-tree's there to this day an' all. Johnnie sets such store on it as you'd never believe. "It wou'n't last a lot longer," 'e says to me only a day or two ago. "But you may depend upon it, when one of us goes, so will the other."

'The Rector 'as 'ad another bad turn,' she said. 'They 'ad to git Dr Henderson to 'im early this morning. Thirz' met me as I were comin' to work, and said as 'ow they don't give 'im much chance, this time.' She went, heavy-footed and sighing, into my study.

Another change that she could well have done without. The poor old man had been tottering on the edge of the grave for so long that it could hardly cause surprise if he stumbled into it now. He was well over eighty. I doubted if Old Swithinford would be granted a new Rector. Without the Thackerays, the congregation regulars had dwindled to about ten people, the most constant being Thirzah, Sophie and Daniel.

'When does she start work for Choppen then?' asked Sophie, reappearing suddenly from my study with her arms full of my waste paper basket.

'Oh, fairly soon, surely. I really don't know.'

She looked grimmer than ever, because she suspected I was not telling her the truth. 'It don't matter to me,' she said. 'I only asked out of politeness, like.'

I felt as if Kezia had slapped me. It wasn't like Sophie to take her bruised feelings out on me. I couldn't help the Thackerays leaving, Choppen coming, Jess taking a job, or the Rector dying. But of course it wasn't just that. I had been very surprised that she had said no more to me about the threat to her home, for instance. Something I didn't know about had caused this morning's mood. She would come out with it when she was ready, I judged – and she did. She came and perched on the edge of a chair.

'Now as my little 'ome belongs to that there Choppen,' she said, her lapse into broad dialect warning me of her distress, 'where do you reckon I shall have to goo to pay my rent come Lady Day?'

'How have you paid it before?'

'Took it down and put it in Old Thack'ray's 'and – well till last year, that is. Michael took it in 'is office last time.'

'Take it to the office again, then.'

'And put it into Jess's 'and, and 'er all starched and blue-bagged like one o' them secerrtarries from up London? Her as I played with as soon as we could both do our own buttons up? Still, even that'll be better than handing it over to that Pamela-Balls-as-was!'

She was now passing beyond the bounds of my sympathy. I simply could not think it mattered very much to whom you actually handed your rent. But there was no doubt about Sophie's distress. 'To think that that lousy little wench as my Mam wouldn't let me set next to in school should ever come be my landlord!' she said bitterly. 'If my Jelly hadn't been killed, we could have 'ad our own 'ouse built, and I could 'ave 'eld my 'ead up as 'igh as she does.' She paused, head down, and hands clasped tightly on the table, as if desperately trying to hold back thoughts and words that were overwhelming her. And the dam burst.

'Oh, Fran! Why did He ever let it 'appen like it 'as? Why does He let a wicked woman like her get everything as she wants, even my own little 'ouse as is all I've got left? I keep thinking as it's in the Bible, and that 'E knows what 'E's doing. "The wicked shall flourish like the green bay tree." That's her! And then, "To him that hath shall be given and from him that hath not shall be taken away, even that which he hath." That's my dear little 'ome. If I'm turned out, what'll 'appen to me? Go into one o' them council 'ouses I will not!'

I had not been prepared for anything so serious as this. I wished she would cry, because I felt I could deal with simple sorrow better than with her anger against God — so real and so unexpected that no platitudes could possibly be of any use. If she couldn't turn to the church, she would be absolutely adrift.

I stretched my hand over the table towards her, and to my great relief she laid her own in it.

'Sophie,' I said, 'are you sure that what you are saying is the truth? I don't think you can blame God for what hasn't happened. Wait till it does.'

'It's all too much to bear,' she said. 'Though I knowed from the start as she were only telling me about it 'cos she wanted to upset me as much as ever she could.'

I thought she must mean Jess. 'Don't grudge Jess her little bit of luck, Sophie,' I said. 'You don't know, because we haven't told you, just how bad things have been for her till now. She simply had to get a job, and it seems almost as if this one has been made just for her. We are all jumping to conclusions a bit about Mr Choppen, you know. Don't make him into a devil just because Jess is going to work for him. He may do some good things, yet. We don't know. It may turn out well enough for us all to be happy again.'

'Nobody, not even 'Im Above 'isself, can bring my Jelly back to 'elp me,' she said.

So that was what I was really dealing with. Whatever it was that had set her off this morning, it was also delayed shock and grief at Jelly's death that was at last breaking through her iron reserve. Perhaps she had expected to find me in tears at parting with William, and had told herself that I had no right to be sorry for myself, because William would be coming back – but her Jelly, never! It took a comparison like that to make anybody understand the agony of desolation she must have endured.

I could not help thinking that perhaps in the long run it would prove a good thing that she had at last let some of her anguish out. She was beginning to calm down a little, and I sought to divert her. I asked her how she had found out about Jess and her job.

If it would save my life, I could find no words that were as eloquent as the expression on Sophie's face as she replied.

'Our Het!' was all she said.

'How on earth did she know?'

She looked at me quizzically, to make sure I was asking a genuine question, and not just pretending not to know. She was 'putting herself to rights' by smoothing her hair, straightening her apron front, and thrusting the wet ball of handkerchief deep into her apron pocket.

'So they've kept you in the dark as well as me and Thirz',' she said. 'Jess and Het are as thick as thieves a'ready. Het's never got over me being able to come back here to work, and be happy here with you. She's been so nasty about it all the while that both me and Thirzah have took her to task more'n once.

'Well, I told you 'ow Het's all'us pushing that little old boy of Wend's about in his pram. By all accounts, soon as ever Jess – Mis' Tolly-whatever-'er-name-is – got into that blessed bungalow, if Het didn't set out to go and call on her. For all the world like Pamela Balls-as-was daring to come and call on you, when you first come back 'ere.' The indignation poured like sweat over Sophie's face.

'She told Thirz' how she had made herself known to Je– to Mis' Tolly, as she was Mam's daughter, and how she remembered your grandfather – which she couldn't ha' done – and how she was my sister what done your work for you, and sich-like. She went on to say as *she* was married, and didn't have to go out to work. And this was her little grandson, and a lot more la-di-da talk. Now I don't want to say nothing to upset you about Mis' Tallyhofearo – 'cos I know as she's his 'alf-sister and your own cousin, but I must tell the truth as I see it, whosoever to. And I say as Jess's never been quite the same as you two. And when I see her again, just lately, I

384

thought so more'n ever. She were *too* nice, if you know what I mean. Sort of all over you, like treacle is if you happen to get a bit on your 'ands. A little o' such stuff goes a long way wi' me. And that's how I felt about her. Though I liked her 'usband a lot better than I ever thought I could. Well — accordin' to Thirz', she oozed with it all over more'n usual when our Het called on 'er. And as for young Stephen! Seems as she would hev 'im took out of 'is pram, and kissed him and cuddled 'im and slobbered over 'im and talked a lot o' posh baby-talk to 'im in that croodling sort o' way as she used to talk to your cat in –.'

It was such an accurate picture of Jess putting on that 'sweet' act of hers that I thought it probably was as near the truth as anything could be that had been jackballed from mouth to mouth so many times.

'Well, Thirz' says that after that first time, Het took to callin' most days, and if she didn't go in for a cup of tea. Mis' Tolly-do-da put 'er coat on and went for a walk with 'er. You can picture for yourself what sort of a swelled 'ead our silly Het would get, to be seen walking up Hen Street with the old squire's granddaughter pushing 'er grandchild's pram, poor fatherless little mite as 'e may be! In fact, Thirz' said Het 'ad told Jess as 'ow Wend' 'ad been deceived by a young motor mechanic in Swithinford as 'ad promised to marry 'er, and then took 'is 'ook when she'd told 'im she were expecting 'is child.

'Me and Thirz' was ashamed of one of our fam'ly putting herself for'ard like that; and I didn't want to be mixed up in it, if I could 'elp it. But next time I see Thirz' to talk to, a-Sunday that was, she said I'd better goo 'ome with her so she could tell me the latest. Het had been to see Thirz' Sat'day, when she'd come straight from a visit to the bungalow. And Jess — I wish as I'd never called her that, 'cos she's no friend o' mine from now on — had emptied a bucketful o' news all over her, as you might say, only it were more like a pail o' pig-swill. First there was that new job; then there was all that Choppen had told Jess what he was going to do with all such cottages as mine.'

She was embarrassed now, and I wondered idly if the next disclosure was that Greg had pinched Hetty's bottom, or winked at her on the sly. That it was something within a sexual context I could foresee, because by now I knew all the signs. But I was not prepared for what was to come.

Sophie was breathing deep, and bringing her courage to the

sticking point. 'Fran,' she said (she never called me that except under the stress of great emotion), 'I don't know 'ow to tell you this, but tell you I must. Thirz' and me prayed about it, and Thirz' said truth is always best told straight off, afore it's 'ad time to get twisted. Het said as Jess 'ad told 'er that William was goin' to America this time especially to find 'is wife and make it up with 'er so as he could bring her back with him when he comes. Now, o' course Thirz don't know as much about you and William as I do, and I didn't want to talk about it. But it seems as Thirz' was inclined to take all Het said for gospel about that, because she had had it straight from Jess. What Jess told Het was that she thought it was all your fault, 'cos you was all'us trying to tempt him, like, against 'is will, and that she, Jess that is, had had a long talk to him and he'd agreed to go and find his wife again and be seen to be a respectable man afore it was too late in case he lost his job because 'e slept with you out o' wedlock! There! Now I've told you, I shall soon feel better. But I were so put out that I told Thirz' outright as it was not the truth about you sleeping together, though if any two ought to be man and wife it was you. And I told her straight that if the time ever come when it got the better of you, as you might say, it would make no difference to me. So she'd better think about that, instead o' Jess's tales. But I do know as it 'll be all round the village, and Hen Street, 'cos Het's got a mouth like an old hen with the gapes. And I were so upset I told Thirz' she 'adn't got the right to judge nobody else — hadn't she been to bed wi' Dan'el as was the man she loved, even if they was married? And I said as none of us 'ould be 'ere to talk about it if our Mam hadn't been to bed with our Dad. (She actually smiled, a smile so wan and pathetic that it hurt.) Do you know, Fran, I thought as Thirz' would have a fit to hear me mentioning such things! She told me I'd better go 'ome and wash my mouth out with garbolic, speakin' o' the dead like that. So I come out, and I ain't seen Thirz' since till this morning. I was glad as I did see her, though. 'Cos when I got up this morning, I wondered what I had done. I thought as how I shall never have a man, now Jelly's gone, and I soon shouldn't have a home, and very like I hadn't got no sisters left as would own me no more. But I did do the right thing, didn't I, Fran? Standing up to 'em all like that, I mean?'

I squeezed the hand I was holding. 'I think you couldn't do wrong if you tried,' I said. 'You certainly did right but you have given me a lot to think about. We'll talk it over later and see what's best to do.'

I went to my study like an animal to its den. The breakdown in Sophie's fortitude had been very hard to cope with: the inter-dependence between us was something very real. I must think things out and be prepared to stand behind her like the rock she had been to me.

With regard to the threat to her home, we could but wait and see; there was always Eeyore's Tail as a temporary, if not a permanent refuge. There was nothing wrong in Jess's friendship with Hetty, but it wasn't natural, so there had to be some ulterior motive. Jess and Hetty made a very curious twosome. Hetty was, as Sophie had said, probably feeling flattered; but what on earth could be Jess's reason for reciprocating? She certainly had nothing in common with Sophie's 'sterrickle' sister.

There could really only be one explanation. It provided her with a news channel about us. She was using Hetty as a spy, on Benedict's in general, on me and on William, but most of all on the two of us together. With a single thread of gossip and a spindle of truth, she could weave a dark veil to throw over my character and reputation. My sense of distaste was so strong that I could almost feel my lip curling — but common-sense told me there was only one way to combat jealousy, which was to take no notice of it at all; to scorn it absolutely as beneath notice, and dismiss it with the contempt it deserved. She should not weave a shroud for my happiness. If Sophie would go along with me, Hetty would get no further reaction out of her, whatever tales she spread, and Jess none whatsoever out of me.

But I was angry, all the same. Jess was as clever as Hetty was simple. Everything she had told Het had a tiny grain of truth in it, making it harder to ignore or live down than a downright lie. As a close member of my family, Jess could be expected to be 'in the know'; whatever she said would be taken as gospel-truth. She *had* talked to William about his wife — and had been subtle enough in her reporting to admit that here and there she was only expressing what she *surmised*, not what she *knew*. That gave wonderful scope for others to pass the tale on 'with advantages', as Shakespeare so wonderfully phrased it. If Jess was going to become a permanent resident of Hen Street, we should be silly to allow her to make an enemy of herself. What was it the Anglo-Saxons used to say? 'If you save a man from drowning, he will be the death of you.'

Where William was concerned, I had no worry at all. That was one aspect I shouldn't need to make clear to Sophie. My thoughts turned again to why I was so much against the neglect or destruction of old customs? Against such 'progress' as Choppen and Co. were proposing, for example? Jess wasn't.

I could only suppose it was because I had a streak of sentiment in me that she hadn't — or, if she ever had had, that it had been knocked out of her by hard experience.

Until the disappearance of the Thackeray family, the village hierarchy had still existed, even though it had been beheaded long before. Now it had collapsed, especially if the Rector was about to vacate his rung on the ladder, too. It wouldn't vanish altogether till Sophie and her generation were dead, but I had never thought of myself as upholding it. And yet had it not been partly due to my sense of *noblesse oblige* that I had not let William share my bed? And was it not because of his, too, that he had accepted my dictum without fuss?

Well, if we were truly now all equal, William and I were freed of the *noblesse oblige* that had been drummed into us when children. How ironic: Hetty and Jess between them had dragged me right up to date, and done me a good turn. So said my reason.

Instinct still had to be brought into line. The truth was that I wanted all that was best of the old as well as all that was best of the new. That was selfish as well as impracticable; but I could not let go of the belief that if there was one place on earth where it was possible to enjoy the best of both worlds, Benedict's was it. And Benedict's was mine. No, correction — it was ours: mine, and William's and Sophie's.

I went back into the kitchen to talk to Sophie, beginning on the point I thought she could best comprehend.

'We are dealing with two spiteful women,' I said, 'as different as chalk and cheese from each other. One is very clever, and the other very silly, and I don't have to tell you which is which.'

'That you don't,' said Sophie with vehemence. 'I hate to say it, but our Het 'as all'us acted like a simpleton. Now she's going on as if she don't know which way 'er behind hangs.'

'But she's still your sister,' I said. 'I'm sure you don't want to fall out with her any more than you can help.'

'That's what Thirz' said, 'cos o' what we promised Mam.'

'Well, I don't want to fall out with Jess, either, specially as she's William's sister. So I am going to try to take no notice of their silly tales at all. Gossip can't harm us — especially if we make up our minds not to listen. So just let's agree to take no notice of whatever Jess and Hetty say.'

She didn't hesitate. 'We ain't got nothing to be ashamed of, as I know. It's them as will have guilty consciences, or ought to, if they ain't got 'em a'ready,' she said.

There was going to be no battle of wills. She was feeling better herself for having got a lot off her chest, and very willing to be mollified if that is what I wanted. I found it a bit more difficult to get through to Sophie that though she couldn't 'go along with it', life in the twentieth century was not necessarily wrong. We had just got to get used to things being different, because whatever we did now, the changes had come, and we could do nothing about it. If we tried, we should only make ourselves look silly. She didn't argue, but hunched her shoulders in a gesture of defiant defeat. I thought perhaps that I had said enough for today, and got up to go and wash my hands in the sink.

Looking down the garden, I saw Ned suddenly straighten himself up, pull off his cap, throw down his hoe, and stand bare-headed to attention. Sophie sprang to her feet, pulled the kitchen door wide open, and listened.

'Hark!' she said, holding up a finger for silence.

The strong, mellow boom of a deep-toned bell rolled across the tops of the trees between us and the church. Then came a pause, in which Sophie said, 'The Rector's gone. That's George Bridgefoot a-tolling the passing-bell for 'im, like was always done till a few year ago for everybody.' The long, slow, hollow, vibrating sound came again. Boom. Boom. Boom. Then another threefold silence.

'That's right,' said Sophie. 'Three for a man, two for a woman, and one for a child.'

We stood as still as statues as the bell made the air shiver with its three booms alternating with aching three-beat gaps. Then, at last, fell an eerie silence. I moved, but Sophie put out her hand to stop me.

'Wait,' she said. 'Now George'll toll once for every year of 'is age. We can spare 'im that amount o' time, can't we?'

The strokes began, and involuntarily we counted. Eighty, eighty-one, eighty-two, eighty-three, eighty-four — the quivering sound hung throbbing on the air, lingered humming far away, and stopped.

'God rest his soul,' said Sophie, and no power on earth could have prevented me from adding 'Amen.'

Sophie closed the door softly. Ned put on his cap, and took up his hoe. Life would go on.

45

I had failed Sophie by not being at home when Jelly was killed. I could not let it happen again, so while there was doubt about her cottage, I could not go visiting. She had taken the death of the Rector with typical rural philosophy. The funeral was arranged for Saturday, and she took it for granted that I should attend. The customary rites must be observed.

'We shan't put Het's name on our wreath to the Rector. Not this time. After all, she's never been to 'is church since she went to live in Hen Street and started going to that other place.'

How that dereliction on Hetty's part still rankled! But I noted with surprise that Sophie's decision had not been in deference either to Thirzah or, much more significantly, to what their dead mother would have preferred. Jelly's death had left a little rod of steel in Sophie's personality that had not been in evidence before.

So I attended the funeral, and as I left the churchyard on Saturday afternoon, I resolved to walk to Hen Street and visit Jess. She had made no attempt to get in touch with me, though Greg had collected William's car. I knew she was busy, and would soon be busier still. It should not be my fault if the gap between us grew too great to be easily bridged.

It required more courage than I had thought it would to turn into the gate of Bryony Cottage, but Jess had seen me approaching, and had the door open for me. As far as I could tell, she was truly pleased to see me. I went up the little hall, and into the sitting-room I knew so well, half-expecting the ghost of Johanna to be sitting with Madge Ellis's knitting on the settee. Instead, there sat Hetty Noble, dancing her grandson on her knee, and beside her sat — surely that fine-looking young lady couldn't be *Wendy*? But it was, there was no doubt about it. We all greeted each other, and I admired the baby, and said (I hope) all the right things. Jess was being as good a hostess as ever Johanna had been, and was soon chatting easily, putting me into the picture regarding her two other visitors.

'Hetty is coming to my rescue,' she said, with a Mata Hari smile that reminded me of Johanna talking to Ned. 'Greg is really getting on so well with his book that I don't want him to have to stop work to be the housewife, as he did the last time I had a full-time job. But Hetty has solved our problem. She suggested that she should come a couple of hours for three days a week to help me out — keep the house clean, and do bits of shopping for me, and so on.'

Hetty, dressed in her best, at that moment appeared as little like a charlady as Johanna had ever looked like a landlady. She was also putting on an act of 'refinement', both in speech and deportment, that was very different from the hysterical Hetty I knew. She volunteered the information that the idea had come to her as being only right, like, seeing as Sophie 'did' for me, and her mother had 'done' for Grandfather. I thought it was a good thing that there would be no further generation at hand for Wendy to do for, because she didn't look much like the sort of person who would 'oblige' anybody. She had not spoken, but sat by her mother wearing a strained expression on a slightly sullen face. I guessed she had been dragged there by Hetty to visit Jess, and had found too many memories there for comfort. My intrusion could not have helped.

When they stood up to go, I had my first good look at her, and was quite surprised at the change in her from what I remembered. Gone was the rather dumpy girl with the round rosy face and the 'country lass' air. She had grown tall during the last year. The skin was just as I remembered it, peaches and cream without blemish, like her mother's, though she was expertly made up; so well, in fact, that I knew at once who had coaxed her to stop daubing crimson lipstick and thick cheap powder on. Wendy's eyes, which I had thought so much like Sophie's, had lost their brilliance, and were now rather dull and expressionless, like those of a doll; windows into an empty house. She was still only eighteen but her figure had lost all its puppy-fat, and was now slim with just a hint of seductive feminine roundness. Apart from her lacklustre expression, she was a beauty. Yet I liked the girl I remembered better. The Wendy I had first known was full of the fire of youth. This made-up creature was an empty shell. What must the poor child have gone through, to have left her so flat and hopeless!

As I put out my hand to her as I said goodbye, I felt I could not stay another minute in the house that for all its changes was still redolent of Johanna. I hated her at that moment. In spite of all she had made of the girl, to satisfy her own desires vicariously perhaps, Wendy was no more to Johanna than one of the country bumpkins she so despised. It seemed to me that the fuse that Johanna and

Birch between them had lit was still smouldering in this listless, immature woman. This room was making her wounds smart.

'Don't go yet, Fran,' Jess said. 'I want to talk to you. And Greg will be upset if he misses you. Let me get you some tea.'

But I declined, because Johanna's ghost had been raised by Wendy, and I wanted to go home. Besides, I now felt in no mood to hear about Choppen's plans, or to answer any searching questions 'innocently' put to me about William.

I spent much of the weekend pouring out words on paper to William — not dealing with any problems, but just letting my pen flow with descriptions on small things at Benedict's, what Cat was doing, the sound of the passing bell, the people at the Rector's funeral, and my visit to Jess. I knew he would be pleased about that, and to get a letter that carried 'home' with it.

As time in his absence passed gently along, I enjoyed the first of the spring sunshine, and looked at all the bulbs and blossoms in the garden, searched the roadside verges for a solitary primrose where once there would have been hundreds, and rejoiced in my own island of peace and comfort in general. I ought to have known it couldn't last. April's sunshine usually gives way to showers.

We had got round to Lady Day, which happened to be a Monday. Sophie, who had been more like her usual self recently, arrived late, looking very put out. As always, she withheld her news until she had put on her apron and fetched out her cleaning apparatus. I was in my study, though I had seen her set face as she passed my window, and judged from the way she was shutting drawers and by her extra-firm tread that something was amiss. When she opened my door with a cup of coffee in her hand quite half an hour before it was due, I knew I had to stop working, turn my chair towards her, and listen.

'Fetch your own drink in here, Sophie,' I said, 'and then tell me quick what is the matter.'

'That Choppen!' she said, before she had got her bottom down on the chair 'Bein' as it's Lady Day, and my rent due, I knowed as you wouldn't mind if I went round that way and took it in to the office, same as you said. So I did. Jess were in there, busy, like, at a desk, and Mr Choppen set aside her. So I told 'im what I'd gone for, and took the envelope with the money in out o' my bag to give 'im.'

'"Put it back," 'e says. "I ain't taking no rent from nobody till I'm 'ad a chance to go and see 'em, in their 'ouses. I want to see the condition of every 'ouse as belongs to us afore we go any further."'

And I 'ad to put it back in my bag, and come away! I don't like the sound of it. I reckon 'e's got some nasty plan up 'is sleeve. Do you think Jess'll know?'

'She probably knows already,' I said. 'But she won't tell us. You wouldn't tell anybody my business, you know. Why should you expect Jess to tell us what is Mr Choppen's business?'

'That's what don't seem right,' she said. 'She 'adn't ought to be working against us.'

'But we don't know what Mr Choppen means to do,' I argued. 'He may mean well.'

'Wash the dog and comb the dog but that'll still be a dog when you're finished,' she said. 'I feel in my bones as 'e means trouble, and 'as done from the start. If 'e don't, why didn't he do as other folks would, an' take my rent when it was offered?' She didn't expect an answer, because she knew I couldn't give one, so she emptied her cup, and marched out with the tray. She was back again next minute, having forgotten my cup. 'They are putting electric into that old barn, this morning,' she added. 'Nobody knows what for, but you depend upon it that it's for no good. What's young Choppen going to do in it? Make cobwebs into ropes to 'ang folks with, I shouldn't be surprised.'

The news was all round the village next day, that every cottage owned by Manor Farms Ltd would be visited personally by Mr Choppen whether or not the occupant was still in his employ.

His message was quite explicit; the days when they could expect to live out their lives in such primitive conditions and peace of mind were numbered. All those dwellings that were now the property of Manor Farms Ltd were to be 'improved', whether the tenants agreed or not. Every cottage, however small, was to have a bathroom added, with a proper 'toilet'; was therefore to be connected with both water and electricity mains; and was to have its corrugated iron or zinc roof stripped off, the old thatch removed, and replaced with new thatch.

The cost was going to be great, and they must understand that their landlord had a legal right to charge a proportional rent for improvement. When asked how much, he named a figure which in most cases was double or treble the four or five shillings a week they were now paying. To those who protested that they did not *want* a bathroom or a flush toilet, and that 'the little 'ouse' at the end of the garden had been good enough for them all their lives, or to the octogenarians who viewed aghast the awful prospect of the

393

disturbance, he was sweet reason personified. He quite understood, and even sympathized – but farming now was different from what it used to be. He had partners with a lot of money invested who had never seen the village. They made the policy; he only carried out their wishes. To those who cried that they couldn't or wouldn't pay the new rent, he gave advice – to ask the council to rehouse them. Had they no children with whom they could go to live?

'It'll be the Union for us!' said more than one old couple.

He did not believe in the terror of 'the Union'. A lot of his taxes went towards funding homes and care for the elderly.

'I'll tell you what I'll do,' he was reported to be saying, 'you get your family to fix you up somewhere, and you can have your last year's rent back if you get out before I want to start.'

Stick and carrot combined. What could they do but give in?

The village seethed like boiling mud. There were many who saw eye to eye with Choppen, smallholders who had tied cottages on their own land and who had not been able to make use of them to get young workmen because the larger and better-off farmers had set standards of compassion they feared to go against. The older half of the people were scandalized. Choppen was Evil personified, the Big Bad Wolf at the door of peace and tranquillity. Ned told me that the visits had started, timing his information to get it in before Sophie came the next Monday morning, knowing that she, too, had had a visit from her landlord.

When she arrived, her expression and general mien denoted excitement and aggression rather than misery or distress. She sat down, looked straight at me, and said, 'I suppose as you've 'eard?'

I nodded.

'Up 'e comes,' she said, 'large as life, and told 'is tale, same as 'e 'as done to everybody. I let 'im 'ave 'is say, and then I asked 'im, "What are you a-going to do," I says, "if I won't *be* moved?"

'"You'll 'ave to pay more rent than I reckon you can afford," 'e says. "'Cos you may as well know as I intend to do as I like with what is our property now."

'"Put your rent up," I says. "It won't worrit me. But I ain't 'aving no changes made to my 'ome as I don't want. It may be your property," I says, "but it's my 'ome."

'"I'll 'ave the law on you," 'e says, "if you hobstruct my workmen. If you don't like the 'eat," 'e says, "get out o' the kitchen."

'"Ah!" I says. "That's just what you want, ain't it? You want me out, so as you can titivate it a bit and then sell it to some poor fool who's got more money than sense. For a lot more than it's worth."

394

'"I won't deny it," 'e says. "You've 'it the nail on the 'ead."

'"I warn't born yist'day," I says. "So, if you are set on selling it, what's your price — as it stands?"

'"More than you can afford, my good woman," 'e says — and laughs such a nasty laugh as you never did 'ear. I'm sure, Fran, I never felt so near to 'itting a man over the 'ead with a flat-iron in all my life afore, not even that 'Ector Birch!'

She was enjoying herself hugely, as I could see. Her clear grey eyes sparkled and glinted, and her unconscious easy use of my name showed how far she was from her normal Monday work-a-day self.

'"Name your price," I says. "And don't you 'good woman' me! I am a good woman," I says, "so you won't hinsult me by calling me one."

'I swear Fran, as I could *feel* Jelly standing right there beside me, and 'ear 'is voice, like, egging me on! 'Cos I'm never spoke to nobody like that in all my life afore, not that I know of. I just don't know what come over me. Well, 'e looked so took aback, I thought as I should laugh in 'is face. "Name your price for it," I says, "as it stands, afore you start mucking it about," I says.

'"Five 'undred, then," 'e says.

'I were a bit shook by that, I must say, 'cos it ain't worth a penny more than £300 at the very most. But there were Jelly again, right in my ear, telling me 'ow 'e 'ad enough money to build us a brand new 'ouse, whatever I wanted, and me telling 'im 'ow I would rather 'ave my own little 'ome done up for us. "'Old your ground, gal," Jelly's voice said, "Don't you give in now."

'"You're a thief and a robber," I says, same as it says in the Bible. "'E that entereth not in by the door but climbeth in some other way, the same is a thief and a robber. There ain't no truth at all in your tale," I says. "You just mean to get us all out, so as you can sell to fools out o' the towns as quick as you can, and get 'old o' their money! So why ain't my money as good as their'n?"

'"It would be," 'e says. "If you could find it."

'"Stand you still," I says, "while I go upstairs." So up I went, and came down with a couple o' tins in my apron. I knowed 'ow much there were in one of 'em, 'cos I'm been saving in that one ever since I were fourteen, and first left school. Since I'm been working for you, and 'aving a lot o' my meals 'ere, I ain't 'ad no call to spend 'alf what I get, let alone that extra as I keep getting from what Jelly left me. I asked the man in the bank to let me 'ave it all'us in cash, week by week, 'cos I felt as if I wanted to 'andle it, and make out to

myself as it were Jelly giving me the 'ousekeeping, like. And then I
put it away in that tin with all the other. So I pulled the lid off the
biscuit tin, and begun to count the bundles o' notes out, in 'undreds,
afore 'is very eyes. When I got to five 'undred, I stopped, and said,
"I am offering to buy my 'ome 'ere and now. And if you don't let
me 'ave it," I says, "it'll be me as goes to law. I am a sitting tenant, I
am," I says.

'I could see as 'e were flummoxed, an' 'e kept looking sideways at
the rest o' the money left in the tin.

'"I am thinking o' putting it up for auction," 'e says. "Likely it'll
make more'n five 'undred pound that way."

'"Not wi' me in it, it won't," I says. "They'd want vacant possession." He knowed when 'e were beat, I'll say that for 'im, but 'e still
didn't like it.

'"I shall 'ave to 'ave a lawyer to see about the sale," 'e says. "I
'ope as you realize it'll cost you a goodish bit in lawyer's fees for
the conveniencing and such."

'"I shall 'and it all over to my solicitor," I says, wi' my nose in the
air as if I done such deals every day o' my life. "And if you are frit as I
shan't 'ave enough left to pay my dues and demands when I am
paid you," I says, "you just take a look in this 'ere." And I opened the
other tin, only it weren't a tin exactly, being as it was my great-
grandmother's tea-caddy. I unlocked it and pushed it under 'is nose.
I reckon 'e 'adn't never seen nothing like that in all 'is born days!
You see, when Grandad Berridge died, they found that there tea-
caddy under 'is bed, where 'e 'ad kept it with 'is savings in, to bury
'im decent with. But 'e 'ad a fair bit put by, one way or another, so it
weren't ever used. So it come to Mam, and when she and Dad were
married, they added to it whenever they could spare anything, so as
to be able to give us all a bit in turn when we got married. But after
Dad died, like, Mam thought she 'ad better keep it for 'er own
burial. But we didn't need it for 'er, neither, and so I left it where it
were. I never told 'em about it, but I ain't never touched a penny of
it. And I ain't likely to 'ave to now, seeing as after all I did 'ave a
man to look after me, and leave me a fortune.'

She sat back, a picture of womanhood triumphant. '"Im and 'is
"good woman!"' she said, puffing out her chest like a pouter-pigeon.

I hugged her, rejoicing that Choppen and all his up-to-date econ-
omic power was helpless when faced with one indomitable ageing
spinster who was sure of her ground.

'But Sophie,' I said, aghast, 'are you telling me that you have been alone all this time with a tin with hundreds of pounds in it under your bed? It is a wonder you haven't been murdered!'

She smiled placidly. 'Nobody knowed as it were there, did they?' she said.

'No. But they do now.'

'Ah, well. It ain't there now,' she said. 'If that Choppen tells folks, and I do get burgled you'll know who to set the police on, anyways.' She looked as if the thought of Choppen in the hands of the police would be worth the inconvenience of having her throat cut.

'What do you mean, it isn't there now? Where is it, then?'

''Ere,' she said, and fished into a deep brown American-cloth shopping bag that she had leaned up against the leg of her chair. From it she extracted a battered old biscuit tin, its paper covering browned and scuffed with age and usage. Pulling off the top, she disclosed the bundles of treasury notes, few worth more than £1, that filled it. That was the sort of currency she understood.

'But you'll look after this 'ere yourself, won't you?' she said, drawing from the bag a most beautiful antique double tea-caddy. She produced a tiny key, unlocked it and lifted the lid. Each of the metal-lined tea-containers was brimful of sovereigns and half-sovereigns. No longer legal tender, of course, but each and every one of them worth far more than its face value. Me take care of that? Only if I was allowed to put it in my safe-deposit box at the bank unopened!

The sight of the gold made me gasp, and I visualized Mr Choppen's face when confronted by it. I could see every detail of the scene as Sophie had described it to me, and more. That overcrowded little room with its lop-sided walls, and Sophie's Bible lying open in full view. Sophie herself, aproned and tidy, still sturdily booted, standing on her pegged hearth-rug to fight for her territory like any other trapped and therefore dangerous female of any species. I saw the incongruous Mr Choppen, pink-faced and so smoothly sure of himself, suddenly peering down into that little well of riches, and feeling himself out of his depth.

It was too much for me. Struggle as I might, I could not swallow the bubble of laughter that was threatening to choke me if I didn't let it out. When finally it got the better of me, I gave way to it and laughed till I was breathless. Sophie's face was a study that only set the peals ringing again every time I thought I had mine under control. The thought that she was well used to Hetty's 'sterricks' only set me off again. Sophie's face was tight-lipped and grim —

but it was as if we were both compelled by that gleaming gold to bend over it and peer down at it again like twin puppets. I felt the irrepressible bubble rising in my throat again, and let out another peal, stuffing my handkerchief against my mouth to stop another attack lest Sophie should misunderstand and be hurt. But my ears caught the sound of a tiny, choked-back snigger, and turning my head sideways, I saw that her face had broken up into one I didn't recognize as she fought against her own desire to laugh. Then she lost control of her face as well as her throat, and let out her own joy and triumph, joining me laugh for laugh till we were both exhausted.

'That's done me good!' she said. 'I ain't 'ad a good laugh like that 'ardly since I'm been growed up!'

I took Sophie's hoard to the bank that very afternoon.

I had barely finished my supper the same evening, when Ned knocked gently on the door and asked if he might come in for a minute or two.

'I thought as I'd better come up specially to tell you,' he said, 'afore Soph' comes in the morning, 'cos she'll be so upset. They found poor old Johnnie Cullup 'ung on his own apple tree this afternoon, while you and Sophie was gone out. It appears as Choppen went to see 'im, and told him he could only stop in his house a little while longer, 'cos they plan to turn the whull row o' them cottages into riding-stables. But they are going to plough up all them gardens straight off like, and throw 'em in with the field at the back, and lay it down for pasture for the 'osses.

'"And what about my apple-tree?" asks old Johnnie.

'"Coming down afore the week's out," says Choppen.

'That were Saturday. And as soon as ever old Johnnie had seen Soph' clear this morning, he went into the barn-place next door to his house and found a halter as had got left there, and went straight to his tree draggin' a pair o' steps with him, and strung hisself up from the tree with the halter.'

'Oh dear!' I cried. 'It's like a row of dominoes pushing each other over. What next?'

Ned was regarding me with a sober eye. 'Bill Edgeley,' he answered, though I hadn't meant it as a question. 'Choppen went to give him a year's notice to quit. Wants to throw all the land into one farm, he says. And he's bidding for the ffranksbridge place, an' all, from what I hear.'

'But surely Bill Edgeley must have tenant's rights after all this long time,' I said. 'Need he go?'

'I daresay he has,' Ned said, 'but it wouldn't be no good trying to keep going if you were all'us going to be at logger'eads wi' your landlord. And in any case it's too late, now. It appears that when Choppen went and faced Bill with it so sudden, he were that worried as he just couldn't think straight no more. I reckon he'd got hisself so worked up 'cos he'd been expecting it. And without really knowing what he was doing, he tells Choppen that the land weren't no good without the coal business, there not being enough of it, like, nor the other way about if Bill had got to find hisself new premises to run it from. So he tells Choppen the best thing would be for him to buy Bill out o' the whull lot, there and then, and he'd get out at the end o' the quarter. "Done!" says Choppen, and he writ out a paper for Bill to sign then and there, in front o' two witnesses, afore he left.

'Now poor old Bill's in a terrible state, and so's his missus. They ain't short of a bob or two, so they'll be all right once they get over it, 'cos it is time Bill didn't have to work so hard. But it were the way it were done as they can't get over.'

'I don't wonder,' I said. 'He really is a dreadful man!'

'If you was to ask me,' said Ned, carefully fitting his cap back on his head as he went to the door, 'I should say he ain't a man at all. He's a bloody locust.'

46

While down in the village all was uncertainty and chaos, up at Benedict's we appeared to be in a state of limbo. Sophie was triumphant, Ned independent and there was nothing I could do.

Benedict's had been drifting farther and farther away from the rest of the village, like a lifeboat lowered from a ship, ever since the night of Mary's horkey. Once upon a time, Benedict's had been a kind of rallying point when things went wrong, because when everybody worked to the rhythms of the seasons, they depended on each other to help over the bad patches caused by the arbitrary whims of Nature. Now, the Choppens of the world had got nature under control, and the welfare state provided the helping hand. I supposed that this was all for the best; in fact, if I had to vote in a referendum about it, I could not in all honesty say I thought the clock should be put back.

No actual date had been set for William's return; he had other things to see to after the actual seminar was over, particularly with regard to the publication of his last bit of research.

I tried not to take account of time. What was time, anyway? A convention, not a reality. I had *lived* more actual life since I came back to Benedict's than I had done in the previous four decades put together — war and all. Since I had been here, every one of my senses had been sharpened, every wit made more acute, every emotion magnified.

Sophie brought items of news to my island of quiet. One was that Choppen was negotiating for the purchase of all the old de ffranks-bridge land, (Sophie's tone was scandalized) that he wasn't going to farm it, but plough it all up and lay it down for something altogether different. Well, that is, if he could get permission. 'That Choppen means to own everything hereabouts, it seems,' Sophie said. 'Only there is one bit as 'e shan't lay 'is 'ands on, thanks to my Jelly.'

'Two bits,' I said. 'Yours and mine.'

'And Ned's,' she said. 'Like it says in the Bible, "the little things o' the earth confound the mighty."' We looked at each other like a couple of small children sharing a big bag of toffee.

I had begun to feel a bit guilty about Jess, because I didn't want any uncomfortable feeling between us to spoil William's homecoming. It was time I made another move. After all, I was now the leisured one, even if I was 'at work'.

As it happened, though, she dropped in one afternoon. She looked fit and well, though a bit tired. I was honestly pleased to see her, and started pouring tea as soon as she arrived, knowing she would not be able to stay long.

'Where's the faithful Sophie?' she asked.

I knew that Sophie had excused herself early because she was no longer sure of her ground with Jess. I had been a bit irritated with her, in fact. I didn't want a re-run of the Johanna situation. But I would rather she went, than have had to conduct tea with Jess in an atmosphere of armed neutrality between them.

'She's gone home early to get herself ready for a visit to the solicitor about her house tomorrow,' I answered truthfully.

'She hasn't forgiven me for having anything to do with Choppen and Co,' said Jess. 'Hetty told me so. I really didn't think anybody could be so stupid, nowadays. I am only the firm's secretary, anyway. It isn't anything to do with me.'

I knew that she meant that for me as much as for Sophie.

'Nobody blames you,' I said. 'I think it's just a bit sad that you happen to have got involved "on the wrong side", so to speak, as far as people like Sophie are concerned. It is an awful blow to a lot of old folks — and you know how inter-related they all are in such small rural communities as this. They feel for each other.'

'Well, as far as I can see, Sophie's the last one who ought to grumble. Apparently she's all right. Well, according to Hetty.'

'I'm afraid "our Het" is a little careless with regard to the ninth commandment,' I said. 'I think she actually enjoys bearing a bit of false witness. I wouldn't take all she tells you for gospel truth, if I were you.'

Jess put down her cup and bit into a scone with deliberation that warned me I was on dangerous ground.

'Is that Sophie's tale, or are you speaking from experience?' she asked — and there was quite a barb in her voice.

'Both,' I said. I was not prepared to make an issue of it with her, but neither was I prepared to back down. I kept it as light as I could. 'I gather from Sophie that Hetty has fed you with some pretty tall tales with regard to young Wendy's baby,' I said. 'If she can invent things like that just to suit herself, she could make trouble. Real trouble.'

'I find her quite amusing and certainly she's a great help to us at the present,' Jess said. 'And I couldn't care less who the child's father was, so why should I worry?'

I changed the subject. 'Do tell about all the personalities up at Monastery Farm.'

'Manor Farms Ltd,' she said, sounding more like 'my' Jess again.

'What's Choppen like? To work for, I mean?'

'Hard as nails. After every penny. A typical business man. He thinks I'm a machine. He certainly doesn't consider me as a human female. Women simply have their uses where he is concerned, and my place is at a typewriter.'

'Perhaps you should wear a fetching frock, and cry prettily into a tiny lace handkerchief.'

She snorted — the sound that brought back childhood and made me love her again instantly.

'You wouldn't advise that if you knew our other working partner, Mr Bartrum,' she said. 'My ski-pants are useful as a chastity-belt where he's concerned.'

'I do know him,' I said, 'or, at least, I have met him. My friend who used to live in Bryony Cottage had much the same view of him. But I thought being married to Pamela — Thackeray-as-was — might have tamed him a bit.'

'Really? But didn't she ask for it? According to Hetty, she was the prototype for the Whore of Babylon.'

I was angry. I looked straight at her, and said, rather coldly, 'I have just called her my friend, Jess. And I asked you not to believe all Hetty says. All I will say is that Johanna did have trouble keeping Bartrum at bay.'

'I don't encourage him,' said Jess, shortly.

'Nor did Johanna,' I said. 'Look, Jess, Johanna Brooke was a townee who hated the country, but you belong. You ought to understand that no *femme sole* is safe in a village unless she's an old maid like Sophie or a widow like me. Safe neither from the Jack Bartrums nor from the women's tongues. Johanna's husband wasn't present to protect her reputation. Yours is. I haven't got one.'

'A husband, or a reputation?'

'Neither, apparently, if Hetty has her way,' I said lightly. 'Well, that is if what Sophie tells me Hetty is broadcasting is right.' I was glad to note that she had the grace to colour. In spite of ourselves, we were still sparring. How right William had been to warn me that we might not be able to take up again where we had left off our loving comradeship so many years ago.

'Tell me about the young Choppens,' I said.

'Nothing at all like him. I haven't seen a great deal of either. Young Gavin is really rather nice. A group musician who wants to run a recording company. Then there is Monique, Choppen's daughter. She's a dress designer, absolutely charming and prepared to be friendly. Goodness! Is that the time? I shall catch it if I'm a minute late back. I was only allowed out because I have agreed to do two hours overtime.'

She came back from the bathroom with new make-up in place and had lost a bit of the tired look. 'Thanks, Fran,' she said, kissing me with genuine warmth. 'It is lovely just to be able to drop in here, you know. I shall be glad when William's back.'

'I shan't be sorry to see him again,' I said.

'I expect he's having a whale of a time among those glossy

American female academics,' she said. 'I hope so. He's still such a virile, handsome man. He needs women. I shall be glad if he finds one he can call his own again.'

I let her out. 'So shall I,' I said.

The weather continued to be very cold, but dry enough to let Choppen get on with the 'improvements' of five cottages. There were harrowing tales of the anger and unhappiness caused, and of one old widow's death, though that could not necessarily be laid at Choppen's door: old people do die. Then came the first breath of real spring, and I was torn between wanting to be out in the sunshine, and wanting to stay at my desk. The latter won, most of the time, because my fictional family was complete and tempted me into letting them get on with their lives, largely because without them I began to feel incomplete, and more than a little solitary.

Time, even so little of it according to the calendar, resettled the village reluctantly into its new pattern, and the ferment died down day by day to a resigned acceptance by some, and vociferous approval by others. Quite apart from the misery of those directly involved, the issue had split the community right down the middle, as if Old Swithinford might be in the throes of a micro-civil-war. None of the usual summer events, such as the annual Red Cross coffee morning or the garden fête in the Rectory garden for the church restoration fund, had been attempted this year.

Sophie was preoccupied with plans for her house as soon as it was legally her own. It gave her a lot of satisfaction to keep Choppen waiting, and she didn't bother to hide the fact; but I had a sneaking suspicion that she was in no hurry till she saw what Choppen was doing with other cottages, meaning to show him that anything he could do, she could do as well if not better. She was, also sticking up for herself against Thirzah who put her spoke in all the time.

I recalled that winter day down by the washes. It seemed to have been taken for granted that Thirz' was the only one with a hot-line to the Almighty, and spoke for them all. Sophie must almost have felt guilty of sedition, trying to to make contact direct and without Thirz' as the operator. The thought of Thirzah dialling Heaven on Sophie's behalf, and finding Jelly at the switchboard, made me smile; but it was no laughing matter for Sophie. The threat to her home had been the last straw added to her load of grief, but it had brought home to her the full extent of Jelly's love and devotion to her; moreover, as she had since told me, she felt that he was hers now as he had never been in life, because nobody could deny her the access to him she had found in prayer. She did not have to share her memories of him with anybody. So she had gained comfort, as well as independence, from what had happened.

Unfortunately for family solidarity, the blatant proof of Sophie's financial independence was too much for Hetty. She broke her word to Joe and told everybody who would listen the true identity of Ben Fisher, hoping to stir up trouble with Jelly's family. But the heat had gone out of that affair. Ken had more sense than to consult any lawyer again, however Beryl might rail at him; besides, his parents had come in for all of Jelly's estate that Sophie had not had, and he was not going to jeopardize the chance of getting most of it second-hand. So the only consequence of Hetty's betrayal was a very definite cooling of her relationship with both her sisters. Another sign of the times. The tablets of Kezia's law had been broken.

The sun tempted me out into a chair in the garden, and I had dropped into a doze when the familiar sound of a car's wheels on the gravel roused me, though there was no cheering dot-dot-dash-dot signal. It could only be Greg, because in mid-afternoon, Jess would be at work.

'Fetch another chair out, and join me,' I called. He did so, and after greeting me with a kiss, sat down beside me. 'This is a pleasure,' I said. 'Has the sun turned you into an idle layabout, too?'

When there was no immediate Greg-like answer, I turned to look at him. Something was quite seriously wrong, I could tell at a glance.

Panic gripped me. How cold fear strikes, even on the sunniest day! Something had happened to William, and Greg had been sent to break the news.

'Greg! What's the matter? What's happened?' I cried.

He took both my hands in his, and said, 'Now Fran, nothing for you to panic about. As far as I know, there's nothing the matter with William that getting back to you as fast as he can won't cure.'

I squeezed the hands I was still clinging to, weak with relief. 'So you do know? I thought you did. Who told you? William, before he went?'

'Not in so many words – but my good girl, I have eyes and ears, and some sense. Anybody who sees the two of you together at close quarters and doesn't see how things stand must be blind, or jealous or both.'

I found it difficult to answer. He could only be referring to Jess. 'Perhaps they don't want to see,' I said.

'So why are you keeping it so dark?'

'There really isn't anything to keep dark. William is still married. I'm too much of a puritan, and he's too much of a gentleman for us to have done anything we should have to hide – yet. Jess wouldn't approve, I fear. But I'm glad that you know, and don't regard us as awful sinners because we can't help still loving each other.'

'That's where you're wrong, Fran. I do think you are both miserable sinners: wasting love, or throwing it away, is a deadly sin. But there's always a chance of redemption for those who repent in time.' He grinned, and kissed me again.

'I hope so,' I said. 'But you didn't come here today to give me advice about that. So what is wrong?'

'I don't know. Jess,' he answered. 'Something's gone wrong.'

'It's no use asking me,' I said. 'She's very cool towards me just at present. I've hardly seen her.'

'She's jealous of you,' he said, bluntly. 'Terribly, insanely jealous.'

He was evidently in earnest, and very distressed. I made up my mind to speak as frankly as he obviously wanted and needed me to.

'William rather foresaw that this might happen,' I said. 'That's the reason he didn't tell her more than he did. He didn't want her to make comparisons till she had had time to settle down.'

'She can't help it. Her jealousy is malignant, like a cancer – growing in all directions. If I as much as mention your name, she flies off the handle. I am accused of making up to you, apparently with some ulterior motive of eventually exchanging my residence in Hen Street for Benedict's.'

Really! He couldn't be reporting truthfully, surely, I asked.

He nodded. 'After that, I had no option but to make it plain to her that she was insulting me as well as you, because whatever else I may be in the way of a lazy good-for-nothing, I am not a cad and she knows it. Then I said that if anything so caddish had ever occurred to me, I should have been out of luck anyway, because it was as plain as a pikestaff that your affections were already very much engaged with William, and what's more, as far as I could see, entirely reciprocated.'

He got up and began to stride about the lawn, finally coming back to stand in front of me. 'Well, she threw such a temper that I was scared – not for myself, but for her. She was nearly out of her mind. I just don't understand.' He sat down again.

I was trying hard to keep calm, though the anger inside me was rising hot in my chest like heartburn, and was difficult to swallow. This wasn't just a bit of partly-justified envy. This was pure hatred.

'William warned me that she might claim a proprietory interest in him, and that I mustn't allow myself to be upset by it,' I said. 'She sees me as having everything she hasn't got, or had, in material terms, but she could always comfort herself by gloating that she had one thing I hadn't got and in her view was never likely to have again — a man of my own. You shattered that illusion by telling her that she was wrong. Not only a man, but one who happened to be her precious brother. It adds up, Greg. She'll do anything — *anything* — in her power to spoil it for me. I wondered why she was so anxious to get Janice back into the fold all of a sudden. I see, now. That would put me out into the cold, if anything could. Then you tell her that in your opinion it's too late — and add insult to injury by insinuating that you rather like the idea, and that you are certainly not going to help her break William away from me. In fact, you make it fairly plain that you rather approve, and that you are on our side, not hers. So she turns on you, as well. That's how it seems to me.'

He nodded again. He got up and walked about, as if trying to make up his mind whether to say more.

'Fran, I'm really worried. I don't think you understand. She's up to something I don't know about, except that I guess it is an attempt to put a spoke in your wheel with regard to William. Don't underestimate her. She's diabolically clever. Oh dear, I do hate having to say these things. But I'm getting the rough end of the stick, too.'

'Shall I bring your tea out there?' shouted Sophie from the door. We made desultory conversation till Sophie was out of range again.

'How? Why?' I asked.

'Well, you know I have a deadline for my book, which I intend to make, this time. I have at last got conditions I can work properly in, but she makes it a complete impossibility for me to use them. She has just stopped me in my tracks.'

'How?'

'She has persuaded Choppen to give that Wendy female a job in her office — female office-boy. So Hetty is forced to bring that brat of Wendy's with her when she comes to work, which is every day, now. He's just at the stage when he wants attention all the time. He's either screaming at the top of his voice, or Hetty's bawling at him at the top of hers, or he has been sick on the settee or wetted on the hearth rug or locked himself in the bathroom or crawled through to my studio and tipped my water-pot all over a finished drawing or . . .' Words failed him. 'It would be bad enough if I didn't suspect that she was doing it all on purpose. That's why I'm so worried. If she can do that to me, what can she think up to do to you?'

I had enough sense to understand that in coming to tell me of my danger, he had gone against every principle in him as a husband who genuinely loved his wife. I tried to soothe him.

'I think you might be right. I don't think she can do much, honestly, so try not to worry too much, until we know. My guess is that once William is back, she'll accept what she can't alter.'

He had sat down, and I could see that he felt better for having done what he felt he ought to do, and because I had not shown as much distress as he had expected me to. So he got up, leaned over and kissed me, and went without saying another word.

He had left me with a nasty problem, though; much worse than William had anticipated, well as he knew her.

It wasn't fair of Jess to turn against me like this – but there it was. 'If you save a man from drowning . . .'

How well those old Vikings understood human nature!

If Sophie knew about Wendy's job, she hadn't told me. So I told her.

'I don't know what's come over 'em,' she said, taking it all more calmly than I had expected. 'It's as though it was all meant to be. Het'll pride herself on having a job every day, same as me. She's lucky to find somebody as'll put up with 'er taking that child with 'er, though. Most folks wouldn't. I ain't seen 'im now for – well, 'ardly since Jelly died – but Thirz' has, and she says 'e's a right spoilt little 'umbug as won't only do as he likes. But that's their business.' She wiped her hands on the duster in her lap, like Pontius Pilate washing his hands of all future responsibility.

'I didn't think as he – Mr Tallyhofearo I mean – looked hisself yest'day,' she said. 'Never opened 'is mouth to me, like 'e usually does to 'ave a bit of a joke, like. Is that book of 'is coming along all right?'

'Oh yes, I think so,' I answered, not prepared to divulge anything more to her, but she had the most uncanny knack of sensing any trouble, and interpreting the cause of it.

'I should ha' been surprised if they had been altogether satisfied, living where they do,' she said. 'Especially in that 'ouse. Some 'ouses get a sort of evil spirit in 'em, and that bungalow's one such. But I reckon as we shall be lucky if we've 'eard the last of it.'

'Dear Sophie,' I said. 'You are usually right about such things, I know, so I'm glad you don't blame me for it. But I'm sure there must have been times when the chain of events has turned out lucky in the long run. Let's wait and see, shall we?'

47

It was still only spring, but the weather had suddenly turned quite hot and muggy. Sophie's washing hung limply on the line like a row of hanged criminals, because there was so little movement of air. Both she and Ned predicted a storm.

'What, so early in the year?' I asked.

> 'Thunder in March, thunder in May,
> Thunder right up until Michaelmas Day,'

quoted Sophie.

'It's going to be one o' them there years,' Ned agreed with her. 'Once it starts like this, it goes on,' he said. 'Likely there'll be a storm any day.'

They were proved right.

On Sunday afternoon I was surprised to see Jess hurrying down the drive towards Benedict's, where I was enjoying my own company and a book. Every Sunday now was a milestone towards William's return, even though the date had not been fixed. He had stayed longer than he had thought he would have to because he had to see to the details of the publication of the report of the conference, and while doing so had agreed to stand in for a colleague who had had a car accident and couldn't complete his lecture tour. As he had written, it was really a sprat to catch a mackerel. If he stayed and got everything finalized while he was there, he wouldn't have to go back in the long vacation. If it hadn't been for my apprehension as to what Jess was up to, I should have welcomed his decision wholeheartedly. I had given him a promise, before he went, and the last thing I wanted was for us to have to be parted again for any reason. I did not want there to be any excuse whatsoever for me to prevaricate any longer. I knew myself too well not to fear that my resolution might waver, even yet, given what I considered good cause.

I was not at all pleased to see Jess approaching. I did not feel in the least well-disposed towards her. But if she was coming to see me in a spirit of reconciliation, for William's sake I should have to reciprocate. So I went to open the front door to her; and as I did so, I heard the first heavy rumble of thunder. I remembered – Jess was petrified with fright at the first hint of a thunder-storm. So had she come to visit me, or was she seeking shelter and company, having been caught while out walking?

'Are you alone?' I asked, ushering her inside. 'Come in, quickly. I know how you hate thunder.'

She barely greeted me. As she stood in the hall while I closed the heavy door again, I could see that she seemed drained of colour – but she had always behaved like a scared rabbit when it thundered.

I led the way to the sitting-room, and offered her a chair. Then the first vivid flash of lightning ripped across the sky, where through the long windows I could see that the storm was coming our way, and showed signs of being a violent one. However we felt about each other, Jess would have to stay till it was over.

'Draw the curtains,' she said. It was almost an order, and I wanted to retort; but she looked, somehow, so desperate that I wondered if the purpose of her visit in the first place could have been 'to have things out with me'. If so, she was liable to find the storm inside as bad as the raging outside.

'What's the matter?' I asked, flatly, having done as she wanted and covered the windows. 'I mean, have you come to visit me, or are you merely taking refuge from the storm? If it is a social occasion, I'm truly pleased to see you. I had begun to think you were deliberately avoiding me.'

To my chagrin, she burst into tears, and began on a long story which was punctuated by whimpers every time a lightning flash showed through the heavily lined curtains, and muffled by the fact that every time it thundered, she shoved her head into a cushion and pulled the corners of it up round her ears. But even so, I got the gist of it. Greg, it seemed, had met and, she suspected, had fallen for Choppen's daughter, Monique. As fellow artists, they had hatched some sort of plan of collaborating on some advertisements for her clothes designs. This had caused her to have a flaming row with Greg last Thursday; and on Friday he had taken off by car with Monique to London, and had not since returned.

'You asked where he is,' she said. 'With her, in her London flat I should think. They are probably in bed together at this very moment.'

An extra-vivid flash of lightning rather spoiled the effect of this meant-to-be so tragic conjecture, because it tailed off into a whimpering squeak which she tried to stifle with a cushion. It was all too reminiscent of Johanna's histrionics to have much effect on me.

'What, at four o'clock in the afternoon? Really, Jess! You are just letting jealousy of everything and everybody get the better of your common sense.'

She turned and flashed at me, for all the world 'like Johanna come again' as Sophie would have said. 'Goody-goody Fran, don't you know anything? We've been to bed in the afternoon many a time — if we got as far as the bedroom! People do make love in other places than between pink silk sheets in the dark, you know.'

My anger swelled with the thunder that rolled round the house till I thought it would choke me. Why did everybody take it for granted that no man had ever wanted me enough to take me wherever we happened to be? I felt William's lips on my neck again, and the hard edge of the piano in my back. What really angered me was Jess's condescending expression, as if she were having to tell a grown-up half-wit facts of life that she would never, could never, possibly find out for herself. There it was again. That modern worm in the bud, the belief that sex and love were one and the same thing.

'You haven't a shred of evidence that he has done anything more than give an acquaintance a lift to London,' I said. 'Is that all?'

'He hasn't come back!' she said. 'So where is he, if not with her?'

'I'm going to make tea,' I said, too angry to sit still. 'Come with me if you want to.'

She did, because she dare not be left alone. In spite of myself I felt sorry for her in this predicament. I was finding out the truth of Sophie's constantly repeated maxim that 'blood is thicker than water'. She was, after all, still Jess, still my childhood companion and cousin, still William's half-sister. Bitter as I felt, I had to try to control my tongue so as not to make matters worse if I could help it.

We carried the tea back to the sitting-room.

'I expect you are exaggerating Greg's friendship with Monique out of all proportion,' I said. 'There is probably some perfectly ordinary reason for his staying away longer than you expected.'

'Then why didn't he phone?'

'Why don't you? I suppose you know her address and telephone number?'

'No, of course not. And I don't want to.' She had stopped crying, and angry pride was taking over. 'I shan't ask him to come back,' she said. 'So I don't care where he is.'

'Well, I do,' I said. 'For one thing, he's gone off with William's car.'

Jess looked positively affronted. She turned her hackles, metaphorically speaking, against me, and prepared to defend Greg's by now somewhat doubtful honour. 'Whatever else he may be,' she said curtly, 'he isn't a thief. And as to him having William's car, I fail to see what concern it can be of yours.'

I was again furiously angry. I was doing my best to be patient with her, but her change of mood had put us back where we had started — I was somebody of whom she was jealous and to whom she would do mischief if the chance arose. But I had feelings, too, and they had already been bruised by her enough. I was utterly fed up with other people's troubles, too. I could no longer choke back my fury at being disregarded as anything but 'old Fran' who could not possibly know how Jess felt at having to do without 'her' man.

'Then I had better tell you why it concerns me,' I said. 'Though you already know. What Greg is to you, William is to me, and always has been. Don't tell me it surprises you. What concerns him concerns me now, and there are no secrets between us. I know that when Greg came to fetch the car before William went, William lent him £500 to make sure you would be OK till he got back. That's nearly as much as he will earn by this extra lecture tour that's keeping him from coming home now.'

Jess sneered. 'If there's one thing I can't stand,' she said, 'it's hypocrisy. So Fran the Righteous, the Lady Bountiful of Benedict's, has been slipping into bed with her tenant all this time, and thinking nobody knew.'

'Wrong on both counts, as it happens,' I said. 'But you knew what we have always meant to each other. You hated us for it when we were children. I never expected to deceive you about anything — I just hoped that being four instead of three would have made all the difference.'

'Of course I knew,' she said. 'Poor old William! How he must hate

411

having got himself mixed up in such a sordid *affaire*! I could see at once how unhappy he is – and I guessed why. If he manages to find Janice, and bring her back, he'll be able to extricate himself. That's one comfort.'

I could hardly believe the concentrated hate. 'Jess,' I said, 'do you really mean that?'

'I didn't know how much I did mean it till yesterday when Greg didn't come home,' she said. 'I know now. Why? Because there's no difference between you and any other woman who steals somebody else's husband. Don't tell me it's different in your case, because you played together as children. It's always different for some reason or other. Greg couldn't have gone off with Monique Choppen if she hadn't been willing. William's been trying for years to get Janice to come back to him – would have been still, till now, if you hadn't been a willing substitute.'

She turned her back on me, literally, making her derision and dislike plain in every line of her taut figure. I would not – *not* – offer her a single word of information or explanation. Let her think whatever she chose to think. In future, it would be true anyway. Because now, nothing, absolutely nothing, should or would prevent me from being to William whatever he wanted me to be. Little did Jess know what she had achieved! Without that turning away in revulsion, that sneering mouth and that scornful glint in her eye, I might still have gone to my consummation with William veiled in guilt. But not now. She had freed me at one stroke from all the moral strictures laid upon me in my youth, which had been irking me all the time since I had stepped off the train and found 'my' William waiting for me. I had put my submission to them down to my reluctance to break the seventh commandment – as Sophie might have done. Except that she hadn't. *She* had seen through them. It occurred to me in a flash why that particular commandment had always been made to seem so much more important than the rest. It had been very convenient to married women to cling to it in this century, when two wars had depleted the stock of men. It was a conspiracy amongst those women who 'possessed' men they could call theirs by right of a wedding ring against any other female who for any reason whatever was manless, and therefore potentially dangerous. Love didn't enter into their reasoning at all. Those who had men could keep what they had – even if they hated the sight of each other – by right of the seventh commandment, and the laws that still upheld it. Legal status and moral righteousness had reinforced each other.

Well, let Janice keep her legal possession of William. A fat lot I cared about that, now. So flushed with triumph did I feel at having at last burst through my self-spun cocoon of Victorian morality that I didn't want William to come home with any promise of his legal freedom to offer me. I wanted to be able to show him that he meant more to me than my upbringing, my reputation, the scorn of women like Jess, or anything else on earth.

The storm had reached its height, and was now centred over the village. It had been teeming with rain, but now it came down so fast that I thought it must surely be a cloudburst. There was an extra-brilliant flash, and a crack of thunder so loud that I flinched.

Jess screamed, and rushed into the hall where she pulled open the door of the coat cupboard under the stairs and squeezed herself into it. She had always done exactly that when we were children. I let her stop there by herself while I went into the kitchen and tried to still the tempest inside me. I felt as if I had two Jesses in my house. It really is difficult to hate somebody you remember cringing in a coat cupboard forty years ago, exactly as she was doing now. But the other Jess, who was doing her best to ruin everything for me for no other reason as far as I could see than an attack of rabid jealousy – she I detested, and wanted to get rid of as soon as ever possible.

The moment the storm and the rain began to ease up, I went to the cupboard, wrenched open the door, and took out my own boots and mackintosh.

'Where are you going?' Jess squeaked, cowering like a mouse in the darkest corner, afraid I might be going to leave her alone.

'To get my car and drive you home,' I answered brutally. 'The storm's gone over. You can wait for Greg there by yourself. I shall come back here and wait for William to come home to me.'

'And what if Janice is with him?'

'She'll see with her own eyes, instead of yours, who it is he loves,' I answered serenely.

'She knows about you,' Jess said. 'I wrote and told her.'

'How pleased with you your generous half-brother will be,' I said. 'Not that it will make a ha'porth of difference to anything except that you'll have to manage without his help in future. That will be a nice change for him.'

'You selfish, conceited, self-righteous bitch!' said my childhood friend and erstwhile loving cousin.

It was a ludicrous situation. She wouldn't come out of the safety of the cupboard of her own accord, so in the end I more or less dragged her out, and manhandled her, with her coat pulled up right over her head, through the rain and into my car.

Then I drove like a maniac to Hen Street. As soon as ever I had turned into the gate of Bryony Cottage, the front door was opened and Greg stood there waiting to welcome her. I didn't wait to speak to him. I turned round, revved up my car till it sounded like a Formula One at Brand's Hatch, and made for Benedict's — and the safety of home.

48

I was soaked by the torrential rain, just getting in and out of the car.

Cat followed me about as I inspected the garden from several windows. There were no fallen or broken branches, as far as I could see, and no stripped roofs. Benedict's had escaped lightly.

The sky was still dark with rolling banks of purply-blue across which little frills of wispy white cloud showed up like lace trimming. I looked at the clock: it was half-past six. I felt exhausted, and sat down in my chair in the sitting-room.

Usually, I was quite happy to be alone there with my thoughts and memories, but this evening I couldn't settle. With nothing to do but think, I gave myself up to what Sophie would have called 'a good old maunch'.

No family escapes quarrels. If a married couple say they've never had a cross word, it seems to me that they can never have had a tender one either. Love has to be stretched at both ends to make it meet in the perfect circle such as I had felt when I stood in William's arms the day we had so nearly surrendered to passion.

The quarrel between me and Jess would have happened sooner or later. Maybe it was a good thing it had happened now, before William had to be involved. But all the same, I was still smarting from it.

Looking back Jess had always been wont to go into rages in which she let drive with her tongue just as she had done today. Children don't take such insults much to heart, and can be friends again in half a hour. We were no longer children. I had taken her bitterness towards me today very much to heart, and was in no mood to forgive or forget.

She had let the cat out of the bag; I had been so angry this afternoon, so determined that I would now be everything to William come what might, that I had not stopped to take in the implications of Jess's interference. William and I had agreed to leave Janice on the sideline – but Jess had thrown her back into the game. It was possible that she could still win, and I lose, in this last little bit of injury-time.

My spirits sagged. I was lonely and miserable. I felt too washed out to go and prepare the food I needed, so I just went on sitting. 'Cat,' I said, stroking her exquisite little muzzle with my fingertip, 'I do wish you could talk. I want somebody to talk to now, to sort it all out with, and there's only you.'

She purred till she sneezed, and at least that made me smile. But she didn't miraculously answer.

The rain had now turned to a long, steady shower, but the storm had cleared the atmosphere and at least there was an ample supply of fresh air again. I stood in the doorway and breathed deep, and felt a little less like a wrung-out dishcloth than I had done earlier; but all the same the evening was long and lonely. I went to bed early and did not sleep well, but I woke to a blue sky with the prospect of a clear summer day washed clean by the rain.

Sophie came full of talk about the storm. I went to my desk, but I couldn't create fiction with so much reality still on my mind. At about eleven o'clock I got up to go and pour myself a stiff whisky, but, as I did so, the telephone rang. I pushed Cat listlessly off the instrument and lifted the receiver, giving my number in a flat voice I barely recognized as my own.

'Frances?' said the voice at the other end. 'Is that you, Frances?'

'Mary!' I gasped. 'Where are you?'

'Where would I be but at home? In the Schoolhouse, in case you have forgotten.'

'I can't believe it! When did you arrive?'

'About an hour ago. And I have a favour to ask. I came in to find my house awash and my carpets sodden, to say nothing of my bed. I don't seem to have any electricity, and there is nothing fit to eat in the place. I'm much too tired to start to deal with all this. Could you possibly give me refuge for a day or two until I can get this mess cleared up?'

'I'll be round to fetch you within ten minutes,' I said, and dropped

415

the receiver before she could argue. I went to the bottom of the stairs and called to Sophie.

'*Now* what's the matter?' she called over the banister. 'Who's a-dying this time?'

I laughed aloud. She would never have phrased her inquiry like that if she had really expected trouble. My voice must have given my joy at Mary's return away.

'Miss Budd is home! She needs a warm, dry bed and some food till she gets straight again. Can you make up the guest-room bed and get lunch for three? I'm going to fetch her now.'

Sophie allowed herself a smile at the good news, but characteristically thought it best to add a pinch of censure as an antidote to too much heady pleasure.

'You know as well as I do that I all'us keep all the beds ready for use at a moment's notice,' she said.

Mary was browned by the antipodean sun, having decided while in Canada to make a good job of it and visit her other brother in New Zealand before returning. Her tan made her hair appear whiter than ever, and though she looked very tired, her eyes still exuded the twinkle that expressed her tolerant and amused if somewhat critical view of the world. She gave me a shrewd look that informed me at once that she had noticed the signs of strain in me; but she said nothing, and neither did I.

Once in the car, I asked, 'Why didn't you let us know you were coming?'

'Because I didn't know myself. I woke up a few days ago feeling homesick. So I went to my hosts and told them I was taking the first flight home that I could get a seat on. And here I am.'

'We're very glad to have you back,' I said. 'A lot has happened while you've been away.'

'Yes,' she said.

Well, I had written and told her some of it — but that could not really have prepared her to take it all in. The changes would hurt her more than most, except that her great gift of logical reasoning would help her to come to terms with the inevitable. I knew she was in her eighth decade, but while she lived, I had a kindred spirit. My heart soared, and my spirits rose with it.

We fed her, and for Sophie's sake she kept going long enough to tell us a few details of her trip; but she then retired to her bed. Having Mary upstairs seemed to make anything possible again.

Mary slept late next morning, coming down just as Sophie and I were about to take our morning break. Sophie was scandalized at my offering Mary her breakfast in the kitchen with us, but she insisted and Sophie had to give way.

'And now,' said Mary, when we were alone, 'tell me what is wrong with you, Frances — if you want to, that is. I don't need telling that something is amiss. Your *joie de vivre* is conspicuous by its absence.'

'I can't wait to tell you,' I said — and I let myself go and told her all. She didn't interrupt, or comment. When I paused at last, she said, 'So Jess has upset your apple-cart by bringing William's wife right back into the picture. So what? Which part of it all do you want me to direct my thoughts to?'

'To me!' I cried. 'To William and me! Have we been stupid, romantic, old-fashioned, puritanical, *frightened* fools, just kidding ourselves that we were "honourable"? Or have we just been playing at being "good" and "moral" and made ourselves into a couple of Early Christian martyrs, sacrifices to our own pride and self-esteem? Nobody else was involved, really, and in any case nobody would have cared tuppence! Did *you* think we were sleeping together? And if it did ever cross your mind to wonder, did you care a brass farthing one way or the other?'

'Yes,' she said firmly. 'I hoped you were. I wanted you both to be happy.'

'We have been happy,' I said. 'That's part of the problem. If Janice walks in and claims him now, I shall lose all that we have had — never mind about what I might have had. We've said we would climb the peak of love together when he came back — but I doubt if we shall ever see the view from up there now. And we've lost the base camp as well. The only consolation I'll have is that I have never brought myself down to Pamela Thackeray's level. Some consolation.'

She pursed her lips and stood up, standing motionless by the window with her back turned to me. I felt in awe of her — just as her old pupils did.

'Well?' I said, almost afraid. She turned.

'I was thinking of Hamlet,' she said. 'His tragedy was that he was Hamlet. If Horatio had been born in Hamlet's shoes, there would have been no play for Shakespeare to write. You are Frances, not Pamela; and William is William. You did what you thought you had to do. But I think you have both been silly. And now, Frances, *you* are being just plain stupid! You are adopting the attitude of the burglar who believes that the theft itself isn't a crime, but allowing

417

himself to be caught is. As if Janice has called your bluff. She hasn't, because she can't. She doesn't own William, so she can't "claim" him as you put it, as if he were an object. Not if he doesn't want her to. *That's* what you fear, you know! You have held back partly because you couldn't be sure you wouldn't be only second best – at least in bed. And you may now have lost everything by not giving yourself a chance to find out whether or not your fears were valid.'

I heard myself gasp, and rushed in to defend myself. 'But surely *you* can't go along with all this modern sex-crazed permissiveness, that makes the instant gratification of sexual desire the be-all and end-all of existence?'

'I think you are confusing animal reproductive urge with love,' she said. 'What the young of today indulge in is the former. The female yowls, and a male appears from somewhere to mate her. God only knows where it will all lead to in future, but that is not the point. From all that you have just been telling me, what you and William have for each other is love. Quite different. You have had something rare and beautiful held out to you by the only god I have ever really believed in, whose name is Love. You both wanted to take it – but what did you do? You said virtuously, "Get thee behind me, Satan!" Self-righteously proud of your will-power. I just hope it isn't too late now. I wouldn't like you to die without experiencing my god's greatest gift to all mankind – that of being one flesh as well as one soul with the man you love more than you love your own self-image.'

She was being brutal, and I was almost drowning in misery. I hit back.

'How on earth should you know?' I said.

Her dark eyes, far from being offended, for a moment took on their habitual twinkle.

'Ah! Like Miss Prism, I must now declare, "Alas! I am unmarried!" So I am, but that doesn't necessarily mean that I don't know what I am talking about, does it? My William – yes, his name was William too – was killed one day before the Armistice was signed in 1918. We had been secretly engaged to each other but nobody would agree to our marriage. They insisted that we both finish our training first, he as a doctor and I as a teacher. Our parents had the financial whip-hand over us with regard to marriage but nobody could prevent us from being lovers, when the crux came. He came home on leave about two weeks before he was killed. We had four days. He – we – died on the mountain top. I had to find my own way down alone. A bit of me has remained up there with him ever since. Nothing can ever take from me the memory of the view from up there. That's what I have. It's what poor Sophie never had. It's what you could have had, and refused. I don't feel guilty. Far from it. *"Non, je regrette rien!"* Now do you understand?'

I was crushed. 'Forgive me,' I said.

'Oh, for heaven's sake, don't be so trite!' she snapped. 'Keep your sympathy for yourself and William – if he deserves it. He seems to have been as much of an old woman wrapping himself up in moral red flannel as you have. Unless, of course, he has been kidding you along while waiting till Janice was ready to come back to him.'

'No!' I cried, bursting with furious indignation. She was just like Kezia, making me open my mouth to take in a huge spoonful of brimstone and treacle, 'to do me good'.

'No, I don't think so, either. You have got yourself into a proper old lash-up, all the same, haven't you? If you are expecting me to sort your problem out, you are backing the wrong horse. I have no idea where to begin. It depends on what happens now, from day to day, almost from minute to minute. You have just got to wait and see.'

'Your dinner's getting cold,' said Sophie from the door. 'I've put it in the dining-room. And Kid Bean's just been here, Miss, to say as 'ow 'e reckons your 'ouse must ha' been struck by lightning o' Sunday. It's going to mean 'e's got to get a 'lectrician in to put it all right for you. 'E'll be back this afternoon to talk to you about it.'

Well if you've got to come down from the high reaches of soul-searching philosophy to the mundane things of ordinary life, you might as well land on a plate filled with beautifully cooked cold gammon flanked with salad and new potatoes as anywhere else. We attacked as if our previous conversation had never been.

'You'll have to stay here with me,' I said gleefully. She ruefully accepted the inevitable. 'Until there is the first whisper of William's return,' she said. 'Then I go home, even if I die of pneumonia from having slept in a wet bed.'

I was not scared by such a threat. If ever there was a woman with plain common sense, it was Mary.

Sophie brought in our second course, a summer pudding in which lush bottled raspberries from my own garden were wedged tightly in thickly whipped cream held together by a good helping of icing sugar, and all enclosed in a basin-shape of white bread marbled with raspberry juice. She set it down before me with a thump, catching my eye as she did so, in defiance of any remark I might make as to its richness. She was going to feed her 'Miss' in the way she thought suitable for such a happy return. (She had said often that she 'didn't 'old with these 'ere calories and such'.)

'There's nothing like a good meal when there's trouble about,' she said.

'So she has picked up that there's trouble,' I said, trifling only with the delicious creamy mess.

'She means my flooded house,' said Mary shortly, licking the back of her spoon. 'How can she know anything at all about Sunday if you haven't told her yourself? Of course, if you were looking like a dying duck in a thunderstorm when she arrived yesterday morning, she may have put two and two together. But I think she has far more sense than you have, if you'll forgive me for saying so. She will only make four. You are, as usual, using two and two as the base of a geometrical progression. I agree that Jess putting her finger into your pie may stir things up in a way you didn't expect,' said Mary, 'and perhaps there is a troubled period to get through before all is rosy again for you. Till William actually gets home, you may have a little more cause for apprehension than you hoped for. But it can't amount to tragedy if you have told me the truth and William is the man I think he is. I don't know Janice and I don't particularly want to – but from all that's gone before I should say any man will do for her as long as he can shell out enough shekels. Which means that William really has the situation wholly in his hands. If he'd simply stop shelling out, she wouldn't care if the cat ate him. What I am trying to get into your thick self-pitying head is that you are handing her all the advantages by making even the thought of her into an ogre. I think you are just being maudlin because he has stayed away a month longer than you expected him to, and because you are tired and flaked out. I also think you are being very unfair to a good man. Eat your pudding up, girl! Do you think William will care a tuppenny damn how many inches farther round the waist you are than she is? That's a field you can't compete in, so don't try. As long as he can still get his arms round it, I don't suppose he has ever given a moment's thought to the size of your waist. You seem to me to have an absolute genius for making mountains out of molehills. So as far as I am concerned, it is no use you starting to go around like a broken-hearted relic, just yet.'

I knew she was right, but I felt a bit sore at her waspishness all the same. Her astringency could sting and smart quite a lot, as I guessed she was well aware. She eyed me calmly, helping herself to another wedge of pudding.

'There! I've said what I had to say. So after lunch, if you will excuse me, I will go and lie down with a book. And if I were you, I should either go for a long walk, or get on with some work.' She rose.

I must have been looking like a disappointed and chastened child, I think, because she paused on her way to the door, and came back to stand quite close to me. Her voice was gentle and soft when she spoke again.

'Leave it to the gods,' she said. 'Till now, you and William have been trying to do their job for them. Be still, and let them take over. The god you profess to believe in may still be on your side.'

She put her hand on mine, and I was shocked to notice how old and gnarled it was beside my own. I bent my head and rubbed my cheek against the swollen knuckles, in a gesture of gratitude that included submission. I was thoroughly ashamed of myself. My William was coming back – in my heart, I knew it.

Mary and I had finished breakfast next morning when Sophie came to tell her that Kid Bean had been to ask if she would be ready for him to pick her up in his new car at ten o'clock to take her to her house about the repairs. She did not return until late in the evening, and she was obviously tired and depressed. She looked old and rather miserable. The afternoon had not been a success.

'Kenneth has done well,' she volunteered. 'I shall be able to go home after next weekend.'

'So what has upset you?' I said, handing her a cup of hot, strong tea.

'Kenneth thought he was being kind. He took me on a tour of the village to show me "the improvements". I can't believe it.' Her voice quivered for a moment. 'My village has gone. And I am an anachronism neither needed nor wanted. All my old friends are gone – either dead or moved out to "homes". All my old pupils either leaving or happily going along with this so-called progress. I'm too old to change. I'm glad I'm nearly eighty.'

I had never before seen her so miserable, or heard any complaint from her.

'I think the change has been too long reaching us here,' I said. 'When it did hit us, it was all too sudden. Don't let it upset you too much.'

'There's *nothing* left!' she said. 'Everything just vanished – while I have been away. Most of the people I really cared about. All the old values! How could it happen so fast?'

'I think it had begun to happen before you went,' I said. 'I think it was already in evidence the night of your last horkey. Maybe you felt it without realizing it, and that is why you gave up and went away. You are seeing it all at once now, with keener eyes just because you have been away.'

'It's horrible,' she said. 'I feel as if I have worked all my life for nothing. Nothing I have striven for has lasted.'

'Drink your tea,' I said. 'I'll go and get you a tot of whisky, too. It didn't happen because you went away, you know. It would have been just the same if you had been here. It is just history in the making. I wonder what the 1980s will be like?'

'Hell, no doubt,' she said, tersely. 'But that won't matter to me. I shall probably be there already.'

'You'll still have plenty of friends,' I said. 'So don't go, at least, not for a long time yet!'

The twinkle was definitely coming back into her eyes. The whisky was doing her good.

'I can't go for a little while,' she said. 'I can see that I have just one more important task to perform before I quit altogether.'

'Only one?'

'One immediate one. After that, I propose to turn my little house into the same sort of island as yours here is, and let the rest of the world pass me by. I feel like a castaway, out of touch with everything already. I am a stranger in my own land.'

There was a great sadness in what she was saying, and a lot of truth as well. But since my encounter with the swans, I was wary of believing I knew what truth was. Mary had been a great power for good here in the past – but it was the past.

Her time of influence had gone, and she was shrewd enough to acknowledge and accept it. I could only guess that there had been something in Kenneth Bean's attitude towards her today, along with his new-found affluence, that had signalled the message to her very clearly. Sadly, in spite of myself, I felt the need to pity her, so suddenly becalmed while still so vigorous and forceful a personality. She would reject pity as a duck's feathers reject water so I hid my feelings.

She sighed, wholly unconscious that I was aware of it. It seemed to me like the dying breath of village life as I had till now known it. No use to repine. Neither grief nor anger would restore it to life again even if it were wise to try.

'Let's go and see what Sophie has left us for our supper,' I said. 'Even castaways must eat.'

49

Mary's ability to look facts in the eye and then go steadily ahead one day at a time had taken the edge off my anxiety. Try as I might, though, I could not quite accept Mary's sanguine view of Jess's interference as a storm in a teacup. My fear was that William's sense of 'honour' might oblige him to honour his promise to Janice, rather than to drag me through a divorce court. But I did my best not to let my anxiety show.

I had a visit from Greg, who had obviously been put into the picture. He was his usual charming self, and asked me how I was coping with waiting for William's return.

'Not so well as I might have been, if Jess had let our affairs alone,' I said. 'What about you?'

'We are all right again, except that I am worried about what she wrote to Janice. If she could undo it, she would. As she can't she won't admit to being at fault. Have you heard from William?'

There was the rub. William was now moving all the time from one place to another, and all I had had was a couple of postcards saying nothing, instead of his long weekly letter. I tried to think there was no reason for it except lack of time, but in the circumstances, it was difficult to keep my sense of proportion. I shook my head.

'Greg,' I said at last, 'I think I would feel better if I knew exactly what Jess said in her letter to Janice. Do you know?'

Yes, he did. He had asked her, and more or less made her tell him. I felt cruel to have to drag such things out of him because he was trying so hard to defend Jess. But he had hinted that he felt bad about it, and simply could not condone what she had done. He owed it to me to help me if he could.

'Tell me,' I commanded.

'As far as I can remember, she said that she had told Janice that she had seen a good deal of William and although he was well, he was obviously not as happy as he might be. He was wanting something he hadn't got, and to put it bluntly, Jess guessed that he was finding his celibate life a strain. She pointed out to Janice that he had always wanted her to go back to him. As he was now in the States and she could give his address, wouldn't it be a good idea for Janice to make the first move, and go to see him? Because he was now living under the same roof as his step-cousin and childhood friend, Frances, and she, Jess, considered the situation dangerous. Fran had always "been after" William – and what man was there who would not, in such circumstances, take what was offered to him on a plate, as it were. So if Janice did not move fairly rapidly to establish her claim on him, she might find she had left it too long.' He related all this in a deadpan sort of voice, while I fought to keep down my rising anger.

'Thank you for telling me,' I said.

'I wish you hadn't asked.'

'Forewarned is forearmed,' I said.

I was dismissing him, and he understood. I liked him, and was sorry that for the time being, at any rate, there would have to be a state of armed neutrality between us. It would not be long now, before William was in England again, and the whole matter resolved. I felt less bitter towards Jess when I remembered that it had been she who without meaning to had made me see at last that there were no absolutes of right and wrong with regard to sexual matters. It depended on the circumstances. Snow falling against the light appeared to be black, but once it landed it was white.

Mary and I had spent our time together talking, about anything and everything except her feelings and mine, which by her decree were banned. She told me of her travels and adventures, making them very vivid because of her acute observation of people wherever they were, and because of her intelligent assessment and caustic wit. She had given me a perfectly valid excuse not to try to force myself to work, and at her suggestion I had fished out bits of tapestry and embroidery that had not seen the light of day for years. So we sat together in the sunshine, talking, dozing, and now and then doing a few stitches of her knitting or my needlework.

On one such occasion, Ned, who was usually working somewhere near, took off his cap and came across to us for a brief chat. He had news. The rumour was that Manor Farms Ltd had asked for planning permission to turn the old de ffranksbridge estate into an eighteen-hole golf course. 'Then they plan to rebuild the old Hall as much like it was afore the fire as they can, only a lot bigger, and turn that into a hotel, with grounds and a swimming-pool and tennis courts and I-don't-know-what-all. Some say as there'll be a football field and a cricket pitch an' all, but you know as well as I do how tales get about. The next one who tells me about it 'll no doubt say as there'll be a tiddly-wink pitch and a snakes-and-ladders room into the bargain.'

'Very wise, too, if the hotel is going to cater for families with children,' said Mary. Rumour though it might still be, neither she nor I actually doubted that there was some truth behind it. I had no adverse reaction to this idea of Choppen's at all. It would link Old Swithinford with Swithinford, of course, but that had to happen some time. A sports centre was infinitely better than an awful new estate of little red-brick houses. If it was set up as a link, it could also be a buffer.

While we were digesting this piece of news, Sophie came out of the house and hurried across the lawn. Her face was white and she said nothing as she put a telegram into my hands. To those who had lived through the war, or in Mary's case, two wars, telegrams could only mean bad news. Both watched me intently as reluctantly I slit the envelope and stared down at the writing: 'HEATHROW 11 A.M. FRIDAY.'

If all had been exactly as it was when William left, it would have been a message from Heaven. As it was, and with Mary looking expectant on one side of me, and Sophie pale with fear on the other, I experienced nothing but a sense of confusion.

'It's a cable from William,' I said, as if announcing that tea was ready. 'He will be at Heathrow at eleven o'clock on Friday morning.'

Sophie beamed a great smile and relaxed so evidently that for a moment she looked more like a home-made rag-doll than the Dutch doll her prim rosy solidity usually resembled.

'I'd better be a-getting things ready for 'im, then,' she said. 'Will 'e be going back into He-horse Tail, or still be using the guest room?'

That's what I didn't know. If Janice were in the offing – where? Even if she weren't, where? Sophie stood waiting for my answer.

'Get the flat ready, and make up the bed,' I answered. 'Miss Budd is occupying the guest room, so he can't go back in there.'

Mary had opened her mouth to speak, but shut it again, mainly because Sophie got in first.

'Anybody 'd think this was one o' them semis down Hen Street,' she said. 'Ain't we got no more than one guest room, then? Seems to me as if I can count at least three others as I all'us keep clean and ready.'

Mary said gently, 'I told you I should go home as soon as we knew when the Professor was coming back.' (She never called him anything but the Professor in front of Sophie.)

I began to protest, vehemently. I wanted Mary to be here, as a shield against too much emotion; as a preventor of any disclosures, one way or the other; as a delaying force against the showdown that now must come.

Mary caught Sophie's eye, and held it. 'I shall get Kenneth to come up and fetch me home on Friday morning. That will give you plenty of time to change my bed and get the room ready for the Professor, won't it, Sophie?'

'Yes, Miss,' said Sophie, looking satisfied.

'Very well. That's settled,' said Mary.

I should have been quite nettled by these decisions being taken over my head, if I hadn't been so confused both in mind and spirit. I tried to think.

'Don't be so silly, Mary,' I said. 'What on earth are you thinking of, talking about getting Kenneth Bean to fetch you home? Of course I shall take you myself.'

'On Friday morning? Surely you will be on your way to Heathrow to meet William?'

Sophie was still there, listening. What could I say?

'I don't know,' I said at last, weakly and reluctantly. 'He hasn't given me any details at all.'

'Really?' said Mary, witheringly. 'If I can get myself round the world, approaching eighty as I am, I should have expected you to be able to locate an incoming flight from New York, given the time of arrival. The various airlines don't have to conduct dog fights for a landing strip! Of course you will be there to meet him.'

'That's right,' said Sophie, decidedly. As if she, of all people, knew anything whatsoever about airports!

'I think Greg is the one who ought to go,' I said, having just had what I regarded as a triumphant idea. 'He has William's car, and men are so much better than women at that sort of thing.'

Mary looked at me as she might have done at an infant she suspected of having wet his pants. 'How very nice for William!' she said sarcastically. 'He will be absolutely overjoyed to see Mr Talia-

426

ferro's face held up to be kissed as he struggles through the crowd!' She turned and took up her knitting in the way a grand Edwardian lady might have picked up a fine china tea-cup – the most elegant expression of disdain that I had ever witnessed. Sophie understood it perfectly, and permitted herself the luxury of an audible chuckle as she turned back towards the house. She knew the issue was settled.

'Really, Mary!' I expostulated, as soon as Sophie was out of hearing. 'Suppose I go, and find Janice there with him?'

'Suppose pigs had wings! She could have crossed the Atlantic piggy-back!' In spite of myself, I laughed; but when I looked at her again, she had become quite serious.

'I am afraid, Frances, that you are showing a streak of cowardice that I never expected of you, or indeed of any of old Mr Wagstaffe's family. And your declarations of faith in William, with which you have been bolstering yourself since the row with Jess, are beginning to look very thin and weak. It wouldn't even take a straw to pierce them! If Janice is there with him, then it can only be because he has brought her, in which case he is not your William at all, but hers. So why should he have bothered to send you a cable? But if you believe Professor Burbage to be such a heel, such a cad as that, your protestations of love for him are as false as you seem to believe his to be. You know perfectly well that it isn't so. You are just plain scared – and there is no other soul on earth who can cure you of that but Frances Catherwood, If you let yourself down now over this small matter, you will have lost your self-respect for ever. And probably everything else as well. The choice is yours.'

'I'll go,' I said.

'Of course you will. And you will greet your man as if that thunderstorm had never happened. You will not let out a hint of it till it is absolutely necessary – if it ever is. Just keep it all to yourself.'

'And what will be William's attitude about it when he finds out that I have been keeping a secret from him? We vowed we would have none between us, ever.'

'He will know how much you love him, that you didn't want to worry him or spoil his homecoming,' she said.

There spoke the village Wise Woman. She went on placidly knitting, and Sophie brought out our tea.

When Friday came, all preparations had been made, though not so much by me as by Sophie with Mary's encouragement.

'It'll hev to be a casserole,' Sophie had said. 'So as I can leave it in the slow oven of the Aga and it'll be ready for you whatever time you want it. What time do you reckon on being back?'

'Heavens! I just don't know. Not, I should think, much before four o'clock.'

'I shan't wait, then,' said Sophie. I was surprised, and even a bit hurt. I almost had to push Sophie out of the door to get her to go home most days, especially if there was any sort of occasion involving any member of my family. It was quite uncharacteristic of her not to offer to stay and serve up the meal. But this time, when what I needed was someone to act as buffer between me and an awkward evening, both she and Mary were determined to desert me. In Sophie's case, no doubt because she honestly believed I should want William all to myself. Mary knew better.

'Oh! Won't you stay?' I said. 'William will be so tired, and so shall I.'

'You won't want a cooked meal at four o'clock in the afternoon, surely?' Sophie countered. 'And I shall leave a tray ready for your tea. As it 'appens, I've got affairs of my own to see to.'

The implied reproof that I cared for nobody's affairs but my own irritated me. It was they who had more or less forced me to go on this long uncertain journey.

'Have it your own way,' I said, and began to get ready to set out.

They stood together at the front door as I left. Mary expressed her sincere thanks, while Sophie hovered behind her. She was a tall and stately figure well able to see over the top of Mary's head.

'Good luck,' said Mary, kissing me as I passed her on my way out to the car. I looked back as I drove off, to see Sophie waving a yellow duster over Mary's head. I wondered whatever had got into them both. They were certainly not so apprehensive as I was. I thought of the old Viking proverb:

> Judge a fair day in the evening: a battle
> when it's over, and a woman when she's old.

Once at the airport, my nerves were eased slightly as I became caught up in the drama provided by others waiting in the airport lounge. That middle-aged couple next to me, looking so anxious, and yet so excited: who were they waiting to greet? They must be professional people, I thought, judging by their determined efforts not to show any emotion as the arrival of the plane was announced and the first of the passengers came through the door. I heard the man say, 'She will have to wait until all the first-class passengers are off.'

And then, miraculously, there 'she' was, among the very first to come through the doors, a young mother with a baby in her arms; and the whole family simply melted into one, three heads close together, three bodies utterly entwined, three faces wet with tears, and a crowing baby boy jammed in the middle of them. All upper-middle-class decorum had been swept aside by pure joy and such happiness that I was enthralled, feeling myself so much a part of their reunion that I almost missed my own, for William suddenly was standing in front of me, dropping his hand luggage to raise his hat before holding out his arms and folding me into them.

'You came!' he said.

I laid my face against his chest, and felt a volcano erupt inside me as he held me close and then kissed me. We had survived. I stole a glance at the reunited family close by. They had come apart again, and the new grandparents were making the acquaintance of the baby they had never seen before. I just hoped all the groups, now thick around us, were as happy as we and they; but the black-and-white pattern of life forbade such a possibility. For every arrival, there must be a counterweight of departure: for every greeting, a farewell.

I tried to be practical. 'What now?' I asked.

'Home — unless you are absolutely starving.' I shook my head. Everything I wanted stood on two feet beside me. When, after what seemed hours, we found the car, I said, 'You drive,' but he shook his head. 'I don't think I'm safe, for all sorts of different reasons. You'll make the journey quicker.'

I had to give all my attention to the traffic, then, but once we were clear of London, William laid his hand over mine on the steering-wheel for a moment, then transferred it to my thigh and left it there. The current between us was switched on, and words were unnecessary. We indulged in none of the usual chatter about the flight or anything else. While we were in this car, close together and silent, he was mine alone. Words were the only thing that could rob me of him. They should not be spoken by me.

We reached Benedict's in the bright glare of the afternoon sun, and when I opened the door, the cool softened light bathed everything in welcome, just as the huge bowl of roses on the hall table bathed everything with their scent. But before we had reached the bottom of the staircase, Cat flowed down the stairs almost choking herself with ecstatic mewing, and launched herself from the fourth step at William's chest. She missed her hold, and he had to drop everything to catch her. I went to them and was enfolded into the group. We were together again, like the family in the airport lounge. A happy omen, surely.

'Leave everything in the hall' I said. 'We can deal with anything that's necessary later. Let's go and see what Sophie has left us for tea.'

William made the tea with a good deal of assistance from Cat that he could have done without, while I carried the tray into the sitting-room.

He sank into his chair and eyed everything with wonder, like a child on Christmas morning, as if surprised to see there all he had asked for.

'You are wonderful, Fran. You have just let me soak it all in until I'm able to believe it. Benedict's *is* real! So are you. All I want to do is just to sit and look ... But I suppose I ought to ask how everybody else is?'

'Let all that wait. There'll be plenty of time. You aren't going away again tomorrow, are you?'

'Never again, if it's left to me,' he answered fervently.

I went out with the tray to the kitchen, washed up, and then took a look in the Aga and laid the table for our supper. Sophie had left the dining-room table all ready, but we should be happier in the kitchen — a kitchen spells 'home'. When I went back to the sitting-room, William had fallen asleep in his chair, with Cat on his chest, one silky chocolate-dipped paw on each side of his neck and her dark little muzzle tucked right up under his chin. I stole as quietly as I could to my own chair opposite, and silently took up my embroidery, but I didn't do any. I just sat and looked across at William. He bore no signs of stress or worry. On the contrary, there was such an aura of peace and contentment around him that it reflected the evening sun like a halo.

Let him sleep as long as he needed to. Supper, and everything else, could wait. I was, after all, a fairly practised hand at waiting.

After about two hours, I went back into the kitchen and took the Chicken Marengo — one of William's favourite dishes — out of the oven and sprinkled the lemon-zest and chopped fresh parsley over it. It would spoil if left much longer but I put it back into the slowest of the four ovens and poured out whisky just as William liked it. Then I sat down on the arm of his chair and stroked his hair and face till at last he opened his eyes. He gazed around him like a child transported to Wonderland, unbelieving and bewildered. Then he leapt to his feet, pulling me up to throw his arms round me as if to make sure I was solid as I looked.

'Have I been asleep? How unpardonably rude of me!'

'Only about two hours,' I said. 'Our supper will spoil if we keep it waiting any longer. Careful – you'll spill your whisky! Drink it or bring it into the kitchen with you.'

'I'm home again. And after that wonderful sleep, I feel as if I've never been away.' He held out his whisky glass, and I clinked mine against it.

'Just one more thing before we go to eat,' he said. 'You haven't changed your mind about anything while I've been away, have you?'

'Not if you haven't,' I answered, meeting his eyes and keeping my voice calm and steady.

'Then let's go and have our supper,' he said.

We ate in the lovely intimacy we had established before he left. I realized that we were both deliberately playing it cool, and I was glad. With his usual sensitivity and tact, he had sensed that it would be a mistake to cut our wedding-cake before we got through the rest of the pledges again.

By the time we had sampled all the nectar and ambrosia Sophie had left for us, the sun had set and the moon was rising. We walked together to the back door, and watched it turn from reddish amber to silver as it climbed above the trees at the end of the garden.

'Why is an English moon so much better than an American one?' he said, winding an arm round my waist.

'Because it's ours, I suppose.'

'And because it matters so much who is with you as you watch it rise,' he added. That lyric again – 'We stroll about together, 'neath the magical moon above, just making conversation . . .'

'Be still,' said Mary's voice in my ear. 'Leave it to the gods.'

'I will,' I promised her silently.

We went back inside and I drew the curtains. William stretched luxuriously. 'I suppose I must unpack,' he said. 'Where have you put me? Back in my own quarters?'

I shook my head. 'Neither Mary nor Sophie would hear of such a thing,' I said.

'Good.' There is no way of expressing the amount of satisfaction contained in that one word.

'Need you bother to unpack tonight?' I asked. 'Why not leave it till daylight?'

'Anything you say, my precious one,' he said. It was the first endearment he had uttered. We were feeling our way back to each other very gently, but very surely. 'I've got all my washing things in my hand-luggage.' William said. 'All I need is a pair of pyjamas.'

I laughed. 'I could bet my life that Sophie has laid them all out for you, with clean towels,' I said. 'She wouldn't sleep a wink tonight if she remembered one single thing she hadn't done to make your homecoming just as it should be.'

We sat down again in the sitting-room, only this time he took up his accustomed place on the floor at my feet. Then he began to tell me about the conference, which had apparently been a huge success. 'But let's forget it,' he said. 'I don't want to go out of the gate again for at least a week.' He rubbed his head against my hand, and printed a kiss on my palm. That had become our secret, ritual sign that we belonged only to each other.

We sat late, unwilling to break up that first wonderful feeling of togetherness. But we rose at last, and William said, 'I'll go and have a bath, if you don't mind, Fran darling. I need to wash the journey off me — and America out of my hair. I'll come down again and lock up before we have our last drink.'

If he was going to indulge in a long, luxurious bath, there would be plenty of time for me to take a quick shower, too.

I slipped up to my own private bathroom *en suite* with my bedroom. I put my dressing-gown over my summer nightie, and looked at myself in the long mirror. That housecoat really was rather a gorgeous garment! It was a Jaegar creation of the finest black wool, embroidered all over with flowers of multicoloured real silk. I had bought it in a mad, flush moment years ago, and it had cost so much that I felt guilty (as usual), so I had put it away and forgotten it, until it had come to light again by chance a week or two ago. But I adored it, because it made me feel expensive and exclusive, like itself.

I had to admit I liked what I saw in the mirror now. My still black hair had a slight tendency to curl when damp, and I noticed with surprise that my cheeks were glowing, I supposed with steam and happiness, since I had applied no make-up at this time of night.

I could hear William tramping about, and made myself ready to go down and stun him with my exquisite taste in dressing-gowns. I was quite startled when he tapped on my door.

'Fran? Are you there?'

'Coming,' I called. I found him standing outside my door clutching an old dressing-gown round him and looking distinctly puzzled.

'Where did you say you had put me?' he asked. 'I thought you said in the guest room I used to have, next to yours. But the bed in there isn't made up.'

'But we agreed, Sophie and I . . . I suppose she must have misunderstood. Or perhaps there was some chance, after I left, that Mary might not be able to go home after all.'

I strode into the bedroom in question and halted, dumbfounded, just inside the door. The mattress had been stripped right down to the ticking, and the blankets and eiderdown were turned back over the foot of the bed, just like old-fashioned spring-cleaning. Sophie *never* left a bed like that! She must be in a terrible state of distress because of something I did not yet know. But why hadn't she left me a note?

'She probably decided I should be in less moral danger in Eeyore's Tail after all,' said William with a wry smile. 'But I think she must have been put out of her stride by something, because I found the clean towels in the bathroom, and my pyjama trousers. I have searched in vain for the top half.'

'Curiouser and curiouser,' I said, as we made our way downstairs and unlocked the door to the flat. The bed had been left exactly like the one in the guest room, though Sophie had actually kept it made up all the time William had been away.

'Well,' I said. 'We did have quite a lengthy conversation on the subject, in case anything should happen to prevent Mary leaving, and Sophie pointed out that we had three other bedrooms always kept aired and ready.'

'I've looked,' said William. 'The beds are all stripped.'

'Sophie must have taken leave of her senses!' I exclaimed, by this time completely bewildered. 'But at least I know where to find some clean linen. She always makes me keep a clean set in the little airing cupboard in my bathroom. I'll go and get it.'

We were back outside my door. 'Come in,' I called from the bathroom, 'while I unearth them.'

I still had my head in the airing cupboard when I heard him say, 'Fran, what's happened to the hedge of thorns? Have you taken it down, my darling?'

I came out, and found him sitting on my bed.

'That's a wonderfully becoming garment you're wearing,' he said. 'Come closer, so that I can see it properly.'

Clasping the bundle of clean sheets in my arms, I pirouetted in front of him to show off the full skirt, but he caught me and pulled me down beside him. I dropped the linen on the floor as I responded to his kiss, and when he reluctantly let me go, we stood up and I stooped to pick up the linen; but an exclamation from William stopped me, and I turned back to the bed again. My movement had disturbed the light summer coverlet, and we were both looking down upon two sets of pillows side by side. On top of the pillows lay William's neatly folded pyjama jacket.

The hands that drew off my housecoat and dropped it on the floor were infinitely gentle, but the arms that almost lifted me back on to the bed were strong and not to be denied.

'I told you,' said William with his lips against my throat, 'I said we should spend our honeymoon at Benedict's.'

The whole world was sparkling with sunshine, though before dawn there must have been a shower. From where I lay, I could see through the window to my left a garden newly washed and trees from which occasional crystal drops were still falling. The morning sun cast shadows of Virginia creeper leaves on to the opposite wall, patterning it with movement like a fairy ballet. My bedside clock told me it was only six o'clock. Too early yet to creep out and make a cup of tea. I sat up on one elbow and looked down at William lying beside me. The moment I moved, I was caught in his arms as he opened his eyes and looked up at me.

'You old fox!' I said. 'You were awake all the time.'

'Mm. I have been sitting up on my elbow looking at you, and wanting you to wake up.' He sat up, performing his eyebrow trick with just enough exaggeration to warn me of slight apprehension in him.

'And how is Her Majesty this morning?' he asked. 'Does your crown fit, I wonder, or are you feeling already that it may be too heavy a burden?'

Beneath the loving banter I detected a note of genuine anxiety.

'It was made to measure thirty odd years ago,' I said.

He kissed me now, not like the passionate lover of last night, but gently, courteously, a knight paying homage to his lady.

'Why don't you hate me, Fran? It's all my fault that we've wasted so much precious life.'

'We'll make up for it,' I said, reaching up to smooth the lines of regret across his forehead. 'Don't think about what's gone. Just look what a gorgeous morning it is.'

'It is the most wonderful morning of my life,' he said, burying his head against me to muffle the emotion in his voice. I groped under the pillows for the handkerchief I was going to need, even if he didn't. The golden moment of pure love unalloyed by passion glided by and fell, like every other passing moment, into the lap of eternity: never, though, to be forgotten, and ever to be recalled at will for as long as memory lasts.

I had not found the handkerchief. Instead, I held in my hand a neatly folded sheet of notepaper.

William sat up and took it from me to open it, falling back with his head beside mine and holding it above us so that we could both see it. Mary's beautiful copperplate hand needed no spectacles to decipher:

Somebody had to play God.

We were both so overcome that we could only cling closer and closer in wordless devotion that still held no passion. Then he put me gently away from him.

'I brought you a present,' he said. 'I was keeping it until I could go down on my knees before you and beg you to really be my wife. But I want you to have it now. Just stay there while I go and get it.' He got out and stood by the bed and stretched, like Adam reaching to pluck a blossom in the garden of Eden. I saw how broadchested he was, how slim-waisted, how lithe of thigh and leg – things I had never thought about before. When he had fastened his dressing-gown round him, he came back to kiss me again, and I noticed that the slight academic stoop of his shoulders seemed to have disappeared.

'Shall I put the kettle on while I find your present?' he asked.

He didn't wait for me to answer, but went off whistling 'Your coffee in the morning' and I heard him holding exultant dialogue with Cat.

I lay where I was, with Mary's note in my hand, trying to envisage my nearly-eighty-year-old friend and my placid, prim, virgin Sophie as reincarnations of Venus and Aphrodite. How on earth had Mary persuaded Sophie into alliance in such a momentous plot?

William came back with a tray and poured out two cups of tea, bringing one round to my bedside table. He took off his dressing-gown and climbed back into bed again.

'I had to shut Cat in the kitchen,' he said. 'I didn't even want her, this morning. I have just realized that it is Saturday, and that we have got till Monday morning all to ourselves. Not even Sophie about. I don't know how I could have faced her, this morning.'

'She must have been in the plot,' I said. 'Mary couldn't have managed it without her help.'

'Polytheism,' said the learned professor in my bed, 'is as old as mankind.'

I laughed. It was always going to be like this. We should never run out of things to talk about, if we both lived to be a hundred.

'I went down to fetch your present,' he said. 'Don't you want to see it?'

He snapped open a little box and there in a nest of black velvet lay an eternity ring of heavy Victorian gold set right round with rubies flanked on each side with rows of diamonds. He took it from its box, and picking up my hand, pulled off the heavy signet ring covering my 'wedding' ring and slid the exquisite Victorian hoop into its place. He held the hand that bore it a moment to the light before kissing the ring and letting my hand go. 'I think,' he said, 'that the gods will understand.'

I couldn't speak. I just lay holding my hand where I could see it. I knew he didn't want me to thank him in anything so banal as words.

'So what shall I do with this?' he said.

I took Grandfather's ring from him, kissed it, and slipped it on to the ring finger of his left hand. It fitted perfectly.

'There. Grandfather has given us his blessing,' I said. 'I know he would rather you wore the Wagstaffe bloodstone than anyone else alive.'

We held our ringed hands together as I lay with my head against his chest. Then he turned on to his side to look down at me again.

He stroked my face, and ran his long fingers into my hair, and round my ear, and over my lips. The look in his eyes was shortening my breath and his touch setting the blood throbbing through me.

'Oh Fran . . . how beautiful you are,' he said, his voice lowered to a husky whisper. 'My beautiful Fran. Mine at last. And I love you so. I love you . . .'

50

'I suppose,' said William, as we finished our late breakfast, 'that even on such a day as this there are chores to do?'

'One or two,' I said. 'I must do something about our lunch, and maybe you ought to clear up the mess in the hall — at least before Sophie comes tomorrow morning.'

'Where shall I put my things in future?' he asked.

I hadn't given such mundane things much thought, so I reviewed the situation at speed.

'No half-measures, now,' I said. 'We'll call the main guest room "William's room" in future, and you can leave your clothes in there because there really isn't room in my wardrobe for both. But I think we ought to leave the flat more or less as it is for visitors.'

'Need I keep on my other flat in town?'

'Of course not. That would be silly.'

He looked very relieved, but laughed. 'In that case, I'll go and start unpacking.'

We went about our separate tasks and didn't meet again until I called him into the sitting-room at mid-morning. I took him his drink as he sat in his usual chair, and was about to carry mine to my own chair when he said, 'Stay close to me, Fran. Sit on the floor.' I did.

'But this is the wrong way round,' I said. 'Does it mean that you intend to be lord and master in future?'

He set his coffee cup down, and stroked my head, holding it close to his knee. 'I still can't believe it,' he said. 'While you've been out of my sight, I thought I must have been day-dreaming. Was last night true, darling?'

He leaned down to me, and put his right hand under my chin to turn up my face so that he could look into my eyes. The other hand slipped caressingly down my neck and into the opening of my dress, pushing off the straps of my bra and then creeping still lower. I knew he didn't want to withdraw his hand any more than I wanted him to, but he did. Then he kissed me, gently and tenderly, sighed contentedly, and picked up his cup.

'Sorry, my darling. That was quite deliberate. I just had to make sure the purse was not full of faery gold after all. I half expected you to jump up and rush away screaming.' I hugged his leg.

'And what prompted Jess to involve Janice?' he said. 'I daren't ask until I knew the gold was real.' (If he had mentioned that name yesterday, Mary and Sophie's magic wouldn't have worked.)

'How did you know?' I asked. 'You tell me, and then I'll tell you.'

'She turned up — Janice, I mean — on the last day of the seminar.' He grimaced at the memory. 'It is a long time since we saw each other, you know — and I don't know which of us had the worst shock. Did I ever say *she* was beautiful? I suppose she hadn't really changed all that much, but I had got used to looking at you. She was dressed like a fashion model, and very made-up and actually she looked ghastly — brassy and hard and — and — well, *passée*.'

He paused, as if very reluctant to go on. 'Sweetheart, I was horrified! I couldn't believe that I had ever thought I loved that woman. How can you ever forgive me, Fran, for being such an idiot?'

I hugged his leg again.

'She took Jess's letter out of her handbag and handed it to me to read . . . Then she asked me if it was true. I knew I had to shoot her down before she could manoeuvre herself into a position to down me — us. So I simply said yes, every word, except that it was too late for her to stop whatever Jess suspected, because I was already living with you. I told her bluntly that she could sue for divorce as soon as she liked — but that in English law she hadn't a leg to stand on. OK. Neither had I. So the result would be a stalemate, anyhow. Only the lawyers would benefit.

'I could see I wasn't telling her anything she didn't already know, on the legal score, anyway. I think she was trailing her coat to find out if the mention of divorce scared me — either because of my academic reputation, or because I would not want to involve you. You learn a lot about tactics in a Spitfire. You blaze away with every shot you've got before the enemy gets out of range.' He grinned. 'I told her you were a thoroughly modern woman whose name was a household word because you write plays for TV and that a divorce or two would probably only raise your viewing rating. I could see how hipped she was, so I pressed on with my tissue of lies. I reminded her that divorce in staid old England, even now, is not like the same thing in Las Vegas.

'I must say she was extraordinarily shrewd. That gave me another clue or two about her purpose in reacting to Jess's letter as she had done. So I asked with whom she was living now, and what his attitude was. I could tell she wasn't quite sure how to deal with me, because she had discovered that I was no longer the compliant fool I have been. But in the end she did tell me – a budding politician.

'I wonder I didn't whoop with joy, or try a victory-roll by somersaulting two or three times on the carpet. The very last man who could afford to get mixed up in any open scandal. That gave me the whip-hand! Whatever does happen in future, it mustn't get into the American press. Quick thinking is something else being a pilot teaches you.

'It seemed not to have occurred to her at all that Jess's information that I was pining for her might not be gospel truth. Well, you can imagine Johanna in the same situation, except that compared with Johanna, Janice is a has-been, or perhaps, a never-was. The shock to her was that I was not clutching her skirts and begging her to come back to me – in fact, that I had made it pretty plain I did not want her.'

'I don't care what she does, as long as you don't want her. I'm not afraid of anything else.'

'Fran! My darling! Have you really been afraid of that? As well as all your other scruples?' His incredulous tone made me feel ashamed of my doubt of him, but his incredulity was like Jove's shower of gold. 'What caused Jess to write that silly letter?' he said.

I related as briefly as I could what had passed during his absence, reporting the quarrel in some detail, especially when I came to the bit when Jess's sneers at me about 'being a willing substitute for Janice' had finally swept aside the last of my reservations. During my recital, the fondling hand had slipped gently back again down inside my dress, and my only reaction was to shift my position to make it easier for him. (So much for Jess's sneers and Johanna's unspoken pity.) We were both diverted from bothering further about Jess or Janice.

'Don't move – I still need reassurance – often, and soon. Last night all my dreams came true. This morning took me to the very gates of Heaven ... but I was still afraid, all the same. You didn't know what I have just told you, and I was afraid you would think I had cheated. But now — Now ...?'

'We have all the time there is now, and I had planned something other before lunch.' We stayed as we were for another blissful minute.

'Tell me what,' he said, as if jealous, even of Cat or the Aga.

'I should like to write to Kate and Roland. May I?'

'If I may put a note in to each of them too,' he said.

We might have been parting for ever, so lingeringly did we cling before going off to our respective studies.

When Sophie opened the door on Monday morning, William leapt to his feet, as he would have done for any woman, queen or kitchen-maid. She was slightly flushed, but otherwise her normal self.

'So you got 'ome safe,' she said, with an air of relief and general satisfaction. She regarded any venture into 'foreign parts' as the equivalent of Livingstone's search for the source of the Nile.

William put his arms round her, and hugged her. 'Safe home – at last. Thanks to you and Miss Budd,' he said.

She coloured, then, her face turning from rosy red to deep crimson that ran down her long but sturdy neck. Such a head-on approach was more than she had bargained for. Without letting go of her, William fished with his other hand into his pocket and brought out a necklace of cultured pearls with a handsome diamanté clasp, which he contrived deftly to hang round her neck, still keeping her within the circle of his arms as he did so.

They hung down over her work-overall front and glowed against her still flushed throat. Then, still keeping one arm round her, he put out the other hand to me, in mute invitation for me to rise and admire them. He pulled me towards them, and enclosed both of us women within his arms, and bent his head to plant a kiss right on Sophie's lips, then on mine, and then back again to give Sophie another.

She looked steadily at William, then at me, and put up her hand to feel the pearls, as if to make sure they were real. (How was it that William had known that it was the one item of jewellery that she considered 'right', even for Sundays?) Then she broke from the circle, trying to find words, but all she could do was to imitate Thirzah in a tight, slightly muffled, 'Thenks.' But after a gulp or two, she turned to face us again, and said, 'That's something as I've all'us longed for. Just fancy you bringing 'em 'ome for me from America! And now,' she went on, 'I'd better be a-goo'in to get all them beds as I stripped a-Friday put to rights again. Like as not we shall need 'em all afore very long.'

I knew from that all-inclusive 'we' that the events of the weekend had sealed her into our family for ever.

I was consumed with female curiosity to know what drama had been enacted between Sophie and Mary on Friday after I had left. Mary would never speak of it again, so that left only Sophie. Intuition told me that she would probably welcome a chance to talk a somewhat uneasy conscience clear again. During the afternoon, William took himself into the study in the flat to begin to sort out his notes for the paper he had to write about the seminar, while it was still fresh in his mind; and once she had closed the connecting door, she sought an excuse to find me in my study. She was having some difficulty in finding a way of leading up to such a personal topic, but since we had on one or two occasions in the past managed to get over such obstacles, I decided to force the issue.

'Sophie, how on earth did Miss Budd persuade you to help her do what she did?'

'I 'ope I didn't do no wrong,' she said, blushing again to a bright pink that showed up William's pearls quite delightfully.

'Wrong?' I said. 'Of course it wasn't wrong. It was right — absolutely right. You said so yourself, once, just after Jelly was killed. It is William and I who have been doing wrong until now. Thanks to Miss Budd and you, we can start afresh.'

'Ah. I'm sure I 'ope so. It was all done for the best.'

Having broken the ice, she was prepared to tell me everything, if I was prepared to let her tell it in her own way.

From the moment we had known that William's return was arranged, Mary had begun a sort of softening-up process on Sophie, from what I could make out, by telling her that she was planning a secret surprise for us, which would require Sophie's help.

'So by that, I agreed to 'elp 'er, but I didn't know till you 'ad gone a-Friday morning what it was she 'ad in mind. I were took aback! I didn't know what to do. I couldn't believe as Miss would ever do anything as was wicked, like, but all the same I kept on thinking whatever my Mam would ha' said at me conniving at such a thing as that there. So I said as I should like to go away and think about it. And Miss said let's sit down, so as she could tell me what she thought, like.'

To be in partnership with her old mentor in a secret or enterprise of any nature was gratifying to Sophie's pride, as I knew. So she had agreed.

'Then she begun to talk to me about Jelly, Sophie went on. 'Seems she had knowed 'ow we felt about each other since we was at school.' She sat silent for a minute. Then she went on, 'And she told me about 'er own young man, told me everything, she did! Fancy! If Mam had a-knowed about that, she'd never a-let me goo to Miss's school no more. Then Miss said, "Sophie, I know how fond you are of Frances. So am I. Do we want her to go on for the rest of her life without her man, like you and me have got to? It's hard enough for us," she said, "but just think 'ow much 'arder it is for 'er, with 'er man living and breathing, seein' 'im day in, day out! You don't need to be told 'ow much them two love each other. But while 'is wife is still above ground, they'll never take no step o' their own accord."

'"No, Miss,"' I said, '"that they never will, much as they may want to."'

'"Then we must push them,"' she says — and told me the plan she'd got worked out.

'"Miss," I said, "can I go away by meself for a few minutes, to think about it?"'

'So I went upstairs, and I knelt down aside o' your bed, and prayed for guidance — like we 'ave all'us done when we needed 'elp. 'Im Above 'as never failed me yet. It were queer, though, 'cos just lately whenever I pray, all I can think about is Jelly. It were as if Jelly was there, in the room with me. I could 'ear 'is voice so plain. "Do you do as Miss says, gel," he said. "Whenever did Miss ever ask any of us to do what was wrong?"

'Well I stopped there a long while, mostly 'cos I didn't want Jelly to go away and leave me again. After a goodish while, I felt Jelly sort of drifting away from me again, but my mind were made up by then. I went straight away and done everything just as Miss had planned, afore I ever told 'er.'

'What did Miss Budd say, when you told her?' I asked.

Sophie coloured again, but this time it was with pride and pleasure. '"Sophie," she said, "I am very proud of you. As proud as I have ever been of anybody as I've ever teached in my life. You are able to think for yourself," she said. "That's why you know right from wrong." And then she kissed me. I shan't forget it.'

'Dear Sophie,' I said. 'I think just as Miss Budd thinks. Thank you for telling me.'

She was herself again in a moment. 'Lawks!' she exclaimed, scandalized by a glance at the clock. 'Look at that time! If I don't go and get on 'eavensard there'll be no scones for 'is tea!'

We seemed to have agreed by tacit consent to regard this week as a

442

honeymoon. We were both saturated with contentment as well rapturous happiness, and made the most of every passing hour.

On Friday, much to my surprise, Sophie asked if I should need any special preparations for the weekend, 'In case Miss Tolly and 'im might be a-coming up to see you,' she said. She had caught me out. I had begun to wonder how we were going to get over that particular hurdle.

'I'll talk to William and let you know,' I said. It could not go on as it was. William was still Jess's half-brother; they still owed William a lot of money, and were still using his car, which he would soon need. The affair of Jess and Greg looked like being the agent of our return to the everyday world of work and problems that to be solved.

I sat back in my office chair, and as William would have said, 'let the wheels buzz round'.

Once we could get Jess back to an even keel, Greg would come up trumps.

O? So we were going to do what we could for Jess, were we? We — not William alone. I must sort out my present feelings towards Jess, before I talked to William, because with all our other emotions at so high a pitch, a row, even a disagreement, would be disastrous. I wasn't going to risk it.

I was sorry to have hurt Greg, for whom my feelings were warm and unequivocal. But although I had been glad to welcome Jess back, and had loved her, in spite of some reservations at finding her so changed, I knew myself well enough to admit that I never had been a soft-centred magnanimous creature who forgave unwarranted insults easily. There was a core of hardness in me that sometimes went against all reason, but — I must not think only of myself.

William was down in the garden, talking to Ned, in view from my study window. I looked out at him and relived the wonder of the last week over again. I had thought that I had known everything there was to know about him — and how wrong I had been! Till last Friday, I had never known him as a lover — and how wonderful a lover I had never even suspected, because I had never before experienced the subtleties of such lovemaking. There was William the passionate, breathtaking, almost ruthless in his desire, making me feel like Cleopatra to his Antony. There was William the humble petitioner, the beggar at my gates, the supplicant for my favours, the knight in thrall to his lady; there was William the artist, playing a beloved instrument to perfection, and William the infinitely tender, ringing my soul out of me as well as my heart; or best of all, all of them combined, when I was no longer Fran, or he William, but so completely one that we were lifted like the Anglo-Saxon swan high over the rest of mankind, a new creation like a satellite in our own space, with no taint of Earth upon us at all. This love was mine alone, a gem honed and polished to perfection by longing and time. I looked at him again as he laughed at something Ned had said, and knew that I could not deny him anything he asked of me. Should he so demand, I would humble my pride and ask forgiveness from Jess for what in fact had been all her doing, and no fault of mine.

I could not grudge her her part in him, because it was not taking anything from me. I did not understand why she should grudge me what I had of him, because that was not hers, and never had been. Her nastiness had to be the result of a sudden, and perhaps only temporary breakdown, not a permanent change of character. I owed it to her, to Greg, and above all to William to give her the benefit of the doubt at least until we had met again. I did not hope that all could be as it might have been between us, but if she would come halfway to meet me, I would do my best to make us friends again.

I brought up the subject at lunchtime and William was hesitant in his reply, searching my face as he trod delicately among the thorns he saw by the wayside.

'I know we can't go on in this lovely seclusion much longer,' he said, 'and I already feel a bit guilty at not having rung to tell them I am back.'

'Which they will have heard,' I said. 'So I think we must make the first move. Shall I ask them up for the day on Sunday? I think that's probably what Sophie had in mind.'

He considered it well before answering. 'No, I'll ring up this afternoon, to break the ice and ask a few things I want to know. Then if it isn't too badly received, I'll suggest that you and I walk down to see them tomorrow afternoon, and we'll bring the car back. It is, I feel, they who owe us something.'

He reached a hand across the table inviting me to put my own into it — which of course I did. 'And I have my wife to think of, now,' he said. 'They have to learn that, too. So will you come walking with me as far as Hen Street?'

'You sound like the old folksong,' I said, determined to keep the discussion light.

'Madam, will you walk?
Madam, will you talk?
Madam, will you walk and talk with me?'

'If I remember, she wouldn't until he offered her what she really wanted!' And he took up the tune from me, and sang:

'Oh I will give you the keys of my heart,
To lock it up for ever that we never more may part.
Now Madam, will you walk,
Madam, will you talk,
Madam, will you walk and talk with me?'

'Both,' I said, happily, charmed by his ability to meet me on every level.

It was a clear, sunny afternoon, but the heat of the sun was tempered by a gentle breeze that made the conditions for walking as good as they could be. I slid my hand into William's, needing comfort and courage. We were already passing the first few semis of Hen Street, and I thought it might be wiser not to be seen actually hand-in-hand, but William would not let go. It was the intrepid pilot, not the circumspect academic, Jess would have to deal with today. In spite of my fears, my heart lifted, as Bryony Cottage came into view.

51

As we turned into the gate, William held on to my hand tightly. 'Remember what you said: "No half-measures now".'

William's Rover stood facing the gate, ready to be driven off; and in the garage, the doors of which had been left open on purpose for us to see, stood what had once been Johanna's small green Morris 1300. I had had barely time to take it in before Greg, who had been keeping a watch for us came out of the front door to meet and greet us.

'Jess is busy in the kitchen preparing tea,' he said. 'Why don't you go and find her, Bill?' It had obviously been carefully planned, and I think both William and I were relieved that it should be so.

Greg took my hand, and squeezed it. 'Sorry about that, Fran — but I do think it wise, don't you? May I kiss you?'

'Don't be daft!' I said, hugging him with a good deal of warmth, which immediately communicated itself to him. He and I had no quarrel with each other. He picked up my left hand, on which the beautiful eternity ring sparkled and glowed in the sunshine. 'Congratulations,' he said. 'I gather that all is well.'

'Very, very well,' I answered.

'Then if you are happy, perhaps it won't be too difficult to meet Jess again,' he said, coming directly to the point. 'Shall we go and sit in the garden? I want to talk to you while those two are sorting things out together.' We strolled to sit down in the very spot where I had sat with Johanna on the very first day I had arrived there. He went on calmly once he had made sure I was comfortable. 'I think there must be some reason for Jess's nastiness and jealousy,' he said. 'It may be her age. I'll get her to go and see a quack. But till then, Fran, can you go easy with her? It's a lot to ask, I know. But none of the four of us is going to be really happy till it's forgotten.'

'I was terribly hurt, Greg,' I said, 'but I have been healed. Grandfather used to say, if we quarrelled when we were little, "Never let the sun go down on your anger." That's where I made the mistake. I should have trusted William, and taken Jess into my confidence.'

I got up, and put my arms round his neck. 'Welcome to the Wagstaffe family,' I said.

He didn't speak, probably because he couldn't, so we just stood and held each other. Then at last he said, 'Do you think they have had time to untangle the skein?' Well, we had to face it some time, so why not at once? I nodded, and we went in through the back door, up the hall and into the sitting-room. It was uncanny. There Jess sat, on Johanna's settee, looking lovingly up at William, who was sitting on the arm of it with his arm round her. Except that this was Jess, not Johanna, and no cheque book was in sight, it might have been a replay of that awful cold Wednesday evening when I had peeped through the curtains.

They both jumped up at our entrance, and Greg said, 'Bill, come and help get the tea. You and I have a lot to talk about.'

It would have been so much easier to try to be natural with Jess anywhere else but in that room. The whole bungalow gave me the creeps. As Sophie said, some houses do seem inimical to some people.

She waved me vaguely to a chair, but I only perched on the edge of it. Neither of us could find anything to say. When it was becoɴ really painful, I thought about William's account of his encounɬ with Janice, and decided that it was no use weaving about jockeying for position. So I took my courage in both hands, and said, 'This is all very childish, Jess. We used to do it when we were ten, but we're both old enough to know better now.'

'Children can forget easily,' she answered. 'I haven't much to forgive, but you have. If you can't forget, there isn't much point in either of us trying.'

We were interrupted by Greg's cheery voice calling 'Tea's made!' and we rose to go back out into the garden, where the men had set out the tea things. I met her at the door, and took her hand for a moment. 'Let's at least try,' I said urgently, 'for their sakes.'

She had made an effort with her preparations for our tea, and I accepted it as an unspoken gesture of underlying goodwill. It was the sort of tea that Kezia would have produced for what she called ''igh days and 'olidays'. As we ate, we all made small talk, till William asked Jess how her job was going now. It was like the magician's 'Hey Presto'. Suddenly turned away from our own private tensions and anxieties, we all became much more our ordinary selves — especially Jess. She stopped with the teapot in the air, held over a cup, and said in a voice that immediately brought three of the four of us close together again, for it was Kezia mimicked to a 't', 'Sich doings as never was!'

'Tell!' exclaimed William and I together, on safe ground at last.

She turned and addressed me directly for the first time that afternoon. 'Choppen isn't really at all a bad chap, once you get to know him. He is first and foremost a business man, and I think he put his foot in it up to the elbow by not understanding at all what he was up against in the first place. He tackled it like a bull at a gate — I honestly don't think he would take that line now, if he could start again. He has had enough sense to learn from things that have happened. Bartrum is a first-class boor with just enough veneer to let him get by as a gentleman.' Her lip curled with distaste. 'But she — his wife, I mean — she's the very end! I have heard from Hetty who she is and what she is, and of course, from keeping the accounts I know that she is the actual partner, not him. I have been wondering how long it would be before she caused a bust-up of some sort. It happened late yesterday afternoon.'

We were both agog. Jess had learned from Hetty in confidence all that had really happened with Wendy, and of course that it had all

..t Johanna's fault. It hadn't taken Jess long to realize that the ..ungalow itself was still like a magnet to Wendy, and that to some extent she had become a sort of substitute for Johanna. So she had quite deliberately taken the step to encourage Wendy to think about going back to work again, and had secured for her the job down at Manor Farms. She was, Jess reported, far more intelligent than might have been expected, and had soon caught on to what was required of her. As far as looks and youth went, she was definitely an asset, and so, apparently, was the fact that she was 'of' a family that had its roots in Old Swithinford.

'I hadn't realized quite why you were so upset, Fran,' she said, 'until I actually started work there. Those poor old folk who didn't know what had hit them — I felt ashamed when they came into the office to plead with Mr Choppen. They didn't remember me, but I belonged to the Wagstaffes — and that was enough. In a curious way, even Wendy helped to bridge the gap between them and Choppen a bit.'

But Wendy's good looks, combined with her reputation, had not been long in giving Jack Bartrum ideas. 'He isn't to be trusted with any female, from nine to ninety, if you ask me,' Jess said scornfully. 'He's got the morals of a goat and the technique of a bull, I imagine.' (How full of memories this horrible little bungalow was always going to be! Johanna hadn't put it so neatly, but her experience bore Jess out.)

Jess had been worried, because she felt responsible. It was part of Wendy's duties to collect all such things as receipts and delivery-notes and such from one of the farm buildings, the harness-room, that was also being used as an office, every Friday afternoon and take them back for Jess to file. Bartrum managed to be there when Wendy went over on Friday afternoons. Jess had become very uneasy, but had noted with some surprise and a lot of relief that Choppen had also cottoned on, and for the last two weeks had made a point of being over in the harness-room himself, with Bartrum, when Wendy went across. But yesterday afternoon, he had been caught in Jess's office by an important telephone call.

'You can't see the harness-room from my office,' Jess said, 'and I had begun to get very worried because Wendy was gone so long. I was just about to go across myself, when Choppen slammed the telephone down in the middle of a sentence and said to me, "I think you'd better come along as well". I didn't know what he was talking about, but I followed him out and round the corner into the yard,

and there was poor Wendy, with her hair pulled down and the fr
of her blouse all open struggling to get free — not from Bartrum, b
from his lady wife! She was clawing and scratching at the poor kid's
face, and screaming such filthy abuse at her that I have rarely heard
anywhere. Bartrum appeared from the harness-room looking as if he
had had to stop to do his trousers up. He's a pretty hefty specimen
— Wendy must have fought like a young tiger to have got away
from him. Mrs Bartrum let go of Wendy as soon as she saw
Choppen there, and the poor girl ran to me for protection. Bartrum
went to his wife, and started swearing at her, so she turned her
stream of abuse on him. I have to say I admired Choppen. He
simply took charge — with orders that were meant to be obeyed.

'"Get out of the yard," he said to Bartrum's wife. "It's Jack I want to
talk to!" And she went! Then he ordered Bartrum back into the little
office as if he had been a rookie caught AWOL, and simply said,
"I'll deal with you later". After which he turned to where I was still
trying to soothe Wendy, who was in nearly the same state of
hysterics as her mother gets into, and apologized to her, and to me.
He has always had a lot of difficulty about what to call me, but
yesterday he solved the problem without thinking about it. "Jess,"
he said. "It is only a little after four o'clock, but I want you to leave
everything, and take Wendy home in the little green car — it is
yours now, anyway. Get the poor child home as soon as you can."
And off he strode into the harness-room. I advised Wendy not to
tell her mother anything at all about it, and she agreed. I think she
has enough sense now not to. And that's where it stands. I must say
I would have liked to know what happened between those two after
I left. My contempt for both Bartrums is now such that I feel
contaminated by being anywhere near them — but my opinion of
Choppen has gone up in proportion.'

We were, of course, fascinated by her tale; I caught William's eye,
and what we read in each other's was the same thought: in telling
her dramatic story, Jess had become her old self again. All tension
had gone out of the gathering, and we were just us, together again.

We were just about to say goodbye when Jess acknowledged for the
first time that she had noticed my ring. 'What a beautiful ring, Fran,' she
said, without a touch of either malice or envy. 'No wonder you look so
happy! And I notice that William is wearing the Wagstaffe bloodstone.'

Greg, sensitive to every nuance, slipped in before I had a chance
to reply. 'William,' he said, solemnly, but with the twinkle very
much back in his eyes again, 'how did you finally manage it?'

blushed furiously, and wondered how William would deal with such a personal approach. I needn't have worried.

'Oh,' he said lightly. 'No problem. I simply remembered my Kipling: "There are more ways of coming at a sweetheart than butting down the wall with thy head."'

We ran off, laughing, to the car, and got away before anything more could be said.

52

For once, the rumpus at Manor Farm on Friday had not become common knowledge overnight. Maybe it was because for a lot of people the fictional communities of *Coronation Street* and *The Archers* had replaced interest in what was going on around them in their own community.

William wanted to get back into harness again, and to give in the notice for his rented flat. I went back to my desk as well – not at all reluctantly, because I was recharged with a zest for life in whatever form it came, which included 'work'. Besides, I never wrote what I didn't want to because of any financial motive. Now, for the first time for several years, I was likely to have regular financial help from another source. William had been adamant that as I had restored one part of manhood to him, I should now restore the complementary part, the right of a husband to support his wife and household.

I had received replies to my notes to my children. There had been a 'Congratulations' card from Roland and Sue, signed by both of them, which had pleased me, because I was never quite sure where I stood in regard to Roland's wife. There was also a letter in Kate's big, generous handwriting. She never beat about the bush!

Darlings,
Welcome to the twentieth century. And about time, too! See you both soon.
With all our love,
Kate and Jerry.

William had reported that Greg had told him they had had a visit from Monty Ellington when the lease William had paid in advance had run out. Poor old Ernie Ambrose had died, leaving what he had to Ellington.

Lying beside William in bed, with my head resting on his shoulder, I reminded him of the horkey, and how wonderful it had been. He agreed.

'Do you think that was the end of an era, or the beginning of a new one?' he said.

'Must be both, surely. I think it was a second beginning for you and me.'

He laughed. 'You didn't know how near you came to being raped, that night,' he said. 'I think it was the first time that I really admitted to myself that I just couldn't go on without you – as my bedfellow, I mean. But you see, unfortunately I was brought up to be a gentleman, and subdue all such base instincts.' He was teasing me, and I knew it.

'Thank heaven,' I said. 'In the end, we timed it nicely. It took all that time to wear down my old-fashioned principles.'

He ruffled my hair, and kissed the top of my head. 'Mm ... Sometimes I'm so happy that I'm frightened, Fran. Truly.'

'Now who is being the puritan? That's exactly how I used to feel, afraid that if we grabbed anything more, all that we already had would vanish! Now I don't feel that any longer. I think we paid in advance – with all that agonizing holding off. We've paid off the mortgage. Everything we have now is ours to keep. Go to sleep. You needn't listen to me.'

I lay thinking about anything and everything, and just before I slept too, made up my mind that we must invite Jess and Greg up to Benedict's very soon, before the ice had time to form again between me and Jess. I would issue an invitation, if William agreed, for the very next weekend.

I decided on a very homely meal in the kitchen, which was a wise choice. Greg wandered about the house and garden, enjoying everything just as he had when they had first come back from the north. Jess was in one of her practical moods, and made all sorts of suggestions with regard to the disposal of such bits of nice furniture as William did not want to part with. She had made up her mind to accept the *fait accompli* with good grace, now that she had failed to prevent it; I made an effort, too, when I ushered them into the kitchen for lunch.

'I do apologize for this,' I said to both of them. 'It's so much cosier in here for what is, after all, a family gathering.'

'Sit down, William,' Jess said, immediately picking up the tone. 'I'll help Fran to dish up.' It was both an apology and a plea for forgiveness. I found, to my surprise, that I was more than willing to meet her.

When we were all served, I asked the question I had been wanting to know the answer to for so long. 'What happened after the Choppen–Bartrum row?' I said. 'It had all the makings of such drama, and then just fizzled out. I was quite disappointed.'

There was a flash of eye contact, question and answer, between Jess and Greg.

'Go on, tell them everything,' Greg said. 'Who has a better right to know – and they certainly won't go spreading confidential business round the village.'

'It has led to great hopes,' said Jess, 'but they are only hopes yet. As Greg says, it is all very confidential, but I can't help knowing, of course, and there's quite a lot in it for us if it comes off.

Pamela was not a Thackeray in anything but name – she had no farming background. But Choppen wanted a parcel of land big enough to be the nucleus of a really large enterprise, by no means all connected with farming. He bought the main Thackeray farm, though it wasn't really big enough by itself to suit the plans he had; but Pamela's and Bartrum's bits added made the scheme possible. What the scheme was, in the long run, was to turn Old Swithinford into a "showplace", a bit of Old England – a picturesque relic, if you like, almost a museum, with plenty of holiday cottages to rent, and a chance for townees to spend their holidays haymaking and so on. Choppen had hoped to buy Pamela and Bartrum right out – but that's where he came unstuck. They knew that during and after the war, there had been a lot of money in farming. They wouldn't sell unless they could come in on the scheme as a whole. And of course, that's where *they* came unstuck. They didn't understand big business. It seems incredible, but they appeared to think they could actually have their cake and eat it. They went back into the Thackeray new house, and began to act as if they still owned the land in their own right. Bartrum threw his weight about as the farmer who knew the land – and perhaps Choppen was glad of him in the first few weeks. But the fact remains that Bartrum and his wife are only tiny shareholders in what is likely to become very big business indeed. The other shareholders are mainly landowners or business men with a taste for

country living, and a lot of money to invest. The Bartrums are v[*]
small fishes in a very big bowl. And the other big fishes, when the[*]
got to know them, didn't care much for either of them. Once the
deal for the de ffranksbridge estate had gone through, the company
was reorganized. Choppen remains as managing director, but both
Bartrums will lose their directorships. This has not actually been
agreed by the rest, you understand, except in private – but none of
the other likely directors wants such as the Bartrums. I told you
Choppen had begun to learn – he has picked up the fact that if he
doesn't have the village more or less on his side, his scheme won't
work. It would be like setting up a zoo with no animals. And chief
among the objections to his plans was not just a few individuals' but
everybody's dislike of Jack and Pamela Bartrum. By this time, though,
Choppen himself had enough experience to understand why. So
when Jack started his tricks with Wendy, and when Pamela showed
what lay under her fine feathers, he blew his top.'

She paused to drink her coffee, and let us take in what she had
said so far.

So Pamela Balls-as-was was about to get her comeuppance! I
couldn't help but feel glad, not for my own sake, because she
certainly was nothing one way or the other to me, but I rejoiced for
Sophie, Mary, and for Johanna – though she, sadly, would never
know.

'All the rest is still in the future,' Jess went on. 'Which is why it
really is absolutely confidential. The other large shareholders want
both the Bartrums out – but they are tough bargainers. The latest
offer is that if the ffranksbridge sports centre scheme is passed by
the planners – and it looks hopeful – they will be offered the chance
to take a handsome lump sum for their land, and become the joint
managers of the ffranksbridge hotel.'

Extraordinary! Just what Ned had foreseen. You could not fool
people like Ned and Sophie. To them the laws of humanity were as
immutable as the laws of physics. Cream will rise, and dross will
sink.

'So there we are! But there's one more bit of good news as well,
for us personally. I have been officially promoted to company secretary – the managing director's secretary till the sports centre is in
being, and then the company secretary . . . with a house thrown in.'

William jumped up to kiss her, and I hugged Greg.

'On the Centre, I suppose?' I said.

Jess grinned in a way that reminded me of Johanna at her most

pish. 'Not on your nelly,' she said, inelegantly. 'Mr and Mrs
ally-ho-fearo are to occupy the Bartrum residence, to be on the spot
at the centre of operations.'

We still had to face the possibility that Janice might sue for divorce, to be free to marry her politician. One morning William
said, 'If the headline across the *Swithinford Star* one day were to
be of my divorce, citing you, what would it do to Sophie? Benedict's would never be the same without her. And it would hurt
her so much that we hadn't even warned her what just possibly
might happen.'

He was right. I wouldn't mention it to her that day, because I
didn't want to spoil her pleasure in the ceremony we had planned of
making the Christmas cake. But on Monday I would explain it all to
her, just in case our luck ran out and she had to face up to a sexual
scandal on account of her close association with us.

'I promise to tell her on Monday.'

I kept my word to William and broached the subject to Sophie on
Monday morning.

'There's always a chance that William's legal wife will try to spoil
everything for us,' I said. 'She may file a divorce, bringing me into
it. It won't make any difference now to us, but it may cause an awful
scandal. If the local papers got hold of it − as they surely would − it
wouldn't be at all nice for you. What about Thirzah, and Hetty?
They wouldn't like you to be mixed up in a juicy divorce case,
would they?'

She thought about it with her usual unhurried calm, brushing
biscuit crumbs from the table on to a plate with studied deliberation.
Then she stood up, and took up the broom she had laid aside before
sitting down.

When she looked back at me, her eyes were steady, if a bit
sterner than usual, and held a challenge in their grey depths. She
pulled her overalled shoulders back, and planted her black-booted
feet firmly side by side, for all the world like a parading soldier
standing 'at ease'.

'Het can hev' all the 'sterricks she likes,' she said. 'She goes her
own way now, and I goo mine. Besides, them as live in glass 'ouses
'ave to be careful where they throw their stones. And as for Thirz'
. . .' She brought her gaze down to meet mine again, and smiled, a
grim, heroic, but nevertheless triumphant smile. 'Let 'em all say what
they blame well like!' she said. 'Thanks be to God and Jelly, I don't

'ave to ask them, no' nobody else, for nothing. And I don't have think or do the same as they do no more. It won't worrit me, whatever the papers say.'

She snapped herself to attention, and quick-marched herself out of the kitchen.

I didn't know whether to be glad or sorry that the twentieth century had at last claimed Sophie too, but there was no denying that it had. She had crossed her Rubicon on the day of William's return.

What Sophie had at last come to terms with was the fact that we no longer lived in the same world as that we had been born into. Old Swithinford had clung desperately to its roots in the pre-war world; it had been one of the very last to ring out the old, and ring in the new. It had become a sort of antique. That was the quality that Mr Choppen had seen in it, and had decided to exploit, because antiques grow in value as time passes. He had proposed to embalm it like a fly in synthetic amber; but there was no way of giving back life to the fly. He could preserve the outward appearance of the village, but he could not conserve the spirit of its past. Those of us who straddled both the pre-war and post-war periods really had no choice. To live in the past was impossible; we all had to go forward and accept the present even if we had our doubts about the future.

I did not have to live in the tarted-up village, nor surrender altogether to the welfare state that proud independence which had been part of the heritage of all indigenous villagers. I was happy as I had rarely been before. But Fate or Fortune or whatever it was in charge of our lives still had one more trick to play before this extraordinary period came to an end, determined, it seemed, to bring the wheel full circle.

Term was in full swing for William, and I was taking a break from my work before starting on something new, when Jess rang up to say she would like to see us. I suggested they came to Benedict's.

'There are all sorts of goings on to report that will make your eyes stick out like chapel hat-pegs,' Jess warned.

Jess knew she was on safe ground when quoting Kezia. It was the glue that could hold even a bad break in our relationship together without a hairline crack showing. So they came; and between them they launched into the story.

Jess said how much easier things had been down at the farm after the Bartrums had been put in their place. Pending them being able to move off the premises to a hotel that did not yet exist other than ı an architect's drawing board, they were staying in what had been ⌐oddy's house and would eventually become Jess and Greg's home. But Jack had been found employment that kept him – and therefore Pamela – out of the offices. From that time on, Jess said, her relationship with Choppen himself had been much more comfortable, and she had even begun to like him because he had quite another side to him when and where his children were concerned. He was proud of both of them in every way, but particularly because he believed that both had inherited his business acumen and entrepreneurial spirit. Jess had already become quite attached to Monique – or 'Monica' as her father called her. The younger woman, in her turn, had become even more attached to Jess. When Monica was not based in London, she made a habit of going across to the office at such time that Jess took her tea-time break, and Mr Choppen himself quite often joined them.

They had all been sitting in the office one day at just such a tea break when the internal telephone had rung. This was an intercom system linking the main office with the harness room, Mr Choppen's private office-study, Monique, her brother Gavin who was still involved in his band, the barn – and previously, the Bartrums (who now been cut off the circuit). Jess had answered the call and said to Monique, 'It's your brother. Will you have a word with him?' Wendy had been making the tea, and had just set all their cups in front of them and retired to her own desk over in the corner.

'Oh, all right,' they heard Monique said, 'I can't come, but we'll send somebody across.' She put down the receiver and said, 'Gavin is setting up all the equipment for their first trial run tomorrow. He wants an extra pair of hands – just to hold something or other for about ten minutes, he said.'

'Send Wendy,' Mr Choppen suggested. 'She's not doing anything very productive here.'

Wendy had been a most reluctant helper, protesting that she didn't want to leave her tea, and 'was too shy to open the barn door and go in' until Choppen had actually ordered her out.

(I couldn't wonder at her reluctance – she had no reason to trust any man, and her memory of Bartrum in the harness room was all too recent. Nobody else seemed to have thought of that.)

Then they had gone on talking, and had forgotten Wendy, when, quite a while later when the tea-break had already been extended to twice or thrice its normal length, the office door burst open and Gavin appeared in great excitement, hugging his sister and yelling,

'Well done Monque!' ('Monque' appeared to be his comprom. between the Monica his sister had been and the Monique she was now.) 'Thanks a million! Dad, Monque's done the trick. I think we're made!'

'What on earth are you babbling about?' Monique asked, in obvious surprise.

'Come off it, Monque! Your find is tremendous!'

'What find? What do you mean?'

Gavin sat down and stared, searching their faces for the truth. 'That girl you sent across,' he said.

'Wendy? She's the office-girl, the one who makes the tea and posts the letters.'

'It isn't possible!' he said, slowly. 'Who is pulling my leg?'

It was Mr Choppen who cut in briskly, suggesting that if Gavin were to enlighten everybody about the cause of his excitement, it might be useful, because otherwise he would be called upon to explain his state of intoxication at this hour of the day.

So Gavin told them. 'I asked old Monque some time ago if with all her contacts and travels she would keep her ears open for me and my new group,' he said. 'At present there are only three of us good enough for what I want. We've got a variety of instrumental skills between us, but no lead-singer besides me, and I'm only second-rate as a singer. There have been hundreds of applicants for our fourth place, but not one among 'em who could supply the something different I'm looking for.

'Anyway, I haven't been able to get on with setting up the recording studio half as fast as I had hoped to because of the commitments I had agreed to with the Catskins. But as you have probably read last week, the Catskins have bust now. So I got the two friends I had already made up my mind about to come down, and the sound engineers, and we planned today as a try-out at recording – moving the instruments about till we got absolutely the best angle for acoustics, and so on. Then we got down to finer details, and set the stage up with the piano on it, and the drums and the double bass and the chairs, and we were ready to try it out as a recording. But we still weren't sure where I as the vocalist would be best placed among the others. Then Harry suggested that if we all played and got somebody else to walk about with the hand microphone, even if they only said the alphabet backwards, we should find out the balance between the voice and the band. That's why I asked Monique to come. But after that, I thought she was having me on.'

'Why?'

'Well, that girl was such a looker, in the first place! Then she was playing at being all shy and village-maidenish, and I still thought Monque had put her up to it. So I sat down at the piano and shoved the microphone into her hand and said, "Let's hear you sing!" – and she did! My God, she did! Whatever it is that makes a vocalist people remember, she's got it. Oh, come on! You are not going to kid me that a girl from the village has got that amount of expertise! Her diction is perfect – not a sound of a pseudo-American croon, not a slurred vowel or a dropped final consonant – not a sign of hesitation or embarrassment. She's been trained. I swear it. She's got stage-presence too. Where did your office-girl learn all that?'

'Jess brought her here,' Choppen said. 'Ask her. She probably knows the answer.'

Jess told us what a dreadful quandary she had been in. She had heard all too often of Wendy's calamitous friendship with Johanna Brooke, and the shattering consequences that followed. She could guess what sort of reception Wendy would get if she ever dared mention singing or being on a stage again. All the same, there was no doubt that young Gavin was in earnest. As Jess said, she simply could not be the cause of robbing Wendy of a chance like this.

And so, encouraged by Greg, Jess had told them all she knew and, knowing the family inside out, she could guarantee what solidarity of feeling and opposition there would be to any suggestion of Wendy using her musical gift anywhere but in church. Jess said she had nearly had to go down on her knees and plead with them to make them believe such an attitude could possibly exist in the 1960s. But Greg had backed her up, and in the end they had agreed not to tell Wendy anything but that they might want her to go and sing with them again, and if she would like to she could sing with them when they took part in a charity concert in Swithinford before Christmas. Jess thought that there would have to be a family conference before even so much was grudgingly allowed. Should she, Jess, break the ice to Wendy's mother, but warn Wendy not to say anything at home about her adventure today until Jess had cleared the way?

The assembled company had had no option but to agree – though Gavin said that he'd see to it that he got Wendy as his vocalist if he had to kidnap her.

Jess said she had been amazed at the bitter vindictiveness in Wendy when she talked to her. She had agreed, but had added,

'They didn't stop me last time, hard as they tried. And nobody sh[a]
stop me now! I shall do as I like.'

'What is going to happen now?' I said. 'Or has it already happened?'

Jess said she had broached the subject with Hetty the very next day. There had been a frightful scene, which had ended with Greg appearing from somewhere with a wet towel and sloshing Het's face with it. It had had the desired effect of stopping her hysterics, but Jess thought that he had blotted his copy-book for ever and maybe done more harm than good. He didn't agree. He said that if it had done anything to harm Wendy, he was sorry, but it had done him a power of good because it was something he had been longing to do from the very first moment he had ever set eyes on her mother. The grin that passed from face to face showed that he spoke for us all.

Hetty had said stiffly that she would tell Joe, and perhaps ask Thirzah. Jess had advised strongly that as Wendy could no longer be regarded as a child although still legally a minor, she should be allowed to take part in any family conference, and Jess had offered to go with her to bear witness that she was telling the truth.

'They know they will never get Wendy there without me,' she said, 'or none of them would ever have agreed to that! But we are bid to Thirzah's tomorrow night as ever is. Baby Stephen is to be put to bed in our bedroom, with Greg as baby-sitter.'

'I shall take my punishment like a man,' he put in. Jess squeezed his hand, and went on.

'Once I have delivered Wendy and made the points only I can make, I shall go home. They can talk. They don't know me like they do you, Fran, and I'm sure it would be best to leave them to it.'

Up at Benedict's we could only wait. William begged me not to worry, and I tried not to. It wasn't all that difficult to forget everything else, when I had him all to myself till Monday morning.

The morning after the family conference Sophie marched straight into my study, without even stopping to put on her apron. The fat was in the fire — I could see that; but her manner was more like that she had displayed after Choppen's visit to her than that of a down-trodden sister or a cast-off aunt. She was bursting to talk, so I waved her into a chair close by me and asked (as if I didn't know) what was amiss.

'You know as well as I do what's going on with Wend' and her inging,' she said. 'Jess told me as she'd been up here Friday night. And she come to Thirz's Sat'day, dragging Wend' with 'er. But when she had said what there was to say, 'ow it 'ad 'appened, like, and what a chance in a lifetime it could be for Wendy, she upped and went again, and left us by ourselves to deal with Wend'.'

She dropped her head suddenly, and tears began to fall on to the handkerchief clasped between her hands in her lap. 'Oh, Fran,' she said. 'I never thought I should live to see anything to do with our family that were as bad as what went on at Thirz's that night. It were terrible!'

'Do you want to tell me?' I said. She nodded.

'Well, there were all of us there – Thirz' and Daniel, and Hetty and Joe, and Wend' and me. Thirz' had set herself down in the chair at one end of the table, and I could see straight away as she had took it on herself to have all the say, whatever the rest of us might think. But she ain't got me quite as much under 'er thumb as she used to have, so I set down aside Wend' at the other end, 'cos I could see she were on 'er own like, with nobody else to stick up for 'er.

'Het 'ad been crying, you could see that – though she looked sort of wild, and excited, and not 'erself. For one thing, she had bedizened herself out in all her Sunday best, just to go down to Thirz's in the dark. Whatever has come over her lately, I can't make out. I sometimes wonder if Mam knowed there were something a bit queer, like, about Hetty, for all she were so pretty. She can't deal with nothing a bit out o' the ordinary, if you know what I mean. I'm sure we was all glad when she got such a good and steady 'usband as Joe Noble. He's all'us been real good to 'er, and put up with 'er tantrums better than most men would, though he could put his foot down with her if she went too far.'

There was nothing for it but to let Sophie run on in her own way. Not that I minded. I was curious to know every tiny detail.

'As soon as ever the door 'ad shut be'ind Jess, Thirz' says straight out to Wend', "So that's what you are been up to! Same as afore, only this time it's Choppen's son. I make no doubt as you're in the family way again, else we shouldn't be told nothing. You ain't been nowhere near us lately – till you want us to 'elp again." Dan'el tried to shush 'er, but she took no notice of 'im at all.

'Well, it took my breath away, 'cos I had never thought o' such a thing. Jess hadn't said nothing o' the sort, only about the singing and such. I couldn't believe it. I looked at Wend', and there she were

sitting looking straight back at Thirz', with 'er 'ead 'eld up 'igh a
proud, like — not the sort o' way you'd expect from a gal as were in
disgrace again. She just sat, and wouldn't open her mouth. Joe
looked as if 'e could do murder, and Het fired up and told Thirz' as
she'd better mind what she was saying. But you know Thirz'! She
all'us 'as to be right, and nobody 'as ever gone against 'er.

'"Well," Thirz' says, "at least he's free to marry 'er, this time. And
marry 'er 'e shall! Else 'im and 'is family'll have to face up in court to
one o' them maternity orders. 'E shan't get away with it, that 'e
shan't. We'll see to that."

'Then Het begun to squeal like a pig with its 'ead in a gate, like
she all'us does when she's goin' to have a fit o' 'sterricks, and Joe got
up and stood over her and told her to shut up or he'd shove 'er
outside and lock the door on 'er. And still Wend' never answered,
not a word. I can't 'elp but think as tha's what made Thirz' so mad.
She ain't used to folks not being scared of her. Wend' wouldn't
speak, and she didn't cry, and she didn't even look ashamed of
herself. She just set there looking straight back at Thirz', and I
couldn't understand it. She may ha' growed up away from me, like,
lately, but I couldn't believe she could ha' changed all that much —
to be so bold and brazen, like, I mean. So I took 'old of 'er 'and
under the tablecloth, and she squeezed mine back, and looked at me,
and 'er eyes was as innocent as a newborn babe's. I could ha' swore
on my Bible as Thirz' had got it all wrong. And nobody else seemed
as if they dare contradict her. We have all got into the 'abit of
taking Thirz's word for gospel truth, and letting 'er rule the lot of
us. But somebody had got to stick up for Wendy, and if nobody
else was going to, it had got to be me. So I started to speak, but
Thirz' held her hand up to stop me, like she's all'us done before.

'"You shut up!" she said. "What do you know about such things,
a old maid like you. You leave it to them as does know."

'And then Thirz' pointed down the table where me and Wend' set
together, and said, "She's a whore, tha's what she is. A whore!"

'Poor Wend' grabbed my 'and again, but she still didn't say
nothing. Then Hetty started giggling — and sort o' crowing — and
we all expected she were going to have a fit o' 'sterricks there and
then. But she didn't — she just pointed and screamed out, "Yis, that
she is! I'm knowed it all along! Why else should Jelly Bean goo and
leave 'er all 'is winnings? He used to goo and visit 'er by night. I
know somebody as seed 'im coming out one night, just afore 'e got
killed. She ain't no better than that Mis' Catherwood as she works

461

, as lives with her cousin though 'e 'as got a proper wife still. They're as thick as thieves, her and Soph, an' that's why. Birds of a feather all'us stick together."'

Sophie looked up at me to see if she had reported too truthfully, but it was for her, not myself, that my indignation was choking me.

'Fran, I'm never been so near fainting in all my life afore. Hetty thought Thirz' had been pointing 'er finger at me! And I don't know what I should ha' done, only Wendy done it for me. She just stood up and reached across the table, and slapped her mother's face so 'ard she knocked 'er 'at off.

'"Don't you dare say things like that about my Aunt Sophie!" she said. "She's worth two o' you, any day! And don't any of you dare to say such things about me, neither, 'cos none of you know what you're talking about. You lot can only ever think about one thing. As far as I can make out, it's about the only thing as you know anything about, 'cos it's the only thing you can find to talk about. Even Aunt Thirz' — though she's never 'ad no gel of her own to worry about. If she had had, she perhaps wouldn't have had time to try and keep other folks's daughters in order." Well, Thirz' went purple, and I thought she was going to 'eve a fit. Nobody had ever spoke like that afore to her! I tried to stop Wend', and so did Joe and Dan'el, but she shouted us all down.

'"You can take back all you said about Aunt Sophie, and what you think about me. It ain't the truth, anyway. It's all lies! I never in my life spoke to Gavin Choppen till yesterday. Mr Choppen sent me over to the barn, and young Choppen told me to stand against the piano. Then he told me to sing, and I did. As far as anybody's ever told me, you don't get babies that way. And if they want me to go and sing with 'em again, I shall. And nobody 'ere is going to stop me."

'If I 'adn't been so upset, I'm sure I should ha' laughed! Joe had stood up, and looked as if he didn't know which to hit first, Het or Wend'. Het were still making funny little squeaky noises as if she was choking, so in the end he hit 'er on her back as 'ard as he could, like a man mazed. And Thirz' set there all of a heap, with 'er eyes rolled up as if she might 'ave 'ad a stroke — but I knowed as she were only busting with temper. She kept opening and shutting 'er mouth, and when Wend' had finished, I upped and said to Thirz', "If tha's your own words as you're tryin' to swaller," I says, "then I don't wonder they stick in your throat! Calling your own niece such names, and saying such things about a poor innocent gal as hadn't had no chance at all to speak for 'erself! You ought all ashamed o' yourselves," I said. "And if our gal 'as got a chanc get 'erself out of a pig's 'ole like this, I 'ope she'll make the most it. And if none o' you will stir a 'and to 'elp 'er, I shall. I'm got enough and to spare, thanks to Jelly. If Wend' had been 'is child," I said, looking straight at Joe, "he wouldn't ha' stood by and let 'er be called such names to 'er face as 'as been used tonight."'

Sophie actually chuckled, having by this time got past the worst bit of what had been said about me. After that, she felt freer to enjoy the telling of her own open bid for independence.

'You should ha' seen the look Joe give me! They were all so took aback by me having my say as they were struck dumb, like.

'I could see that Joe believed me though, but didn't know what to do for the best. So he set down again by Hetty, and tried to stop her from making such a row. She shoved him away. "Don't you 'now Het' me," Het said to Joe. "Get up and give that gal a good threshing. If you'd ha' done that years ago, she'd never ha' dared to strike her own mother. You jest set there and let 'er do it! She *is* a whore, as Thirz' said. Ain't we got proof of it? Who is it that 'as to look after the base-born child as she's got a'ready? She can't deny that!" And then she turned to Wend' and shouted, "Who do you think's a-gooing to look after 'im while you goo a singin' and play-acting with young Choppen, eh?"

'"I don't know," says Wend', cool as a cucumber, "and I don't care!"

'"You wicked gal! Oh, you wicked gal!" Thirz kept saying, over and over again. And when Het had got her breath back, she joined in. "However dare you stand there and say that!" she said. "'Im Above can 'ear every word you say! Don't you forget that! Saying as you don't care what 'appens to that poor fatherless little mite as you brought into the world, disgracing us all like you did! And you dare to stand there and say as you don't care now what 'appens to 'im!"

'"No," says Wendy. "I don't. So now you know! I hate the very sight of 'im, so there!"

'Well, if I hadn't been there and heard and see it all, I never would ha' believed such things could happen to anybody, specially us. But there was worse to come. Wend' were still standing up there at the end o' the table, like she might ha' been saying her collect for the day at Sunday breakfast time afore she went to Sunday School when she was little. Nobody else spoke, 'cos we were all dumbfounded, even Het. We couldn't believe as we was 'earing right. So Wend' just kept on.

...nd afore any of you asks me, I'll tell you why! 'Cos he ain't no ...e fatherless than any other baby as is born is! He had a father all ...ght, same as everybody else, and you all know who it were, whatever tales you choose to tell folks. And that baby is so much like his father as I can't bear to look at him! That man as Mother set such store by! Him as pretended to be a parson! If any of you had ever told me about such men as him when I were growing up instead o' making me go to Sunday school where he could catch me and kiss me if I got there early, by myself — I should have known better. And then when I found as I was going to have a baby by him, it was all my fault. Not his. He cleared off and left me to it. But he couldn't do no wrong, so it all had to be my fault. It wasn't my fault. It was yours — all of you!"

'I never took it as she meant me — 'cos as I've told you many a time, nobody had ever spoke to me about such things, so they surely hadn't expected me to tell Wend' things she ought to have knowed. And to think that man—' She cried again, quietly, into her handkerchief. It had been for her far worse than just a family row. The very foundations of her faith in the church had been shaken, even though she had always declared that Hen Street's 'place' was not a proper church nor Birch a proper parson. But she soon dried her eyes again, and went on with her tale.

'"So if anybody is going to look after his child," Wend' says, "it ain't going to be me, 'cos likely I shan't be 'ere." And she looked straight at her mother, and said, "So it'll have to be you. He couldn't do no wrong for you, could he? All'us hanging about our house he was, having cups o' tea and such — till Johanna Brooke come. She put your nose out o' joint, didn't she? That's why you hated her so much. And why you hated me when I were carrying — not like Dad, 'cos you were so ashamed o' me, but because you were jealous of me. And even after he'd cleared off, you used to be round there at his church on your knees pretending to be praying for me — but you was only thinking about him and praying as God would send him back. You know what I'm saying's true, don't you Dad? You didn't know till after the baby come, but you could see it then. The way Mam took him away from me, and pretended she was his mother, and went about so proud of him. I had had a lot of time shut up to think things out for myself — and I had growed up as well," she said. "I knowed then why Mam had had 'sterricks every day and made my life a misery. And if you don't believe me, ask Dad." Then she sat down and begun to cry. I hope I never have to see anythink like

464

that again. Joe was as white as a sheet, and Dan'el got up o...
place and went and got the brandy bottle as Thirz' all'us keep
medicine, like, and give Joe a good dose. Hetty 'ad put 'er '...
down on the table and was sobbing and trying to take 'old of Joe,
but he pushed her away. I stroked Wendy's hair and tried to pacify
her – but we couldn't ha' been more knocked to pieces if a bomb
had dropped among us.

'Then Joe said, "Ah, I knowed. I thought at fust that Het's queer
goings on were because o' the shame Wendy had brought on us.
But she never would say a word against him, only what a good man
he was, and she never believed Wendy when she said as he were
the baby's father. She were always taking the child to church – well,
to that place as she calls church – and when young Stevie begun to
look like Birch, she pushed Wendy aside, like, right out of her
proper place as his mother. She wanted him all to herself. I drawed
the same conclusions as Wendy has, only I never thought as she
could think such a thing, so I kep' it all to myself. What else had I
got to do? He were gone, and I'd got Wendy to think about, and
the baby. So I pretended I didn't know, and looked after Het as well
as I could. You all know how she is."'

'Oh, Sophie,' I cried. 'Don't tell me any more. I can't bear it.'

'So we all thought, Sat'day night,' she said. 'We all set there as if
we was dead and turned to stone. But the funny thing to me now is
that I could see we all believed it, now it had been pointed out to
us. We had all been blind, except Wendy and poor Joe, because it
never entered our heads as such a thing might 'appen to anybody in
our family. Joe was doing 'is level best to soothe Hetty. "Don't take
on, Het," he was saying. "He's gone for good now, but you've still
got me. And we've both got the littl'un. And Wendy."'

I entered Joe Noble's name down on my private list of saints.
Noble by name, and noble by nature.

'Hetty set up then, and said, "Do what you will, Joe Noble, but I
ain't heving that bloody, whoring little bitch under my roof no
more! She can go to the Devil, for all I care! Bad'll become of her,
and the sooner the better."

'We had all been trying to comfort Wendy, and all of us was
crying except Joe, but when Het said that, Dan'el, who hadn't said
nothing till then, banged his fist down on the table, and said, "Who
is master in this 'ouse? *I am*. And now I'm going to have my say.
Hetty, unless you want to be took to the 'sylum, like poor Eth
Merriman, pull yourself together and listen to me. I will not have

ge like that spoke in my house never. I never have used such ..age myself, and I never will. And more shan't anybody else in y 'earing. Don't you cry no more, Wendy my gal. You've 'eard your Aunt Soph say as she'll 'elp you all she can. And so will your old Uncle Dan'el. Your Dad 'as got about as much on his plate as he can manage, I reckon. Don't you worrit, Joe! Sophie and me'll look arter Wendy and see as she's all right."

'I could see as Thirz' were going red in the face again, and so could Dan'el. He looked Thirz' right in the eye and she quailed. I could see 'er. Dan'el had never crossed her in public like, afore, as far as I knowed. "Let me finish what I'm got to say," he said. "Then you can have your say if you want. You get more like your mother every day – and I had plenty of her before she died. You took over from her, and it's a pity for all of us as we ever let you! You've 'ad your way all along," he says, "and although you done it for the best, you was wrong in some things. I ought to ha' spoke out afore, I know. But I'm a peaceable man – till the time comes as I can't stand by no more. Sophie could have had a good husband if it hadn't been for you, after your mother died. It never were fair to expect her to stop at 'ome and look after the old woman just 'cos it was convenient to you and Het. What we've got put by now, I've earned – and you've saved; 'cos you never would spend a penny if a ha'penny would do. And what good is it doing to anybody now, in the Co-op? And if I say as it shall go to 'elp Wendy, if that's what she wants, that's where it'll go. And that's what we all come 'ere tonight to find out, ain't it? She's right, such as us don't understand. So you tell us, Wendy. I can't see nothing wrong with singing, meself. I sing loud enough, when I'm in church, or about in the cowsheds. And Wend's all'us been one for singing. She takes after Joe's sister Emma, what died. Sung like a hangel, Emma did.'

(Sophie actually laughed.) 'I wish you could ha' seen Thirz's face, Fran! You see, Dan'el had been sweet on Emma, till she died, poor gel. It were only after that he'd courted our Thirz'. And I just couldn't help putting my spoke in there. "So she did," I said. "And Wend' never got her voice from our side, we all know that. Het a-singing sounds like a rusty old saw as is just come across a six-inch nail." And even Wendy laughed. And after that, things settled down so as we could hear what Wendy had to tell us. I can't say as I goo along of it with a very good heart, but then, I know I'm old-fashioned. I don't understand it, you see, and I don't like it. But there. Things do change. What can't be cured must be endured, as our Mam always said.'

466

'And what happened, after all?' I asked.

'Well, it seems as if nothing is going to happen, like, s—away. Wendy'll keep her job with Choppen, in Jess's office, when young Choppen wants her over in the barn to sing or practise, she'll be allowed to go – and get extra money if they keep 'er late. So that's one good thing.'

'And was she allowed to go home?'

'Joe told Het much the same as Dan'el had told Thirz', so they both had their combs cut.' There was a good deal, of satisfaction in her voice. 'He said Wend' could stop at home as long as she wanted to. She said that wouldn't be long!'

Sophie got up, and the next time I saw her she had put on her overall, and was bearing a tray.

'I don't know as if we shall ever meet again, as a family, like,' she said, philosophically. 'There was too much said that night for it to be easy mended. We all agreed that as long as none of us didn't tell nobody, nobody else need know what had been said. I'm told you, and you'll tell William, but you won't let it go no further. But things have to change some time, don't they? And it ain't all'us for the worse. I'm made tea, this morning. It's better than coffee to set you up again, ain't it?'

It had all passed into history, then. Jess reported to Mr Choppen, who solved Wendy's problem by suggesting that she should take up residence in one of the back rooms of his own house, close to both her work and to the barn when needed. The main condition of Wendy's living there was stated clearly: that he would keep a strict eye on her, not for her own sake but for his son's. At the first intimation of any association other than a strictly professional one, her job as well as her chance of a singing career would be gone. 'But from what I have seen and heard of her so far,' he said to Jess recently, 'the last thing she is interested in is men. She might as well be a nun, so Gavin says. He calls her "Sister Anne".'

Which in turn had had a consequence. When the charity concert at Swithinford took place a couple of weeks ago, Gavin's musicians had contributed. For the second half, they had donned dinner jackets, and Wendy had stood by the piano, and sung as only she could. But it was Monique who had added the final, stunning touch. She had designed and had made up a dress especially for the occasion – a long, sweeping robe in black moiré silk, with wide sleeves lined with white over tight-fitting medieval ones of white lace. Around

slim waist a belt of white corded silk hung down, ending
o huge, magnificent tassels. The wide low collar was also
te, but was filled in, right up to the chin, with boned tucks of
ne same exquisite lace, which in turn almost met the coif of the same
material that sat so demurely on Wendy's flax-golden curly head.

'SISTER ANNE: STAR OF THE FUTURE' read the *Star's* headline, over
a full page photograph. 'Local girl's triumphant début.'

Sophie held it long before she could find her voice.

'It's beautiful,' she said. 'But I do wonder what Mam would have
said. After this, she'll never be our gel no more. And I still don't
hold with it. None of it would ever have come about if it hadn't
been for that red-headed dink-me-doll up at Hen Street who didn't
know when to mind her own business.'

Well, I knew that somehow there would be another side to
Wendy's triumph, and that Johanna would get the blame. But *'Che
sera sera.'* The future was not ours to see.

53

*Cat woke from her snooze, and climbed up on to my chest, asking in a
subdued voice why I was being idle for so long.*

*On a little table by my side the opened Christmas cards still lay.
Tucked between me and the side of my chair was the unopened envelope
from Johanna.*

*The card that lay on top of the pile was from Mary. Not for her the
cheap and meaningless greetings cards splashed with stars and angels and
Christmas trees and bought in their thousands from any stationer's shop.
Mary had made her own, sending, as it were, a bit of herself specially for
me and William. I took it up and examined it again, appreciating the
love and the thought and the time and the skill she had expended on it
as her rheumatic old hands had plied the needle that had executed it
in such tiny, perfect stitches. It was her own design, too, a message
that we could not but understand: an emblem of Love, below which she
had added, in minute cross-stitches, a bit of medieval philosophy she
was fond of quoting:*

Yesterday returneth not.
Mayhap to-morrow cometh not.
There is to-day; mis-use it not.

I had been lost in thought of a past that would never return — except in memory. Even memories could be double-sided, made up of sweet and sour, like the most popular of the dishes now available from the ubiquitous Chinese Takeaways springing up everywhere, even in such small places as Swithinford. The flavour of sorrow enhanced the taste of joy. I had had more than my fair share of joy — balanced, sadly, by Sophie's unequal share of sorrow in the year that was just coming to an end. For Mary, there could only be little future left, even if she lived to be very old. But there was to-day — and every day as it came — one day at a time.

We should not misuse these next few lovely days. It was the first Christmas ever that William and I would not be parted by the clock striking bedtime, or by anything else except our duties as host and hostess to our guests. Well — guests only because they were under our roof, since they were all 'family', including Mary by adoption and Sophie by choice, because she seemed to be as much a part of Benedict's as the landing window or the beautiful staircase. We were dearer to her now than the shattered remnants of Kezia's family, though there had already been signs, this very morning, that perhaps Time would help them all to forgive and forget. As Jess and I had managed to do, though forgiving was so much easier to accomplish than forgetting. Leave it to the gods — who had magic herbs for all our ills, even death. I hoped they would not take Mary from me for many years yet.

One friend gained, and one friend lost. I did not know why I feared to open that envelope, except that I did not want any sorrow or distress it might contain to stain my own bright happiness; because in spite of everything, I still thought of her as a friend — and one whose welfare I cared for. In fact, I still loved her. I couldn't help it. Now and then when something reminded me of her, I longed to see her again, just for a few minutes. Only for a few minutes, though. She was too dangerous.

Love has so many sides to it, so many qualities that make it, like Time, beyond human understanding. It doesn't die when people you have really loved die; you can't kill it, even if or when you want to; you can neglect it and let it wilt like a plant without water, but the first meeting or the first sound of a voice will revive it instantly. If it won't stand up to those tests, then it isn't and never has been, Love.

I had admitted to myself that I could not help loving the memory of Johanna . . . Perhaps that is what I was afraid of — that she might once more become more than a memory? I had to face up to finding out. I fished *ope from its hiding-place down in the side of my chair, and slit it*

here was a Christmas card, Italianate and, of course, mainly pink. here was a photograph and a four-page letter tucked inside the card.

I studied the photograph. It was in colour, and showed Johanna as ravishing as I had ever seen her, in a dress with a slit at the side that let the skirt fall away to reveal one of those perfect legs thigh-high. Her head was half-turned towards her companion, a middle-aged, well-groomed, stocky but intelligent-looking man rather like Greg, though obviously Italian.

Whoever he was, he could not be the faithful Dave! I looked again at the glowing woman in the photograph. She was such a many-sided personality, and as Shakespeare had said of Cleopatra,

> Age cannot wither her, nor custom stale
> Her infinite variety.

I thought of her patiently 'unmuddling' Madge Ellis's knitting, and of the genuine care she had lavished on old Ernie until the silly old man himself had ruined the harmless relationship. I thought of the fun we had had together when she had entertained me with her lightning impersonations, of the verve and joie de vivre she created round her when she was happy. It was only when insecurity brought out the ruthlessness of her that she was, as William had said, 'as treacherous as cat-ice'. I liked the look of the man beside her; while she was in such company, I had no need to fear her. I opened the letter. There was no date, no address. She just started straight in.

My dear Fran,

If you hoped never to hear from me again, I shouldn't be surprised after the way I treated you. Forgive me if you can. Dave couldn't, so I had to start yet again.

I won't bore you by giving you a blow-by-blow account of how I managed to survive — you can see by the photo that I did.

I have been living with Seppi in Italy for six months now — long may it last. I am happy. Apart from Seppi himself — and his oodles of boodle — he happens to be an impresario, so the smell of grease-paint is never far away, and I love it. In fact, I am beginning to think I couldn't live long without it.

We came to England recently, and I had a sudden longing to see you, and to show Seppi what he had rescued me from. We drove down – but at the last minute, my heart failed me. I did not know what might have happened to you in the meantime, and you might not have wanted to see me. So I tried to disguise myself, covering up ny hair, and wearing a huge pair of dark sunglasses, in the hope that no one would recognize me.

We went first to look at Hen Street, and had a look at Bryony Cottage. There was a nice-looking man in the garden – I learned afterwards that he was one of your home-spun cousins, who now live there. And who should come past us by but Madge Ellis, driving an old goose along the street with a stick. She peered at the car, but she didn't recognize me, so I felt fairly safe. Then we went through the village. What a transformation! If it had looked like that when I was there, I might have been reconciled to it. Then I thought that before trying to see you, we would go for a drink and a bite to the pub, to gain a bit of info. That's how we knew who it was at Bryony, and all that had happened, and was likely to happen in the old village. I told Seppi to ask about 'the big old house off the road', and heard about you and 'the man who lives there with her, who is her cousin. But you never see one of 'em without the other, and some folks say'—

Fran dear, I can't say how pleased I am. I knew I was right. I guess you are truly happy. Too much so to want me butting in. Give my love to William, and may you both go on being as happy as you deserve.

And then somebody came in with the local paper – full of the news about Wendy Noble, and with that photo of her. What a looker! What a dress! Talk about an ugly caterpillar turning into a butterfly. I shall give myself the credit for it, because I know her family won't. My miserable years in Hen Street did some good, after all. I'm glad.

I never had a lot of luck in my life, as you know. But luck did send you to me – I think the only true friend that I have ever had. And a woman, too! The one who knew all about me, and loved me just the same. So I send you my love in return.

Johanna.

P.S. I brought the soapstone with me. Seppi actually likes it. Maybe my luck has changed!

I was still staring at it, wet-eyed and regretful, when I heard William's signal as he drove in. Dot-dot-dash-dot. Get-your-hair-cut. William didn't mean me to take it literally, as I knew. He had encouraged me to grow it again, so that I could once again coil the bun in the nape of my neck, as he had remembered it. It had remained as dark, so far, as his own had once been.

He came in with his arms full of huge chrysanthemums, which he laid in my lap as he bent to kiss me.

'It's the wrong time of the year for red roses,' he said. 'But they mean just the same. Who's the letter from?'

'Read it,' I said. He perched on the arm of my chair, read through it, and looked at the photograph. Then he handed it back to me without comment.

'Shall I put the card up with the others?' he asked.

'No,' I said. I was making up my mind. She had not put her address on the letter, and she had not come to call when so near. She was as intelligent as she was beautiful, and had too much sense to try to persuade the past to return. She had said her farewell – and I could see that it was all for the best. If I left her card, or her photograph about, it would act like a tiny splinter in the thumb of Benedict's this Christmas. It would wrench at Sophie's heart; it would remind Kate of the only time her relationship with me had been seriously threatened; and could William ever glance at it without thinking how much she was like Janice? Photograph or no photograph, I should not forget her.

I tore the letter into tiny shreds, and I took one long last look at that alluring figure and the demon-angel face framed by that halo of hell-fire-red hair. Then I put the photo with the card and the torn-up letter back into the envelope, and handed it to William.

'Burn it. Now,' I said.

He squatted down without a word, leaned forward and tucked it right into the heart of the glowing log fire, while I held the tawny red petals of William's chrysanthemums where I could bury my face in them.

We watched as the paper singed, and curled, and blackened, and then crumpled away to white ash before it became one with the rest of the living, leaping feathers and petals of the flames.